# THE CHILDREN OF THE GODS SERIES BOOKS 14-16

### DARK ANGEL TRILOGY

I. T LUCAS

Copyright © 2020 by I. T. Lucas

All rights reserved.
No part of this book may be reproduced in any form or by any electronic or mechanical means, including information storage and retrieval systems, without written permission from the author, except for the use of brief quotations in a book review.

**NOTE FROM THE AUTHOR:**
**Dark Angel Trilogy This is a work of fiction!**
Names, characters, places and incidents are products of the author's imagination or are used fictitiously and are not to be construed as real. Any similarity to actual persons, organizations and/or events is purely coincidental.

## CONTENTS

### DARK ANGEL'S OBSESSION

1. Callie — 3
2. Callie — 8
3. Brundar — 12
4. Losham — 16
5. Callie — 20
6. Jackson — 23
7. Brundar — 27
8. Callie — 32
9. Brundar — 36
10. Callie — 39
11. Roni — 44
12. Brundar — 48
13. Callie — 53
14. Brundar — 57
15. Tessa — 60
16. Jackson — 63
17. Tessa — 67
18. Callie — 71
19. Brundar — 75
20. Callie — 80
21. Brundar — 85
22. Kian — 88
23. Syssi — 90
24. Brundar — 94
25. Brundar — 97
26. Callie — 100
27. Brundar — 104
28. Callie — 108
29. Roni — 112
30. Kian — 116
31. Brundar — 119
32. Callie — 122

| | |
|---|---:|
| 33. Brundar | 126 |
| 34. Roni | 129 |
| 35. Brundar | 133 |
| 36. Tessa | 137 |
| 37. Jackson | 141 |
| 38. Tessa | 144 |
| 39. Brundar | 148 |
| 40. Callie | 151 |
| 41. Brundar | 155 |
| 42. Callie | 158 |
| 43. Brundar | 161 |
| 44. Brundar | 165 |
| 45. Callie | 169 |
| 46. Brundar | 172 |
| 47. Callie | 175 |
| 48. Brundar | 179 |
| 49. Callie | 183 |
| 50. Brundar | 186 |
| 51. Callie | 189 |
| 52. Brundar | 192 |
| 53. Callie | 195 |
| 54. Brundar | 197 |
| 55. Callie | 200 |
| 56. Brundar | 203 |
| 57. Roni | 205 |

## DARK ANGEL'S SEDUCTION

| | |
|---|---:|
| 1. Brundar | 211 |
| 2. Callie | 214 |
| 3. Roni | 219 |
| 4. Callie | 223 |
| 5. Brundar | 227 |
| 6. Callie | 230 |
| 7. Kian | 233 |
| 8. Roni | 236 |
| 9. Brundar | 240 |
| 10. Callie | 243 |
| 11. Brundar | 246 |
| 12. Callie | 250 |
| 13. Brundar | 253 |

| | |
|---|---|
| 14. Callie | 258 |
| 15. Shawn | 261 |
| 16. Tessa | 263 |
| 17. Jackson | 268 |
| 18. Roni | 271 |
| 19. Callie | 275 |
| 20. Brundar | 278 |
| 21. Tessa | 282 |
| 22. Jackson | 285 |
| 23. Callie | 289 |
| 24. Brundar | 293 |
| 25. Callie | 298 |
| 26. Brundar | 302 |
| 27. Roni | 305 |
| 28. Carol | 308 |
| 29. Brundar | 311 |
| 30. Callie | 314 |
| 31. Roni | 319 |
| 32. Shawn | 323 |
| 33. Callie | 326 |
| 34. Brundar | 330 |
| 35. Callie | 333 |
| 36. Brundar | 338 |
| 37. Roni | 341 |
| 38. Jackson | 345 |
| 39. Tessa | 349 |
| 40. Anandur | 353 |
| 41. Callie | 357 |
| 42. Brundar | 359 |
| 43. Callie | 362 |
| 44. Losham | 365 |
| 45. Callie | 369 |
| 46. Anandur | 372 |
| 47. Shawn | 375 |
| 48. Callie | 378 |
| 49. Brundar | 381 |
| 50. Callie | 385 |
| 51. Brundar | 388 |
| 52. Callie | 391 |
| 53. Shawn | 392 |
| 54. Callie | 394 |

| | |
|---|---|
| 55. Brundar | 396 |
| 56. Callie | 398 |
| 57. Brundar | 400 |
| 58. Callie | 402 |
| 59. Brundar | 404 |
| 60. Callie | 407 |

## DARK ANGEL'S SURRENDER

| | |
|---|---|
| 1. Anandur | 413 |
| 2. Callie | 416 |
| 3. Brundar | 419 |
| 4. Callie | 422 |
| 5. Callie | 425 |
| 6. Tessa | 429 |
| 7. Jackson | 432 |
| 8. Anandur | 436 |
| 9. Brundar | 440 |
| 10. Callie | 443 |
| 11. Brundar | 446 |
| 12. Anandur | 449 |
| 13. Callie | 453 |
| 14. Brundar | 456 |
| 15. Roni | 460 |
| 16. Anandur | 463 |
| 17. Amanda | 467 |
| 18. Callie | 470 |
| 19. Brundar | 473 |
| 20. Losham | 476 |
| 21. Brundar | 478 |
| 22. Callie | 481 |
| 23. Brundar | 485 |
| 24. Roni | 489 |
| 25. Kian | 491 |
| 26. Brundar | 493 |
| 27. Callie | 497 |
| 28. Roni | 500 |
| 29. Callie | 503 |
| 30. Brundar | 507 |
| 31. Callie | 510 |
| 32. Kian | 512 |

| | |
|---|---|
| 33. Brundar | 515 |
| 34. Roni | 518 |
| 35. Jackson | 522 |
| 36. Tessa | 526 |
| 37. Jackson | 529 |
| 38. Tessa | 532 |
| 39. Kian | 536 |
| 40. Anandur | 539 |
| 41. Callie | 542 |
| 42. Brundar | 545 |
| 43. Callie | 548 |
| 44. Brundar | 551 |
| 45. Tessa | 554 |
| 46. Jackson | 558 |
| 47. Kian | 561 |
| 48. Losham | 564 |
| 49. Callie | 567 |
| 50. Brundar | 571 |
| 51. Jackson | 574 |
| 52. Brundar | 577 |
| 53. Callie | 581 |
| 54. Brundar | 584 |
| 55. Callie | 587 |
| 56. Brundar | 590 |
| 57. Jackson | 593 |
| 58. Brundar | 595 |
| 59. Callie | 599 |
| 60. Brundar | 602 |
| 61. Callie | 604 |
| 62. Brundar | 607 |
| 63. Callie | 609 |
| 64. Brundar | 613 |
| 65. Turner | 616 |
| Dark Operative A Shadow of Death | 621 |
| The Children of the Gods Series | 635 |
| The Perfect Match Series | 645 |
| Also by I. T. Lucas | 647 |
| FOR EXCLUSIVE PEEKS | 651 |

# DARK ANGEL'S OBSESSION

# 1

# CALLIE

*Twenty-two months ago.*

"What's wrong? You look green." Iris's worried eyes met Callie's in the mirror.

Ugh. The nausea should have passed by now. Morning sickness at two in the afternoon was unacceptable. But then her queasy stomach might have had less to do with her pregnancy and more to do with her upcoming nuptials.

"I think I'm going to be sick again." The train of her wedding dress clutched in her hand, Callie bolted for the bathroom.

Locking the door behind her, she eyed the toilet and contemplated kneeling on the floor, but doing so in a white, voluminous dress was asking for trouble. It could get dirty or wrinkled, and she didn't need the extra stress.

Instead, she put a protective hand over the plunging neckline and leaned over the sink, trying to purge the swirling sensation from her gut. Nothing came up, only painful dry heaves.

"Are you okay in there?" Iris knocked on the door. "Can I help? Do you want me to call Donald?"

"No. Just give me a minute," Callie called out.

The last thing she needed was for her father to freak out. The man couldn't deal with anything female related.

She still remembered his reaction to her first period. It was good that the supermarket had been walking distance from their house. There was no way her father would have survived buying her tampons.

It was a freaking miracle that man had managed to raise a daughter on his own since she was a tiny toddler.

Another knock. "Callie, let me in. I can at least hold your hair back while you puke," Iris pleaded.

"I'm fine. I'll be out in a minute." *Gah.* The woman was so irritating.

Iris meant well, but she was too young to play mother of the bride. A big sister, maybe, but not really. Less than a year ago, when her father had finally remarried, Callie had been genuinely happy and excited to welcome Iris into their lives, even though the woman was only eleven years older than Callie and thirteen years younger than Donald.

Iris was chatty and smiley and filled their quiet home with life.

Callie had hoped for a sisterly relationship with her new stepmother, but things hadn't worked out that way. Though not for lack of trying on both sides. They were just two very different people. The only thing they had in common was their love for her father.

Iris made Donald happy.

Before she'd tumbled into his life, he had rarely smiled, which made Callie wonder whether he'd been a happier man when her mother was still alive.

Getting him to talk about her was impossible. It made him too sad. But the many pictures and few home movies told a story of a perfectly normal little family, with two doting parents and a chubby baby girl whom they'd seemed to adore.

Callie sighed and leaned her forehead against the cool mirror.

One tragic moment had shattered their family forever, taking away her mother from them and leaving Donald a broken, sad man to raise a daughter on his own.

"Callie, are you okay?" Her father's voice.

*Damn it, Iris.* She'd told her not to bother him.

"I'm fine. I'll be out in a moment."

If she could work magic, she would've gotten rid of them both, sent them to mingle with the guests and let her breathe for a few moments, but the best she could do was get rid of at least one. Temporarily.

"Can either of you bring me a coke?"

"Sure thing." Her father jumped at the opportunity to be useful doing something other than dealing with his daughter's prenuptial jitters. Or worse, her pregnancy nausea.

Callie waited another moment before opening the door.

"Feeling better?" Iris asked.

She forced a smile. "Much. Can you do me a favor and bring me some saltines from the kitchen?"

Iris patted her arm. "That's a splendid idea. Saltines work miracles on nausea." She rushed to the kitchen, or rather attempted to. Hindered by her spiky heels and long tight dress, it was more of a waddle than a fast walk.

Alone at last, Callie sat down in front of her vanity and picked up the pink lipstick, hoping the bright color would help offset the green hue of her skin.

Pregnancy should have made her glow with health, not look pale and sickly. Except, that was likely true for those overjoyed by the prospect of motherhood, not those tricked into it at nineteen.

Too young.

She hadn't done anything with her life yet.

*No regrets, Callie.* It was the mantra she'd adopted after the shock of discovering she was pregnant had worn off.

It was all happening a little sooner than she would've preferred, but she was going to make it work. Her life was going to be great. She was going to build a cozy home for her sweet, adorable baby and loving husband.

Except, Callie wasn't so sure about that last one.

Did Shawn really love her?

Did loving people trick their partners into marriage?

Relationships were supposed to be built on trust.

Theirs wasn't.

Callie had no proof that he'd gotten her pregnant on purpose. After all, condom failure was not unheard of. But from what she'd read online, it was mostly due to mishandling. At twenty-seven, Shawn should've had plenty of experience in handling one properly.

As the door to her bedroom opened, Callie took a deep breath, bracing for more of Iris's prattle, but it wasn't her stepmother.

"Dawn!" Callie jumped and turned, almost tripping on the gown's long train. "You made it!"

"Of course, I made it. You think I would miss my best friend's wedding?" Dawn handed her a Coke can and a pack of saltines. "I told your dad and Iris that I'm taking over and that they should stop neglecting their guests."

"Thank you." The tears prickling the back of Callie's eyes were threatening to ruin Iris's carefully applied makeup. "Aren't you missing finals?"

"All done. I took the last one yesterday."

"How did it go?"

Dawn waved a hand. "Easy peasy lemon squeezy."

Callie laughed. "You are probably the only one that can say that about MIT's electrical engineering department finals."

"Not really. To my utter horror, I discovered I wasn't the smartest thing to ever grace the lecture halls of that prestigious institution."

Callie pretended to gasp. "Get out of here. Really? It can't be."

Dawn shook her head. "Sadly, it is. But enough about me. How are you holding up?"

"I want to throw up."

"That's to be expected from one who is expecting."

Callie sat back on her vanity stool. "I don't want to marry Shawn."

"I don't blame you." Dawn knelt in front of her and clasped her hands. "You can still call it off. I'll go out there and tell everyone to go home including Shawn, who, by the way, is strutting around like a peacock, happy as can be."

"I bet. He got his way, the bastard. He's been pestering me to marry him since the day he popped my cherry, obsessed by the idea of marrying a girl who's never been touched by another."

Dawn's eyes narrowed. "Do you think he did it on purpose?"

"I can't be sure, but I have my suspicions."

"So why the hell do you refuse to get an abortion?"

Cradling her middle protectively, Callie shook her head. "I can't. It's not this little one's fault that his or her father is an underhanded jerk. Besides, you know I love children. I'm going to be a great mother."

"I know, sweetie, but is Shawn going to be a great father? Or husband?"

"I don't know," Callie whispered.

He'd been so charming and attentive when they'd first met three months ago. Still was. But Callie couldn't shake the feeling that Shawn was putting on a very convincing act, hiding a darker, more sinister side underneath all that smooth talk.

The thing was, when he turned it on full force, it was hard to hang on to that suspicion. It was much easier to believe that she was worried for no good reason, scared by nonexistent shadows.

Shawn was older, bossy and dominant. It was what had attracted her to him in the first place. Except, that bossy attitude was getting annoying. Especially when his dishonesty and manipulative behavior brought about disillusion and disappointment.

The thing was, blinded by her attraction to him, she hadn't noticed any of it until it was too late and she was carrying his child.

Callie had never been drawn to guys her age. Ever since she had become sexually aware, she'd craved something that for the longest time she couldn't define or name. Naturally, she'd assumed it was what every woman craved and hadn't been overly bothered by it. But the sweet romances she'd sneaked under the blanket at night had painted a different picture.

Much later, she'd found a series of books that had opened her eyes. As a high fantasy it was mostly about adventure, not about romance, and the few intimate scenes were by no means descriptive, but the tapestry it had woven contained many more shades than Callie had been aware of.

"Love as thy wilt." That imagined society's main motto was that nothing was taboo as long as it was consensual.

Easier said than done.

It had been difficult to accept that she wasn't like everyone else, and that the things she craved were somewhat outside the norm.

Why the hell did she crave sexual dominance?

Callie wasn't combative, but she wasn't timorous either. She didn't accept authority without question, and had her own opinions about pretty much everything, which she never shied away from expressing.

She was a strong, capable, and independent woman.

She had no other choice.

With no mother and a father who worked long days, she had been basically left to her own devices since she was a very young girl. No one had ever supervised her schoolwork, and yet she had always been a straight A student. No one had ever moderated her behavior, and yet she had always been polite. No one had told her how to dress, and yet she had always dressed modestly.

Perhaps the reason for her good-girl model behavior was that she had never had a reason to rebel. Why would she? And against whom or what?

With no one to tell her otherwise, Callie could do whatever she wanted whenever she wanted.

Her father had trusted her with running the household from a very young age, giving her a bank card and a checkbook filled with signed checks. Callie had done all the grocery shopping and paid the bills. It was a lot of responsibility, but she'd never shied away from it. Her father needed her help, and she'd given it freely, glad she was able to do it.

So why the hell did she crave sexual domination?
Why did nothing else turn her on as much? Or at all?
Those were questions she'd grown tired of asking.
It just was.

2

# CALLIE

*One year ago.*

Shawn parked the car behind the club, cut the engine, and turned to regard Callie with a deep scowl. All during the drive she'd watched his simmering irritation intensify. She knew how to manage his anger tantrums and violent outbursts, but they still made her anxious.

"Are you sure you want to go through with this?" he grated.

No, she wasn't, but she needed an answer to a question that had been bothering her for months, and the club was the only place she could think of that could provide it. A lot of self-talk and nerve had gone into suggesting the visit. "We are not going to do anything in there. We're just checking it out, and if it's gross, we'll leave."

"How do you even know about a place like that?"

"I told you, Dawn's ex-boyfriend took her there."

Dawn had been her best friend since middle school, though Callie hadn't confided in her about her unorthodox preferences. It was too embarrassing. But after Dawn had told her about the club, Callie jumped at the opportunity in the name of adventurous experimentation. It had been so good to finally talk to someone about it without fear of being judged or humiliated.

It shouldn't have taken her so long. Dawn had no qualms about sharing her most intimate experiences with Callie. It wasn't that her friend was promiscuous, so far Dawn had had only two serious boyfriends, but she liked to live dangerously and experiment—perhaps as a way to dispel her dorky reputation.

"She is a bad influence on you."

Yeah, Shawn thought everyone was a bad influence, doing his best to isolate Callie.

"Don't be silly. Dawn just has an open mind and likes to get a taste of different things. Anyway, she said it is pretty tame, with a clientele of mostly committed couples and nothing overly kinky going on in the open." Supposedly, the club held nightly lectures and presentations on different techniques. The demonstrations were being done on fully dressed volunteers. Shawn should have no problem with that.

"She said it was very educational and that we were going to like it." In fact, her words were more along the lines of Callie getting turned on as hell watching whatever subject was taught that night and wanting to jump the next available male, which unfortunately was going to be Shawn.

There was no love lost between those two.

"Fine." He gritted his teeth and opened his door. "I don't understand why we need this crap. Am I not enough for you?" His voice had risen in volume.

Damn it, just as she'd managed to calm him down, Shawn was working himself up again. The only way to defuse the upcoming storm was to stroke his ego. She patted his arm. "You're my stud muffin. I'm doing it for us. We might learn something new to spice things up. Aren't you curious?"

The ruddy color leaving his cheeks, Shawn's chest inflated with self-importance as he pointed a finger at her. "I'm only going because you want to. There is nothing these people can show me that I haven't seen already. But you'd better not forget who you're with and who you belong to."

Callie stifled the urge to roll her eyes. For a guy who believed he was the big bad wolf, Shawn was ridiculously predictable and easy to manipulate.

Flattery worked on him like a charm.

"Never." She shook her head dramatically. "How could I?" He was so full of himself that there was no chance he'd detect her mocking tone. "You're the best."

Out of necessity, Callie had gotten very good at acting over the past year.

Shawn was a big guy, and with his volatile mood swings and aggression, he could turn really scary really quick. Defusing and deflecting his rage was an exercise in survival.

So far, she'd been lucky.

During his temper tantrums, Shawn had taken out his rage on the walls, the furniture, the appliances, the dishes, and other inanimate objects, but not on her.

Not yet.

It hadn't taken her long to realize that her husband was a bully who thrived on belittling her, manipulating her into bending to his will, and generally pushing her around. The funny thing was that he didn't see it that way. Shawn was convinced that he was a great husband and that she should be grateful for him.

It was easier to just let him believe that.

Instead of fighting an outward war, which she was sure to lose, Callie learned to roll with the punches and get what she wanted in a roundabout way.

Shawn believed he had a subdued, agreeable wife, when in fact she was only letting him win the small things while going after what was really important to her.

When he'd said she couldn't go to college because she needed to help pay the mortgage, she'd taken a waitressing job at the Aussie Steak House where Dawn's sister was a manager, and the tips were more than generous. Working only four evenings a week, including weekends, she made decent money, and could still take college classes with enough free time left over for homework and housework. As a car salesman, Shawn also worked evenings and weekends. As long as she brought the money home and deposited everything into their joint account, he had no problem with her schedule. As with everything else, he wanted complete control over their finances.

Whatever. It wasn't all that important.

She made their marriage work, but the effort that went into it was becoming more and more exhausting.

Were all marriages like that?

One big compromise?

Other than books and movies, which romanticized the reality of everyday life, Callie had nothing to compare her marriage to. Growing up in a single-parent household, she could only imagine what a loving partnership was like.

Perhaps what she and Shawn had was as good as it got?

Still, she couldn't help thinking that it shouldn't be so difficult, and that power games, lies, and manipulations shouldn't be part of a good marriage.

Then again, it was possible that in her youth and naïveté she was imagining an ideal that was unattainable, and she should be thankful for what she had.

Shawn wrapped his arm around her shoulders. "Instead of watching perverts in a kink club, we should go home and work on putting another baby in here." He rubbed a hand over her flat belly.

As devastating as losing the baby had been, Callie was grateful for her apparent difficulty in conceiving. Given that they weren't using contraceptives, though, it was only a matter of time. Ever since her miscarriage, Shawn had been obsessed with getting her pregnant again.

She rested her head on his chest. "There is no reason to rush, Shawn. It will happen when it happens."

He tightened his hold. "God willing."

She hated when he talked like that. Shawn wasn't a religious man, and those kinds of sayings just rolled off his tongue without any real meaning behind them. Growing up in a devout home, he hated anything and everything to do with religion.

He wasn't a believer, and neither was Callie.

When he'd knocked her up, her refusal to consider abortion was not because of the dictums of some scriptures; she'd followed what was in her heart. Even though she was now smarter and somewhat disillusioned, if faced with the same decision today, she wouldn't act differently.

At the time, she'd believed that if they nurtured their attraction and infatuation with each other, they would grow and mature into love. A year later, she was less hopeful but not ready to give up yet.

Not everything was lost.

In his own convoluted way, Shawn loved her. She didn't love him back, but she didn't hate him either. Their marriage was salvageable. In Callie's opinion, people were giving up on their marriages too easily and for the most trivial of reasons.

Besides, giving up was not an option.

The truth was that Shawn would never let her go voluntarily. Aside from his temper, which was worrisome enough on its own, she could sense that something was off with him. She couldn't put her finger on it, but there was a darkness lurking inside him—just waiting for the right catalyst to manifest.

Leaving him would unleash it with a vengeance.

She would have to run—flee to either South Carolina, where her father had been transferred, or Massachusetts, where Dawn was still attending MIT.

The situation with Shawn was far from desperate enough to make her do either.

She would make it work.

Somehow.

The problem was that she had no clue how to tame Shawn. Instead of getting better, he was getting worse. His newest control freak-out was demanding to know where she was and what she was doing every minute of the day. He didn't even try to hide the fact that he was tracking her by her phone's GPS.

Whatever. The tracking had at least ended the baseless accusations.

Before that ingenious solution, he used to put her through a merciless interrogation every time she'd left the house, and then not believe anything she'd said.

Some battles were just not worth fighting.

Compromise was the name of the game.

# 3

# BRUNDAR

*One year ago.*

"Boss, can you come up front? I have a situation." The receptionist sounded annoyed and just a little scared.

"On my way," Brundar spoke into the microphone attached to his T-shirt.

One of the biggest hassles of being a part owner of a nightclub was throwing out undesirables. After the last idiot who'd harassed the girl, Brundar had bought a taser gun and instructed her and her weekend counterpart on how to use it in case he and Franco were both occupied elsewhere.

Buying half of Franco's club hadn't been a financial or business decision. Brundar had done it to help the guy out of a tight spot in exchange for a share of the profits—if there were any—and had had no intentions of getting involved in the day to day management of the place. His Guardian job wasn't the kind that allowed time for a side business.

As the saying went, no good deed went unpunished. Whether he liked it or not, time and again Brundar found himself stepping in.

The financial rescue hadn't been a favor to a friend. Brundar didn't have any. He liked Franco, but the guy was little more than an acquaintance.

Brundar's reasons had been entirely selfish. Finally finding a place where he was comfortable, he refused to let it go bust. When Franco needed an infusion of cash to keep it running, Brundar came up with the dough in exchange for fifty percent ownership just so he wouldn't have to search for a new club.

What made the place different than others was Franco himself. He started it as a regular nightclub, adding the private basement level much later to provide a safe space for himself and a group of like-minded friends to socialize and play. Over time, his friends brought along other friends and membership had expanded, but Franco still treated it as his private playground and was very picky about who he allowed in there.

The upstairs clubgoers didn't even know about the lower level.

Making most of his money from charging entry to the nightclub, selling drinks, and renting the place out for private parties, Franco kept the membership fees to a bare minimum. The guy was more concerned with the quality of his clientele than with their ability to pay.

The upstairs club subsidized the maintenance of the lower level.

Unfortunately, Franco's business acumen left a lot to be desired, and Brundar was slowly getting sucked into getting more and more involved, implementing changes that would make the member portion of the club if not profitable, then at least self-sustainable.

Most of the time Brundar didn't mind helping, but occasionally he had to get involved in inconsequential crap. Drunks and the like were handled by a bouncer, but sober paying customers were usually not turned away unless a private party was going on. He wondered what it could possibly be that required his intervention.

Hopefully, it wasn't another nosy journalist like the one he'd kicked out a week before.

As he neared the anteroom, the waves of aggression wafting from the receptionist station had Brundar's fangs throbbing and lengthening even before he pushed the door open. "What seems to be the problem, Belinda?" he asked in his usual icy tone.

The troublemaker turned around, his face red with anger. "This bitch you have sitting here refuses my wife entrance," he spat.

That was unusual. Women were never turned away from the nightclub. On the contrary, twice a week they got in free. There were always more guys than girls.

The lady in question was hiding behind her husband's broad shoulders, but Brundar could smell her embarrassment. It wasn't an unpleasant scent like the stink coming from the husband; in fact, it was quite alluring despite her discomfort. A mix of soft femininity and strength of character. The last was not a scent most immortals could detect, but it was one Brundar was especially attuned to.

"I tried to explain that no one under twenty-one is allowed in the nightclub or in Franco's basement," Belinda said. "And that it doesn't matter that they have a member's recommendation."

Sidestepping the angry jerk, he peeked at the slender woman standing behind him.

To call her a woman was an exaggeration, and yet she took his breath away—a beautiful, delicate flower that had no business in the club above let alone the one below.

She was still a child. No wonder Belinda refused her entry. The girl looked eighteen at the most.

Why the hell was she married at such a young age and to that asshole?

"This is ridiculous. She is a married woman, for fuck's sake," the jerk fumed.

*Yeah, and you should get flogged for robbing her of her childhood.* The thing was, Brundar had the sense that the girl wasn't scared of the big bully, only embarrassed by his behavior.

"That's okay, Shawn, let's go." She tried to thread her arm through his.

He shook her arm off. "Stay out of it, Callie." He turned to Brundar. "So what is it going to be? Huh? If you don't let us in, I'm going to trash your club on every review site and every newspaper I can get to." The guy inflated his chest, thinking to intimidate Brundar.

So that was why Belinda had asked him to intervene. The jerk had probably threatened her with the same crap. Bad reviews were bad for business, and one jerk with a vendetta could do a lot of damage.

Behind the desk, Belinda groaned in frustration.

Brundar affected a tight-lipped smile. "I don't think that will be necessary. We can resolve this misunderstanding in a mutually beneficial way." He imbued his tone with influence.

Trying to resist the command, the guy pinched his forehead between his thumb and forefinger. A few seconds later, he faltered. "Yes, that would be better." His chest deflated.

"Come. I'll escort you to your car." Brundar opened the front door.

The girl named Callie cast him a perplexed glance. To resist the influence, her brain must've been stronger than her husband's.

What was a smart girl like her doing with a moron like that?

"Sometimes a calm tone is all that's needed," Brundar whispered in her ear.

Staring at him, she shook her head, once, and then again. Perhaps she was wondering about her husband's uncharacteristic response, or still feeling the influence and fighting it.

As they reached the couple's Honda Civic, the husband unlocked the doors with the remote and got behind the wheel, leaving his young wife standing on the sidewalk.

Brundar walked around to the passenger side and opened the door for her. "My lady." Without thinking, he offered Callie his hand, a rare gesture for him. He hardly ever shook hands with a woman and never with a man.

"Thank you," she whispered, her eyes trained on his face, his offered hand outside her peripheral vision. "Can I have your name, sir?"

"Brad." He gave her the name he was known by in the club. "A pleasure to make your acquaintance, Callie."

She smiled shyly. "It's Calypso, but I go by Callie." She shook her head. "I don't know why I'm telling you this. I never use my real name." Pink flooding her cheeks, she looked down.

Unable to resist, he hooked a finger under her chin and lifted her head. "Calypso. It suits you better. A unique name for a unique girl. One of a kind and beautiful."

She chuckled, blushing again. "Funny that you would say that about me. Talk about unique." She waved a hand at him. For a moment, it seemed like she wanted to say more, but then she decided against it.

"Look at me, Calypso," Brundar commanded softly.

She did, her green eyes losing focus as he delved into her mind. "You're beautiful, and I'm just a guy who is way too old for you. Forget about me."

"I'm not a kid. I'm twenty," she protested.

A little older than he'd thought, but still a child. One with a strong mind, though.

Curious, Brundar delved a little deeper.

He didn't like what that little glimpse he'd allowed himself revealed. The girl wasn't safe with the man she called her husband. Brundar knew the type well. For now, Shawn was just a controlling bastard and a verbally abusive jerk, but his behavior was going to escalate. It always did with bullies.

"Get in the car, Calypso." He waited for her to buckle up before closing her door and going around to the driver's side.

The guy was still in a trance-like compliance.

*Weak mind.*

"Look at me, Shawn," Brundar commanded.

The guy raised a pair of unfocused eyes.

"You're going to pay attention to the road and drive home safely. You're going to take care of Callie and treat her well. Do you understand?"

"Yes, sir."

Brundar closed the door, then waited for Shawn to turn on the engine, put the transmission in drive, and ease out of the parking lot.

As he watched the car disappear from view, he committed the license plate number to memory. The thrall he'd put on Shawn was going to hold for a while, but not indefinitely.

Once it wore off, Calypso would be in danger.

## 4

## LOSHAM

*The present.*

Losham poured himself a shot of whiskey and walked out the French doors to the presidential suite's balcony. Nothing but the best for him and Rami. The twelve men Navuh had grudgingly allotted for his use were comfortable enough in a nearby extended-stay hotel.

Leaning over the railing, he took a sip and held it in his mouth to savor the flavor. It wasn't the best there was, just the best the hotel had. Decent, but not what he was used to drinking at home. And to think the place promoted itself as the fanciest in town.

Rami followed him outside. "What are we going to do with the new men?"

Losham knew what he meant. Navuh had authorized less than one fifth of the personnel Losham had asked for. "That's not nearly enough for all the clubs, but it is for one. I'm going to keep them here. We know that at least part of the clan is residing somewhere in this area. It makes sense for them to hide in a big city. San Francisco with its tech hub is also a good bet. But I have a hunch their leadership's base is in Los Angeles. If it were me, I'd have chosen the larger city as my command center too."

"As always, you are right, sir." Rami glanced at his watch. "We should head out. The men are waiting."

"Yes." Losham finished his drink and handed Rami the empty glass. "Call the valet and have the car ready."

"Yes, sir."

After much deliberation, Losham had decided that the best place for holding meetings with his men was in a rented warehouse in an nondescript industrial park, one of the hundreds scattered throughout the large city. Keeping his operation low key was prudent on top of saving him money.

The place was the size of a classroom, with a kickboxing class as a neighbor on one side, and a spinning class on the other, where sweaty humans exerted themselves on stationary bikes to the screeching sounds of loud music.

Perfect for his needs.

With various fitness trainers renting spaces in the park, there were plenty of people coming and going. His men wouldn't stand out.

Rami parked next to the two minivans he'd rented for the men. Through the windows, Losham could see them sitting inside.

"Rami, transparency doesn't lend itself to covert activities."

His assistant followed his gaze. "The rented vans are a temporary solution. I'll make sure that the cars they get have tinted windows."

"Indeed."

As Rami unlocked the door, Losham motioned for them to come out of the vehicles. "Welcome," he greeted each one, offering a handshake.

Following instructions, the men didn't salute.

When everyone was inside, Rami locked the door behind them and lowered the shades, then walked over to the stack of folding chairs leaning against the wall. "Make yourselves comfortable," he said, pointing for the men to make use of them.

Forming a semi-circle, they sat facing Losham and Rami.

"Welcome," Losham greeted them. "Let's get straight to the purpose of your deployment. As you were all briefed, the Brotherhood now owns a chain of luxury sex clubs. The original goal was to lure rich clan members, with the intent of capturing and torturing them for information about the location of their leaders. Unfortunately, it seems that the civilians have no idea where the clan's command center is located. Therefore, we need to catch a Guardian."

Twelve apprehensive sets of eyes met his gaze.

Losham raised his palm to forestall questions. "I know these warriors are fearsome, but even the best fighter can't overpower twelve well-trained men. All we need is to catch one. That's why I'm keeping all of you here in one location instead of distributing you as reinforcements between the clubs."

The team's commander raised his hand.

"Yes, Gommed." Losham gave him permission to speak.

"Are we going to wait around until a Guardian shows up? It might never happen, sir."

"Good point. That's why we need to make sure one of them comes to investigate. I don't know their procedures, or if they usually send one or two. I'm betting on one. With such a small force, they can't afford to send more."

"Investigate what, sir?"

"Either another civilian that we catch and kill, or several of their human pets."

Gommed frowned. "I don't understand, sir. You want us to start killing random humans? Why would the Guardians care?"

Losham smiled indulgently. Simple soldiers needed to be fed information like baby birds. Their deductive skills were nonexistent. "They would care if the humans bled to death from two puncture wounds to the neck." He put two fingers on his carotid artery to demonstrate.

"Are we to instigate fights? Seek out gang members and other violent human scum to kill?"

The question was so naive it bordered on embarrassing.

His men were not going to like his idea, but they were soldiers, and they were going to obey orders. Nevertheless, Losham would pretend the course of action he was about to set was as unpalatable for him as it would be for the men.

"I wish it was that simple. But the clan leaders are not going to care about us eliminating random human scum. They might even think we've been reformed and come to care for the humans."

He smirked, making quotation marks with his fingers. "Your victims will have to be female. When several are found dead in a pool of their own blood, obvious bite marks on their necks, it will make the news. Naturally, the Guardians will know who's responsible. When they send one to snoop around, he will follow a trail of false clues that will lead him into a trap."

"What kind of a trap, sir?"

"I'm working on it. I'll let you know as soon as the plan is finalized."

"Yes, sir."

Gommed was a good soldier who didn't ask unnecessary questions like why and if there was another way. Except, it was written all over his face, as well as those of the others.

Although Mortdh's teachings held females in low esteem, they were considered a crucial resource. Since the soldiers' early years in the training camp, it had been drilled into their heads that human females were fragile and were to be used with care so as to not harm their breeding capabilities.

"Killing young fertile females is wasteful, but that's the nature of war. Sacrificing resources is unavoidable. If there were another way, I would've gladly taken it."

He got some approving nods but also some involuntary grimaces.

They would adjust.

"What are our orders, sir?" Gommed asked.

"First order of things is to get you settled. You need to buy cars, used ones from private owners. Rami will give you the cash needed, explain how to go about it, and take care of registration and insurance. When it's time for you to go to work, I want you to spread out and cover a wide area."

After several more questions had been answered and instructions clarified, the men left.

"Should I find us a nice restaurant, sir, or do you prefer to dine at the hotel?" Rami opened the sedan's door for Losham.

"Let's go back to the hotel. I find their culinary offerings acceptable."

"As you wish, sir." Rami closed the passenger's door and walked around to take his place at the driver's seat.

"Have you made any progress with your cult idea?"

Rami turned on the ignition and eased out of the parking spot. "I've spent some time thinking it through, and I think I have a solid plan."

"Please proceed."

"The men we want to recruit into the cult should be true women haters. I'm not talking about men like you, sir, who consider women inferior but still enjoy their company, or womanizers who use them, or men like me who are just not into them. I'm talking about those who've gotten rejected, thrown out, emasculated. Western society and the freedom of choice it affords women ensures that there is no shortage of those."

Very astute observation for a man who'd never had a relationship with a woman in a sexual, romantic, professional, or any other capacity. Doomers interacted with females only on a sexual basis, and Rami wasn't interested in that.

"I agree. How do you propose we find those angry rejects?"

Rami's lips turned up in a lopsided smirk. "You know how Americans have all those silly support groups? We make one for recently divorced men, men who were kicked out by their girlfriends, or simply all those who got rejected over and over again. There will be an avalanche of applicants."

"A brilliant idea, my friend. But how are we going to promote it?"

"Facebook. Paid advertisements can be targeted to a certain age group, gender, and other factors. We can employ an expert to help us narrow the selection."

"And who will lead that fake support group?"

Rami shrugged. "We either hire an actor or a quack therapist with women issues himself."

"What about the cult leader?"

"I thought you would want to do that yourself, sir."

Losham shook his head. "I'm a thinker, not a motivator. We need someone charismatic, someone who can incite men to violence. We either hire another actor, one with charisma and no scruples, or we choose one of the participants. We can observe a few of the initial meetings and look for someone who fits the role."

5

# CALLIE

*H*ands trembling with equal part excitement and anxiety, Callie opened the letter from UCLA.

*Dear Ms. Davidson,*

*I am pleased to congratulate you on behalf of University of California – Los Angeles upon our acceptance of your application. As you know, UCLA has a long tradition of academic excellence and reviews the many applications it receives with the highest standards.*

CALLIE SKIPPED over to the next part.

*You will find all the necessary forms for your enrollment included with this letter. We request that you fill them out and return them to us no later than October 1, 2018. This will help us to ensure that your spot remains open and facilitate the enrollment process. Please contact us if you have any questions or problems regarding this letter.*

OH BOY, did she have problems, but none that a call to the university's admissions office could solve. Tuition was tenfold what she'd paid at the community college, and there was no way Shawn would agree to the expense. Not because they couldn't afford it, after all she could apply for a student loan, but because he would use it as an excuse and throw a tantrum if she insisted.

It had crossed her mind to ask her father for a loan, but she'd rejected it out of hand.

Donald would gladly give her the tuition money if he had it, but after buying the house in South Carolina, she knew he was short on cash. Besides, with Iris ready to pop at any moment, they would need whatever was left over from his paycheck to buy things for the baby.

As of late, the little half-brother she was expecting was the only bright spot in Callie's life. Hopefully, Shawn wouldn't object to her going to see the baby. Not that it would stop her. There was only so much jerkiness she was willing to put up with.

No way was she missing out on holding her newborn brother and cuddling with him as much as Iris allowed.

"What do you have there?" Shawn looked over her shoulder at the letter in her hands.

She would rather have waited to tell him after having some time to think of the best way to spin it in her favor. On the other hand it was better to get it done and not obsess over it for days. "I got in. This is from the UCLA admissions office."

"Did it come with a scholarship?"

Callie sighed and folded the letter. "We don't qualify for financial aid, Shawn. Between your paycheck and mine, we make too much."

He snorted. "Right, as if there is that much left over after the mortgage and the car payments and all the other bills."

She wanted to tell him that leasing a car for close to a thousand dollars a month was not considered a life necessity, and that the difference between the payments on his luxury BMW and her basic Honda Civic would've paid for half of her tuition, but she knew it was no use. He would go into a whole tirade as to why he needed to drive the BMW because he was selling them and how would it look if he drove something else.

As if any of his customers cared what car he was driving.

Shawn was a selfish prick, that's all.

"I could take out a student loan," she said softly. "I got the credits from the community college transferred, which means I only have two or three years of tuition left."

"With the interest those fuckers are charging on student loans, even that is a lot. We will never get out of debt. And for what? So you can become a teacher and make even less money than you make waiting tables? I don't think so."

It was hard to argue with that logic. Except, waiting tables was not her life goal. Teaching was. Callie loved kids, and working in an elementary school, preferably with kindergarteners, was her dream job.

"Yeah, I guess you're right," she said, to get him to leave her alone.

He looked disappointed. She'd robbed him of the opportunity to argue and work himself up so he could wreak havoc on the house and terrorize her.

Over the past year, Shawn had gotten worse. The anger tantrums were becoming more frequent and more violent. Most everything in their house was either broken or scratched, the walls covered with discount store framed art to hide the many holes he'd made in them.

Sadly, Callie was reaching the end of her rope. She couldn't save their marriage no matter how hard she tried, and frankly, she was tired of trying. Changing Shawn for the better was not going to happen.

Quite the opposite. The harder she tried, the worse he got.

If she wanted any kind of life for herself, she had to leave.

Grabbing a can of soda from the fridge, Callie walked over to the living room window and pulled the curtain back. There was something oddly calming about doing that, as if by gazing out on their quiet suburban street she could pretend that their home was as peaceful as the grassy lawns and young trees lining the sidewalk, their skinny, pliable trunks swaying in the light breeze.

It was a sorry state of affairs when the outside of her home felt safer than the inside.

Away from the suffocating confinement of those hole-ridden walls, she could breathe. Out there she felt whole, capable, free. Working, grocery shopping, or just taking a walk, it didn't matter where she was or what she was doing as long as she was out.

That good feeling would gradually evaporate the closer she got back to her house. Returning from work, her heart would skip a beat as she pressed the remote and waited for the garage door to lift.

Whether Shawn's car was there or not determined if her pulse sped up or slowed down. The times he was gone, the adrenaline drop that came on the heels of the relief would often make her dizzy.

It was no way to live.

Callie hated the thought of being alone, but staying with Shawn was like living inside a horror film. She knew the boogieman, she knew he was coming for her, she just didn't know when.

Except, until she figured out her route to freedom, Callie had to pretend that everything was all right. In order for her to escape unharmed, Shawn couldn't suspect that she was unhappy and planning to leave.

## 6

# JACKSON

Jackson parked in the keep's guest parking garage and took the public elevator to the lobby, wondering what would it take to get in. But when he stopped at the guard station, the guy buzzed him in without question.

"Go ahead. We have you on file."

"Thanks." Jackson gave the guy a two finger salute and proceeded to the concealed side door marked as maintenance. It clicked open as soon as he pressed his thumb to the scanner.

Right. He'd almost forgotten about the mandatory sex-ed class he and his buddies had participated in so long ago. They had been granted a security clearance to enter the underground facilities, and apparently it was still good.

At the time, he'd been pissed at Kian for forcing him to endure Bhathian's lectures, but that class had ended up changing his life in unexpected ways.

Jackson must've left an impression on Bhathian because the guy introduced him to his daughter Nathalie, which turned out to be a great business opportunity for Jackson. More than that. While managing Nathalie's café, he'd met Tessa.

If not for that sex-ed class, he might have missed his one chance at a true-love match. It might have come and gone without him knowing it had been so close.

Must've been fated.

A nasty prank that had gotten him in shitloads of trouble ended up bringing him the love of his life.

Taking the clan's private elevator down to the basement, Jackson stepped out on the clinic's level.

Hopefully, Dr. Bridget wasn't busy and would agree to see him. He would've made an appointment, but he didn't have her private phone number, only the keep's emergency hotline, and there was no way he was explaining to whoever was answering the phone why he needed to see the doctor.

In fact, he was hoping no one other than Bridget was there to see him come in. He could count on the doctor to keep their conversation confidential, but not anyone else. The last thing he needed was for the gossip machine to start spinning.

Knocking on the door, he pushed it open a crack. "Dr. Bridget, do you have a moment?"

She waved him in. "Of course. Come in, Jackson."

"Thank you." He closed the door behind him.

"Please, take a seat and tell me what brings you here."

"My mate," he started, and stopped at Bridget's surprised expression. "I mean my girlfriend, but she is so much more than that."

Bridget smiled. "Tessa, right?"

"Yeah. So I guess the rumor machine is already working."

"I don't know about that. Per my request, or rather demand, I get informed about all possible Dormants. Actually, I would appreciate it if Tessa would come in and give a few blood samples before her transition starts. Have you bitten her already? And if yes, how many times?"

Jackson pinched his forehead between his thumb and forefinger. "Enough to induce her transition. But it's not happening."

Bridget's eyes filled with pity. "I'm so sorry, Jackson. Maybe she is not a Dormant. We are so eager to find new ones that we are grasping at straws. I was told that she doesn't have any special abilities, so it was a long shot from the start."

"No, she doesn't. But I'm sure she is my fated mate. I don't want to sound like a sap and tell you all the reasons why I believe that. But I think I know why she isn't transitioning, and I need to run it by you."

"Of course."

By her compassionate doctor's tone, it was obvious that Bridget was just humoring him. She'd already removed Tessa from her potentials list.

He pinched his forehead again. "Tessa has issues. I don't want to get into details without her being here or giving me her consent to talk about it with you." He sighed. "We haven't had sex yet."

Bridget looked puzzled. "What about the biting? How did you get so close to orgasm without having sex?"

Jackson tilted his head sideways and narrowed his eyes. Did the doctor need him to explain about the birds and the bees?

Her eyes widened, and she slapped her forehead. "Duh. I just didn't expect you to pull a Clinton. Oral sex is sex, you know."

He chuckled. "We are not even there yet, but we've done some heavy necking. When that's all there is, it's enough stimulation to get my venom glands primed."

"And you think that's the reason?"

"Yeah. Maybe the bite works together with intercourse or something. Some hormonal interaction. I'm not a doctor or a scientist, but it makes sense to me."

"Hmm..." Bridget tapped her keyboard with one finger without typing anything. "According to Annani's stories, the Dormant girls of her time transitioned from just the bite. But it was done at the peak of puberty. Perhaps that's why it was enough. The adult Dormant females that transitioned under my care were all sexually active with their mates. The biting was congruent with not only intercourse, but also insemination. You might be on to something."

Jackson slumped in his chair, his arms dropping to his sides. "Thank you. You've just given me hope."

Bridget smiled. "You're welcome. It's only a hypothesis though. Time will tell. By the way, is Tessa getting professional help with those issues you mentioned?"

"No. She refuses."

"You should encourage her to at least talk to your mom. Whatever trauma Tessa has been through, it should be treated by a professional."

"I suggested seeing either my mother or one of her colleagues, but Tessa vetoed it. I'm not pressuring her because she is making progress without any outside help. In the beginning, she couldn't tolerate any intimacy at all, not even a kiss. Things are much better now. I learned the trick is to go slow, holding back even when she wants to push forward, and not scare her or overwhelm her. Patience is the key."

Bridget put a hand over her heart. "You're such a sweet guy, and so mature for your age."

The tips of his ears tingled in embarrassment. Jackson didn't like compliments like that. He wasn't doing anything special. If he wanted a future with Tessa, there was no other way. He didn't volunteer for the task out of the goodness of his heart. He was doing it for selfish reasons. Helping the woman he loved to heal was like helping himself, and no one would've called him sweet for that.

"Did I embarrass you?" Bridget asked. "I'm sorry. It's just that I envy you a little."

"Envy me? Why?"

"I envy your youth. Only the very young can love with such passion. Your heart is still wide open, and you gaze with hope upon the future. I'm jaded. Even if I found my true-love match, I don't think I could fall so deeply in love."

"What about Bhathian and Eva? Syssi and Kian?"

She nodded. "Yeah. I guess it's a lot like having a first baby. No matter how much everyone around you gushes about their love for their children, you can't imagine the intensity and the power of that love until you hold your own child in your arms."

Jackson lifted both hands in the air. "One thing at a time, doctor. I'm only eighteen. All this talk about babies is freaking me out."

Bridget laughed as she rose to her feet. "Let me escort you out. I'm going to the café." She waited for him to join her then threaded her arm through his.

The mighty doctor was petite, the top of her head reaching a few inches below his shoulder. Jackson smiled down at her. "You would like Tessa. She is tiny, like you."

Bridget wasn't as skinny, though, and had flaming red hair. But he was smart enough to know it wasn't something a guy should remark on. Women took offense to the silliest of things.

Jackson liked females of all shapes and sizes, and in his eyes beauty didn't equate with skinny or tall, or the other way around.

Her lips pursed in mock affront. The doctor managed to look down her nose at him even though she had to crank her head way up. "The correct term, young man, is vertically challenged."

He snorted. "Good to know. I'll keep it in mind."

# 7

# BRUNDAR

*P*arked on the street across from Calypso's house, Brundar heard her husband's irate voice. "What do you think you're doing?"

"I'm filling in paperwork."

"What for? I thought we agreed that you're not going to waste your time studying a worthless profession like teaching." His voice got louder.

"I know. But what if I can get several scholarships that together will cover the tuition? I can still work my shifts at Aussie and make the same money I'm making now."

"And what about the house? Who is going to clean and cook, huh?"

"I've been managing that just fine with work and classes at the community college."

"No one is going to give you money so you can play at being a student. But by all means, go ahead and play pretend. Maybe you should buy a lottery ticket too. Who knows? Maybe you'll win?" he mocked her.

*Asshole.* Brundar didn't need to delve into the guy's sick mind to know what this was all about. It wasn't about money, or Calypso earning less as a teacher than as a waitress. It was about control. A moment later Brundar heard the door slam, then the garage door lifted and Shawn backed his fancy car into the street.

It was so tempting to arrange an accident. All Brundar had to do was project an illusion, something that would cause the jerk to hit the brakes, put the car into a spin, and hit a tree. The problem was that the neighborhood was new, and the trees were mere saplings.

The lamppost wasn't sturdy enough either.

Besides, Brundar couldn't do it. He was a Guardian, a law enforcer, and arranging an accident was the same as murder. Regrettably, Shawn's behavior and nasty intentions didn't justify an execution.

Not yet.

The problem was that when they did, it would be too late.

Calypso's husband was a sick fuck. She needed to leave him as soon as possible and run as far away as she could.

If he could only talk to her and convince her of that. But knocking on her door and getting invited inside wasn't happening. She wouldn't remember him. Calypso had seen Brundar only once, almost a year ago, and he'd made sure to muddle her memory of the entire incident before sending her on her way.

The garage door opened again, this time to let Calypso out.

Brundar frowned. Why was she wearing the steak house's red T-shirt on her day off?

The girl must have switched shifts with another waiter again. She'd been doing it a lot lately. Probably to get out of the house and away from the abusive jerk.

*Verbally abusive*. Brundar ordered his fangs to retract. Shawn hadn't abused her physically yet, that was why he was still alive. Nevertheless, he was systematically squashing her spirit. But one of these days, he was going to snap and hit her. With men like him, once that mental barrier was breached it never went down again.

Brundar couldn't let it happen.

It was time to take action.

He would follow Calypso to work, walk in as a customer, order a steak, and strike up a conversation while gently returning her memory of their first and only meeting.

But what if the reminder embarrassed her, and she refused to talk to him?

Trying to get into a kink club and getting thrown out because she was underage at the time probably wasn't her proudest memory.

What if she wanted to forget about it?

He could always take a peek at her mind and gauge her reaction, but it was a dishonorable thing to do. An invasion of privacy. The clan had very strict rules about what, when, how and why it was allowed.

The rules of conduct Brundar lived by were even stricter.

Protecting the clan and the secret of its existence was basically the only reason thralling a human was allowed. Not that everyone adhered to the letter of the law. But as long as the thrall was minimal and not done to gain an unfair advantage, it was considered more of a misdemeanor than a criminal offense.

He'd done it himself before, but it was to protect her, not for his own benefit. Brundar couldn't claim that defense in this case.

Driving slow, he got to the Aussie Steak House a few minutes behind Calypso and parked his car at the other end of the restaurant's parking lot, as far away from her Honda as he could.

There was a small chance Calypso might recognize his car from the many times he'd been parked across the street from her house. Continuous shrouding took a mental toll, and sometimes he'd been too tired to bother. Besides, even if Calypso had noticed the same car coming around and parking next to one of her neighbors' houses once or twice a week, she probably assumed he was their guest.

Pulling a leather string from his pocket, Brundar gathered his hair back in a tight ponytail and tied it. He liked eating steaks, but not smelling them on his hair.

Aussie was a trendy steak house. Even at seven in the evening on a weekday, there was a twenty-minute wait. Brundar slipped the hostess a twenty, asking to be seated in Calypso's section, took the pager she'd given him, and went back to sit in his car. There were class schedules to check, updates to read, and once it was all done he even had time to catch up on the headline news before the pager went off.

The hostess escorted him to his table. "You look so familiar. Are you an actor?" she asked as she handed him the menu.

He got it a lot. It was the hair. He reminded people of a character in that *Lord of the Rings* saga—the elf guy with the pointed ears.

"No." He opened the menu, making it clear that the conversation was over. It was pointless to humor people with lies or idle chitchat. A simple no didn't waste anyone's time.

"Well, enjoy your dinner." The hostess sounded cheerful despite what she must've perceived as rudeness. The girl probably assumed he was an actor who didn't want to be bothered.

From behind the large menu, Brundar observed Calypso interacting with the other customers. The bright smile she offered everyone wasn't faked even though she had no reason for smiling today, or the day before, or the one before that.

Her husband was a mean and angry jerk, and between her classes, work, homework, and keeping the house the way the asshole liked it, she had no time for friends.

Or maybe she was just reluctant to have anyone she knew meet Shawn and witness how he was treating her.

As she got nearer, Brundar's breath caught in anticipation, but then she stopped by the couple sitting one table over, and he had to wait a moment longer.

Damnation, the girl was making him nervous. He couldn't remember being so anxious in centuries.

*Bloody battles? Bring them on.*

*Outnumbered and surrounded by enemies? No problem.*

Before Calypso had entered his life over a year ago, Brundar hadn't needed to slip into the zone to be at his best. He'd lived in it. A well-oiled, efficient, killing machine who experienced no fear, no hatred, no emotion at all.

It had been his shield, staving off mistakes, keeping him alive, and making him invincible.

But one young woman had managed to ruin all that. She was stirring a storm of emotions within him that he had no idea what to do with. Between one spying visit and the next, he had to work hard on blocking thoughts of her and getting back into the zone.

Being here, talking to her would only make it worse. He should just get up and go.

*Too late.*

She was coming over, that bright smile of hers searing him like a beam of sunshine on a vampire.

"Good evening, sir. What can I offer you to drink?"

"Whiskey."

"Sure thing. Which one would you like? We have Johnnie Walker, Chattanooga, Jameson, Crown Royal, Jim Beam, Chivas Regal, and Jack Daniel's."

"Chivas."

"Neat?"

"Is there any other way?" Ice cubes had no place in a whiskey. It wasn't a bloody soda.

She smiled. "You've got it. Some bread to munch on while you wait for your steak?"

"How did you know I was going to order a steak?"

She tapped her temple. "I'm a mind reader."

Strange, she was teasing, not intimidated by him at all. That didn't happen often.

Calypso laughed, the sound going straight to his balls. "Just joking. It's not like there is anything else on the menu, and you don't look like the type who orders an appetizer salad."

"No, I'm not." He debated whether he should release her memory of him now or later. "You look familiar. I think we've met before."

She put a hand on her hip. "Yeah, you look familiar too. But that's probably because you look a lot like Legolas."

Brundar frowned. "Who?"

She rolled her eyes. "The elf prince from *Lord of the Rings*."

He nodded. "I've been told that before. Though the only thing we have in common is the hair."

She looked a little closer, examining his features. "You're right. You're much better looking than Orlando."

"Who?" He was starting to sound like a broken record.

"Didn't you see the movie? That's the name of the actor who played Legolas. I used to have a huge crush on him."

It was good she'd used the past tense. Otherwise...

What? Why was it even bothering him that Calypso liked that Orlando guy? "I don't watch movies," he grumbled.

"Well, you should watch that one and see why everyone thinks you look like him."

"Do we have the same eyes?"

As Callie bent down to take a closer look, he trapped her gaze and went in.

Sifting through a year's worth of memories took time, but he was good, speeding through them as if it was a fast forward movie and taking care not to peek at the many scenes flashing by. Not only to protect her privacy, but also to save himself from seeing things that would incite him into a murderous rage. No amount of self-talk and restraint would save Shawn then.

He held her captive for a good two minutes before finding the one buried memory he needed to flush out.

When Brundar released Calypso, she swayed on her feet, her hand going to her head. "Wow, where did this headache come from?"

He got up, ready to catch her if she fell. "Do you need to sit down?"

She shook her head. "No, I'm fine. It was just a weird moment. It's already getting better." She lifted her eyes to him. "Now I remember where I've seen you before. You were the guy at that club…"

He pretended surprise. "That's why you look so familiar."

# 8

# CALLIE

*The guy from the club.*
She should've remembered him. Not only was he the best-looking man she'd ever seen, but the circumstances of meeting him were quite memorable.

Except, for some reason, everything from that night had been hazy.

Shawn hadn't remembered much either.

Maybe they had both suppressed the details of the episode because it was an uncomfortable memory. Getting thrown out like a couple of trespassing teenagers had been embarrassing, and they hadn't even made it into the kinky area. The receptionist had refused them admission into the nightclub that everyone else over twenty-one could get into.

After that night, things had been good between Shawn and her for a while, so maybe that was the reason she'd pushed that memory into some dark corner of her mind where it had joined other unpleasant moments she wasn't keen on remembering.

At the time, Callie had hoped that they were on the right track, that they had reached a turning point and that their marriage was going to survive. But the good times hadn't lasted long. Shawn's anger tantrums had returned and then worsened. It had taken her a while, but eventually she realized that more than an expression of his inner turmoil and fury, the tantrums were a tool meant to intimidate her and control her.

"Did you ever try again?" the guy asked.

She knew he didn't mean going to a nightclub. Callie shook her head. "No." She was spending way too long talking to this customer, Brad, if she remembered his name right. A quick, friendly chitchat was part of her job description, but this conversation was going places she'd rather not talk about in the middle of the restaurant. "Did you decide on a steak?"

Brad didn't look at the menu. "The largest you have. Medium well."

"Fries or mash potatoes?"
"What do you recommend?"
"We are famous for our mash potatoes."
"Then that's what I'll have."
"Anything else I can get you?"
"Food wise, no. But I would like to talk to you after your shift ends. If you're so inclined," he tacked on at the end as if remembering to mind his manners.

Callie wasn't sure about that. He was a stranger she'd only met once before and under peculiar circumstances.

Was he safe?

Logically, no, he wasn't. Take away his good looks, and his demeanor was straight up creepy.

And yet, her gut told her differently.

Or was that her hormones?

He was incredibly attractive.

"My shift ends at midnight. I'm sure you have better things to do than waiting around for me." She collected his menu.

He caught her hand. "I only want to talk. We can sit out on the patio and have a drink. I checked, and the bar stays open until two in the morning. We will not be alone out there."

She shrugged as if it didn't matter to her one way or another, but the truth was that his offer was more than enticing. She wanted to sit out on the patio with him and talk, find out more about this mysterious man. "If you're there when I'm done, I'll stay for a few minutes."

"That's all I'm asking for, Calypso."

Callie smiled a fake little smile and walked away on shaky legs.

He remembered more about her than he'd let her believe. Her name tag said Callie, the name everyone knew her by. She'd told this stranger her real one a year ago, and he remembered. Which meant he'd been faking the whole 'you look familiar' thing. He knew exactly who she was.

She should stay away from him.

What if he was a crazy stalker?

*Yeah, right. And he waited almost a year to approach me.*

*Not likely.*

Why would a movie-star-gorgeous guy stalk a Plain Jane like her?

He wouldn't.

Maybe his strangeness was the result of a personality disorder?

Who talked like that?

Clipped answers spoken in a flat computer-like voice. Heck, the text-to-speech on her phone sounded more human than Brad.

Maybe he had a speech impediment?

She shouldn't be afraid of him because of a disability. As someone who had dreams of teaching kids with learning difficulties, she should be more open-minded than that.

When she brought him his drink, Callie made sure to serve it with a smile. "Here you go, Brad. It's Brad, right?"

For a split second, he looked uncomfortable. "That's the name I use in the club."

*Okay?*

*And?*

At that point, any normal person would have offered the name he wanted her to know him by.

The guy was definitely on the spectrum.

She should encourage him. "What's your real name?"

"Brundar."

For some reason, she thought it fitted him better. A warrior's name. Not that she knew what it meant, but it sounded like it. "Is it Nordic?"

"Scottish." He said it with an accent.

She was a sucker for foreign accents, especially Scottish. "It's a good name. It suits you."

He nodded in agreement.

"I'll go check on your steak."

He nodded again.

Not a man of many words.

When he was done with his meal, Brundar rose to his feet, put cash into the padded folder she'd handed him, and walked outside without saying a word to her.

Spectrum or not, the guy definitely needed help with his social skills.

Unfortunately, she was in no position to offer him or anyone else help. Not until she resolved the situation with Shawn.

---

As her shift drew to an end, Callie got nervous.

Was he going to be there?

Waiting for her?

God, she hoped he was.

Brundar was such a mystery. The man she'd remembered from the club was self-assured and dominant in a way that had resonated with her on a primitive wavelength of sexual attraction.

Maybe that was why she'd suppressed the memory of him? At the time she'd still thought of herself as a married woman who shouldn't have naughty thoughts about another man.

Nothing had changed about his looks, he was still sinfully attractive, but he wasn't projecting as much dominance as he had that night. In fact, she sensed vulnerability in him, and that resonated with another facet of her—the caretaker.

In short, she was confused as heck.

"Callie, are you just going to stand there? Go home!" Katharine slapped her arm.

Right. She'd zoned out in the middle of the employee break room, standing like a zombie with her purse in her hand and her jacket draped over her arm.

She smiled at her friend. "Goodnight, Kati."

"You too. Are you okay to drive? If you're not, I can take you home after my shift ends in an hour."

"Thanks, but I'm fine. I just have a lot on my mind."

"Yeah, just make sure you pay attention to the road and don't zone out while driving."

"I will."

But not right away.

First, she would indulge in a rendezvous with the mysterious guy waiting for her on the patio.

# 9

# BRUNDAR

Out on the patio, Brundar sat with his back to the other diners, thinking about Callie, or Calypso as he preferred to call her.

The two names represented two different aspects of her personality.

Not personas. She wasn't pretending to be one thing and then another. They were more like modes she was switching between depending on the situation. Most people did it to some degree.

There was that saying about a perfect wife human males liked. A lady in the living room, a cook in the kitchen, and a harlot in bed, or something crass like that.

Maybe that was what he was observing.

But he had a feeling that Calypso's demarcation lines were clearer and deeper. The partitions she erected between the different roles she assumed were thick and solid.

Not that he was such an expert on human emotions, but she was so different here from how she was at home. Yet another reason to free her of the asshole she'd married. Hopefully, Brundar could persuade her to leave the jerk. Otherwise he would have to kill him—and the clan's penalty for murder was entombment.

Nevertheless, one way or another he was going to make sure Calypso was free.

Her time was running out.

He felt her the moment she stepped out on the patio and turned around to look at her.

"Hi, you waited," she said.

Brundar cast her a puzzled glance. "I said I would."

"You did."

He stood up and pulled out a chair for her.

"Thank you." Calypso draped her jacket over the back of the chair and sat down. "But often enough people don't mean what they say or change their minds."

"Not me."

She smiled. "No, I guess you don't. With how little you say, I bet you mean every single word."

"I do."

Damnation. He was so used to talking in monosyllables that it was difficult for him to articulate his thoughts in complete sentences. He needed to do better than that if he wanted a sliver of a chance convincing Calypso to listen to him.

Looking at him expectantly, she was waiting for him to say something.

"Are you twenty-one yet?" He knew she was, but that was the first conversation starter that popped into his head.

"Yes. I turned twenty-one a couple of months after the incident."

"Why didn't you try again? Did I scare you away?"

Not that he would've allowed her inside the lower level even after she'd turned twenty-one. At Brundar's prompting, Franco had changed the minimum age to twenty-eight for anyone seeking admission to the lower level. Another club in town had been involved in a case of minors using fake identification, and Brundar used it as an excuse to raise the age to one that would be more difficult to fake.

She shook her head. "No. It's just that things came up and experimenting was the furthest thing from my mind."

"So you didn't go to other clubs either?"

"No. I dropped the whole thing. It was a silly idea to begin with." She blushed and looked away.

"How about your husband? Didn't he want to try again?" The last thing Brundar wanted was to hear about that jerk, but he needed her to start talking about her marriage.

Her cringe spoke louder than words. "Believe it or not, it was my idea, not his. He didn't want to go that first time, and after what happened, I never mentioned it again."

As with everything else in her life, Callie had shelved her needs and wants in the pursuit of marital peace. She must've been so frustrated, and not only sexually.

He leaned forward and clasped her hand, surprised again by the urge to do so. It had been the same the first time they'd met. When Calypso didn't pull away, allowing him the small touch, it encouraged him to say something that was too personal for people who'd just met. "You can't ignore your needs forever. It's like letting a part of you wither away and die."

Sucking in a breath, she leaned away from him. "It's a choice, not a life necessity or a compulsion. I don't have to have it."

Her naïveté was endearing.

"Would you say homosexuality was a choice?"

Taken aback, Callie's eyes widened. "Of course not. But it's not the same."

"That's where you're wrong. Denying yourself because you think you should, or because others don't understand it, is not going to make the need go away. As long as it is not harmful, emotionally or otherwise, there is nothing wrong with wanting something different with another consenting adult."

Calypso crossed her arms over her chest. "Wow. I was under the impression that you have a problem expressing yourself, but evidently I was wrong. Did you have that speech memorized? Do you recite it to new club members?" She kept her voice low, casting worried glances at the people sitting next to them.

Her outburst didn't offend him. Clearly, the subject was making her uncomfortable, and she was getting defensive.

Brundar leaned forward, making sure no one other than Calypso heard him. For her sake. Not his. "That's not part of my job. Do I look like someone who makes people comfortable?"

Her smile was back. "No, you don't. So what is your job? Are you the bouncer? The scary dude who throws undesirables out?"

"Sometimes, when those whose job it is are not available, or when the situation demands it. I'm not an employee of the club. I'm a member turned silent partner. It was an investment, a way to help out the owner and keep the business afloat. Except, I find myself doing things I didn't sign up for."

Why was he telling her all that?

Her eyes were full of understanding. "Of course you do. I'm surprised you expected it to go differently."

That was news to him. "What makes you say that?"

Uncrossing her arms, she leaned forward. "You're the kind of guy that takes charge," she said. "You can't just let things go and wait for others to fix them. You either tell someone to do it and then verify it's done or do it yourself."

He chuckled. "You're right. I should have known I'd get involved. Instead of buying half of Franco's business, I should've offered him a loan."

"But you didn't. Which means that subconsciously you wanted to change how he was doing things."

"You're a very smart young lady, Calypso. You figured me out."

# 10

# CALLIE

Callie snorted. "Right."

As if. She might have peeled away one layer out of a hundred. And the way he'd called her young lady, as if he was an old man and not a twenty- or thirty-something-year-old guy, was odd, but she liked it anyway.

Still, she knew her insight and his acknowledgment of it was no small achievement. Brundar wasn't the type who let people get close to him.

"It's true. I didn't realize it until you spelled it out for me."

She shrugged. "Glad I could help. Talking with others about things clarifies bothersome issues. While you're too bogged down by the minutiae, you can't see the big picture."

"Smart girl. Do you know how smart you are?"

She wasn't sure how she felt about him calling her a girl, but she liked the other part.

Well, she'd always gotten good grades, but book smart wasn't life smart, as evidenced by her ill-fated marriage. "I don't know about that. I did my share of dumb things. If I were so smart, I wouldn't be in the mess I am in now."

"Perhaps I can help. What is your minutiae, Calypso?"

A chuckle escaped her throat. "Mine is not a minutiae, it's a bigutiae. Here, I invented a new word. Does that make me smart?"

Brundar didn't laugh at her joke. Not even a tiny smile. What would it take for this guy to loosen up?

"Talk to me, Calypso."

She was tempted. Yeah, he was a stranger, but in a way that was easier. She probably wouldn't see him after tonight, and getting things off her chest might ease the vice constricting her lungs.

Taking a napkin, she wiped the table clean of a few drops of condensation. "I don't want to burden you with my problems. I'm sure you have enough of your own."

"No."

Again with the one-word responses. "No what? You need to talk in complete sentences to me. I know you can." Contrary to what she'd thought before, Brundar had proven that he had no speech impediment and no personality disorder. He was just a tight-lipped guy who was stingy with words.

"I don't have any problems."

"You see? That was a clear answer."

One corner of his lips twitched in a smile. "Yes, teacher."

Callie sighed. "I want to be."

"What's stopping you?"

"Not what, who. My husband."

"You want me to beat him up?"

Lifting her eyes, she was prepared to answer with a joke, but Brundar looked dead serious.

Was he acting?

She tilted her head, narrowing her eyes at him. "If I said yes, you would. Wouldn't you?"

"I always do as I say."

"Good to know." For some reason, his answer and the tone he'd used evoked a few erotic scenarios that had no place in this conversation.

Brundar's nostrils flared and he shifted in his chair.

Callie sniffed but detected nothing unusual. Not surprisingly, the steak house always smelled like steaks.

"What is it? What do you smell? Is it smoke? A few days ago, there was a brushfire nearby, and the wind carried the smell of smoke for miles."

He shook his head. "Not that kind of fire. Do you want a drink?"

"Sure. Another whiskey for you? I'll go get it." She started to lift off the chair.

Brundar caught her hand and pulled her down. "You're not working now, Calypso. Let others do their job."

"They are my friends. I'd feel weird ordering drinks from them. And besides, they all know I'm married. There will be a few raised brows."

"I'll order the drinks, and you can introduce me as your cousin."

Not a bad idea. That would kill two birds with one stone. Brundar would order them drinks, and she'd stop the rumors before they started.

"Where should I say you came from?"

Brundar spread his arms. "Scotland, of course," he said with a lilt.

"God, I love your accent," she husked.

Ignoring her comment, Brundar turned around and waved Kati over.

"Hello…" Kati looked from Brundar to Callie and back.

"Kati, meet my cousin Brundar."

Kati smiled and offered her hand. "Nice to meet you, Brundar, cousin of Callie who she never told me about and should have."

Callie rolled her eyes. Kati knew she wasn't supposed to flirt with customers. Especially not this one.

"Nice to meet you." Brundar didn't take her hand.

Some people didn't do handshakes—germophobes and the like.

Kati frowned and retracted her offered hand. "What can I get you, guys?"

"I'll have an apple ginger, and Brundar will have Chivas, no ice. Right?" Her cheeks warmed as she realized her faux pas.

He nodded.

"I apologize for ordering for you," she said after Kati had left. "I shouldn't have done it. It's a waitressing reflex."

"You knew what I wanted, so why not?"

Why not? Because if she'd done something like that to Shawn, he would have thrown an anger tantrum.

"As long as it's okay with you."

"It is. Back to my offer. It still stands."

"Thank you, but no. It won't solve my problems. I need to get a divorce, that's all."

"What's stopping you?"

Where to begin? And did she want to pour her heart out to this sexy stranger? Not really. He would think her weak. He would ask why she hadn't left Shawn a long time ago.

Brundar wouldn't understand.

Callie didn't consider herself weak for staying, she considered herself strong. Quitters ran at the first sign of trouble, and Callie was no quitter.

But she wasn't blind either.

All the effort in the world wasn't going to fix what was wrong in her marriage because nothing and no one could change another person. Shawn was who he was and she couldn't see herself enduring him for the rest of her life, or worse, having children with him.

*Someone kill me now.*

"Calypso?" Brundar snapped her out of her head.

"I'm sorry. I zoned out a little. I was thinking of how to answer that in a way that wouldn't portray me as the victim." She looked away. "I'm not weak, you know."

He took her hand. "I know you aren't."

The sound of truth in his words was like a benediction, his hand offering comfort and support she hadn't had in forever. Regrettably, a moment later he dropped her hand.

Fast.

Kati came back with the drinks.

"Apple ginger for Callie, and a Chivas no ice for Brundar." She put down the drinks. "Anything else I can get you?"

"No." Brundar's one-word answer was delivered in such a commanding tone that Kati dropped her flirtatious smile and beat feet back inside.

"You don't have to be so rude to people," Callie blurted.

"I'm not rude. I'm efficient."

"It's not what you think that matters, it's how your communication is perceived."

"Don't try to fix me, Calypso."

Oh shit. Now she'd made him mad. Instinctively, Callie shrank back in her chair. She saw a flash of anger in his blue eyes, but it was gone in a split second.

"I hate to see you scared like that. Does that jerk you're married to get violent with you? Does he hit you?"

She shook her head and grabbed a napkin. "No. But if I tell him I want a divorce he will."

In the moment of strained silence that followed, Brundar took the napkin out of her hands and clasped them. "Trust your instincts, Calypso. You need to leave. The sooner the better. Don't tell him your intentions. Go out the door and hide somewhere safe until the divorce is final."

"There is nowhere safe," she whispered. "Shawn knows that there are only two people I can turn to. My father and my friend Dawn. He'll find me. But that's not the worst part. If I go to either of them, I'd be putting them in danger. I'm afraid of what he'd do." She looked into Brundar's pale eyes. "I don't know why I fear him so. Other than destroying our house he never hit me. And yet I expect the worst."

"As I said before, trust your instincts. You need to run. I'll help you. I'll hide you and protect you until you're free of him. You'll be safe with me."

She narrowed her eyes at him. "Why? Why would you do that for me? You don't know me." People didn't just offer help out of the goodness of their heart. There was always a hidden agenda, an ulterior motive.

Brundar closed his eyes as if she was tormenting him. "I don't know why, Calypso. But I know I'd protect you and shield you with all I have. And trust me when I say that there is no one in the world who can do a better job of it than me. That's what I do best."

"You're a bodyguard?"

"Yes, that's exactly who I am. The best there is."

From anyone else, it would have sounded like boasting, but she knew that Brundar was just stating facts as he saw them.

"I need to think about it. I need to get an appointment with a lawyer, so I know what to expect. The problem is that Shawn monitors every penny I spend and tracks my every movement." She lifted her phone from her pocket. "He has this tracked. And you know what? I don't mind because when he knows where I am at all times, he has fewer reasons for exploding. Like now. He thinks I'm still working because the signal is coming from the steak house. That's how I can sit here and talk to you without worrying."

"You'll have to leave your phone here while I take you to a friend of mine. Edna is a great attorney. She can answer all your questions. But if you want my opinion, you need to run first and do everything else later. The longer you stay, the more dangerous it is for you. Go to the bank, take all the cash you can, leave your credit cards and your phone at home and drive off. I'll meet you somewhere where you can leave your car, and I'll take you to a safe place. Edna will take care of the divorce papers. Clean exit."

No one went to so much effort to help another unless they were family, or they wanted something. But that didn't make sense. Brundar could've snapped his fingers at Kati, and she would've gone home with him. Heck, if Callie weren't still married she would've gladly accepted an invitation too.

Brundar was sexy as sin. But she was done letting her hormones lead her astray. That was what had gotten her in trouble in the first place. She'd thought Shawn was sexy too, and that didn't end well.

Not at all.

Once she got free, she should find herself a nice guy, an accountant or an engineer or a teacher. Someone mellow and agreeable with whom she could have a nice, peaceful life.

Contrary to what Brundar believed, sex wasn't all that important.

"What are you thinking, Calypso? What's going through your head?"

She looked up and gazed upon his perfect face. Sincere blue eyes the color of a clear sky were tracking her every movement, every expression. He probably knew what she was thinking just from observing her so intently.

"What do you want, Brundar? For real. Because for the life of me I can't understand why you would go to all that trouble to help me." She had the passing thought that he might be after her money, telling her to empty her bank account and take all the cash she could before meeting him. Without a phone or money, he could leave her somewhere stranded.

"I want to set you free."

"Why?"

"Because I have to."

"That's not an answer."

"That's the only answer I have. If you're asking whether I'm attracted to you, the answer is yes. You're a beautiful, smart, and kind woman. Do I expect anything in return for my help? The answer is no. Even if offered freely, I would turn you down, or at least try to. Is that a full and satisfactory answer?"

"Yes." Not really, but she wasn't about to tell him she suspected him of staging a heist.

"When is your next shift?" Brundar asked.

She found herself answering him even though she was still suspicious. "Thursday. Same time. Five in the evening until eight, an hour break, and then until midnight when the kitchen closes."

"I'll be here for your break. Have an answer ready for me."

"I can't decide so quickly."

"You can, and you will. It's not complicated. If you want to leave him, that's the only way to do it safely. Don't procrastinate, Calypso. The first rule of survival is to strike fast and strike hard." He punched his fist into his other palm. "No hesitation, and no mercy."

"No mercy," she repeated.

## 11

# RONI

Entwining the fingers of his hands behind his head, Roni leaned back in his throne-like chair.

The backdoor he'd programmed was working beautifully. He'd been testing it over the past week with no alarms going off.

As long as the current security protocol was used, he had nothing to worry about—at least for a couple of years. The guys upstairs hated making changes. A new system cost millions and wreaked havoc until every last issue got debugged.

The question was what he would do once it was eventually changed, because it would be changed. The race between the hackers and the protectors made it an unavoidable necessity. Every time the hackers gained an upper hand, the protectors had to come up with new solutions, and the race began anew, keeping everyone in business.

Through the glass enclosure, Roni glanced at his handler. The guy wasn't so bad. Most of the time he was just bored. Not that Roni could blame him. Babysitting him was a job an agent got as a punishment for a major screw-up, or in Barty's case failing the physical exams.

On purpose.

Barty was tired and wanted more time at home while still earning an agent's salary, not the reduced retirement pay.

As unbelievable as he found it, Roni realized that he was going to miss Barty. He'd gotten used to the sarcastic old goon.

But no more excuses.

It was time to leave this prison that had become his home and give Andrew the green light.

Roni was going to relinquish his seat of power for an unknown future.

He was scared shitless.

Scared of getting out into the real world he'd never been equipped to handle, scared of having to interact with people other than agents, most of whom were old enough to be his parents.

Would he have to shop for groceries? Take care of his own laundry? Roni had no idea how to do all those basic things that came naturally to other people. He understood code. Real life baffled him.

Most of all, though, he was terrified of Anandur. The guy was a giant, and not the gentle type. Sure, he was friendly, even funny sometimes, but he had muscles on top of muscles and knew how to use them. There would be pain even if the guy did his best to hold back and treat Roni like a fragile little girl.

Roni didn't like pain.

So what if he was a wuss. He had no problem admitting it. Brains were worth more than brawn, especially one like his. There were plenty of goons on the planet, but only a handful of geniuses.

The only problem he had with that was Sylvia.

No woman wanted her guy to be a weakling. Even Einstein's wife had divorced him. Not necessarily for that reason, but who knew. Maybe.

With a sigh, he pushed out of his chair and walked out of the glass enclosure that was his war room. It was dojo time.

"You're ready, Barty?" Roni asked his handler.

"Yep." Barty put his feet down. "Let's go, boyo."

"Where is your karate-gi, Barty? Didn't we agree that you would join the class today? You can't participate unless you wear the uniform." Roni loved teasing the guy.

"Up yours," Barty returned the favor. "While you are sweating, I'll be watching the girls. It's the highlight of my week. Just so we're clear." Barty pointed a finger at him. "I'm counting on you to stick with this class. If you dare quit on me, I'm going to pull you there by your overlarge ears."

"My ears are not big." They weren't. He had normal ears. Didn't he? Maybe they stuck out a little… Roni couldn't help himself, touching them to make sure.

"Just kidding. Don't take everything so seriously."

"You're not funny. What happened, did you run out of jokes?" He was counting on Barty's lame jokes to distract him from thinking about what was waiting for him in the dojo.

*Think about lots of sex with Sylvia.*

That was his main impetus for going ahead with the crazy plan. Immortality was not Roni's top priority. Sex with Sylvia was.

Especially since she claimed his stamina would quadruple. Roni smirked. They would be going at each other like rabbits.

"What kind of bagel can fly?" Barty started as soon as he eased the car into traffic.

Roni rolled his eyes. "A plane bagel. Ha, ha."

"You heard that one before?"

"No. It's so stupid a four-year-old can guess the answer."

"Okay. How about this one. What does one plate say to the other?"

"I don't know."

"Come on, boy genius. Dinner is on me." Barty laughed at his own stupid joke. "Get it? Dinner is on me." He demonstrated with a palm up as if Roni needed visuals to understand it.

"Not funny."

"I have a smart one for you. What do you get if you divide the circumference of a pumpkin by its diameter?"

"Pi."

"Yeah, but what kind?"

"There is only one kind of pi. It's a number."

"Wrong. You get pumpkin pie." Barty's huge belly heaved along with his snorts.

That was a little funny.

The best part about Barty's jokes was that they filled the time until they arrived at the dojo, and for a few minutes Roni had forgotten about the giant redhead with huge muscles and scary fangs.

"Hey, guys," Sylvia said. "How are you doing, Barty?" She gave him a hug and kissed his cheek, as always, and her friends lined up to do the same.

Barty was in heaven. Roni felt a pang of guilt. The dude was going to miss all the attention he was getting from the young hotties—as he liked to call them.

If he only knew...

"Roni! Over here!" Anandur called.

*Oh, boy.* Were his knees shaking?

"Are you ready?" Andrew asked.

Reluctantly, Roni nodded.

"Okay!" Anandur clapped his hands. "Let's do it. It's actual sparring time."

Barty tilted his head, looking at Anandur and Roni with interest. The jerk probably wanted to see Roni getting annihilated by the red giant.

Any traces of guilt for the agent went *poof.*

Roni imagined a boxing ring with the announcer going, "*In this corner, we have the Red Giant, and over there is the Scrawny Chicken! Which one is going to win?*"

"Barty, I have a funny story for you." Sylvia plopped on a chair next to the handler. "So, yesterday..." In less than a minute, she got him enthralled in her story.

Anandur got in position and motioned for Roni to do the same. They circled each other for a few moments, with Roni bracing for the pain and Anandur waiting for God knew what.

Finally, Anandur stopped and put his hands on his hips. "I can't do it." He waved a hand at Roni. "How am I supposed to get aggressive with that?"

Andrew shook his head. "Wait until he opens his mouth. Show him what you got, Roni."

Roni flipped him the bird. If Andrew thought he was going to goad Anandur he was dead wrong.

"You'll have to do it, Andrew," Anandur said.

"I've never done it before."

Anandur chuckled. "Oh yeah? Should I give your wife a call?"

"You're such an asshole. I mean with another guy."

Anandur feigned shock, his fingers splayed over his gaping mouth. "You don't say. You don't know what you're missing." Anandur batted his eyelashes.

Roni chuckled, enjoying the show. Now, that was funny.

Andrew looked like he was about to punch Anandur, but then thought better of it. Smart man.

Waving a finger at the big guy, he said, "I've heard about you and your antics. I'm not going to get tricked into issuing a challenge to spar with you."

Anandur pointed a finger back. "That's a shame. Because you could've gotten me worked up, tough guy."

"Oh."

"Yeah, oh. You either man up and do it, or I'm calling Brundar."

Andrew looked horrified. Who was this Brundar guy that his name made the formidable Andrew cringe?

"Not Brundar. Are you nuts? The kid will shit his pants."

"He's the only one on duty right now. It's either you or him."

With a deflated sigh, Andrew hung his head. "I'll do it." He then turned to Roni. "Make me mad, kid. You don't want the alternative."

They assumed positions and started circling each other. Andrew wasn't as scary as Anandur, but he was a big guy too with at least eighty pounds over Roni's one hundred and thirty.

The easiest way to annoy the guy was to say nasty things about his wife. "How is the old ball and chain, Andrew? Still finds you attractive? I bet she is sick of waking up to the sight of your ugly puss every morning…"

Andrew was on him in a blur of movement, and before he knew it, Roni found himself face down on the mat, one of Andrew's hands pinning his arm painfully behind his back, the other on his neck, holding his head down.

If he could, Roni would have rolled over and offered his vulnerable belly, but in lieu of that he stopped struggling and closed his eyes.

Andrew hit fast like a cobra, which was a mercy because the anticipation was worse than the bite…

On second thought, no. The bite hurt and burned like a son-of-a-bitch, for about two seconds.

And then there was bliss.

## 12

# BRUNDAR

*P*arked across the street from Calypso's home, Brundar kept a solid shroud around his car. Not so much to camouflage the vehicle as the driver. She remembered him now, and seeing him there would understandably scare her.

As it was, she was rightfully suspicious of his motives. He was sincere and meant every word he'd told her, but she wasn't a mind reader or an empath who could check the veracity of his words. Suspecting an ulterior motive was natural, and proceeding with caution was smart.

Offering her his help had seemed so natural, the right thing to do, but her questions made him realize that he might have not acted out of pure altruism. He wasn't in the habit of helping random people.

What was in it for him?

Brundar wasn't sure. Emotional entanglement wasn't something he was familiar with. As was the case for all his clansmen, his interactions with women were purely sexual. Before he'd found a solution to his particular needs in the clubs, he'd never had the same one twice, and more often than not he'd paid for the services. For a price, most hookers agreed to get tied up and blindfolded, which wasn't the case with the vast majority of nonprofessionals. Relinquishing control to a stranger was stupid, and most women had more sense than that.

The clubs, at least the good ones, provided a safe environment. What Brundar disliked about them were the labels attached to the different sexual roles people played. As an immortal male, dominance came naturally to him, but it didn't define him. It wasn't who he was.

It just happened that his specific needs fit the role.

He didn't need his partner's obedience, and he didn't need her to be subservient to him. All he needed was to tie her up so she couldn't touch him and blindfold her so she wouldn't see his glowing eyes and protruding fangs.

But contrary to popular belief, it wasn't all about his needs.

The women he partnered with in the club had needs of their own, and it was his responsibility to meet them. Brundar was fine with delivering pain when needed, but it didn't turn him on. Or off.

What did it for him was the immense pleasure his partners derived from it, and the heights they reached with his help. According to some, subspace was better than any drug-induced trip, and a lot healthier.

That state was unattainable for the vanilla crowd or those holding the flogger or the paddle. The rewards were only for those on the receiving end. The exchange of power was well worth it.

For him, though, there was another fringe benefit that was even more important than the satisfaction he derived from pleasuring women into soaring up into subspace. When tied up and blindfolded, soaring on a cloud of post-orgasmic euphoria, his partner was oblivious to his bite, which he usually delivered to her inner thigh. Later, when she came down, there was no sign of it. She either didn't remember it at all or thought that the small pain was part of the scene.

No thralling required.

A big advantage since most of the women he partnered with were regulars. Still, he tried to keep the frequency to a minimum. Brain damage from thralling wasn't the only risk. Emotional entanglement was an even greater one. The intensity of the acts, the highs and the lows, played tricks on the participants' minds. As cold and as detached as he was, Brundar wasn't made from stone.

The most he'd scened with the same partner was once a month. For their sake and his. In case his stoic attitude wasn't enough of a deterrent, playing with a variety of partners sent a clear message that he wasn't interested in a relationship.

It wasn't that he didn't care; on the contrary, he was doing his best to protect their feelings. His partners trusted him to see to their pleasure and their well-being, and he was very serious about ensuring both. But that was the extent of his obligations. Nothing more.

With Calypso, the emotional entanglement was already there, at least on his part. Not to mention that she was a green-as-grass newbie who needed a slow and gentle introduction that should be spread over several consecutive sessions with someone who knew what the fuck he was doing. She had no idea what she liked or didn't like, what scared her and what excited her. The only way to find out was to experiment. But only with someone who was patient and completely focused on her and her experience.

It was an intimate and emotionally intense journey, necessitating a prolonged relationship. Trust, which was a crucial component, wasn't built in a day, or a week. Under these circumstances, preventing a bond from forming was difficult for the initiator as well as the initiated.

He could do none of that. Even if a relationship between an immortal and a human was possible, Brundar didn't have what it took.

The problem was, he couldn't conceive of anyone else introducing Calypso to that unique brand of pleasure either.

It would drive him insane.

He had to distance himself from her. After her divorce was final and she was free, he would sever contact with her and let her make the journey of discovery on her own. Not in his club, though. He'd provide her with a list of others that were just as good—small, tame, and with long-term members who'd been properly vetted.

"What's that?" Brundar heard Shawn asking.

Up until that moment, the only sounds coming from Calypso's house belonged to the football game Shawn was watching, and the intermittent bursts of commercials.

"Oh, it's nothing. I'm filling in applications for scholarships. Who knows? Maybe I'll get lucky and collect enough to cover the tuition? I heard that it's good practice to apply to as many as I can. A few small scholarships can add up. I probably won't get anything, but I thought it was worth a try."

Brundar approved. She was pretending a dismissive attitude toward her wish to attend the university, which should make the scumbag happy.

Shawn snorted. "You're wasting your time. No one is going to give you money. I don't know why you even bother. College education is worthless these days. I'm doing perfectly fine without it."

Aha. That was the crux of it. Shawn didn't want his "little wife" gaining a college degree because he didn't have one.

Asshole. Just for that Brundar should slit his throat. Hell, slicing his head clean off would be even more satisfying.

Why in damnation had Calypso married someone like that?

She seemed like a sensible woman, insightful, a good judge of character. Tomorrow he would ask her what prompted her to say yes when she should've said hell no and run as fast and as far as she could.

Had she ever loved him?

Had Shawn charmed her into believing that he was worthy of her love?

Her youth and innocence must've blinded her.

How old was she then?

Eighteen?

Nineteen?

Truth be told, at that age Brundar was already a hardened warrior, but then his innocence and naïveté had been shattered years before. He was only twelve when he'd learned his lesson the hard way. Sometimes evil was so well masked by a charming face that even the most guarded and suspicious couldn't detect it until it was too late.

To this day, the betrayal hurt more than the violation that had followed.

Closing his eyes, Brundar brought up the memory that had been forever playing on a loop in his head. It was what had kept him training when every muscle burned with fatigue and he could barely move his legs. When anyone else would have collapsed from exhaustion, the anger had given him the extra fuel needed to push himself harder.

That memory had helped shape him into the lethal weapon he was.

He had to become invincible.

Fates, he'd been such a soft boy. A gentle soul that wouldn't have harmed a butterfly. No wonder the human village boys had called him a girl.

His looks hadn't helped either.

He was too pretty for a boy, they'd said. He should've been born a girl, they'd teased. He was a mistake. A freak.

Lachlann had been the only one who befriended him, probably because he'd been as much of an outcast as Brundar, though for different reasons that Brundar had been too young to understand at the time.

His mother had told him to stay away from the human boys. She'd told him they were up to no good. But like every other teenager throughout history, Brundar hadn't listened.

As the only boy in their small community of immortals, he was lonely. Besides, at the time he was still a human. At twelve, he'd had an entire year ahead of him before he could transition.

Anandur was a grown man, a warrior, who'd considered Brundar a nuisance —a kid too scrawny and weak to bother even with sword practice.

"You should think of becoming a scholar," Anandur said. "You don't have the heart of a warrior."

Brundar chuckled. He'd proven his brother wrong and then some. Not only was he a warrior, he was the best. And as for his heart? It beat steady in his chest during the most vicious of fights.

Calm, cold, calculated, and lethal.

But he hadn't been born this way. He'd been made. A living proof that even the lowliest of beginnings can produce a champion.

There was a price to pay, but Brundar hadn't minded giving up his so-called humanity. It was a good thing. He had done so gladly. Humans were traitorous, deceitful, and cruel.

Not all of them, but enough.

"Let's go fishing," Lachlann offered.

Brundar would've loved nothing better than to join his best friend at the lake. "I cannae. My mam forbids it."

"Do ye always do what your mam tells ye?"

"I dinnae." Brundar puffed out his chest. "Wait for me by the lake," he told Lachlann. "I'm going to sneak out."

He'd lied. Brundar had usually listened to his mother, and to Anandur. But to admit it would've made him look even more of a wuss than everyone had accused him of being.

He'd waited until his mother went out, grabbed his fishing pole, and sprinted for the lake.

Sitting side by side on a big rock protruding from the shallow water, Lachlann and Brundar waited patiently for a fish to get hooked like they had done many times before.

Lachlann had moved a little closer, draping his arm over Brundar's slim shoulders.

"You know you are my best friend? Right?"

"I know. And you are mine."

"You have such pretty hair." Lachlann grabbed a fistful of Brundar's chin-length hair and brought it to his nose. "You smell nice too."

Brundar shrugged. "I wash myself."

"I know. I saw you."

*"So?" That summer, they had swum naked in the lake almost every day. All the boys were doing it with nothing on.*

*"Nothing." Lachlann dropped Brundar's hair.*

He should've seen the signs, but he hadn't known about things like that yet. Brundar had had a good idea about what went on between a man and a woman. Living with animals, most everyone had those days, but not that the same could happen between two men.

# 13

# CALLIE

Just as he'd promised, Brundar walked into Aussie exactly at eight, turning everyone's heads, men and women alike.

It wasn't every day that a gorgeous man with waist-long, pale-blond hair walked into the restaurant. He looked more like a movie star or a rocker than a bodyguard. But that was only upon casual observation. Those who dared to look at him for a little longer noticed his hard expression and cold as ice gaze, quickly averting their eyes.

There was a deadly aura around him that should've terrified her, but instead it made her feel safer. Brundar was putting all that lethal power at Callie's disposal. He was going to hold her within the bounds of that aura, where no one and nothing could hurt her.

There was no safer place for her than at his side. Or behind his back. Whatever spot worked.

The question was what price he'd demand for his protection services. Frankly, she would be more than happy to pay up. Whatever he wanted was his.

In fact, she was hoping he would make the demand and was afraid he wouldn't.

"Are you ready?" Brundar asked, not bothering with a hello.

*Efficient, not rude*, Callie reminded herself.

She'd already transferred the care of her customers to another waiter and was ready to go on her break.

"Hi, and yes, I'm ready."

He nodded.

"Do you want to sit out on the patio again?"

He nodded again.

Today Brundar was communicating with even less than the monosyllables from the day before yesterday. Was it a sign of stress? Was he more talkative when relaxed?

Callie hoped she would get to know him well enough to figure that out.

"Come on." She threaded her arm through his.

For a moment, he looked surprised, glancing at her hand on his arm, but then pulled her a little closer so their sides touched, but not as close as a lover would.

Out on the patio, she found them a table in a semi-secluded corner, signaling Suzan, whose shift had just started, that she was claiming it.

With a wink, Suzan gave her the thumbs up.

Her astute coworkers weren't buying the cousin from Scotland story.

"Are you hungry?" she asked Brundar.

"Always."

Callie waved her friend over. "My cousin would like to order dinner."

Suzan pulled out her best smile for him. "What would you like?"

"Your largest steak, medium well, mash potatoes, and a Chivas."

"Excellent choices, sir. And for you, Callie?"

"A mojito, but tell Tony to make it light. I still have a shift to finish."

"Anything to eat?"

"No, thank you."

"Perfect. I'll get your drinks."

"Have you decided?" Brundar asked the moment Suzan was out of earshot.

The guy didn't beat around the bush and neither would she. He'd probably get annoyed if she did. "Yes. I'm going to take you up on your offer."

His stoic mask slipped for a moment, showing relief. "Good."

"I have a few concerns, though, that I would like to run by you."

"Naturally."

"My father and my best friend. How do I ensure their safety? The first place Shawn will look for me is at my father's and then at Dawn's. What if he threatens them? Or worse, harms them?"

"It's a valid concern. Where do they reside?"

"My father is in South Carolina, and Dawn in Massachusetts."

"Good. It means that Shawn would have to buy a plane ticket to get to either of them. I have a friend who can put an alert on him."

Brundar sure had useful friends, but it wasn't surprising given what he did for a living. He probably had the whole protection thing figured out.

"Just out of curiosity, how is your friend going to do that? Don't you have to work for the government?"

A smile tugged at the corner of Brundar's lips, which in his case meant that he was very amused. "Who said my friend is not working for the government?" He leaned closer and whispered, "He'll flag your soon to be ex-husband as a suspected terrorist."

Callie chuckled. "I love it. It's perfect."

Suzan arrived with their drinks and a bread basket. "I'll have your dinner ready in a few minutes." She winked. "I put a rush on it."

"You're the best, Suzan."

"I know." She sauntered over to the next table. "What can I get you, folks?"

"Any other concerns?" Brundar asked.

She sighed. "Where do I start?"

"The order doesn't matter."

Sheesh, the guy was so literal. "Where do I stay? What about my car? What if Shawn goes to the police and files a missing persons report? Where will I work? How will I get to work if I don't have a car? And if I find work in another restaurant, will he be able to find me there?"

"I'll find you a place to stay."

"Where?"

"Leave it to me. I know a lot of people. I'll ask around if anyone needs a house sitter."

"What if no one does?"

"Then I'll give you a room at the club."

*The kinky portion?*

Not something she was comfortable with, but as the saying went—beggars can't be choosers.

"I don't want to dump all of my problems on you, but I really don't know what else I'm going to do. It would've been so much simpler if I didn't need to hide. But I know I do. I'm going to take half of what's in our savings account, but it's not much. I need to work."

"You can work at the nightclub. Serve drinks. I'll have Franco pay you cash. The car is not a problem either, the same person who needs a house sitter will probably have a car idling in the garage. You can borrow it until the divorce is final."

If it all sounded too good to be true, it probably was.

But what choice did she have?

It was either accept the help or stay with Shawn and be miserable and scared for the rest of her life.

The deciding factor was that she felt safer with this stranger than with her husband.

Brundar was dangerous, even lethal, but not to her and not to any other decent person. His enemies, however, or any who earned his wrath should be terrified.

The problem was that she was basing it all on a gut feeling, and it was difficult to read a man who displayed no emotions. Brundar's usual expression was an impassive mask, and when he spoke, it was in a flat tone with no inflection. In a movie, he could've played the part of a robot. She was betting her safety on the little glimpses of humanity she'd caught, and a sixth sense that was telling her Brundar wasn't evil.

Shawn, on the other hand, reeked of it, metaphorically speaking. Not from the very start, though. When she'd first met him, he was just a bully who pushed and manipulated to get his way.

He'd changed. Was he on something? Was he doing drugs?

She knew for a fact that on occasion he'd lied about going to work and had gone someplace else. He wasn't making as much in commissions as he used to either. Lately, his pay had dwindled down.

Was that the reason for his nasty moods? Men associated their self-worth with success at work. Maybe he was feeling insecure and taking it out on her?

Except, the decline in earnings had started about the time she'd given up, and Callie no longer cared. Besides, confronting him about it would have resulted in another temper tantrum.

"Calypso? Are you with me?"

She shook her head. "Yes, I'm sorry. Where were we?"

"The last item on your list of concerns. Shawn reporting you missing. You call your father and your friend and tell them you left and that you fear for your life. He'll call them, looking for you. They'll tell him that you left."

And incur his wrath.

But Brundar had this covered too. They would have plenty of advance warning if Shawn made travel plans.

Callie let out a breath. "Okay."

"When?"

"A week from now. Will you meet me here?"

"What time?"

"Five. When my shift is supposed to start. I'll stop by the bank on my way and take out half the money. I'll leave my phone here. Shawn will think I'm at work. It will give me a few hours' head start."

"Why take only half? You're leaving everything else behind. Shouldn't you take more?"

Callie shook her head. "If I could afford to, I would have left that behind as well. The fewer reasons he has to come after me the better. I'm not going to ask for anything in the divorce settlement either. I just want my freedom."

# 14

# BRUNDAR

On his way back to the keep, Brundar went over the list of things he needed to prepare for Calypso by next Thursday.

First, he needed to rent her an apartment or a house, furnished if possible and if not, do it post haste, and plant fake personal items to make it look as if it belonged to someone who was coming back, giving it a lived in look.

As it was, she had a hard time accepting his help. He needed to keep up the façade of a Good Samaritan who wanted nothing in return.

A lie, because he wanted her like he'd never wanted a woman before, but that was beside the point. He wasn't going to act on it. Not even if he were human or she an immortal. He wasn't what she needed and would never be.

The thing was, it would be impossible to convince Calypso of that if she ever found out that he'd lied to her about the friend who needed a house sitter, and rented an apartment for her instead.

The car was a problem. He could buy her one, but his name would appear on the registration. Unless he asked Kian for another set of fake papers, or Anandur to buy it for him.

Brundar didn't want his brother or anyone else from the clan involved.

Another possible solution was to find her a place to live within walking distance of the club so she wouldn't need a car.

Or maybe he could give Franco the money and ask him to buy it as part of her compensation package.

Yeah, like that wouldn't start a thousand questions.

As it was, they didn't need another waitress in the nightclub, and he was not letting Calypso anywhere near the basement level, even if she weren't way under the new age limit they insisted on.

What he'd said about giving her a room in the club was another lie. If by next week he still didn't have a place for her, he'd put her in a hotel.

It wasn't that Brundar felt the club was inappropriate for Calypso; she could probably benefit from hanging around there. Franco didn't allow public scenes, and everything happened in private rooms. The public area was a place to hang out and talk with others, with the benefit of being able to discuss openly experiences, preferences, and lifestyles. Different classes were held almost nightly.

Members could learn bondage techniques, and get introduced to the latest toys and their use. Classes were held on everything from proper etiquette and safety measures all the way to lectures on the psychology and physiology involved. Most were taught either by Franco or other experienced club members, but on occasion Franco brought in guest speakers.

Brundar himself had learned a thing or two over the four years he'd been a member.

The real reason he didn't want Calypso there was that she wasn't ready. It would be a long time before she felt safe enough to trust a man again. Her bad experience with Shawn had to fade first.

Except, it might not.

Time didn't do a thing for Brundar. He still didn't trust anyone aside from Anandur, and he didn't trust his brother with everything either.

Brundar's experience, however, had been much more traumatic, which might explain why he needed complete control in sexual situations. Hell, who was he kidding? There was no situation he could think of where he could let go, but it was most apparent with sex.

Brundar liked his partners tied up, blindfolded, and facing away from him.

Everything else was negotiable. But not that.

If a woman refused his demands, he walked out.

Needs and wants didn't always align, and that was fine. He respected the hell out of those who were clear on what they wanted and didn't want and weren't afraid of saying no.

It still left many who liked what he had to give, as evidenced by his popularity. Brundar never had a shortage of willing partners or repeat requests. Within the limitations of what he would and wouldn't do, he left his partners fully satisfied and craving the next time.

He, on the other hand, was always left with a sense that something was missing. Brundar suspected the culprit was his muted ability to feel. Even casual sex required some sort of connection, which he was incapable of.

He was hollow, empty, untouchable, and it went deeper than the physical level.

*Brundar lifted the bundle of five fish strung together with a length of twine. "'Tis enough," he said. "I should be getting back before my mam notices I'm gone."*

*Lachlann cast him a sidelong glance, a strangely unsettling expression making him look older than his thirteen years. He was smiling, but it was not a friendly smile. "Not yet. A few more."*

*The small hairs on the back of Brundar's neck prickled. Something was not right about Lachlann. His friend was not himself today. He seemed twitchy.*

*"I cannae. I need to go." Brundar rose to his feet, balancing on the smooth rock by gripping it with his toes. "You keep the fish." He dropped the bundle next to Lachlann.*

*His friend looked up at the sky, his eyes following the sun's position. "Aye, you are right.*

'Tis time to go." He grabbed the fish in one hand and his pole in the other, and stuffed the jar of bait into his pocket.

The uneasy feeling didn't abate as they traipsed through the forest heading toward the safety of Brundar's home. Instead, it intensified. Lachlann's eyes kept darting left and right as if he was afraid of a bear or a wild boar coming at them.

Lachlann hadn't been expecting wild animals. He'd been expecting something much worse.

*Several older boys emerged from behind the trees, the evil smiles on their faces portending trouble.*

*Brundar's instincts kicked in. "Run, Lachlann!" he shouted at his friend as he broke into a sprint. If he made it back home to Anandur and his two uncles, he would be safe.*

*"Run, little girl, run as fast as ye can, but we are gonna catch ye!"*

*Brundar ran faster, ignoring the tree branches slapping at him and tearing into his skin, but the boys were gaining on him. He could hear them getting closer. His only hope was that Lachlann had gone the other way.*

*Lachlann was a fast runner. Mayhap he would bring help...*

*But the first hand grabbing at him and shoving him face down onto the ground, the heavy body landing on top of him, and the strong hands pinning his arms behind his back, shattered that hope.*

*Brundar froze in shock as a familiar voice whispered in his ear, "I know you want it, bonnie lass. Ye've been asking for it for a very long time and I'm gonna give it to ye real good."*

*"Lachlann? What are ye doing?"*

*Brundar started thrashing anew, trying to buck off the body on top of him. Lachlann was only a year older. He could take him...*

*"Grab his hands!" Lachlann called out.*

*Someone did.*

*Brundar fought, but there were too many of them.*

*He was helpless.*

At first, Brundar had thought they were going to kill him, or beat him up, but he couldn't understand why. He hadn't done anything to any of them.

His first inkling of what was coming had been Lachlann pulling Brundar's pants down.

*"Dinnae do it, Lachlann, I am yer friend, please!" He wasn't above begging, even though he knew it wouldn't help.*

*"My bitch, ye mean. And 'tis time ye put out."*

*Brundar felt something thick press against his rear hole.*

*"Nae!!!" he screamed as his body got violated, the pain unimaginable. He hadn't known such pain existed.*

And then it had gotten worse.

## 15

# TESSA

*E*very muscle in her body aching, her light exercise shirt soaked through with sweat, Tessa felt amazing.

"Okay, girls!" Karen clapped her hands. "Listen up! Your homework is lifting weights. You are all pitifully weak."

Several of the women dared to snort and giggle.

"Pitiful, I tell you!" Karen repeated with more oomph. "Here is a printed page with all the exercises I want you to do between classes, and I don't want to hear any excuses like, 'I didn't know how'." She imitated a valley-girl whiny tone. "It has pictures." She lifted the flyer and tapped it with a finger, then stared each of them down. "Understood?"

"Yes, Karen," they all replied in unison.

Tessa rolled her eyes. Karen had told them all about her military background, but it would've been obvious even if she hadn't.

The 'Yes, Karen' was a lot like 'Yes, commander,', and Karen insisted they say it after each instruction. Serving three years in the Israeli army as a fitness trainer of an elite commando unit, she'd developed the attitude of a drill sergeant.

She treated the women in her Krav Maga class as if they were warriors and not a bunch of out-of-shape suburbanites. Karen was dead serious about teaching them real self-defense, the kind that might actually work against rapists and other abusers. It wasn't fancy, it wasn't pretty, and it wasn't sportsmanlike.

The merciless fighting style went against every feminine and compassionate instinct they had.

It was crude but effective.

A set of skills that could save lives.

"Eva was smart to wiggle out of it." Sharon wiped her face with a towel. "The pregnancy is just an excuse. Pregnant women can exercise."

Tessa knew the real reason for Eva's refusal to join the class was her unnatural strength, but she couldn't share it with Sharon. The same way she couldn't share Eva and Bhathian's romantic love story, or that it was not going to be their first baby, and that their older daughter was already a mother herself. It was hard to be the keeper of secrets. Especially when she had to keep things from people she cared about.

Hopefully, Nick and Sharon would be paired with nice immortal partners soon, and be told about their potential dormancy.

"How are you doing, girls?" Karen slapped Tessa's back.

"Great. Everything hurts, but in a good way."

Karen beamed with satisfaction. "You'll see. By the time I'm done with you, you'll be able to take down guys twice your size. Krav Maga teaches real fighting skills. It's not an elegant dance like martial arts, but it gets the job done."

"That's why I'm here. I want to kick ass."

Karen smiled like a proud mother. "Good for you." She clapped Tessa's shoulder, then repeated, "Good for you."

She did it a lot, repeating words and whole phrases in her guttural and harsh accent, often more than twice.

"How about you, Sharon?"

"Oy vey." Sharon groaned.

Karen laughed, slapping Sharon's back much harder than she had Tessa's. "Hang in there. My mission is to turn women into fighters, so they are victims no more. Understand?" She looked into Sharon's eyes.

"I do, I really do." Sharon was too smart to get into an argument with Karen.

Their neighbor didn't hold back punches—the verbal kind. Tessa suspected the woman could knock any of them unconscious with one jab.

Karen nodded. "It's not easy, and not only because women are not as strong as men. Women are softhearted. They don't want to hurt anyone. And what do they get for it? They get hurt instead. So be strong, be merciless, and protect yourself. Understand?"

"Yes, Karen." They both answered as one.

"As you were, ladies." Karen turned on her heel and walked up to another group.

"Sheesh, bossy woman," Sharon whispered in Tessa's ear.

"I like her. Heck, I want to be her. Imagine going through life with that much confidence and attitude. I bet no one ever dreams of messing with Karen."

Sharon pulled her shoes out of the cubby and slipped them on. "Not me. I don't want to look like her. She has more muscles than most of the guys I date, which is disturbing. Besides, imagine the endless hours of training that went into that body. Karen is a natural athlete. Neither one of us is."

"I know. And that's a shame." Tessa would not have minded a strong body like Karen's, even if it made her look more masculine. The confidence and absence of fear would've more than compensated for a little loss of femininity.

As she put on her shoes and followed Sharon out of the studio, Tessa filled her lungs with the cool evening air. It was dark outside, but for once she didn't feel a tightness in her chest when stepping into a darkened street. "You know what's weird?"

"What?" Sharon clicked the locks open.

"It's only my second class, and I already feel different. Not as fearful." She chuckled. "I'm no longer a shaking Chihuahua. I graduated to a fluffy poodle."

"Woof, woof. Congrats." Sharon turned the engine on.

"Thank you."

"Are you going to Jackson's tonight?"

"Yeah, why?"

Sharon shrugged. "It's late, that's all. Why don't you invite him over to our place? He can spend the night. You guys can sleep together, as in actual sleep. Should be nice."

"Yeah, much better than trying to squeeze onto Jackson's couch. But my room is sandwiched between yours and Nick's, and the walls are thin." Tessa felt her cheeks get warm.

"That's how you wanted it."

"I know. But things are different now. I'm not as scared anymore. Especially with Bhathian in the house."

Sharon chuckled. "How much of a badass you think he really is? All those incredible muscles could be just for show."

"Trust me, they are not for show."

"Well, he does work for some law enforcement agency, right?"

"Yes."

Sharon huffed out a breath. "Fine. I know you're all keeping secrets from me, and I'm kind of sick of it. But whatever."

Guilt churning in her gut, Tessa didn't respond.

"Can you at least tell me what the deal with you and Jackson is? Do you love him? Does he love you back?"

A week ago she would have been afraid to admit it, but after two of Karen's classes in which woman power was infused in every move and every sentence, Tessa felt a little bit like a badass herself.

"Yes and yes."

"How about, you know..." Sharon waggled her brows.

Tessa blushed and shook her head.

Sharon cast her a sidelong glance. "What are you waiting for?"

What indeed?

Sharon didn't know the whole story. She might have suspected what Tessa had been through but not the extent of it. Nevertheless, she was right.

Tessa forced a smile and fibbed a little. "I'm waiting for the perfect moment."

"If you ask me, the Nike commercial got it right: just do it." She winked at Tessa. "Just do it, girl. Just do it," she repeated, parroting Karen's harsh accent.

Good advice.

Tessa pulled out her phone and texted Jackson. *How about you come over to my place and we spend the night together in my comfortable BIG BED.*

A moment later he texted back. No words, just three emoticons: a thumbs up, a heart, and a smiling face.

# 16

# JACKSON

Jackson put down the phone, wondering what had prompted Tessa's invitation. They had talked about him coming over to her place before but had decided against it.

His place offered more privacy. But on the other hand, Tessa had a larger room and, what was more important, a larger bed. Up until now, the only night she'd stayed over at his place had been that one time she'd fallen asleep on his couch. He'd ended up sleeping on the floor because there was no way they could both squeeze in there. Tessa was tiny and didn't take up much space, but he did.

Jackson had thought about buying a mattress to replace the couch, but that was before the option of having a brand new house at the new development had come up. There was no point in buying new furniture when the houses came furnished with much better things than he could afford.

Besides, he didn't want to put pressure on Tessa, and a new bed might have done just that.

Should he bring a change of clothes and a toothbrush?

It wasn't as if he was moving in.

In the end, he packed a bag, deciding that he was going to leave it in the car. In the morning, while everyone was still asleep, he would retrieve the bag, take a shower, put on a fresh change of clothes, and put it back in his trunk before anyone woke up. Or, he would just drive back to his place and shower there. But then he would miss a chance to have breakfast with Tessa.

As he turned into her street, Jackson saw Tessa sitting outside on the steps. He parked and got out.

"What are you doing out here?" Sitting next to her, he wrapped his arm around her. "Did you change your mind?"

"Not at all. But I didn't want you to knock or ring the bell. Sharon and Nick are out, and Eva and Bhathian are in their room. You can sneak in with no one any the wiser."

Jackson frowned. "Why do I need to sneak in? Are you embarrassed about me staying over?"

She shook her head. "No. But I don't want to answer questions or endure the smirking looks. I'm sure you don't either."

Jackson shrugged. "I don't mind. They are going to know eventually. Unless you want me to sneak out in the early hours of the morning." He cocked a brow.

"I don't. When they see you at breakfast, it's going to be like stating a fact. You slept over. End of story. Somehow it's different."

"I'll probably be gone by the time anyone wakes up. I need to be at the coffee shop before seven."

"I'll just tell them that you stayed the night after the fact."

"Eva and Bhathian would know. Did you forget? Immortal hearing."

"It's not as if I want to hide it. I just want to avoid the looks."

"In that case, I'll go get my overnight bag from the car. I was planning on sneaking out in the morning for it."

Tessa snuggled closer. "You see? We were both thinking along the same lines. Way to make me feel guilty for nothing."

He kissed the top of her head. "I'm sorry. I'm looking forward to spending the night with you. Even if it's just to hold you close."

Tessa lifted her head with the sexiest come hither smile he'd ever seen on her. "I have plans for much more than cuddling."

Jackson was hard in an instant. "Oh, yeah? What plans?"

She humphed. "I'm not going to tell you. What's the fun in that?"

Was she talking about going all the way?

Damn, curiosity was eating at him. "Let me get my bag."

Tessa waited as he retrieved it from his car, holding the door open while he climbed the three steps.

"Let's keep it down," she whispered, taking his hand and pulling him behind her up the stairs.

With a slight hitch in her breath, she opened the door to her room and motioned for him to go ahead.

*Oh, wow.* Tessa had been busy.

Soft music was playing, and several lit candles cast their gentle glow on the room. On one nightstand, a bottle of wine and two glasses sat on a tray, and on the other a platter of cut fruit.

She'd gone all out preparing for tonight.

"Come here." He dropped his bag on the floor and pulled her into his arms, lifting her up for a kiss. He did it a lot. With their height difference and how little Tessa weighed, it was more comfortable for both of them. Besides, he liked to kiss her while holding her up.

Especially since it seemed to turn her on. But this was the first time she had lifted her legs and wrapped them around his torso, returning his kiss with abandon.

Sexy as hell.

Carrying her to the bed, he sat down with her still wrapped around him. Except, now that he didn't need to hold her up, his hands were free to explore. Reaching under her loose T-shirt, Jackson cupped her perky little breasts over her flimsy bra and kissed her again.

Tessa moaned into his mouth, her hips moving restlessly and rubbing against his groin. A moment later she grabbed the bottom of her T-shirt, pulled it over her head, and tossed it to the floor.

Jackson buried his nose in the valley between her breasts, inhaling her sweet feminine aroma mingled with the strong scent of her arousal.

Her small hands cupping his cheeks, Tessa lifted his head and kissed him again, her tongue sliding inside his mouth.

Jackson's eyes felt like rolling back in his head. Never before had Tessa been so assertive, so demanding, and it was hot as hell. But was she pushing too hard? Going too fast?

"Slow down, kitten. There is no rush," he murmured into her mouth.

"Says who?"

With her lips red and swollen from their kisses, and her eyes glazed with desire, she'd never looked more ready. And yet, Jackson hesitated. He'd read her wrong before.

It was so easy to get swept away in her desire and enthusiasm, but he knew better now. Tessa's limits were in flux, and if they weren't careful, she'd overreach only to get snapped back to the starting point.

"Says I." He took her shoulders and steadied her. "I love your passion, and I would like nothing more than to get you naked and under me, but I'd rather take it slow and steady, so you can have all the time you need to process every little step and decide if you're ready for the next one."

With a sigh, she leaned her forehead on his. "You're right. But I feel stronger now, and I want to get a little further. I want you to see all of me. Touch all of me. And I want to do the same to you. Can we do that?"

"Of course, baby, but slowly."

She shook her head. "I don't want slow."

"What if I show you how amazing slow can be?"

Lifting her head, she nodded. "Show me."

The yearning and hope in her eyes as she said that made Jackson anxious. He wanted to give her every pleasure imaginable, but he'd just set the bar up high. What if she expected more than he could deliver? What if he disappointed her?

Closing his eyes, he shook the momentary insecurity off. He wasn't an inexperienced virgin. He knew what he was doing and had a well-earned reputation as an extraordinary lover. Quite an achievement for a guy his age. But then it always felt as if he was born to provide pleasure. The knowledge was almost instinctive.

With deft fingers, Jackson unclasped Tessa's bra and slid the straps down her arms, removing the last barrier between him and her bare breasts. His fangs elongated at the sight of her sweet little nipples, pebbled with need and aching for his touch.

Slowly, he extended his tongue and licked around one, then the other, then went back to the first one and sucked it carefully into his mouth, making sure not to nick it with his fangs.

On a moan, Tessa arched her back, stretched her arms behind her and put her hands on his knees to brace herself. There was nothing timid or unsure about the blatant invitation, and it made Jackson's heart swell with gratitude.

His Tessa was healing.

With a hand between her shoulder blades, he held her to him firmly as he licked and sucked until she was squirming in his lap, her little mewls getting louder and more demanding.

His kitten needed more.

With his hands still on her back, he lifted her off his lap and laid her on the bed. "Ready to take these off?" He tugged on her leggings.

"Yes." No hesitation.

He hooked his thumbs in the elastic band and pulled down. Pulling off her panties and leggings slowly, one inch at a time, Jackson gave her every opportunity to stop him the moment she felt uncomfortable.

As Tessa lifted her butt off the bed, making it easier for him to continue, Jackson pulled a little faster, hungry for his first glimpse of her fully naked.

His breath caught.

She was completely bare.

Tessa hadn't been the last time he'd touched her under her panties.

"Do you like it?" she asked.

"I fucking love it. When did you do it?"

"Today. I wanted to look pretty for you."

He caressed her moist bare folds with the tip of his finger. "So smooth. Did you wax?" The thought made him cringe. She shook her head. "It was on the spur of a moment, so it's only a close shave. Next time I'll wax."

"Don't. I heard it hurts like hell." Just thinking about someone pulling on her soft and delicate tissues made him wince.

"But you like it, don't you?"

"I do, but not if it causes you pain." He smoothed the tips of two fingers down her center. "If you allow me, I'll gladly shave you here anytime you want." As far as he knew, immortal females had no body hair. But he didn't know if a grown Dormant lost it after her transition. He wasn't going to ask Syssi or Nathalie such an intimate question. As former humans, they might still hold onto human sensibilities. Besides, their mates would not be happy about him sticking his nose where it didn't belong. But he could ask Bridget.

Tessa moaned, her eyelids fluttering shut as an outpour of moisture coated his exploring fingertips. The idea excited her.

"I'd like that," she husked.

# 17

# TESSA

Tessa would've never expected Jackson's offer to give her such a delicious thrill. As someone with major intimacy issues, the idea of being exposed and vulnerable to him while he glided a razor blade over the most sensitive place on her body should have terrified her, but it didn't.

It was the sexiest thing ever.

She would be embarrassed, no doubt about it. Nevertheless, when it was time for the next shave, she would let Jackson do it. The ultimate gesture of trust would be the perfect gift for his patience and selflessness.

Hopefully, she wouldn't freak out. In her mind and in her heart she was more than ready, but her subconscious, which still bore the scars of her past, might interfere.

The bed dipped as Jackson climbed on and stretched on his side next to her.

For a moment, his eyes roamed her body, the hunger in them making her feel beautiful, desired. Under his gaze, Tessa didn't feel too small, or too skinny. She didn't feel like a scared little girl. Jackson's burning desire brought out the woman in her.

The one she was born to be—confident and strong.

"I'll never get my fill of looking at you," he said, his fingertips tracing the line from her shoulder down to her arm.

As he reached the inside of her elbow, the sensation part ticklish, part arousing, she shivered in anticipation. Tessa wished for his knuckles to brush against the side of her breast, and then for his warm palms to cover her wet, hard nipples. But he'd done none of that, leaving her aching with need.

Was it deliberate?

A way to ramp up her desire by depriving her of touch?

She arched her back a little, hoping he'd get the message.

Jackson chuckled. "Not very patient, are you?" He dipped his head and took the nipple closest to him between his lips, his fingers closing around the other.

Fire shot from the twin points of pleasure straight to the juncture of her thighs, her butt lifting involuntarily off the bed.

His breathing got heavier, and after a moment his hand abandoned her breast to scorch an excruciatingly slow path down her belly, skimming her hip and sliding around to her inner thigh.

God, would he touch her there already?

As his hand moved up in what seemed like increments of a fraction of an inch, her breathing got more and more ragged.

Jackson hadn't been kidding about going slow, or how good it would feel.

A most exquisite torture.

Tessa felt needy and achy, but there was something to be said for savoring every little touch, every sensation, for being acutely aware of the coil inside her tightening with growing want. The buildup of anticipation.

Instinctively, she knew that the slower he made the climb up to the steep edge of the cliff, the higher and longer she would soar when she leaped off.

When his fingertips finally reached her wet folds, Tessa's hips jerked up and her eyes popped open, straight into the twin pools of light Jackson's emitted.

"So beautiful." She cupped his cheek.

Drawing lazy circles around and around, he steered clear of her most needy place. "Would you allow me to kiss you there?" he asked.

Kiss her there?

It was something she'd only heard about. Did men actually do it for women? It wasn't another urban legend?

Tessa wondered if Jackson was the one in a million who was willing to pleasure a woman orally, or was it as common as women pleasuring men that way.

In the world of Internet pornography and open talk about sex, she was the anomaly. Ignorant though not innocent. Outside the safe bubble Jackson provided, anything sexual repulsed her.

Tessa didn't read about it and she didn't talk about it.

The downside was that she knew next to nothing about the different ways a woman could be pleasured. She was an expert on the reverse. Tessa knew all about the many ways men derived pleasure from using women with no regard for their pleasure or pain.

*Not all men*, she reminded herself. Not her Jackson.

"Am I going to like it?"

"I'll make sure you do."

"Then yes," she whispered.

Jackson kneeled on the bed at her feet and put a hand on either knee, applying light pressure to push them apart. "Don't be afraid. You're going to love it." He kissed each knee.

Quivering, her excitement tinged with a little apprehension, Tessa allowed her legs to part.

With a gentle push, Jackson spread them further and lowered his face, kissing the inside of one thigh, then the other.

As he kissed and nipped, working his way down, the tension inside Tessa coiled tighter and tighter, until she was sure she'd explode the moment he arrived at his final destination.

She was ready to scream when his mouth hovered ever so close over her quivering folds, pushing up to meet it, but he clamped his hands on her thighs and held her in place.

"Patience, kitten." He blew air on her overheated flesh, cooling it down a little before flicking the tip of his tongue to tease her folds, setting them on fire again.

The repeated cooling and heating was the most exquisite torture imaginable. Tessa was torn between begging Jackson to stop and begging him to continue.

It was hard to think when every nerve ending in her body tingled with sensation.

"Please," she begged for something, anything.

The next lick was followed by another and then another, delving between her folds and teasing them gently until suddenly his tongue drove inside her, catching her by surprise.

Tessa's hands fisted the bed sheet. "Oh, God, Jackson… yes…"

She was close. One flick of his tongue over the right spot and she would go off like a rocket.

As his tongue thrust in and out of her sheath, Tessa bucked and writhed as much as his gentle hold on her thighs allowed. The small part of her brain that still functioned realized that he was guiding her rather than restraining her movements and that she should follow his guidance because he knew what he was doing.

She whimpered as he withdrew his tongue, but then as he pressed the flat of it over that most sensitive bundle of nerves, her lower body surged up and she had to bite down on her lip to stifle the scream that built up in her throat.

Not moving his tongue, Jackson let her ride out the initial jolt of finally being touched there, waiting for the tremors to subside before replacing his tongue with his lips and delivering the gentlest of kisses.

So sweet, so loving, and so not what she wanted at that moment.

Or did she?

As she was discovering, Jackson was more attuned to her needs than she was.

The loving touch had brought the intensity level a notch down but provided priceless reassurance and a powerful sense of being cared for.

She probably needed this as much as climaxing, if not more.

His hands on her inner thighs moved to caress the muscles she hadn't known were tensed, and she relaxed even further, letting her buttocks unclench and rest fully on the bed.

The reprieve didn't last long, though. Apparently, Jackson's intention was to move her away from the brink so that he could bring her there again.

Closing his lips around her clit, he sucked gently and pushed a finger inside her. Her opening, which the swollen inner walls had made impossibly tight, stretched, and then he added another one.

Jackson's fingers working in tandem with his gentle sucking, he brought her back to the precipice and held her hovering above it for long moments.

Panting, head thrashing, sweat dripping between her breasts, Tessa was mindless with pleasure and the need to catapult over that edge. Once she did, she was going to shatter into a million pieces.

"Jackson…" she pleaded.

"I've got you, kitten."

He sucked harder and curled his fingers inside her, touching a sensitive spot she didn't know existed, bringing the pleasure to the point of no return.

Tessa erupted with a brilliant explosion of light behind her closed eyelids. It shimmered for a moment then flicked out of existence, and all she saw was darkness.

Later, when she came to, Jackson's lips were trailing a path from the hollow of her throat up to her mouth.

His kiss was gentle, appreciative. "Thank you," he whispered.

She cupped his cheek. "Why are you thanking me? I should be the one thanking you. It was indescribable. I didn't even feel your bite."

He touched her inner thigh. "I bit you there."

"But I climaxed like an exploding volcano before that. You're amazing."

Jackson couldn't have looked prouder if she had handed him a Nobel Prize. "Thank you for the gift of your pleasure. For me, there is nothing more precious. Except for your love, that is."

"Oh, Jackson," she whispered, tears stinging the back of her eyes. "I love you. More than anything."

## 18

## CALLIE

Yesterday, as she'd planned today's escape while keeping her mask firmly in place, must have been one of the toughest days in Callie's life, topped only by the day she'd lost her baby.

Keeping calm and pretending that nothing was going on had been so difficult. She'd pulled out the best acting of her life, but Shawn had been suspicious nonetheless.

The thing was, he was always suspicious, and with how nervous she'd been, Callie couldn't ascertain if he was acting more suspicious than usual or just the same.

She'd been relieved beyond measure when he'd left for work and had told her he would be late because they had a sales meeting after closing. Not trusting him, she'd called the dealership and talked to Shawn's manager. She'd asked him how long he thought the meeting would last because she was planning a surprise for her husband and needed to know when he'd be back.

That way she'd verified that there actually was a meeting, and made sure the manager wouldn't tell Shawn she'd called. Even if he did, it would be no big deal. Her excuse was good enough to fool Shawn too.

Callie chuckled.

He was in for a surprise all right. Just not a pleasant one.

As she packed her suitcase, it was quite shocking to see how little really mattered to her. She still remembered the care with which she'd chosen the perfect place setting and best bedding she could afford. None of that meant anything to her. In fact, other than the photo albums containing her childhood memories, she could've walked out in the clothes on her back and not missed a thing.

Callie hadn't taken much, packing only the newest and most useful articles of clothing, all of her photo albums, the books she'd purchased for her classes that had cost a bundle, her laptop, the little jewelry she owned, and miscellaneous toiletries.

She regretted not thinking ahead and scanning all those old photographs and storing them on a flash drive. Her suitcase would've been so much lighter.

Now all that remained was to call her dad and Dawn.

The question was which phone to use. It might have been paranoia, but she feared using the house phone or her cell. If Shawn was using her phone to track her location, it was possible that he was somehow tracking her calls as well.

A better idea was to wait and call from the restaurant's landline.

Taking one last glance at the home she'd shared with Shawn for close to two years, she felt nothing but relief as she stepped out the front door and locked it.

At the bank, she took out the seven thousand one hundred and thirty-two dollars that represented half of their savings. Stuffing the cash inside an old makeup bag she'd brought with her just for that purpose, she put it all the way at the bottom of her oversized satchel, then covered it with whatever else was there. Not much of a protection, but it was the best she could do.

Once Brundar picked her up, it would no longer be a concern. Her personal bodyguard was formidable enough to protect her and her money.

Arriving at the restaurant earlier than planned, Callie stashed the satchel inside her locker in the employee lounge.

"Hey, Callie. You're early." Suzan plunked her butt in one of the chairs.

"So are you."

Callie had arranged with Kati to take over her shift, but had asked her not to tell anyone. As far as everybody at the restaurant was concerned, Callie was working her shift as usual.

Paranoid or not, she refused to let seemingly unimportant details give her away.

Suzan stretched her arms. "Yeah. My mom got there early to babysit my kids, and I grabbed the opportunity to have a few quiet moments for myself, put my feet up, and read a raunchy romance." She pulled out her reader and propped it against the napkin dispenser on the table.

"Sounds like a plan. Enjoy."

Crap. Callie was hoping to have the lounge to herself when she called her father and Dawn with the news. Then an idea struck her.

"Suzan, can I borrow your cellphone? Mine is low on power."

"Sure thing. Just don't call China. My plan doesn't cover whatever is beyond the Great Wall." She winked as she pulled her new Nebula phone out of her purse and handed it to Callie. "Be careful with my baby."

"I will."

Now, where to call from?

The bathrooms were too public, and there were always a few tables occupied out on the patio, especially on a hot day like this one. She could either find a shaded spot out in the parking lot, or hide in the storage room.

Given the hundred-degree heatwave, the storage room seemed like a better choice.

Ducking inside, she went all the way to the back and sat on the floor in the little corner niche between the two tall shelving units housing the restaurant's miscellaneous cleaning and paper supplies.

She called her father first.

Huffing like she'd run the marathon, Iris answered. "Callie, how are you? Is everything all right? We haven't heard from you in way too long."

That was Iris's usual line of questioning. It had nothing to do with a sixth sense or anything resembling one.

"I'm fine. What about you? Did you run to the phone?" She didn't want to tell Iris her story and send a nine-months-pregnant woman into hysterics. Her father could relay the news later.

Iris snorted. "Me? Running? I get winded from climbing the stairs. And I'm talking about the five steps leading up to the front door, not the ones going up to the second floor. I regret buying a two-story house."

"Cheer up. Only a little bit longer, and then you're going to be a mommy."

"I know. You should see my ankles, though."

"What about them?"

"It looks like I don't have any. Anyway, I'm sure you didn't call to hear me kvetch. I'll put Donald on the line."

"Thank you."

"Hi, cupcake. How is the world treating my girl? Did you hear back from UCLA?"

Damn, it was going to be hard.

"I got in."

"She got in, Iris!" Donald called out.

"Yay!!" She heard Iris clap her hands. Her father's young wife wasn't best friend material, but she was a good person.

"When do you start?"

"I don't. Not yet, anyway."

"Why? Is it a money problem?"

"That's what student loans are for, dad. It's a Shawn problem."

Her father had never been thrilled about her marrying Shawn, but he hadn't been too distraught over it either. Donald had no idea how bad it had become for her. Not his fault, though. She didn't share her mistakes and failures with others.

Not even her father.

"What's going on, Callie?"

"I left him."

There was a moment of silence. "How did he take it?" By her father's tone, the news didn't come as a big surprise. He sounded worried. Which meant that he wasn't as clueless as she'd thought he was.

"He doesn't know yet. That's why I'm calling. I don't want you to freak out when he calls looking for me."

"Where are you going?"

"A friend is helping me out. I need to go underground, so to speak, until my divorce is finalized. I'm afraid of what Shawn might do to me when he finds out I left him."

"Tell me the truth, Callie, did he raise his hand to you?" Her father's voice quivered with anger.

"No. But he raged a lot and destroyed things. I felt it was only a matter of time before he turned that anger on me. I didn't want to wait around for it to happen. The last straw was when he refused to pay a dime for my studies, as if I wasn't working and had no say in it. He also refused to hear about taking out a student loan. I don't qualify for a scholarship, not with our combined earnings. But as a single woman, I might. And if not, I'll take out a loan."

"Do you need help? Iris and I can chip in for the tuition, and you can come stay with us until the storm passes."

His offer brought tears to her eyes. Just knowing that help was there if she needed it meant so much to her. "I'm good. I took out half of our savings and it should tide me over. But you and Iris need to be careful. I'm afraid that Shawn might go after you guys and after Dawn. He'll try to intimidate you into telling him where I am. Or worse, threaten to harm you if I don't come back to him."

"Don't you worry about us, Callie. I'll buy myself a shotgun and put a hole in that asshole if he comes anywhere near us. You can come here and I'll make sure you're safe."

Callie barely stifled a snort. Her father was incapable of harming a mouse, let alone a human being, and he'd never held a weapon in his life. Still, it felt good to hear him getting so protective.

"Thanks, Daddy. I really appreciate the offer, but it's better this way. As a precaution, I'm not going to call anytime soon, but I don't want you to worry about me. It's better that you don't know where I am. I'll send postcards. You get anything with a picture of a sunset, you'll know it's from me and that I'm fine."

Her father chuckled. "You are really going deep into cloak and dagger territory, aren't you?"

"Better safe than sorry, right?"

"Always."

19

# BRUNDAR

When Brundar arrived at the restaurant, Calypso was already waiting for him on the patio, a cocktail clasped in her hands. He glanced at his watch even though he knew he wasn't late. In fact, he was early.

"Have you been waiting long?" he asked.

"I was impatient."

"Understandable. Are you ready to go or do you want to finish your drink."

"No, I want to get going. The sooner it is done the better."

"Agreed." He offered her a hand up.

She took it, swaying a little on her feet.

Steadying her, he lifted a brow. "Drink or nerves?"

"A little bit of both."

"Are you okay to drive?"

"I'm good."

"Perhaps you should get some coffee to go."

"I have water in the car."

He nodded. "Follow me to the parking lot of the Galleria."

"Okay." Calypso seemed a little dazed.

Had she remembered the fine details of the plan? There weren't many, but in the state she was in she could've forgotten something important.

"Did you leave your phone behind?"

"Yes. It's in my locker."

"Good." He took her elbow. "Which car is yours?" He knew, but there was no reason to alert her to the fact that he'd been stalking her for months.

She pointed. "The Honda."

He helped her in. "Do you have everything you need?"

She patted the large satchel she'd deposited on the passenger seat. "All my money is in here."

Any thug could snatch it from there while she was stopped at an intersection, taking all her worldly possessions.

"Put your bag on the floor and push it under the seat."

"Yes, sir." She followed his instructions.

Her slurred speech worried him.

"Touch your finger to your nose."

She did just fine. But he was still worried.

"On second thought, I'll follow you. Do you know the way?"

"Sure. Everyone knows where the Galleria is." She rolled her eyes at him as if he'd asked her the dumbest question.

"Drive carefully."

"Yes, sir." She saluted.

As he drove behind her, Brundar was relieved to see Calypso driving steadily and obeying all traffic laws despite her mild inebriation. Still, he was uncommonly agitated until they arrived at their destination and he eased his car next to hers in the sprawling underground parking structure of the mall.

When Calypso popped the trunk, he glanced at her single suitcase. "Is that all?" he asked as she got out and joined him.

"Yeah. I travel light. Most of the stuff in my house isn't worth much. When I start earning money again, I'm going to get rid of the clothes I took and buy everything new. I want to erase that period of time from my life. No reminders."

"A clean slate."

"You got it."

He lifted the suitcase and carried it over to his Escalade. When he opened the passenger door for her, she got in without a second glance at her car and put her large satchel on her lap.

Evidently, his Calypso wasn't a material girl.

*Where in damnation did that come from?* Brundar shook his head. She wasn't his. Not now, not ever.

She was a human, and even if she weren't, the only thing he could offer her was keeping her safe for a short period of time. No woman wanted an emotionally handicapped male at her side.

Undeniably, he felt something for her, and it was more than he'd ever felt for anyone else, different from the familial bonds he had with Anandur and their mother. But even though it was a lot for him, it was not enough to satisfy a woman's need for love.

The best explanation for what was happening to him was that his protective instincts were kicking in full force. The strong physical attraction might have something to do with it as well.

But the thing was, he liked her as a person, which was significant since Brundar couldn't stand most people.

"Do you have any special abilities?" he blurted out.

Amanda had recently added affinity as a possible Dormant indicator.

Was that what he was feeling for Calypso?

She cast him a perplexed glance. "Like what?"

"Can you tell if someone's lying? Or sense someone else's emotions?"

She shrugged. "Not unless they are very obvious about it. Why?"

"Just curious. I read an article about extrasensory perception. It said that some people have it but are not aware of it. I know a guy who can always tell the truth from a lie."

Calypso chuckled. "I wish I had that ability. If I had, maybe I wouldn't have married Shawn."

Brundar intended to ask her about it, and she'd just provided him with the perfect opening. "Why did you?"

Looking down at the satchel in her lap she shrugged again. "The oldest reason in the world. He'd knocked me up."

That didn't add up. She didn't have a child. Maybe he was misinterpreting the phrase? It happened to him sometimes. "I'm not sure I understand."

Calypso sighed. "I was young and stupid and trusted him to take care of us both. We had never done it without protection, but a condom must've been defective and tore." The bitterness of her tone made it clear she didn't believe it had been an accident.

"Did he do it to entrap you?"

"I have no proof, but I suspect that he did. He was so enamored with the idea of being my first, and he wanted to be my last."

Brundar didn't want to drag up old hurts, but he needed to know. "What happened with the baby?"

"I miscarried six weeks into the pregnancy. It was terrible. I cried my eyes out for months. But I guess it was not meant to be. I never conceived again, though not for lack of trying on Shawn's part. He was obsessed with getting me pregnant. I, on the other hand, thanked God every time my period came on time."

"Did you use contraceptives?"

Calypso shook her head. "When I realized that there was no hope for us, I wanted to but didn't dare. If Shawn found out, I was sure he would lose it and do something horrible to me. So all I did was pray to God not to let it happen. My prayers must've been heard."

It was a surprising revelation. Brundar was under the impression that Calypso's dissatisfaction with her marriage was a recent development. When he'd kicked her and her husband out of the club, she'd seemed embarrassed by Shawn's behavior but hadn't harbored animosity toward him. Brundar would've sensed it if she had.

As far as he knew, the situation had started its downward spiral only a few months back. That's when Shawn began to show more and more of his true colors, and Callie started looking out the window with a sad expression on her face.

"When I first saw you at the club, you didn't look like you wanted to be free of your husband."

She sighed. "I was still hoping to salvage our marriage. Things were good between us for a little while, but then slowly deteriorated over time. At some point I realized that I didn't want to bring a child into the world before I knew for sure that it would be born into a healthy, loving family."

"When did you give up on that dream?"

"It didn't happen overnight. I'm stubborn, and admitting failure is not easy for me. It happened gradually over time. I think the last straw was when he tried to stop me from attending UCLA. I wasn't willing to give up on my dream of becoming a teacher."

Before he knew what he was doing, Brundar reached for her hand and clasped it. "You did the right thing. He is dangerous. Eventually, he would've harmed you." Or worse. But Brundar couldn't tell Calypso how he knew her husband was unstable and capable of murder.

She would've said he was overreacting.

Her lips twisted in a sad smile. "Do you have special abilities yourself, Brundar? Can you see the future?"

"No, I can't. But I'm a good judge of human nature, especially the rotten side of it. And Shawn is rotten," he bit out.

Calypso tilted her head and gazed at him appraisingly. "Part of the job, I assume? As a bodyguard you probably encounter a lot of bad people."

"I do."

Unfortunately, not only on the job. He'd been exposed to evil way before he'd become the warrior he was now. In fact, that experience had shaped him into who he was today. On that day, he'd vowed never to be a helpless victim again.

Brundar had spent his life honing his skills and ensuring he could cut down anyone who threatened him or his.

"I forgot to ask, where are you taking me?"

Brundar stifled a wince. He didn't like lying to her. Hell, he didn't like lying period. But it was necessary. "My friend is teaching a semester abroad. I told him that you are a trustworthy house sitter."

The furnished one-bedroom apartment he'd rented for her was a great find. It wasn't fancy, but it was walking distance from the club, and the building had a good security system in place. The front door was always locked, and visitors had to call and show their faces to the camera to be let in, reducing the chances of undesirables making it inside the building without invitation.

"Did your friend leave a car behind by any chance?"

"No. But his place is ten minutes walking distance from the club, and there is a grocery shop nearby that makes deliveries. You don't need a car. I would advise against visiting friends until your divorce is final."

Calypso grimaced. "Other than Dawn, I have no close friends. Shawn made sure none wanted to keep in touch."

His anger rising, Brundar's hands tightened on the steering wheel. It was a classic bully strategy. By isolating her, Shawn ensured she had no one to turn to.

"Brundar?"

He cast her a sidelong glance.

"Promise me you're not going to arrange an accident for Shawn."

He chuckled, because it was exactly what had crossed his mind. "Are you sure you have no paranormal talents?"

"I'm sure. But I'm starting to read the tiny nuances in your expressions. You looked like you had murder on your mind."

"It would solve all of your problems."

She shivered. "I don't hate him so much that I would like to see him dead. I just want to be free. He never actually harmed me, not physically. Suspecting that he was about to doesn't justify harming him."

Brundar couldn't argue with that statement.

His own code of honor demanded the same.

20

# CALLIE

*H*efting her suitcase in one hand like it weighed no more than a grocery bag, Brundar pulled out a key from his pocket and opened the glass door to the building's lobby. It looked old and a bit rundown, but it was clean.

"You see the camera up there?" He pointed before entering.

She lifted her head. "Yes."

"The feed from it goes to each apartment. You can see on the screen who is buzzing you from downstairs." He held the door open for her. "It's an old building. Only one elevator."

"What does your friend teach?" she asked as they entered the lift.

"I don't know." Brundar pressed the button for the third floor.

Callie frowned. How come he didn't know something so basic about a friend who was close enough to entrust him with finding a sitter for his apartment?

Her suspicions only intensified when they entered the apartment. The furniture wasn't new, but then most hotel rooms' furniture wasn't either. And like in a hotel, there were no personal touches to indicate someone lived there, other than a few books that looked brand new, several DVDs and one potted plant. No throw blanket on the couch, and no framed family photos on the mantel. A quick look at the kitchen cabinets confirmed it. A matching service for six, all pieces included and none chipped, was neatly organized on the shelves.

Then again, Brundar's friend might have been a neat freak. Or had OCD about matching place settings. No chipped or mismatched mugs like in her own kitchen.

*Not mine anymore.*

"Come see the bedroom." Brundar opened one of the three doors clustered in the barely there hallway.

Callie opened the one across from the bedroom. It was a coat closet. The other one led to a bathroom. She peeked inside, then walked in and crossed to the door on the opposite side that opened into the bedroom.

As Brundar pulled the closet doors open and put her suitcase inside, Callie dropped her satchel on the queen-sized bed that took up most of the space. A six-drawer dresser with a flat screen on top leaned against the opposite wall. The remote was on the nightstand.

Just like in a hotel.

Three decorative pillows against the slatted iron headboard and a folded blanket on a chair seemed like a feeble attempt at making this room look more lived in.

The best part, however, were the sliding glass doors that opened to a nice-sized balcony, which the bedroom shared with the living room. It was furnished with a lounge chair and a side table.

"It's a very nice apartment. Thank you."

"It's safe."

It didn't escape her notice that he didn't answer with a 'you're welcome,' or that she should thank his friend and not him.

Pushing her hands into her pockets, she glanced at her rescuer. "What now?"

"Grocery shopping. Then the club."

"When do I start working?"

"Tonight."

That was a pleasant surprise. "Really? So soon?"

He misinterpreted her question. "Tomorrow then."

"No. Today is fine. I don't want to sit around this empty apartment all by myself. I'd rather be working."

Brundar acknowledged her with a nod and headed for the front door.

The grocery store was packed with customers, most everyone casting curious glances at Brundar and basically ignoring her. Callie wasn't a great beauty, but she was used to at least a few appreciative look-overs from guys. This felt like hanging with a supermodel. A male supermodel.

Brundar seemed oblivious to the attention he was garnering, his stoic expression unchanging even when the cashier blushed all shades of pink while ringing up their stuff.

Not theirs, hers, Callie corrected herself.

"Please, let me pay for my own groceries."

Brundar shook his head. "Next time. This one is on me."

Not wanting to make a scene, Callie decided to repay him by cooking him dinner.

But wait, what if he had someone waiting for him at home?

A guy as handsome as him probably had a girlfriend. Or even a wife. Which would explain why he wasn't interested in her. That little speech about being attracted to her had probably meant nothing.

Empty words to make her feel good.

Except, it wasn't Brundar's way. He wasn't polite. He didn't say things just to put someone else at ease. He didn't say much at all.

Callie spent the short drive back to her new apartment planning dinner. When they got there, Brundar insisted on carrying all the bags up to her apartment, not letting her pick up even one.

"You're a chauvinist," she accused.

He lifted a brow, waiting for her to open the door, then carried the bags to the kitchen and deposited them on the counter.

"Can I invite you to dinner? Or do you need to be at the club?" *Or home with your significant other?*

Brundar looked surprised, but in a good way. "Will it take long?"

Good. He wasn't going home to anyone. "Not at all. I'm a devil in the kitchen."

She expected some witty comeback, but there was none. Instead, he pulled out a stool and sat down on the other side of the kitchen counter.

"I guess that means you accept."

He nodded.

"Do you like Mexican?"

He shrugged.

"I guess it's a yes." Callie wondered if that's how all their conversations were going to be—with her talking and him either nodding or shrugging or grunting in response.

After rinsing the vegetables, she pulled out a cutting board and started chopping onions and bell peppers. "So what exactly am I going to do at the club?"

"Serve drinks."

"Yeah, you said that before. But I couldn't help wondering which portion of the club I will be serving the drinks in. The upstairs or the downstairs?"

"Upstairs. I'm not letting you inside the kink club."

Callie paused mid chopping. "Why?"

"You're too young."

She put a hand on her hip. "I'm twenty-one."

"You need to be twenty-eight."

"Since when? My friend Dawn is only a year older, and she was allowed in."

"It was a recent change."

"Why?"

"To prevent kids with fake identification from getting in. It's harder to fake being twenty-eight than twenty-one."

"But I'm not going in as a participant. As an employee I'll need to provide my social security number, and you can easily verify my age."

Brundar cast her a hard look. "You're not working down there. End of story."

He was such a freaking chauvinist.

Swallowing the arguments that were on the tip of her tongue, she pulled out a skillet and put it on the stove. The man was helping her out of the goodness of his heart. Arguing the terms of that help would be the epitome of ungratefulness.

"What made you come to the club in the first place?" he asked.

Callie felt the blush creep up her cheeks. "I was curious."

Brundar arched a brow. "I remember you telling me that it was your idea, not your husband's."

She turned around, adding oil to the skillet. "He didn't want to go. I convinced him to."

"That's unusual for first timers."

Callie dropped a package of beef strips into the skillet, the sizzling meat filling the small kitchen with an appetizing smell as she stirred them around with a wooden spoon.

"Let me ask you something." She turned to Brundar. "How can I tell the difference between a bully and a dominant?"

His stoic expression revealed nothing. "Respect and consent."

He was driving her crazy with those one- or two-word answers. "Can you please elaborate? Give examples?"

Brundar rubbed a hand over his clean-shaven jaw. "A bully demands your obedience and submission. He thinks of it as his right and doesn't care what you want."

That was a little better, but it still left a lot of questions unanswered. Brundar was like a web browser. She had to ask precise questions to get relevant answers from him. He didn't extrapolate what else he could tell her, or answer questions she didn't know to ask.

"Okay, so if I understand it correctly, a dominant asks for my permission and cares for what I want. Isn't that what any normal guy should do?"

"Yes."

Ugh. He was so frustrating.

"That doesn't tell me anything."

If she had a sliver of hope that Brundar might be interested in her, his cold and detached tone made it clear he wasn't.

"Your meat is burning."

"What?"

He pointed at the stovetop behind her.

She'd forgotten all about the skillet. Snatching it off the burner, Callie tossed the smoking strips around. "I hope you don't mind well-done bordering on charred." She speared a piece on a fork and tasted it. "Still good."

"Smells fine."

Was he being nice? Not likely. Brundar probably found the smell appetizing. Otherwise he wouldn't have said anything.

Callie added the chopped vegetables to the skillet. "I guess I'll have to come to the club and observe how it works. You're not telling me much."

"You can read about it."

"Yeah, I did. But the problem with that is that I don't know how much of it is true."

Brundar pinned her with a hard stare. "Tell me what prompted you to come to the club."

*Gah.* She'd never talked about it with anyone but Dawn, and even then it was half-jokingly.

"I'm not into pain." She wanted to make that clear. "I'm not a masochist. But dominance excites me. Always has. Ever since I started having naughty thoughts." She turned around and got busy with the wooden spoon, stirring fajita sauce into the meat and vegetable mixture.

"A lot of females are excited by it. It's not unusual."

"I guess."

Maybe not. But she was willing to bet that most of those women enjoyed purely vanilla sex as well.

She didn't.

Unless she added a fantasy of dominance to the act, she didn't get aroused, let alone reach a climax. It didn't have to be anything extreme. Imagining her arms held over her head, or a little erotic spanking would do the trick.

The images her brain conjured up had the expected effect, especially since her fantasy dominant was replaced by the very real Brundar who was sitting no more than four feet away from her.

Her curiosity be damned, this conversation had to end, or she would be forced to excuse herself and make a dash for the bathroom. Callie turned her back to Brundar and got busy with the skillet.

## 21

# BRUNDAR

She was killing him.

Whatever Calypso was imagining, it was exciting her—the scent of her arousal was overpowering that of the cooking meat.

Was she thinking of him?

Gazing at her shapely ass encased in those tight-fitting jeans, Brundar's own imagination went to work. He would walk up to her and clasp her wrists so she couldn't touch him. With her arms twisted behind her back, her ample breasts would get pushed forward, and he would cup one, then the other, tweaking her nipples through her bra as he kissed her neck. She would melt into him and beg him to take her to bed…

To master her…

Brundar closed his eyes. Not going to happen. He was already too emotionally entangled to risk the intimacy of a scene. The only way to stay detached was to engage with partners who weren't seeking an exclusive playmate.

That wasn't Calypso. He didn't know her well, but a girl who'd married the first guy she'd had sex with wasn't the type to do casual.

She needed guidance, though. Without it she could fall prey to another jerk like her soon to be ex-husband. The club was a safe place for her to dip her toes. The problem was that he couldn't stomach letting anyone else show her the ropes, literally speaking, and he couldn't do it himself.

"It's ready," she announced with fake cheer as she placed a plate of sizzling fajitas in front of him. "Would you like a beer?"

He shook his head. "Water will do." To an immortal, the Hawaiian beer she'd bought would taste like piss water.

She poured him a cup. "Ice?"

"No."

Calypso put a much smaller portion on her own plate and sat next to him.

"Dig in." She grabbed one of the warmed tortillas and heaped some of the mixture onto it, then added a tablespoon of ready-made salsa.

Brundar followed her lead. A home cooked meal was a novelty for him. He and Anandur ate out except for the rare occasions they mooched off Okidu's cooking.

Taking a bite, he wasn't expecting it to taste as good as it did.

"How is it?" Calypso asked.

"Good."

She chuckled. "You sound surprised."

Brundar wiped his mouth with a napkin. "I'm not used to home cooking. I didn't know what to expect."

"Do you live alone?"

"No."

"Oh." She sounded disappointed.

"I live with my brother."

"Oh." The 'oh' sounded peppier. Had she been asking to find out if he had a girlfriend?

Finishing one tortilla, he reached for another. Calypso smiled. So he ate a third and a fourth.

"You were hungry." She collected his plate and took it to the sink.

"I wasn't. But it was really good."

His words brought a bright smile to her beautiful face. A stuffed to bursting stomach was worth the sacrifice.

Calypso finished washing the dishes and wiped her hands with a paper towel. "Ready to go?"

"Yes." *No.* He wanted to stay and have her all to himself, even if it was only to talk or watch a movie on the television. It didn't really matter what.

But that was another lie. What he wanted was to take her to the bedroom, tie her to the bedposts, and show her pleasure like she hadn't known before.

"By the way. What do you suggest I do with the cash? I don't want to carry it with me, but I'm afraid of leaving it here."

"You can use the safe in the club."

She looked unsure.

"Or I can help you find a good hiding spot right here."

She fiddled with the dishrag. "It's not that I don't trust you. I do. But I want access to it whenever I need it."

"Understood. Give me the money."

She went into the bedroom and returned with her satchel. Taking out the bundles of hundreds, she put them one by one on the counter.

Brundar opened the Ziploc box they'd bought and pulled out several bags. Wrapping each bundle in paper towels, he stuffed it inside a Ziploc, closed it, and stuffed it inside another one. When all were done, he opened the freezer and put everything on the bottom of the ice cube compartment, then piled the ice on top of the bags.

"It will do for now. I'll get you a safe tomorrow and install it for you."

She eyed the freezer. "That's clever. No one would think to look under the ice cubes."

He wasn't so sure of that. But he trusted the building's security system to prevent anyone from getting in and looking. "It's a temporary solution. Let's go."

She followed him out and locked the door behind them.

"Are we taking your car or walking?"

"We're walking. I want to show you how close it is."

The walk would do them both good, cooling some of the heat that had been generated in Calypso's kitchen. What he hadn't counted on, however, was how awkward the short walk to the club would be.

As they strode in silence, Brundar had the strange impulse to wrap his arm around her shoulders, but then she would wrap hers around his middle like he'd seen other couples do, and he wouldn't like it.

Except, what if he did?

Better not to test it. He'd lived with his limitations for hundreds of years and managed just fine. There was no need to change a thing.

As it was, the girl had done enough damage already.

A master fighter like him needed to exist in the zone, which was impossible when feelings were battering against the walls he'd built around his psyche. Calypso was dangerous to him.

His Achilles heel.

## 22

# KIAN

Robert's heavy footsteps announced his arrival long before the guy knocked on the glass doors of Kian's office.

"Come in, Robert."

He walked in with a newspaper tucked under his arm.

Apparently, Robert still preferred the old fashioned way of reading the news, as did Kian. But he had a feeling Robert preferred it for other reasons—like using it as a shield when relaxing in the downstairs coffee shop. Reading news on a smartphone wasn't as effective in that capacity.

"I thought you'd find this interesting." Robert put the newspaper in front of him. A story about a new string of murders was circled with a red sharpie.

Frowning, Kian speed read the article.

Over the past week, five women had been found dead. They'd bled to death from twin arterial puncture wounds to the neck. There were no signs of struggle, and autopsies revealed no drugs or high levels of alcohol in four out of the five. The similarities had the authorities suspecting that the murders were the work of a serial killer.

Kian dropped the paper on his desk. "Doomers?"

Robert shook his head. "Doomers don't go around killing women. They are considered too valuable to waste. This is the work of a crazy person. Probably an immortal male, but not necessarily a Doomer. He could be one of us."

It didn't escape Kian's notice that Robert had referred to the clan as us. Should he be glad that the guy was counting himself as one of them?

Kian wasn't sure how he felt about it.

"Thank you for bringing it to my attention. I'll start an investigation."

Robert rose to his feet. "I guess you'll be keeping the paper?" He looked at the thing longingly.

"I don't need the whole thing. Just leave the article about the murders. Unless there is something else you think I should read?"

"Are you interested in sports?"
"Not really."
"Stocks?"
"Shai keeps me updated."
"Then I can think of nothing else." With careful precision, Robert tore out the relevant section, folded it neatly, and handed it to Kian.
"Thank you."
As soon as Robert left his office, Kian called Onegus.
The chief Guardian arrived a few minutes later.
"Doomers." He shook his head as he read the article.
"Not necessarily. Robert argued that even Doomers don't kill women indiscriminately. He thinks it's an immortal male gone insane. Which means the murderer could be anyone. Even one of ours."
Onegus scratched his tight blond curls. "It happened before."
"Vlad."
"Yeah. What a clusterfuck that was."
In those days, there had been no newspapers to deliver news almost instantly. News had traveled slowly. By the time they'd become aware of what their deranged relative had been doing, the body count had been staggering.
"I'm putting you in charge of the investigation. If you need help, we can contact Turner and have him send out one of his contractors to snoop around."
"We could use Eva's help."
Kian pointed a finger at the Guardian. "Don't even breathe a word of it in front of her. Bhathian would lose his ever-loving shit if we involved his pregnant mate in an immortal-gone-rogue manhunt."
"I have no intentions of getting her physically on the case. Just as an advisor."
"And you think she'd be satisfied with that? I've dealt with her. Other than my mother and Amanda, she is the most strong-headed female I've ever dealt with."
Onegus chuckled. "I can sweet-talk her like I do every other woman."
"No, you can't. Just drop it. We don't need her help with this. Am I clear?"
"Yes, sir." Onegus saluted with a grimace.
Fuck. The Guardians needed a reminder that he was their leader and his orders were not suggestions or friendly requests.
Kian expected them to be obeyed.

## 23

# SYSSI

"Let's go out." Kian pulled Syssi into his arms. "You need a change of atmosphere."

As always, the feel of his strong, warm body provided a sense of well-being. But even that wasn't enough to improve her mood. Which was probably why Kian was suggesting an outing.

"Where to?"

"How about your favorite, that cheese place?"

"I thought you didn't like how crowded it was."

"I don't. But you like it, and that's good enough for me."

It was sweet of him, but she didn't want him cringing under the hungry gazes of covetous humans. She wasn't happy about those either.

They shouldn't have bothered her. Kian had eyes only for her and patently ignored all others, but when it happened more than once or twice it became annoying.

No wonder movie stars stayed away from public places.

"We can go to By Invitation Only."

His bright smile confirmed his preference. "You sure? I don't mind the cheese place."

"I'm sure. I like the idea of dressing fancy for a change."

The gleam in his eye meant he had something naughty on his mind. "Wear your diamond choker for me."

She smirked. "I thought I was supposed to wear it only in the bedroom with nothing else on."

"After dinner, it will be exactly what you'll be wearing. Or rather not wearing." He cupped her rear and gave it a squeeze. "I've been remiss lately." He slapped her butt playfully.

It was true. With how down she'd been, it was no wonder Kian had been in no mood to play. It started with the vision and had gotten worse after Eva's announcement. The twinkle of hope that the little boy in her dream had brought had been snuffed out, and the disappointment was devastating.

"What else should I wear? Besides the choker?"

Kian shrugged. "Something that's easy to take off."

"You're so romantic..." she mocked.

"Never claimed to be." He kissed her lightly. "Go get dressed." He turned her around and slapped her butt again.

God, she missed it—that delicious tingle and tightening. Tonight they were going to play, and she was going to forget all about the disturbing vision and her silly yearning for a baby.

What had gotten into her anyway?

She and Kian had time in abundance to become parents, and in the meantime she was getting her baby fix babysitting Phoenix. Soon there would be another little one to babysit. Eva and Bhathian would be living next door in the new compound, or village as everyone had started referring to it, and she could enjoy their baby boy whenever she pleased.

As to the visions, she was done with that. No more courting those. She could do nothing about them when they came out of the blue, but there was no reason to actively seek them.

No more visits to the famous medium either.

When Nathalie was ready, she could go see Madam Salinka and learn how to deal with her ghosts. As of late, Mark was her only visitor. Nathalie was perfectly fine with him popping in and out of her head, but his comments about keeping the bad spirits at bay had scared the crap out of her. Not that Syssi blamed her. Mark could cross over at any moment and leave Nathalie exposed. The sooner she learned how to block those nasty ghosts the better.

It didn't take Syssi long to get ready, and an hour later they were sitting in their favorite private enclave and going over the revamped menu.

Syssi shook her head. "Gerard must've gone through another of his culinary crises. I don't recognize any of these items."

Kian seemed unfazed. "He can't afford to become boring or predictable. His finicky clientele would abandon him."

"After the membership fee they paid? I don't think so. It was a brilliant move. Guaranteed repeat business."

A chuckle bubbled up from Kian's chest. "For most of the people here, the cost is insignificant."

She crossed her arms under her chest. "If they are so rich, they should donate that money to charity."

"The world doesn't work that way. Most of them donate plenty. That's what all those charity balls are for. What's the fun of donating extravagant amounts if they can't show off to their rich friends?"

Syssi uncrossed her arms. "I don't mind that. Whatever they get out of it is fine. Fame, admiration, I don't begrudge them these thrills. What's important is that the people who need the help get it."

Kian reached across the table and took her hand. "My sweet Syssi. I love how practical and level-headed you are."

She smiled at her husband and squeezed his hand back.

He would disagree, but Kian was so sweet. He never failed to compliment her on every little thing. So yeah, he was often late to dinner, and sometimes he worked in his home office long after she'd fallen asleep, but his love for her was ever present and unwavering. For a guy that didn't smile much and had a quick temper, the joy he expressed at just being with her was all the more precious.

"Thank you for taking me out. I needed that."

"I should have done so sooner. But you know me, I want to make you happy, but sometimes I just don't know how. Clueless as usual."

"Oh, Kian." She reached for his other hand. "You make me happy just by loving me. You don't need to do anything special. Some things are just beyond your control." She smirked. "I know how hard it is for you to accept that you're not omnipotent and all knowing."

His eyes peeled wide as he pretended shock. "I'm not? I think I'm plenty potent." He waggled his brows.

"You are plenty potent, just not omnipotent."

"I wish I was." His expression got serious. "I wish I could protect you from your visions. And more than anything I wish I could give you the baby you want."

It dawned on her then that she hadn't been the only one suffering. Her misery had been affecting Kian as well.

*Time to toughen up, girl.*

It was one thing to wallow in self-pity all by her lonesome, but dragging Kian down was another. It was her duty as the clan leader's mate to provide him support, not weaken him.

They were a team.

"We will have our baby. Eva pointed out that she was forty-five when she got pregnant for the first time, and she hadn't been using any contraceptives because she'd thought she was barren. I'm still young, even in human terms. I shouldn't be obsessing about babies yet."

Kian looked as if a weight had been lifted off his shoulders, and he winked. "I don't mind keeping trying."

"Me neither."

"Good. Let's go home and practice."

She laughed. "We didn't eat yet."

"Right. After we eat. You'll need your energy."

When their dinner arrived, Kian wolfed down everything on his plate in record time. The new menu items they'd ordered were unsurprisingly excellent, but Syssi had a feeling his haste had more to do with wanting to get her home than with hunger.

"Gerard is a true culinary genius," she said, wiping her mouth with a napkin.

Kian nodded. "An unparalleled talent with an attitude to match." He leaned closer. "To call him a prima donna is a polite understatement."

True. The guy was a pompous ass. The way he'd treated Carol when she asked for an apprenticeship had been despicable. If Gerard had been more accommodating and less insulting, Carol might have not chosen a new career path as a spy.

It was so scary to think of the pixie blond in the midst of the hornets' nest that was the Doomers' base, alone, with no support and no one to rescue her if needed.

"I worry about Carol. If there is one reason I would consider courting visions again, it would be to try and foresee her future."

"Carol is not going anywhere yet. First, she's not ready. Second, until we figure out how to communicate with her and find a means to extract her if necessary, I'm not green-lighting the mission."

"Good. Please keep me in the loop. I'll sleep better knowing what's going on with her."

"I will."

An uneasy expression flitted across Kian's handsome features, and Syssi wondered what he was trying to shield her from.

"What is it? What are you hiding from me?"

"I don't want to upset you."

She rolled her eyes. "Come on, out with it."

"Robert came to see me today and showed me a news article about a series of murders. Someone is biting women and leaving them to bleed to death."

That was horrible. "Doomers?"

"That was my first thought too, but Robert pointed out that killing females is not their way. He said that it could be any immortal male gone crazy, and I had to agree since it's not the first time something like that has happened."

"Are you talking about Dracula?"

"It was a dark time in our history."

Syssi frowned. "Where were the bodies found?"

"The article didn't say. The police are not releasing much information yet. Why?"

"Maybe the deaths in my vision were of these women? The first victims I saw were all female. After that the vision got blurry, and I couldn't tell anymore. I was so sure the vision was about us, but maybe it was about what's going on now."

"It could be. I put Onegus in charge of the investigation, and Andrew is looking into it as well, trying to dig out whatever information the authorities are hiding. We will know more tomorrow."

As a shiver ran through her, Syssi rubbed at her exposed arms. "Poor women. I hope he is not one of ours."

## 24

# BRUNDAR

"What's up with you, bro?" Anandur opened the bathroom door and leaned on the jamb.

His brother had no respect for personal boundaries.

"Get out." Brundar snapped a towel off the hanger and wrapped it around his hips.

"If I do, you'll just slink out like a shadow, and I'll miss the opportunity to bond with my little brother."

"What do you want, Anandur?"

"You're acting strange lately. Let me rephrase. You're acting stranger than usual."

"I don't know what you're talking about." Denial was the best defense. Telling Anandur anything was like announcing it to the entire clan.

To be fair, the guy knew how to keep a secret when it was important, but anything involving Brundar and a woman was too juicy a bit of gossip for Anandur to keep to himself.

"I'm smelling a woman."

Without thinking, Brundar sniffed at his body, searching for Calypso's scent. It dawned on him then how ridiculously he was acting. He'd just stepped out of the shower. Besides, like any other immortal male, he often returned home smelling of a woman. Nothing unusual about that. But the only one who came to his mind was Calypso, even though they never touched more than hands.

He frowned at his brother. "What if I am?"

Anandur chuckled. "I meant figuratively. Wrap a towel over that hair of yours. You're dripping all over the floor."

He was. Catching the long strands, Brundar leaned over the sink and wrung his hair out.

"Want me to blow dry it for you?" Anandur teased.

Brundar ignored the obnoxious oaf and stepped into his closet to get dressed.

Looking at his sparse selection, he wondered what should he wear for his appointment with the judge.

Should he put on dress slacks?

Edna always managed to unnerve him and disturb his equilibrium. Though not as much as Calypso, and for different reasons. Brundar did his best to stay as far away as possible from the Alien Probe.

His secrets were no one's business, and Edna didn't always ask before probing people's emotions and intentions. It was different from thralling, and in her defense, she only did it for the right reasons, but it was disconcerting nonetheless.

When it came to the clan's safety, Edna had no qualms about probing. She'd done it to Syssi without the girl's permission. Worse, she hadn't even asked Kian's. Apparently, even their almighty regent was afraid of reprimanding the judge, because, as far as Brundar knew, Kian hadn't done anything about it. Not publicly. Maybe he'd had words with Edna privately.

Anandur followed Brundar into the closet, eyeing the gray dress slacks he was pulling on. "Where are you going?"

"None of your business." Brundar grabbed a white button-down off the hanger and shrugged it over his shoulders.

Anandur crossed his arms over his chest. "You're neglecting Carol's training."

Brundar stopped with his fingers poised over a button. It was true. Over the past week, he'd canceled three training sessions in a row. Then again, Carol wasn't taking the training as seriously as she should.

Until she was willing to kill, he wasn't going to invest more time in her training and definitely not going to authorize her for any missions. "She needs to make up her mind whether she is in all the way or not."

Anandur frowned. "I thought she was."

"She did too. Until I told her she would need to kill an animal and take its heart out."

Anandur cringed. "Ouch. No wonder she is having second thoughts. Carol is a lover, not a fighter."

"She needs to be both to have a chance in hell to get out alive from where she is going." His dress socks in hand, Brundar glanced at his brother. "No objections?"

"No. You're right. Target practice and real life are two different things. She needs to toughen up."

Brundar pulled a pair of black loafers off the shelf and blew on them to remove the dust. He hadn't worn those since the last wedding he'd attended.

Should he wear a jacket? The only place he could hide knives under his dressy outfit was strapping them to his calves. If he put a jacket on, he could strap some to his back and front as well.

"Feeling naked without your toys?" Anandur knew him well.

Brundar tapped the numbers on the combination lock securing his metal weapons closet and took out only two small blades. Edna would appreciate him showing up practically unarmed.

"Not now, I don't." Brundar adjusted his pants over the hidden weapons.

"Do you want me to help with Carol?"

"Doing what?"

"I can get her to kill something."

Maybe. But Brundar didn't trust the big softie. Anandur would do the killing and give Carol credit.

"No. Kian entrusted her training to me." Using his fingers, Brundar combed his long hair away from his face and secured the long ponytail with a stretchy piece of leather string.

"I promise I won't cheat. It's going to be her kill."

Brundar eyed his brother suspiciously. "What makes you think you'll succeed in convincing her to do it while I couldn't?"

"A little humor and supportive attitude will help ease her into it. The first time is the toughest. The next one is not going to be as difficult. It takes time to turn someone into a cold-hearted killer. Especially a female."

Brundar arched a brow. He'd been turned into one overnight. Except it had been in his nature, and only needed the right catalyst. Carol, on the other hand, had suffered much worse than he had but was still averse to killing. She wasn't born with the right instincts.

It was an interesting thought. "Maybe she doesn't have it in her? If we push her too hard, she'll break. Carol needs to decide for herself."

Anandur scratched his bushy beard. "As unbelievable as I find you having such insight, I have to agree. I'll talk to Vanessa, and ask her if I should bring Carol for an evaluation. We need a professional's opinion."

"Thank you." Brundar passed his brother on his way out.

"You're welcome. You know I always have your back."

Brundar stopped with his hand on the door handle and turned around. "I know."

25

# BRUNDAR

"Come in," Edna called out when Brundar knocked on her office door.

He pushed it open and strode in. "Thank you for agreeing to see me on such short notice." Brundar's tongue twisted in his mouth as he forced himself to address the judge politely. Not only because he needed to ask a favor, but because she'd chewed him out for his laconic speech patterns before. As an attorney, Edna appreciated clarity and exact usage of language.

He'd do all the tongue twisting necessary, including reciting poetry if it helped him avoid the trap of her hypnotic eyes. Even without actively probing, the woman saw too much.

"That's what I'm here for. What can I help you with, Brundar?"

"A friend of mine needs to file for a divorce, and she's short on cash."

Edna's brows lifted in sync with the corners of her lips. "You've got a friend?"

Brundar shifted in the uncomfortable chair. Everyone knew he didn't have any.

Was Calypso a friend?

Probably the closest he'd got to anyone since he was a kid, but that didn't make her a friend. "An acquaintance."

"You need to tell me more, Brundar."

He'd been expecting that. "She is married to an abusive jerk and fears for her life. I helped her make a clean exit, and I'm helping her hide from him. She wants a quick divorce. There are no children involved. She took half of their cash savings and wants nothing more from him. The house they bought together can stay his, and she is not asking for support."

As Edna regarded him with her old, pale blue eyes, Brundar focused his gaze on the top of her forehead.

"What is your involvement with her? Did you influence her in any way to leave her husband?"

He'd been expecting that line of questioning as well. Hopefully, Edna would believe him and not try to push her ghostly tentacles into his head to check his veracity.

"I didn't thrall her. I only told her what she already knew. Her husband is manipulative, controlling, dangerous, and unstable. Up until now he has only taken out his anger on inanimate objects, but that's about to change. I allowed myself a quick peek into his mind. He'd rather kill her than let her go."

Edna nodded. "With no kids and no property to divide it's going to be a simple procedure. I can file the paperwork for her."

"Thank you."

"Naturally, I need her to come see me."

"I can bring her to your outside office." The one she kept for her dealings with humans.

The judge brought up her schedule on the screen. "Can she come at two o'clock?"

"Yes."

"Good." Edna smiled. "I'm glad you finally found someone."

"It's not like that. I'm just helping her out. She is human."

"No special talents?"

He shook his head. "None. She is an ordinary, young human female." Calypso was anything but ordinary to him, but Edna didn't need to know that.

"I'll see you both tomorrow." She rose to her feet, her baggy slacks too long, their bottoms pooling over her sensible Oxfords. "I'm curious to see the girl that managed to penetrate the shields of our most formidable warrior."

Brundar couldn't help the wince that twisted his lips. His strategy hadn't worked, and Edna had read him as if he was an open book.

*Unnerving woman.*

"As I said, she is only an acquaintance. Someone who needs my help."

Edna patted his arm, her sad eyes getting sadder as he flinched away from her touch. "Sometimes all that's needed is a small initial spark. You deserve to have someone care for you. Other than your brother, that is."

"Goodbye, Edna. And thank you again."

Out in the corridor, Brundar exhaled the breath he'd been holding, his shoulders sagging in relief. The worst part was over. Tomorrow, when he brought Calypso with him, Edna was going to focus on the girl and leave him alone.

The next step was to ask Onegus for a half day off. Filling in the paperwork would probably take up the entire afternoon.

When he entered the chief Guardian's office, Onegus looked him over. "Going to a funeral?"

"I need half a day off tomorrow. I can be here until one o'clock, but someone needs to take over my evening classes, or I can cancel them."

Onegus knew better than to ask what Brundar needed the time off for, but his eyes were full of curiosity. "I don't have anyone to fill in for you. You'll have to cancel."

Brundar nodded. "I'll take care of it." He walked out of Onegus's office and pulled out his phone to send a message to his trainees.

On second thought, though, there was someone who could teach a couple of self-defense classes for him.

She answered on the third ring.

"Carol."

"Yes, my absentee sensei."

"How do you feel about taking over my classes this evening?" His talk with Edna had left a residual polite tone.

"Brundar? Is that you?"

"If you feel you're not up to it, I'll cancel them."

"It's not that. I can pretend to be you and whip those trainees into shape. But I'm shocked that you asked me how I felt. What happened to you? I'm thinking an alien invasion of the body snatchers."

Brundar rolled his eyes. "Thank you. I'll text you the times and room numbers."

"You're thanking me! I'm about to faint!"

Brundar clicked the call off.

*Silly girl.*

Carol and Anandur would get along great. The question was whether they would get anything done, or spend all their time horsing around.

26

# CALLIE

*A*s they left Edna's office, Callie felt ten pounds lighter. Heck, it was more like twenty. Brundar's cousin, the woman he'd failed to mention he was related to, seemed super capable. With those smart eyes of hers and her gentle tone, she'd projected calm and confidence that Callie had desperately needed.

"I can't believe the divorce can be finalized in a month." That was what Edna had said, but Callie doubted it would go so smoothly. Shawn would not let her go so easily, not even for her share of their house. Edna had suggested offering Callie's half in the equity in exchange for agreeing to the expedited process.

"If Edna says it will be done in a month, it will be probably done even sooner." Brundar opened the passenger door for her and waited until she buckled up to close it.

He looked so different today in his fancy appointment-with-the-lawyer clothes, like some model from a menswear magazine.

Callie slumped in the passenger chair. It was such a shame he was uninterested in her. Maybe if she had more experience, she could've done more to seduce him.

Except, he might have responded negatively to her taking the initiative. Dominant men liked to be the hunters, not the hunted.

But didn't all men enjoy feeling wanted?

Was she supposed to play coy and give out hints like a damsel from a different era?

Callie wished she knew the rules of the game, but Brundar refused to tell her even the bare minimum.

Last night, she'd tried snooping around the club to find someone who was willing to talk to her, preferably a woman, but it seemed as if the two portions of Franco's sprawling domain were completely separated.

"Edna liked you," Brundar said.

"She did? How do you know?"

The woman had been accommodating in a professional manner, but she didn't smile enough for Callie to feel comfortable around her. Compared to Brundar, though, Edna was like a fluffy blanket of warmth.

He'd treated his cousin with such cold detachment.

Callie was grateful that he acted a shade warmer with her. She couldn't have dealt with him if he treated her the same way.

"She didn't interrogate you." Brundar turned into the onramp, easing into the freeway's slow traffic.

"Funny you would say that, because I felt like she did. She asked me a lot of questions."

"None of them intrusive. Trust me, Edna could make anyone squirm."

Callie lifted a brow. "Even you?"

He nodded. "Those eyes of hers. They see too much."

Wow, Brundar not only admitted to having a weakness but had expressed a genuine feeling.

He wasn't a lost cause.

She wondered what was he hiding from his cousin's knowing eyes. "Edna can look to her heart's content. I have nothing to hide." It was true. There were no dark secrets lurking in Callie's head and no skeletons hanging in her proverbial closet.

"Must be nice." Brundar stopped in front of her apartment building and killed the engine.

Was he coming upstairs?

God, she hoped he did. Not that there was any chance of him touching her, and it would be pure torture to think about it and imagine it while he was there, indifferent, or at least pretending to be. But she wanted to spend some time with him, have him near.

Was it because she had no one else?

Because she was lonely?

Her yearning for Brundar's company didn't make sense. He barely talked and almost never smiled. He reminded her of an old science fiction story she'd once read. It was about a humanoid robot that was made to look like a very handsome man. The thing was, the robot in the story knew how to mimic human emotions. If the story were about Brundar, the robot would've been a defective one.

*Broken.*

Was that what was wrong with him?

Was he broken?

Or was he perfect the way he was?

Callie shook her head. She was confusing herself.

"Are you coming?"

She lifted her eyes to see him standing on the sidewalk with her door open, waiting for her to come out. "I'm sorry. I zoned out again."

A big box under one arm, he offered her his other hand.

"What's that?" Callie pointed at the box as she took his offered hand.

"A safe."

"Thank you. I forgot all about that."

"The meeting with Edna must've been stressful for you."

Callie smiled tightly. "Yeah. It was. A life-altering event." A second one. The first one was Brundar walking into Aussie and making her an offer she couldn't resist.

Or perhaps it had happened even before that.

In the club.

Life was funny that way. Something seemingly trivial could lead to unexpected consequences. Alter the course of one's life.

"Your keys." Brundar held his palm out.

Feeling around her purse, she found the jingling pair. One to the building's front door and another to her apartment.

Only two keys, and neither belonging to her.

But those keys were what separated her from the truly homeless. Tears pooled at the corner of her eyes as she pulled them out and handed them to Brundar. Standing a step behind him as he opened the door, she wiped them discreetly on the sleeve of her shirt.

He cast her a curious glance as he held the door open for her. "What's wrong, Calypso?"

She shrugged, her lungs constricting as she watched him press the button for the elevator. Spending even a few short moments with him in such a confined space would be too much.

"Do you mind taking the stairs? I hate that clunky old thing." She wasn't lying. Besides being claustrophobically small, the noises it made were frightening. Going up and down the three flights of stairs was nothing.

"No."

It was good that he headed for the door to the staircase, otherwise she wouldn't have known if he'd said *no* to the stairs or *no* to not minding them.

*Frustrating man.*

She followed him up the stairs, getting an eyeful of his fabulous ass muscles moving under the thin fabric of his dress slacks. His movements were so graceful, so fluid. Compared to him she felt clumsy. Callie was glad to be in a good enough shape to not get winded by the climb. It would've been so embarrassing.

Spending long hours on her feet had been good for more than getting paid.

Her keys still in his hand, Brundar opened the door to her apartment. "Go sit on the couch and put your feet up. I'll install the safe in your closet and bring you a glass of wine to relax with."

"Thank you. You're an angel." In more ways than one.

She hadn't been pampered like that in... well, never. Callie had always been the one telling others to relax while she brought them things. Her father, when he would return tired from work, or when he would get sad. And then Shawn, who'd expected her to wait on him hand and foot.

Closing her eyes, Callie heard banging noises coming from her bedroom. A few minutes later Brundar came back with an open wine bottle and two wine glasses.

The man sure worked fast.

"The safe is secured to the floor, and I left the instructions on top." Brundar lifted the bottle with a grimace and poured the red wine into the glasses. "I should get you better stuff than this."

"Thank you." She took the glass he handed her. "What's wrong with that? It's not a cheap wine. I think it was like almost twenty bucks." At home, she used to drink the ones from the Trader's market that went for less than four bucks and were very good for the price.

"Let me spoil you. I think I would like it." He frowned as if he wasn't sure.

She took a sip and looked at him from under her eyelashes. "You sound like you've never spoiled a girl before."

"I haven't."

"Oh." She'd forgotten.

Dominants probably didn't pamper their girlfriends. She should strike that stupid sexual fantasy of hers for just that reason alone. When Callie started dating again, she wanted to be treated like a princess. Not the maid.

Even at the cost of sexual satisfaction.

She could always resort to her fantasies to carry her over. Having a nice guy who treated her well was more important than how she got her orgasms.

*Love as thy wilt.* She remembered the book that had changed her outlook on sexuality, liberating her from feeling ashamed because her fantasies didn't conform to the norm.

"Next time I'm here, in addition to the wine I'll bring some Chivas for me and cocktail fixings for you. I know you like the sweet stuff."

The wine was starting to work, relaxing more than her muscles. "You're so sweet for noticing."

Brundar winced as if she'd offended him.

Callie laughed. "You're funny."

Now he really looked perplexed.

## 27

# BRUNDAR

No one had called Brundar sweet or funny other than his mother, and that was a very long time ago.

He used to love making Helena laugh. As a little boy, he'd thought his mother's laughter was the most beautiful sound in the world.

Anandur had gotten her sense of humor, her propensity for mischief, and her love of gossip. The red hair and his size must've come from his sire. Brundar had inherited their mother's looks. Her pale blond hair, her slim build, her perfectly symmetrical features. She was a stunningly beautiful woman.

On a male, though, that beauty was a curse.

He should call her.

But what would he say?

Sorry for not calling?

Nah. Anandur was doing the honors for both of them. His brother updated their mother on the latest keep gossip, and she returned the favor by supplying the same about the Scottish arm of the clan.

Every Sunday, on their once a week call, Brundar would hear them talking and laughing.

Yeah, it was better if he didn't call. Ever since he'd been irrevocably changed, talking to Helena only dampened her spirits. She could do without his calls.

According to his brother, Brundar was a dry stick who had no sense of humor.

"How am I funny?" he asked.

Calypso waved a hand. "You got that confused look on your face when I called you sweet. That's funny. You're funny."

She was slurring her words after three-quarters of one glass of crappy wine. The woman was not a lightweight; she was a featherweight.

"Are you okay?" He frowned. "I think you're drunk."

She nodded with a smile. "I am, a little, and it feels wonderful. Don't be mad." She pouted.

The woman was so sexy when she loosened up. Leaning against the sofa's back pillows, Calypso let her head drop back, which had the effect of elongating her creamy neck and pushing her breasts out.

Like a ripe peach, sweet and succulent, she looked ready for the taking.

"Why would I be mad?" His own words came out somewhat slurred, though in his case it wasn't due to inebriation.

She shrugged. "I don't know. You're weird. Difficult to figure out. I don't know what makes you happy, what makes you sad, what gets you aroused... and your eyes glow." She pointed with a finger.

He bet they did. Every part of his immortal male anatomy was responding to Calypso's unintentional come-hither body language.

She giggled. "Did little Red ask the big bad wolf about his glowing eyes? Or was it their size?" She glanced down at his very obvious bulge and giggled again, covering her mouth with her hand. "Do you think it was a metaphor for something else?"

"So now I'm the big bad wolf?"

She shook her head. "You're way too pretty." She appraised him with mischief in her eyes. "You are Prince Charming." The mischief extended to her lips, lifting the corners in a sexy smirk. "But unlike in the fairy tale. I didn't get a kiss, yet." She waggled her brows.

He narrowed his eyes at her. Was she really that drunk from one miserly glass of cheap wine? Or was she angling for a kiss?

*Tempting, so very tempting.*

But if he kissed her, he would be crossing the point of no return.

After kissing her, he would lift her into his arms, carry her to the bedroom, tie her spread-eagled to the bedposts, and pleasure her until she forgot her own name.

*A stupendously bad idea.*

"Don't do this, Calypso. You don't know what you're courting."

Swishing around what little remained of the wine in her glass, she took a moment to lift her head and look into his eyes. "I love it when you call me Calypso. I used to hate that name, but not anymore. On your lips it sounds like sex."

Fates, he was losing the battle to this little girl. The mighty warrior was helpless against the charms of a woman barely out of childhood.

She was setting his blood on fire and scrambling his brain.

He watched with morbid fascination as she reached her finger and touched his lower lip, the scent of her arousal drowning out the last vestiges of reason and restraint.

The predator in him surged to the surface, demanding he take over and teach her everything there was about yielding, starting with that impudent finger. Catching it between his blunt front teeth, he bit down gently, then licked the little hurt away.

Calypso didn't cower and pull back as he'd expected her to. Instead, her eyes hooded with desire, and her lips parted on a moan.

He shook his head, dispelling the momentary loss of control. This wasn't right. She was drunk, and he hadn't explained anything, hadn't laid out the rules. That was not how it worked in his world.

But he couldn't reject her either. It would crush her spirits. The wine had given her the courage to voice her wants, and if refused she might never have the guts to be so forward again.

It would be unforgivable.

He should kiss her, even if it could go no further than that. Just one kiss with no strings attached. Give the girl a taste of how it could be. Give her the courage to seek her pleasure and not shy away from it.

Cupping the back of her neck, he leaned closer, his mouth inches away from her lips. "Sweetling, there is so much I need to tell you, but it will have to wait until you sober up. Remember what I told you about respect and consent? Those are not present when your brain is even marginally incapacitated."

She blushed but didn't shy away from his gaze. "I might not have the courage then. I know what I want, what I need." Her temporary bravado spent, she lowered her eyes. "Sometimes, though, I wonder if it's worth the risk or the consequences. It would be so much easier to leave it as a fantasy. It took me forever to admit my cravings. I don't know why I have them. I wish I didn't. It's hard on my self-respect. I'm not weak, and I'm not a pushover, but that's the first thing that comes to mind."

He shook his head. "This is a misconception. There is a stigma attached to the women and men who enjoy submitting sexually, but those who pity or look down on them should be envious instead. Vanilla, even at its best, can't compare. The heights of pleasure a submissive can climb are unparalleled."

She chuckled and gulped the last of her wine. "So what are you saying? That I'm lucky to be like that?"

"That's exactly what I'm saying. This is a gift, not a curse. Don't deny yourself because of what others think. You shouldn't deprive yourself of the experience. But make sure you do it with a deserving partner. Safety is paramount. Don't bestow this gift on just anyone. The right man should understand that your pleasure and your needs dictate the scene. Not his."

"I don't get it. You make it sound as if it's all about me. What do you get out of it?"

By replacing the hypothetical placeholder partner with him, she was turning it personal and making it extremely difficult for Brundar to leash his raging need.

They weren't talking about him.

This was about her.

He continued as if he wasn't part of the equation. Because he couldn't be. "What people fail to understand is that the dominant partner should serve the needs of the submissive and not the other way around. The pleasure the dominant derives is in direct proportion to the pleasure he or she delivers. I'm not saying that it's like that for everyone, not even the majority of them. But the good ones know that it's their responsibility, and that it should never be taken lightly."

Franco had taught him that. It was that philosophy that had made the place a second home for him as well as for the other members.

For Brundar, there was no greater satisfaction than bringing his partners to the peak of ecstasy, and not by pumping them full of his venom. That came after—an unexpected bonus he ensured they had no recollection of.

By this point in the explanation, most novices' emotions would be all over the place, hovering between lust and embarrassment, even fearfulness. Not Calypso, though. She was still gazing at him with desire in her eyes, and if he was reading her right, determination.

Damn. The lady knew what she wanted, and whom she wanted it with.

"Can I at least get a kiss? I'm sure you don't need a signed contract for that." She didn't even try to hide the sarcasm in her tone.

Was she making fun of him?

Did she think he was making too big of a deal of something that wasn't?

Brundar was tempted to show her the error of her ways. One light punishment would drive the point home. Leaning closer, he whispered in her ear, "I should spank you for not taking this seriously. And for that disrespectful tone."

Instead of jerking away, Calypso closed her eyes and let her head fall back into his loose grip. "Oh, God. Yes. Please."

He nuzzled her neck. "Not shy, are you, lass? Is that the wine talking?"

"It's not the wine. I'm tired of waiting around for what I want."

Brundar had to admire her honesty. "Good for you."

Encouraged by his praise, she lifted her hands to his chest. He could tolerate a female's hands on him; it was only another male's touch that repulsed him, but that didn't mean he was comfortable with it. Gripping her wrists in one hand, he held her hands down on her lap.

She whimpered, her arousal rising.

Damnation. Not taking it further than a kiss was going to strain his formidable self-control to its utmost limits.

Could he survive just kissing her for the next hour until she sobered up?

Or should he give her the one kiss she'd asked for and leave?

That would be the smartest course of action. The problem was, for a change, Brundar wasn't thinking with his head. His gut and his lust were screaming so loudly for him to take her that he could barely pay attention to what his brain was trying to tell him.

# 28

# CALLIE

Callie should've been shaking like a leaf. How the hell had she summoned the courage to proposition Brundar, the most dangerous man she'd ever met, and goad him into taking the first step?

Was it liquid courage?

Or was she certifiable?

Looking for the baddest of the bad boys?

First Shawn, and now this deadly angel of a man who made Shawn look like nothing more than a sandbox bully.

Where Shawn was quick to anger, making as much noise as possible and breaking things while at it, Brundar's silent control gave the impression of real and mortal danger. The analogy that came to her mind was a bulldog versus a tiger. One raged and barked loudly, the other delivered justice stealthily, swiftly, and emotionlessly.

One was a potential criminal, the other a lawful executioner.

The paradox was that Brundar's leashed power didn't scare her. Not much anyway. She had a strong feeling that if he only let her in, it would be like taking shelter in the eye of the storm. The world could rage around her, but she would be safe.

Naturally, there was a price to pay for that security.

She was more than willing to pay. Ceding control to the only man who could ever live up to her fantasies was no hardship at all.

His thumb stroked the back of her neck where his large hand held her in a loose grip.

"You're a beautiful woman, Calypso," he said as he closed the distance between their lips and kissed her.

As lights exploded behind her closed lids, sizzling energy flooded her body, frying her synapses and making her limbs feel limp.

She'd been waiting for this for so long.

How many times had she fantasized about being held immobile and taken by a man she trusted implicitly?

But the reality of Brundar being that man was so much better than the fantasy. For the next few minutes her choices were no longer hers, but only because she agreed to the transfer of power and was a hundred percent sure she could get it back anytime she wanted to. A contradiction, a paradox, but somehow it all made sense to her.

His lips were firm, but gentle, and as his tongue licked at the seam of her mouth, the fingers holding her nape tightened. On a gasp, her lips parted, granting him entry. Keeping her immobile with a firm yet careful grip on her neck, his other hand holding down both of her wrists, he plundered her mouth expertly, thoroughly.

She was being taken and loving everything about it.

As Brundar possessed her mouth, the fire burning inside her got so hot she felt like she was melting. For a few precious moments, Callie experienced something so new, so different, that it was outside her sphere of reference. Nothing compared to this.

When his mouth abandoned hers, she was ready to cry from disappointment, but then Brundar lifted her into his lap and closed his arms around her, cocooning her in his warmth.

The iceman wasn't cold at all.

But why had he stopped?

The hard length prodding her backside proved that he'd been just as affected.

Callie's experience with guys wasn't extensive, limited to Shawn and what she heard or read about, but it was enough to know that stopping in the middle of something so hot was not what the vast majority of men would do.

To have a willing woman they were obviously attracted to and refuse her?

"Is it because I'm not on the pill?" she blurted. It was something Callie intended on taking care of as soon as she could.

Brundar rested his chin on the top of her head. "No, sweetling. It's because of what I told you before. Alcohol impairs judgment."

"I'm not drunk. I can prove it to you. I can touch my nose with my finger." She tried to release one of her hands, which he had trapped between their bodies.

His arms tightened around her. "Don't."

The edge of command in his tone sent a wave of heat rushing through her.

"Okay," she reluctantly acquiesced.

Were they done?

Would he ever allow her to touch him? Just a casual touch when they were not in what he called a scene?

A chilling thought occurred to her. What if he never did anything with a woman outside of those parameters?

Was he one of those who demanded obedience at all times?

Talk about a splash of ice-cold water.

The disappointment was so deep that it almost felt like grief. Already, she was mourning the loss of him.

Callie could never tolerate a relationship like that. No matter how amazingly sexy the guy was, or how much he'd done for her, her freedom was not something she was willing to barter for a few moments of passion. This was not how she wanted to live her life.

Brundar's hold on her loosened. "What's going through your head, Calypso?" He sounded worried.

She shook her head. For someone who appeared so stoic, he was way too perceptive. He felt her emotions changing even without observing her expressions.

She couldn't tell him, though. It wasn't fair to him. This was all on her.

She'd been the one to initiate, to push him into something he didn't want or would only participate in under strict conditions.

No wonder going over the rules was so important to him.

"I'm sorry. I shouldn't have pushed."

He chuckled. "If I didn't want to kiss you, it wouldn't have mattered how much you pushed."

The compulsion to ask was too strong for her to ignore, even if the answer she was expecting would hurt like hell. "Why can't I touch you? I understand when it's part of a scene. But we are done, aren't we?"

"Yes, we are."

When he didn't continue, she thought he wasn't going to answer her, but then he sighed and put his chin on top of her head again. "I don't like being touched. I don't even shake hands."

Was he talking about his sexual partners or in general? "With no one?"

"No one."

Okay, so it wasn't about sex with him. Some kind of a phobia?

"But you're touching me. You offered me your hand several times."

He chuckled. "I have no problem with touching you. I love having my hands on you."

She could live with that. Maybe not forever, but in the meantime, until she helped him work out whatever issues he had with being touched.

*Listen to yourself. After one kiss you're already planning on fixing the guy? What if he doesn't want to be fixed?*

Relaxing in Brundar's arms, she rested her cheek on his hard chest muscles, listening to the steady beat of his heart. He was so strong. Yes, he'd just revealed vulnerability, but that required strength as well. It was hard to imagine a powerful man like him having trouble with such a simple thing as a handshake.

"You're a bodyguard. What happens in a fight? Like in hand-to-hand combat?"

"I'm very good with knives, swords, and guns. You name it; I mastered the use of it. No one ever gets close enough to touch me."

Callie shivered. She could totally imagine Brundar with a sword like some medieval knight.

Curiosity demanded that she ask why, but compassion overpowered that need. He didn't know her well enough to share such a personal thing with her. That being said, she could at least sate her curiosity regarding his relationship preferences.

"Forgive me for asking," she started and felt him tense. "What kind of a relationship are you into?"

"What do you mean?"

"I read about the lifestyle and I know some dominants like to be in charge at all times. Are you one of those?" She held her breath as she waited for his response.

And waited.

The guy took his sweet time.

"I don't think so, no."

He'd sounded unsure, which was weird. He either was or wasn't. Brundar seemed to be in his late twenties or early thirties. A guy as handsome as he probably had a lineup of ex-girlfriends. He should have some idea of what he liked in a relationship.

"Think back. What did you like or not like about your relationships with women?"

"I never had any."

That couldn't be true. He must've misunderstood her meaning.

"Your other girlfriends. Did you want to dominate them twenty-four-seven?"

He sighed, sounding exasperated. "I've never had a girlfriend. I only do hookups."

She looked at him. "Do you mean to tell me that all you had your entire life were fuck-buddies?"

"That would be correct."

"So..." she started.

"That's enough, Calypso. Don't try to fit me into a box, and forget all you've read about on the Internet. It doesn't apply to me."

"But you told me to read—" His disapproving expression shut her up.

It was true he'd told her that, but what she could learn from reading about others would tell her nothing about Brundar. Every person was different. The only way she would find out what made him tick, what he liked or disliked, was by getting to know him.

The question was whether he'd ever let her get close enough.

## 29

# RONI

Two weeks and nothing.

Roni knocked on the glass, letting Barty know he was ready to go.

Maybe Andrew's venom was too weak?

The last time they'd met at the dojo, Andrew had said something about bringing another immortal male. Hopefully it wasn't that scary Brundar guy.

Was he even bigger than Anandur?

Were all immortal males big?

Sylvia was of average height, and none of her girlfriends were huge, so it made sense that the men were of average height too. Maybe Anandur was the anomaly.

He could hope.

Crap. He wasn't looking for a repeat round of getting thrown to the mat and bitten. Then again, now that he knew what was coming it wasn't as scary. The bite had stung like a son-of-a-bitch, and being overpowered so easily by Andrew had been humiliating, but the after effects hadn't been so bad.

Hell, if he cared to be honest it had been fucking awesome.

A psychedelic trip.

Roni wondered if it was what smoking pot felt like.

From movies and books it seemed that his entire generation was doing it and he was the only one not partaking in the fun because he was a prisoner. A pampered and respected one, with a nice crib and all, but not free to do what other guys his age took for granted.

He was beyond lucky that Andrew had agreed to help him get laid, otherwise he would have still been a virgin. And he was luckier still that Sylvia liked him enough to stick around.

"Ready for some ass whooping, boy genius?" Barty asked as he opened the door for him.

"Fuck you, Barty. Put your fat ass on the mat and let's see how well you do."

Barty shook his head. "Touchy, touchy." He slapped Roni's back. "There is nothing wrong about getting your ass handed to you by someone better trained. That's how you learn."

Yeah, if he was training to become a fighter that would've been true, but Roni was fighting a war with a different set of tools. His were much more valuable than the muscles needed for simple hand-to-hand combat.

One day, in the not too distant future, he would be able to topple regimes without firing a single shot. Working for the government, with the best hardware in the world at his disposal, Roni's skill had grown exponentially over the years.

Anandur, Andrew, and their like had nothing on him.

This was the new reality. The world belonged to geeks and nerds, not the strong of arm. The days of might making right were over.

On the drive to the dojo, Roni distracted himself by reading a book. The old fashioned paper kind because his supervisors refused to let him use a smartphone or a tablet outside his secure glass enclosure.

God, he couldn't wait to be free.

"Who's the new guy?" Barty asked when Roni opened the door to the dojo.

"I don't know."

The new immortal they'd brought in looked less intimidating than Anandur, but not by much.

Anandur beckoned him over. "Roni, my man, come meet Onegus. Your new sparring partner."

The guy cracked a smile and winked as he offered his hand. "Don't worry, kid. I'll go easy on you."

"Don't," Barty called from the peanut gallery.

"Asshole." Roni turned around and flipped him the bird.

"Don't mind him." Onegus wrapped his arm around Roni's shoulders and leaned closer. "Let's give him a good show," he whispered.

Roni groaned. It might be a show for Onegus, but it sure as hell wasn't going to be for him. "Yeah. Let's."

Onegus assumed the stance and Roni mirrored it.

"Barty, you're not listening," Sylvia complained.

"I want to watch the new guy." The handler waved for her to move.

That was a problem.

"Pay attention to Sylvia," the one called Rachel said, compelling both Barty and Roni to look at Sylvia.

Onegus snapped his fingers. "Eyes on me, kid."

Roni shook his head and turned to face his sparring partner. There had been something weird in both Onegus and Rachel's voices, a sort of vibration that had an almost hypnotic quality. Was that thralling?

"Last warning, Roni. Pay attention." Anandur said. "Let's start with a warmup, going through the katas you've learned."

"Okay."

"Onegus, you're on the offense."

The guy moved in slow motion, broadcasting his move so Roni could prepare the appropriate block. They went through several sequences until Anandur clapped his hands.

"Okay, boys. Warm up is done."

Roni glanced in Barty's direction. The handler had forgotten all about him and was giving his undivided attention to Sylvia, who was telling him about her imaginary brother who wanted to become an agent.

The girls must've been thralling Barty all along for the guy not to realize that it was strange they never joined the guys for practice, or that Sylvia was spending most of her time entertaining him with stories instead of training.

"Don't worry about him," Onegus said. "A bomb could detonate next to him and he wouldn't notice."

Roni nodded.

Onegus smiled again, this time flashing a pair of elongated fangs. Interesting. The warm up had been enough to spur aggression in the immortal. There was so much Roni still had to learn about these people. Just as humans, each one was an individual—different and unique. Onegus was nothing like Anandur, and Andrew was nothing like either one of them.

Getting in position, he waited for Onegus to make the first move, but the guy motioned for Roni to start.

Roni attacked, and Onegus blocked but didn't attack back. For a few minutes, he let Roni practice his moves and then started a slow attack. Roni managed to block a few, but the guy was so strong that blocking him nearly shattered Roni's bones. When this match was over, he would be bruised black and blue.

"Finish it," Roni said quietly.

Onegus shook his head. "You have to work for it, buddy."

Crap. The immortal was toying with him.

"Showing off to impress the ladies?" He taunted the guy, hoping to make him angry.

"Always." Onegus smiled again. The guy used that smile of his like a weapon. "But these ladies are my cousins. So no, I'm not showing off to impress them. Come on, boy. Show me what you got. You can do better than that."

Frustrated, Roni forgot all about the damn katas and just charged forward, yelling as he barreled into Onegus.

He barely managed to move the guy an inch, let alone topple him. Roni's miserly one hundred and thirty pounds were to the immortal what a fly was to a wolf.

With a sigh, Onegus grabbed Roni as if he was going to give him a hug, picked him up and slammed him down to the mat, turning him around midair.

The air rushed out of his lungs and his ribs hurt, but Roni didn't stay down. Rolling sideways, he kept Onegus off him for another split second.

The immortal didn't pounce on him. He grabbed him like a rag doll, turned him around and slammed him back face down. A powerful hand closed over the back of his neck. "Stop squirming and make like a possum," Onegus hissed, his hot breath bathing Roni's neck.

Easier said than done.

Roni's brain was telling him to submit and have this over with, but his instincts screamed for him to get away and avoid the mouth with those sharp fangs poised for attack, hovering an inch away from his neck.

"Stay!" Onegus's hand squeezed tight, cutting off Roni's air supply.

Roni bucked harder.

"Oh, for fuck's sake." Onegus loosened his fingers, moving his palm to the back of Roni's head.

A moment later Roni felt the guy's tongue on his neck.

*What the hell?* He hadn't signed on for any tongue action.

But when the sharp points of Onegus's fangs penetrated his skin, the burn wasn't as bad as when Andrew had done it. Or maybe it was just less of a shock.

"Hey? What the hell are you doing to him?" Roni heard Barty yell, the cloud of euphoria spreading throughout his body, making his limbs feel as soft as clouds.

"He is fine. Give him a moment," Anandur said.

The venom's effect was milder this time. Roni was aware of what was going on around him but too loopy to respond. It took him a few minutes to regain control of his arms and push himself up to a sitting position.

"Are you okay, boy?" Barty tried to push Anandur aside.

*Yeah, good luck with that, buddy.* Moving a semitrailer was easier.

"I'm good, Barty. Just got the air knocked out of me for a moment." Roni took several deep breaths, then pushed up to his feet.

He walked over to Barty, his wobbly legs making him sway from side to side as if he was drunk. "I'm touched, old man. You care." He pulled Barty into his arms in a weak embrace. "I love you, man."

Awkwardly, Barty patted his back. "You must've banged your head damn hard, boy." The handler turned an angry glare at Onegus. "Are you out of your fucking mind? Do you know what his brain is worth?"

Barty pushed Roni off him but wrapped his arm around his waist to help him stand straight. "That's it. This class is officially over. These people are morons."

"No, Barty. I'm fine. Really. Ask me something hard."

"How much is sixty-four times seventy-three?"

Roni rolled his eyes. "That's what you call hard? I can do this with half of my brain missing."

"Just answer the question, smart ass."

"Four thousand, six hundred and seventy-two."

Barty pulled out his phone. "Hey, Siri, what's sixty-four times seventy-three?"

Naturally, Siri confirmed Roni's answer.

"Okay, so you can still do head math. But I still think something is wrong with you. You're way too relaxed and mushy. My Roni is a prickly pear."

"Oh, you called me your Roni." Roni leaned his head on Barty's shoulder.

"Well, kid, if getting beat up gets you in such a good mood, I'm willing to slap you around anytime."

"Stand in line," Andrew muttered.

Roni flipped them both off. "I feel the love, assholes."

"And... he's back." Barty clapped him on the shoulder.

## 30

# KIAN

From his seat at the head of the conference table, Kian glanced at William and Andrew who had joined the weekly Guardians meeting. Their respective expertise was needed.

"What's the status with the cars, William?" he asked.

The poor guy looked like he had lost a lot of weight, but it had done nothing to improve his looks. On the contrary. The dark circles under his eyes had gotten worse, and he looked even paler than usual. Kian was of a mind to send the guy to Bridget for a checkup. Or even better, to Vanessa.

William seemed depressed. Ever since his girlfriend had left, he hadn't been his cheerful old self and had been spending his days and nights in his lab, working. By the looks of him, the guy hadn't slept for days.

"I'm told that the model works fine. The design firm shipped it to us for a test drive, and once we approve it, they'll send a rep to incorporate the technology into our manufacturing process. After that, it's a matter of how fast we can build them."

"Tell them to send the rep right away. I want them to modify the production line even before the test model gets here. If they say it works fine, then it probably does. If I'm not happy with something, they should be able to make adjustments on the fly."

"I'll let them know." William started typing on his tablet.

"What about the hacker?" Kian asked Andrew.

"Onegus treated Roni to another bite yesterday. I haven't heard anything from the kid yet."

Kian tapped his pen on his notepad. "A young guy like him should've transitioned after the first bite. I think we need to accept that he is not a Dormant."

Andrew shook his head. "Not possible. He has more indicators than all of us newly initiated immortals put together."

"That's true. But it could be a coincidence."

Andrew lifted a brow. "Including the grandmother?"

"Who knows. Maybe there is another explanation for that. In any case, if he doesn't transition in a couple of days, we venom him one last time. If that doesn't work either, it's memory clean time."

Andrew grimaced. "Can we keep him even if he doesn't turn immortal? The kid is a fucking genius. He is going to be a huge asset to us. Besides, taking chances with that brain of his…" He shook his head. "It would be like exposing a masterpiece to smoke. If we damage his brain even a smidgen, it would be unforgivable."

Bracing his elbows on the table, Kian raked his fingers through his hair. "If we do that, we will have to keep him locked up for the rest of his life. That's not a good deal."

"He would be exchanging one prison for another, with the added benefit of being with Sylvia whenever he wants. I think it's a better deal than the one he has now."

"True. But his current imprisonment is temporary. How long does he have left?"

"Don't be naive, Kian. They will not let Roni go unless they find someone better to replace him. They will dig out more charges or make some up as an excuse to keep him locked up. He is too valuable on the inside and too dangerous on the outside."

"Guys," Kri interjected. "This whole discussion is premature. Wait until we know for sure that he is not turning."

"Right." Kian waved a hand. "We'll discuss Roni again at our next meeting." He turned to Onegus. "Any news on the police investigation?"

"There was another murder at the beginning of the week."

"Fuck," Bhathian grumbled.

"The police are trying to keep it under wraps to prevent panic, but they are suspecting a satanic cult or something similar. They're thinking along the lines of ritual sacrifices."

Kian nodded. "What about your investigation?"

"Still working on it. I'm checking every male's alibi for the time frame of the last one's murder."

"Any suspects?" Kian asked.

Onegus smirked. "The only one who sneaks around like he has something to hide is our friend Brundar."

Kri snorted, and all eyes turned to the Guardian.

Brundar crossed his arms over his chest and lifted a brow. "Should I get legal representation?"

Fates, the guy really didn't have a sense of humor. "No, Brundar. Just tell us where you were."

"No."

"Leave him alone." Anandur put a hand on his brother's shoulder, which earned him a deep scowl and a growl. He took it off. "Brundar is seeing some mystery woman. That's all."

Several pairs of incredulous eyes landed on the stoic warrior.

"Is that true?" Onegus asked.
"None of your fucking business."
*I'll be damned.* Kian stifled a smile.

## 31

# BRUNDAR

Fucking Anandur and his big mouth.

Brundar shook his head as he walked out. It served him right for trying to crack a joke. He sucked at it. Legal representation. It wasn't even funny.

What had possessed Anandur to come to his rescue when none had been needed?

He'd known Onegus hadn't been serious.

His brother was supposed to be the trickster, the funny one; he should've recognized a joke for what it was. But no, he had to do the brotherly thing.

Brundar got in his car and slammed the door shut.

For a few moments, he sat motionless, trying to calm down. Ever since Calypso had reentered his life, not that she'd ever really left, his quiet Zen-like attitude had evaporated. He was restless, agitated, and itching for a fight.

If only he could find someone to offer him a challenge.

It probably had something to do with his self-imposed abstinence. He wasn't like William who could do without. Brundar was only four generations removed from the source, which made him one horny bastard who needed a steady supply of sex.

Normally, it wasn't a problem; he had plenty of willing takers in the club and elsewhere. But he wanted none of them. There was only one woman he wanted, and he couldn't have her.

What a clusterfuck.

Brundar turned on the ignition and backed out of his parking spot. There was a small matter that he needed to take care of, and it couldn't wait.

Tomorrow, Shawn was getting served with the divorce papers. Brundar intended to make sure the guy signed on the dotted line.

He was about to break clan law, and he didn't give a damn. He was allowed one fucking transgression after all his years of service.

No, he wasn't. All the excuses in the world would not make it right.

Brundar sighed. As a Guardian, he had an obligation to adhere to the letter of the law, and until now he had. Thralling was not allowed for personal benefit.

Out of necessity and in the spirit of keeping immortals' existence secret, it was allowed after a venom bite and any other incident which could lead to their discovery. Naturally, everyone cheated a little, and as long as it was harmless no one made a big fuss about it. But as a Guardian Brundar held himself to higher standards. He'd already bent the law when he'd thralled Shawn a year ago. Except, at that time there had been no personal benefit to Brundar. He'd done it to protect Calypso.

Not even Edna, the strictest judge the clan ever had, would fault him for doing so. Or maybe she would. Edna believed that the laws the clan had put in place over its many years of existence were crucial to its continuing survival and the welfare of its members.

It was fine with him if she took that stance. As far as Brundar was concerned she could judge him for that infraction and impose whatever penalty she believed he deserved. But the one he was about to commit was not an infraction, it was a straight out violation. So yeah, in a way he was protecting Calypso again, but Brundar couldn't pretend he had no personal stake in it.

He would do the crime and serve the time, or have it taken out of his hide as the case was. After the deed was done, he would march himself to Edna's office, confess, and get the whipping she would no doubt sentence him to.

Not a big deal. Pain didn't scare him. On the contrary, he would welcome it. The punishment would help clear the guilt.

Nothing was going to deter him from the course of action he'd decided on.

Hopefully, the asshole was home. If not, Brundar was going to wait as long as it took until he got there.

Last night, Brundar had listened to the recordings of Shawn's phone calls over the past week. He owed William a favor for that.

The guy had fumed and raged when Calypso's father had informed him she'd left, and that he had no idea where she was. Shawn had made some threats, but fortunately for him, he hadn't followed through on them.

Calypso's friend had been next. When she'd told him the same thing, Shawn had changed tactics. He'd asked Dawn to deliver a message: to tell Calypso that she was going to crawl back to him and beg him to take her back because she was a worthless piece of whoring shit and no one else would ever want her.

The jerk deserved a slow and excruciating death just for that. But that was Brundar's opinion, not the law's. Not the clan's and not the humans'. Hateful words were allowed by law, and punishing someone for uttering them wasn't.

Brundar only wondered how many victims' lives could have been spared if the law saw things differently.

Shawn wasn't home when Brundar got there, but he didn't have to wait long until the guy arrived and his expensive car pulled into the garage.

A minute later Brundar knocked on the door.

Shawn threw it open, his eyes narrowing. "What do you want?" Obviously, he'd been waiting for someone else. "I don't want to buy anything." He tried to slam the door shut in Brundar's face.

Brundar blocked the door from closing with his booted foot, then gave it a push, sending Shawn staggering back.

"What the fuck?"

"I only need a minute of your time." Brundar walked in and shut the door behind him.

They were more or less the same height, and getting Shawn's beady eyes to focus on his was easier than Brundar had expected.

*Weak mind.* He was reminded of his first impression of the guy.

"Listen and remember." He took hold of Shawn's suit jacket, which the guy hadn't had time to take off yet. "Tomorrow, you'll be served with divorce papers. You are going to accept all the terms and sign them immediately. You're getting one hell of a deal. Callie is leaving you the house and asks for nothing. You are very happy about that. She is gone, and you get to keep the house. You don't care where she goes or what she does. You don't want to even think about her. After you sign the papers, you will barely remember ever being married to her. Do you understand?"

Eyes glazed over, Shawn nodded.

"Repeat what I said."

"I'm very happy about the deal I'm getting. I get to keep the house, and I don't care what Callie does or where she goes."

"Very good. Now go sit on the couch and repeat that twenty times."

Shawn shuffled to the couch and plopped down. "I'm very happy—"

Brundar let himself out.

That had been one hell of an invasive thrall. Some brain damage was inevitable, but Brundar couldn't care less. With Shawn's twisted mind, anything would be an improvement. The important thing was that it should hold for at least a couple of months. By then Shawn would forget why his wife leaving him had upset him.

The thing was, Brundar still felt uneasy. Killing Shawn would've eliminated the threat not only to Calypso, but to any other woman the guy might get involved with in the future. But the law tied Brundar's hands.

As he drove back to the keep, Brundar debated the wisdom of the laws he followed. Today he'd done the right thing, and yet he was going to get punished for it.

Was it right? Or was it wrong?

Was the law flawed?

Or was his reasoning erroneous?

There were no right answers, and greater minds than his had struggled with these issues. Right and wrong were not black and white, they were many shades of gray.

## 32

## CALLIE

"Miri, I'm taking my break now," Callie told the barmaid.

"No problem, take your time. It's a slow night."

"Thanks."

It was her second week working at the club. Even though she was an experienced waitress, it had taken some adjusting to. The level of noise was deafening. She'd tried wearing earplugs to reduce the damage to her hearing, but it was counterproductive to taking drink orders, and she'd taken them out.

Other than that Franco and his crew were good people who treated her as part of the family from day one, which was very much appreciated given how lonely and isolated she was.

Customers were the same everywhere; some were nice, some were jerks and some tried to flirt with her. But she'd encountered none who had been overly rude or handsy. The tips, as she'd discovered, were much better than at Aussie.

As always, she took her break outside to give her ears a reprieve from the noise.

"Hey, Callie girl, how ya doin'?" Donnie the bouncer closed his massive hand on her shoulder and gently tugged her to stand next to him. Wandering away from the club without an escort was not happening. Neither Donnie nor Salvatore would let her out of their sights.

"Fine." She cast him a glance. "Tell me something, Donnie. Did Brad tell all of you to keep an eye on me or is it standard procedure?"

Donnie added his second hand to her other shoulder and started kneading her sore muscles. "It's the middle of the night, girl, and this is no Beverly Hills. Not that I would've let you walk alone in the dark even if it was."

"Oh, Donnie, this feels great. But you didn't answer my question."

He exhaled an exasperated breath. "I did. Even if Brad didn't ask, I would be keeping you right here by my side."

So he did ask. Figures.

Every night after her shift ended, Brundar walked her home, and if he wasn't available, Franco or one of the bouncers did.

The problem was that it always ended at her door. He never came in.

Brundar had given her a taste with that one kiss and that was it. At the club, he treated her the same as any other employee, and the only one who talked on their short walk to her apartment was her. He was very careful not to give her the slightest opening, keeping her at arm's length.

Donnie let go of her shoulders and pulled out a cigarette. "You want one?" he asked as he always did even though she'd told him she didn't smoke.

As frustrated as she was, maybe the coffin nail would do her some good. She was so sick of being a good girl. Perhaps that was why Brundar was staying away from her. She was too naive, too green, etc., etc.

"Yeah, I'll take one. But you need to tell me what to do. I never smoked before."

He handed her the cigarette and pulled another one for himself. "Easy, it's just like smoking a joint."

"I never smoked pot either."

Donnie chuckled. "Where did you grow up? An Amish farm, or a convent?"

"Stop it." She slapped his arm. "Not everyone does it. I chose not to."

Lighting his cigarette, Donnie shook his head. "I knew there was something strange about you. You're a time traveler from the fifties."

Callie laughed and slapped his arm again. "Doofus. You keep it up, and I'll tell everyone that the big scary Donnie is a sci-fi and comic books nerd."

"See if I care." He flipped the lighter again and held it up for her. "Put just the tip to the flame and inhale. Don't take it in too deep. You'll choke." He winked.

"Pervert."

She followed his instructions and immediately started coughing. "This is horrible."

"I told you not to inhale too deeply. You didn't listen. Try it again and hold the smoke in your mouth. Don't inhale at all."

After two more drags, she dropped the cigarette and stamped it out. "Blah. It left a bad taste in my mouth."

Donnie's massive shoulders heaved with laughter.

"It's not funny." What a one-track mind. Were all guys like that?

She narrowed her eyes at him, her anger giving her courage. "Do you ever work or play downstairs?"

He shook his head. "Not in the way you think. Sometimes I help carry chairs and other furniture down there, but they have their own bouncers, or monitors as they call them." He smirked. "Why? Are you curious?"

"Yes. But Brad won't let me even take a peek. What do they do there that's so bad?"

Donnie waggled his brows. "Maybe he doesn't want you to see because what they do there is so good, eh?" He gently elbowed her side.

"If it is, why aren't you there?"

"It's not my thing. I'm as vanilla as they get, baby. Your boyfriend, however, has quite the reputation."

"He is not my boyfriend."

Donnie lifted a brow.

"He is a friend who happens to be a boy. Not the same. And what do you mean by reputation?"

Donnie shrugged. "He is very popular with the ladies. That's all I know."

Right. Donnie was a terrible liar.

"I know you know more. Spill."

"And get in trouble with Brad? I like my face the way it is, and I like my job."

Okay. She could understand that. Brundar was intimidating as hell. Though for a mountain of muscle like Donnie to fear him, he must've done more than glare.

"Is he violent? Did he ever get into a fight in the club?"

Donnie shook his head. "Not that I know of. He doesn't need to get physical. He just needs to show up. You know what we call him behind his back?"

"What?"

"The Grim Reaper."

She snorted. "He is too beautiful to be evil."

Donnie crossed his arms over his chest. "The Grim Reaper is not evil. He just does his job. And he is God's emissary, which means that he is an angel. And angels are supposed to be pretty."

"When you put it like that… I guess. He might be a little intimidating, but he is a good man. He is helping me, a lot, and expects nothing in return."

Donnie's brow lifted. "You sure about that?"

"Well, yeah. You said it yourself." She grimaced. "He is very popular with the ladies. He doesn't need to go out of his way to get, you know… laid."

Donnie remained silent for a few seconds, which wasn't like him. The big guy was a chatter bug. Taking one drag after the other from his cigarette, he blew smoke out into the cold night air.

"He doesn't look at anyone the way he looks at you."

"What do you mean?" Callie didn't notice Brundar looking at her at all. He'd been avoiding her as much as he could. He didn't look at her even on their walks home.

"He sneaks peeks at you like some teenager with a crush. And when he sees guys ogling you, he treats them to his deadly stare. I haven't seen him do that before. Until you came along, I thought he was made of granite. Like a statue or like that Edward guy from the vampire movie. Super pale face and all." Donnie bent from his considerable height and whispered in her ear. "Maybe he is a vampire. Did you notice his canines? They are fucking huge."

They were a little longer than usual, but a far cry from qualifying as fangs.

Callie patted Donnie's arm. "You have one hell of an imagination."

He shrugged. "Can you blame me? Most of the time I'm so bored standing here that I count the bricks on the building across the street. I have lots of free time to think."

"Why don't you get another job, then?"

"Who says I don't have one," he said in a tone that implied it was something interesting.

"What is it?"

"I draw comics." Donnie squared his big shoulders.

"Really? Which one?" No wonder he'd been telling her so much about them. He probably worked on one.

"Mine is not published yet. But it's going to be. Guess who's my superhero?"

"How would I know?"

"Your boyfriend. Bud, the slayer of rogue vampires."

Callie put her hand over her mouth to stifle a laugh. "He's going to kill you if he ever finds out." She didn't know Brundar well, but he seemed a very private person. Not the type who would appreciate starring in a comic.

Donnie put a finger to his lips. "If you don't tell him, he never will."

## 33

# BRUNDAR

*E*dna sighed, her shoulders slumping. "I understand why you did it, Brundar. But the law is the law. However, given the mitigating circumstances, I can reduce the severity of your penance. One week of incarceration."

Brundar shook his head. "I appreciate your leniency, but I can't do jail time. We are short on Guardians as it is, and putting me away will put an extra strain on the others. Besides, I need to keep an eye on Calypso. I'll take the whipping."

Edna regarded him with her soul-probing eyes. "Can I ask you a question?"

He nodded.

"Are you a masochist?"

Interesting. It seemed the Alien Probe couldn't read him as well as he thought she could. Good to know.

"No, I'm not."

Her lips lifted in a smile. "Good. I wouldn't want your punishment to be a reward."

Damn rumors. "I know what they whisper behind my back and I don't give a f… fig. I'm not looking forward to it, but I don't tremble in my pants either."

Her smile got wider. "I can't see you trembling in your pants for any reason. You have the strongest hold on your emotions of anyone I know. And it's more than skin deep."

Brundar stifled a smirk. Edna wasn't the all-powerful empath and soul searcher everyone thought she was because for the past two weeks his emotions had been all over the place. It was a daily struggle to drag himself back into the zone.

"Thank you."

"You're welcome, though I'm not sure it's a compliment."

"For me it is."

She nodded. "I bet. Back to the issue of your penance. Because you are a Guardian, only another Guardian can deliver it. But given the mitigating circumstances, I leave it up to you to choose which one. Also, I'll keep it a private affair with only Kian and the Guardians present. The last thing we need is for a rumor to spread of a Guardian breaking the law."

"Right. I appreciate it." He would've hated a public whipping. On the other hand, it could've been beneficial to show that Guardians were not above the law and got punished for breaking it the same as any other clan member.

"Normally, I prefer to execute the sentence immediately, but I'm willing to accommodate you. When would you prefer it done?"

"Tomorrow night if it's okay with you. I want to deliver the papers to Calypso's husband personally and make sure he signs them."

Edna tilted her head. "You know you're compounding your punishment. That's another violation to tag on."

He shrugged. "I want to see this brought to a conclusion as soon as possible, and I'm willing to suffer the consequences. Well worth it for me."

"You need his signature notarized. Are you going to drag a notary with you?"

He hadn't thought of that. "If I must, I will."

"You can use my secretary. She is human, but she knows not to ask questions."

"Good. And thank you."

Edna opened a drawer and handed him a brown envelope. "Everything he needs to sign is in here." She lifted her desk phone and pressed the intercom button. "Lora, could you please come in here? I have a short errand for you."

"Of course."

A moment later a rotund older woman entered Edna's office.

"Lora, this is my cousin Brundar. He is a friend of the lady who I took on as the pro bono divorce case. I need you to go with him to the husband's home and notarize his signature."

Lora shifted from foot to foot. "Hmm, you said he is the violent type. Wouldn't it be better to send a guy?"

Brundar rose to his feet. "That's why I'm delivering the documents. You have nothing to worry about with me around."

Lora looked him over. Once, then again. "You look like someone who can handle himself in a fistfight. But what if the guy has a weapon? A knife or a gun?"

"I'm trained to deal with situations like that. You're perfectly safe."

"Special Forces?"

"Yes. You'll wait in my car until I'm sure he is going to behave. You'll come in only when I call for you."

Lora exhaled the breath she'd been holding. "Okay. That I can do."

He waited for her to get her briefcase, then escorted her out of Edna's office and down to the parking garage of the high-rise.

"Thank you," she smiled as he opened the passenger door for her, then huffed as she climbed up into the seat.

"That's a big car you got," she said as he got in. "Do you have a large family?"

"Huge." He knew she was referring to a wife and kids and not to his extended family. But telling her that would have started another cascade of questions. Like how come he wasn't married and what was he waiting for?

"I have five grown kids and eleven grandchildren." She pulled out her phone and started showing him pictures.

Brundar pretended to glance at what she was showing him, nodding from time to time so as not to appear rude.

"My husband, may his soul rest in peace, he was the silent type too."

Sure he was. With her talking nonstop, the guy hadn't had a chance to stick a word in between.

"I didn't mind." She chuckled. "I talk a lot, as you surely noticed. So it was nice to have someone who was happy to just listen. I miss him dearly." She wiped at her eyes.

Poor woman, she must've lost her husband recently. He should say something. "I'm sorry for your loss."

Lora waved a chubby hand. "Oh, my Larry, God bless his soul, has been gone for more than a decade now. He was a good husband and a good father. The kids and I miss him so."

Surprisingly, Lora's love for her dead husband tugged at Brundar's heart. He'd witnessed his share of misery and loss, but he always managed to remain detached.

So why the hell had this story saddened him?

It wasn't a bad story. Lora and her Larry had had a good life together, which was more than most people got.

Was it because Lora was sitting right next to him?

Was it because she was a nice woman who wore her emotions on her sleeve?

Or was it envy for her deceased husband?

She'd compared Brundar to her Larry, and it made him think. The guy had been dead for over a decade but was still loved by his wife and children. It was something Brundar couldn't even imagine. He never thought of himself as worthy of love.

No, that wasn't true.

As a boy he'd been loved and cherished by his mother, probably still was in some small way. But he'd lost the ability to feel that love.

He didn't deserve it.

He'd been a foolish boy who should have listened to his elders instead of trusting the wrong people. He'd been so fucking naive.

Because of him, his family had suffered.

## 34

# RONI

Standing by the window, Roni looked out on the night cityscape visible from his building. Not much of a view. A row of office buildings, four to five stories high, one bench across the street with a poster of a smiling real estate agent glued to its back, two lampposts. He'd been staring at the same thing for way too long. And it seemed like he'd be staring at it for a whole while longer.

Fourth day since the bite and nothing. Roni sighed.

It had been a pleasant dream. Freedom, Sylvia, immortality. Maybe even good money so he could buy a car, a convertible, and go traveling.

With Sylvia, of course.

He'd leave the top down. Her hair blowing in the wind, she would be smiling the whole way. Maybe even singing.

Could she sing?

He didn't know.

They would stop for the night at roadside motels and make love for hours, then in the morning get in the car and keep going.

A fantasy.

Turning away from the window, Roni walked over to the couch, grabbed a comic book off the coffee table and lay down. Barty had brought him a stack of them. The agent claimed that he'd found them while cleaning up the attic. Tucked away in a box that had been gathering dust and spider webs, they were beautifully preserved because Barty's nephew had put each one in a plastic sleeve to protect them.

There must've been over a hundred of them, and Roni intended to read until his eyes got tired and he fell asleep. He needed to take his mind off what was not happening to him.

His eyes started drooping sooner than he'd expected. By the second comic his vision blurred and he had to close them. Maybe he needed reading glasses?

It was cold, and Roni covered himself with the throw blanket Barty's wife had crocheted for him. She'd never met him, and yet she'd gifted him with something that must've taken her days or even weeks to make.

The handler and his wife acted more like parents to Roni than his real ones.

What if he was adopted?

Maybe that was why his parents didn't care about him?

That would explain why he wasn't transitioning even though his grandmother almost certainly was an immortal. Other than that the only indicator that he was a Dormant was the fact that Sylvia liked him. True, the odds that a hot girl like her would fall for a scrawny guy like him were slim, but women were strange that way. Maybe she was attracted to his brain.

Could happen. Like Stephen Hawking's second wife. It wasn't as if she'd left her husband and married the dude in the wheelchair, the one her poor shmuck of a husband had designed for Hawking, because the scientist was such a hunk or a charmer. The only thing the guy had going for him was his brain.

Damn, it was getting cold in his apartment.

Too lazy to go get another blanket, or drag his ass to bed, Roni tucked the throw tighter around him and pushed himself deeper into the couch, pressing his back against the cushions.

He was still cold.

Why was his apartment freezing? It was the middle of summer for fuck's sake, and this was Los Angeles. Not a city known for its cool weather. Fucking climate change. It was supposed to be global warming, not cooling.

When the shivers started, Roni realized it wasn't cold in his apartment, but that he must be sick and running a fever.

Wait a minute, Andrew had warned him that the first symptoms of transition were flu like.

Fucking hell. If he was transitioning, it meant that he wasn't adopted, just not lovable enough for his parents to give a damn. True, his legal defense had ruined them financially, but weren't parents supposed to love their kids no matter what?

He hadn't killed anyone for God's sake. And until his eighteenth birthday, his pay checks went straight to his parents' account. That should've compensated nicely for their losses.

They had been relieved when he moved out, taking his handler with him and giving them their lives back. In the beginning, they'd still called once or twice a week, visiting once or twice a month, but soon the phone calls and visits had dwindled down to once every few months.

Fuckers.

Not a nice thing to say about one's parents, but they deserved it for abandoning him like that.

Whatever, he was getting a new family now.

Yeah. Like they were doing it out of love for him. The only reason the immortals were interested in him was his talent.

Did Sylvia really have feelings for him? Or was she bait to lure him in?

Paranoid much?

It was too late to start second guessing things now. He should call the front desk and tell them he wasn't feeling well. For his extraction to work, he had to get transferred to a hospital.

With a shaking hand, Roni picked up the cordless and dialed zero for the internal switchboard.

"What's up, Roni? Want us to order you pizza?"

He groaned. "Not this time. I'm sick. I need you guys to call a doctor or take me to the hospital."

"What's wrong with you?"

"I have a fever, and I shake all over. Please, hurry." He made himself sound more pitiful than he really felt.

"I'm on it. Hold it together, kid. We will take care of you."

"Thanks, man."

Disconnecting the call, Roni slumped into the couch cushions. Hopefully, they would call Barty to come sit with him. Roni doubted they would allow him to use the hospital's phone, while Barty wouldn't mind calling Sylvia for him, which would start the ball rolling.

Images of Sylvia swirling in his feverish head, Roni dozed off, only to wake up when someone pounded on his door.

"Roni, are you alive in there? We are coming in."

*About fucking time.*

He didn't answer, not because he didn't want to, but because his mouth was too dried out to talk.

The next moment, Jerome walked in. It was good that Roni's door had a keypad and not a regular lock. There was no need to break it down. Jerome could've done it, the guy must've weighed over three hundred pounds. Most of it was muscle, but a good layer of fat provided padding on top.

"I'm taking you to the hospital. Boss's orders." The guy scooped Roni into his arms as if he weighed nothing.

"Kevin, bring the kid a glass of water," Jerome told his buddy.

A couple of moments later the other security guard held a plastic cup to Roni's lips. "Try to drink some, kid."

The water felt heavenly and he emptied the entire cup. "Thanks. Can you get me another?"

"Sure thing, kiddo." Kevin walked over to the kitchen to refill the cup.

"Put me down, Jerome, I'm fine."

Jerome shook his head. "I put you down, you crumple like a rag doll."

Kevin held the cup to Roni's lips. He emptied it as well.

"Okay, princess. Let's get you to the hospital," Jerome said.

"Screw you."

"See?" Jerome turned to Kevin. "I told you he is not as sick as he looks. Roni is still the jerk we all know and love." He hoisted Roni higher. "You always act like such a prima donna, at least now you have a good excuse."

"Just don't mistake me for a football, and toss me to Kevin." Jerome used to play football in college.

"I just might. Doesn't his big head look like a football?" Jerome asked Kevin as he carried Roni out.

"It does. But how do we separate it from that scrawny string attached to it? What is it? Is it a neck?"

They might have had more fun at his expense, but Roni decided that it was okay to check out for at least a few minutes. Everything was working according to plan, and he was on his way to the hospital. His head resting on Jerome's padded chest, he closed his eyes and let sleep claim him.

## 35

# BRUNDAR

"Are you okay here on your own?" Brundar asked Lora, peering at her through the open passenger-side window.

"Perfectly. Better here than there." She pointed at Calypso's house.

"Expect my call in a few minutes."

"Yes, boss." She lifted her phone, showing him she was ready.

"Good."

Once again he was striding up to that house, readying for a confrontation with Calypso's soon to be ex-husband. Hopefully, for the last time and not because he killed the bastard.

Since Brundar had set the divorce papers as the trigger, the thrall he'd implanted in the guy's head was not in effect yet. Once Shawn was served, he would be compelled to agree to all the terms and sign, but until that moment a lot could happen.

Itching for the guy to give him a good reason to beat the hell out of him, Brundar knocked on the door. He couldn't kill the asshole, but beating him within an inch of his life would do.

No answer.

He pressed the bell button.

A moment later the door flew open. "What do you want? I'm not buying anything."

The small additional thrall to forget Brundar seemed to have worked exceptionally well. There wasn't even a shard of recognition in Shawn's booze-shot eyes. By the smell of alcohol wafting off of him, the guy had been drinking for a while.

Brundar rolled his eyes as Shawn tried to slam the door in his face again.

So predictable.

His hand bracing against the door, Brundar was ready this time. "Get inside." He shoved it open.

Shawn swayed on his feet, his balance further impaired by his inebriation. "What the hell? I'm calling the cops," he slurred.

"No, you're not. Sit down." Brundar pointed at the couch. "And turn off the dumb box." He imbued his tone with influence, compelling Shawn to obey.

"What do you want, man? I have no money or jewelry because my fucking whore of a wife left me and took everything with her." The guy's face twisted into an ugly grimace.

Brundar didn't need to delve deep to get hit with the jerk's ugly thoughts. He was practically projecting them like a damn telepath.

*I'm going to find her, and when I do, I'm going to beat the shit out of the fucking, cheating bitch until her pretty face is pretty no more. And after I kill the fucker she's fucking, I'm going to rearrange her face, so no one will ever want her. She'll come crawling back to me. I'll take the whore back, but I'll make her pay for the rest of her fucking life.*

In two long strides, Brundar closed the distance between himself and the piece of shit, hauled him up by his ratty T-shirt, closed his hands around the guy's thick neck, and squeezed.

Shawn tried to pry Brundar's fingers off, but even though he was strong for a human, he stood no chance against a pissed immortal.

When the guy's face started turning purple, Brundar forced himself to let go, dropping the scum on the couch.

If he killed every psychotic piece of shit for what they were thinking, there would be a trail of dead bodies in his wake. Ugly thoughts and nefarious intentions were not considered criminal until perpetrated.

As the guy wheezed and sputtered, Brundar picked up the yellow envelope from where he'd dropped it on the floor, and pulled the divorce papers out.

"Read, motherfucker." He shoved them at Shawn's trembling hands, then stood over the guy until he'd read every last paragraph.

"I don't have a pen," the jerk wheezed, tears running down his purple cheeks as he frantically looked around for one.

Brundar pulled out his phone and dialed Lora's number. Hopefully, the woman wasn't squeamish and wouldn't faint when she saw the black fingermarks on Shawn's neck and the purple hue of his face.

"You can come in now."

A few moments later, Lora knocked on the door. Brundar opened the way. "I had to use a little persuasion. I hope you're not the fainting type."

"Don't worry about me. Whatever you show me, I've seen worse. I volunteer at a battered women's shelter."

Brundar dipped his head in respect. "Then you'll appreciate my work here. I promise you that he earned it."

She regarded him with a serious expression in her eyes. "I believe you. Lead the way."

Five minutes later they walked out with the signed papers, everything properly notarized.

"Is he going to report you to the police?" Lora asked as he opened the passenger door for her.

"No."

"You sure?"

"I'm sure."

"Do I want to know why you're so sure?"

"No."

"Okay."

Brundar walked around and got behind the steering wheel.

Lora buckled herself in and smiled at him. "You didn't work him up as bad as I thought you would."

He lifted a brow. "What were you expecting?"

"By your grim expression, I was expecting at least a broken nose and plenty of blood."

Was it his imagination, or was this soft-looking grandma of eleven bloodthirsty and vengeful?

"Did you want me to?"

She shrugged. "It depends on what he'd done to deserve it."

Brundar didn't answer because he couldn't. How could he explain that Shawn hadn't committed any crimes aside from bullying his wife, and that he'd earned Brundar's wrath by plotting to do her harm?

Instead, he changed the subject. "Is there a personal reason you volunteer at the shelter?"

"Yes, there is. My sister was abused by her husband for years. She was hiding it, coming up with all kind of excuses for her bruises and her broken limbs. I should've guessed what was going on, but it was such a foreign concept to me that the thought never even crossed my mind. I believed her. The last beating before he was finally arrested has left her with permanent brain damage."

"I hope that monster is either dead or behind bars."

Her lips pressed into a tight line, Lora shook her head. "He did some time, but not enough for what he did. No length of time can pay for that. Not even execution."

"An execution would have at least saved his next victim."

Lora nodded. "You'll hear no argument from me. If we lived in different times, my sister's family could've avenged her and rid the world of that monster."

Brundar nodded. He'd lived in those olden times when family avenged family. Was it a better system than what humanity had devised in modern times? Or was it worse?

*The monster behind Brundar, the one he used to call a friend, started thrusting in and out of him to the loud cheers of his buddies.*

*No!!! A roar sounded from not too far away.*

*A moment later the body above Brundar disappeared, and a sickening breaking noise followed. After that, there were a few more screams, sounds of pursuit, and then nothing.*

*Throughout it all Brundar lay with his tear-stricken face to the ground, the pain and humiliation he'd been subjected to making him wish for death. There was no coming back from that. It would haunt him for the rest of his life. Mayhap he could end it before his transition. Before he was doomed to carry on endlessly.*

*Gentle hands pulled his pants up, and strong arms lifted him up, cradling him against a familiar muscular chest.*

As Brundar turned his head to look at the carnage, bile rose in his throat and he tilted his head away from his brother's chest to vomit.

Anandur wiped his mouth with his sleeve. "Dinnae look," he said. "It's over."

A drop of water landed on Brundar's cheek, but it wasn't his. He was all out of tears. Lifting his eyes to his brother's face, he saw that the big man was crying.

"I'm so sorry, laddie. I should've come sooner. I didnae know."

"Are they dead?"

Anandur nodded. "To the last one. They will never hurt anyone again."

## 36

# TESSA

"Can you at least give me a hint?" Tessa asked.

Jackson cast her a mysterious smile, then put the blinker on and eased his car into the quiet Venice street. "Nope."

Pouting, Tessa crossed her arms over her chest and tried to guess. Maybe he was taking her to a Sunday brunch?

It was too early for the movies, and it wasn't the beach because he hadn't said anything about a bathing suit or towels.

"I don't like surprises."

"You'll like this one."

Ugh, she was discovering that her sweet, accommodating Jackson had a stubborn streak a mile long.

Over two weeks had passed since he'd kissed her and licked her into her most powerful climax yet, then refused to take the final step and go all the way.

She was more than ready, but he insisted on waiting. Not that she'd been deprived in the meantime. Jackson had been treating her to more of those mind-blowing orgasms nightly.

Tessa had to admit, though, that his caution wasn't baseless. Even though she pleasured him with her hands and her tongue, she still couldn't take him into her mouth. And if she couldn't do that, Jackson wasn't off base assuming that she wasn't ready for intercourse either.

Distracted by her thoughts, she hadn't noticed that they'd exited the freeway at downtown. Was he taking her to the keep? Was someone throwing her a surprise party? But it wasn't her birthday, and no parties started at nine in the morning on a Sunday.

"Are you taking me to the keep?"

"Just a stopover. We need to change cars."

"Why?"

"If I tell you, it will ruin the surprise."

Ugh, she hated not knowing what was coming. Even if it was a good thing.

Jackson parked his car next to a fancy black limousine and got out.

"Hi, Okidu. Thanks for taking us," he greeted the driver, who rushed to open her door for her.

"Madam." He offered his hand.

She recognized him as the same guy who'd served refreshments on her first visit to the keep. Kian's butler. Was he his driver as well?

"Thank you." She let him help her up.

The butler opened the limousine's passenger door, and as she got in, Jackson followed her inside and sat next to her, grinning from ear to ear.

"Why are the windows opaque?" Limousine windows were darkened, so the interior wasn't visible from the outside, but she'd never heard of one with windows that made the exterior invisible from the inside.

He wrapped an arm around her shoulders. "To keep where we're going a surprise."

The partition between them and the driver was raised, and it was opaque too. Given the impressive soundproofing of the cabin and the lack of visuals, the interior felt like a luxurious sealed container. Tessa's stress level began climbing, and all the self-talk trying to convince herself that she was safe with Jackson, and that Kian's driver wasn't aiding in her kidnapping, wasn't helping.

Tessa felt the limousine climbing up the ramp from the underground garage level and then turning into the street. Sensing the movement helped to reduce her anxiety, as did Jackson's warm body pressed against hers.

"I don't like not seeing where I'm going."

He leaned closer and nuzzled her neck. "I can distract you."

As much as she liked him touching her, Tessa was too stressed to enjoy it.

As always, Jackson was attuned to the slightest of her responses. "Or we can watch a movie." He pressed a button, and a screen rose from the panel separating the passengers from the driver. "You can pretend we are in a movie theater."

Tessa let out a breath. "What movies do you have?"

"Anything your heart desires. This thing has all the streaming channels."

"Do they have *Guardians of the Galaxy* number two?"

"Let's see." Jackson got busy on the tablet that apparently served as the remote for the screen. "Found it." He selected the movie. "It's not long enough of a drive to see the whole thing."

"We can watch some on the way to your surprise, whatever it is, and then on the way back. If it's still not over, we can ask Okidu to let us stay in the limo until it ends."

A few minutes into the movie, Tessa got so immersed in it that it felt like no time at all had passed before the limousine stopped and Okidu opened the door for her.

Jackson paused the film and followed her out.

"Where are we?"

They were in a parking garage similar to the keep's, just much larger. The question was where.

Jackson ushered her into the elevator. "Count to twenty, and you'll see."

The doors opened before she reached fifteen, and she stepped out. Outside, beyond the glass sliding doors of the building they were in, she saw lush landscaping and several buildings that looked as if they were in the last stages of construction, with the scaffolding still attached.

Jackson waved a hand toward the glass doors. "Welcome to the village, Tessa."

"I feel so stupid. The car switch and the limousine with its opaque windows should've clued me in." Jackson had promised to arrange a visit to the village weeks ago.

A wide grin on his handsome face, Jackson circled her waist with his arm and led her toward the exit doors. "I'm glad I was able to surprise you."

"Have you been here before?"

He shook his head. "I asked Kian if we could see the place, and he said he'd let me know when he had time to show us around. I kept reminding him, but he was too busy and finally told me we could go by ourselves. He gave me a schematic of the layout so we could find our way around. I could've asked Okidu, but I thought it be would more fun to explore by ourselves."

Pulling out a folded printout from his back pocket, Jackson straightened the page and showed it to her. "The houses that are already taken are marked with a red X, and Kian even wrote next to each one the initials of the couple it's assigned to. All the rest are up for grabs." He smirked. "We can choose the one we want."

For a moment, Tessa was speechless. He wanted them to choose a house? Together? Wasn't it a little premature?

Apparently, Jackson wasn't kidding about the fated mates thing. He truly believed that they were it for each other. Forever.

The thought was wonderful and scary at the same time.

"Didn't you say that young bachelors would be the last ones to pick?"

"Yes. But couples get first dibs."

"We are not married."

"We don't have to be. Amanda and Dalhu aren't married either, and they got to choose a house already."

Tessa rolled her eyes. "You can't compare us to them. First of all, Amanda is Kian's sister and a member of the council, and second of all they have been living together for a while."

His face fell, but then he lifted his head with a mischievous glint in his eyes. "That's true. But to be considered an official couple all we have to do is pledge our love and devotion to each other in front of two witnesses. According to clan law, that's a lawful marriage."

That didn't sound right. Marriage required someone to preside over the ceremony to make it official, legal documents to be filled and signed, a blood test, and maybe more. She never had reason to look into it, and wasn't sure about what exactly was involved in the process, but it was certainly more than pledging love in front of witnesses.

Tessa arched a brow. "Really?"

Jackson dipped his head and kissed the top of her nose. "Really. That was what Bhathian and Eva did."

A stab of hurt pierced her heart. Eva hadn't told her anything. "Are you sure? Eva said they were planning a big wedding."

"They are because they want to celebrate their union, but it's not required."

What was going on?

Was he seriously talking about them getting married? So they could get a house?

No, no, no. First of all, they were way too young to be even talking about marriage, and second of all it was the least romantic proposal she'd heard of.

Tessa stopped and turned to face him. "Is that your roundabout way of asking me to marry you?"

Jackson shrugged. "What if it is?"

Tessa lifted her eyes to the sky, praying for patience. "Don't you think this is too early to be talking about it?"

"Why?"

Casting a glance at the Chinese construction workers, who for some reason were eyeing her with open hostility, Tessa lowered her voice. "There are a few things that need to happen first. Like sex and me transitioning before we can seriously talk about getting married. But even if, or rather when both those conditions are met, you're still eighteen, Jackson." She waved her hands in the air. "This is crazy talk. I'm not willing to take such a huge step just because you want dibs on a house."

## 37

## JACKSON

*J*ackson shook his head and pulled the bristling Tessa into his arms. "Don't get all worked up over nothing. We don't have to even make a pledge to be considered a couple. Everyone knows we are together."

She punched his chest. "So why did you start with that whole thing if you knew it wasn't necessary?"

He kissed the top of her head. "Sheath your little claws, kitten. I'm the one who should be upset. As far as I'm concerned I already pledged myself to you, the only thing missing were witnesses. But your refusal to do the same hurts."

She stopped her struggles and wrapped her arms around his neck, stretching on the tips of her toes to reach him. "I love you. Never doubt it. And I pledge that I always will. But I'm not ready for any official announcements just so we can get priority on a house or any other material benefit. It cheapens what we feel for each other. Don't you agree?"

He didn't. One had nothing to do with the other. The house was a side benefit, and he saw no reason not to take advantage of their status as a couple to secure it for them. "It doesn't matter if I agree or not. The only thing that matters is how you feel about it. We will do whatever you want, Tessa. I'm not pressuring you into anything."

She sighed. "I know. Let's forget about this whole discussion and look at houses just for the fun of it."

"I'm all for it."

As they walked down the winding pathway between the buildings, Jackson couldn't shake the tinge of unease Tessa's rejection had caused. She loved him, he didn't doubt that, but she still wasn't one hundred percent committed the way he was.

Why?

Looking back, he couldn't think of a single thing he'd done wrong. He'd been gentle, patient, supportive, and loving. Everything women supposedly wanted.

Had he gotten it wrong?

Jackson had always made fun of the guys who couldn't figure women out. He'd believed himself an expert, priding himself on knowing exactly what women wanted and needed but were too coy or too confused to ask for.

The problem between most men and women was communication.

Men accepted things at face value, listening half-heartedly beyond the first sentence or two. They ignored subtle clues like the tone of voice and the body language, which betrayed so much more. Women were more attuned to those clues, and they expected their men to be as astute, getting upset when the poor schmucks didn't get it.

Apparently, he wasn't getting it either.

"Is that one taken?" Tessa pointed to a two-story house with a wrap-around porch.

Jackson checked his map. "Yes. That one is Nathalie and Andrew's."

They walked down the lane with Jackson checking each house. "This one is available." He pointed to a one-story ranch style house with a front porch.

"Then let's take a look." Tessa marched toward the door pulling him behind her.

For someone who'd just a few minutes ago bashed him for wanting to secure a good home for them, she was sure eager to explore.

"Nice," he said as they walked inside. He loved the open plan combining the living room, dining room and kitchen into one big space. A perfect layout for hanging out with friends.

"How many bedrooms does it have?" Tessa asked while pulling the pantry door open and peeking inside.

Jackson looked at the printout. "Two bedrooms, two bathrooms and a study that can be converted into a bedroom."

Tessa closed the pantry door. "Perfect." She strode toward the hallway and opened the first door. "It's gorgeous. Come take a look."

He followed her into the master bedroom. Long and narrow, it was big enough for a king-sized bed against its narrow back wall, and a sitting area in front of it, facing a fireplace. But the nicest part was the private patio and the French doors leading to it. Jackson could imagine Tessa and him drinking their morning coffees out there.

"We can hang a television screen above the mantel." Tessa pointed.

She was already taking ownership of the house. Funny girl. Jackson opened the double door to the bathroom and smiled. "A whirlpool tub, a glass enclosed shower for two, two sinks." He opened another door. "And a separate room with a toilet and a bidet. I'm in."

"I love it." Tessa turned in a circle, then opened the next set of double doors. "Look at this closet, Jackson. We can make an office out of it. It's huge."

He walked up to her, wrapped his arms around her front, and pulled her back into him, resting his chin on the top of her head. "We can't. Where are you going to hang all the sexy outfits I'm going to buy for you?"

She turned around in his arms, a happy smile brightening her small face. "I could manage with less than half of the space, but there is no window, so no office."

"Hmm, no window, you say. So if we close those doors we will have total privacy." He didn't shut them, leaving a wide crack to admit some light. Tessa didn't like total darkness.

She narrowed her eyes at him. "What do you have in mind?"

He picked her up, waiting for her to wrap her legs around his waist before carrying her to the nearest wall. "Just a little necking." He kissed her neck.

"Just a little?"

"Hmm, let's see." He pulled her T-shirt up, exposing her bra-covered breasts, and kissed the tops before unhooking it and pushing it up as well.

Perky breasts topped with small puckered nipples made his mouth water. Jackson licked his lips. "Sweet berries." He dipped his head and treated one to several long licks.

On a moan, Tessa let her head drop back, her hands coming up to fist his hair and hold him to her.

"Lift your arms, baby."

When she did, he pulled her shirt and bra off. "That's better." He swiped his tongue around her other nipple.

"Jackson."

It was a throaty whisper that could've meant so many things. After their previous argument, he was no longer sure he could guess what she wanted.

"What, kitten? Tell me what you need."

She cupped his cheeks and brought his mouth to hers, kissing him with passion and abandon that a few weeks ago he would've never believed she could summon.

Her spark hadn't been extinguished; it had remained hidden somewhere beneath the wreckage, under the scars and the fears. Freed, it was burning bright.

Had it been his gentle coaxing that had nurtured that spark into a healthy flame? Could he at least take partial credit for that miraculous transformation?

Yesterday, he would've claimed it as his doing without batting an eyelid. Yesterday, he would have said that he was born to be the best lover of women a man could be.

Today, he wasn't so sure.

## 38

## TESSA

"What, kitten? Tell me what you need."

Tessa didn't know.

She wanted so many things.

She wanted to kiss Jackson until he forgot the hurtful words she'd hurled at him because she was afraid to hope too much.

She wanted this house to become their home.

She wanted to raise children with the man she loved even though they were both too young to even think of such things.

She wanted Jackson to lower her to the carpet-covered floor and make love to her and plant a baby inside her right now.

Tessa wanted a lot of things she couldn't have.

Not today and not tomorrow, but maybe someday.

There was one thing she could do today, though. She could give back at least a fraction of what he'd given her.

"I love you, Jackson, and I want to spend the rest of my life with you. I'm sorry if what I said before hurt your feelings. That wasn't my intention."

He sighed and rested his forehead on hers. "You know that I love you and that I'll wait as long as it takes. I'm an immortal. Time and chronological age have little meaning to me."

She hadn't thought of that.

Of course he would have a different perspective than her.

But even if the thought had crossed her mind, she would've thought that an immortal would feel like a teenager at sixty, not that an eighteen-year-old would feel mature enough to commit to a lifelong relationship.

Maybe it really wasn't about chronological age. Maybe Jackson's soul was old. Some people were like that. Sometimes children possessed wisdom that the adults around them lacked.

Perhaps he was really ready, and she was too close-minded to see that, blindly following society's inflexible rules, when she was the last one who should feel bound by them. Society hadn't been kind to her. The rules governing what was decent and what was not hadn't been applied to her.

She should make her own rules to live by. Simple ones. The first rule she'd follow was to give back as much as she was given. Vengeance for wrongdoing, love for love, and pleasure for pleasure.

"Put me down."

Jackson frowned but did as she asked.

He always did.

Tessa continued her descent until her knees touched the floor, then reached for his belt buckle.

He caught her hands and pulled them away. "What are you doing?"

She smirked. "What does it look like I'm doing?"

"I don't want you to."

"Oh, yeah? You don't like oral sex?"

"Of course I do, but not like this. Not on your knees." He whispered the last words with a pained expression on his face.

She pulled her hands out of his grasp and stroked his thighs. "I know you think this is degrading, but it's not. Not with you, not when you've only ever shown me love and respect. We have no bed to lie on, no couch to snuggle on. And this works. Can you let me do this?"

He nodded, even though given his pinched expression he was still unsure.

Sweet guy. Jackson was the universe's way of righting the wrong, rewarding her after screwing her over so badly.

Leaning against the wall, Jackson let his arms fall at his sides, submitting to her and what she wanted to do to him.

Even before she unbuckled his belt and pulled on the zipper, it was quite obvious that his arousal was gone. Her suspicion was confirmed when she pulled his pants and his boxer shorts down.

He hadn't been kidding when he'd said he didn't want it like this.

Jackson must've been the only healthy male alive who went limp at the prospect of a blow job.

She regretted pressuring him into something he felt uncomfortable about. He'd never done it to her even when he'd thought she'd enjoy it. But it was too late to retreat now. Tessa had a point to prove—more to herself than to Jackson.

First, she kissed the tip to let him know she was doing this out of love. Then she kissed another spot and another until he hardened in her hand. When she treated him to a long lick, starting at the tip and going all the way down to the base, Jackson groaned and got even harder.

She got him.

At first, Tessa just licked and pumped, stopping only to pepper him with small teasing kisses before resuming her ministrations. It wasn't the way she'd been taught to do this, but that was the whole point. Nor was it the first time Tessa had been on her knees in front of a man, but this was the first time she was doing it because she wanted to and not because someone was forcing her.

Tessa intended to make it as different of an experience as possible, wiping the slate clean by doing it her way.

His palms glued to the wall behind him, Jackson held himself still as a statue.

The only signs that he was enjoying this were his harsh breaths and the hard length pulsating in her hand.

Lifting her gaze to him, she took the tip into her mouth.

He sucked in a breath, his hooded eyes blazing with an inner light that was enough to illuminate the darkened interior of the closet.

There was no more doubt that Jackson loved what she was doing.

For a few moments, Tessa sucked, licked and pumped, enjoying the taste and the feel of him in her mouth. Sweet and tangy, hard but covered in velvety softness, he was perfect in every way a man could be.

Jackson groaned, his strong thigh muscles straining against his need to thrust.

Should she take him all the way to the back of her throat?

Could she?

Tessa had done this countless times before, but then it had been part of her torture. Could the same act bring about different sensations when done willingly?

Could it actually turn her on?

It was time to find out.

Bracing a hand on Jackson's hip in an instinctual attempt to hold him in place, preventing him from thrusting before she was ready, Tessa closed her eyes and took him a little deeper. Then a little deeper yet.

Jackson's breathing became ragged, but he still didn't move an inch.

Filling her lungs with air, Tessa loosened her throat muscles and took him as far as he would go.

Jackson jerked, trying to pull back, but with his butt against the wall, he had nowhere to go. His next move was the least expected of all. He went flaccid, his erection shrinking inside her mouth.

Why?

Did she accidentally scrape him with her teeth?

Letting go of him in a rush, she expected to see a scratch. But there was nothing. He was as smooth and as perfect as always.

"What happened?" she asked.

Jackson glided down until his butt hit the floor, then reached for her, cradling her in his arms. "A bad thought." He hugged her closer.

What kind of a bad thought could've ruined his mood like that?

Had he remembered a bad experience?

Had some nasty girl bitten him?

Then it dawned on her. It wasn't about something Jackson had experienced himself. It was about what she'd experienced. What she'd done wasn't something a novice could do. It had taken a lot of practice and beatings to conquer her gag reflex. Was he disgusted by her? Had her expertise driven the point home that she wasn't clean?

How could he hold on to her with such ferocity while being disgusted by her?

"Let me go, Jackson," she croaked as tears started running down her cheeks.

His arms around her tightened even more. "I'm not letting you move an inch."

She struggled even though she knew it was futile. "Let me go! I'm disgusting to you!"

"What?" His grip on her loosened just enough so he could look at her face. "What are you talking about? And why the hell are you crying?"

God, what had happened to him? Why did he want to humiliate her further by forcing her to spell it out?

"You went soft on me. I thought I hurt you, scraped you with my teeth or something, but that wasn't the reason. You finally internalized how soiled I am. Didn't you?"

Jackson crushed her to him with a force that had the air in her lungs leave with a whoosh. "Oh, baby, you're so wrong, I could never think that of you. You're my love and my sunshine. You're everything to me."

He sounded so sincere that she had to believe him. "So what happened?"

Jackson sighed. "You're so tiny, Tessa. I've been with girls a foot taller than you who were experienced as hell and still couldn't take me as far as you did. I couldn't help thinking about what you had to go through to be able to do that. I can't think about you suffering and stay aroused. I'm just not wired that way."

"I know."

She put her head on his chest, and as he held her close, the tears kept coming, and there was nothing she could do to stop them.

"I'm sorry," she hiccupped. "I can't stop."

Jackson stroked her hair. "It's okay. Let it all out, kitten, I got you."

## 39

# BRUNDAR

Her hands braced on her hips, her head lowered to avoid Brundar's eyes, Kri shook it from side to side. "Please don't ask me to do that. I've never even held a whip in my hand."

He'd expected her to balk at his request, but she was his only option. Only another Guardian could deliver his penance, and she was the only female Guardian.

Having a male at his back might override his logic circuits and lead to disastrous results. Some reactions were instinctive and too powerful to control.

If he wasn't capable of tolerating even a casual touch from his own brother, there was no chance he could tolerate a male with a whip executing his punishment.

Brundar would never forgive himself if he attacked a fellow Guardian. He wasn't sure anyone could pry him off the guy before he delivered a deadly dose of venom.

"I'll show you how."

She shook her head again. "Why me? Why not Bhathian? He's done it before."

Damnation. Revealing his true reasons was not an option. No one other than Anandur knew what had happened to him. But he had to tell her something to convince her. Perhaps his reputation would come in handy for once.

"I prefer a woman with a whip."

Kri's face twisted in a grimace. "Ugh, Brundar, that's gross. I'm your cousin. I'm not going to help get your rocks off."

That hadn't come out as intended. "Get your head out of the gutter, Kri. This is not a sex game."

"So what is it? You have to give me a reason to do something I really don't want to do."

Brundar held her gaze. "If a male delivers the punishment, I'm afraid the pain would cloud my reasoning and evoke an instinctive, aggressive response. I don't want to kill one of my friends."

"How do you know you're not going to attack me?"

"The instinct is not going to kick in with a female at my back."

"You sure about that?"

"A hundred percent."

Kri let her head drop down. "Fine. But don't blame me if you end up with a back that looks like ground meat. You really should pick someone experienced."

"I'll take a shredded back over a dead friend any day."

Taking a deep breath, Kri exhaled through her mouth. "Where do you want to train me?"

"Same place you're going to do it an hour from now."

With a groan, Kri nodded.

"Thank you."

"You owe me. And if after this I can't sleep, you owe me more."

"Think of it as an exercise in toughening up."

She waved a hand. "Yeah, yeah."

---

AN HOUR LATER, Kri had mastered the basics of wielding a whip, but she was still far from skilled. It didn't matter. Where Brundar prided himself on never breaking the skin, Kri was expected to do just that. She was supposed to deliver a punishment, not satisfy a kink.

She looked like she was going to a funeral. He owed Kri a big favor for this.

"Don't overthink it." He patted her shoulder. "Remember that I asked for it. I could've taken jail time instead and refused because I didn't want to waste time. Besides, I'm going to be as good as new in forty-eight hours or less."

She squared her shoulders. "Don't worry, I'm not going to faint on you."

"I know you won't."

Edna entered the chamber followed by Kian. Trailing behind them were the rest of the Guardians, including his brother who looked even more pissed now than during Brundar's earlier sentencing.

Per Brundar's request, Edna omitted the details of his personal involvement in the matter, only stating that he'd confessed to using an unlawful thrall, and the punishment appropriate for such transgression according to their law.

"No mitigating circumstances?" Anandur had tried to argue in Brundar's defense.

"Declined by the offender." Edna hadn't elaborated, protecting Brundar's privacy.

When Anandur's attempts to drag the details of what he'd done out of him had failed, he'd made it clear in so many words that he was done with Brundar and his shitty attitude.

He'd get over it. Even though Brundar didn't deserve it, his brother always forgave him.

Taking his shirt off, he dropped it on the floor, then disarmed, pulling out every one of the knives he carried on his body and putting them down on the shirt. When he was done, he wrapped them into a tight bundle and handed it to Anandur. "Keep them safe and try not to cut yourself."

Anandur growled. "Now you're making a joke? Screw you."

Brundar turned around and faced Edna. "I'm ready. I chose the Guardian Kri to deliver my penance."

Edna nodded. "Proceed. Ten strokes."

Given his repeat offense, it was a merciful number, and he'd made the mistake of pointing it out to Edna.

Never a good thing to piss off the judge.

With a chilling smile, she'd informed him that she could still slap a week of incarceration on top of the whipping. That had shut him up.

Bracing his hands against the cool stone, Brundar closed his eyes and slipped into the zone. The soft murmurs of the Guardians faded away, and all that was left was quiet. Ready, he dipped his head once, giving Kri the signal they'd agreed on.

# 40

# CALLIE

Working at Franco's, Callie's schedule consisted of waking up at ten in the morning, two hours of studying, and then lunch. After that, she was free to do as she pleased until her shift started at eight in the evening.

Plenty of time to do nothing.

She'd downloaded a bunch of books on her tablet, spending several blissful afternoons curled up on the couch reading. But the novelty of having so much free time had worn off soon.

Callie was bored and lonely.

No one ever came in.

Brundar, Franco, and the bouncers who sometimes walked her home after her shift never crossed the threshold of her apartment.

When her buzzer went off at four in the afternoon, it was a pleasant surprise. She padded barefoot to the monitor by the door and pressed the intercom.

"Hi, Brundar." She tried to sound casual even though her heart started thudding in her rib cage the moment she saw who it was.

"Let me in, Calypso."

"Of course."

For a few seconds she couldn't tear her eyes away from Brundar, watching him push the lobby's door open and walk in until he disappeared from the camera's view. Only then did she make a mad dash for her bedroom to brush her hair and put a bra on. There was no time to change out of her pajama pants or look for a better T-shirt.

He'd never just popped in before. But at least he'd given her a few moments' notice by buzzing her intercom. Callie was sure Brundar had another set of keys, but it was decent of him not to use it.

Her stoic, indifferent protector was a man of honor.

She wished he had a little less of all three qualities. Less stoic and more feeling, less indifferent and more interested, less honorable and more forward.

It should've been illegal to be so attractive and so cold at the same time.

He hadn't been cold that one time he kissed her, though.

Callie sighed and rushed back to the living room to open the door.

"Hi," she said as she let him in.

Brundar smiled, actually smiled, showing a little bit of teeth. It was so shocking that she had to ask, "What are you so happy about?"

"I have a present for you." He handed her a large envelope.

"What is it?" She started opening the flap.

"Your freedom."

Her hands trembled as she finished pulling out the stack of papers. "How?"

It had been only two weeks since Shawn had been served. She hadn't known he'd even signed them, interpreting the silence from the attorney to mean nothing was happening yet.

"A little persuasion."

"Did you beat him up to have him sign so fast?" She leveled Brundar with a hard stare. Not that she minded terribly if he had, but she did mind that he hadn't told her about it.

Brundar shrugged. "I didn't have to beat him up to have him sign. As I told you before, I can be very persuasive."

He wasn't lying, but he wasn't telling her the whole truth either. "Is he okay?"

"That depends on what you consider okay."

She rolled her eyes. A question addressed to Brundar needed to be precise. "Is he in the morgue? Or in a hospital with broken bones?"

"No."

Exasperated, she threw her hands in the air. "Please, just tell me what you mean without me having to drag every freaking word out of you."

He seemed taken aback by her outburst, his pale blue eyes widening for a moment. "Shawn's mind is twisted. The world would be a better place without him. But my hands are tied by the law and by your request not to harm him."

Letting out a breath, Callie let her head drop. She felt so bad for snapping at him. It was no way to repay the guy after all he'd done for her. "Thank you. For everything."

He nodded.

"Please, would you like to take a seat?" She pointed at the couch.

Without answering, he walked over and sat down, his back straight as an arrow, his legs crossed at the knee.

"Can I offer you a drink? Coffee?" He'd never made good on his promise to bring her a good wine. After their kiss, Brundar had turned from cold to icy. Not in an angry way, or dismissive, just remote and indifferent. He might as well have painted a sign on his forehead saying, 'I'm not interested.'

"Do you want to have dinner with me?" he asked.

It took a great effort not to let her jaw drop. Brundar was asking her out? Impossible.

Maybe he wanted her to make him dinner? He liked her cooking. "Would you like me to whip up something quick for us instead?"

His eyes brightened. "Your fajitas were exceptional."

Callie guessed it was a yes. "I don't have the ingredients for fajitas, but I can make something else. If you'd given me advance notice, I would have cooked you a gourmet five-course meal."

"You can do that?"

She chuckled. He was so literal. "I'm a good cook, but calling what I do gourmet is a slight exaggeration." To demonstrate, she put two fingers together with barely any space between them.

Brundar smiled again.

Wow, at this rate she might make him laugh. Wouldn't that be a great achievement? Worthy of a mention in *The Guinness Book of World Records?*

"Let me see what I have to work with." She turned around and headed for the refrigerator.

Brundar followed, taking a seat on the same barstool he'd sat on the other time she'd cooked for him.

Maybe that was the ticket.

Wasn't there a saying that the way to a man's heart was through his stomach?

"I could make lasagna, but it would take too long. Do you like Thai?" Holding the fridge door open she turned her head around, catching him ogling her ass.

If he was embarrassed about getting caught, he didn't show it. Brundar's austere, handsome face was expressionless as ever.

"I will like anything you make."

It was such a nice thing to say, and if it were anyone else she would have interpreted it as flirting. But Brundar meant it literally.

Either way, she knew it was a compliment. That didn't mean, however, that she couldn't tease him about it.

"Did you mean to say that you think I'm a good cook and that you're sure everything I make tastes good, or that you're not particular about what you put in your mouth?" She pulled out a few ingredients from the fridge, then opened the pantry in search of a can of coconut cream.

"You know the answer. I told you I liked your fajitas."

Callie winked. "I'm just teasing you. Trying to loosen you up a bit."

He pinned her with a hard stare she couldn't decipher, sending shivers of desire dancing along her spine. She waited for him to say something, admonish her for suggesting he wasn't loose enough, or for teasing him, but he remained silent.

*Oh, well.*

Pulling out a cutting board, she started chopping vegetables into large chunks. The way Brundar was following her every move, as if he was her apprentice and was trying to commit every detail to memory, it was a miracle she didn't slice off a finger.

Having his undivided attention was doing strange things to her. She'd never had anyone focus on her like that. Even during the good times with Shawn, when he'd still been charming and attentive, the focus had always been on him, not her.

He'd talked and she listened, he'd told jokes and she'd laughed.

In a way, it had suited her. To be with Shawn hadn't taken much effort on her part. Not in the beginning. But then he'd changed, or maybe she'd just started seeing him more clearly. Being around him had felt like being next to a black hole—he'd sucked the life out of her.

With Brundar it was the opposite. It was all up to her. With laser-like focus, he listened and he watched as she talked, as she made jokes. Being around him was like getting hooked to an electrical outlet, the sizzling current between them filling her with energy, with life.

The powerful vibe he exuded wasn't stifling, it was like pure oxygen to a smoldering fire, igniting a dangerous flame.

## 41

# BRUNDAR

He shouldn't have stayed.

It was pure torture pretending he didn't know Calypso wanted him, ignoring the scent of her arousal. But she'd looked so relieved, with her beautiful face relaxed and happy for the first time in months, that he wanted to gaze at her for a little longer.

Brundar's idea had been to celebrate Calypso's freedom by taking her out to a nice restaurant, but when she'd suggested cooking for him, he could not bring himself to refuse.

Being alone with her, watching her do this for him, was too precious to squander. For a couple of hours, he could pretend she was his. That he was normal. That he was sharing his life with her.

That he had a mate.

Brundar shook his head. A human couldn't be his mate. And hoping Calypso was a Dormant was like hoping to win the lottery by buying the first ticket.

She had none of the indicators. Not unless cooking could be considered a paranormal talent.

"Do you think I'm safe from Shawn now? Do you think he could still come after me?"

Not in the very near future, but unless Brundar thralled the jerk every couple of weeks, the last thrall he'd put over him would eventually fade. Regrettably, other than Annani none of the clan members had the ability to place a permanent compulsion on a human, and the goddess couldn't be bothered with every abusive asshole. She would end up doing nothing but.

"No."

Calypso arched a brow, indicating his answer wasn't satisfactory. It wasn't. But he was so used to brushing everyone off with his terse answers that he had to relearn how to talk to someone he didn't want to push away. "His mind is not right. I don't know how long he is going to hold a grudge against you, but I don't expect him to forget about it anytime soon."

She nodded, satisfied with the completeness of his answer, but not with the implication. "What am I going to do in the meantime? I want to get my teaching degree, maybe even continue and get a Master's. I can't do it if I can't attend classes."

"You can. With caution."

She lowered the flame under the wok and leaned against the other side of the cooktop. "Meaning?"

Brundar's lips twitched. He was starting to rub off on her. Did she notice that she had just used a one word sentence?

"To start with, you'll need to change your name."

She shook her head. "I was admitted as Calypso Davidson."

"I'm sure the university's administration will have no problem with a new name once you explain the circumstances. I can get you a legit new identification. I know a guy."

"Sure you do. You know a lot of people in the right places."

"It's my job."

"And other than changing my name?"

"A few small changes in appearance. Different hair color and cut, large glasses, different style of clothing."

She pondered his suggestions for a moment, then nodded. "It won't fool Shawn up close, but it might from a distance."

"That's the idea."

Calypso let out a breath and uncrossed her arms. "I can live with that. And with a different name, I can open a new bank account, and Franco can start paying me with checks. I can even get myself a car, a cheap, used one I can buy with cash."

She took out two clean plates from the dishwasher and heaped them with what was in the wok.

"What would you like to drink with that? I only have Diet Coke and orange juice."

"Water is fine."

She put the plates on the counter, took out a can of Coke from the fridge and poured him a glass of water from a pitcher she'd kept there.

"Thank you."

He waited to take the first bite until Calypso sat next to him.

"I hope you don't mind tofu," she said.

"I don't."

Calypso watched him as he forked a cube together with a few pieces of vegetables and stuffed it in his mouth.

"How is it?"

"Very good." It was the truth. He wasn't crazy about tofu, but the dish was so full of flavor it compensated for the tofu's bland taste.

Calypso chuckled. "I would've never pegged you as someone who eats tofu. Not after the steaks you wolfed down at Aussie."

"My cousin is vegan, and his butler cooks vegan dishes for him. Sometimes my brother and I invite ourselves for lunch."

She shook her head. "You have a cousin who has a butler? Who has butlers these days? Is he royalty?"

In a way, Kian was royalty. But it would be difficult to explain without revealing too much. "He is a businessman."

"A very successful one, I assume."

"Yes." Brundar stuffed his mouth with another forkful before Calypso threw more questions at him. In the short time he'd spent with her, he'd talked more than he usually talked in a year. It was tiring. He wasn't used to that.

Thankfully, she dug into her own plate and for a few minutes they ate in blissful quiet.

It didn't last long. Calypso put her fork down and wiped her mouth with a napkin. "I should start looking for an apartment. Your friend will want this one back."

Brundar scrambled for a passable lie. He remembered telling her that his made-up friend was teaching a semester abroad. "He is not coming back anytime soon. They offered him a two-year stint. He is very happy that you're staying here and making sure his place doesn't get vandalized."

She narrowed her eyes at him. "He told you that?"

Brundar nodded. Fates, he hated lying.

"When you speak with him again, please tell him I'm grateful and that I'm more than happy to pay him rent."

If she knew how much the rent was, she would have thought twice before suggesting it. She wasn't making that kind of money at the club.

"He doesn't want a tenant. He wants a house sitter. And besides, you need to save up the money you're making to pay tuition."

She lowered her head. "Right. I forgot about that."

Her embarrassment made him uncomfortable. She'd seemed so upbeat and hopeful about her prospects until he'd mentioned the tuition. Maybe what she was making at Franco's wasn't enough.

"If you need help with that, I can loan you the money. Interest free."

She lifted her eyes to him. "Thank you, but I'll manage. I'm living rent free." She ran a hand through her hair. "God, Brundar, how will I ever repay you for all this?"

Brundar could've said that it was nothing, and heaped on more lies about his nonexistent friend, but he didn't want to. Instead, he changed the subject. "I would advise against visiting your father and your friend. If Shawn is plotting revenge, he will keep tabs on them, waiting for you to show up."

"Yeah. I know. Maybe I can get them to meet me somewhere."

"Wait a few months until you do. Don't call them from here or the club either. I'll get you a burner phone."

"I have one."

Not the kind he was talking about. "I'll get you a safer one. You can trust me to know which one is best."

Her green eyes pinned his with an unreadable expression. "I trust you with my life."

## 42

## CALLIE

Brundar gazed at her as if she'd grown horns. But Callie had meant it.

"Don't look at me as if I'm missing a screw. I still don't know why you're doing all of this for me, but I know that without you none of this would have been possible. You gave me my life back. If not for you, I would've been still trapped with Shawn, and one day he might've snapped and beaten me to death. So yeah, I trust you with my life. Deal with it." She grabbed his plate and hers and carried both to the sink.

She'd never met a more frustrating and confusing man.

He was her angel, but there was palpable darkness in him. It was leashed and contained, but for better or worse it was there. She could deal with it, even embrace it, because without it Brundar would not be who he was—her fierce protector.

That wasn't the problem, though. She needed to understand his motives, she needed him to open up to her, she needed to have him.

It was a need more than a want. On some primitive level, she felt that he belonged to her, and she was more than willing to give herself to him. The attraction didn't make sense. So yeah, he was criminally handsome, and right now he was her only friend, but it was like falling for a robot. A capable, helpful creature like one of the cyborgs she'd read about in her sci-fi romance novels.

"Why are you angry?" He seemed truly perplexed.

She dropped the plate she was rinsing into the soapy water and turned around to glare at him. "You want to know why I am angry?"

It was a rhetorical question, but he answered it anyway. "Yes. I just asked you that."

God, what was wrong with this man?

"I'm frustrated."

"With me?"

"Yes, with you." She walked up to him, invading his personal space. "Are you attracted to me, Brundar?"

He swallowed. "Of course I am. Who wouldn't be?"

"Good." She took a step closer, crowding him. "Then you won't mind this." She cupped his cheeks and kissed him.

He stiffened, not responding to her kiss, keeping his lips tightly pressed and not allowing her tongue inside.

Crap. What the hell had gotten into her? Was she trying to dominate a dominant?

No wonder he didn't want that.

Callie took a step back. "I'm sorry. I shouldn't have." She turned, intending to flee into the bedroom and bury her flaming face in a pillow.

He caught her elbow. "Wait."

Embarrassed, she closed her eyes as he turned her around, refusing to look at him.

"Look at me, Calypso," he commanded.

She shook her head.

His fingers closed on her chin.

"Open your beautiful green eyes and look at me," Brundar repeated softly.

He thought her eyes were beautiful? Gathering her courage, she opened her eyes.

"I want you. But not like that."

"Not like what?"

"I have to be in total control. Do you understand?"

She nodded.

"I can't have you kiss me. I can't even have you touch me."

"I know you don't want to be touched, and I'm sorry I did. Well, I'm not. But you know what I mean. It was an impulse. But are you going to touch me? Because I really need you to. Is that okay for me to say? Or is it not allowed either? You never told me the rules. I don't know what's okay and what's not. It's all so confusing. You're so confusing. I don't know what you want from me—" She was blabbering, but she was so sick of holding it all in.

He put a finger to her lips to shush her. "Yes. I'm going to touch you. But you might not like my rules. And that's okay. The only way this works is if your rules and mine don't conflict."

Callie let out a breath. That made sense, and it made her feel more in control. Somehow she'd managed to push him a tiny step closer. "Tell me."

He sighed. "First rule. No emotional entanglement. Not because you're not great but because I can't. There are things about me I can never tell you that make a relationship impossible."

He might as well have stabbed her heart with a knife. The pain of his rejection was sharp and all consuming. She needed to at least understand why.

"Is it something personal? Something about me? Am I missing something?"

He shook his head and parted his legs, wrapping his arms around her and pulling her closer.

She remembered he didn't want her to touch him, and even though her hands itched to burrow into his beautiful blond hair, she fisted them by her sides.

"You're perfect. And if I were free to do as I please, I would make you mine and never let you go. But I'm not."

He had told her that he lived with his brother. Had he lied? "Are you married? Do you have someone?"

He chuckled. "I'm married to my job and my duties."

An excuse if she'd ever heard one.

"A lot of people have demanding jobs."

"My job prohibits a relationship with a—" He stopped. "A woman."

She humphed. "Does it allow a relationship with a man?"

He smacked her butt, igniting her arousal. "Don't be a smart ass, Calypso."

She narrowed her eyes at him. "Or what? You'll spank me? I'm shaking in my proverbial boots."

Another smack followed, harder than the first. "At this rate, you won't be able to sit by the time I finish the list of rules."

She shrugged.

Brundar shook his head. "You're enjoying this too much for it to be effective."

He had that right. If she could think of another smart-ass remark, she would make it. "I'm listening."

"Good girl." He patted her behind. "Rule number two. You're not allowed to touch me, which brings me to the last rule. If we get intimate, you'll be tied up and blindfolded. That's the only way I play."

Callie frowned. It required a lot of trust, especially since all they had done until now was kiss. What if she got scared? She'd never been tied up or blindfolded before. Still, his list of rules was surprisingly short.

"That's it? I don't have to call you sir or anything?" She could deal with calling him sir, but she was never going to call him master.

A smile tugged at one corner of his lips. "Only if you feel like it."

"How about treating you with respect and stuff like that?"

"You already do. Most of the time. But that has nothing to do with playtime. I expect respect from everyone I come in contact with, and provided they do, I respond in kind."

Funny he would say that. Apparently, Brundar didn't realize how his curt answers could be perceived as rude. His definition of respectful was very different than hers.

"I like that. Being polite is important to me."

"Good, any other questions? Anything you disagree with?"

"No. I'm game. But what if I get scared? Or overwhelmed? I like you, and I trust you, but we've never done anything aside from kissing. Which by the way, was amazing. But it's difficult for me to leap from that straight to bondage. Do you know what I mean?"

## 43

## BRUNDAR

Brundar knew exactly what she meant. A newbie wasn't ready for bondage. Not with someone she didn't know well and didn't spend a lot of time with.

Telling her that it was the only way he did things would hopefully deter her from her tenacious pursuit of him. Brundar wasn't strong enough to keep pushing her away. It was difficult enough to control his attraction to her, doing it on two fronts was impossible even for a fighter like him.

The only way to stop that thing between them from moving forward was for Calypso to realize that he wasn't what she wanted. The other option was him walking out the door and never coming back.

He'd tried to distance himself from her, but it didn't work. The pull was too strong.

"I know, sweetling. You're not ready for someone like me."

Eyes cast down, Calypso chewed on her lower lip. "I want to try. If I tell you to stop, will you?"

Fates, why the hell was he so relieved that she still wanted him?

He could've said that he wouldn't, scaring her off. Instead, he told her the truth. "Yes. Immediately."

She nodded, then sighed. "I know you don't like to talk a lot, but there is so much I don't know, and so much you can tell me."

Sweet girl. She was so brave.

Calypso deserved so much more than he had to offer. The least he could do was sate her curiosity. For her, he would make an effort and talk. Hell, if it made her happy, he would talk from now until next morning.

The thing was, he wasn't sure he could answer all of her questions.

Brundar didn't dwell on the psychology of the various kinks people engaged in. He couldn't explain them to her even if he tried. He wasn't even sure if his particular kink was the result of what had happened to him as a boy, or if the need for control was just a part of who he was, his genetic makeup.

Pushing to his feet he took her hand, walked her over to the couch, sat down, and pulled her onto his lap.

The world righted itself.

Calypso leaned against him, her body molding into his. Without him having to remind her, she tucked her hands between her thighs.

Good girl.

"I'll do my best to answer your questions. But the truth is that I'm not an expert."

"You're not?"

"I know a hundred ways to tie a woman up, and just as many to bring her pleasure. I'm also an expert with the whip."

Callie shivered, and he tightened his arms around her. "I know how to use it correctly, but it's not something I enjoy doing. I'm not a sadist."

She let out a breath. "Thank God. I can't even imagine the pain. Why would anyone want that?"

He chuckled. "That's one of the questions I'm not qualified to answer. For myself, I know that a punishment like that can be cathartic, but it's not something that excites me sexually."

She frowned. "Have you ever been whipped? Or are you talking hypothetically?"

He shifted, the almost healed scars on his back more itchy than painful. Kri had tried her best, but she had a lot to learn about wielding a whip.

"The first one."

She looked at him with horrified eyes. "Why? Who did it to you?"

Fates, how could he explain this to her in a way she could understand?

"It was ceremonial."

"What do you mean? Like hazing?"

Not exactly, but it would do. "Yeah. Something like that."

She shook her head, her eyes blazing with anger. "God. Men are such morons, always coming up with crazier and crazier ideas to prove worthy of their dicks."

He smacked her flank. "Watch it. That wasn't cordial or respectful in the least."

Calypso wiggled on his lap. "I don't remember spanking on your very short list."

It wasn't, but the scent of her arousal intensified after each smack. Sweet Calypso enjoyed a little playful spanking.

"It's not on mine. But it's on yours."

A deep blush bloomed on her cheeks. "How do you know what's on my list?"

Another thing he couldn't tell her. "An educated guess. You just squirmed on my lap, and it wasn't because you were in pain. I didn't smack you hard enough for it to hurt."

She pouted. "It did."

He might need to add another rule. Honesty was not something he required from his playmates, but he needed it from Calypso. It was hypocritical of him to demand truth from her while he piled lie after lie, but that was different. He lied to protect his people; she lied because she was embarrassed to admit what turned her on.

It wasn't going to work unless she talked to him.

"Don't lie to me. That's another rule."

She wiggled again. "What are you going to do about it?" Her voice got husky.

"I'm going to turn you over my knee and spank your cute little ass until you admit the lie, say you're sorry, and mean it." He teased her, knowing it turned her on.

"What if I like it?"

"I promise you will not."

"You'll punish me? For real?" She looked worried.

"Only if you want me to."

Closing her eyes, she put her head on his chest. "This is all so confusing. Why would I want you to punish me?"

"The why isn't important. Only the what. You make your own rules, and it's okay to change them and make adjustments as you go. You might think you like something and then realize you don't, or the other way around. But you won't know until you try."

"It's all a big game. Isn't it?"

"That's why I call it playing."

"Is everyone in the club like that? Or is it just you?"

He shrugged. "As with every type of game, some take it more seriously than others. Some like to play twenty-four-seven, while others like to play once a month, and everything in between."

She seemed confused. "I don't know what my rules are. And what happens if I refuse one of yours or you refuse one of mine?"

"There are hard rules and soft rules. The rules I laid out for you are my hard rules. If you refuse, we don't play, and the same goes for you."

"Is there a chance your hard rules will one day become soft rules?" she whispered.

Fates, there had been so much hope in that whisper, he knew he was going to disappoint her no matter how hard he tried not to.

It wasn't that he hadn't harbored the same insane hope, a hope that one day he would find his fated mate and would crave her touch as much as she craved his. But Calypso could never be that mate. All she could be was a transitional lover he would have to abandon sooner rather than later.

The only reason he was succumbing to her was that she needed guidance and he hated the idea of her falling into the hands of some pervert who might hurt her. He would teach her the right way to go about it, help her explore her needs and once she was ready he would disappear from her life.

"Not likely. If you can't accept them, we'd better stop right now."

She lifted her eyes to him. "You're not getting rid of me that easily. I'll take whatever you can give me and love every moment of it."

He lifted a brow. "And you know this because?"

"I just do. Call it a woman's intuition."

Right. A woman's intuition. Calypso's was obviously malfunctioning. If it were working right, she would not be sitting in his lap, hoping for a future that couldn't be.

His phone buzzed, and he pulled it out of his pocket.

"It's not a good time, Anandur."

"We need you at County. Roni is transitioning."

Damnation. They needed him for the extraction. Other than Yamanu, his shrouding and thralling abilities were the strongest. "Take Yamanu."

"Are you serious? And miss all the fun?"

Yeah. It was a rare opportunity to practice his skills, but he had more important things to do.

"Yes. Is he okay to go?"

"Of course he is. I just wanted to save this for you."

"Some other time."

"There won't be another time."

"There always is." He clicked the call off.

"What was that about?" Calypso asked.

"My brother wanted me to take part in a prank."

She lifted a brow. "You? Pranking someone? Boy, did he choose the wrong man."

"My thoughts exactly."

## 44

# BRUNDAR

The phone call had been a most welcome pattern interrupt. Brundar had allowed himself to get carried away.

What the hell was he thinking, sitting with her in his lap as if they were lovers?

She needed information and he was more than willing to provide it, but he shouldn't have done it in such an intimate setting. Calypso's arousal was playing a number on him. He was hard as a rock, and it hadn't gone unnoticed.

Calypso's cheeks were flushed, her eyes glazed in desire. They both needed a splash of cold water to break the spell.

"Come on." He lifted her off his lap and helped her to her feet.

She looked confused for a moment, then glanced at her watch before lifting her gaze to him with a frown wrinkling her forehead. "It's not time for my shift yet."

"I know. You need a tour." He stood up.

Her breath hitched. "You're taking me to the club? I mean to the lower level?"

"Yes."

"I thought not being twenty-eight I wasn't allowed in there."

"Not as a member and not as an employee, but there is nothing prohibiting me from taking you on a tour. There is no one there this time of day during midweek."

She swallowed. "I need to get dressed first."

"Take your time." He sat back and crossed his legs. "I'll wait."

"I won't be long." She hurried off to her bedroom.

As he waited for Calypso to get ready, Brundar wondered what would scare her off. He could show her the various rooms and the equipment they housed. Some of them were set up for those with darker tastes, the instruments of torture sure to terrify her.

Calypso wasn't a masochist, and she seemed fairly empathic. Just imagining what went on in those rooms should cool her off.

By the time the tour was over, sex would be the farthest thing from her mind.

Which was his goal. The scent of her arousal was scrambling his brain. It was impossible to be around her and resist such a powerful and blatant invitation.

"I'm ready." She came back, the strap of her purse slung over her shoulder, wearing the club's informal uniform of black jeans and black T-shirt with Franco's logo embossed in red on the right breast.

*Don't look at her breasts!*

Brundar stood up and headed for the front door, opening it and waiting for her to step out before closing it. "Lock it."

"Yes, of course." Calypso pulled out her key, her hand a little unsteady as she tried to fit it inside the lock.

"Let me." He took it from her.

She was unsettled. Exactly as he wanted her to be.

They took the stairs, the short burst of activity clearing his mind. He walked over to his car and unlocked it with his fob, then pulled the passenger door open for Calypso.

They passed the short drive in silence, with Calypso sneaking surreptitious glances at him when she thought he wasn't looking.

Poor girl, he was confusing her with the mixed signals he was sending her. Letting his cold mask slip had been an unforgivable mistake. It wasn't her fault he couldn't give her what she needed. Stringing her along had been cruel.

The thing was, Brundar was swimming in unfamiliar waters. Calypso had a way of infiltrating his shields and bringing about sensations that were completely foreign to him.

Most of which had nothing to do with sex.

If it were only sexual attraction he could've dealt with it just fine, satisfying his needs and hers.

But it wasn't.

Calypso felt like home. When he was with her, watching her cook, talking with her, sharing a meal with her, he didn't want to leave.

Ever.

As he pulled his car into the club's parking lot, Brundar took stock of who else was there at that time of day. Franco's red pickup was there, a delivery van that belonged to the laundry service they used, and two other cars he didn't recognize. Hopefully, those didn't belong to members. He didn't want anyone to interrupt the tour he was about to take Calypso on.

He frowned as she opened the passenger door before he had the chance to open it for her. "I was about to do that."

"I can open my own door and get out of a parked car without assistance," she gritted. The lady wasn't happy, and he couldn't blame her. He'd been the worst kind of tease, getting her all worked up and then dropping her like a sack of potatoes.

"I know you can. That's beside the point. It's okay to let others do nice things for you even if you don't need them to."

"Look who's talking," she murmured under her breath, thinking he couldn't hear her.

She was upset. He would let it pass this time.

Damnation. Once again he was losing his focus. This was about driving Calypso away, not thinking about an impossible future with her.

He strode in the direction of the club's back entrance, leaving her to stomp behind him.

Calypso was getting angrier by the minute. Perfect. The angrier she got, the easier it would be for her to walk away from him.

He didn't waste time looking for Franco before crossing the club's main level to the locked door that led to the basement. A few clicks on the keypad opened the way, and he waited for Calypso to go in before letting it snap closed.

There was no elevator to the lower level, only a narrow staircase. The basement used to be a storage area before Franco converted it into his sprawling playroom.

"It's dark in here," she said, reminding him he'd forgotten to turn the lights on.

He flipped the switch on, and a lineup of shaded sconces bathed the staircase in soft light. "Better?"

"Yes, thank you." Her voice betrayed a slight tremble.

Without thinking, he offered her his hand. "It's not scary. The main room looks like a giant living room, with a bar in the middle and a bunch of soft couches thrown around."

She exhaled the breath she'd been holding, letting him lead her down the stairs.

At the bottom of the staircase, he flicked another switch. "See? Just as I told you, a bar and a lot of couches."

She glanced around nervously. "What happens when there are people here?"

"Same as at any other gathering. Drinks, snacks, chitchat, and gossip."

"You mean to say that no one is, you know, getting busy on those couches?"

He chuckled. "I didn't say that. There is a lot of necking going on. But Franco doesn't allow nudity in here. That's what the private rooms are for. If anyone is into public play, there is a larger private room where they can invite guests."

"Can you show me? I mean a regular room. Not the one for exhibitionists."

Well, one more thing he was certain of. Calypso wasn't into public play. "Sure. I promised you a tour."

Leading her out of the main area into a hallway lined with doors on both sides, Brundar opened the first one using his master code.

She took a look around and exhaled. "This doesn't look so scary. There is only a bed and a couple of nightstands in here. Is that a bathroom?" She pointed at a door."

"Yes. Each room comes with a basic bathroom. Nothing fancy." He opened the door. "A shower, a sink, and a toilet."

"Does it cost to rent a room?"

"There is a cleanup fee."

"I see."

Brundar closed the door, walked over to one of the nightstands, and pulled out the first drawer. "There is a price for each of the toys. For health reasons, if you use them you buy them." He pulled out a wrapped paddle and smacked it against his palm. "Even this."

Calypso jumped. "Oh."

"Would you like to take a peek?"

She hesitated for about two seconds, then came closer and leaned to take a look, her hands clasped behind her back as if she was examining a museum display.

Her eyes widened. "Wow. That's... yeah..." She stepped back. "I think I've seen enough."

Brundar stifled a chuckle. If a paddle, a flogger, and a strap were enough to scare her off, he wouldn't even need to show her the other rooms. His work was done.

"Do you want to go upstairs and have a drink?"

She shook her head. "Not yet. Are all the rooms the same?"

"No. This is the tamest one."

She blushed. "I want to see."

"Are you sure? You just said you'd seen enough."

Calypso waved a dismissive hand. "Of what's in the drawers. I want to see what's in the other rooms."

"Okay." She had only seen the contents of one drawer. The one below her would have made her blush several shades deeper.

The good thing was that he could scent no arousal on her. Brundar wasn't sure he could've been so nonchalant otherwise.

"Let's get a look at another room."

She waved a hand again, pretending bravado she didn't feel. "After you, sir."

## 45

## CALLIE

It was meant as a tease, a joke, but calling Brundar sir had caused something to shift inside her, washing her in a wave of arousal Callie had managed to hold at bay until now.

The spanking implements inside that drawer had helped. There was nothing sexy about those instruments of pain. The most Callie could conceive of was a light, erotic hand spanking, but not paddles, floggers and the like. Just thinking about it made her shiver and not in a good way.

How could anyone enjoy that?

*You're such a hypocrite,* she admonished herself. Others would think the same about her deviant desires, tame as they were. It reminded her of a funny definition of a religious fanatic—*anyone more religious than me.*

Change the subject, and that definition would work perfectly for kink as well.

Opening the next door, Brundar cast her a questioning glance. "Ready?"

She nodded and stepped in.

He closed the door behind them.

This room was larger than the previous one. The four-poster bed was taller, and the bedding was a different color, blue as opposed to the white in the other room. The nightstands were also taller to fit the bed, narrower. But the thing that stood out the most was the bench. She'd seen one of those on the Internet—a spanking bench.

As an image of her bent over the contraption with Brundar behind her skittered through her head, Callie felt her core clench. He wouldn't use any of the implements from the other room, just his hand, caressing her heated flesh after every smack…

Next to her, Brundar sucked in a breath. Had the same image flashed through his mind? Or had it been an image of a different woman bent over the thing?

A wave of intense jealousy washed through her, constricting her airways. She fisted her hands, digging her nails into the skin of her palms, hoping the sting would chase away the other hurt.

"What's the matter, Calypso? Is it too much? Do you want to leave?"

What was his game plan? Why did he keep asking her if she wanted to leave? Was he hoping to scare her off? Was it a test to see if she was serious about this?

"You said something about contracts."

"What about them?"

"Shouldn't I sign one? You're showing me all of this, and I didn't even sign a confidentiality agreement. Isn't it against the rules?"

"It is if anyone were here. But it's just the two of us. The confidentiality agreement is to protect the privacy of our members."

She turned to face him. "What if someone walks in while we are still here?"

Brundar frowned, his eyes boring into hers. "Follow me." He turned around and left the room.

"Where to?" She had a hard time keeping up with his long strides.

"You wanted paperwork. I'm just fulfilling your wishes."

Behind his back, Callie rolled her eyes. If he were into wish fulfillment, he would strip her naked, tie her to that four-poster bed, and give her the best sex of her life.

Brundar typed the code into another keypad and opened the door to an office. One desk, two chairs, a filing cabinet. An old style desktop computer that had seen better days sat on top of the neatly organized desk, the keyboard yellowed from years of use. Apparently, Franco was still struggling financially. Or maybe he just didn't care about having the latest technology.

"Does that thing even work?" She pointed at the bulky screen. "It belongs in a museum. Or a junkyard."

Brundar shrugged. "I think Franco keeps it as a desk ornament. It's not really needed here since the contracts are done on paper and kept in the filing cabinet. Franco is old school. Computers can be hacked, and members' privacy could be compromised. Paper is still the safest way to go." He pulled a folder out of one of the drawers and dropped it on the desk. "Have fun."

Callie draped her purse on the back of the chair, sat down and opened the folder. The confidentiality agreement was on top, and she skimmed through it before signing on the bottom and putting it aside. The next several pages explained about consent and limits, and what was permitted in the public areas of the club and what was not.

From the looks of it, Franco's main concern was ensuring members' privacy and safety. Very few things were explicitly disallowed in the private rooms, which left an overwhelming variety of options, some of them quite shocking. Most sexual activities were disallowed in the public area, but there was no restriction on what could be discussed there.

*Must be interesting to be a fly on the wall in that room.*

The next section contained a long list of activities, three boxes to check off next to each. Okay, soft limit, and hard limit.

She lifted her eyes to look at Brundar who had taken a seat on the other side of the desk, watching her intently.

"Do I need to fill in all of this? There are like five hundred items here."

"Do you want to play, Calypso?" His voice had never sounded so deep.

She swallowed and nodded, the words sticking in her throat. For the first time since she'd met him, Brundar intimidated her. His pale eyes seemed to glow in the poorly illuminated office, and the shadows painted his austere features even harsher.

"Then fill it out." Sensing her trepidation, Brundar softened his tone. "When you are done, we will go over it together. Going through all these items will clarify things for you."

God, she had no idea. When she was done, the hard limit row had most of the check marks, the soft limit a few, and the okay one even less. As far as kink went, she was just a darker shade of vanilla. If this club was as tame as Brundar had said it was, she shuddered to think what went on in others.

This whole idea, which had been fueling her sexual fantasies for years, suddenly seemed extremely foolish.

Turning the folder around for Brundar to read, she leaned back in her chair and crossed her arms over her chest. She wouldn't be surprised if he told her she shouldn't be there. That she didn't belong.

He would be right, of course.

But if not here and not in the vanilla world, where did she fit in?

A sinking feeling in her belly whispered that she didn't fit in anywhere.

It wasn't the end of the world, though. Sex wasn't all that important. In fact, she would be better off forgetting this silly quest and focusing on more important things like getting the education she needed to fulfill her dream, or finding a decent guy to share her life with, complete with the house with a white picket fence and two and a half kids.

The thing was, Brundar was a guy who walked in the shadows. He didn't fit in that sunny picture.

For reasons she couldn't fully understand, Callie felt that she would be better off in his dark and stormy landscape than under the bright sun.

Perhaps her company would make his landscape just a little bit sunnier.

# 46

# BRUNDAR

Brundar wasn't surprised as he looked over Calypso's list. It was exactly what he'd expected. What he hadn't expected, though, was for her to remain seated and gaze at him with hope in her eyes.

While going over the questionnaire, her arousal had slowly dissipated, until the scent was completely gone. He'd been sure she would get up and leave as fast as her legs could carry her.

"Any questions?"

"I'm all out. There is some scary shit in there." She pointed at the papers. "I know it's supposed to cover everything, but I didn't know half of it even existed. Probably more. I feel like such a fool for entertaining the notion that I could belong in here." She waved a hand around.

Her honesty and courage impressed him. It hadn't been easy to admit that she was in over her head. On the other hand, he didn't want her so completely discouraged.

"It's okay, Calypso. I didn't know more than half of it either when I first discovered this world."

With a sigh, she slumped in her chair. "Thank you for telling me that."

Brundar rubbed at his jaw. Calypso deserved better than what he was doing to her.

Hell, whom was he fooling?

If he wanted to be honest with himself, he should admit he was looking for an excuse to backtrack from his previous decision to stay away from this woman who was pushing all of his buttons and tugging at all of his strings. For the first time in his adult life, Brundar felt he was more than a weapon. Not an automaton, but a man who was flesh and blood and, most surprisingly, heart.

He pulled a blank piece of paper from the drawer and handed it to the amazing woman gazing at him with eyes that saw him clearer than he saw himself. "List your rules, Calypso. Now that you have a better understanding, you should know what you want."

She took the blank page, looked at it for a moment, than looked up again. "I can't. It's too embarrassing."

"Do you want me to do it for you? You can cross out anything that I've gotten wrong and add anything that I've missed."

"Yes, please."

Brundar went through the motions of checking her answers again, even though he had them seared into his brain from the quick scan he'd done before.

Calypso was perfect for him, and he was going to let her know that before he touched her in any way.

"You're okay with bondage." He glanced at her and she nodded.

"You're not so sure about a blindfold, but you're willing to try." She nodded again.

"You're okay with a light spanking, but only with a hand." He chuckled as he added, "Paddles, floggers, and straps are all hard limits." She might change her mind about that once she got a taste.

Nodding, Calypso blushed deep crimson, the musk of her arousal perfuming the air.

"You have no problem with obeying orders as long as they don't breach any of your hard limits." Which was almost everything. Calypso didn't belong in the club. Her tastes were too tame even for Franco's soft-core establishment.

She nodded.

"You chose red as your safe word." He looked up and smiled. "Given your short list, I don't think you need one."

She smiled sheepishly. "I know. But it was one of the few questions I could actually answer positively."

Brundar turned the page over to her. "Feel free to make changes, then sign at the bottom."

She looked it over and then scribbled her name. "My list is just as short as yours," she said as she handed him the page.

He took it, adding it to her file. "Which is perfect."

"I agree." Calypso smiled, her facial muscles losing some of their tension.

He rose to his feet and offered her his hand.

She took it, letting him pull her up and bring her flush against his body.

He stroked her hair, then kissed her lightly, not wanting to overwhelm her when she was already overwhelmed.

His courageous girl.

He was done fighting a losing battle. She was his. Not to keep, that was impossible, but at least for a little while. He was too weak to deny himself the rare pleasure of a kindred soul.

"Are you taking me to one of the rooms?" The quiver in her voice betrayed both hope and anxiety.

"Would you prefer I took you home?"

She shook her head. "No. I'm afraid you'll change your mind again."

Poor girl. He'd toyed with her enough. "It's not that I didn't want you. I did, from the very first time I saw you, but you were married."

"Is that why you helped me get free?"

"No, sweetling. I did it for you. Now, same as then, I have nothing to offer you except a few nights of passion. I wish things were different, but that's still true. Are you okay with that?"

"I'll take whatever you can give me. I need you."

*Fates, I need you too.*

He took her to the one room with a private exit to the outside. Soon, the regulars would start arriving, and she would be embarrassed to be seen walking out of there when they were done.

Hell, whom was he fooling? He didn't want anyone seeing her with him and imagining what they'd done. Calypso and everything about her belonged to him. No one other than him was allowed to have sexual fantasies about her. Not while he was around.

Walking into the room, Calypso took a quick glance around, her eyes lingering on the specially designed contraption in the corner.

"What is that?" She pointed.

He wrapped his arm around her waist, holding her to his side. Not because he was afraid she'd bolt—Calypso had made her decision, and nothing short of an explosion was going to deter her from it—but she was scared and unsure and physical contact would make her feel safer. "I think you can guess."

"Are you going to tie me up to this?"

He scented her anxiety, but it was overwhelmed by the scent of her desire. This was turning her on.

"It's either that or face down on the bed. Your choice. But I think you'll enjoy the bench more."

Resembling a weight-lifting bench, the front part was raised to its maximum height, while the back was lowered. Dangling from the other side of it, the leather straps that were lined with fake fur would secure her comfortably in place, while the extra padding on the almost vertical support would ensure she was comfortable enough for an extended play.

Trying to look at it through her eyes, Brundar didn't think the piece of equipment looked particularly ominous. But assumption was the mother of all fuckups, and it was always better to ask.

He stroked her hair, gentling her. "You're okay with that? Or does it scare you?"

"I think it's fine," she whispered.

## 47

# CALLIE

That was not how Callie wanted her first time with Brundar to be.

The first time was supposed to be tender, explorative, which wasn't going to happen while she was tied up and blindfolded with her back turned to him.

She wasn't scared, trusting him to be gentle with her and lead her slowly into this new world of darker pleasures. But she yearned for the intimacy he couldn't give her.

His rules prohibited that.

"Calypso." Brundar pulled her into his hard body, his warmth and his strength easing her turmoil. A finger under her chin, he lifted her head, so she was looking into his smoldering eyes. "Don't think so much, just feel." His large palm stroked small circles on her back as he lowered his head and kissed her.

His gentle hold on her contrasted with the ferocity of his possessive passion as he took her mouth, his lips firm, his tongue stroking and gliding against hers.

Lost to the passion, to the kiss she'd been dreaming about since that first time he'd kissed her and had left her with a taste for more, Callie moaned. Her hands ached to thread through the curtain of his silky hair, but she had to respect his hard limits, the same way she expected him to respect hers.

There was so little she'd agreed to. Would it be enough?

Any moment now, he could demand her to strip for him, and she'd have to do it, with grace, because she'd given him that power. She'd promised to obey as long as he respected her rules.

The thought mortified and excited her at the same time.

Callie wasn't shy, but to strip on command for a man who was going to see her nude for the first time would mean stretching her courage and determination to the max.

Brundar deepened the kiss, a growl rumbling in his muscular chest as his hand, which up to that moment had been so gentle on her back, fisted her hair and pulled her head back, opening her for him.

The dominance of the act more than the slight sting had her nipples pebble and moisture gather in her panties, which hadn't been dry since he'd shown her the room with the spanking bench.

She rubbed her achy peaks against his chest, hoping it wasn't against his rules, and if it was, she didn't care. Worst case scenario it would earn her a spanking, and that wouldn't be bad at all.

But given the tightening of his hold on her and the way he rubbed his erection against her belly, it seemed Brundar was fine with that.

Lost to the sensations bombarding her starved body, Callie felt her legs go soft, and if not for Brundar's firm hold on her, she would've collapsed into him.

With one last swipe of his tongue against her kiss-swollen lips, he made sure she was stable enough to stand on her own before catching the bottom of her T-shirt and pulling it over her head in one swift motion.

"Thank you." She was so grateful he wasn't forcing her to strip.

He chuckled, though she wasn't sure he'd caught her meaning. "You're welcome." He unzipped her jeans and pulled them down. She stepped out of them.

If she weren't so embarrassed, she would've thanked him again for not stripping her in one go, leaving her in her bra and panties.

His palm splayed on the naked expanse of her belly, warm, possessive, reassuring. His other hand stroked her hip, his fingers curling around the curve of her ass.

"You're beautiful, Calypso."

"Thank you," she blurted, feeling foolish for sounding like a broken record. Where was the rich vocabulary she prided herself on? But her mouth was dry, and the words were swirling in her head in an incoherent jumble she couldn't make sense of.

Her breath hitched as the hand on her belly stroked up, reaching the bottom curve of her breast. Panting, she looked up at Brundar, startled at the intensity he regarded her with.

Slowly, he ran a finger at the bottom of her breast, the sensation electrifying but far from what she needed. With a light squeeze, he abandoned her butt cheek, his hand reaching for the back clasp of her bra. He didn't snap it open right away as she'd expected. His fingers caressing the skin around the clasp, he looked into her eyes and waited for her acquiescence.

Callie might have not known much about dominants, but she very much doubted they sought approval before every move. Wasn't he supposed to order her to do things? Take what he wanted as long as it wasn't against her rules?

Not that she was complaining. This was perfect, exactly like it should be between a man and a woman. It just didn't fit the profile she'd imagined.

Except, Brundar wasn't like anyone she'd ever met. He didn't fit into any neat category. He was different in almost every way.

Snapping the clasp open, he hooked his fingers in the shoulder straps and lowered them down in slow motion, treating her as if she was a spooked little kitten he didn't want to scare off.

Which made her aware that her initial anxiety was gone. With his slow and careful treatment of her, he was easing her into the scene. It was exactly what she needed to loosen up.

Brundar sucked in a breath when he bared her breasts, letting the bra slide down to the floor.

As he stared at her practically nude body, Callie forced herself to stand straight, her hands fisted by her sides to remind herself she wasn't allowed to touch this incredibly handsome man who was looking at her as if she was special, beautiful.

With her shoes gone, she felt tiny next to him even though she wasn't short. Callie couldn't help feeling a little intimidated by Brundar's sheer size. He wasn't bulky or heavily muscled. But his height and the breadth of his shoulders were impressive. That he was powerful, she had no doubt.

If she were allowed to touch him, Callie would've divested him of his shirt and run her hands all over his taut muscles—the six-pack she'd felt when he'd held her close.

"Beautiful," he hissed, lifting his hands to her breasts and stroking his thumbs over both of her nipples, running lazy circles around the pebbled peaks.

Involuntarily, her back arched in a silent invitation for him to take more, to cup her breasts, knead them, lick and suck on the achy twin points of gnawing need.

When his thumbs finally brushed over the tips, the moan she'd been trying to hold in escaped her throat in a rush, and she closed her eyes.

God, it was becoming impossible to keep her hands off of him. If he didn't tie her up soon, she was in danger of breaking the rules. Maybe he wasn't going to do it after all? He didn't seem to be in any rush.

"I'm proud of you, sweetling," he whispered in her ear, a moment before nuzzling her neck. "Such a good girl for keeping your hands at your sides."

His words of praise elicited another soft moan, and she tilted her head, giving him easier access. "If I promise to keep my hands to myself, can we forgo the bondage?"

"Nice try." He tweaked her nipples hard, the small pain sending a zing of desire straight down between her legs.

"Turn around, Calypso," he commanded.

She obeyed in an instant.

His thumbs hooked inside the elastic of her panties, pulling them down past her hips and letting them drop to the floor.

Her cheeks flared with heat as she imagined him seeing how soaked through they were, grateful for having her back to him.

"Look at you, sweetling, so wet for me."

His finger sliding over her sleek folds from behind, she almost came right there and then, her impending climax halted only by the sharp smack he delivered to her naked ass. "Not yet."

Unbidden, the words she'd never imagined uttering of her own accord in a sexual situation left her mouth. "Yes, sir."

"Good girl." His palm caressed the sting away, making her hungry for more.

"Get on the bench, Calypso." He tapped her butt cheek lightly.

*Here it comes.* Callie closed her eyes for a split moment, then took in a fortifying breath and stepped closer to the contraption Brundar was about to strap her to.

"Don't be afraid." He kissed her neck as his hand on her shoulder guided her onto the thing.

The pose was awkward to say the least. On the top, the bench reached only up to under her breasts, supporting her torso but leaving them exposed. On the bottom Brundar pulled out two knee supports and guided her to kneel on them, her thighs spread wide lewdly. In seconds, he had her strapped in, fiddling with the buckles to ensure she was secured but comfortably so.

Her thighs were strapped to the supports, her torso to the bench, and her arms to the strap that secured her torso. Her range of motion was limited to less than an inch in each direction.

"Okay?" Brundar's warm hand caressed her back.

Surprisingly, it was. She was comfortable, nothing pinched or pulled, and Brundar's hand on her was reassuring, as was his soft tone.

"Uh-huh."

"Words, sweetling," he leaned over her, pressing his front to her back.

"I'm good."

He dangled a long piece of black silk in front of her eyes. "I'm going to blindfold you now."

She took in a long breath and closed her eyes. "Okay."

## 48

# BRUNDAR

"Okay, sweetling?" Brundar asked after tying the end of the black silk scarf at the back of her head.

"Perfect," Calypso husked.

The entire room was perfumed with her arousal.

Brundar still couldn't get over how trusting she was with him. Did she feel the same deep connection that had battered at his shields, bringing him to his knees?

Was she as helpless against the irresistible pull between them as he was?

Looking at her golden hair spilling in soft waves down her slender back, he felt like an awestruck boy, flummoxed that a beauty like her found him worthy of her trust, her surrender.

She shivered when he lifted the golden strands, shifting them to the side and exposing the long expanse of her back. She was slender, but not thin, small-boned, as his mother would have described her.

Calypso was a tapestry of contradictions. She was soft yet firm, her skin the softest silk spread tight over taut muscles honed by long hours of working on her feet. She was delicate yet strong. She was determined yet flexible, demanding yet yielding.

He loved the many facets of her.

It would take a lifetime to learn all her nuances, discover all her passions, test all her limits—soft and hard. He would have gladly committed himself to the exploration. Unfortunately, Calypso's lifespan was painfully too short for him to unravel all of her secrets.

He'd better remember that before letting the ice shields surrounding his heart melt for her.

Closing his eyes, he made a decision that was going to cause him agony in the short run but save his heart from shattering in the long run. Brundar could not afford a meltdown. He wouldn't survive it, and the clan would not survive without him.

For the foreseeable future, he was indispensable. Until new blood fortified the Guardian ranks, the clan needed him.

He would pleasure Calypso until she forgot her own name, but he would hold back. It wasn't an impossible task. He'd done it before. His overriding need was to bite, and he could do it without taking his pleasure inside her.

Caressing her back, he kissed her neck, nipping the soft spot where it connected to her shoulder, then circling his arms around her to cup her breasts. She moaned and bucked as much as her restraints allowed, while he tweaked and pulled, torturing her hard nipples and ratcheting her desire to a fever pitch.

"Please, Brundar, I can't, please..." She wasn't coherent in her pleas, but then he wasn't expecting her to be. He knew what she wanted, what she needed better than she could articulate in her current state.

He cupped her breasts, his warm palms easing the ache he'd caused, letting her catch her breath.

However, the reprieve he granted her was short. Now that her front was soothed, he intended to warm her backside—one of the few things she'd listed.

The first smack caught her by surprise.

"Ow, that hurt."

He rubbed the small ache away. "Do you want me to stop?"

She shook her head.

"Words, Calypso." He delivered another smack to her other butt cheek, immediately rubbing the sting away.

"No. More."

He chuckled. "I didn't understand that." He teased. "Is it no more, or give me more?"

"Give me more."

"That was what I thought. But I wasn't sure."

She snickered, which earned her a harder smack.

"Ouch. Was that your hand or did you switch to a paddle?"

The impudent remark earned her a volley of smacks, leaving her heart-shaped behind slightly pinked, and her sex blooming with desire.

His Calypso wasn't much of a submissive, but that was perfectly fine with him. He didn't need her to submit to him, just yield for the duration of their playtime. In fact, her sass was making the game more fun.

He leaned over her, pressing his aching hardness to her warmed behind. "Do you still doubt me, little girl?"

He heard her stifle a chuckle. "No, sir. I wouldn't dare. I'm sure my fanny bears your paddle-like handprints."

"Hmm, let's see." He rubbed one cheek and then the other. "I don't think you've had enough."

Calypso shivered at the loss of his body heat as he pulled back and delivered another volley of light smacks. She was panting now, not because she was in any real pain, but because she was on the verge of climaxing.

"Not yet, sweetling."

"Please, I'm so close."

"I know, just a little bit longer. Can you do that for me?"

She nodded.

"Good girl. Wait for my permission." He kissed her neck, his palm caressing her warmed cheeks.

She stiffened, his command apparently not sitting well with her, nevertheless when his finger brushed over her drenched folds, she groaned but held herself back.

He rewarded her by pushing his finger inside her wet heat, then pulling out and coming back with two, slowly stretching her sheath. She was so tight, it must've been a while for her. He wondered how she'd managed to avoid her asshole husband's advances.

It had been a while for Brundar as well.

Ever since he'd revealed himself to Calypso, he hadn't been with anyone else. His abstinence didn't make sense since he'd had no intentions of having any kind of a relationship with her, but the thought of being with another woman had felt like a betrayal.

Which meant that even though he was still fully dressed, and his painfully stiff cock was still imprisoned inside his jeans, he was just as close to climaxing as she was.

In two quick moves, he freed himself. The fingers of one hand still pumping in and out of Calypso's drenched sheath, he palmed the hard length with the other, stroking it in sync with his thrusting fingers.

Unable to resist, he rubbed the tip in her wetness, coating himself in her fragrant cream before pumping into his fist.

"Brundar..." She whispered his name like a plea.

He wasn't going to last and neither was she. After pining for one another for weeks, they were both too close to the edge to try to prolong this first time.

"I've got you, sweetling," he hissed through protruding fangs and pressed his thumb to the seat of her pleasure.

Her sheath convulsed around his fingers, the loud keening moan leaving her throat sounding tortured and euphoric at the same time.

Pressing himself to her, his seed shot out, covering her ass and her back in one hot stream after another. He gripped her hair, pulling her head back and elongating her neck before sinking his fangs into it.

She climaxed again, and so did he, bathing her backside in more cum.

As he'd expected, she blacked out, going limp under him, the first venom bite the most potent of all.

Giving himself only a moment to catch his breath, Brundar untied Calypso and carried her to the bed, laying her down on her belly. She was a mess. The sight of her back and her ass and the back of her thighs covered with his seed brought him a sense of odd satisfaction. He hadn't come inside her, but he'd marked her as his nonetheless.

Where had that primitive response come from? It was like nothing he'd experienced before. Nonetheless, he wasn't embarrassed by it. On the contrary, he felt like pounding his chest caveman style and shouting 'mine.'

An odd feeling, but not unpleasant.

Calypso was changing him.

For the better, Brundar decided.

A caveman was a marked improvement over an iceman.

In the bathroom, he wetted several washcloths in warm water, then went back and gently wiped the evidence of his possession off her.

To the naked eye, she might've appeared clean, but his scent was all over her, warning any immortal male to stay away because she belonged to him.

It was a nonsensical sentiment, as no immortal male would care if Brundar claimed a human as his own, but it was significant to him, as was the fact that for the first time ever he'd bitten a woman's neck instead of the inside of her thigh.

## 49

## CALLIE

"Brundar." His name was on Callie's lips the moment she woke up.

No longer tied to the bench, she was lying face down, tucked inside the blankets burrito style. Brundar was next to her on the bed, sitting with his back propped against several pillows, his eyes trained on her with that unwavering focus she was becoming accustomed to.

"Here." He lifted a water bottle off the nightstand, unscrewed the cap, and held it out for her.

Freeing one arm from the tight bundle of blankets he'd wrapped her in, she took the bottle and lifted it to her parched lips. After the first few gulps wet her dry throat, she wiggled out of the burrito style wrapping and sat up, holding a blanket to cover her nakedness while she drank the whole thing up.

"Thank you." She handed him the empty bottle. "Do you happen to have another one?"

"I do."

She drank half of the second bottle before her thirst was finally sated. "Thanks." She handed it back.

"You're welcome." He reached to cup her cheek, then leaned and kissed her lips chastely. "How are you feeling?"

A sheepish smile lifted the corners of her lips. "Like a woman who had the best orgasm of her life." Amazing, considering that he hadn't even been inside her. Which raised the question, why?

Had Brundar remembered what she'd told him about not using birth control with Shawn? Or had it been what she'd told him about getting pregnant because of a defective condom?

Brundar smiled, a real smile and not the slightest lifting of lips that barely passed as one. "I'm glad."

It seemed that pleasuring her into oblivion made the guy not only happy but proud. His male ego had probably inflated to the size of a zeppelin.

"I'm sure you are. I never passed out from one before."

Callie had been so out of it that she hadn't felt him cleaning her up, which he obviously had done because she didn't feel sticky. She hadn't heard him showering either, but it was obvious that he had. Brundar's long hair was swept away from his face and tied at his nape, the wet ends leaving water spots on the pillows behind him. She must've slept for a while.

"How long was I out?"

"About an hour."

"Shit." She lifted her other arm and glanced at her watch. "I'm late." She slid off the bed, dragging the blanket with her.

Brundar caught the end of it, fisting the fabric and twisting it away from her. "You're not late. I told Franco you're off tonight."

Yanking on the blanket, she turned around, the sharp movement making her head spin. "Why? I need the hours, Brundar."

"Because you need to rest more. He'll give you another shift."

"I'm not tired."

He lifted a brow. "Are you steady on your feet, Calypso?"

About to answer in the affirmative, she remembered his new rule about lying. As fun as the erotic spanking he'd given her had been, she didn't want another one right away.

Tomorrow? Heck, yeah.

"No, I'm not. You're right." She wrapped the blanket around her, tucking one corner in. "It's so weird. I'm tired and dizzy as if I ran a marathon when I did basically nothing." She chuckled, lifting her fingers. "I didn't move an inch."

"Come here." He patted the spot next to him.

She did, snuggling up close and almost purring when he wrapped his arm around her and brought her even closer. She needed the intimacy. That's what had been lacking before. As hot as it was, it had been a scene, a sexual experience, a physical coming together of desires, not souls.

Resting her head against his pectoral, Callie sighed. The only thing missing now was her touching him, but she wasn't even going to mention it. He obviously had a problem with that, and she was in no position to ask when it would be okay for her to do so just because they'd had sex.

Sort of.

As far as the simple mechanics, what they had done was heavy necking. Except, they had both orgasmed, which in her opinion counted as sex.

"Scening is intense. That's why you're exhausted."

Hmm, he might be right. "Was it for you? Exhausting, I mean?"

"Less so. It's always more intense for the one on the receiving end."

She lifted her head to look at him. "You mean the submissive?"

He shook his head. "I don't like the term, the same way I hate being called a Dom. People don't fit into neat categories or same size containers, and words have power. Your sexual preferences do not define who you are. You're not submissive, Calypso. In fact, you're quite bossy. But you enjoy yielding sexually."

Lifting a finger, he rubbed it over her lower lip, awakening her desire. "If I order you to do my laundry, or pick up my stuff from the dry cleaners, it's not going to turn you on, and you're not going to obey. But if I order you to strip, you probably will. Do you get the difference?"

The small touch and the desire she saw in Brundar's eyes were playing a number on her. Her nipples tight beneath the blanket, she wanted him to kiss her, to fondle her. In the sexual haze of arousal, Callie had a feeling she would've agreed to do a lot more than wash his dirty clothes. She wanted to do things for him, to please him.

Was it wrong?

"If you ask nicely, I might do your laundry and pick up your stuff from the dry cleaners. People do nice things for each other when they care." She'd meant to say it teasingly; instead, her words came out sounding throaty and needy.

He tugged at the blanket, and she let it drop, her breasts exposed to his smoldering gaze.

Cupping one, he lazily thumbed the nipple. "And I would do the same for you. If you ask nicely." He bent his head and flicked his tongue over her other nipple.

"Oh, God." Callie moaned. Crossing her legs, she clenched her core in a futile attempt to relieve the ache that had started down there.

But all too soon Brundar sat up, taking his talented tongue and fingers away. "At this rate, we will never get out of here. Get dressed. I'm taking you home."

*Bossy man, ordering me around.*

Disappointed, Callie felt like reminding him of his little speech from before. It wasn't that she didn't agree they should leave the room. Franco probably needed it for his members, and whoever did the cleaning needed time to replace the bedding and the towels and to wipe all the surfaces clean. But a different phrasing would have made all the difference, turning an order into a request.

Perhaps, though, such subtleties were lost on Brundar. He was a military man, used to issuing and taking commands. For him, it might have been the only way he knew how to communicate.

She knew so little about him, especially about his past. Had he been in the service? And if yes, doing what? A Marine? A navy SEAL? A demanding physical fitness trainer?

Their shared experience didn't give her the right to question his aversion to being touched, but it did allow for at least a few questions as long as they weren't overly intrusive.

Once they got back to her place, she was going to lull him with a good meal and start a carefully worded interrogation.

## 50

# BRUNDAR

"Can you stop by the supermarket?" Calypso asked when Brundar backed out from the club's parking lot.

"Sure." He stifled a smile.

The girl was more resilient than he'd given her credit for. He had underestimated her and her resolve. Apparently, when Calypso set her eyes on a goal, nothing and no one was going to deter her from it. Not even him.

She'd wanted him, and she'd had him.

Case closed.

He'd been mistaken thinking he could scare her off by showing her a few spanking implements or letting her read the long list of kinks Franco allowed in his club. It was by no means exhaustive, but it should've been enough to send a newbie with tastes as mellow as hers running.

Not Calypso.

She'd cornered him into doing exactly what she'd wanted. Obviously, he hadn't been a helpless victim, nothing would have happened if his restraint had held, but he wanted her too much to keep fighting on both fronts.

"I'll be just a moment." Calypso opened the door as soon as he parked next to the small neighborhood supermarket.

"I'll come with you."

"No, it's okay. I know what I need. Give me three minutes."

"If you're not out in five, I'm coming in."

She rolled her eyes and closed the door.

Why did he have the sense she was plotting something? But what the hell could it be that required a trip to the supermarket?

It wasn't as if the place had a lingerie section, and she was planning the next step in her seduction by getting herself something sexy to wear. But even if it weren't the stupidest idea that had ever crossed his mind, and she really was going to buy sexy lingerie, he could have told her that she didn't need anything special to entice him.

Calypso could've been wearing a potato sack, and he would've found her irresistible.

Especially if it was one of those made from a thin plastic mesh…

Her small nipples peeking through the weave…

Fates, he was a goner.

The iceman had melted. The tin man had gotten a heart, or as was the case, a hard-on. Brundar cursed under his breath and adjusted himself in a failed attempt to relieve the pressure. What was the last part? Something about a lion and courage?

As promised, the passenger door opened a few minutes later, and Calypso slid inside holding a brown paper bag.

With his acute sense of smell, Brundar didn't need to ask her what she'd gotten. There were steaks in that bag, rib-eye, his favorite. By the heft of it, though, there was more in the bag, but he couldn't smell anything other than the meat. Maybe she'd bought several pounds of it and was planning a block party to celebrate her victory.

"What's the smirk for?" Calypso asked.

He shook his head. "Nothing I care to share."

With a humph, she crossed her arms over her chest and murmured, "Nothing new there."

Her building was only several hundred yards away from the store, and a few moments later Brundar was sitting at her counter, watching Calypso unpack her groceries.

"I hope you're hungry. I got four steaks. Three of them are for you."

"Feeding me to ensure I have my strength for later?" He lifted a brow.

Calypso stopped and looked up at him, amusement making her green eyes sparkle. "Brundar, did you just make a joke? Are you okay?"

He hadn't. He'd been dead serious, questioning her motives for treating him to another meal in the same day. But if it made her happy, he could play along.

Maybe. He was rusty, but once upon a time he'd had a sense of humor. "It's a legitimate question. I have a feisty, lustful redhead cooking me dinner. Can you blame me for being suspicious?"

A soft scent of guilt wafted from her. Had he been right?

"I'm not a redhead."

An evasive answer if he'd ever heard one. "What do you call the color of your hair? Gold?"

"Light brown with red undertones." She unwrapped the steaks, spreading them over a cutting board.

"That's too complicated for me."

Calypso salted and peppered the meat, then pulled out a head of lettuce and a few tomatoes from the fridge.

"I like cooking for you. You enjoy everything I make, and it's a pleasure to watch you eat. But the truth is that I had an ulterior motive for splurging on steaks."

With a fake frown, Brundar crossed his arms over his chest. "I knew it." If the woman wanted to fortify his energy level so he could pleasure her again, there was nothing wrong with that. But he was glad she felt the need to be honest with him.

"I know so little about you." She dropped the steaks on a large skillet.

"I know that you're of Scottish descent, but I don't know if you were born there or here. I know you have a brother you live with, a cousin who is a superb attorney and another one who is some big shot businessman who has a butler, but nothing about your parents or other family." She rinsed the cutting board, the lettuce and tomatoes, and then started chopping the vegetables for a salad.

"I know that you work as a bodyguard, but I also know that you have a lot of connections in law enforcement and other government agencies, which leads me to believe that you're much more than a simple bodyguard." She flipped the steaks to the other side.

The woman had been listening to every little morsel of information he'd told her. Should he feel flattered?

"I thought if I fed you, you'd be more inclined to talk."

Brundar didn't like where this was going. He would either have to lie or tell her half-truths. He pinned her with a hard stare. "Did it work on Shawn?"

Calypso blushed. "I knew all there was to know about him. I knew his parents. I knew where he went to school. I knew the people he worked with. There was no reason for me to butter him up for information."

Brundar hated that she had anything positive to say about the sick bastard. "What about other things? Did you cook for him so he wouldn't throw tantrums and scare you?" He was hurting her with those questions, and he didn't even know why he was doing it. Was he trying to push her away again?

Calypso wiped her hands with a kitchen towel and then threw it on the counter. "So what if I did? You have a problem with how I survived a marriage that was becoming more and more hellish? Are you going to lecture me about it?" Her voice quivered with unshed tears, tearing him apart.

Brundar pushed the stool back, strode to the other side of the counter, and pulled her into his arms. "I'm sorry. You don't deserve me treating you like that."

Forgetting she wasn't supposed to touch him, Calypso pounded her fist on his chest, not hard, her aim wasn't to hurt, just to make a point. "You're damn right I don't deserve that. Not from Shawn, not from you, and not from anyone else. I don't care if talking about yourself scares the shit out of you. If you can't treat me with respect and kindness, you'd better leave now."

She couldn't have hurt him more if she'd plunged a serrated blade into his black heart.

"You're right. I'd better go." He released her.

The best thing he could do for Calypso was to walk out the door and never come back.

## 51

## CALLIE

*What?*

He thought he was leaving?

*The coward.*

Callie fisted Brundar's T-shirt and pulled him back. "I can't believe you, Brundar. You're not going anywhere. You're going to apologize and promise to be nice and mean it. Then you're going to eat the dinner I cooked for you, tell me about yourself as much or as little as you want, and then you're going to make love to me. And I mean the real thing. Is that clear? Sir?"

Wow. What had gotten into her?

Callie had never talked like that to anyone. Ever. Not to her father, not to Shawn, not to her friends, and not even to any of the pissy customers who'd been rude to her. She was too polite, too reserved to raise her voice and make demands.

Why the hell had she goaded Brundar?

But the ease with which he was willing to give up on her had made her so angry that her head had started pounding from the stress of it.

The thing was, she wanted this strange, broken man with a passion and an obsessive need that was terrifying in its intensity. There was nothing she wouldn't do to make him hers, but it was going to be on her terms. She would give him her body, her heart, and her soul, but only if he gave the same back.

Deep in her gut she knew they belonged together, and she was going to do everything in her power to make that happen.

In the end, he might still walk away, but not before she'd given it her best. Callie wasn't going to spend the rest of her life wondering what if she'd tried harder. If he walked, it would hurt like hell, but at least she'd know it was not for lack of effort on her part.

Brundar was doing a great impression of a pillar of salt, frozen in place with his eyes peeled wide and mouth gaping. Apparently, no one had ever spoken to him like that before.

Calypso reached behind herself and turned the burner off, then snapped her fingers in front of Brundar's face. "Did I shock you? Do you need smelling salts?"

A moment later his palm landed on her butt with a loud smack. "Watch it, young lady. That wasn't very respectful of you." He wrapped his arms around her and dipped his head to look into her eyes. "I apologize. I promise no more snide remarks or questions. I'm going to eat the dinner you cooked for me, and then I'm going to make love to you until you pass out again. Is that clear? Ma'am?"

The relief his words brought about was so profound that it made her feel lightheaded. She wanted to laugh, or cry, she wasn't sure. Instead, she buried her face in his T-shirt.

"But." Brundar put a finger under her chin and lifted her head, his pale blue eyes boring into hers. "It's gonna be my way—with you tied up and blindfolded. Are you okay with that? Because that's not negotiable."

She nodded enthusiastically. "Yes. Definitely yes."

His lips twitched. "Aren't you going to tack on the 'sir'?"

Callie straightened her back and saluted. "Sir! Yes, sir!"

"Good. Now let's eat. I'm starving." He rubbed at the flat expanse of his stomach.

"How about we take our dinner to the dining table? The steaks deserve a more formal setting than the counter."

"No problem."

Brundar helped set the table, while she arranged the steaks on a platter and tossed the salad with some olive oil and lemon juice.

A bottle of mango-flavored vodka, a container of lemonade, and a bottle of Chivas completed the setup.

"Thank you for the Scotch." Brundar pulled the bottle closer to him. "What are you going to do with the vodka and the juice?"

"Mix them, of course. The recipe says one shot of vodka to two shots of lemonade, but I double on the lemonade. As you've noticed, I'm a very light drinker." She reached for the vodka.

He grabbed the bottle with a speed that seemed almost unnatural. "Let me mix it for you."

"Oh, I forgot the mint. I'll be right back." The drink wasn't the same without that last finishing touch.

When she got back, she dropped the leaves inside the drink he'd mixed for her, and for the next few minutes, they ate in silence.

Watching Brundar eat was fascinating. He was so methodical and precise. Every cut was the same size, and each forkful of salad had the same precise combination of lettuce and tomatoes. She wondered what it said about him. Was he as meticulous in everything? Was the apartment he shared with his brother pristine?

"You never told me your brother's name."

"Anandur."

"Can you tell me a little bit about him?"

Brundar halted with a piece of steak speared on his fork. "Imagine the opposite of me and you get Anandur."

Callie smirked. "You mean ugly, short, and talkative?"

That got a smile out of him. "You got the talkative right. If you want a rumor to spread at maximum velocity, tell it to my brother. He isn't ugly or short. He is bigger than me and covered in way too much crinkly red hair. Beard, mustache, legs, chest, he looks like a Viking."

She would've liked to meet Brundar's brother. Anandur sounded like fun. "Is he in the same business as you? Personal protection?"

Brundar nodded. "We work for our cousin, the big shot businessman with the butler."

That explained how they got to share the guy's vegan meals. If they were his bodyguards, they were spending a lot of time with him.

"Your cousin is smart to employ family. I'm sure you guys are more dedicated to his safety than some random security firm."

Chewing, Brundar nodded again.

"Why does he need bodyguards? Does he conduct business in Third World countries or other dangerous places?"

Brundar hesitated, taking a moment to formulate his answer. "Sometimes. His dealings are confidential. I can't share details."

That was reasonable. "What about your parents?"

"When Anandur and I moved to the States, our mother remained in Scotland."

"What about your father?"

"Fathers. Anandur and I each had a different sire. They died a long time ago."

Sire was a strange way to refer to one's father. It sounded like a sperm donor. Maybe it was a cultural thing, and all Scots referred to their fathers as sires? She wondered if Brundar's mother had been widowed twice.

"How is she doing? Did she get married again?"

Brundar finished chewing. "She was never married. Anandur and I are both bastards."

Callie's hand flew to her chest. "Oh my God, Brundar. What a nasty thing to say. Why would you talk about your brother and yourself like that?"

He shrugged. "It's the truth. Nothing nasty about it."

"You can say that you're a lovechild, or that you were born out of wedlock. You told me yourself that words have power. Why use a derogatory term like that?"

He pinned her with his pale eyes. "When I was growing up, those euphemisms didn't exist. We were simply bastards."

That had to have been another cultural difference. No one called children born to single mothers bastards anymore. She found it hard to believe that things were all that different in Scotland.

"Did you grow up in some small mountain village?"

Brundar dropped his fork, his eyes hardening, and his pale, austere face darkening as if night had descended above his head. "How did you know?"

"Just a guess."

There was a story there, but Callie sensed it was better left alone.

## 52

# BRUNDAR

Calypso was asking too many questions. At first, Brundar tried to humor her, telling her details that revealed no dangerous secrets or even hinted at them, but enough was enough. He wasn't comfortable talking about himself, especially not about his childhood. It was a subject best left buried.

"Why do you keep your hair so long? Not that I don't find it beautiful and sexy, I do, but it's uncommon. You don't strike me as a guy who likes to attract attention to himself." She chuckled. "Though I don't think you could avoid it even if you shaved your head bald. You're strikingly good-looking."

She'd gotten that right. Even without the hair, his good looks had been the bane of his existence, but no more. No one could touch him. No one could get close enough to hurt him. He dared anyone to try.

Brundar put his fork and knife down and wiped his mouth with a napkin. "Thank you for dinner, Calypso. It was very good." He pushed his chair back to lounge more comfortably.

"You're most welcome." She rose to her feet and collected her plate, and then reached for his.

He caught her wrist. "Leave it."

She looked up at him with questioning eyes.

"Put the other one down too."

Without taking her eyes off him, she did as he'd asked. Under his thumb, her pulse sped up. Her breaths became shallow.

Brundar grabbed her other wrist and pulled her onto his lap. Transferring both into one hand, he threaded the fingers of his other one in her hair and kissed her—the taste of the sweet drink she'd had with dinner mingling with her own sweetness.

In moments, the scent of her desire permeated the room.

It didn't take much to arouse Calypso. She was the most responsive female he'd ever been with. Brundar wondered whether it was his effect on her, or had she responded the same way to others.

Her husband had been her first, but that didn't mean she hadn't snogged with others before him.

Had other males touched her intimately before she'd surrendered her virginity to that asshole?

Had she responded to any of them with such lustful abandon?

One thing Brundar knew for certain: No other woman had ever affected him the way Calypso did. He couldn't conceive of her responding to anyone else the way she responded to him.

Jealousy washed over him like hot acid, scalding, scarring, blurring his vision.

As his fangs punched over his lower lip, his venom glands pulsing with venom, he tightened his grip on her hair, pulling her head back to expose her neck. The need to bite her, to possess her, was overwhelming—a primitive urge he fought with every last bit of reason he had left.

Thousands of years of civilization were no match for the powerful animal instinct gripping him. A less disciplined man would have succumbed.

"Close your eyes, Calypso," he hissed.

She tried to turn her head and look at him, but he tightened his grip on her hair until she whimpered. He let go. "Don't argue. Keep them closed." He used his most commanding tone. Her obedience was not negotiable this time. She couldn't see him like that. He'd already thralled her once today; another thrall so soon might cause damage.

"Yes, sir," she breathed without a shred of mocking in her tone.

Letting go of her wrists, one arm around her waist and the other under her thighs, he lifted Calypso as he pushed to his feet and carried her to her bedroom.

"Keep your eyes closed, and don't move," he reminded her as he laid her on top of the comforter, face down.

"Okay," she murmured, sounding a little scared.

He didn't want her afraid of him, but right now it was better that she was. It would keep her from trying to peek at him, which would force him to thrall her again if she did. He treasured her mind even more than he treasured her trust. He could regain the latter, but damage to the former was irreversible.

Rummaging through her drawers, he found a silk scarf in one and an unopened hosiery four-pack in another.

He blindfolded her first, then helped her out of her clothes.

"Back on your stomach, sweetling," he commanded when he'd divested her of the last article of clothing.

Sitting naked on the bed, her sight obscured by the colorful silk tied around her eyes, one leg folded under her delectable ass, Calypso worried her lower lip. "Do I have to?"

Stocking in hand, Brundar paused, letting it dangle from the bedpost he was tying it to.

But before he could make up his mind, she continued. "I can't see you, and you're going to tie me up so I can't touch you either. Can I at least have the intimacy of chest to chest?"

In a last ditch effort to keep up his crumbling shields, Brundar had planned to keep intimacy to a minimum, but he couldn't deny Calypso her request. "You may."

Exhaling a relieved breath, she lay down on her back and stretched her arms over her head.

Spread out before him, trusting him, she was all woman, perfect in every way, and all his. He had to spend a moment just drinking in the sight of her. "You're beautiful, Calypso."

She smiled. "Thank you."

"No, thank you." He wrapped a stocking around one wrist, tying it loosely so she was comfortable, then repeated with the other. Stroking the inside of her arms, he went all the way up to her bound wrists then entwined their fingers. "I left a lot of give in the bindings. If you really want to, you can get free. The ties are meant as a reminder to keep your arms up."

She nodded and let out a breath, the little trepidation that still lingered in her expression vanishing.

Good. Brundar wanted her aroused and hungry for his touch, but not afraid.

He kissed her parted lips, sliding his tongue for a quick taste before getting up to continue his work on the other side. Wrapping his palm around one slender ankle, he pulled it sideways and secured it in place with a stocking, then did the same with the other one.

Spread-eagled, pliable and obedient, Calypso was a wet dream come true. For the next hour or two, this beautiful, strong woman was going to give herself over to him to do with as he pleased, trusting him with her pleasure.

Was there anything sexier than that?

Nothing compared to this.

His prowess as a fighter and a swordsman was legendary, but his prowess as a lover who could bring a woman to the highest possible ecstasy was what Brundar prided himself on most. It didn't matter that none of his clan members would ever know this about him. It was enough that he knew. And now Calypso would know that too.

Like a master musician, he tugged at the strings until he found the right combination of touch and pull to bring the most out of the particular instrument he was playing. Because no woman was the same as another, and each deserved her particular code deciphered.

Just like his swordsmanship, it required singular focus and dedication, prohibiting the intrusion of any rambling thoughts about his disturbing past or his uninspiring future.

Except, Brundar had a feeling that all his prior performances were nothing but practice runs, preparing him for the masterpiece that was Calypso.

## 53

# CALLIE

Callie might have been deprived of sight, but she could sense Brundar watching her. For long moments he just stood at the foot of the bed.

What was he thinking about?

Was he admiring his handiwork?

Was he admiring her?

Callie wasn't shy, but she wasn't an exhibitionist either. She had a healthy body image, knowing she wasn't too thin or overly padded, nor was she flabby or overly muscular, and even though her proportions weren't perfect, they weren't bad either. With the right clothes and the right bra, she could hide the fact that her butt was too scrawny and her hips too boyish in proportion to her bust, or that her breasts were too big for her delicate frame.

Naturally, she couldn't hide those imperfections while in the nude, but it was nothing she felt embarrassed about.

Not with the way Brundar looked at her.

Callie had never felt as beautiful and as feminine as she did under Brundar's gaze. It was so intense that even now, blindfolded, she felt it as if it was a physical caress.

It infused her with power.

"I can't get enough of looking at you," he admitted.

"You can look as much as you want, touch too." She reminded him that she wasn't an exhibition piece but a hot mess of sexual need that couldn't wait to be sated.

Warm and strong, his palm wrapped around her calf, the small touch sending a zing of desire straight to her center.

She was already starved for his touch, even though he'd brought her to the heights of pleasure only a couple of hours ago.

This man was turning her into a nymphomaniac.

"What's that mysterious smile for?" he asked.

"I can't get enough of you either."

He chuckled. "That's good because you're going to get a lot of me, and I'm not sure you can handle it all."

"Try me," she issued a challenge.

He caressed her knee, circling to her inner thigh, his touch feather-light, stopping an inch from her moist folds and moving to her other thigh, feathering his way down.

Calypso shivered, her arms tugging on her bonds.

"You need to learn patience, sweetling. All good things come to those who wait."

Not in her experience. "Do you actually believe that?"

Brundar's hand stilled on her thigh. "No, I don't. Not out there. But in here, you can bet on it." He continued his lazy caress.

Could she?

Brundar had proven to be a man of his word. Except for the wine bottle he'd promised and must have forgotten about, he'd come through for her on every front, not asking for anything in return.

He was her savior, her guardian angel, and she trusted him without reserve—as evidenced by her current state. There was no one else she would've ever let tie her up and blindfold her.

It was a huge step for her. Life had taught Callie not to give her trust lightly, and lowering her shields for Brundar was her biggest leap of faith yet.

And her last.

If Brundar ever betrayed that trust, she would never give it to anyone again. "I bet on you, Brundar. Don't let me down."

He groaned. "I'll make your body sing for me, Calypso. That's a promise, but it's the only one I can make. No entanglement, no strings."

She stifled a smirk. "I expect nothing more."

*For now.*

## 54

# BRUNDAR

That was a lie.

Calypso wanted so much more from him—things he could never give her.

It didn't matter that he'd never promised to stay or be anything other than a guide on her journey of sexual discovery. She wasn't the only one caught in an emotional whirlpool, either. They were both trapped and sinking fast.

When it was done, and he was gone from her life, Calypso would hurt, and so would he. But at least he would know the reason why.

She would be left wondering what she'd done wrong.

The only thing he could do to mitigate her pain was to show her that she was perfect, and teach her to reach for what she deserved.

Later, he would come up with an excuse for why he couldn't stay—fabricate a story that would leave no room for her to doubt herself. Like a deployment to a Third World country on some secret mission he would never come back from.

She'd mourn him for a while, but eventually she'd get over it and move on with her life, secure in the knowledge that she was desirable and worthy of love.

With that plausible scenario alleviating some of his guilt and his worry, Brundar returned his focus to the naked beauty sprawled before him, her sex slick and glistening with the evidence of her desire.

He'd made her a promise that he would make her body sing for him.

It was time he delivered on that promise.

It had been so long since Brundar had pleasured a woman with her front to him and not her back that he had to stop and think for a moment how to go about it.

Calypso wanted chest to chest contact.

It seemed that he would have to learn some new bedroom skills.

Pulling his shirt over his head, he dropped it on the floor, then climbed on the bed and knelt between her spread legs.

Calypso parted her lips, her heartbeat speeding in anticipation.

He lowered himself gently over her, careful not to crush her under him as he dipped his head and kissed her.

She moaned into his mouth, wrapping her tongue around his as soon as he penetrated her mouth.

His torso still braced on his elbows, he threaded his fingers through her lush hair, cradling her head and lifting it for his kiss.

Arching into him, Calypso groaned in pleasure as soon as their chests touched. The hosiery tying her to the bed limited her range of motion, but the things stretched enough so she could rub her tight nipples against his chest.

The pose must've been extremely uncomfortable to maintain.

"My poor girl, her sweet little nipples so desperate for my attention." The words that had tumbled out of his mouth surprised him. Brundar wasn't much of a talker in general and during sexual play in particular. But he was starting to realize that being with Calypso was changing him in more ways than one.

She wasn't letting him get away with his Spartan speech patterns. She demanded he talk to her, tell her things, and little by little he was getting better at it. It no longer felt like such a tremendous effort to form whole sentences, to express his thoughts and what little feelings he had.

No one had challenged him in so long. Even Anandur had given up on coaxing him out of his shell. But Calypso refused to back down. Refused to accept that it was all he had to give.

She mewled in agreement, rubbing against him one last time before collapsing back down on the bed.

Untangling his fingers from her hair, Brundar moved his hands down to her breasts. For a moment, he just cupped both, enjoying the heft of them filling his hands to overflowing. Her hard nipples poked his palms, reminding him where his girl needed his attention most.

She was sensitive there; he remembered it from their previous interlude that day. Nevertheless, she wasn't averse to a little rough play. A tiny dose of pain was a sure way to ratchet her pleasure.

He started with his thumbs, circling round and round and barely touching the turgid nubs. When his fingers finally closed on them and pinched, Calypso's chest pushed up on a strangled moan.

Sliding down, he licked the small pain away, first one, then the other. When she relaxed, lowering her back, he pinched and tugged again.

"Aw," she complained.

He didn't let go. "Do you want me to stop?"

Biting on her lower lip, her eyelids pressed tight, she shook her head, the scent of her arousal intensifying and proving him right.

When she started thrashing her head from side to side, he knew she'd had enough. Letting go, he plumped her breasts and licked her nipples, alternating between the two until he soothed the pain away.

He had only just begun, and Calypso was already on the cusp of climax.

Trailing small kisses down her belly, he slid further down until his mouth was level with her molten heat.

Fates. How had he thought of denying himself this pleasure?

Spreading her folds with his thumbs, he treated her to a long lick that had her arching off the bed again. She had such a small ass that Brundar could keep her spread with his thumbs, while cupping it with his other fingers and holding her down.

She wiggled in his possessive grip, but it wasn't because she was sore from the light spanking he'd treated her to earlier. There was no trace left of it. Calypso was just loving what he was doing to her.

After a venom bite, even a harsher spanking would've left no residual soreness or marks, which was one of the main reasons he was in such high demand at the club. Those who enjoyed the spicier spectrum of tastes couldn't understand how he did it, only that he was the only one who could.

Brundar had a feeling that his former partners were going to be very disappointed. He was no longer on the market.

For the near future, he belonged to Calypso.

## 55

## CALLIE

This was the most intimate sexual act imaginable, and Callie was glad Brundar was the first one she was sharing it with.

Shawn had made a half-hearted offer to pleasure her this way, once, but his lack of enthusiasm had made it far from appealing. It wasn't something she'd craved anyway. Too intimate of an act with a man she'd never fully trusted—not even when she'd been still trying to make their marriage work. Subconsciously, or even consciously, Callie had known all along that he wasn't the right man for her.

Only later, she'd also realized he was mentally unstable and dangerous.

And here she was, blissful in her surrender, unafraid even though she had been tied up and blindfolded by a man she knew very little about, who was kissing and licking the most intimate and vulnerable spot on her body.

At first, she'd agreed to the blindfold as a concession to Brundar, but she was discovering that by depriving one of her senses, she was feeling everything more acutely with the others.

Callie could hear Brundar smacking his lips as if he was tasting something delectable, feel the reverence with which he held her open, his thumbs gentle on her folds, his tongue rimming her trembling flesh in slow, careful licks, applying the exact pressure to bring her the most pleasure.

At the same time, his other fingers were digging into her ass muscles, possessive and strong.

The combination pushed all of her buttons—physical and mental.

Or were they one and the same?

A self-feeding loop of sorts?

"Okay, sweetling?"

She loved that he checked with her at every stage even though her body's responses were telling him all he needed to know.

"Amazing. More."

He chuckled, smacking his lips again.

Was he doing it on purpose to let her know he was enjoying eating her up?

Brundar spread her even wider, his thumbs parting her folds and holding her open for his tongue. As he speared it inside her, the need to move and undulate around that penetrating tongue was overwhelming. But the iron grip Brundar had on her buttocks prevented even the smallest of movements. She was helpless and open for his ministrations.

Damn, it was hot.

Giving her bindings a small tug, Callie reassured herself that she truly was at Brundar's mercy.

God, it felt so good to surrender everything and just feel.

In the back of her mind, she was well aware that it was all an illusion. One word from her would stop Brundar immediately. And the binds were loose and stretchy enough for her to pull her hands out without much effort.

She was learning. It was all a game, and perception was everything.

Would it feel different if it wasn't?

What if she really was at this man's mercy with no safe word and ties she couldn't get out of?

Arousing as hell and just as dangerous. The fear would have been too intense to enjoy anything. It was like parasailing for real versus a ride in an amusement park. Same sensations but without taking a risk.

One thick finger replaced Brundar's tongue, filling her in a different way. Then he added another, curving both to massage a particularly tender spot.

The coil inside her getting tighter, Callie moaned, her involuntary undulations thwarted even though Brundar was holding her down with only one hand.

"More," she groaned.

Pressing his mouth over her pulsating clit, he drew it between his lips, detonating an explosion that sucked a scream out of her throat.

Brundar slowed down, planting a gentle kiss on her clit, his fingers moving in and out of her in a slow rhythm, letting her catch her breath.

"You're magnificent when you come."

His words of praise pleased her to no end. So much so that she didn't even come back with the snarky remark that was on the tip of her tongue. He'd given her too much for her to repay him with anything less than profound gratitude.

She was about to say something to that effect, when Brundar resumed his assault, driving away any and all coherent thoughts.

The only movement available to her was thrashing her head from side to side. She tried to form the words to tell him that it was too much, that she was too sensitive and couldn't take any more, but something inside her didn't want him to stop, trusting him to know what she needed. If he thought she could come again then she would.

She wasn't wrong. In moments, she was once again climbing toward another climax.

"Brundar!" Callie keened as another explosion rocked through her.

Her body trembling from the aftershocks, she had a vague impression of his fingers on her ankles. A moment later her wrists were unbound, and he was holding her to him in a fierce embrace.

Warm in his arms, Callie stopped shivering, and her mind's frazzled gears came back online. Brundar was shirtless, but his jeans were still on, and she was no longer bound.

Which meant that as far as he was concerned sex was over.

"What's wrong? Why did you stop?" She hated how needy she sounded.

"I didn't bring a condom."

God, she was so stupid. She should've bought a pack while at the supermarket.

On the one hand, she was touched that he hadn't presumed anything when he'd brought her home. Most guys Brundar's age carried at least one condom in their wallet just in case they got lucky.

"You didn't ask if I have one."

He chuckled. "I know you don't."

She hated for their time to end like that. Being on the receiving end of pleasure was fun, but it didn't sit well with her not to reciprocate.

"Can I return the favor?" She wasn't nearly as good at oral as Brundar, but she would give it her best.

Gentle fingers removed her blindfold, and he leaned to plant a chaste kiss on her lips. "Not tonight. You're exhausted."

It was true. Callie felt as if she'd just finished running a marathon and could sleep for two days straight. Who knew that orgasming several times in the same day would be so tiring?

After all, she hadn't done anything other than cook two quick and easy meals.

"Tomorrow, then?"

"Maybe." Gazing at her as if he wanted to memorize every detail of her face, he leaned and kissed her forehead. "Sleep. I'll see you tomorrow at the club." He slid out of bed.

Callie wanted to reach for his hand and stop him, but then remembered she wasn't allowed.

"Please, can you stay a little bit and hold me?" He didn't seem like the type of guy who cuddled, but she was desperate for the closeness.

He looked conflicted, standing beside her bed and looking at her with hungry eyes.

Of course, he did. He hadn't climaxed. Brundar was considerate, but that didn't mean he had no needs of his own. He probably couldn't wait to get home and jerk off to relieve the pressure.

"I would understand if you couldn't stay." She let her eyes glide over the bulge in his pants. It must be painful.

His jaw muscles hardened and he nodded. "I'll stay."

"Thank you." She burrowed under the blanket and lifted it for him to get in.

Brundar eyed the space she'd made for him as if it was dangerous territory.

"Do you want to stay on top of the blankets?"

He shook his head and got in, pulling her into his arms.

Heaven.

Callie belonged inside those strong arms. Her cheek pressed against his hard chest, she listened to the steady beat of Brundar's heart for as long as she managed to keep herself awake. Every moment was precious, and she refused to squander even one. Eventually though, sleep won.

## 56

## BRUNDAR

Brundar couldn't refuse Calypso's plea. The temptation to hold her in his arms as she fell asleep had been too strong.

He'd never held a woman in bed, never had anyone fall asleep in his arms. Before today, he'd never felt the need. To want something, he had to be aware of its existence first. Otherwise, how would he know he lacked anything?

Calypso was showing him a lot of things he hadn't known were missing from his life.

Relationships between men and women were not only about sex and procreation. There was more to it than that. There was partnership, companionship, and togetherness.

A simple thing like sharing a meal with Calypso was so much more than just a meal. It wasn't the same as having dinner with his brother, or the other Guardians.

Except, he could have none of those things with Calypso. Not long term.

One day, Amanda might find him a Dormant, and he could try and recreate what he had with Calypso, but Brundar had a feeling he could never feel the same about another female.

Fates knew he tried to keep himself from sinking deeper. But each time he managed to distance himself, Calypso pulled him right back, and he was helpless to deny her anything.

If he'd thought of bringing a damn condom, he would've been inside her a moment after she'd climaxed on his tongue. He carried no diseases, and getting her pregnant was a one in a million chance. But he'd already thralled her once that day, and he couldn't thrall her again to make her think he had protection.

As much as she wanted him, Calypso would've panicked. Especially given what her ex-husband had done to her.

It was better that way.

Brundar would survive a case of blue balls.

The question was what was he going to do tomorrow. Continue from where they'd left off?

Put in motion the story about getting deployed on a mission and cut his ties to her before they were impossible to sever?

Or claim her as his own and keep her locked up in the keep?

No one needed to know. He would ask Ingrid to arrange a new apartment for him, sneak Calypso in, and never invite anyone over.

Would she mind?

Yeah, she would.

Calypso had dreams and aspiration beyond being his pet.

*Dear Fates, I could use some divine intervention.*

# 57

# RONI

*L*ifting his eyelids was a struggle, so Roni didn't. It felt as if they were glued shut with sticky slime.

Trying to remember what had happened to him, he couldn't manage to distinguish between what had really happened and the dream he'd woken from. In the dream, he'd been abducted by aliens. One of them had carried him off, and the bastard must've spat on Roni's eyes, gluing them shut. They were playing irritating alien music to get Roni to talk. All that clicking and beeping was giving him a headache.

"I'm not telling you anything, you alien slime," he murmured through cracked lips and dry throat. Part of the torture must've been water deprivation.

"He's delirious again, dear. Should I call the nurse?" It was an unfamiliar kind voice. Grandmotherly.

Was that another torture tactic? An alien disguised as a friendly grandmother who Roni would trust?

"He is getting intravenous. He's fine, Mildred. Stop fretting."

Mildred; the name sounded familiar, as did the gruff voice belonging to the guy she'd called dear.

"How are you doing, kid?" Dear's coffee breath smelled very human. Had Dear and Mildred also been abducted?

"Eyes," Roni croaked. "Sticky."

The coffee breath shifted away. "Mildred, get me a wet washcloth from the bathroom. Cold."

"Of course, dear."

A moment later Roni felt Dear wipe his face, careful around his eyelids.

"Open them now, kid."

At first, everything was blurry, but soon Dear's pudgy face came into focus. "I know you." Roni tried to lift a finger. "Your name is not Dear."

The pudgy face got closer. "It's Barty, you moron. Don't you recognize me?"

There was a shocked intake of breath from behind Barty's bulk.

"Bartholomew Edward Gorkin, don't you talk to the boy like that. He is sick with a high fever. Be kind to him, you hear?"

Barty smirked. "That's my wife, Mildred. Thirty years she is trying to make me into less of an ass. Unsuccessfully, might I add, but she never stops."

"He is a lost cause, Mildred," Roni said.

"I know. But I love him anyway." Mildred brought a cup of ice water to Roni's lips. "The doctor said you can drink a little when you wake up."

Roni lifted his neck and took a few grateful sips, wetting his chin, some of it dripping on his hospital gown. "How long have I been in here?"

"A little over eight hours. The doctor says you have pneumonia."

Crap. As the cobwebs of sleep or fever or whatever it was started to lift, Roni remembered why he was here, and it wasn't pneumonia.

"Where is Sylvia?" he asked, looking around for his rescue squad.

Had he been too out of it to ask for her?

"She is here, dear, taking a potty break." Mildred patted his hand. "You asked for her and for Barty. The nice security guy who brought you here called Barty, and Barty called Sylvia. She didn't leave your side other than to grab something to eat and bathroom breaks. Such a nice young woman." Mildred leaned closer. "She is a keeper. Don't let her get away." She winked, her kind round face beaming.

Roni decided that he liked Mildred. She was a lot nicer than her dear husband. But Barty was okay too. Had they been here the entire time?

"Why are you guys here?"

Mildred frowned. "Somebody needs to keep an eye on you. Barty tried to reach your parents, but they are not home. He tried several times but no one is picking up."

Yeah, they were probably on one of their cruises, spending the money he'd earned while underage.

"Thank you for staying with me."

Mildred squeezed his hand. "Think nothing of it. I'm glad we could be here for you."

The door opened, and a moment later Sylvia's arms were around him. "Roni. I'm so glad you're awake. I was so worried about you." She planted a kiss on one cheek, then the other.

"Barty, dear, let's give these young people some privacy, shall we?" Mildred tugged on Barty's sleeve jacket.

"Yeah, why not." Barty winked at Roni. "You're only young once. Enjoy it while you can." He wrapped his arm around his wife's rounded shoulders. "How about I invite you for a cup of coffee, Mrs. Gorkin?"

"I'd be much obliged, Mr. Gorkin."

Sylvia smiled. "They are a cute couple. Barty is such an old lecher, I never expected him to love his wife so much."

"You know he is harmless. He just likes to watch you girls."

"I know." Sylvia sat next to him on the hospital bed. "How are you feeling?"

"Horrible. Where is my rescue team?"

Sylvia's smile vanished. "I called them off for the time being. Barty and Mildred wouldn't leave your side. By the way, I don't want you to worry about your parents. They are not answering their phones because we are rerouting the calls, not because something happened to them."

"I'm not worried. Can't you guys take care of Barty and his wife?"

She shook her head. "Too risky. We are waiting for them to go home and the night shift to start. The fewer people who are familiar with you, the easier it will be to thrall them and get you out unnoticed. That way we will have the entire night head start before anyone starts looking for you."

That made sense. "Then we wait."

Sylvia still seemed bothered.

"What's wrong?"

"You have viral pneumonia."

"Or so they think."

"No, you really have pneumonia. The doctor took X-rays."

Roni frowned as an uncomfortable feeling started deep in his gut. "Meaning?"

"Meaning that it might be a false alarm and you're not transitioning. Actually, that's what our doctor thinks. A transition is not accompanied by pneumonia."

"So what do we do? Do we continue with the extraction plan, or abort?"

"You tell me. It's up to you."

# DARK ANGEL'S SEDUCTION

# 1

# BRUNDAR

Faith.

Brundar had lost his so long ago, he couldn't remember ever believing that there was any good in people.

Betrayal by someone you considered a brother, someone you loved and trusted with not only your heart but your very life, would do that to a guy.

He'd learned his lesson the hard way.

He trusted no one, depended on no one, except himself and his sword arm and his aim.

Deadly.

It was more than a description, it was his essence.

He was the Grim Reaper.

Or at least he had been until Calypso had turned his world upside down. The sense of vertigo was disturbing, destructive, dangerous to a warrior who depended on a quiet mind to maintain the focus crucial to his survival.

The only antidote was distance.

Not his resolve because his was worth shit, and not his logical mind because it barely functioned in Calypso's presence.

The further away from her he got, the more time that passed since he'd been with her, the clearer his thoughts became.

One would think that he would utilize the one remedy available to him and stay the hell away from her. But no, apparently he was a glutton for the fucking vertigo because time and again he returned for more.

If Brundar had had any faith left in him, he would have prayed to the Fates for guidance. But the bitches were a myth, existing only in the minds of fools. As to those made of flesh and blood, he had no friends, and the only one even remotely close to him was his brother, who was the equivalent of an old yenta and the last person Brundar wanted to confide in or ask for help. Anandur would do anything for him, he never doubted it, but he would exact a payment in the form of information to feed his insatiable hunger for fresh gossip he could spread around.

With a sigh, Brundar filled the carafe with water from the filter and poured it into the coffeemaker.

"What's that grim face for?" Anandur asked as he entered the kitchen.

Brundar ignored him.

But naturally, Anandur wouldn't let it go. "You seem gloomier than usual. What's the matter, no food?" He pulled the fridge door open. "Do not despair, bro. We have leftover Italian." He took out the container.

Brundar regarded his brother with a grimace. "Only you can eat pasta for breakfast."

"You're welcome to cook. I would like an omelet with a side of hash and four pieces of toast," Anandur teased. "But since you won't…" he shrugged. Forking a swirl of cold spaghetti straight from the container, he stuffed it into his mouth.

The guy could eat anything, including a week-old moldy pizza and food leftovers on other people's plates.

Charming and easygoing, Anandur had the capacity to feel for his partners and yet never get attached or possessive. No woman ever harbored ill feelings toward him, and not because he made sure they didn't remember him. The guy's thrall was so pathetically weak that he could barely erase the memory of his bite.

How the hell did he manage to keep his heart open while protecting it from emotional attachment?

"Let me ask you something." Brundar poured himself coffee.

"Ask," Anandur said with a mouthful of pasta.

"You were fond of that Russian you pumped for information, right?"

Out of all the Guardians, Anandur was the only one who would take on a mission like that. He had no qualms about pretending to be a lowly deck boy or seducing one of Alex's all-female Russian yacht crew.

Acting the bum was one thing. Anandur probably had fun with that. But agreeing to whore himself out was another.

Thankfully, Kian had never asked Brundar to do anything even remotely of that nature. He was a lousy actor, and using sex as a tool was abhorrent to him. Give him a weapon, point out an enemy to kill, and he'd deal with it.

Even if he hadn't had issues with the morality of such underhanded acts, he was too rigid for subterfuge.

"Yeah, she was a fine piece of ass. Not the sharpest brain, but the shapeliest legs. Beautiful and strong." Anandur flexed his biceps. "I mean muscle strong. When she wrapped those around me and squeezed, believe me, I felt it." Anandur shifted himself in his pants.

Evidently, he remembered Lana quite fondly.

"But even though you liked her and spent a few weeks with her, you had no problem saying goodbye."

Anandur grabbed a mug and filled it from the carafe. "Not entirely true. I was worried about how she would take it. But Lana is a tough cookie and life-smart. She said she didn't feel it either. It wasn't love. We parted as good friends." He took a sip of coffee.

"What would you have done if she'd clung to you?"

"Then it would have been a bitch. I don't like hurting people. Not unless they earned it, that is. Alex, for example, I had no problem hurting. The scumbag got off easy with entombment. I would have flayed his skin off first."

"I would have helped."

They nodded to each other in agreement.

It warmed Brundar's cold heart that his brother wasn't all that different from him. On the outside, the guy might have appeared the charming and good-natured one; on the inside, though, he was just as bloodthirsty and cruel as Brundar.

But unlike those they hunted, he and his brother reserved their wrath for those who'd earned it. Alex and other scum like him who kidnapped people and sold them into slavery didn't deserve mercy. They deserved eternal damnation in the deepest, most fiery pits of hell, in the company of other soulless creatures who preyed on the weak.

Anandur put the mug on the counter and lifted the box of leftovers, taking another forkful. "Why all the questions? Do you need advice on how to dump someone?"

"No."

Anandur's smile turned into a frown. "When you actually want to talk, come find me." He stood up and threw the empty container in the trash.

If Brundar wanted advice, he needed to keep talking. "Did you ever feel like you wanted to keep one of the human women you hooked up with?"

Anandur shook his head. "No. Do you want to keep yours?"

Brundar should have known better than to turn to his brother. He needed answers, not more questions. Anandur was as blunt as ever, but not helpful in the least.

"As what? A pet? Keep her locked up until she gets old and dies?"

With a sigh, Anandur patted his shoulder. "It's tough to have feelings for a human. I can't believe I'm saying that to you, not when I've been waiting for centuries to hear your heart beating again, but you need to get rid of the girl sooner rather than later. It's a shame because I'm glad to see you finally thawing, but the longer you wait, the harder it's going to be. I don't want to see you break."

Regrettably, Anandur had no magical solution. His words echoed Brundar's thoughts to the letter.

"Can I trust you not to breathe a word of this to anyone?"

"All you have to do is ask, and it's done. Did you ever know me to reveal a secret I was asked to keep?"

Brundar thought back to Anandur's many years of gossiping, and the truth was that he'd never betrayed the confidence of anyone who'd asked him to keep a secret.

He dipped his head in a slight bow. "My apologies for insinuating a flaw of character. The insult was unwarranted."

Anandur rolled his eyes. "Sheesh, so formal. Apology accepted." He clapped Brundar on the shoulder. "Good luck with your lady friend. Whatever you decide to do, you can count on me to back you up."

"I know."

"Good. Sometimes I'm not sure you remember that."

## 2

## CALLIE

Waking up alone wasn't a big surprise. But it was disappointing nonetheless. Callie hadn't expected Brundar to stay the night, but a tiny part of her had wished he would.

This morning, her heart and her mind were in an even greater state of sensory overload than the day before. Probably because she'd had time to process. She needed to talk about what had happened between them. She needed to feel connected to the man with whom she'd shared so many firsts.

The girl who had married the first guy she'd had sex with had celebrated her divorce by seducing a dangerous man who was so far from the norm he was practically an alien. And she wasn't referring to Brundar's sexual proclivities, which were strange to say the least.

*Look who's talking.*

As if she'd been an innocent lamb who had no idea what she was getting herself into. Brundar had been honest and upfront about everything, and yet, fully informed of his preferences, Callie had pursued him with a single-minded determination. On his side, he had done everything he could to deter her.

Was that why she'd gone after him like she'd never gone after any guy before?

Perhaps she'd subconsciously considered his reluctance a challenge?

Or was it something else?

What did it say about her that she'd chosen a bondage aficionado as her first after Shawn?

*Way to come out with a bang, Callie.*

It had been amazing.

She hadn't known such heights of sensory pleasure were even possible. And she hadn't expected a guy who kept his heart locked in an impenetrable box to be so completely selfless either.

Knowing that without a condom he couldn't take it any further, he'd pleasured her into oblivion and then refused her offer to reciprocate orally because she'd been exhausted by the experience.

On the other hand, had the lack of a condom been an excuse? And if yes, why?

Callie had no plausible answer for that.

Why would a guy deliberately choose to go home with a giant case of blue balls? And it wasn't as if Brundar hadn't been affected. She'd seen the evidence of his arousal even though he'd never taken off his pants.

One thing Callie knew for sure, as soon as she made it to a pharmacy, she was going to buy a bunch of them.

The thing was, it wasn't all about sex, and emotionally Callie had been left bereft. She needed more from a relationship, even a casual one. But then, she should've been prepared for that. What had she expected from a guy whose range of emotions spanned between indifferent to marginally interested, or from stoic to mildly amused?

Nevertheless, Brundar's quiet presence had been reassuring. She loved having him around even though she was the one doing all the talking and his responses were limited to an occasional nod or a single word.

It was strange how this man who seemed as cold as a marble statue had managed to fill the apartment with warmth. In his absence, the place felt like the temporary shelter it was and not a home.

Maybe she could call Brundar and invite him to stop by and have lunch with her. They could talk, or rather she would talk and Brundar would do his statue impersonation. It was better than the silence, better than the vacuum in which her thoughts ran in circles with no anchor.

She had his number, but he'd given it with explicit instructions to use only in emergencies. Was there a way she could claim her need to see him was an emergency?

For her it was.

Right. The last thing she should do was to appear clingy and needy, not unless she wanted to see him run leaving skid marks on the sidewalk.

He would be at the club tonight. She could hold out until then.

A cup of coffee in hand, Callie sat down at her dining table and opened a book, ready to put in her two hours of studying.

After half an hour she gave up. At the rate she'd been going, it would've taken her double the time to go over the same material. She couldn't concentrate, reading the same paragraph over and over again and still not getting what she was reading because thoughts of Brundar kept interfering.

Crap. She needed someone to talk to before her head exploded.

Calling Brundar was out, and calling Dawn was still dangerous, which left only one person.

Miriam. Or Miri as the barmaid liked to be called.

They'd exchanged numbers with the vague promise to hang out sometimes. Maybe she should take her new friend up on that offer.

With spiked blue hair, arms that were covered in tattoos starting at the wrist and going all the way up to her shoulders, a nose stud, and a dirty mouth, Miri wasn't the type Callie would've normally befriended.

But that was the old Callie who for the past two years had been living under a rock. The new Callie was all about grabbing life by the horns, which translated into taking chances, experimenting with new sensations, and getting to know new people.

Pulling her phone out of her purse, she rang Miri.

"Yeah."

"Hi, it's Callie. Do you want to hang out before work?"

"I do, but I have a nail appointment."

Miri's nails were tiny works of arts, and she changed the designs on a weekly basis.

"How about after your appointment?"

"I have a better idea. Come with me."

"To the nail place?"

"Yeah. Yours could use some decorations."

Callie had had her nails done exactly once. For her wedding. "Don't I need an appointment?"

"Nah. You're with me. Get ready. I'll come get you in half an hour. And wear flip-flops if you want your toes done too."

"Thanks. You're awesome." Not having a car was a drag. She was lucky Miri didn't mind picking her up.

Dressed in a pair of old faded jeans, a plain T-shirt, and flip-flops, Callie waited for Miri's call. She was excited. Since Dawn had left for MIT, Callie hadn't done anything fun with a friend.

When the call came, she ran down the stairs taking two at a time, her flip-flops making a ruckus that echoed through the stairwell.

"Are you going to get acrylics?" Miri asked as Callie got in. "They are durable." She wiggled her fingers, tapping the steering wheel to demonstrate how tough her nails were. This week it was butterflies—a different one for each nail.

"I think I'll start with a manicure and a clear nail polish."

Miri smirked. "A nail virgin, eh?"

"No, but almost. I had them done once. For my wedding."

"You're married?"

"Not anymore."

"High five, sister."

They clapped palms.

"What about you?"

Miri shrugged. "I dumped my boyfriend's sorry ass after three years of living together. Got tired of watching him sit around the apartment and do nothing, while I worked and paid the bills and did everything else. Supposedly, he was pursuing his true calling." She rolled her eyes, making air quotes with her fingers while holding the steering wheel with her thumbs.

"What was it?" Callie asked.

"His true calling? He claimed it was music. But the only thing he excelled at was bumming, while I was the idiot enabling him. Took me three fucking years to get smart and realize that the motherfucker was using me."

With a screech of tires, Miri turned into a parking spot that had just been vacated.

The *salon* occupied a corner of a tattoo shop and had only one beautician, a woman who was covered in even more tattoos than Miri, displaying them proudly by wearing a muscle shirt and shorts.

"Hey, Lisa, can you squeeze in a manicure for Callie here before your next appointment?"

"What's up, Callie?" Lisa smiled before turning back to Miri. "Depends on what you have in mind for today. If it's something elaborate then no."

Miri plopped down on a chair and pointed for Callie to sit next to her. "I'm in a patriotic mood. Stars and stripes. That shouldn't take too long."

"Then yeah." Lisa put a folded towel over her workstation.

Sitting sideways and facing Callie, Miri offered Lisa her hand. "So, what's the story with you and Donnie?"

*What?* That came out of nowhere.

"Donnie the bouncer? Nothing."

"You spend all your breaks outside with him. And I know that he walks you home sometimes. I was wondering if you guys had something going on."

"I go outside to give my eardrums a break from the hellish sound levels in the club, not to hang out with Donnie, although he is a nice guy and I enjoy his company. But he is only a friend. Nothing more."

Miri narrowed her eyes at Callie. "What about when he walks you home? Do you ever invite him to come in?"

"No, I don't."

The girl wasn't buying it. Her eyes were still full of suspicion. "Why not? You're single, and you think he is cool. Not too shabby to look at either."

Aha. So that was the reason Miri had invited her to come have her nails done. Not because she wanted to be friends, but because she wanted to grill Callie about Donnie.

Barely stifling a laugh, Callie crossed her arms over her chest and returned Miri's glower. "I think someone has a crush on our hunky bouncer."

Miri waved her free hand. "Your lingo is so high school. No one over eighteen calls it a crush."

"What do they call it then?"

"Doesn't matter. I think he's hot. Don't you think?" Miri was still fishing.

"I think he is a great guy, and he is all yours. The only reason he walks me home is that Brun… I mean Brad asked him to. Franco walks me home too. Do you think I have something going on with him as well?"

Miri shrugged. "Some girls like variety. I don't judge."

*Yeah, right.* "Well, I don't. One is more than enough for me."

"And who's that one?"

Wasn't it obvious? Or was Miri playing dumb to have Callie admit it?

Whatever, she had no reason to hide their involvement. Brundar hadn't told her to keep whatever was going on between them a secret. He might have implied it by ignoring her at the club, but she could play dumb as well as the next girl. The bottom line was that she needed someone to talk to, and Miri was the only one available. Even if she had her own agenda.

"Brad."

Miri's eyes widened. "I heard rumors, but I didn't believe them. You have the hots for the Grim Reaper?"

Ouch, what a nasty nickname. "You know how it goes. The heart wants what the heart wants. It might not make sense to anyone else, but he is the only one I'm interested in."

"Poor girl." Miri reached with her free hand and patted Callie's knee. "He is a looker, I'll give him that. And I hear he is good with the whip. So I guess he appeals to a certain type. I just didn't think you were into that stuff. You sure don't look it with your innocent girl-next-door looks."

"Kinky," Lisa butted in, which earned her a hard stare from Miri.

Callie felt her cheeks heat up. "I'm not." She shivered just thinking about it. "Not whips and stuff like that."

Miri smirked. "I don't judge, girl." She lifted her tattoo-covered arm. "It's not like I don't get it. I don't do tats just for the ink."

"You don't?"

Lisa snorted. "Nope."

They were both weird. "I have no idea what you're trying to say, but whatever. Brad helped me a lot while expecting nothing in return. In my book, it makes him a good guy. He might appear cold and indifferent, but I think it's only a mask to hide who he really is inside."

Miri lifted a pierced brow. "And what if it isn't? What if what you see is what you get? Would you still want him?"

Callie didn't need to think about it. The answer was instantaneous. "Yes."

Lisa shook her head, while Miri made a show of mock crossing herself. "May God have mercy on your soul, my child."

3

# RONI

"Goodnight, Roni." Mildred kissed his forehead. "Are you sure you don't want us to stay with you?"

She was such a sweetheart.

His handler and his wife had spent all day sitting in Roni's hospital room. Barty was there to keep an eye on him, making sure he didn't get his hands on a computer, but Mildred was there because she cared.

What did his bosses think he could do? Hack the Pentagon from his hospital bed?

Maybe. If he had a reason to.

Even feverish with pneumonia and weak like a newborn, Roni could still wreak havoc if allowed access to the Internet.

The paranoia was justified.

After all, the government had been holding Roni captive for years and he had a score to settle. But even if he had the opportunity, he wouldn't hack the system with malicious intent. To use the backdoor he'd programmed, he needed the system up and working fine.

Roni patted her hand. "I'm sure. Besides, you have to go. Visiting hours are over."

The bossy bird of a nurse had informed them that everyone needed to leave. Sylvia was allowed to stay only because Roni had told everyone who cared to listen that she was his fiancée.

Rising to his feet, Barty hiked his pants up. "I'll be back tomorrow morning, kid. If you need anything, you can call me. Jerome is just outside your door. You can ask him to make the call." He clapped Roni on the shoulder, so gently that it was almost a pat.

God, he was going to miss the old jerk and his kindly wife.

"Yeah, okay. See you tomorrow morning," Roni said, his voice quivering a little.

The fever was making him mushy. That's what it was. Because no way in hell would he shed a tear because that old asshole and his wife, who really was a sweetheart, were leaving and he wasn't going to see them ever again.

Once they were finally gone, Sylvia's crew would arrive and spring him free.

In the long hours he'd been waiting for Barty and Mildred to leave, Roni had made up his mind. It was a no-brainer. To stay meant that he would keep doing what he loved doing but have no life. To go with Sylvia, even with no chance of ever turning immortal, still meant doing what he loved doing, but with perks.

Either way, he would be a prisoner.

As long as the immortals kept him pampered and Sylvia warmed his bed, he didn't mind never leaving their lair, or whatever they called their home. As it was, he spent most of his days in front of monitors, and it didn't really matter to him where he was doing it.

"Thank the merciful Fates." Sylvia let out a breath. "I thought they would never leave."

"Yeah. I'm ready to get going."

"I'm glad you decided to take the chance." Sylvia sounded relieved.

Good, it meant she wanted him even as a human, but he needed to make sure. "What happens if I don't turn?"

She looked away. "I'm not sure. Normally, someone who is really good at thralling would get into your head and make you forget everything you've learned about us. But I'm hoping our regent would allow you to stay. First of all, because we need you, and second of all because I doubt anyone would dare mess with that brilliant brain of yours—it's too valuable. And if that's not enough to convince him to let you stay, I'm going to plead and beg and do whatever I can until he does."

Roni took her hand. "You really care about me."

"Of course, I do, dummy."

He smirked. "Hey, a minute ago you called me brilliant."

"You're both. But seriously, you know that if you stay with us as a human, it's like a life sentence. You can never leave."

"As long as I have you, I don't mind. It's not like I want to go anywhere without you."

A tear slid down Sylvia's cheek. "Don't give up yet. I'm not. I'm going to implore the Fates every day all day long until they get sick of hearing my prayers and turn you. I don't want to watch you get old and die. I can't."

He squeezed her hand. "I'm not giving up. I don't care if I have to let all the males of your clan take turns beating me up and biting me until it happens."

It wasn't an idle promise. For Sylvia, Roni would even face that Brundar dude Andrew thought was so mean and scary. One of the males must have the right venom composition to turn him. Because there was no way Roni wasn't a Dormant. Not with his grandma surfacing decades after her supposed death by drowning, looking not a day older than she did at twenty-five.

Sylvia nodded and squeezed his hand back. "That's the spirit. Never give up, never surrender."

"I'm with you, baby. Call your posse."

Pulling out her phone, Sylvia sent the text.

"What about Jerome?" Roni asked.

The guy knew him well, which meant it wouldn't be easy to thrall him to forget why he was there, and who he was guarding.

"We will take care of him."

"You're not going to do anything to him? Right? I like the guy."

With a smile, Sylvia leaned and kissed his cheek. "I wish everyone got to see this side of you. Underneath that prickly exterior, you're a nice guy."

Roni shifted up, making himself more comfortable. "Don't read too much into it. I don't want to see Jerome hurt, but that doesn't make me a good guy. I'm not violent, that's all."

Sylvia patted his arm. "Yeah, yeah, keep telling yourself that. Anyway, one of the guys is going to thrall him to believe that his shift is over and someone is coming to replace him."

"He is not going to leave his post until his replacement arrives."

"Don't worry about it. He'll be convinced it's okay to leave. Let me just send them a text with instructions." Her fingers flew over the screen.

"Why does it have to be one of the guys? Can't you do it?"

Sylvia shrugged. "I can, but I don't have as much practice. The guys do it all the time. Once they bite a woman, which they do almost every time they have sex, they have to make her forget the fangs. Immortal females don't have such problems. We don't bite. Much." She winked.

"Good. Because I don't think I would've liked being a pincushion, even for your cute little fangs. Those fuckers hurt."

"I don't know about that. Supposedly, the ladies enjoy it very much." Her eyes lit up the way they did when she was turned on.

Good. Because for some reason, being the one doing the biting sounded way more sexy than being the one bitten. If Sylvia didn't share his opinion, Roni would've felt guilty about having such seemingly misogynistic thoughts. "I hope you'll find out soon."

"I do too. But even if you turn tonight, it will take up to six months for your fangs to become fully operational."

"Bummer."

She waved a hand. "I can wait."

Hopefully, she wouldn't end up waiting for nothing.

"Tell me more about where I'm going. If I'm to spend the rest of my life locked up, at least I hope to spend it in luxury."

Her smile wilted, but then she put a brave face on. "You will. And the lockup is only temporary. We are building a new place that has large open areas. It's going to be ready in a couple of months. You won't have to spend all of your time indoors."

He chuckled. "You forget who you're talking to. Hackers are like vampires. We shun the sun and lurk in our lairs."

"I'm not going to let you do that."

"Oh, yeah?"

"Yeah. You're going to eat right, move your ass every couple of hours, and spend at least an hour a day outdoors. Even if you don't turn, I'm going to make sure you live long and prosper."

He loved when Sylvia made *Star Trek* references, and more than that he loved that she cared. Still, he had an image to protect.

Roni glowered at her, pretending to be mad. "I'm not even there yet, and you're already bossing me around?"

"Trouble in paradise?" Anandur sauntered into the room accompanied by a freaky looking dude who was more handsome than humanly possible.

"Yamanu at your service." He offered Roni his hand.

"Roni." He shook it, hypnotized by the guy's pale blue eyes and singsong voice. "You're the thrall master, right?"

"Very astute observation," Anandur replied. "Get dressed. We are moving out." He handed Roni a plastic bag.

Glancing at the various tubes and monitoring wires sticking to him, Roni wondered how he was supposed to manage that.

"I'll unhook you," Yamanu offered.

With fingers that were much gentler than their size implied, Yamanu had Roni unplugged from everything, while Sylvia took care of the equipment with her special magic, so none of it sounded the alert.

His girlfriend had some impressive skills.

A few minutes later, they left the hospital room. Yamanu and Sylvia stepped out first, with Yamanu making sure no one spared them a second glance, while Roni and Anandur trailed behind with him leaning heavily on the big guy.

Roni would've felt better about starting this new phase of his life walking unaided, but in a way, it was symbolic of the future awaiting him. As a hacker he'd always worked alone, and as a prisoner he'd lived alone.

But from this day onward, he'd have to learn to work with others while living with an entire clan.

# 4

# CALLIE

While waiting for Miri to fill her drink order, Callie leaned on the bar and observed the crowd. Another couple had just disappeared into the side corridor, on their way to the basement. Something was going on down there tonight.

Were they having a party?

"There is a lot of traffic today." She pointed her chin in their direction.

Miri put two drinks on Callie's tray. "It's Wednesday."

"So?"

"Demonstration day. Must be something super interesting to attract so many."

"I wonder what it's about." Callie lifted the tray.

"Who knows?" Miri leaned closer, her chest almost touching the bar. "Maybe your boyfriend is demonstrating whipping techniques?"

"Ha, ha," Callie chuckled while nervously glancing around. "He is not my boyfriend," she whispered.

"Right."

After delivering the drinks, Callie stopped by a couple of tables and collected new orders.

"I'm dying of curiosity." She handed Miri the tickets. "Do you think they will let me watch during my break?"

Miri shrugged. "You can ask your boyfriend. He is the boss and what he says goes."

Good idea. If she could find him. When she'd gotten to work, Brundar was already down in the basement, and he hadn't surfaced yet.

Was he busy?

Or was he avoiding her?

She had a strong suspicion it was the second one.

*Coward.*

If he didn't want to hook up with her anymore, all he had to do was say so. This hide and seek game was ridiculous.

Callie felt her cheeks heating up, but this time it was anger and not awkwardness that was causing the blush. She'd give him another hour, and if he didn't come up by then, she would call him, using the emergency number he'd given her.

The hour was almost up when Callie spotted Franco emerging from the side corridor. Pushing people out of her way, she rushed over to him.

"Franco! Wait up!" she called as he opened the door to the supply room.

On the other side of it was the employee entrance, and if she didn't stop him, he would leave before she had a chance to talk to him.

Holding the door opened, Franco turned and scanned the crowd for his caller.

She waved at him.

He lifted a brow.

"Do you have a moment? Or are you in a super hurry to get out of here?"

He smiled. "For you, I can spare a moment." He opened the door wider. "Please, step into my office." He waved her on into the supply room.

"I heard you guys are holding a class down there. Can I watch? I mean, during my break."

He shook his head and patted her shoulder. "I'm sorry, Callie, but I have a policy about keeping the nightclub's personnel and that of the lower level separate. If you worked downstairs, it would have been a different story. But you're not old enough."

Disappointing to say the least. "Any chance you'd change your mind about the age limit? I know that until recently it used to be twenty-one."

He shook his head again. "It works better this way. Most of the members are older. And we want to make sure no one gets in with a fake ID. Other nightclubs have gotten in trouble because of nonsense like that, and those were just regular clubs."

"But you know me. You know I'm over twenty-one."

"That's enough, Callie." Franco used his drill sergeant's tone. "I don't have time for this."

That commanding tone and that stern look might have scared most people into compliance, but not Callie. Not while she was mad and on a mission.

Another day? Maybe?

"Can you at least tell Brad to call me? Or come up and see me?"

He cast her a curious look. "I will when I come back."

"Thank you. And sorry for bothering you, sir."

The formal address seemed to mollify him. "It's okay."

The thing was, Franco didn't come back. Or if he had, Callie had missed him.

She'd waited and watched people leave from that freaking side corridor all night, but there had been no sign of Brundar or Franco.

"Come on, Callie." Donnie looked impatient. He'd been waiting outside and then came in looking for her.

She buttoned up her light jacket. "Let's go."

"Finally."

It was after closing time, and she was taking her sweet time getting ready to head home, just in case Brundar finally showed up. But it wasn't fair to Donnie. With both Franco and Brundar busy elsewhere, he was stuck with walking her home.

"You can drive me home. It will take less time." It wasn't fair of her to take more of Donnie's time than necessary, but after the noise and the smells of the nightclub, Callie preferred walking. The ten minutes' stroll in the crisp night air was relaxing, and listening to Donnie talk about his latest comic starring Bud, the mighty slayer of rogue vampires, was fun.

Most nights Donnie seemed to enjoy it too.

He wrapped his arm around her shoulders. "Are you kidding me? Walking you home is the best part of the night for me."

Talk about awkward. Maybe Miri was right.

Had Callie been too preoccupied with her own problems to notice that Donnie wanted to be more than a friend?

"I want to ask you something, Donnie. What do you think of Miri?"

He shrugged. "I'm thinking of a comic she could star in. She'd make the visuals stand out. But I can't think of a story for her."

That wasn't what Callie had in mind. But maybe she could steer him in the right direction. "She could be Bud's girlfriend."

Donnie shook his head. "Nah. They don't fit. A comic needs contrast. The strange looking guy with an ordinary looking girl or the other way around. You can be Bud's girlfriend in the story."

She lifted her hand. "Please, don't. I need my privacy."

"Don't worry, I'll change the way you look. But I can base a character on you."

"I can live with that. Who would you cast as Miri's boyfriend?"

"Let me think…"

Donnie looked up to the sky for inspiration, which meant he didn't see himself in that role. A pity.

"I know. A computer nerd. Maybe a hacker."

A more direct approach was needed. "How about a comic book nerd?"

It took him a moment to catch her meaning. He laughed, his big body shaking. "Me? No way. Miri is cool, but she is too cool for me."

"What's your type?"

"Someone like you, or Fran." The way his voice got all soft when he said Fran's name said it all.

"Fran is cute." The girl was a student and worked only on weekends.

"Yeah. But she ignores me. Probably thinks I'm a dumb bouncer. All muscle and no brains."

"She doesn't know you. You need to talk to her. Show her that you're much more than muscle."

"How can I do it when she barely says hi to me?"

"Easy, give her one of your comics. With a dedication."

"What, just shove it in her hand?"

"Yeah. Bring a few to give to other employees too if it makes you feel less awkward."

Donnie nodded. "It wouldn't hurt to do some PR."

"Exactly. That way everyone will know how extremely talented you are. Just don't bring the ones starring Brad."

"No way. Even I wouldn't want to mess with your boyfriend."

And just like that her good mood vanished. "Stop saying that. He is not my boyfriend."

"Then what is he to you?"

"I wish I knew. For a few days, I was stupid enough to think he was. But how can he be when he spends nearly all his evenings and nights downstairs? Playing with other women? That's not my definition of a boyfriend. I have no wish to become one of his many whatever he calls them. His playmates or scene partners or whatever."

Donnie stopped and turned to face her. "He owns half of the club, and he is into that shit. A guy like that can't be monogamous. Part of his job is to teach and demonstrate, and he can't do that while keeping his hands off. What did you expect? That he would quit everything because he likes you?"

"Yeah, I kind of did. Silly me."

"Come here." Donnie pulled her into a bear hug. "You can either accept Brad the way he is or find someone else. Those are your only two options. You can't change him into who you want him to be."

"I know."

5

# BRUNDAR

Brundar collected his equipment and put everything into a large gym bag. His demonstrations always drew a crowd, and this evening was no different. He liked that part. Teaching others how to do it right. Hopefully, this time Gloria's husband was paying attention to what Brundar had been doing to his wife and would be able to replicate the intricate knots in their private play. Next class would be a hands-on for the participants, with the couples experimenting and Brundar only supervising.

It would be interesting to see how much they remembered. Worst case scenario, if they messed it up so badly that the knots couldn't be untied and they couldn't get their partners free, the ropes could be cut off.

"Brad, can you come into my office? I need to run a couple of things by you."

Brundar lifted his head and regarded Franco. "About?"

"Your expansion plans."

"You said you didn't want the hassle."

"I changed my mind."

"Good." Brundar's ideas would bring much needed additional profit to the club. Franco's reluctance hadn't made sense. Just because they were finally breaking even didn't mean that everything was going great. In business, not moving forward didn't mean staying in place—it meant going backwards.

Besides, if Brundar stayed to talk to Franco after closing, he couldn't see Calypso as he'd intended, which was a good thing. He needed time to think, and if he went home with her, thinking would be the last thing he'd do.

It was shameful that he needed outside help to stay away from her. He had no willpower when it came to Calypso.

Gym bag in hand, Brundar followed Franco into his cramped office. The memory of Calypso sitting in the same chair he now took was playing a number on him. Franco said something, but Brundar wasn't with him. All he could think of was Calypso's lips as she worried them while going through the paperwork, and what they'd done after that.

"Callie asked me to tell you to call her, but you were busy. So I'm telling you now."

"Did she tell you why?"

Franco smirked. "She tried to convince me to let her see the demonstration. I told her no. Obviously, she is going to try you next. Tenacious little thing."

"You have no idea."

Franco shook his head. "Pretty girl, but too mouthy for my taste."

Brundar stifled a growl. "You have nothing to worry about. She is not after you."

"Didn't think she was, my friend." Franco smirked. "Not for a moment. I'm just commenting on the fact that she is mouthy and far from submissive. I saw that you had her fill out paperwork."

Damnation. He'd forgotten to destroy that file. "Shred it. She was curious. The paperwork was meant as a scare tactic. I had no intention of making her a member. Too young."

"And too vanilla," Franco added.

Brundar closed his eyes and counted to five, waiting for his fury to subside. Franco read Calypso's file. It was worse than if he'd seen her naked. Her soul was bared on that questionnaire. But it wasn't Franco's fault. It was Brundar's.

"Give me her file."

When Franco just looked at him, Brundar felt like baring his fangs. Instead, he repeated, "Now, Franco."

His tone must've penetrated Franco's momentary stupor, and the man scrambled to riffle through the files in his filing cabinet.

"Here." He threw the file to Brundar as if it was about to catch fire.

Franco was an ex-Marine, not a guy who spooked easily. Brundar must have looked terrifying.

"Thank you," he said, his speech sounding like something between a slur and a hiss.

"Your eyes are glowing." Franco pointed at Brundar's face.

"Contact lenses reflecting the light."

"Don't give me that bullshit. Your eyes fucking glow. What are you?"

*Hell and damnation.*

Brundar leaned closer. "Look at them now. Do they look like they are glowing?"

"Yes."

But it was too late for Franco. Brundar had him in a thrall. Justified this time. But as long as he was already in the guy's head, he might as well erase the memory of that fucking file. In fact, he was going to erase this entire conversation.

In the time it took Franco's eyes to regain focus, Brundar stashed the file in his gym bag.

Franco rubbed his temples. "Where were we?"

"Expansion plans."

"Right. The liquor store next door is willing to let us have their basement.

They are not using it, and we can connect ours to theirs by cutting out a doorway."

"How much do they want for it?"

"That's not a problem. A few hundred bucks a month. The remodeling is. I don't have the funds for that, you know that. Are you willing to invest more?"

"I will invest my share and lend you enough for yours. I don't want to own more than half of the club. But first, let me crunch the numbers again."

Franco nodded, then rubbed his temples. "I know there was something else I wanted to talk to you about, but I can't remember what it was. I must be getting old."

"Are we done?"

"Yeah. We can talk about the other thing tomorrow if I remember what it is."

"Goodnight, Franco." Brundar lifted his gym bag and walked out.

Pulling out of the club's parking lot, Brundar had every intention of going home. Instead, he drove to Calypso's.

Not wanting to wake the girl, he let himself in using the spare set of keys the landlady had given him.

His careful steps were soundless as he entered Calypso's bedroom. For a few moments, he just looked at her, but then the compulsion to get closer animated his feet. He took a few steps and stood by the bed, watching her beautiful sleeping face for a few moments longer.

But that wasn't enough either.

Defeated, Brundar took off his boots and his socks and climbed on the bed next to Calypso, lying on top of the comforter while she was bundled underneath it.

Better.

Some of the tightness in his chest eased. Brundar inhaled Calypso's scent, feeling as if he was drawing his first full breath of the day. The thing was, he hadn't been aware of the tightness and the shallow breathing until he came home to her.

A moment later, she turned in her sleep and threw an arm over him, then sighed as if until now she hadn't been able to take a full breath either.

## 6

## CALLIE

Callie had slept better than she had in years. There had been no tossing and turning, no disturbing dreams about running away from monsters, no impossible puzzles to solve, only complete relaxation.

If not for the sudden loss of warmth, she would have kept sleeping, refusing to wake up and lose that peaceful feeling.

As it was, she reached her hand for the spot beside her, searching for the source of warmth. There was no one there, but there had been. The top of the comforter wasn't cold.

She popped her eyes open to see Brundar's back. Holding his boots in one hand and his socks in the other, he was trying to sneak soundlessly out of her room.

*I knew it! He has an extra set of keys.*

The thought should have bothered her, but it didn't.

How could it?

To come in the middle of the night and just lie in bed next to her meant that he couldn't stay away. Callie felt like pumping her fist in victory.

The change in her breathing pattern must have alerted him to the fact that she was awake, and he turned his head. "Did I wake you?"

"I guess you did. But I don't mind. Why are you leaving?"

"I need to be at work."

"Guarding your big shot cousin?"

He nodded.

"Can you at least stay for breakfast?"

"I don't have time."

"Coffee?"

He glanced at his watch, then nodded.

"Great. Give me two minutes to get ready. Do you know how to work the coffee machine?"

A small smile pulled on one corner of his lips. "That's the only thing I know how to make. I'll get on it."

If she hurried, she could make him a quick breakfast, and not send him on his way with an empty stomach.

After a quick visit to the bathroom, Callie pulled on a pair of leggings and an oversized T-shirt, ran a brush through her hair and padded to the kitchen.

The coffee machine was just starting to make hissing sounds, which meant she had a couple more minutes before it was ready. Plenty of time to stick a few bread slices into the toaster and scramble some eggs.

Passing him by, she kissed Brundar's cheek. "Thank you for coming and keeping my bed warm." She loaded the toaster first, then grabbed a frying pan.

"You're not mad that I let myself in?"

"No. I figured you had another set of keys. You're welcome to come in anytime you want. It's not like I'm afraid you'll catch me naked." She winked at him.

If Callie hadn't been so attuned to the slightest change in Brundar's expression, she wouldn't have noticed the impact that what she'd said had had on him.

He looked stunned, though to anyone else he would've looked as impassive as always. The guy wasn't as unfeeling as he pretended to be. A lot was going on underneath that stoic exterior. She just wished he would lower his guard around her, just a little, and let her glimpse the man inside.

"You're too trusting, Calypso. The world is full of evildoers, and it's difficult to tell the good guys from the bad."

Callie cracked two eggs into the pan, then reached for two more. "I know. But you're not one of them. If you wanted to hurt me, you could've done it anytime. Besides, I seriously doubt that this building's security system or the locks on my door would've posed much of a challenge for you. Right?"

Getting up to tend to the coffee, Brundar nodded. "You happen to be right about me. But promise me you'll be much more careful with everyone else. Don't let anyone in here without telling me first."

Callie lifted a brow. "Now, that sounds creepy, Brundar. Don't you think?" That was something Callie would have expected Shawn to say. She loaded Brundar's plate with most of the scrambled eggs and added three pieces of toast. "Butter?"

He nodded. "It's not what you think. You live alone, and anyone who comes in here knows it. You'll be safer if they hear you call a friend and tell him or her who you're with. Right now I'm the only one you can call."

That made sense. But there was one problem with that. "You told me to call you only in case of emergencies. If I invite Miri over does that count as an emergency? Or Donnie?" She cast him a sidelong glance, checking his reaction to her mention of the hunky bouncer.

*Bingo!*

Brundar's jaw tightened. "Why would you invite Donnie?"

She shrugged. "He walks me home. I feel like I should at least offer him coffee." Callie stifled a smile. She was willing to bet that from now on Brundar would be the only one walking her home.

"I can't always answer calls. But you can text me anytime. Just make sure that whoever you let in knows you're texting me about them."

Well, well, wasn't that a major breakthrough? He was allowing her to text him.

"How are the eggs?" she asked.

"Excellent. Everything you make is."

Callie waved a hand. "You've seen nothing yet. All you've had until now were quick impromptu meals. How about I invite you to dinner this evening and show you what I can really do?"

Brundar barely managed to keep his stoic mask on. But Callie caught the excited gleam in his eyes.

"That is an offer I can't refuse. What time?"

A point for Brundar, even though she was a little disappointed. At least the guy was honest, admitting that he was excited about the meal and not about seeing her. "Is five too early? I want us to have plenty of time before I have to leave for my shift at the club."

"I can be here at four if you want. I'll ask to be released from duty earlier."

Again with the military lingo. She wondered where he'd served and in what capacity.

"Perfect. Now eat your eggs before they get cold."

While Brundar got busy cleaning his plate, Callie went through a mental list of her best recipes. She didn't dare try something new in case it didn't work out. Not all recipes were as good as they looked on the screen.

The same applied to plans. Not all worked out as well as anticipated. An idea that seemed great in theory could crash and burn when implemented.

Her seduction plans aside, Callie still owed Brundar a huge debt of gratitude, and the only way she knew how to repay even a fraction of what he'd done for her was to cook him dinners every night from now until about forever.

It wasn't as if she had much else to offer him.

She would've gladly done his laundry and picked up his dry cleaning too, but she knew he would be offended if she offered.

Brundar would refuse any attempt on her part to repay his kindness.

Callie didn't like being in his debt or anyone else's. But there were several factors at work forcing her to swallow her pride and just say thank you.

One was that she couldn't have done it without Brundar's help, and that cooking him dinners would never come close to repaying that debt.

But more importantly, Brundar deserved to feel good about what he'd done and was still doing for her. To look for convoluted ways to repay him was like telling him she felt bad about accepting his help, and therefore taking away from his pleasure of providing it.

Oftentimes, the giver got more out of the giving than the receiver got from the receiving.

7

# KIAN

Kian tapped his hand on the conference table to get everyone's attention.

When they quieted down, he began. "We have two topics on the agenda for this meeting. One is the progress with the autonomous cars, and the other is the continuing murders. Let's start with the easy one. The cars."

William pushed his glasses up his nose. "They sent a rep to the factory in Sweden. The prototype should arrive here the day after tomorrow."

The guy's face had gotten so gaunt that it no longer fit the frame, and the glasses kept sliding down. William needed a new pair. But more than that he needed a change of pace.

"We will test the prototype as soon as it arrives. Once we know what changes are needed, I want you to book a flight to Stockholm and supervise the production line. At least until the first batch is ready to ship."

William looked uncomfortable. "I hate flying."

Bhathian clapped William on the shoulder. "Then load up on Snake's Venom before you board and sleep throughout the entire trip. First class has seats that recline all the way. They turn into very comfortable beds."

William shook his head. "I don't like getting drunk either. I'll figure something out."

Kian nodded. Council members and Guardians alike could not afford to have quirks like aversion to flying. They had a job to do. "Good. Let's move on to the murders. Onegus?"

"Our men are all clear, thank the merciful Fates. All have alibis for the time of at least one of the murders. I think it's safe to assume that we don't have a madman in our midst, let alone two who went on a simultaneous killing spree. Which leaves either a Doomer or a random, unaffiliated immortal."

Kian raked his fingers through his hair. "True, now that we know there are more than two players in this game, we need to take it into account. It can be a lone immortal, unaffiliated with any group, maybe a member of Kalugal's crew."

Onegus reclined in his chair and crossed his arms over his chest. "I wish we could find him, see if we could work together. Think how much stronger we could be with an additional group of highly trained warriors. We could continue their training until they reached Guardian level. A lot easier than starting with newbies who have no prior training or combat experience."

Kian leaned forward. "You would trust ex-Doomers?"

Onegus shrugged. "We have two who've proved themselves quite helpful."

"Not the same, Onegus. If Kalugal indeed managed to defect with an entire platoon, he and his men can take us on with ease. Are you willing to risk it? Because I'm not."

Onegus let his arms drop. "Of course not. It was just wishful thinking on my part. I'm tired of trying to manage with only six Guardians. That's more than enough when nothing is going on, but not nearly enough in time of trouble."

"Which is the big conundrum." Kian sighed. "Most of the time Guardians have little to do. But when you are needed there are not enough of you to do the job. I want to start patrolling the areas where the murders occurred."

"Can't do it." Onegus shook his head. "They were spread out, and the way Los Angeles is built, it's not like there is a center where everything happens. You need a lot of men to do that."

"Hey!" Kri called out. "Chauvinist much?"

Onegus pinned her with a hard stare. "We are talking about an immortal male gone rogue. I would never send a female Guardian after him. And if it makes me a chauvinist, I can live with that."

Kri humphed. "I can take on most immortal males."

"Civilians," Kian said. "If this is an ex or active Doomer, he is not a civilian. Do you think you can take on Dalhu? Or Robert?"

"Not Dalhu, I've seen him fight. But maybe I can take on Robert."

"Match! Match! Match! I want to see a match," Yamanu singsonged while drumming his hand on the table and making the whole thing shake.

Kian groaned. Sometimes his Guardians behaved like high schoolers. Correction. Kindergarteners. "You're welcome to invite him to spar with you in the gym. I'm sure he would love it. I'm just not sure what Michael would think of you getting physical with an immortal bachelor who is not a relative of yours."

"I don't care what he thinks. He can watch if he wants."

Yamanu rubbed his palms together. "That would be one hell of a show. I call dibs on a first-row seat."

"Enough!" Kian raised his voice.

Everyone quieted instantly.

"This is an official meeting, not a social gathering. I need suggestions for patrolling the murder areas. If we believe this is the work of an immortal male, it is our responsibility to deal with him. The human authorities can't and should not have to take care of it."

The door opened, and Okidu walked in with a tray. "I brewed fresh coffee, master."

"Thank you, Okidu." Kian waited while the butler put a porcelain cup in front of each person and then poured them coffee from the two thermal carafes he'd brought.

When he was done, Okidu bowed and retreated from the room.

"Any ideas?" Kian glanced at Brundar who hadn't spoken a word yet.

The Guardian who was the master of stoic expressions looked perturbed, his forehead creased and his eyes focused somewhere on his knees. His body was sitting at the conference table, but his mind was miles away.

If Anandur's remark hadn't been a joke, then Brundar had gotten himself a woman. Not a hookup, but someone he saw on a regular basis. Which would explain his peculiar mood. Getting involved with a human was a bad idea, and Brundar was well aware of that.

"I could tap into the surveillance cameras in the area." William brought Kian's attention back to where it needed to be.

"To what end?" Onegus asked. "Someone would have to watch the feed. If something suspicious came up, even if we had men on standby in the area, they wouldn't get there in time to catch the bastard."

"True," Kian conceded. "But they can make it in time to save the woman from bleeding to death. Besides, we will at least have a visual. We can continue the search using the facial recognition program."

"I wonder why the police are not doing that," Kri said.

She had a point, but Kian doubted they had. The police only looked at the feed after they found a victim, not as a prevention method. But William's suggestion gave him an idea.

"Here is what I think we should do. William, go ahead and hack the surveillance cameras. I'll contact Turner and have him find us a contractor to monitor the feed. They will contact us and call an ambulance if needed. We can take up the investigation from there."

William lifted a hand. "It will have to wait until I come back from Sweden. I can't do it all in one day, which is all the time I have before the prototype car arrives and I have to get busy with that."

Anandur snapped his fingers. "Not a problem. We have a new hacker on board."

Kian lifted a brow. "The kid? I understand that he is in the clinic, sick with pneumonia."

"He is. But knowing Roni, he could handle this even sick as a dog." Anandur turned to William. "If you can show him what you need and provide him with the equipment he needs, he can probably do everything from his sickbed."

William shook his head. "That's a lot of equipment."

"Then we move his sickbed to your lab, together with Bridget to keep an eye on him." Kian looked at William for approval.

The computer lab was the guy's whole world. He wouldn't be thrilled about letting the kid in there unsupervised.

"Let me talk with him first. See how good he really is."

Anandur chuckled. "He is good."

# 8

# RONI

*B*eing sick sucked.

Roni was bored out of his mind, and lying in bed all day was getting on his nerves. The trouble was that walking around unaided was still a no-no. Hell, even going to the bathroom required leaning on Sylvia or one of the nurses for support.

He vehemently refused a catheter, which meant no intravenous either.

His pneumonia was viral, so there wasn't much the hot little doctor could do with medications other than fever reducers.

It still bugged the hell out of him that he was younger than the hot-looking doctor's grown son. He had to remember that looks were deceptive as far as immortals went, and some of these people were ancient.

Anandur, who was a major goofball, was fucking one thousand years old. How was it possible?

Roni got the biological explanation, but that was just a small part of the equation. The amount of information the guy must've absorbed over his long life should have made him a genius. But he wasn't. Mentally, he was just an ordinary dude who acted like any twenty-something-year-old.

Well, not exactly. There were a few tells.

Like, forget politically correct. The way the guy talked, every other sentence had something that would offend an average millennial.

And his jokes. Come on, Anandur needed major help in that department. He was almost as bad as Barty.

Fuck. He hoped the guy was okay. Barty was either worried sick or spitting mad and cursing Roni with every vile thing he could think of.

Both Barty and Jerome would get in shitloads of trouble because of him. Mostly Jerome. Barty had done his part in guarding Roni, but Jerome had abandoned his post. No one would believe him that he'd somehow gotten hypnotized.

Guilt was an unfamiliar and unpleasant sensation.

What he wouldn't have given for a laptop right now. There was nothing that could take Roni's mind off life's stinky nuggets like a good hacking session that required his total concentration.

"I brought you soup." Sylvia entered his room with a tray.

"I don't want soup."

"Well, tough, Mr. Grumpy, soup is what you get. Bridget said you need plenty of liquids."

Sylvia pressed the foot pedal, lifting the back of his bed to a sitting position. "Open wide." She brought a spoon to his mouth.

He shook his head.

"Do you want a catheter?"

"No."

"Then open up."

Resistance was futile.

Sylvia smiled. "That's a good boy. Now let's try another."

"Yes, Mommy."

She fed him another spoonful, and another until the bowl was empty.

"All done. See? It wasn't so bad."

Roni grunted in response.

The soup wasn't bad, he was just sick and tired of hospitals, and of bland food, and of nothing to do.

"I need a laptop. Can you get me one?"

Sylvia put the bowl on the tray and hopped on the bed to sit next to him. "I have to ask around who has a laptop to spare."

"Don't you have one?"

"I do. At home. I don't live here."

He glanced at the soup. "Then where did you get that from?" As far as he knew, he was the only occupant of the clinic, and it had no dedicated food service.

"Nathalie, Andrew's wife made it. She sends her love and apologizes for not coming to visit. It's because of the baby. She and Andrew can't get infected, but they are afraid of an airborne virus clinging to their clothes and then attacking little baby Phoenix."

Roni frowned. "When is that baby going to turn immortal?"

Sylvia shrugged. "I don't know," she said while looking away.

He knew exactly why she felt uncomfortable. Did she think he was stupid and wouldn't figure it out?

In case he didn't transition, which seemed most likely at the moment, Sylvia didn't want him to know more than he already did. Fewer memories to wipe away.

"Did anyone talk to Kian about me?" At least they'd finally told him the name of the guy who was in charge of Roni's future. He was sick of calling him the big boss, or the dude on top.

"I'm sure someone did. But we are all waiting to see what happens. If you transition, then there is nothing to talk about."

"Bridget said that the pneumonia might be the reason I'm not transitioning. My body needs to get healthy first." Chances were the doctor was just being nice and trying to give him hope. It made sense, though. Like the way certain diseases stalled the onset of puberty.

"She is absolutely right."

Someone knocked on the door.

"Come in," Roni called out in his sick guy's barely there voice. But for the immortals it should be enough.

"The room is soundproofed. I'll go see who it is." Sylvia hopped down and went to open the door.

"William. What are you doing here?"

"I came to see my new partner."

*Partner?*

The clan's famous science genius was calling Roni a partner? That must mean that they had decided to let him stay no matter what.

"Sure, come in." Sylvia moved aside to let William in.

He was tall, though not as tall as Anandur, more like Andrew's height. But he didn't look so good. The dark circles under his eyes were so deep that even his glasses couldn't hide them.

"Hi, Roni, I'm William." He offered Roni a hand.

Roni shook it. "Usually my handshake is more manly than the limp noodle I can offer you now."

"No worries. How are you feeling?"

"Like shit."

William pulled up a chair and put it next to Roni's bed. "Yeah, me too. I have trouble sleeping lately."

"I can see that."

William looked up at Sylvia who was leaning against the wall. "I'm sorry. Did I take your chair?" He started to get up.

"No, keep it. I usually sit on Roni's bed."

"Oh." William dropped his butt back and pushed his glasses up his nose. "So I hear you have some mad skills?"

"I do."

"I have a job for you."

Roni felt like William had just thrown him a lifeline. "Yes, thank you. I'm going insane with nothing to do."

William smiled. "You came in last night, and it's not even midday yet. Do you always work around the clock?"

"Every moment I can."

"Same here."

Roni liked the guy. A kindred spirit. "High five, dude."

William obliged him, lifting a palm up and holding it close to Roni's so he didn't have to lift his own too high to reach it.

"What's the job?"

"Hacking into surveillance cameras."

"Child's play."

"Hundreds of them. Spread over fifty square miles of densely populated urban area."

"Still child's play, but time-consuming."

"Right. Time that I don't have because I have another project I need to take care of. Anandur suggested I check with you. Are you up to it in your current state?"

"Yes, yes, and yes. Where do I work?"

"Wait a moment." Sylvia pushed off the wall and came to sit on Roni's bed. "You're so sick I have to spoon feed you. And you think you can work?"

"My body is weak. Not my brain."

"You need your hands to type on the keyboard."

"I can manage that."

She shook her head. "Not unless Bridget says it's okay. Even Kian can't go over her head where her patients are involved."

"Then call her in."

Sylvia turned to William. "Can't it wait a few days until Roni feels better?"

William sighed. "Did you read about the string of murders?"

"Of course. They think it's some satanic cult."

"We think it's an immortal male gone insane. Not one of ours, Onegus checked everyone's alibi. It's either a Doomer or an unaffiliated immortal. We have to help catch him. Every day that passes without us doing anything could mean another victim's life."

Well, that put things in a different perspective. Roni's mind went to work.

Sylvia looked like she wanted to say something, then shook her head and got off the bed. "Let me find Bridget." She turned to William. "Should I tell her what's at stake? Or do you want to do it?"

"Makes no difference to me."

"Then I'll tell her."

"Thank you."

When Sylvia left the room, Roni asked the most pertinent question. "Tell me about your equipment. I need to know what I got to work with."

William's face brightened with the first real smile since he'd gotten there. "You're in for a real treat, Roni. I have the best setup in the world."

"I highly doubt it. Until yesterday, I worked with the finest setup the government of the United States of America can put together. I'm sure it's the best in the world. You can't possibly have anything even remotely as powerful."

"You'll be singing a different tune once I tell you what I got."

# 9

# BRUNDAR

Brundar knocked on Onegus's door.
"Come in."
"I'm leaving early today," he said as he walked in, stopping a couple of feet away from Onegus's desk.
"Again? What about your evening classes?"
"Taken care of."
Instead of the reprimand Brundar had been expecting, the chief Guardian smirked. "So it's true. You've got yourself a woman."
Out of respect for his superior, Brundar didn't tell him to fuck off. Instead, he lifted a brow then turned on his heel and walked out.
What a bunch of juvenile busybodies. Given the respect the Guardians were regarded with by the rest of the clan, they should at least behave like the warriors they were supposed to be. In war and in peacetime.
Besides, Brundar didn't have a woman. Calypso wasn't his. She was a temporary distraction he needed to get out of his system. Maybe his obsession with her would end once he finally bedded her.
If he was lucky, it would be the same for her. Once she satisfied her curiosity, she might realize he wasn't the right guy for her. Because he wasn't. He wasn't the right guy for any woman.
It would be best if she pushed him away.
Hell, he had a feeling that as long as it was up to him to break them up, it was not going to happen anytime soon. When Calypso pushed his buttons, he responded. She controlled him as if he had no mind of his own.
Brundar shook his head. It boiled down to two options. Either Calypso stopped pushing those buttons of her own volition, or he ensured she had no access to them.
To prove his newfound resolve or rather lack thereof, he stopped by a liquor store to get the wine and cocktail fixings he'd promised her because he was a

man of his word, and not because he felt as if Calypso's dinner invitation was a date and it would be rude to arrive empty-handed. Leaving everything in the cardboard box the cashier had given him would send the right message—no fancy wrapping paper and no sappy cards to give her the wrong idea.

As Brundar let himself into the building using the extra set of keys and took the stairs up to her apartment, the smell of delicious food made him salivate in anticipation.

He rapped his knuckles on her door.

A moment later, Calypso opened the way, rendering him breathless and speechless.

"Hi." She looked at the box tucked under his arm.

It took him a moment to respond. "You look beautiful." He couldn't stop his eyes from roaming up and down her body.

Her hair was done in big fat waves, her green eyes were emphasized by long lashes painted black, and her perfect body was encased in a knee-length, strapless black dress that had no visible zipper, which meant it could be pulled down or up with a single tug.

A pair of small, gold earrings was all the jewelry she had on, but then Calypso didn't need any decorations to accentuate her beauty. Dressed in that curve-hugging dress, a pair of tall, spiky heels making her legs look amazing, she was sure to cause men to drool and stutter, which meant she was never leaving her apartment in that getup unless escorted by him.

The woman was beautiful in jeans and sneakers, with no makeup and her hair gathered in a ponytail. All decked out she was a stunner.

A smile brightened Calypso's face. "Thank you. You look amazing. But then you always do." She motioned for him to come in.

Brundar had put on the grey slacks and the blue button-down shirt not because this was a date, but out of respect for all the trouble Calypso had gone to in preparing this special dinner.

Damnation. Who was he fooling? It was a date, and they'd both dressed up for the occasion.

Putting the box on the kitchen counter, Brundar started pulling out the assortment of wines, liqueurs, and vodkas he'd bought. "Where do you want me to put these?"

She looked at the number of bottles and shook her head. "One could go on the table, and the rest wherever you find space. I guess the vodka can go into the freezer."

When he was done, Calypso showed him to the dining table. "Please, take a seat."

He remained standing. "Do you need help bringing things from the kitchen?"

"I've got it. You can uncork the wine. Other than that just sit down and prepare to get pampered."

Why did that sound so good?

Had he ever been pampered?

Not even as a boy. His mother was a lovely woman, but she'd been a scatterbrained mother who'd often forgotten to prepare meals for him. Anandur would bring something he'd killed, skinning and roasting it over an open fire, and Brundar had done the same to the fish he'd occasionally caught.

Though after Lachlann's betrayal, he'd never fished or eaten fish again.

Even the smell of anything fishy brought on nausea.

Brundar reached for the wine bottle. This was not the time to bring up bothersome memories. This was a time to enjoy getting pampered by a beautiful woman.

Probably the only time he would, so he'd better enjoy it.

Uncorking the wine, Brundar poured it into the two wine glasses, then sat down and admired the table.

A white tablecloth, two candlesticks, a vase with several cut flowers, and cutlery for two.

He wondered how meals were served in other human households. Was dinner a formal affair like this one? Did families gather around a dining table or eat at the kitchen counter? Did it make a difference?

After all, food was food and how it was served wasn't important. Or was it?

Calypso walked in with a bowl in each hand. "Onion soup with cheese crostini." She placed one in front of Brundar, then sat across from him with the other. "*Bon appetit.*"

"Thank you." Brundar dipped his spoon in the soup and brought it to his mouth. "Delicious," he said after taking two more spoonfuls.

Calypso beamed with pride. "Thank you. This is just a simple dish. Wait until I bring out the next one: spicy grilled shrimp over shaved fennel slaw."

Before he could think better of it, Brundar grimaced.

Calypso's smile wilted. "What's the matter? You don't like fennel? Or shrimps?"

If he could stomach it without getting nauseated, Brundar would have shut up and eaten. But barfing over Calypso's masterpiece was worse than admitting he didn't eat shrimp.

"I don't like seafood. Can you serve the slaw without the shrimp?"

"Certainly. I'm sorry. I should've asked you beforehand if you were allergic to anything, or if there was anything you didn't like. It's just that Shawn ate everything, so it didn't cross my mind."

"I don't like to hear about your ex while eating."

Calypso flushed red. "Oops. Sorry. I don't like it either. It's an appetite spoiler."

Brundar lifted his wine glass. "To a new life. Let the old one be forgotten."

Calypso lifted hers and leaned closer to clink glasses with him. "To a new life."

As they drank the wine, Brundar had a passing thought that he should do as he preached. It was hypocritical of him to ask Calypso to forget about her unfortunate marriage while he still clung to old hurts, letting them define who he was and how he lived his life.

## 10

# CALLIE

*Embarrassing*, Callie thought as she collected the bowls. A good hostess would have checked with her guest about likes and dislikes. She'd been so busy planning the perfect dinner, it hadn't crossed her mind that Brundar might have a problem with any of it.

At least he'd enjoyed the onion soup as evidenced by his empty bowl.

The slaw wasn't really a big deal either. The shrimp and the slaw were stored in separate containers in the fridge, so she could just omit the shrimp. If Brundar didn't like seafood, the smell would probably bother him. She could have them for lunch the next day.

But the slaw on its own was more of a side dish than an appetizer. Serving it as a separate course wouldn't look right. Instead, she decided to go straight to the main course and add the slaw to the plates.

Taking her time to arrange everything the way she'd seen chefs do it on television, Callie looked at her creation with satisfaction. Not perfect, but pretty damn good for a home cook who'd learned her stuff from searching recipes on the Internet and watching YouTube to see how it was done.

"Fennel and rosemary-crusted rack of lamb, with spicy-sweet pepper medley, and fennel slaw," Callie announced as she carried the two plates to the dining room table.

"Sounds fancy." Brundar stood up and took one of the plates off her hands. "Smells good too."

She sat down and pulled a napkin over her knees. *"Bon appetit."*

The look of bliss on Brundar's face was worth the hours of effort Callie had put into preparing this meal.

Would he look as blissed out during sex?

Regrettably, she wasn't going to find out anytime soon. Brundar had made it clear that the blindfold wasn't coming off. Ever.

*We'll see about that.*

After finishing almost everything on his plate, Brundar lifted his head and glanced at her. "Aren't you eating?"

"I'm full."

He looked at her plate. "You've barely touched anything."

"I kept tasting what I was making while cooking it, and I was already quite full when we sat down to eat. The soup finished the job."

She smiled when Brundar glanced at her plate longingly. "Would you like to finish it for me?" She hoped he wasn't grossed out by her offer. Shawn had had no problem polishing her plate clean. But Brundar wasn't Shawn, and thank God for that.

"Are you sure? You could save it for later."

"I'm sure." Callie pushed her plate toward him. "I have plenty left over."

That settled it for him. In a matter of minutes, he cleaned her plate as well.

"Can I get you more?"

He shook his head and leaned back in his chair. "I'm more than full. Thank you. This was the best meal I ever had."

Callie chuckled. "Thank you for the compliment, but I guess you've never eaten in a gourmet restaurant. Not that I ever had the pleasure, but I'm sure I can't compare."

"On the contrary. One of my cousins is a gourmet chef, and until today I considered his cooking the best."

Obviously, he was exaggerating. All she did was find interesting recipes to make. That didn't make her a chef. Those people invented the recipes.

"Thank you." Then the other part of what he'd said registered and she lifted a brow. "Another cousin? How many cousins do you have?"

"Many."

"It must be nice having such a big family."

"In some ways it is. In others, it is not."

"Like what?"

He shrugged. "It's good to have a safety net. As annoying as my family can get, I know they will catch me if I fall. But when those busybodies, who don't understand the concept of privacy and boundaries, meddle in my life, I'm not sure the net is worth it. It can be suffocating."

Callie heard little of what Brundar had said after his first sentence. She was taken by the idea of having a safety net comprised of family members who cared.

It was a rarity in the modern world.

How different would life have been if she'd had that? Not that she would have asked for help. But knowing it was there and available if she needed it desperately enough would've made her life a lot less stressful.

Would her father have recovered sooner after losing her mom if he'd had help?

He might not have sunk into depression if he'd had a support system in place. Brothers, sisters, and cousins who would have taken turns making sure he was okay and helped him raise his daughter.

"I wish I had a large family that actually cares. You should be grateful for yours."

"I am. Defending the clan is my job, and I regard it as both a duty and a privilege."

"A whole clan? And what about your cousin the big shot with the butler whom you guard, isn't he your priority?"

"That's part of my job too. He manages the family business for all of us. My brother and I make sure no harm comes to him."

Fascinating. It almost sounded like a mob organization. But Brundar was too honorable of a man to take part in something illegal.

"I think so too. I mean about it being a duty and a privilege."

Brundar dipped his head. "I'm glad you see it my way."

"I wish I could be part of your clan." She regretted the words the moment they'd left her mouth. The meaning he could attach to them could be very different from what she meant by them. Callie felt her cheeks get hot. "I mean to be under the protective umbrella of it, I didn't mean to say that I wish you'd marry me or anything like that."

A sad smile tugged on Brundar's thin lips. "Of course, not. You're too young to be thinking of marriage. The first one robbed you of your youth. You need to attend college, get your degree, and then get a job doing what you love doing. Not to mention the partying a young woman like you should partake in. All those things need to happen before you settle down again."

All true, except for the partying. The train had left the station on that a long time ago. What the heck did she have in common with a bunch of college kids? They might be the same age as her, but that didn't put them on an equal footing. Life had made her older than her years.

"Speaking of college. I'll take you up on your offer to produce a fake ID for me. I hope you're right about the administration accommodating my situation. It's not like I have a restraining order against Shawn I can show them as proof."

"Don't worry about it. I'll take care of the fake papers, and I'll make sure they don't give you any problems over the name change."

"Don't tell me. You have another cousin working at UCLA."

That got a real smile out of him. "Not as far as I know. But my government contacts can come in handy again."

Callie shook her head. "Amazing. I still can't believe how lucky I am to have you as a friend. Fate must've prompted me to go to your club that night."

Brundar shifted in his chair. "Are we friends, Calypso?"

She winked. "With benefits."

Brundar ignored the suggestive remark, pretending as if he didn't know its meaning. Not his usual style, true, Brundar was quite direct. But she couldn't believe a handsome young guy like him didn't know what the phrase friends with benefits meant.

# 11

# BRUNDAR

Calypso rose to her feet and collected their plates. "Are you ready for dessert?"

"There is dessert?"

"Cinnamon-orange crème brûlée."

Brundar's eyes almost rolled back in his head. "I can't wait to taste it."

Talk about pampering. If she were an immortal, he would've proposed right there—the whole ridiculous thing of dropping to one knee and begging her to become his. Not really, he wasn't husband material, but the thought felt good. Evidently, Anandur was rubbing off on him because that was something his brother would have done.

He should help. Calypso had worked hard to prepare this amazing dinner, and that was pampering enough.

Pushing his chair back, Brundar got up and followed Calypso to the kitchen. "Can I make coffee?"

She smiled up at him. "Sure. You're good with that machine. I liked my coffee this morning."

Yeah, as if putting a pod into the coffeemaker and filling it with water was rocket science.

"I'm good with a lot of things. Anything kitchen related is not one of them."

"Good. Otherwise, there would've been nothing left for me to do for you, which would've bothered me. You did so much for me. You still do."

Brundar wanted to tell her that there was no need but stopped himself in time. For Calypso, it wasn't just about gratitude. She seemed to genuinely like cooking. The right thing to do was to thank her and tell her how much he'd enjoyed himself.

"I need to keep coming up with things I can do for you, just so you keep feeding me."

"It's my pleasure. You're welcome anytime." Calypso removed the foil from two small serving dishes and sprinkled sugar over them. "This should be done at the dinner table, but I'm afraid I'll set the place on fire." She pulled out a gas torch from a drawer.

"I suggest you stand back." She waved the torch.

"What are you going to do?" He stepped back, his eyes following the device in her hand.

"Just watch."

Switching the torch on, Calypso aimed the flame down at one of the dishes. The sugar caught fire, browned, and a moment later the flames died out. She repeated the process with the other one.

"Yay! I did it!" Grabbing her creations, she carried them to the dining room.

Brundar waited until the coffee maker finished brewing, filled two cups and brought them to the table. "I didn't know cooking involved such risks."

"That's only risky in the hands of an amateur, like me. Professional cooks have it down."

She didn't seem like a novice to him.

"How many of those did you make?"

She smiled sheepishly. "That's my second time. Let's see how well they turned out."

Brundar picked up the little spoon and scooped some of the crème into his mouth.

*Bliss.*

"What do you think? Is it any good?"

"It's excellent."

"I'm so glad to hear you say it. That's the only part of the meal I was worried about."

"Everything tasted amazing. Thank you."

"You're welcome."

As he finished the last spoonful, Brundar noticed that Calypso had barely touched her dessert. Perhaps she was saving it for him? After he'd finished everything she'd left on her dinner plate, she might have thought she hadn't made enough.

"Eat your dessert, Calypso." He pointed at her dish.

She shook her head. "I'm full. Do you want to finish it?"

He would've loved to, but he wanted her to have it. "I'm full too. Eat!" To emphasize, he pushed his chair back and rubbed his stomach as if it was overstuffed.

"Sheesh, you're so bossy." She crossed her arms over her chest. "There are like a thousand calories in this. I'm watching my weight."

He cast her an incredulous glance. "You don't need to lose anything. In fact, you could use a few more pounds."

Calypso shook her head. "I'm starting to believe that you really haven't had any girlfriends. For future reference, avoid mentioning weight even if asked. Never tell a woman she needs to gain or lose any pounds. Consider it a taboo subject."

"What should I say, then?"

"That you think she is perfect the way she is."

"You are perfect. And that's not a polite lie."

Her smug smirk and the naughty gleam in her eyes had seduction written all over them. Calypso quickly polished off her dessert and a moment later she pushed to her feet and sauntered over to him.

"You're perfect the way you are too." She sat on his lap and leaned against his chest while tucking her hands between her thighs.

He appreciated that she hadn't tried to get away with touching him and was making sure not to forget by keeping her hands entrapped.

Lifting her head, she kissed the underside of his jaw, then whispered, "I bought lots and lots of condoms."

Brundar's cock surged against the thin fabric of his slacks, poking Calypso's sweet ass.

"You've been a naughty girl, haven't you?" His hand closed on her nape, caging her in place.

She licked at his jaw, sending a bolt of fire straight to his balls. "A well prepared, naughty girl," she breathed.

So it seemed.

The lady wasn't going to take no for an answer, and frankly, he was tired of playing hard to get. With one arm under her thighs and the other wrapped around her waist, holding her tight against his chest, he pushed off the chair and strode to her bedroom.

Taking in the scene before him, Brundar stopped at the doorway.

When Calypso had told him she was well prepared, she'd meant more than the condoms. Four scarves were tied to four corners of the bed's iron scrollwork, and a fifth one was lying on the bed, its bright colors in stark relief on the white bedding.

She'd thought of everything.

Sitting on the bed with Calypso still wrapped in his arms, Brundar wanted to flip her over his knees, expose that beautiful ass of hers, and give her a few teasing spanks. Except, he was swimming in uncharted waters. This wasn't a scene at the club.

Should he thank her for dinner with tenderness?

Or should he give her what he knew she craved?

He didn't know her well enough to choose for her. It would be best to ask.

"Now, what should I do?" He reached behind himself for the scarf and handed it to her. "Should I reward you for an amazing dinner, or punish you for your presumptuousness?"

The scent of her arousal intensifying, Calypso obediently wrapped the scarf over her eyes, tying the ends in a loose knot at the back of her head. "Both."

Brundar smiled. With the blindfold in place, he no longer feared his fangs showing. For some reason, his fangs tended to react sooner and with less stimulation than those of other immortal males, reacting to the slightest provocation, aggression, or conversely arousal. He kissed her tenderly, going for slow and sweet instead of rough and intense.

She moaned, wiggling on his lap, impatient for her funishment.

Taking his time, he caressed her silky face, the long column of her neck, and the tops of her breasts, all while exploring the sweetness of her mouth, tasting the crème brûlée on her tongue.

When he was done with her mouth, he guided her gently to lie belly down over his knees, her cheek resting comfortably on the bed.

Her contented sigh erased the last of his doubts about what Calypso wanted him to do to her next.

This felt very different from any scene he'd ever participated in. Holding Calypso snugly against his middle was all about intimacy and closeness. Not about keeping his partner at a safe distance. Surprisingly, it felt good.

More than good, it felt right.

But only with Calypso.

Somehow, she'd managed to penetrate the shields around his heart and make a home for herself inside it. When he left her, and he didn't kid himself that he could stay, he would have to tear that piece of his heart out and leave it behind because it belonged to her and always would.

Right now, though, he was hers, and she was his, and the future or the past didn't exist at this moment.

Holding the bottom of Calypso's stretchy dress, he prolonged her anticipation by inching it up her thighs in slow motion. She had plenty of time to reconsider if she wanted to. But as with everything else, the lady knew precisely what she wanted and wasn't shy about asking for it.

When the dress finally cleared the bottom swell of her ass, Brundar let out a hiss. Not only did the tiny thong she had on leave her butt cheeks bare, but the gusset was soaked through.

Unable to resist, he snaked a finger under the scrap of fabric, dipping it in Calypso's arousal. The gentle touch had her jerk up, but he held on, keeping her tightly secure against his stomach.

She was in desperate need of relief, but he didn't want her orgasming yet. Still, he couldn't just leave her like that. He could ease her a little until she was primed for the big finale.

A strangled moan escaped her throat as he pushed a finger inside her scorching, tight sheath. Calypso managed to wiggle despite his tight hold. Tightening his arm around her middle, he added another finger, and then another, stretching her to where it must've bordered on discomfort.

Calypso stilled, absorbing the fullness, getting used to the sensation.

He withdrew his fingers and delivered the first smack.

"Oh, God," she hissed, her hands fisting the comforter. The flare of her arousal was so potent, it wreaked havoc on his restraint. Brundar was a hair away from stripping her naked and entering her in one hard thrust.

But this was about Calypso and her needs. His would come later.

A few more smacks and she would orgasm just from the spanking.

Should he let her?

Yeah, this time he would. Calypso was too far gone to survive a drawn-out foreplay. She needed this one now.

"Put your hands behind your back, sweetling," he said as he caressed her perfect globes.

The pose would be less comfortable for her, but it would prevent her from instinctively reaching behind her. He didn't want to accidentally smack her hands. Besides, the confinement would further ratchet up the potency of her arousal.

And his.

## 12

# CALLIE

"Put your hands behind your back, sweetling."

Callie responded to Brundar's command with a pained groan. Already turned on beyond belief, she was almost sent over by his stern tone and what he'd asked her to do.

Gritting her teeth, Callie held it off. There was so much more coming, and she wanted to savor it all. If she climaxed now, he would stop spanking, and she would miss out on it.

As soon as she obeyed, he gripped her wrists with one strong hand and started a steady beat on her upturned behind. The first few smacks were so light they almost felt like caresses, but soon his tempo increased and with it the sting. Still, it was far from painful. He was only teasing her. In the world of kink, this was like foreplay, and she was ready for the real thing.

Brundar stopped and massaged her warmed globes, his finger sliding down to her wet center. "How close are you, sweetling?"

"Close," she husked.

His grip on her wrists tightened, and he pulled her even closer against his body, his warmth and his scent and the feel of his hard abs further scrambling her brain.

The next smack took her by surprise.

It delivered a real sting that had her jerking on Brundar's knees. This was what she imagined a punishment spanking would feel like. Then came another one, just as hard, on her other cheek.

Callie tensed in anticipation, but instead of a smack, Brundar's hand caressed and massaged the ache away.

"Okay? Too much?"

Was it? Callie wasn't sure. "Maybe a little."

His hand kept on caressing. "Remember. One word from you and everything stops. No fear."

"I'm not afraid."

"Good." He kept massaging and caressing, giving her time to process what she was feeling.

In retrospect, those two hard smacks had been more intense but not really painful. It was fear that had made her tense.

She wiggled as much as his iron hold on her allowed, signaling that she was ready for more.

"Words, Calypso."

"Please continue."

He gave her butt cheek an approving squeeze before resuming.

It was perfect. Not too hard and not too soft, it was exactly how she wanted it. Despite the rapid climb of arousal, Callie managed a brief moment of clarity. This had been a test of sorts. Brundar couldn't have known where her sweet spot was without stretching her limits. He was good at reading her responses, but he wasn't a mind reader. The important thing was that she could trust him.

The man was devoted to bringing her maximum pleasure.

With that realization, Callie let herself go in a way she hadn't before.

Complete surrender.

Her orgasm crested, washing over her in wave after wave of languid fire instead of one volcanic eruption.

"Oh, sweetling." Brundar lifted her off his lap as if she weighed no more than a pillow, turned her around and cradled her in his arms as if she was precious to him.

*What a feeling.*

His hand soft on her cheek, he turned her head toward him and kissed her as tenderly as he did before.

"Good?" he asked.

"Excellent."

His arms tightened around her. "There is no more beautiful and titillating sight than you in the throes of climax."

It was on the tip of her tongue to tell him it was unfair of him to deny her the same. Brundar would look magnificent as he reached his peak. But there was no point in bringing it up and ruining the sweet moment between them.

As it was, Brundar had already relaxed his own rules by not tying her up. Instead, he'd held her tightly against his body throughout.

Was it the first time he'd been that intimate with a woman?

Could she ask him that?

Her need to find out was so intense it was undeniable. "Am I the first? I mean like this. Close and personal."

"Yes."

Satisfaction, pure and sweet.

"Good."

Brundar didn't have a monopoly on one-word answers. In fact, she was starting to like them. He was right. It was a more efficient way to communicate if one didn't mind sounding like a Neanderthal.

Next thing she would be using grunts instead of words.

"What's that smug little smile about?"

Callie chuckled. "I was just thinking that we rub off on each other, and that pretty soon I'd be talking in grunts instead of words."

"I don't grunt."

"Yes, you do."

There was a moment of silence, during which Callie regretted not seeing Brundar's expression. It was one thing to have sex blindfolded; conducting a conversation was another. Without the facial cues, she was literally blind.

"Not a lot," he acquiesced.

Carefully, afraid she would bump her nose on his jaw, Callie lifted her head and kissed his cheek. "Thank you."

"For what?"

"Compromising." Callie meant about everything. About relaxing his rules and holding her close, and about agreeing with her on a silly thing like whether he tended to grunt a lot or not.

"Aha." He let go of his grip on her, allowing a few inches between their bodies, and tugged on her dress. "As sexy as this is, I think it's time to get rid of it."

"I agree." She lifted her arms.

He pulled it off with one tug. "I like this dress. You should always wear things that are easy to take off. But only when you're with me."

"Yes, sir." Even though the dress didn't show cleavage and reached down to her knees, the clingy fabric and how easy it was to pull off made it somewhat scandalous. She would've never dared to wear it while going out alone or with a girlfriend.

"I like it when you're so agreeable." Brundar chuckled. "Even though it's only when it suits you." He unclasped her strapless bra, baring her breasts.

Her nipples breathed a sigh of relief, figuratively speaking. The strapless bra had been tight and uncomfortable, especially when her poor little nipples had beaded with arousal but had nowhere to go.

Brundar traced his finger over the bra's compression lines. "Next time you wear this dress, don't wear this instrument of torture beneath it. Even bondage doesn't leave marks like that."

He lifted her and laid her on the bed. "Arms up, baby."

She stretched like a cat on a windowsill on a lazy afternoon.

Brundar tugged off her tiny thong and cupped her molten center. "I'm going to enjoy the hell out of lapping up all the nectar that you've made for me."

Hopefully, he would do more than that. She had no intention of letting him out of her bedroom until he joined them as one.

This strange and wonderful man belonged to her, and she needed to claim him. She would let him believe he was the one doing the claiming, but at the same time, she would be staking her claim on him.

## 13

## BRUNDAR

It hadn't even crossed Brundar's mind to put Calypso face down as was his habit. Her ass was magnificent, but he liked the frontal view better. Taking a long moment to admire the woman sprawled before him, he started with her lush lips that were upturned in a little secretive smile, continued to her slender wrists and ankles that were secured to the bed frame, then back to her face and her beautiful green eyes that were regrettably covered by a silk scarf.

What would it be like to look into those eyes as he made love to her? To watch every expression?

Except, he had little choice in the matter. It wasn't about him seeing her, but the other way around. Besides, she already had him spellbound. Her eyes had the power to cement that spell in place for good.

"Calypso," Brundar uttered her name like a prayer.

No woman had ever looked as beautiful, as majestic, and as powerful as the one spread-eagled on the bed before him.

A goddess.

She had him wrapped around her little finger, and they both knew it. He might have been the one who'd spanked her and tied her up, but there was no question as to who held the power in this exchange—not in his mind, and not in hers, judging by that victorious smile on her lips.

Were men fools for thinking they were ever really in charge?

He was reminded of a passage from the human Bible that had struck him as odd. As a whole, it was hard to claim the Bible as anything but patriarchal, and yet it said, "Therefore shall a man leave his father and his mother and shall cleave unto his wife; and they shall be one flesh."

The reality of the human world Brundar had grown up in was that the wife left her father and mother and followed her husband. Not the other way around. But he was starting to think that the Bible was spot on. For the right woman, a man would leave everything and everyone dear to him because she was the key to his happiness, his future, and without her there was nothing.

Or more accurately, nothing important.

Being a master swordsman and the clan's best fighter provided Brundar with a sense of worth and no small amount of pride, but only Calypso made him feel needed, wanted, and desired.

"Brundar?" There was a note of worry in her tone.

Did she think he'd left?

He would never leave her side after tying her up, but in a way she was right. He'd retreated inside his own head and had stayed there for far too long. "I'm here."

Her smile was back. "Why are you over there and not over here?"

"I had to take a moment to admire your beauty, sweetling."

The smile got wider.

As he started unbuttoning his dress shirt, Brundar wondered if Calypso was listening for clues. Did she hear him shrugging it off and laying it on the dresser?

"Are you taking off your clothes?" She sounded so hopeful.

"Impatient?"

"You bet."

Kneeling beside her on the bed, he caressed her soft cheek.

"Kiss me," Calypso whispered.

He took her sweet lips, licking into her mouth and sliding his tongue along hers in lazy swipes. Even though his impudent cock strongly disagreed, there was no hurry. Brundar intended to take his time feasting on the beauty before him until he got her senseless with need and climaxing all over his face.

She was already panting restlessly, her nipples so stiff they must've ached.

He would be neglecting his duty if he didn't do something about it right away, providing the relief she needed.

Moving to kneel between her spread legs, Brundar lowered his torso and braced on his forearms.

In anticipation, Calypso arched her back.

Not wanting to prolong her torment, he dipped his head and closed his lips around one turgid peak, treating it to a few swipes of his tongue, then moved to the other and repeated.

The first sound Calypso made was a sigh of relief, the second was a throaty moan, and as his fingers gently tugged on one hard peak while he sucked on the other, her moans became louder.

He loved that she was uninhibited this way. Her moans and her cries of pleasure were his rewards, and she was just as generous with those as she was with everything else.

Kissing his way down her flat belly, Brundar closed his eyes and inhaled the unique musk of her arousal. If he could bottle that scent, he would carry it with him everywhere and take whiffs every time he missed her. She was addictive.

Her belly quivered under him, the muscles contracting in anticipation. "Brundar," she whispered his name like a plea.

"I've got you, sweetling." He licked into her, touching the pad of his thumb to her sensitive nub. She bucked, and he pressed his hand to her belly, holding her down as his tongue rimmed her entrance and his thumb moved in slow circles around the second most erogenous part of her body.

What most men didn't realize was that the seat of a woman's pleasure resided between her ears. That was why sex games were more about altering perception than a specific touch, and why pain could in certain situations be interpreted as pleasure but not in others.

A true master manipulated body and mind.

He pushed a finger inside her, then added another and flattened his tongue over the needy button jutting from the top of her sex.

Her head thrashing from side to side, Calypso alternated between needy moans and impatient hisses. Hanging right on the edge, but unable to dive over it, she needed one final push.

Brundar curled his fingers inside her, pressing on that bundle of nerves that was sure to send her flying, and yet she didn't, her frustrated groans sounding pained.

Strange. Up until now, he'd marveled at how responsive Calypso was, how easily she reached her climaxes, but something seemed to bother her, preventing her from letting go.

Female orgasms were finicky.

Slightly too much or too little touch could make the difference between a woman's ability to orgasm or not. And a disturbing thought could have the same effect. Maybe the ties were too tight?

"What's the matter, baby? Are you uncomfortable? Do you need me to loosen the knots?"

Biting on her lower lip, she shook her head.

"Then what is it? You need to tell me."

"I'm afraid," she whispered.

He hadn't smelled fear on her, but then the scent of her arousal was quite overpowering.

"Of me?"

She shook her head again, her cheeks turning bright red. "I'm afraid that you will make me come with your fingers and your tongue and then leave again like you did before."

Poor girl. She was too anxious to climax.

"I have no plans of leaving without sinking my shaft all the way inside you and fucking you into oblivion like I promised. Where do you keep that stash of condoms you mentioned?"

"The nightstand drawer."

Brundar leaned over her and pulled the drawer open. Calypso hadn't been kidding. She must've emptied the store's entire supply of the brand she'd chosen.

He picked a packet up and chuckled. "Should I be flattered? Size extra-large?"

Worrying her lower lip, Calypso smiled. "What I felt through your pants seemed extra large."

Brundar shook his head, pressing his lips together to stifle his retort. What had she used as comparison? Was that jerk of a husband of hers an extra large? Or was he just a large, and Calypso expected Brundar to be larger?

To voice those thoughts would not only be a dicky thing to do, but it would most likely kill her mood. It was sure as hell killing his.

"Let's try it on and see if you were right."

"Like you don't know."

"Different brands have different sizes. Like shoes." Or so he assumed.

He had no need for them. Immortals didn't contract diseases, and the chances of him impregnating a mortal were slim. Besides, most were on the pill or some other form of contraceptive. The last time he'd used a condom was when a partner had handed it to him, insisting that he put it on before blindfolding her. He couldn't remember what size it was, only that it had felt uncomfortable.

Unbuckling his belt, Brundar hoped he remembered how to use the damned rubber. For his first time with Calypso, he would've preferred nothing between them.

Regrettably, it was not to be. Not unless he thralled her right now, which he didn't want to do either. Sober consent aside, he just wanted to be with the real Calypso, to feel her responses, to hear her moan and plead loudly and clearly with nothing to dilute her experience.

Except for the bloody rubber.

Calypso's belly quivered, and a moment later she erupted in giggles.

His pants and boxers hitting the floor, Brundar paused. "What's so funny?"

"I don't know. Maybe comparing condoms to shoes?" She erupted in a new wave of giggles.

It was anxiety. Calypso had been waiting and preparing for this moment, building up her anticipation, while all along fearing that he would back away. Now that he'd reassured her, her relief was coming out as laughter.

He didn't know what to say in response, but he knew how to stop the giggles.

Thankfully, as he carefully rolled down the condom, it wasn't as uncomfortable as the other one, which meant that Calypso's assessment of his size had been accurate.

Climbing back on the bed, he lowered himself on top of her, bracing his weight on his forearms but letting his chest touch hers.

Calypso sighed in contentment, her body soft and giving under his.

"Are you ready for me, sweetling?" He nuzzled her neck.

"I've been ready since the first moment I saw you."

Reaching a hand between their bodies, he stroked along her wet slit, gathering moisture and dragging it up to tease her.

She arched her back. "Please, Brundar, I can't wait any longer. I need you inside me."

How could he refuse her? How could he refuse himself?

Positioning himself, Brundar breached her entrance with just the head and stilled, giving her time to adjust to the invasion.

She pushed her pelvis up, impaling herself on another inch. "More."

His control snapped, and he surged all the way inside her, filling her, stretching her in a way that must've been painful. And yet, Calypso didn't cry out and didn't drop back down. Instead, she kept her pelvis raised as if afraid he would withdraw before she was ready to let him.

He wasn't about to.

Not yet.

Even the rubber couldn't take away from this moment. Being inside Calypso felt like nothing he'd experienced before.

It was a true joining.

It was perfect.

Did it feel this way because he wasn't indifferent to Calypso like he'd been to all the others?

Or was it something else?

The Fates must really hate him for taunting him with the perfect woman, sending him a human he couldn't have instead of a Dormant or an immortal.

Cupping Calypso's cheeks, he kissed her lips, licking inside her mouth, gently at first then with more fervor as holding still became too much.

He retreated and surged again, then again, ramming into her full force.

By the third thrust, her inner muscles fluttered around him, and she screamed her release into his mouth.

By the fifth pump, his own climax came barreling up his shaft, along with the undeniable need to sink his fangs into Calypso's neck. Clasping her head in an iron grip, he hissed and struck her soft flesh. She tensed as his sharp canines broke her skin, but she didn't jerk back, submitting beautifully to his claiming.

A moment later, Calypso's body went lax under him, and her facial muscles relaxed into an angelic, blissful expression.

Brundar retracted his fangs and licked the twin puncture wounds closed, then buried his face in that same spot he'd just bitten—where her neck met her shoulder.

In a little bit, he would enter her mind and erase the memory of his bite. But in the meantime, he would enjoy the incredible sense of connection for a little longer.

## 14

## CALLIE

Confusion greeted Callie as her brain restarted after short-circuiting for several moments, or was it longer?

With her body languid, and her mind working in slow motion, it was hard to grasp the thoughts swirling around her head like croutons in a French onion soup, and concentrate on anything.

The previous time Brundar had worked her up into a mind-bending orgasm, she'd been out of it for nearly an hour, during which Brundar had removed her restraints, carried her to bed, and cleaned her up. She'd felt none of that, waking up wrapped in blankets with Brundar sitting next to her fresh out of the shower.

This time, however, she must've woken up earlier because she could feel him wiping her gently with a warm washcloth.

Was blacking out and passing out from powerful orgasms normal?

Or maybe it only happened to her twice in a row because both times were firsts.

At the club, Brundar had introduced her to bondage and erotic spanking. The experience had been so intense that it was no wonder she'd passed out after orgasming. Heck, afterward, she'd been as exhausted as if she'd run a marathon.

This time had been just as intense or even more so because Brundar had finally joined them.

Had he felt the same thing she had?

The connection?

The indescribable awareness of finding her way home?

It had been so much more than sex. Then again, it could all have been in her head. The buildup of anticipation prompting her to assign meaning to what was nothing more than incredible sex.

One thing Callie was sure of, though. She wanted more of that. Heck, she wanted that every day, preferably more than once, for the rest of her life. But if it were too much to ask for, she would settle for one daily dose of a mind-blowing orgasm, please.

Brundar was turning her into a sex addict. But it was all good. Craving one man a lot couldn't be unhealthy, right?

She felt Brundar move the warm washcloth to her inner thigh.

Was tending to her privates part of the aftercare she'd read about?

The blindfold was still on, but her arms and legs were free. Callie reached for the washcloth. "You don't have to do this."

With a growl that sounded more animal than human, Brundar moved her hand aside and continued his ministrations. "Better get used to it because I'm always going to take care of you."

Oh, she could get used to him taking care of her, no problem.

The question was what he'd meant by that. Caring for her after sex?

For Callie it meant the whole kit and caboodle, like a commitment and a relationship, and all that jazz.

Except, there was something to be said for Brundar's cleaning routine too, especially when he pushed on her knee and spread her thighs wider. The combination of dominance and gentle care was like an erotic Molotov cocktail on Callie's arousal, igniting it and getting her wet all over again.

It hadn't gone unnoticed. The washcloth disappeared, replaced by Brundar's finger.

She chuckled. "Are you going to punish me for ruining all that careful cleanup work?"

His finger traced her slit. "On the contrary. I'm going to reward you." The finger kept doing wicked things to her.

Callie lifted up to get a little more, only to have Brundar's hand push down on her belly. "Arms over your head, Calypso. Grab onto the headboard and don't let go."

"Yes, sir."

She felt like giggling again. Brundar was trusting her to keep her hands away. Not that she minded him tying her up, not at all, it was hot as heck. But she wanted more than that. Eventually, she hoped he would allow her to touch him. In the meantime, leaving her unrestrained was a step in the right direction.

Getting between her upturned knees, he spread her thighs even wider and blew on her heated flesh. Imagining what he saw, Callie felt a blush creeping up her cheeks. She was completely exposed to his gaze, her lower lips spread so wide that she felt his cool breath all the way inside her.

A moment later his tongue speared into her, pulling a ragged moan from her throat. His strong hands holding her thighs spread wide, he licked and sucked like a man possessed.

It was too much. Callie forgot about keeping her hands up above her head and reached for his head, tugging on his hair.

His warning growl reminded her of her mistake.

Immediately, she reached back for the iron scrolls of the headboard, gripping on to them for dear life.

Brundar stopped his attack for a moment to lift her legs and drape them over his wide shoulders, exposing her even more. But at this point, Callie was beyond caring.

"Please."

She didn't have to wait long.

Penetrating her with two fingers, Brundar sucked her clit in.

Her moan sounding more like a strangled, pained cry, Callie exploded, the tightly wound coil inside her springing free.

Through the orgasmic haze, she heard a wrapper tear, and a moment later Brundar was inside her. He wasn't gentle, going hard and deep with one powerful thrust, then pulling almost all the way out only to ram back inside her full force.

Hanging on to the headboard for dear life, all she could do was spread wide and accept his hammering. It was exhilarating to feel Brundar lose control like that. There was nothing cold or reserved about the man on top of her.

Callie would've given anything to see his face lost to the passion. Grunting and growling, Brundar sounded like a rutting animal, and yet she couldn't imagine him as anything less than the beautiful angel he was.

Her dark angel.

It was a heady feeling to be the one who caused this powerful and proud man to lose control.

His grip on her hips was bruising, but Callie didn't care. He was claiming her, leaving his mark on her, and in turn, she was claiming him. As his shaft swelled inside her, stretching her to her limit, another climax rolled over her like a semitrailer going downhill with no brakes.

She screamed.

But this time she didn't black out.

## 15

# SHAWN

Staring at the divorce papers, Shawn couldn't believe that he'd signed them. Served him right for getting wasted. Weed on its own was harmless, and so was alcohol, but they sure as fuck didn't mix well.

When he'd sobered up, he'd found the signed divorce papers on his coffee table, and purple fingermarks on his neck.

Fuck, he must've attacked the delivery guy.

Shawn smiled. If he'd ended up looking the way he had, the other guy had probably ended up in the hospital. True, he hadn't wrestled since high school, but he was as strong as an ox.

Except, he would've expected the weasel to report him to the police. Maybe he didn't do it because of the damage he'd done to Shawn's neck. It would have been hard to prove who started the fight.

Shawn had been in enough brawls to know that. It was his word against the delivery dude. Maybe the guy had a record and couldn't afford to tangle with the police.

Whatever.

The thing that bothered Shawn the most was that until recently he'd been glad that the bitch had left, and couldn't understand why suddenly it had started making him angry again. After all, he got to keep the house, which was worth much more than the measly amount she'd taken by emptying half of their savings.

The ones she knew about.

The real money was in an account only Shawn had access to. The stupid bitch thought he was depositing all of his income into their joint account. Shawn was way too smart for that. Only the base salary went in there. His commissions and his bonuses and money from the deals he'd made on the side went into his private account.

In that regard, signing the divorce papers without a fight had been a smart move on his part. If lawyers had gotten involved, they might have discovered the money he'd hidden from her, and the fucking whore would have walked out with way more money than she'd ever imagined.

If he'd let her out.

She had been smart running off the way she had.

Nah, Callie was a dumb little cunt. She must've had help. Probably the guy who was screwing her. The one she left Shawn for.

Was it one of the waiters at Aussie?

He needed to go there again and talk with her friends. Get some more information out of them. Callie hadn't told anyone that she was running out on him. She hadn't even told her bosses that she was quitting.

But one of the other bitches must have known something. That slut, Kati, had looked at him funny like she suspected he'd been beating Callie up.

Fuck, maybe if he had, the little bitch would've had more respect for him. He'd been too easy on her because he wanted to get her pregnant. Every month he'd hoped she was, and every month he'd been disappointed.

The slut was probably taking some form of contraceptives. But if she was, she must've hidden it damn fucking well. He went through her things almost every day and checked all her credit card purchases. If she'd been seeing a doctor or buying pills, he would've known.

Sneaky little bitch must've found a way. Maybe her friends had gotten it for her?

He was not going to make the same mistake with the next woman he claimed as his. From the very start, he'd show her who was boss, and she would know her place—barefoot and pregnant and jumping to obey his every command.

# 16

# TESSA

Tessa eyed the two guys standing next to Karen with identical conceited smirks on their handsome faces. Both were young, in their mid-twenties, with athletic builds and hair so short they looked practically bald.

"Good evening, ladies. I want to introduce my two friends, Yoram and Gadi." She pointed at each guy as she said his name. "They've graciously volunteered to be your punching dummies."

The one named Yoram flashed a smile, revealing perfectly straight white teeth. "We didn't volunteer. We've been drafted," he said, casting an accusing glance at Karen.

She shrugged. "I figured my generous hospitality deserved a little something in return." She turned to Yoram. "If you want to crash at my place while visiting Los Angeles, you can put in some work. Except for love, and you have mine, nothing in life is free."

At first glance, the guys seemed intimidating. Standing with their hands clasped behind their backs, their feet parted in a military stance, they looked dark and dangerous. But as soon as Yoram smiled and started his friendly banter with Karen, the knot in Tessa's stomach eased.

Sharon elbowed her. "Yum."

"Uh-huh." They were handsome, but neither could hold a candle to Jackson.

"Ladies, as I've said before, you need to practice your moves on real men in real situations," Karen continued. "Yoram and Gadi are both tough commando soldiers. I know because I trained them both. They can take whatever you dish out. They'll be wearing groin protectors, so that area is not off limits. The only thing you shouldn't do is the eye-gouging move I taught the class before last."

Tessa grimaced, and she wasn't the only one. Karen's no-nonsense fighting technique was brutal in the extreme.

"Both men are well trained, are in peak health, and weigh around two hundred pounds each. The odds are that you will never encounter a heavier or stronger assailant. Let's see if you can take them down."

Karen turned to the guys. "Suit up, boys, and protect those family jewels. I want to see babies from both of you."

Their tough Krav Maga instructor was an interesting cross between a drill sergeant and a pushy mother.

Sharon smirked. "I would like a go at those family jewels."

"Stop it," Tessa hissed in her ear. "They'll hear you."

"No, they won't."

"Whatever, it's not my problem. If you want to flirt with Karen's friends, it's your business.

"Sharon, darling, how about you go first?" Karen's mocking tone convinced Tessa that she'd overheard her friend.

"Sure." Sharon sauntered to the mat area.

The instructor took her by the shoulders and turned her around. "You just stand there, like you're waiting for a bus. Gadi will come at you from behind and grab you. Try to get free."

"Got it." Sharon rotated her shoulders as if she was a fighter getting ready for a match.

Tessa rolled her eyes. Her co-worker was one of the worst students in the class. She was in for some major humiliation.

"Go!" Karen gave the command.

Gadi rushed toward Sharon's back. Catching her around her waist, he lifted her off the ground with one arm as if she weighed nothing and closed his other hand over her mouth to prevent her from screaming for help.

The knot in Tessa's stomach tightened, and she swallowed hard to stop bile from rising up her throat.

*It's not real. It's not real,* she kept repeating in her head as Sharon thrashed in a futile attempt to get free, pin-wheeling her legs as if she'd learned nothing.

Gadi pushed her face down to the mat and pounced on top of her, pinning her hands behind her back.

Karen clapped her hands. "Okay, Gadi, that's enough. Sharon, you can get up."

The guy sprang back to his feet and offered a hand up to Sharon, whose face was redder than a ripe tomato.

Addressing the class, Karen waved a hand in Sharon's direction. "See? This was an excellent example of what not to do when someone grabs you from behind."

Hands on her hips, Sharon hung her head in shame.

The instructor clapped her on her back. "Let's try this again. But this time you do what I taught you, eh?"

Sharon nodded.

"Do you need a moment?"

"I'm good."

Karen clapped her on her back again. "Good, good. This time I'll have Yoram come at you, so you won't know what to anticipate. Ready?"

Sharon nodded.

Yoram grabbed her the same way Gadi had, but used both arms around her middle, pinning her arms to her sides.

This time, Sharon didn't panic and dropped down before he had a chance to tighten his grip. From her squatting position, she straightened, elbowed him in his tummy and ran. Exactly like Karen had taught them to do.

After a few steps, she stopped and turned around. "You let me go. I know I couldn't have gotten away from you if you really held on."

Yoram flashed his cute smile again. "I'm stronger and better trained than the average man. So I allowed for that. But if you want, we can do it again."

With a wink, Sharon shook her head. "Maybe after everyone else has a go and you're tired."

He pointed a finger at her. "It's a date."

Sharon turned and sauntered back toward the group, sashaying her hips, then looked back to catch Yoram ogling her ass.

Someone was going to get lucky tonight.

Karen, being the insightful woman she was, kept Tessa for last. The guys were good sports. Even though they were tired and sweaty, they both kept smiling and encouraging the women to do their worst.

"Tessa, you're next." Karen beckoned her to the mat.

Tessa took a deep breath and got in position. After watching Yoram and Gadi with the other women, she was okay with one of them grabbing her.

*Hopefully.*

The last thing she needed was a panic attack in front of all these women.

Karen walked over to her and bent her knees, so they were eye to eye. "You're small, Tessa. But that's actually an advantage. First of all, no one expects you to fight. You look like easy prey. Use it to your advantage. The faster you respond, the better. The moment he grabs you from behind, make yourself limp as a noodle and drop to the ground. Take a step forward, and while you're getting up, use the momentum to kick him in the groin as hard as you can, then run while he's nursing his balls. Got it?"

"Got it." Tessa glanced at Gadi.

He cupped himself, tapping his knuckles on the rigid protection over his family jewels. "Don't be afraid to hurt me. Kick like your life depends on it. Your foot is probably going to hurt more than my nuts. "

She nodded and turned her back to him.

Gadi lunged at her, gripping her not too gently. But Tessa had practiced this move so many times, the response was instinctive. She didn't need to think what to do next, she didn't need to think at all. She just acted. Turning her body limp as a noodle, she dropped the second she felt him coming at her, not giving Gadi a chance to get a good grip. She turned exactly as Karen had told her to, delivering a roundhouse kick to Gadi's protected family jewels.

Somehow, her kick was powerful enough to send the two-hundred-pound man flying back to land on his butt, gripping his injured privates and writhing on the floor.

Shit, he'd lied to her. Her foot hurt only a little, while he looked like he was in real pain. Unless Gadi was pretending to boost her confidence. She eyed him suspiciously, but he was either a very good actor or hurting for real.

Nevertheless, it had been a commendable performance. Hers as well as his.

Karen was the first one to clap, followed by Yoram and then the rest of the class.

Poor Gadi was still on the mat. Had she really hurt him?

Tessa crouched next to him. "Are you okay? Is this for show, or are you really hurt?"

He winked at her. "A little bit of both. Good job, Tessa." He offered her his hand.

Not sure if he wanted her to help him up or shake it, she opted for the safer route and tried to pull him up.

If he hadn't helped, Gadi would still be down on the mat. His two hundred pounds were more than double her weight.

Karen pulled her away from the smiling Gadi, wrapping her arm around Tessa's shoulders.

"You see, ladies? This is what training can do for you if you practice the way you should. If Tessa can do it, so can you, eh?"

Sharon clapped again, and the rest of the class followed. "Way to go, badass!"

Tessa grinned. She was a badass.

Gadi came over and wrapped his arm around her middle, pulling her away from Karen.

"How about we celebrate? Can I interest you in a drink? Or a cup of coffee with a Danish?" He leaned to whisper in her ear. "I'm not much of a drinker. I'm more of a coffee and cake kind of guy."

Unbelievably, Tessa felt flattered by his flirting, and not anxious at all. "If I weren't engaged, I would've loved to. You're an awesome guy."

He made a pouty face, which looked adorable on his rugged face. "That's a shame. Do you have a friend you can hook me up with?"

She glanced at Sharon, who was all over Yoram. "I think your friend called dibs on mine."

Gadi followed her gaze. "I see. Well, it seems like I'm on my own. Do you know which of these ladies are single?"

"I do." Tessa spent the next five minutes giving Gadi a rundown on each one of the unattached women.

"Thanks," he said when she was done. "I'd better get to work before they all scatter." He rubbed his hands, a predatory gleam shining in his eyes.

It seemed like another lady was going to get lucky tonight.

Karen clapped her hands. "Listen up, ladies. I promised you dangerous jewelry, and I brought samples. Come take a look. If there is anything you like, there is a stack of order forms next to the display you can fill out. When you're done, hand them to me."

Tessa had been waiting for that. After Karen had told them about the rings and bracelets that doubled as weapons, everyone had been looking forward to checking them out.

"This one is simple." She lifted a silver-toned ring with a pointy edge. "You use it as a knuckleduster." Karen demonstrated, making a fist and punching the air with the sharp triangle pointing out.

Tessa put it down on her order form.

"This one is special." Karen put on a heavy ring. "It has a retractable blade."

She pressed on one of the fake jewels and a tiny blade popped out. "Now I know what you're thinking. What on earth can you do with such a small blade?"

With a secretive smirk, she looked around at her eager audience, waiting for someone to make a suggestion. When no one had, she turned to Gadi. "Can you give me a hand?"

He walked over, and Karen handed him duct tape. "Wrap it around my wrists."

When he was done, Karen used the tiny blade to cut through the tape. "This could also work on a rope. Or to gouge out an eye." She jabbed the blade in the air at eye level.

Tessa cringed again but added the blade ring to her order form.

"The bracelet." Karen lifted a plain looking metal cuff with several gaudy fake jewels glued to it. "This you can kill with." She tugged on one of the jewels, pulling out a metal wire so thin that it was barely visible.

Moving fast, she caught poor Gadi by surprise, holding the wire a few inches away from his throat.

Gadi froze. "Careful with that, Karen."

Gasps sounded from all around.

"I am, darling." Karen kissed his cheek and carefully withdrew the wire. "This is so thin, you don't need much force to cut someone's neck. Very useful. But there is a caveat. You need to act fast and catch your nemesis by surprise."

Tessa added the deadly bracelet to her order. "Anything else in your bag of tricks?" she asked Karen.

"Oh, there is plenty. But I didn't bring it all. You can have spiky heels that can kill, sneakers with retractable blades, pendants with tracking devices. You tell me what you want, and I'll bring a sample."

Tessa handed Karen the order form. "I don't know what else there is. So how can I ask for it if I don't know if it exists?"

"Good point. I'll bring the catalog next time."

"When will the stuff I ordered get here?"

"A few weeks. Everything is made in China. Slow shipping."

That was a shame. Tessa couldn't wait to have all those gadgets. She'd feel like a real 007.

Casting a quick glance at Sharon, she saw her friend was still busy flirting with Yoram. But it was okay.

After today's lesson, Tessa felt confident enough to go out into the dark street and walk to her car by herself.

17

## JACKSON

"All done," Gordon announced. "I'm ready to hit the sack."
Jackson glanced at his watch. "Dude, it's only eight-thirty." He needed to talk to his friends about their future.
Gordon was leaving at the beginning of the school year for the University of Arizona, and Vlad was starting Santa Monica College. At least he was staying in town.
"I'm tired. I just want to get in bed and watch a few episodes of *Rick and Morty* before I fall asleep."
Both Gordon and Vlad were obsessed with the cartoon. It had a few funny episodes, but Jackson didn't get their fascination with it.
"I want to talk to you guys."
Gordon sighed. "About?"
"What am I going to do when you guys are in college?"
Vlad emerged from the kitchen with a six pack of soda cans. "I'm still here."
"Yeah, but how many hours can you work?"
His friend folded his long and wiry frame into the front booth and popped the lid off one of the sodas. "I can still do the mornings, preparing the dough and doing the baking for the day, but I can't stay after that."
That was better than nothing, but not enough. Jackson pushed his bangs back and slid into the booth next to Vlad. "I'm thinking about closing the café."
Gordon sat across from them and grabbed one of the sodas. "That's extreme. Why don't you hire a couple of humans?"
"It's not going to be the same without you guys."
Gordon put a hand over his heart. "I'm touched. But really, man, life goes on. You can't expect things to stay the same."
"I know. It sucks. Vlad and I will need to find a new drummer for the band."
Jackson had known that one day they would need to part ways, but he'd hoped he had more time.

"What about the new place?" Vlad asked. "The village needs someone to run the café over there."

The thought had crossed his mind. Nathalie couldn't manage it for the foreseeable future, but Carol was doing fine without her.

"Kian will probably close the one in the keep and Carol will manage the new one."

Gordon shook his head. "I overheard Bhathian talking about her training for some secret mission."

Jackson's ears perked up. "And you kept it to yourself? Talk!"

Gordon shrugged. "I don't know what it's about. Bhathian was talking to Andrew about it, and both of them were shaking their heads like it was the dumbest idea ever."

Whatever it was, Carol leaving the café was news to Jackson. Without her, there would be no one to run the old or the new place, and people would be majorly bummed if that happened. Besides, it was a wasted business opportunity.

If he could figure out the logistics, maybe he could jump on it.

"I can't run the place by myself."

Vlad put his empty can on the table. "What about Onidu? He's doing a fine job."

"If Amanda agrees for him to continue, then I might be able to pull it off. But I still need you to bake."

"I said I would."

For a few moments, the three of them sat in silence, thinking.

Gordon lifted his head. "Maybe you could advertise a position on the clan's digital bulletin board. Not everyone works full time. Before Carol took over Nathalie's café, she was a bum. Does Sylvia work?"

Jackson shook his head. "I don't know."

The board was a good idea, though. Maybe some of those who had jobs would want to quit after moving to the village. The commute was going to be much longer. Besides, the place was so nice people would want to hang around.

"Tessa and I applied for a house."

Gordon grinned and lifted his palm for a high five. "Congratulations, man. Moving in together is a big step."

"We didn't hear from Kian yet. Maybe we need to be officially mated first."

Vlad toyed with his empty can, squeezing and bending it into different shapes. "That's an even bigger step. Are you sure about it? You're still a kid."

"I don't feel like a kid. And yes, I'm sure."

Vlad flipped his long bangs back. "Then you're lucky. I wish I could find a girl. I wouldn't even mind a human."

Jackson sighed. "Tessa is still one."

Vlad patted his shoulder. "Don't worry. She will turn. The Fates would not have brought her to you just to dangle happiness in your face and then take it away."

That was exactly what Jackson was afraid of. "The Fates are not always kind. Sometimes I think that they like to play with us. They get bored and look for poor saps like me to mess with."

It felt both good and bad to finally voice his fears. He'd been keeping them inside himself for too long, fronting optimism for Tessa's sake.

Vlad shook his head. "I don't think the Fates are capricious. I think they just have a bigger plan than we can see."

Gordon pushed to his feet. "All this talk about Fates is one big bullshit. I'm going to bed. You guys can discuss philosophy without me."

Jackson nodded. "Goodnight, Gordon."

The guy took a few steps then turned around. "I'm sorry, Jackson. I know that you're scared, and believing in some cosmic order makes you feel better. I shouldn't have said anything."

"No, that's okay. You're right. The moment I start relying on the Fates is the moment I start relying less on myself, which is not good. I will do what I can, and if the Fates want to help, that's great. But if they don't, it's fine too."

Gordon smiled. "That's the Jackson we all know and love. One hell of a cocky bastard who thinks he can take on the world and win."

"You betcha."

# 18

# RONI

Roni's new throne room left a lot to be desired, but considering that it started with a hospital bed and an assortment of medical equipment, he couldn't complain.

In fact, he was so comfortable he was considering adopting the same setup once the doctor cleared him to leave.

William's assistants, a bunch of super nerds Roni felt right at home with, were quite enterprising. They had rigged him up a contraption that suspended two large monitors over his bed, which he could move every which way he pleased. A regular hospital rolling table doubled as his keyboard desk, and the large towers were cooling behind the bed.

Bridget wasn't happy about the freezing temperature in the room; it wasn't the optimal environment for someone sick with pneumonia, but perfect for keeping the equipment running at optimum level.

Roni was used to working in a cold room.

Besides, Sylvia had brought him a sweater, a scarf, a knit beanie, and fingerless cashmere gloves to keep him nice and warm. She was a keeper, just as Mildred had told him.

Damn, he missed Barty and his wife.

Working on and off all morning, Roni had been taking occasional naps when he'd gotten too tired. The fucking pneumonia was making him not only weak like a baby, but melancholy. Otherwise, he wouldn't be thinking about his old crusty handler and his wife, Mildred.

Being sick literally sucked the life out of him. It might have been his imagination, but Roni was convinced his hard-earned muscles were shriveling by the hour. Once he was back on his feet, he would be back to the scrawny scarecrow he was before a year of working out had filled him out a bit.

Fuck. He hated working out.

What a waste of time. The hour a day he spent working on improving his unimpressive physique could've been put to better use hacking and programming.

Someone knocked on the door.

"I'm busy!"

Another disadvantage of working from a hospital room was the doctor or one of her nurses interrupting him with their unnecessary checkups. He really didn't need his temperature and blood pressure taken once an hour every hour, day and night. It wasn't as if pneumonia was a deadly disease, at least he didn't think it was.

Ignoring Roni's clear dismissal, the knocker, a Lord of the Rings elf prince lookalike, opened the door and strode in as if he owned the place.

"I'll be brief," he said in a monotone voice. All that was missing was an Austrian accent, and it would've sounded a lot like the famous "I'll be back."

Roni gave the intruder a once-over. An intimidating dude. "And you are?"

"Brundar." The elf lookalike didn't offer his hand. Instead, he inclined his head in a gesture that looked more like a nod than an attempted introduction.

*Wait a minute...*

Brundar? The guy who gave Andrew the shivers?

It was good Roni was meeting the guy here, where he'd established his position as king, and not at the dojo. Otherwise, he would've felt intimidated as hell.

"I heard about you."

Brundar lifted a brow.

"Anandur threatened Andrew to bring you as my initiator if Andrew refused to do the honors."

Brundar regarded Roni as if he was an ant under a microscope. "Anandur should've done it."

Roni grimaced. "He couldn't get aggressive with me. I was not enough of a challenge."

Brundar nodded. "I can see how that could be a problem for him."

"But not for you?"

The guy affected a chilling smile. "Not for me."

He could see why Andrew didn't like the guy. From now on whenever Roni imagined a cold-hearted assassin, he would see this guy's face. And the fact that Brundar was enviously good-looking, like a fallen angel, only enhanced the chilling effect instead of softening it.

"What can I do for you?" It would be in Roni's best interest to have the guy indebted to him. If he ever needed anyone taken out, Roni would know who to turn to.

"William is not here, and you're supposedly one hell of a hacker."

"Not supposedly. I'm the best."

Brundar's lips twitched. "And modest, I see."

Roni shrugged. "It's not boasting when it's the truth."

"Can you hack into a university's computers and change the name of a student? A friend of mine got accepted, but she needs to go under a different name."

"So you need me to change her records to reflect a different one?"

"Exactly."

"I will need a new social security number for the new name."

"I'm having them done. Birth certificate, social security, driver's license, passport, the works."

"Excellent. When do you need it done?"

"How soon can you do it?"

Roni had a lot on his plate, and hacking into hundreds of security camera feeds was time-consuming. If he waited until he was done with all of that to help Brundar's friend, it would be several days before he could get to it.

"William left a big project for me, but I'm willing to take a short break to help your friend. It will set me back a couple of hours." Let the guy think it was a bigger deal than it really was.

"Thanks. I owe you, kid."

Roni smirked. *Music to my ears.* "Get me her old and new papers."

"I'll come later when I have them. Does it matter to you what time?"

Roni shook his head. "Not really. I'm sick, as you can see, so I need to take short naps from time to time. If I'm sleeping when you come back, wake me up."

Brundar nodded, then smoothed his palm over his blond hair. "I don't know how it works with you being a human. Do I pay you? Can I get you something in return for the favor?"

"I'll take an unspecified IOU."

It was funny to watch the guy who was pale as a vampire to start with getting even paler. "That can be anything."

Roni chuckled. "Don't worry. I don't want your first-born or anything like that. I don't even know what kind of favor you're good for."

"I obey the law. So whatever you have in mind it can't be illegal."

Roni lifted a brow. "Says the guy who just asked me to falsify records."

Brundar shifted, putting his weight on his other foot. "That's different. Think of it as a witness protection program."

"What did she see?" Roni got excited. He was so bored with the project he was working on, he was hungry for a good story.

"It's not like that. Her ex-husband is dangerous. If he finds her, he will harm her."

The smile evaporated from Roni's face. "Say no more, my friend. It shall be done. No future favors required."

For the first time since he'd arrived, Brundar regarded Roni with real respect. Apparently, his hacking skills hadn't impressed the guy as much as his gallantry.

"I appreciate that. Whatever I can help you with, I will. Not as a favor, but as one warrior to another."

Roni snorted. "Warrior?" He looked down at himself. "Damn, this sweater must make me look good." He patted the sleeve. "But regrettably it's all false advertisement. There isn't much underneath."

Brundar didn't laugh at his joke. Hell, the guy looked like he never did.

"We utilize different weapons, but we fight on the same team."

Roni lifted his palm for a high five, but Brundar ignored it.

*Strange dude.*

He let his arm drop. "Thank you. I always thought of myself as a cyber warrior, but you're the first one to acknowledge me as one."

Brundar inclined his head. "I'll be back with the papers." He turned on his heel and walked out without saying goodbye.

Kind of impolite, but then Roni often acted just as rude if not worse. The difference was that Roni was well aware of it and did it on purpose, while Brundar was just weird.

19

# CALLIE

Callie's afternoon walk almost always ended at the neighborhood grocery store. With no car, she could only carry so much back home. The solution was to buy only what was necessary for whatever she planned on cooking for dinner and for breakfast the next day.

Her lunch was usually leftovers from dinner.

Unless Brundar came over, and then she had to stock up on more stuff.

Callie smiled. Feeding him was such a pleasure. The guy ate the way he made love, giving it his complete and undivided attention and savoring every little bite.

Absentmindedly, she rubbed a spot on her neck that held a ghost memory of a bite. She must've dreamt it because her neck was spotless. Brundar hadn't even left a hickey.

Probably a tiny bug bite she couldn't see or feel.

It had been two days since he'd made love to her. He'd said hi at the club, but that had been the extent of their interactions.

The logical part of her brain told her that he was busy. Guarding his cousin during the day and helping Franco run the club evenings and nights counted as two full-time jobs. It was a wonder Brundar had managed the little time he'd spent with her. In fact, he'd told her that he'd asked for a half a day off just so he could have an early dinner with her.

The other part of her brain, the one that was more emotional, felt neglected and unwanted.

He was avoiding her.

Today, Callie was once again eating dinner alone. It was no fun to cook for one, but she needed to eat, and there was no way she was going to stoop to sandwiches or frozen dinners. A simple dish of spaghetti with mushroom sauce that took about fifteen minutes to make was what she was planning for tonight.

It was inexpensive, which was important since she was saving as much as she could to pay for school. Tomorrow, she'd eat the leftovers for lunch.

The only time Callie splurged on food was when cooking for Brundar.

Back at her building, she took the stairs up to her apartment. At her door, she put the grocery bag on the floor and shuffled through her purse looking for her keys.

The sound of the elevator doors opening had her turn around. Maybe it was her next door neighbor. The apartment adjacent to hers had been dark and quiet for the entire time Callie had lived there.

A woman was muscling a suitcase out of the elevator while pushing a carryon in front of her. Callie rushed over to hold the doors from closing on the suitcase.

"Thank you," the woman said, finally getting the heavy luggage past the metal sill. "I always over pack, forgetting I also need to schlep the thing around."

"Let me take this." Callie reached for the carryon.

"Thank you." The woman let go of the handle. "I'm right over here." She pointed at the door to the apartment next to Callie's.

"I thought no one lived there," Callie said as the woman pulled out her keys.

"I travel a lot." She offered her hand. "Hi, I'm Stacy."

Callie shook her hand. "I'm Callie."

Stacy opened her door. "Would you like to come in?"

Callie chuckled. "You just came back from what must've been a long trip. How about you come over to my place and eat dinner with me?"

Stacy looked tempted but shook her head. "Thank you. That's really nice of you, but I need to unpack, take a shower, etc."

It was quite obvious that the only reason Stacy had declined was that she was embarrassed about accepting a dinner invitation from a neighbor she'd just met.

"Come on. You can do it later. I hate eating alone. Besides, you probably have nothing edible in your fridge."

Stacy grimaced. "Don't remind me. I don't want to know what grew in there while I was gone."

"So, does it mean you're coming?"

"Yeah, you twisted my arm. Let me just push that monster inside."

Callie lent Stacy a hand. The suitcase had wheels, but it was so heavy they barely moved. "How much did you have to pay for excess weight?"

Stacy closed the door and followed Callie to her apartment. "The company I work for pays all of my travel expenses."

"Oh, yeah? What do you do, if you don't mind me asking?" Callie put the grocery bag on the counter and motioned for Stacy to take a seat.

"I'm a business consultant. I go in, talk to everyone, see what needs improvement, and sometimes even oversee the implementation."

Callie pulled out the box of spaghetti from the bag. "Sounds fascinating."

"It is."

"I'll brew us some coffee."

"Thank you. I need it."

Filling up a pot with water, Callie put it on the stove, then popped a pod into the machine. "I'm making spaghetti with mushroom sauce. I hope you're not allergic to mushrooms."

Stacy slapped a hand on her thigh. "Not counting the peculiar swelling of my hips, which is a reaction I get to any kind of food, I'm not allergic to anything."

Callie chuckled. "I have a similar allergy. Though in my case the swelling happens in my tummy."

Stacy cast her an incredulous glance. "What are you talking about, girl?"

"I'm a waitress. So I'm on my feet a lot. That's the only reason I don't gain weight."

Stacy frowned, making Callie uncomfortable. Was she one of those snobs who looked down at waiters and cashiers and the like?

"You must be getting excellent tips to afford this place."

Callie relaxed. The frown wasn't about what she'd thought. "I'm apartment sitting for the professor who lives here. He was kind enough not to charge me rent."

"Mike?"

She had no idea. "I guess so. The whole thing was brokered through a friend of his. I don't even know his name."

Stacy shook her head. "Mike moved out over a month ago. He got a job at Arizona State."

"I was under the impression that he was teaching a semester abroad."

"He did. Two years ago."

"Are you sure?"

"Positive."

*What the hell?*

What kind of a story had Brundar invented and why?

"Maybe we are not talking about the same person. Maybe another professor rented this apartment after Mike left and then got an offer to teach abroad."

Stacy crossed her legs. "I guess that's the only plausible explanation. After all, several professors live in this building because it's so close to USC. That's why the rent is so expensive."

Callie put on a smile. "Mystery solved. How do you like your coffee?" She changed the subject.

Frankly, she didn't believe for a moment the explanation she'd offered Stacy. Brundar had rented the apartment for her and concocted the story about the professor. The landlady had probably told him about the previous tenant, and that was where he'd gotten the idea for his lie from.

The question was why?

And if he'd lied about that, what else had he lied about?

"Black, with stevia if you have it."

"Sorry. I only have regular sugar."

"Then one teaspoonful of sugar it is."

## 20

# BRUNDAR

*B*rundar had used his lunch hour to visit the document forger at his downtown studio. Francis's day job was artistic photography, and he was quite famous in the art community, but that didn't mean he was making money. For that he relied on his share in the clan profits, supplementing his income with superb forgeries.

"Did you get the name and social from the hacker? You're aware that I only make the documents, right?" Francis asked.

"I did."

Kian had another source for those. Though with Roni on board, Brundar didn't expect they would need that other hacker for much longer. Right now the kid was too busy with the assignment William had dropped on him, but once he was done with that, he'd be free for all the other things they needed a hacker for.

"I will have them ready for you tomorrow. Should I put it on Kian's tab, or are you paying for that yourself?"

"I'm paying."

"I'll give you the special clan discount. Seven hundred fifty instead of twelve hundred. Cash, of course."

"No problem."

Francis nodded, knowing not to offer a handshake.

Brundar glanced at his watch. He had less than twenty minutes to get back to the keep for Kian's emergency Guardian meeting, which meant he wouldn't have time to grab something to eat. Hopefully, Okidu would serve refreshments.

"Roni already has a wide area covered," Kian opened the meeting. "William's squad is going to monitor the feeds and alert the Guardian on duty if they see anything suspicious. I want you to start rotations. The murders have all happened after dark, so I'm not going to waste your time on that during the day. Onegus has prepared a schedule that requires each one of you to be on the alert five hours every other night."

Brundar groaned. Between his Guardian duty and managing the club, he was already stretched to capacity.

"Is there a problem, Brundar?" Kian asked.

"Could we suspend the self-defense classes until this is over?"

Kian nodded. "I don't like it, but I can't expect you guys to work sixteen hours a day."

Anandur snorted. "As if it ever stopped you before."

"In times of emergency, you bet your ass I expect you to give me everything you got. But this doesn't qualify as one."

Onegus tapped his pen on the conference table. "Should I inform all of our students that classes are suspended until further notice?"

"Carol and Kri can teach a few," Brundar offered.

Kri crossed her arms over her chest. "You guys are chauvinist pigs."

Kian glared at her. "As I said before, I'm not going to risk a female against a Doomer. These are all well trained immortal males."

"Yeah, yeah. The little lady will stay and teach the kids."

"You betcha. Onegus, talk with Carol and see what she can handle, then divide the classes between her and Kri."

Onegus nodded. "I'm going to email you the schedules with the area you should hang around. I also rented motorcycles for all of you so you can get to the scene of the crime faster. The helmets are also good to disguise your features."

Anandur rubbed his hands. "Which ones did you get?"

"BMWs."

"Sweet. Are they here already?"

"In the parking garage."

Anandur pushed his chair back. "Are we done? Can I go check out the new toys?"

"We are done." Kian rose to his feet. "I'll come with you. I need a crash course in riding one."

Anandur wrapped his arm around Kian's shoulder. "I'll teach you all you need to know."

Brundar parted ways with the gang at the elevators. The motorcycles would have to wait until after he'd had a couple of sandwiches from the vending machine in the lobby. At the rate his stomach was rumbling, even the powerful BMW engine wouldn't drown out the noise it was making.

At the café, he bought two readymade sandwiches and a muffin, then walked over to the counter.

"What can I get you, my absentee sensei?" Carol bowed her head in mock respect.

"Coffee. Large."

"Coming up, sir."

"Anandur was supposed to take over your training."

Carol shrugged. "He's busy too. Everyone is. We managed one session this week." She handed him a large paper cup.

"The Guardians are starting nightly rotations. You and Kri will have to take over the self-defense classes."

"Do I have to?" Carol grimaced. "We are seriously understaffed in pretty much every department. I'm voting for employing humans. But of course, no one is asking for my vote."

"If you can figure out how to do it without revealing who we are, I'm sure Kian would love to hear it."

"Humans can run the café. We just need to be careful how we behave around them."

"That doesn't solve the shortage of Guardians problem."

She shook her head. "Kian needs to start using the reserves. Make it mandatory for all ex-Guardians to give one month a year. You know, like the National Guard. They are serving a few weeks every year, and if there is a war, they are called in to serve."

"I like your idea."

Carol beamed. "Thank you. A compliment from you means a lot to me." She put a hand over her heart.

"But I think Kian had trouble convincing the retired Guardians to come in for training. Most are willing to come in case of emergency, but that's all."

Her face fell. "Oh."

Brundar allowed himself a small smile. "See you later, Carol. And don't give Anandur too hard of a time."

She saluted. "Do I ever?"

Not really. She was mouthy and didn't walk on eggshells around him like everyone else, but other than that Carol was a good person. Dedicated. Loyal.

Taking his coffee in one hand, Brundar tucked the two wrapped sandwiches under his other arm, grabbed the muffin, and turned to look for an empty table. There were a few, but on an impulse, he chose to join Robert at his.

"May I?"

Robert glanced at him over his newspaper, a surprised expression on his face. "Go ahead."

Brundar put down his lunch and pulled out a chair. "Any news on the murders?" he asked to start a conversation.

"Thank Mortdh, I mean the Fates, it was quiet for the past several days."

Brundar unwrapped his first sandwich. "We are starting nightly rotations."

"I overheard you talking with Carol. I'm glad. I hope you catch the bastard fast."

With a nod, Brundar bit into his sandwich and thought about what had motivated him to sit with the ex-Doomer.

The truth was that he needed to talk to someone, and none of the males he worked with was a good candidate for a sounding board. Robert was still an outsider. Besides, the guy had an inventive mind. The ideas he'd come up with for the village were all excellent. Robert appeared to be a simpleminded fellow, but surprisingly he had the ability to think outside the box.

"Did you ever have a relationship with a human female?"

Robert frowned. "Aside from sex? No. Why do you ask?" He sounded offended.

Too late, Brundar realized his question might have implied suspicion on his part, somehow connecting Robert to the murders. Which prompted him to be more direct.

"I wondered how an immortal male who grew to care about a human female could end their relationship without hurting her feelings."

"Oh." Robert raked his fingers through his shortly cropped hair. "My only experience is with Carol." He leaned closer and lowered his voice. "Ending it wasn't my choice. Maybe you should ask her how to dump someone. Though I can't say my feelings weren't hurt."

Brave guy. Admitting to having been dumped took courage.

"I appreciate your honesty." Brundar unpacked his second sandwich.

"Sure." Robert smiled. "When Carol and I were in Vegas, I worked on a construction site with a crew of humans. They gave me good advice on how to pursue a woman, but not how to end things with one."

Brundar put the sandwich down on the wrapper. "Did it work? The advice?"

"Yeah, it did. But a man can only pretend for so long to be someone he is not. Carol wasn't interested in the real me."

## 21

## TESSA

Jackson eyed her. "You look different."

"How so?" Tessa patted her hair. Her hairdo hadn't changed since Eva had insisted on a total makeover. The color was still very blond, the cut very blunt, the length just a little longer.

"Your eyes sparkle. You seem upbeat, full of energy."

Her boyfriend, or should she start thinking of him as her fiancé? never missed anything.

"I kicked ass yesterday at Karen's class."

"Oh, yeah? Whose?"

"Karen brought two guys for us to practice on. They were both big, tough soldiers she'd trained herself."

Jackson frowned. "Did they frighten you?"

He knew men intimidated her, especially big ones. She shrugged. "At first, a little. But they were both so friendly. And flirty."

The creases between his brows deepened. "Who flirted with you?"

"His name was Gadi. But he was chill when I told him I'm engaged. He asked me to point out all the single ladies. Sharon called dibs on the other one, Yoram." Tessa smirked. "I'm pretty sure she took him home with her."

Jackson was still glaring at her.

"Are you jealous, baby?"

"You're damn right, I'm jealous. I don't want any guys sniffing you up."

"Ugh, Jackson. That's gross. It sounds like you're talking about dogs."

"Men are dogs."

She lifted a brow. "Are you a dog?"

"Except for me. I'm a prince among men."

He was so cute. Tessa stretched up to her tiptoes and kissed his pouting lips. "Yes, you are."

That seemed to mollify him. But she felt like teasing him some more. "You keep saying that I'm hot. Do you expect no one to notice?"

For a moment, he seemed stumped, and she was ready to declare herself the winner of the teasing contest. But this was Jackson. He always had a comeback.

"Noticing you is a given, but not flirting. You don't go smiling at some guy who just had his hands all over you and expect him not to think of it as an invitation to flirt."

Tessa put her hands on her hips. "So what are you saying? That I can't even smile at anyone?"

"Not if they are male, between the age of seventeen to forty-five for humans, and no limit for immortals."

She lifted her chin. "I'm going to smile at whomever I want."

Jackson grinned wickedly as he dipped his head to look her straight in the eyes. "Is that so? What if I smile at whomever I want too?"

Crap. Jackson's smile could melt the panties off a librarian. Tessa didn't want him turning that charm on any woman, young or old.

She pointed a finger at him. "Don't you dare activate that pussy magnet of yours."

He almost choked on the snort that escaped his throat. "A pussy magnet? Where did that come from?"

She felt her cheeks get warm. Tessa made a point of never using language like that. "That's what Gordon calls you."

"I need to have a talk with Gordon about keeping his mouth clean around my fiancée."

Tessa slapped his bicep. "Oh, no you don't." Gordon and Vlad would never talk freely around her again. She liked that they treated her as one of the gang.

Jackson leaned in again, mirth dancing in his eyes. "Or what?"

Catching his chin between her thumb and forefinger, she mock glared back. "Or I'll kick your butt."

Instead of laughing or coming up with another teasing comeback, he got somber. "Yeah, you should. I should've thought of that sooner. You can practice on me." He patted his chest.

When she looked unsure, he flashed her his panty-melting smile. "Come on, kitten, show me your moves."

The effect of that smile combined with that seductive tone was that Tessa couldn't deny him anything. Besides, she was quite proud of herself and wanted to show off. The problem was that Jackson was way too strong and his reflexes were lightning fast. Her only chance was taking him by surprise.

"Okay. Let's clear some floor space." She lifted the folding tray they used as a coffee table.

Jackson took it out of her hands. "I'll clear the area, you bring the comforter from the couch and spread it on the floor."

She rolled her eyes. He was such a macho guy, never letting her lift anything.

Pushing the TV stand all the way under the window, Jackson cleared even more space.

Tessa took off her shoes and spread the comforter over the hardwood floor. "I'm going to stand here with my back to you as if I'm waiting for a bus. You sneak up behind me and grab me."

Jackson took off his sneakers and went to stand out in the hallway. "I'm very stealthy. Listen to the floor crack. That's how you'll know I'm coming at you."

"Thanks, Sherlock. I'm supposed to figure it out on my own."

"I don't make as much noise as a human because I pay attention to it. My hearing is much more acute."

"Okay." She turned her back to him, her whole body tensing in preparation for his attack. "I'm ready."

He was so fast, she felt the air move like a slight breeze a split second before his arms came around her.

Not giving him the opportunity to tighten them, Tessa twisted and dropped down, slipping through his loose grip. Bracing her crouching form with a hand on the floor, she turned her hips and delivered a roundhouse kick to his groin.

Jackson cupped his injured equipment and crumpled to the floor, his face twisted in pain.

"Oh, my God! I'm so sorry! I didn't think. Crap!" She kneeled next to him. "I should have told you to stuff a pillow in your pants."

It took him a moment until he was able to speak. "It's okay. You're amazing. I didn't expect you to get free, let alone kick me in the nuts."

Tessa winced. "Is there anything I can do?"

"Ice would help."

"Got it."

She rushed downstairs, filled a Ziploc bag with ice cubes, and rushed back, taking the stairs two at a time.

She handed him the ice bag.

"Thank you, baby." Jackson pushed his pants down and held the ice bag over his injured parts with only the thin fabric of his briefs as a barrier. After a few moments, his face relaxed.

"I'm so sorry." Tessa caressed his arm.

"Don't be. You can't harm me. Knowing you can kick ass for real is worth getting my equipment temporarily out of commission. I should come with you to your next class and thank Karen in person for teaching you to fight like that."

"I'm her best student." Tessa felt like she was allowed a little boasting. She was so damn proud of excelling at something she never believed she would.

"I bet you are. Just don't tell the guys that you've taken me down. Instead of a pussy magnet, I'll be called pussy whipped, or just a pussy." He groaned and kicked his pants all the way off. Lying down on the comforter, he lifted his knees so he could apply the ice pack to where he needed it most.

Ogling his powerful thighs and calves, Tessa felt like a lecher. He was in pain, because of what she'd done, and all she could think about was how sexy his body was. Then again, it wasn't her fault that Jackson was built like an Adonis. It was impossible not to ogle.

If she could only find an excuse for him to remove his T-shirt. And his briefs.

## 22

# JACKSON

Nursing his bruised kahunas, Jackson didn't immediately notice Tessa's expression turn from remorseful and concerned to horny and wistful. But luckily for him, he didn't have to rely solely on sight to figure out what his girl was in the mood for.

The faint aroma of her nascent arousal was affecting him even before he'd become aware of it. An immortal male couldn't ignore his female's arousal even if he wanted to. Especially while she was so close, kneeling next to him on the floor, so his nose was mere inches away from that intoxicating smell.

"How are you feeling?" Tessa asked, her voice turning husky. "Do you want me to kiss it all better?"

And just like that Jackson's shaft surged up, forgetting all about the pain and readying for action. "Do you think it would help?" he teased.

"I'm sure it would." Tessa licked her lips. "But for it to work, you need to take off all of your clothes."

He liked the game she was playing. "I heard that for the healing to commence, both the healer and the injured need to get naked."

Tessa stifled a smile, going for a serious face. "Well, if it's in the name of healing, then all right. Should I help you with your briefs? It looks as if it would be difficult to get them past that impressive bulge."

"By all means." Tossing the Ziploc with the semi-melted ice cubes aside, Jackson lifted his torso off the floor, pulled his T-shirt over his head, then lay back down. "At your service, miss."

Tessa hooked her fingers in the elastic band of his boxer briefs and tugged down just a little, then reached inside and freed his aching cock before pulling them all the way down.

Staring, she licked her lips again. Could it be that she really enjoyed taking him in her mouth? He knew plenty of girls who did, but given Tessa's past, he would've never expected her to enjoy this. Especially when it was one-sided giving of pleasure.

"Nah-ah, kitten. You don't get to lick before you take your clothes off. A deal is a deal."

"True."

Jackson crossed his arms under his head, lifting it so he could watch Tessa strip for him.

Holding his eyes, she pulled her shirt over her head and tossed it on the couch, then unhooked her bra and aimed at the couch but missed. "Basketball is not in my future." She smiled sheepishly.

Jackson had a hard time focusing on anything other than her perky breasts. To keep from reaching for them, he laced the fingers behind his head and held on tight.

Her jeans and panties were next, tossed unceremoniously toward the couch, this time making the target.

"Score!" Tessa pumped her little fist in the air.

She was so fucking adorable, Jackson wanted to lick her all over. Which he planned on doing very soon. There was no way he was allowing a repeat of what had happened last time. He would make sure this was as different from any oral she'd experienced in the past as it could get.

"Okay, Mr. Patient, may I proceed with my therapy now?"

"You may."

His cock sprang up, standing at full mast.

Kneeling by his side, Tessa inched closer. She smacked her lips as she wrapped her palm around the base, then lowered her head and flicked her tongue over the head. She looked up, smiled, and then did it again, circling all around in little teasing licks.

Already, this was nothing like the other time.

Yeah, Tessa was kneeling, but over him and not at his feet. This time, she was playful, enjoying tormenting him with little flicks of her wet tongue, and not trying to get him off. But even though she refrained from giving him the pleasure of taking him deep down her throat, Jackson preferred the teasing a hundred times over to that professional display of skill from before.

This was fun.

He was going to let her play for a little bit longer, then show her something new and exciting. "Are you having fun, kitten?"

"Mm-hmm." She took the head into her mouth.

"Then let me show you something that is even more fun." Reaching for her hips, he lifted her up and twisted her around to straddle his head.

She let his cock slide out of her mouth but kept her palm wrapped around the base as if afraid it would flop the moment she let go. Silly girl. His dick knew what was good for him. He wasn't going anywhere other than her hot, welcoming mouth.

Tessa looked at him over her shoulder. "What are you doing?"

In response, Jackson pulled her sweet bottom closer and licked her slit.

She moaned. "Oh. I like this."

He chuckled. "I thought you would. It's called sixty-nine."

She giggled, but her laughter died out when he flicked his tongue over her clit.

"Oh, oh, keep doing that."

Her head thrown back, rocking her sex against his tongue, Tessa was too absorbed in her own pleasure to remember that this was supposed to be simultaneous.

Not one to be petty about things like that, Jackson gave her a few moments of his undivided attention, both of them concentrating solely on her pleasure.

But he wasn't a saint.

With his heels digging into the comforter-covered floor, he thrust up, reminding Tessa that his dick was waiting for some tender, loving care.

She took him into her mouth again, just a small portion of his length, treating the rest of it to up and down pumping with her soft palm.

This was good, better than good. He loved driving her crazy with his mouth and his tongue and his fingers.

The girl who'd been so skittish at the beginning, the one whose expectations had been limited to being able to endure sex as opposed to truly enjoy it, had turned into a most wonderfully responsive woman who loved what he was doing to her and reached climax with ease.

He was lucky beyond belief.

Splaying his hands over her tight little ass, he gripped her and licked in bliss, making growling sounds while at it to let her know how much he loved eating her up.

The growling must've excited Tessa. She moaned around his shaft and took him deeper.

When he let go of one hip and pushed a finger inside her tight wetness, she groaned, the vibrations almost sending him over.

He wasn't going to last. But he'd be damned if he didn't bring her to the finish line first.

Withdrawing his finger, Jackson came back with two and flicked his tongue over her clit. Her juices running down his fingers and onto his chin, Tessa groaned again and took him all the way to the back of her throat.

This time he was all for it.

As he shouted his release and pushed deeper, her tight channel contracted around his fingers. Driven by instinct, Jackson moved his mouth to the side, flicked his tongue over a soft spot on her inner thigh, and bit down.

Tessa climaxed again.

When the fog lifted from his blood-deprived brain, Jackson felt her little tongue licking him clean. The venom wasn't affecting her as strongly as it had the first couple of times. He, on the other hand, was losing his fucking mind every time he bit her.

Damn it. He shouldn't have come inside her mouth.

Lifting her up by her hips, he turned her around and laid her over him like a blanket. Exhausted, she put her head on his chest and sighed.

He cupped her cheeks and lifted her head. "I'm sorry, kitten, can you forgive me?" He looked into her eyes.

A satisfied smile spread over her sweet face. "What am I supposed to forgive you for?"

"I didn't plan on coming in your mouth."

She braced her elbows on his chest and rested her chin in the cradle of her laced fingers. "I know you didn't plan to do it, but I'm glad you did."

From his experience, very few girls actually liked that part.

"Are you sure? Because I don't want you to do anything you don't enjoy. And I don't mean just the things you really hate, but also the stuff you think I like but you could do without. I want you to do only what brings you pleasure."

Tessa smiled and dipped her head to plant a soft kiss on his lips. "I did enjoy it because it was you. Giving you pleasure makes me feel wonderful. I'm sure you get it because I know you feel the same."

"I do."

She kissed him again. "You better marry me, Jackson, because I don't want to ever be with anyone else."

His arms came around her in what would have been a crushing hug if he hadn't reminded himself to be careful with her. "I'm yours, Tessa, forever. There will never be anyone else. For you or for me."

## 23

## CALLIE

"Goodnight, I'll see you tomorrow." Callie waved at Miri before ducking into the employee lounge—a small room with a row of lockers on one wall, hooks for hanging things on the other, and one wooden bench. Not as nice as the one at Aussie's, but then no one ever hung out in there. It was a place to store personal stuff and not much more. Franco couldn't afford a lavish lounge for his employees. Not yet. Maybe once Brundar helped him make the place more profitable he would.

Opening her locker, Callie collected her purse and her light jacket. The club was always warm, but it was getting cold outside at night. Unable to help herself, she pulled her phone out, hoping like an idiot to see a message from Brundar, or maybe even a missed call, but of course there was nothing.

Third day in a row and no Brundar. Not in person or any other way.

After the talk she'd had with her neighbor, Callie itched to confront Brundar about his deception. But after having a full day to cool off, she'd decided to wait and see if he'd confess. Maybe she would drop hints, leading him to talk about it.

The problem was that he was avoiding her again. Just when she'd thought they were making progress, he'd retreated into his shell, and was hiding from her like a coward.

That evening, he hadn't even shown up at the club.

Callie had been waiting to catch Franco and ask him if Brundar had called him. Maybe he was sick and couldn't come in, or something had happened to him…

Crap. She shouldn't give a damn, but she was worried about the jerk.

Except, Franco had been busy in the basement and hadn't surfaced at the nightclub throughout her shift. Unless he had, and she'd missed him because she'd been taking orders or delivering drinks.

Should she text Brundar?

Ask him if he was okay? A bodyguard's job was inherently dangerous.

Now that her thoughts had wandered in that direction, her worry kicked into overdrive. She had to text him. Otherwise she wouldn't be able to sleep.

*Hi, just checking if you're alive.* With her finger hovering over the send button, she decided to add *I'm worried.* Just in case he got mad at her for texting him.

A couple of minutes later he answered, and the tightness in her chest eased.

*Working.*

At least he was alive. But would it have killed him to ask if she was doing okay? Show that he cared even a little?

He was such an infuriating man. When he was near her, she felt that he cared, that he liked her as a person, and that he liked spending time with her. But when he was away, Brundar behaved like she didn't exist, like nothing had happened between them, and like he didn't give a damn about her.

How did the saying go? Absence makes the heart grow fonder? In Brundar's case, it was more like out of sight, out of mind.

She put the phone back in her purse and headed outside.

"Hi, Donnie. Ready to call it a night?"

"I was waiting for you, girl."

"Thanks. Brad was a no-show, and Franco spent the entire night in the basement. So I guess you're stuck with me."

Donnie wrapped his thick arm around her shoulders. "I love walking you home."

The truth was that he never complained and was always upbeat during their walks. He was such a nice guy. Why the hell did she have to go for the complicated and the troubled?

If Donnie were her boyfriend, he would probably call her and text her throughout the day and be happy if she called and texted back. That was what normal couples did. Wasn't it?

But Donnie had his eye on someone else. Besides, as hunky as he was, she wasn't attracted to him.

"Are you going to give Fran your comic this weekend?"

Donnie shook his head. "I'm too big of a chicken."

Callie chuckled. "An enormous chicken. The size of a bull. But seriously, why not?"

"What if she thinks it's stupid?"

Callie patted his bicep. "Then she is not worthy of you, and you should set your sights on someone who thinks your comics are fabulous."

"Would you mind taking a look at it?"

She stopped and put her hands on her hips. "Mind? I've been asking you to show me your work since the night you told me about it. I'm dying to see it."

Donnie patted his jacket. "I have one in here."

"Then you must come up and show me."

He looked unsure. "I don't know about that. Do you think Brad is going to be okay with that?"

Callie pulled out the key to the building's front door and unlocked it. "Brad has no say in who I invite to my apartment."

She held the door open, but Donnie didn't come in. "It's the middle of the night."

She reached for his jacket, grabbing it to pull him in. Not that she was under any illusions that she could've moved that mountain of muscle if he hadn't let her, but it seemed Donnie needed the pretense of being coerced. "Come on. I'll make us coffee, and you'll show me your work."

"Fine. But if Brad rearranges my face, it's on you."

"Donnie, what are you worried about? You don't even need to fight him, you can sit on him. You outweigh him by about a hundred pounds." Callie kept walking, Donnie's sneakers making squeaking sounds behind her.

"I don't know about that. He is freakishly strong."

"How so?" Callie opened the door to the staircase and waited for Donnie to catch up.

"Once, when I was sitting in my car in the club's parking lot, I saw him pick up a Suburban with one hand. He must've dropped something, and it rolled under the car. He just held the thing up and reached with his other hand for whatever was under it, then lowered the Suburban back down as if it was a cardboard box filled with toilet paper."

"Impressive. But I think you could've done it too."

"I could. With two hands and a grunt."

"Nevertheless, as I told you before, Brad has no say in whom I invite over. I can entertain whomever I want, whenever I want."

Subconsciously, Callie suspected Brundar hadn't told her the truth about where he was and what he was doing. Now that Donnie was going on and on about not wanting to anger her so-called boyfriend by coming up to her apartment, her own anger was pushing the subconscious suspicion to the surface.

She could accept that on occasion Brundar's cousin would need his bodyguards in the evenings, or even on an out of town trip. But while in town, this time of night the big shot was most likely asleep in his bed.

For as long as she'd known Brundar, which admittedly wasn't all that long, he worked for the cousin during the day and at Franco's during the evenings and nights, which meant that the cousin didn't need his services while at home.

Only two scenarios could support Brundar's claim of working that late at night. One was that the cousin was making a transaction at night, which implied some illegal activity she knew Brundar wouldn't have taken part in, and the other was that he was partying somewhere and needed his bodyguards with him. Which again, didn't follow the normal pattern of Brundar's employment.

Something smelled fishy.

Callie opened the door to her apartment and flicked the lights on.

Donnie took a look around. "Nice place."

"Thanks." She dropped her purse on the kitchen counter and grabbed the carafe. "Make yourself comfortable while I make coffee."

Donnie sat on the couch, opened his jacket, and pulled a rolled up comic out of an inside pocket that must've been really deep.

Watching him flip through the pages while she loaded the coffeemaker, Callie observed that his sitting pose was nowhere near relaxed. The poor guy was anxious to see her response to his work.

He shouldn't be. She was going to gush all over it even if it wasn't great. Friends didn't put friends down. Not unless she thought it was a complete disaster and he shouldn't waste his time on it. But even then she would only suggest that he take a course to improve his skills.

When the coffee was ready, she loaded a tray with two cups, some sugar cubes, creamer, and a few store-bought cookies. As talented as she was with cooking, Callie sucked at baking.

"Okay. I'm ready for the grand reveal." She lowered the tray to the coffee table.

Donnie handed her the comic, then got busy with the coffee, dropping in several sugar cubes and following with creamer.

As soon as Callie opened the comic, she had to slap her hand over her mouth to stifle a laugh. Not only because it depicted Brundar with uncanny accuracy, but also because she was relieved that Donnie was really good and she wouldn't have to pretend to be impressed.

"That's Brad." She pointed to the comic's hero. Donnie hadn't changed anything. The same long pale hair, the same austere expression, just the clothes were different. The comic hero was wearing leather pants and a muscle shirt.

Donnie nodded. "He is so perfect for the role, I couldn't change a single thing about him."

"And that's Miri." Callie pointed to the hero's sidekick. "But you said she didn't fit as his sidekick, and that you needed someone less colorful."

"I decided she does. What do you think?"

"I think you're amazing. This is so well done. But I have second thoughts about you showing this to Fran. She might tell Brad. Or Miri."

Donnie pretended to shiver. "Right. I don't know who's scarier."

"I have an idea."

He lifted a brow.

"Make a comic strip starring Fran. Nothing elaborate, just a page or two. There is no way she wouldn't go out with you after seeing how much effort you've gone to and how talented you are. Make sure she looks amazing in it. It's a rare woman who is immune to flattery. I'm sure Fran isn't."

Donnie clapped her on the back. "Callie, you're a genius."

## 24

# BRUNDAR

Brundar's rotation had ended when the sun came up at five in the morning. There had been one false alarm, a drunk couple necking in a parking lot, but thankfully no murders.

If he didn't have a full workday ahead of him, Brundar would've gone straight to Calypso. That one text had shattered his resolve to try and stay away from her as much as he possibly could.

She'd been worried about him.

Or perhaps he was just looking for an excuse. Blaming Calypso for his weakness was much easier than admitting he had no willpower where she was concerned.

He was so screwed.

At this stage, no matter what he did, they were both going to get hurt.

There was no elegant solution.

After a quick shower, he lay down in bed, trying to catch a couple of hours of shuteye before having to report to Onegus for his daily duties. But sleep eluded him. All he could think of was Calypso; her sexy smile, her bright green eyes, her laughter.

She'd been through so much, and yet she seemed happy. He would've expected her to be reserved, subdued, maybe even a little sad. But she'd proved to be more resilient than he'd given her credit for. Or maybe it was in her character to be upbeat and positive, and external forces had little to do with how she felt.

Did it mean that he was naturally unhappy and cold? And that what had happened to him hadn't really shaped who he was?

Those were questions better addressed to a professional, and Brundar wasn't planning on visiting Vanessa anytime soon. Or ever. Maybe he could buy a book on the subject. Get some information without visiting a bloody shrink.

Later, while waiting for Kian to be done with his lunch meeting, Brundar was bored enough to actually search the Internet for such a book, but he didn't find anything he was interested in reading. It could have had something to do with Anandur peeking over his shoulder and asking him what he was looking for. The truth was that he wasn't much of a reader. Whatever little free time he had was usually spent training, and lately with Calypso.

Damnation. He couldn't wait for his tasks for the day to be done so he could go to her. So much for willpower.

At four o'clock, after completing a short investigative assignment Onegus had sent him on, Brundar informed the chief Guardian that he was leaving early.

"Go get some sleep. You look like hell." Onegus allowed him to cut one hour off his schedule. After spending most of the night on rotation, he shouldn't even have to ask.

Nevertheless, sleeping was not what Brundar had in mind.

Fighting against Calypso's pull was like resisting an elastic tether, but one that was made of carbon fibers. At first, there had been some give, the pull bearable, but with each passing hour the pull became stronger, and digging his heels in the ground wasn't helping.

Brundar parked his car in front of her building and pulled out the keys to its front door from the glove compartment, but then reconsidered and put them back. After neglecting her for so long, it would be inappropriate for him to come unannounced.

He walked up to the door and punched the buzzer.

A moment later, he heard the door lock release, but not a word from Calypso. She was allowing him in but refusing to acknowledge him. Obviously, she was mad. He couldn't blame her.

Taking the stairs two at a time, he was at her door a couple of moments later. It was ajar, and he pushed it in.

Sitting on the couch, Calypso was watching a show on the tube, ignoring him. Perhaps she hadn't heard him?

Brundar cleared his throat. "May I come in?"

"You're already in."

Yep, she was mad. But that wasn't the only thing that made him tense.

There were two new scents in the apartment. An old one, female, and a recent one, male.

He crossed the distance to the couch and stood in front of Calypso, blocking her view of the television. "Who was here?"

"None of your business."

Damn it. He couldn't tell her that he could smell people's residual scents long after they had left. But then she hadn't denied having someone over.

"I asked you to text me if you invite anyone in here."

"I was in no danger from either."

He crouched, forcing Calypso to look at his face and not his belt buckle. "Are you angry?"

She rolled her eyes. "Duh."

He tilted his head. "About what?"

"Don't play dumb, Brundar. You know exactly why."

"Because I didn't come over for a few days?"

If looks could kill he would've been dead already. Calypso's green eyes were shooting daggers at him. "Because you didn't call. Because you didn't text to let me know you're alive, and because your answer to my text was super jerky." She crossed her arms over her heaving chest.

Scratching his head, he tried to remember what his answer had been. "I said I was working."

"Yeah, you did. And that was it. You didn't ask how I was, or if everything was okay. Nothing. You made me feel like the clingy clueless girlfriend who should've gotten it through her head that you're not interested but didn't." She looked away. "Well, you succeeded."

"Succeeded in doing what?"

"Ugh, you're infuriating. I get it that you're not interested. You can go home." She pointed at the door.

"I don't want to go home. I came because I wanted to be with you."

Calypso shook her head. "Well, I don't want to be with you. I don't want to be with anybody. Men are all jerks and are good only for one thing that I can do without. I'm taking a vow of celibacy."

What happened next was totally unexpected.

Brundar felt laughter bubble up from deep in his belly, and, once he let it out, it just kept coming in wave after wave until there were tears in his eyes and a stitch in his side.

If Calypso had been pissed at him before, now she looked ready to do him harm. Shoving on his chest, she sent him toppling down on his ass. "It's not funny!"

Brundar laughed even harder.

The idea of Calypso taking a vow of celibacy was just ludicrous. She wouldn't last more than a week.

"I'm sorry—" he croaked between peals of laughter, "—it has been so long since I laughed, I forgot how it felt—" He tried to breathe in to stop. "It's bad… It hurts…" He pressed a hand to his middle.

Calypso's lips quivered with an effort to stifle her own laughter. "Good. I want you to suffer."

It took a few forceful inhales and exhales before Brundar regained his composure. "Please forgive me. I meant no disrespect." He pushed up and sat on the couch next to Calypso. "When I got your text, I was in the middle of a situation. But that's not an excuse. I could've texted you later that night or this morning. I'm not adept at social interactions."

Calypso's rigid posture relaxed a fraction. "This is not about social etiquette. I'm allowing for your no-nonsense military style. This is about caring and showing it. But I guess you don't. Not enough, anyway."

*Damnation.*

Brundar cared a lot. More than he should. Except, telling her that might appease her in the short term, but later, when he would be forced to sever the inexplicable bond between them, it would cause her more grief.

"I'm not adept at interpersonal relationships either. Whatever expectations you may have, forget them and save yourself a shitload of disappointment." He had done his best to avoid saying anything that would've sounded as rejection, going for self-deprecating and noncommittal. The less she thought of him, the better.

Calypso sighed, her shoulders slumping. "You're right. You are who you are, and I can either take it or leave it. I told myself a long time ago that I shouldn't try changing anyone because it's a waste of time and energy. The only one I can change is me."

"Smart." Especially for a woman so young. She was a quick learner.

She shrugged. "If I were smart, I would've stayed away from the complicated and the brooding and gone after the simple and upbeat. A nice guy who would treat me right and call me ten times a day to tell me he loves me."

Her words cut deep. Brundar wished he could be that guy she'd described, but even if she were an immortal female, and he loved her dearly, he would've never called her ten times a day to tell her that. Or even once. That just wasn't who he was.

With a frown, Brundar tried to imagine the guy she'd described. Was it anyone he knew? Was it the same man who had visited her last night?

Had she had sex with him?

Anger and jealousy washing over him like a tsunami, Brundar took a deep sniff. If she had, he would smell it.

Thank the merciful Fates, there was no lingering scent of sex. Not even his and Calypso's from several nights ago. Still, he had to know who it was. "Who did you invite over here?"

"I already told you. It's none of your business. Don't play the part of a possessive boyfriend when you keep telling me you're not mine." She waved a hand in the air. "You spend your nights in that dungeon, doing God knows what with God knows who, and I can't even invite anyone for coffee?" She huffed. "Please. Give me a break."

"I haven't been with anyone but you since I helped you leave your husband."

She pinned him with a hard stare. "And I'm supposed to believe that? You are the co-owner of a kink club. It's your job to play." She waved her hand again.

Brundar didn't take offense easily, but being accused of providing sexual services was too much. "I'm not whoring myself out, Calypso. That is not part of my job."

"So what do you do down there all night?"

He itched to repay her in kind and tell her it was none of her business, but that was before he'd scented her distress. Calypso was putting on a brave face, masking her hurt with anger, but her eyes were shining with unshed tears.

"I instruct, I demonstrate, and I monitor. I don't participate in sexual acts unless I want to. And ever since I brought you here, I haven't wanted to play with anyone else."

"Really?"

At first, her doubting his veracity angered him, but on second thought he realized Calypso needed reassurance.

"I can't promise you much, but I can promise you exclusivity as long as we are together, and I demand the same from you. No more inviting men to your apartment without letting me know who and why."

Calypso nodded. "I can live with that." She smirked. "It was Donnie. He walked me home, and I invited him for a cup of coffee."

As if that was supposed to ease his mind. Donnie was a good looking human, with exactly the kind of mellow personality she'd described as desirable in a male.

"Why did you invite him up?"

"What do you mean, why?" Calypso lifted her hands in exasperation. "That's part of the social interactions you don't get. He was kind enough to walk me home, and the least I could do was to offer him a cup of coffee. Besides, you have nothing to get jealous about. Donnie is not interested in me. He has his eyes on Fran. All we talked about was him mustering the nerve to approach her."

That was good. Donnie's face was no longer in danger of getting beaten into a pulp. Except, Calypso hadn't clarified about her interest, or lack thereof, in the bouncer.

But inept as Brundar was at interacting with people, especially women, he knew it would be a mistake to ask her directly. Instead, he could keep her talking about the guy and sniff for arousal. Her body couldn't lie.

"Donnie is handsome. Why would he fear approaching Fran?"

Calypso shrugged. "She is a little snooty to him, barely acknowledging he exists. Donnie believes Fran thinks of him as all brawn and no brain. A dumb muscleman."

No arousal.

Brundar allowed himself to relax. "I can ask her for him."

Calypso shook her head. "Don't. He needs to do it himself."

"What if she says no?"

"So it's a no, and he can move on. Dealing with rejection is part of life. Getting turned down is not as bad as never trying."

"Come here." Brundar leaned and scooped Calypso into his arms, positioning her in his lap. "The lady is both smart and beautiful. A killer combination."

## 25

## CALLIE

Hot and cold. Cold and hot. Brundar was a man of extremes.

It was so satisfying to have seen him getting jealous over Donnie.

As much as he pretended that their relationship was nothing more than a string of exclusive hookups, Brundar wasn't fooling Callie.

He had feelings for her. The problem was his attitude toward those feelings. He regarded them as a curse or a disease and not something wonderful between two people that was rare and special and should have been cherished.

Callie couldn't change him or who he was, but she could change his mind about that—give it her best and hope it would be enough.

She wanted to touch his face, caress his clean-shaven cheeks, run her fingers through his hair. But, of course, she did none of that, keeping her hands tucked between her thighs as a reminder. "This was our second fight. I would say it's an achievement."

Brundar's left brow arched. "You consider an argument a good thing?"

"Sure, I do. Getting a rise from someone as stoic as you means that you care."

Brundar kissed the top of her head. "I think you have things turned around. Both times you got mad at me."

"True. But you took the effort to engage with me. I guess you don't do that with others. You walk away."

"That is correct." Brundar seemed to ponder her observation. "I wonder why that is?"

The guy didn't understand the most basic elements of human interaction.

"Because you don't care what others think or feel toward you. Well, maybe other than respect. I think that is important to you. But with me, you want more than my respect."

"You bet, I do. I want your moans, and your whimpers, and your screams."

His thumb brushed over her puckered nipple, stoking the simmer of desire his words had started.

"So what are you saying? That I make a lot of noise?" Callie teased.

"Music to my ears." He brushed his knuckles over her other nipple.

He was teasing her back, not with his words but with his hands. To touch her over her shirt and bra instead of her naked skin was like letting her smell something delicious but not allowing her to taste it. This was so like him, expressing himself through touch and not speech, probably because he was so good with the first and so inadequate with the latter.

Days without him had created so much pent-up need that Callie felt like crawling out of her skin. Touching herself, which was the only relief she'd gotten for the past few days, had been pleasant at best, but she needed Brundar to take her higher. To make her wild and wanton the way he'd done before.

Sex with him was so intense that everything else seemed devoid of color and flavor in comparison.

It scared her.

What were the chances of her ever finding another man who could so perfectly satisfy her? Who could bring her to such heights of ecstasy?

As inexperienced as she was, Callie figured out that a precise match like theirs was rare. Given the huge spectrum of shades and variations, a perfect alignment was nearly impossible. She was just a slightly darker shade of vanilla, while Brundar was on the lighter shade of kink, and they were both flexible enough to stretch a little and meet where they were both comfortable.

Unless she was reading him wrong and he was holding back to accommodate her.

"Am I enough, Brundar? Tell me the truth. Are you holding back on what you want, what you need?"

He shook his head. "Not in the way you think."

"Please explain, because I'm having an insecure moment here."

Dipping his head, he kissed her forehead. "I told you what I need, and I didn't omit anything. You agreed to it. Why would you think I would want more?"

That was true. The only thing Brundar listed as an absolute must was bondage. The blindfold was probably part of that. But he admitted that something was lacking.

"What are you holding back?"

He chuckled. "I have incredible stamina. If I had my way, you would need a transfusion by the time I was done with you."

"Is that a challenge?"

"No, sweetling. I know when you have had enough."

"But what about you? I hate thinking that you're left unsatisfied."

"Who said anything about not being satisfied? The fact that I can go on doesn't mean I'm unsatisfied."

Callie tilted her head back to have a better look at Brundar's face, wondering how was it possible to want more but at the same time feel satisfied.

Was it like eating chocolate?

She was an unrepentant chocoholic. One or two squares were never enough, and she would keep coming back for more until there was nothing left. But there was a price to pay for the overindulgence, and not only in extra pounds. The nausea and upset stomach were an unpleasant reminder that she should've stopped at no more than one-third of a pack. Except, she usually smartened up only after the fact, not while obsessively devouring one piece after another.

Maybe for Brundar sex was the same. The fact that he could go on didn't mean he should.

"Okay."

"Okay what?"

"Okay, sir?"

Brundar chuckled. "And you were accusing me of unclear communication. Okay as in, I understand? Or okay as in, take me to bed right now?"

"Both. I accept your explanation, and I want you to take me to bed."

"I will. But first, there is the small matter of your punishment."

Callie felt herself melt into a puddle. Except, she needed a cause to make the game fun to play. "Punishment for what?"

"Let me see." Brundar looked up as if he was concentrating on recounting her misdeeds. "First, you didn't believe me when I told you that I haven't been with anyone but you since we got together. Just for that, you deserve a thorough spanking. Then you suggested I was whoring myself out to club members. That's a strapping offense, but you're too green for that."

Callie shivered, and not in a pleasant way. "You mean like with a belt?"

"Yes."

"I will never be ready for that." What could be sexy about that much pain? Not that she would know. No one had ever done that to her, and Callie was adamant about keeping it that way.

"Never say never."

She smiled, thinking he was teasing, but Brundar seemed serious. Her smile turned into a frown. She would've dismissed his remark as nonsense, but the thing was, he seldom made claims about things he wasn't an expert on.

"Why would you say that?"

"I've seen it before. Some start easy and never venture into darker places, while others get the taste and want to experience more. I always try to guess which camp a new member will end up belonging to, but I miss more often than I get it right. Each person is different."

"Which camp do you think I belong to?"

"The second one. But as I said, I'm often wrong."

Callie looked away, embarrassed even though she was sure he was mistaken. Pain wasn't her thing. She liked the feeling she got from submitting, and a little spanking was the perfect catalyst to help her get there; bondage was too, but that was as far as she was willing to go. "I'm curious to hear what makes you think that."

"Mostly because you're gutsy. You don't back away from trying new things even when you're scared."

True, but she was also a reasonable woman. Callie's willingness to stretch her comfort zone in the name of experimentation didn't mean she would abandon it for just any thrill.

If Brundar stayed around for long enough, they might find out who was right. It saddened her to think that he might not.

Callie's arousal dissipated along with her good mood.

"What's going on in your head?"

As usual, Brundar didn't miss the slightest change in her. Which was weird given how obtuse he was about almost everything else.

"I just thought that you need to stick around for a while to find out if you're right about me."

## 26

# BRUNDAR

Brundar felt trapped.
What could he say to her?
Even though he wanted it more than anything, he knew he wasn't going to stick around. And he wasn't about to lie to Calypso either.

Which left him with only one choice. Change the subject and make it about the present, not the future.

"Enough stalling, sweetling. Right now we have some business to attend to." Hands on her waist, he flipped her around, so she was sprawled over his lap, bottom up. He grabbed one of the decorative pillows and put it under her cheek. "Comfortable?"

"I am, but not for long." She wiggled her cute little ass.

Reaching under her, he popped her jeans button, then pulled her pants and panties down to her mid thighs.

Calypso's arousal, which had taken a nosedive during their talk, was back and climbing with each passing moment.

"Do you want to hold my hands?" she asked.

"I'm not going to restrain you. Not unless you want me to. But I want you to close your eyes and not open them under any circumstances. Can you do that for me?"

"Yes, sir." She sounded so happy that he was making a concession and trusting her to follow his rules without enforcing them by tying her up and putting a blindfold over her eyes.

Brundar was well aware that he was taking a risk.

His fangs had already elongated just in response to Calypso's scent of excitement and the sight of her perfect globes. In a few moments, they would reach full length, and his eyes would start glowing. If she disobeyed him and opened her eyes, he would have no choice but to thrall her, and that would end their playtime.

He never engaged with a woman who was drunk or high, and a thrall reduced mental capacity just as much if not more. He wanted Calypso to participate while fully cognizant.

His palm resting on her beautiful ass, he reiterated, "I'm trusting you to follow the rules. If you break them, this playtime will end immediately. Do you understand?"

"I do. I promise not to look and to keep my hands right here." She tucked them under the pillow.

"Good girl." He caressed her butt cheeks. They were so small that he covered both with one hand.

His first smack was more of a love tap. Calypso felt so good draped over his knees, her trust in him tasting so sweet, that he wanted this to last. Getting into an easy rhythm, Brundar tapped her butt cheeks, caressing and kneading after every two or three taps.

It wasn't what she'd expected, but she wasn't complaining. He was stoking the embers of her desire slowly, enjoying the closeness. She seemed to be enjoying it too.

To mix things up a little, he surprised her by delving his finger between her moist folds. Unprepared for the new sensation, she sucked in a breath and arched up, seeking more. He reached with his other hand and pressed the heel against her sensitive nub, then pushed inside her, first with one finger, then with two.

Undulating her hips, Calypso rubbed against his palm, pleasuring herself on it while he slowly pumped his fingers in and out of her.

This wasn't enough to bring her to a climax, but then he was in no hurry.

For a few minutes, Calypso played along, but he knew it wouldn't last. His girl was patient in many ways, but not in this.

"Please, Brundar, I need more."

With a swift tug, he got rid of her pants; her T-shirt and bra were gone next. When she was gloriously nude, he lifted her hips and slid from under her.

"Stay here and don't move. And no peeking either. I want to see your face buried in that pillow when I come back," he commanded, laying her legs back on the couch.

"Where are you going?"

"To the bedroom, to get a condom."

"Okay."

He was back before she'd finished sighing contentedly.

"You're fast," she commented.

*You have no idea.*

With her face firmly pressed into the pillow, he allowed himself to move at his natural speed, shedding his clothes and sheathing himself in the hateful rubber in seconds. This was something he needed to address, the sooner the better. Bridget could produce a clean bill of health for him, and Calypso could get on the pill.

Keeping up the charade was taking pleasure away from both of them.

"Lift." He tapped her bottom while grabbing another pillow, then tucked it under her pelvis. "You're so beautiful. I could just stand here and look at you."

She giggled, the sound muffled by the pillow. "I hope not for long."

"Impudent girl." He smacked her bottom, harder than before.

She moaned.

Fates, that throaty sound went straight to his cock.

Getting into position behind her, he covered her body with his like a blanket, enjoying a moment of skin to skin and prolonging their anticipation. His cock nestled in the crease between her butt cheeks, and he wanted to grab her chin and turn her head around so he could take her mouth before surging inside her, but he didn't dare.

As it was, he was already playing with fire. He couldn't risk her opening her eyes and seeing him in his full alien mode.

That was the disadvantage of not using a blindfold and leaving Calypso unrestrained. He didn't feel as free to do as he pleased, and the underlying stress wasn't conducive to a good experience.

Next time he would go back to business as usual.

Both of them would enjoy it more.

## 27

# RONI

"What's the verdict, doctor?" Roni looked hopefully at Bridget.

"The verdict is that you don't need to stay here. You're still sick, but your symptoms are milder. If Ingrid can find you an apartment, you can move to a more comfortable setting. No exercise and no other strenuous activity for at least two weeks."

Bridget glanced at the contraption William's students had built for him. She'd pushed it aside to conduct her examination, and it was now blocking the entrance to the room. "Take this thing with you. I know you'll not listen to me and rest, so the next best thing is working from bed the same as you did here."

"Thanks. What if Ingrid, whoever she is, can't find me an apartment? Can I stay here?" He'd kind of gotten used to the hospital bed, which he could adjust for maximum comfort with the remote, programming into its memory his two favorite positions, one for working and the other one for resting.

A regular one was never going to be as comfortable. One could only do so much with pillows.

Fuck, would there be pillows? And blankets? And the other things he'd always taken for granted?

And who was going to feed him?

Andrew's wife had been kind enough to send down meals, and the nurses pampered him with sandwiches and other things from nearby restaurants. He had no money, and if he did, he was pretty sure he couldn't leave the building to go shopping. Sylvia would have to buy him groceries until he figured shit out. The problem was that he'd never cooked anything in his life, and as far as he knew neither had Sylvia.

"Don't worry. She'll find you a place."

Yeah, don't worry, right. He was on the verge of panicking.

"Will the apartment come with pillows and blankets and towels and all of that shit? Because I don't have money and I don't know where and how to get things. I've never been on my own."

Bridget patted his shoulder. "Everything you need will be there, and if anything is missing, you can call Ingrid, and she will get it delivered."

Roni exhaled a relieved breath. "That's one less thing to worry about. What about the transition, though? When should I attempt it again?" Not anytime soon, that was for sure. He was so weak that a walk to the bathroom was a strain. Getting on the mat with an immortal was a no-go if he couldn't even stay upright without aid.

"You need to wait at least a month, maybe longer, and not before I give my okay. If you want it to work, you need to let your body get back into peak condition first. You might have been carrying this virus with no symptoms for weeks, and that could be the reason you didn't transition."

Having a plausible explanation for not transitioning was comforting and made his outlook way more optimistic. But waiting so long to try again was going to be a bitch.

"I hate waiting."

"Patience, Roni." Bridget patted his arm again. "I'm going to call Ingrid."

"Thanks."

"You're welcome."

Now that he was about to get discharged, Roni needed to figure out some basic logistics before he could leave. First of all, he needed clothes. With the state he'd been in when snatched from the human hospital, Roni hadn't noticed if anyone had bothered to collect the clothes he'd arrived in. Or if Jerome or Kevin had had the presence of mind to bring his wallet to the hospital.

Fuck. He could probably say goodbye to all the money he had saved up in his bank account. He of all people should know he could never touch it again without giving the feds a way to find him. Money left a trail no matter how carefully it was hidden.

Andrew might have an idea of what was going on, but he was still avoiding contact with Roni. He wouldn't come without a hazmat suit, and Roni doubted the clan kept those on hand.

Or they could talk on the phone.

Reaching for the one next to his bed, Roni pressed zero for the operator. Bridget had told him the line went straight to the keep's security office and nowhere else, but they could connect him with Andrew.

"What can I do for you, Roni?" an unfamiliar male voice answered.

"Do I know you?"

The guy chuckled. "No. But your name is programmed as the occupant of the room you're calling from."

"Obviously." The fever must've destroyed a good number of his brain cells for him to ask a dumb question like that. "Can you connect me to Andrew Spivak?"

"Sure. Let me check if he is home. I'm going to put you on hold."

"No problem."

A few moments later Andrew picked up. "What's up, kid? How are you feeling?"

"Better. Bridget is letting me out of here."

"Good. I'm glad to hear that."

"Yeah. How are things at work? Anyone talking about my disappearance?"

Andrew chuckled. "It is assumed that you hacked your way out of the hospital."

Sylvia had been questioned by Barty the day after Roni's escape, even though Yamanu made sure the staff remembered her leaving shortly after the agent and his wife. According to her, she'd been very convincing, crying about what a jerk Roni was for leaving her without a word.

"Did any of you get my clothes? Or my wallet?"

"Sylvia has them. But what do you need your wallet for?"

"I have a few bucks in there. The money saved up in my bank account is probably gone. I don't want to hack into it because I know they booby-trapped it to hell and back. If they release it to my parents, and providing the bastards will cooperate and not snitch on me, I can then hack into their accounts and take it out."

"How much do you have in there?"

"Close to a hundred thousand. I spent almost none of my pay."

Andrew whistled. "Yeah, that sucks. But I wouldn't touch it anytime soon even if they transferred it to your parents. They will be watching for that. Besides, you can probably make it back in no time."

"If I were free, I could. But I'm not."

"I'm sure some kind of an arrangement could be made."

"I want to talk to the head honcho, Kian. Can you arrange a meeting? I hate not knowing what to expect. And by the way, Dr. Bridget says I need to wait at least a month until I attempt transition again. She says I might have been carrying the virus for weeks without showing symptoms and that's why it didn't work."

"That would explain it. You're the best candidate for transition the clan ever had. Better than I was, that's for sure. I was racking my brain trying to figure a plausible explanation for your grandmother's picture on those driver's licenses other than her being an immortal. But I couldn't find one."

"Yeah, same here. So are you going to talk to the boss for me?"

"Not yet. I think you need to get settled first. If I were you, I would want to be healthy enough not to look like the living dead when I meet him. Well-dressed too. You want to leave a good first impression."

"Yeah, you're right. It's like a job interview."

"The most important one you'll ever have."

"Right."

## 28

## CAROL

"Here you go." Carol handed Anandur the plate with the sandwich he'd ordered. "And just in case you're about to ask, I'm not going hunting with you."

Leaning against the counter, Anandur lifted the sandwich to his mouth and took an enormous bite, shoving in at least one third of it. He chewed and swallowed, then grabbed a napkin and wiped his beard. "It needs to be done, Carol. You know it's a crucial step."

Yeah, Brundar had made it very clear that he wasn't green-lighting her for the mission unless she proved she could kill an animal and remove its heart.

*Crazy asshat.*

Of course, he would think it was critical for the mission. The guy was the deliverer of death. What did he know about the art of seduction and manipulation?

*Absolutely nothing.*

"This is not the place to have this conversation." Carol handed Anandur another paper napkin. "You have mayo on your mustache."

"Thanks." He grabbed it, dabbing at the wrong spot.

"Here, give it to me." She took the napkin and wiped his mustache for him. Men with facial hair, especially as bushy as Anandur's, were walking germ farms. Tiny food particles always landed in there, providing a fertile breeding ground. "You should shave this bush off. It's not sanitary."

"But it's sexy, and the ladies like it." He waggled his red brows.

"If you say so." Carol wasn't a fan. One of the things she'd liked about Robert was that he was always clean shaven.

Had she been too hasty throwing him out?

Probably. After years of living alone, she'd expected the transition back to single life would be smooth and easy, but it hadn't been. As annoying as Robert was, she missed his presence. The apartment felt lonely without him.

Still, it would've been wrong to keep him around just because she couldn't tolerate the silence, or to have a male available for shagging at her disposal. Carol was quite proud of herself for setting him free. Contrary to what everyone else thought, she wasn't a heartless bitch, and freeing Robert to seek his someone special had been a selfless move.

"Can you take a break?" Anandur asked.

She glanced around the café. It wasn't too busy, and Onidu was there in case anyone ordered a sandwich. Everything else was handled by the vending machines.

"Do you want to come up to my place?"

"Nah. Let's take a walk outside."

Imagining herself trotting behind him, Carol grimaced. The guy was huge, especially compared to her. She would have to take two steps for each one of his. "On one condition." She pointed a finger at his chest. "You walk at my pace. I can't compete with your long legs."

"Done."

Removing her apron, she signaled Onidu that she was taking a break.

"Let's go." Carol stuffed her phone in one pocket, her wallet in another.

Anandur waited until they were out of the building. "Did you change your mind about the mission?"

Other than the two of them, there were no pedestrians on the street. Even the traffic was sparse this time of day.

"If I have to kill animals, then yeah. I can't do it. No way."

Anandur stuck his hands into his jeans pockets. "Let me ask you something. Are you a vegetarian?"

"No. I'm an omnivore with a preference for vegetarian dishes."

"If eating a piece of meat that you bought raw in the supermarket or already cooked in a restaurant doesn't bother you, but killing the animal you are going to eat does, it's not a moral issue for you. You're just squeamish."

"I can't argue with that. But knowing that doesn't make it any easier for me. Besides, I'm too busy. I'm running the café during the day and teaching self-defense beginner classes in the evening to free your time for patrolling. I have enough on my plate."

Anandur's strides were getting longer, and Carol found herself trotting behind him. "Slow down, big guy."

He stopped. "I'm sorry. I forgot." Scratching at his beard, he waited until she caught up and was standing next to him. "I'll make you a deal."

Making deals with Anandur could be tricky. The guy was a prankster. The good thing about his brother was that she'd never had to second guess Brundar's motives.

"I'm listening."

"With Brundar so busy lately with whatever he is doing in his off time, I offered to take over your training. Even if you later decide to scrap the mission, I think you should keep on pushing to improve your skills. We will train twice a week, an hour each time. That way you'll stay in shape, I'll fulfill my promise to Brundar, and if you later decide to do what's needed to get green-lighted for the mission, your skills will be where they need to be."

"Sounds very reasonable. Except for the fact that neither of us has any spare time."

Anandur shook his head. "Two hours a week is nothing. We will make the time. This is important."

# 29

# BRUNDAR

Brundar halted in front of Onegus's office and knocked. If the chief was going to chew his ass for taking another half a day off, he would be well justified. Everyone was stretched to the limit, working double shifts. The thing was, Brundar and Anandur's job allowed them more free time than the others.

When Kian didn't have meetings outside the keep, they could choose to help out with other tasks or not.

Lately, Brundar was mostly opting to take time off. Between his second job helping manage Franco's club and seeing Calypso, he just couldn't afford to volunteer any of his free time.

Today, he was taking her to UCLA, even though Roni had made it unnecessary by changing the records. The kid was amazing. Calypso's old name had been replaced by the new one Brundar had chosen for her in each and every one of the admissions records the university kept.

For some reason, this outing was important to him. As a guy who'd never taken a woman anywhere, it would be a first for him. He didn't want to give it up unless he absolutely had to.

"Come in," Onegus called out.

Brundar pushed the door open. "I'm taking the rest of the day off. I'll be back for my night shift."

Onegus shook his head and waved him off without a comment. The dismissal was worse than the chewing Brundar had been expecting.

Closing the door, he wondered whether he should've offered an explanation. But what could he have said? That he was choosing to escort his lady friend over helping his fellow Guardians? Promise that it was the last time?

Both options would have made him look bad. It was better to keep his mouth shut. Anyway, no one expected him to explain, because he never bothered.

Not Calypso, though. She had a way of pulling words out of him like no one before her had managed. Which reminded him that he should text her to get ready.

He pulled out his phone. *On my way. Be there in twenty.*

*I'm waiting*, was her reply.

As he tucked the phone into his back pocket, Brundar frowned, wondering why the text exchange bothered him. For some reason, he felt uncomfortable, as if he was wearing shoes that were rubbing his feet the wrong way or an article of clothing that didn't fit well.

He was still trying to figure it out when he knocked on Calypso's door.

She opened the way, her broad smile taking his breath away. How was it possible for her to look more beautiful every time he saw her? And it wasn't as if she was dressed to kill. The thing was, simple jeans, sneakers, and T-shirt looked better on her than an evening gown on another woman.

"Don't just stand there, come in and give me a kiss."

He could do that.

Taking a step in, Brundar kicked the door closed and wrapped his arms around her middle. Trapping her arms as he lifted her up, he kissed her until she pulled back to suck in a breath.

"You must have huge lungs," she said after catching her breath.

Brundar set her back down. "I do." His lungs could go without air much longer than a human's.

"Can I see the papers?"

He'd kept the name she was going to use a secret, wanting to surprise her.

Reaching inside his pants' back pocket, he pulled out the envelope with her new birth certificate, social, driver's license, and passport.

Calypso walked over to the kitchen counter, upended the envelope, then picked up the driver's license first.

"Heather Wilson?" She grimaced. "That's so boring."

"I agree, which is exactly the reason I chose it. You need a name that's forgettable. A unique name would stand out. You don't want people to remember it."

"Yes, you're right, of course. I need to memorize it."

"Do you want me to start calling you Heather?"

"Oh, God, no. It's weird enough that you call me Calypso when I think of myself as Callie."

She should've told him she didn't like her given name. He thought it was beautiful, like the woman herself.

"If you don't like it, I can start calling you Callie."

"No. For some reason, I like the way you say it. It sounds so regal coming out from your mouth. Calypso." She imitated his serious tone, then chuckled nervously. "Ignore me. I'm talking nonsense."

"No, you are not. I like using your given name because it sounds special. Like you."

"Thank you." Calypso opened her purse and put her new documents inside. "Heather Wilson is ready to tackle the administration offices."

Brundar shifted his weight to his other foot. "I have another surprise for you."

"What is it?"

"My hacker took care of everything, changing your name in the university's database. There is no real need for us to go there. Only if you want to."

Calypso lifted her purse and tucked it under her arm. "First of all, I still want to verify that everything is all right. Secondly, they might keep a paper trail."

He hadn't considered the possibility. "I don't think any institution does that anymore these days. Why waste space on endless paper files?"

"Maybe you're right. But we need to check."

"Agreed."

Brundar pulled the door open for her.

"How long do you have?" she asked while locking it. "Do you need to go back to work? Or just the club?"

Brundar held the door to the stairs open for her. "I have a night shift, so no club. But other than that I have the rest of the day off." He took her hand as they descended the stairs.

"After we are done with the administration, do you want to have an early dinner with me?"

"I would love that."

"I mean out in a restaurant. Like a date. Our first." She cast him a hesitant glance.

A date. He'd never been on one. Did hookups count as dates? Not likely. Not his kind of hookups. The kind that required a signed contract.

Calypso was still waiting for his answer, her heartbeat getting faster by the second. He assumed it wasn't due to physical exertion. Going down the stairs wasn't a strenuous activity.

"Of course. I owe you for all those amazing home-cooked meals."

Her face fell and he knew he'd botched it.

"What I meant by that is that it is my turn to treat you, and since I don't know anything about cooking, I should invite you to a good restaurant."

Calypso smiled, but it was forced.

Could he have said it better? How?

The uncomfortable feeling from before was back.

Calypso was expecting too much from him, and he was feeling trapped by her expectations, trying to accommodate them because he wanted to make her happy. Or at least not sad. That was why he'd felt weird about the texting earlier. With all her talk about caring and showing that he cared, she was trying to turn him into someone he was not and would never be.

He wasn't her boyfriend, and he didn't do the things a boyfriend was expected to do. He would never fit into that mold.

Friends with benefits. That was what she'd called their arrangement. It was a good definition for what they had, and they should never cross that line.

## 30

# CALLIE

The campus was beautiful. Old trees, large grassy areas, and walkways meandering between the various buildings. Callie had been there before, but it was Brundar's first time, and she was excited to show him around.

"Where did you go to college?" she asked as they left the administration building. Just as the hacker had promised Brundar, he'd had her registered as Heather Wilson. She'd picked up a bunch of forms even though everything was available online. Tomorrow she would sort through them and fill out everything needed.

"I didn't." Brundar turned to look at one of the buildings. "Must be stifling to sit in one classroom or another all day."

"Not if you're enjoying the subject you're studying."

He shrugged.

Some people were more physical than cerebral, but for some reason, Brundar struck her as someone who was both. Perhaps circumstances had prevented him from pursuing higher education. Not everyone could afford it. Given that he and his brother had been raised by a single parent, money had probably been tight.

Damn it. What if she'd embarrassed him by asking?

"I guess not everyone likes studying," she offered.

"When I was young, my brother thought I would become a scholar. He said I didn't have the soul of a fighter. But I proved him wrong."

There was a note of pride in Brundar's tone, which was a big deal since he'd rarely expressed any emotion. Apparently, he valued fighting skills more than scholarly pursuits.

Good. It meant he hadn't been offended by her question. "How long did it take you to master swordsmanship?"

"Centuries," he deadpanned.

Callie chuckled. "It must have seemed that way."

"Yes, it did. Endless hours of grueling training. I wanted to be the best."

"Are you?"

"Yes."

No hesitation there. Was it the truth or his ego? "Did you win any tournaments?"

He chuckled. "Many. I'm still alive. My opponents are dead."

Was he joking? No one went to war with a sword anymore. Even if he served during the last one, she doubted he'd killed anyone with a blade. And competitors in fencing tournaments didn't kill each other, either. He must have been talking about mastering a different weapon.

"You must be very good with rifles and machine guns as well."

"I am."

"Which war did you serve in?"

"Not any that you're aware of."

A secret war? He was probably a member of some special commando unit that went on undercover missions.

Casting Brundar a sidelong glance, Callie took in his harsh profile, his straight posture, his determined strides. He was a soldier through and through—from the way he talked to the way he thought. It was like he'd never known anything else, and civilian life with all its loose social rules baffled him.

"Did you go to a military high school?"

"No."

Brundar's curt tone was a good indication that he was starting to get annoyed with her incessant questioning. She'd overdone it. The trick to getting information out of him was to limit her inquiries and spread them out over time, but once again curiosity had gotten the better of her.

On the one hand, it was frustrating to have to do all this careful maneuvering to get Brundar to lower his shields a fraction at a time. On the other hand, it was challenging. Even professional psychologists had to work months and sometimes years to get a person to open up, or deal with problems, or even acknowledge having them.

In fact, Callie was convinced that no psychologist would have been able to make the smallest crack in Brundar's shields, for the simple reason that he didn't think there was anything wrong with them. Furthermore, there was no chance in hell Brundar would have ever consulted one.

The silence that stretched between them felt uncomfortable. Callie needed to fill it with something other than addressing personal questions to Brundar. A strategic change of subject was in order. "I'm thirsty. Do you want to check out the student cafeteria? I would love a cup of coffee."

Brundar scanned the grounds again as he had continually done throughout their walk. Always on high alert, the guy never relaxed his vigilance. "I don't see one, but I can smell food."

"You do? Can you find the source, or should I ask someone for directions?"

His lips compressed, showing his displeasure. Guys were so weird about that. Suggesting that they needed assistance to find a location was like an insult to their manliness. On the other hand, they had no problem getting help finding their socks, their car keys, their wallets, and any other item they misplaced in the house. Somehow that was okay.

Brundar took her hand. "With me around, you'll never need to ask for directions."

She chuckled. "The nose that knows."

"In this case, yes."

Following a smell she couldn't detect, Brundar found the cafeteria with ease. The place was huge, the coffee was meh. But then Callie hadn't expected it to be good.

Brundar tossed his cup after taking one sip without slowing his steps, hitting the trashcan's flap with an unerring accuracy.

"That bad?" she asked.

"I've had better. My cousin's wife bought a fancy cappuccino machine, and she keeps experimenting with it. Naturally, she chooses my brother and me for the taste tests."

Another little tidbit of information. Should she chance a couple more questions?

Not as finicky as Brundar, Callie took another sip of her coffee. "I'm guessing you're talking about the wife of the cousin you work for."

Brundar nodded.

"Do you like working for him? Does he treat your brother and you well?"

"Kian is a good and fair leader. I've never had any grievances with him. My brother, however, finds great satisfaction in aggravating me any chance he gets."

This was another piece of information to add to her collection.

"And yet you choose to work with him every day, and to share an apartment with him."

A ghost of a smile flitted through Brundar's austere features. "Anandur never means to insult. He's a trickster and a joker and he thinks he is funny. As annoying as he is, I wouldn't want anyone else fighting by my side."

That was as close as Brundar got to admitting that he loved his brother.

"I would really like to meet him. Your cousin and his wife too."

Brundar didn't respond. Was he pretending he hadn't heard her? Or maybe he hadn't understood the implied suggestions that she wanted him to arrange a get-together?

Pushing the subject could backfire, but Callie felt compelled to do so despite the possibility of it blowing up in her face. "Do you think we could maybe all go out together to a restaurant? Does your brother have a girlfriend? Because a three couples outing could be fun."

"No."

God, she felt like slapping the infuriating man.

"What do you mean, no? No, as in it's not going to be fun? Or no, as in you don't think we could all go out to dinner? Be more specific."

With a sigh, Brundar pinched his forehead between his thumb and forefinger. "My brother doesn't have a girlfriend. That's the only question I can answer."

*Crap.*

The rest of the walk to the parking lot passed in even heavier silence. Callie searched her brain for something to say, but for once came up with nothing.

She wasn't going to apologize for wanting to meet his family. And she wasn't going to apologize for bringing it up either.

Was he still taking her out to dinner, or was that idea scrapped together with what passed for Brundar's good mood?

When they reached his Escalade, he opened the door for her as he usually did, and she thanked him politely even though the lump in her throat was the size of a frog.

"Are you taking me home?" Callie asked as he turned on the engine.

He lifted a brow. "Do you want to go home? I thought we were going out to dinner."

Well, at least there was that. "I thought you changed your mind."

"Why would I do that?"

The guy seemed genuinely puzzled, but she was not in the mood to spell it out for him. It was getting tiresome. Callie felt like she was the only one putting in the effort for their so-called relationship to work.

Except, even as peeved as she was, she knew it wasn't true.

Brundar was taking days off work to be with her, and he was doing so much to help her out, like taking her to the campus because she didn't have a car and was afraid of going by herself, in case Shawn was stalking the place.

They were both making an effort, each in her or his own way. It was vitally important to remember that, especially when annoying things popped up, making her doubt her resolve.

People had different things going for them, different skills, different comfort zones, and judging everyone by the same standards, usually her own, was wrong. She was verbally competent where Brundar was not. She was outgoing while he was not. On the other hand, where he would bravely meet an enemy head on, she would cower in the darkest hidey-hole she could find.

The most important thing they had in common was loyalty. Callie would do anything for the people she cared for, and she believed Brundar would do so as well.

What about honesty, though?

She had laid herself bare for him, keeping nothing back, while he was still more secretive than an undercover agent in enemy territory.

Maybe that's what he was.

What if that story about being a bodyguard for his businessman cousin was a lie? What if he was a Russian spy?

Callie shook her head. With way too much time on her hands, she was reading too many suspense novels lately. Still, if Brundar were a spy, he would be Russian. With his pale complexion and hair color, he could hardly be spying for anyone else.

As far as she knew, the USA had no conflict with Scotland or any of the Scandinavian countries, and she'd already dismissed the Mafia scenario. A Google search had revealed nothing. No mention of anyone named Brundar or Brad who matched Brundar's description.

What the heck was his last name?

After today's fiasco, Callie wasn't about to ask. She could either search his wallet and check his driver's license, or invent a good reason for needing to know it.

"What are you thinking so hard about?" Brundar asked.

Callie plastered a smile on her face. "I'm trying to guess where you're taking me."

"Do you like Italian?"

"I love it."

"Then I'm taking you to Gino's. Best Italian cuisine in L.A."

## 31

# RONI

"I brought you clothes." Sylvia lifted a hefty shopping bag. "I hope they fit. I went by the sizes of what you had on when they brought you to the hospital."

Fuck. Did he have enough money in his wallet to cover it?

Roni pushed up on the pillows. "Thank you. How much do I owe you?"

"Not a thing. It's a present from me. A welcome to your new home present." She hopped onto his bed and leaned to kiss him. "Do you want to see what I got?"

"Sure."

Upending the huge plastic bag on the bed, she started grouping the items. "Five pairs of jeans, size twenty-nine; ten T-shirts, size medium; three hoodies, size medium as well."

She put the aforementioned items back in the bag and continued with the inventory. "Two nice button-downs, a sweater, two packs of boxer-shorts, five in each pack, and ten pairs of socks." She added those to the bag. "I didn't know if you wear pajamas, but I can get them when I go back to get you training clothes. I forgot about those."

Sylvia had forgotten some other necessities as well, but he was too embarrassed to remind her. As it was, she must've spent a lot of money. She'd bought him an entire new wardrobe.

"Thank you. You have no idea how much I appreciate this. I feel even more helpless here than I felt there. All I had to do to get something was to put in a request. I don't know how things work here. Besides, I can't access my money, which means that all I have are the few dollars in my wallet."

Dr. Bridget had a stash of new toothbrushes and disposable razors. He could ask her to give him some until he settled in. Or maybe he could ask Andrew if he had any he could spare.

Sylvia reached for her purse. "I have your wallet here. Not that you have much use for it. You need a new name and a new driver's license."

"I know." He took the wallet and put it on the table by his bed. It was all he had. Never mind that he hadn't had much use for a driver's license before, and he wouldn't have in the foreseeable future. He was still a prisoner. The dream of touring the country with Sylvia in a convertible was just that. A dream.

"What about shoes? I don't think I was wearing any."

"Right." Sylvia pulled out her phone. "You weren't. Another thing I forgot. What's your shoe size?"

"Ten and a half. And I'm going to pay you back for all of this once I get paid myself. I don't know when that will be, though. Andrew thinks I should get better before talking to Kian."

"He is right. Kian is a cool guy, and I don't think he would mind that you look sickly, but you'll feel more confident, and that's what's important. You just need to remember not to be rude to him. He is not known as a forgiving kind of guy. In fact, he is pretty intense."

Roni had met his share of type A personality assholes. Almost every fucking agent thought he could push the scrawny hacker around. Wrong. The only way to deal with them was the opposite of polite. The ruder he'd been to them, the more respectful they had been. Showing weakness was the worst thing to do with these types.

Except, the agents had had no power over him. If they'd wanted Roni's help, they'd had to grovel, not the other way around. Here, he was at the mercy of that Kian guy, and Roni didn't like that at all.

True, Kian needed him, but Roni needed Kian just as much if not more. Damn it, for a smart guy he'd been incredibly stupid not to consider the precarious position he was putting himself in.

He'd been blinded by fantasies of living with Sylvia. Going to sleep with her each night and waking up with her each morning. The other promises Andrew had made had been just a bonus.

Even the immortality.

Roni had been lonely and friendless for most of his life. Even before the prank he'd pulled that had gotten him in trouble and had taken his freedom away, he'd been the geeky kid who'd spent all of his time alone in his room with only his computer for company. Other kids his age had been dumb and boring. The guys had behaved like adolescent chimps, and the girls had ignored him.

Sylvia was his salvation. Much more than a lover, she was his only friend.

"Knock, knock." A woman sauntered into the room. "I'm Ingrid, the housing fairy." She offered her hand to Roni.

He shook it, painfully aware of how pitifully weak his grip was, while the foxy lady in charge of housing arrangements could smash the bones in his hand if she so wished. "Nice to meet you in person."

They'd spoken on the phone earlier. Ingrid had promised to check the available inventory and then come talk to him.

"I assume you know Sylvia."

Ingrid put her hand on Sylvia's shoulder. "Of course I do. Roni tells me that the two of you are going to share the apartment."

Fuck. He hadn't asked Sylvia about it. But Ingrid had made it clear that there weren't enough vacant apartments and that he would have to share. Roni didn't want to room with some strange guy. He wanted to be with Sylvia and only Sylvia.

"I can't. I wish I could. I'm going to spend as much time with you as I can, but I can't move in with you. I'm sorry."

"Why not?"

Sylvia sighed. "My mother. She is clingy. She'd be devastated if I left. I have to get her used to the idea over a long period of time. Maybe in the new place, she'll have more company and won't feel as lonely."

Ingrid shook her head. "I got you your own apartment under the assumption that Sylvia would be moving in with you. So until I run out of options and have to stick you with a roommate, you can enjoy your solitude."

"Thank you."

"Here are the keys." She handed him two plastic cards like the ones used in hotels. "The apartment number is on the sticker attached to each key. First two numbers indicate the floor it's on. Welcome to the keep, Roni."

When Ingrid left, Sylvia leaned and kissed him again. "I'm sorry, baby. I told you about my mom. I thought you figured out that I'm stuck with her."

"Being with you was the most compelling reason for me to leave my old life behind. I can't help feeling disappointed."

"It will happen. Just not right away." She hopped off the bed. "Come on. Get dressed and let's get out of here."

"What about my equipment?" Roni pointed at the monitor stand.

"I'll ask someone to bring it up."

A few minutes later, dressed in his new clothes and with socks on his feet, Roni came out of the bathroom holding a new toothbrush and a disposable razor.

Sylvia noticed the items and pulled out her phone. "I forgot those too. I'll get them when I go for the other things." She typed on the small screen, adding to her shopping list.

Roni threw them in the plastic bag and lifted it off the bed, pretending it wasn't a huge effort to hold the thing up.

"Give me that." Sylvia snatched the bag away from him.

He was too weak to fight her for it. "Way to make me feel like a man, baby."

Holding the bag in one hand as if it weighed nothing, Sylvia wrapped her arm around his waist and propped him up. "You're a man who is weakened by pneumonia. Once you're back on your feet, I'll let you carry all the heavy things. Deal?"

"Deal. And also let me pay you back."

"Nope. I don't want to hear another word about it."

The arguing continued all the way up to the apartment.

"I'll tell you what." Sylvia inserted the keycard into the lock and pushed the door open. "When you get your first paycheck, I'll order a bunch of stuff for myself, and you'll pay for it. A present from you to me for being an awesome girlfriend."

That sounded reasonable, and it gave him an idea. He didn't need to wait for a paycheck to buy his girlfriend things, or for himself. As one of the best hackers in the States, he could get her anything without paying for it, and no one would ever find out. There were two problems with that. One was the delivery; he didn't know if he was allowed to have things delivered to him in the keep. The other problem would be keeping it a secret from Sylvia. She wouldn't accept stolen gifts.

"Okay?" She put her hands on her hips.

"It's a deal."

Sylvia's face lit up. "Wonderful. Now let's take a look around."

She took his hand and tugged, urging him to follow her to the bank of windows. "Look at this view!"

Roni glanced at the high-rises across the street. It was a better view than the one he'd had before, but nothing spectacular. What interested him more was the big television screen hanging over the low fake fireplace and the comfortable couch facing it.

"The sofa looks comfortable." He tugged on Sylvia's hand.

"Let's check it out."

They plopped down at the same time, bouncing up from the springy cushions. Roni leaned back. "Now, that's what I call a sofa. Every couch potato's dream come true."

Sylvia cast him a smirk. "How about we check out the bed for bounciness?"

"Most important system check. Lead on, captain." Roni imitated *Star Trek* Scotty's accent.

Sylvia tugged her T-shirt down and straightened her back. "So I'm the captain?"

"Who do you want to be?"

"Commander Deanna Troi, of course."

"Not the same *Star Trek*. Troi is from the Next Generation. Scotty is from the old one."

"Then you can be Geordi."

"I don't want to be Geordi. How about Worf? I always wanted to be a Klingon."

Sylvia chuckled. "Works for me. Deanna and Worf had a fling."

"In a hallucination. It wasn't real."

Sadly, in his current state, all Roni could do was hallucinate.

32

# SHAWN

"See you tomorrow, Jerry." Shawn passed his fellow salesman on the lot.

Jerry glanced at his watch. "You're leaving early today. What gives?"

"I have a thing, and I'm late for it." Shawn hurried up his steps.

He wasn't late; in fact, he was leaving an hour earlier than needed, but it was none of Jerry's fucking business where he was going.

If word got out about Shawn joining a support group for jilted men, he would become the laughing stock of the dealership. It would be like admitting that he'd gotten his dick cut off and had grown a pussy.

Deciding to check it out had surprised him too. Something in that Facebook ad had resonated with him, touched a sore spot, and the only way he could think of getting rid of that soreness was to go there and make a mockery out of all the sad saps who showed up.

In the end, the joke was on him. A few of the guys were obvious losers, but the majority were other angry men like him. Shawn had felt right at home. He wasn't the only one who felt like a ticking bomb. There were others like him.

The coolest part was the shrink. That dude not only understood Shawn and the other guys, but he also approved of their anger and their right to vengeance.

There was none of the hippie-dippie nonsense about forgiving and forgetting and moving on. The guy got it that it was not going to happen until revenge had been exacted.

Today was the second meeting, and Shawn couldn't wait for another session. He only hoped that none of the pussies came back.

His trip to Aussie was the first step in tracking his wife. He didn't give a shit about the divorce papers. Callie belonged to him. He owned her and her whoring cunt. She would learn that the hard way.

Her phone was still at the restaurant. The battery was long dead, but he knew where she'd left it. One of the waitresses called asking if she was coming back to work and if not if it was okay to clear her locker. Which meant she hadn't told her coworkers about her plans.

He'd told Kati, or whatever the cunt's name was, that Callie had had an emergency back home, something about her father, and that she'd had to leave unexpectedly, but that he would come to collect her things.

A perfect excuse to question the other cunts working there.

As he entered the restaurant, he stopped by the hostess.

"How many in your party?" She flipped her hair back as she smiled at him.

The cunt was fuckable, and he would've gladly done her if not for the charade he needed to keep up. Callie's devoted husband wouldn't fuck her coworker.

"I'm here for my wife's things. Callie. Is there anyone who can help me with that?"

Her smile turned into concern. "What happened to her? Nothing bad, I hope?"

Not yet, but something bad was going to happen to her soon.

"Callie is fine. It's her father. She had to go home, and she has no idea when she'll be able to come back."

The hostess shook her head. "It must be really bad if she didn't even call to let us know she wasn't coming in for her shift."

Shawn plastered on an apologetic expression. "You know how it is when a family crisis hits and they need you. Everything else gets forgotten."

"Yes, of course. I understand. Let me get Kati for you. She can help you."

"Thank you. Your help is much appreciated."

"Of course." The chick hurried to get the other one.

A few moments later, she came back with another hot piece of ass. He should've come here when Callie had asked him to. She'd failed to mention how hot some of her coworkers were. Apparently, she'd failed to mention a lot of things. Like the guys she'd been screwing on the side.

"I'm Kati. You're Callie's husband?" The hottie offered her hand.

"Shawn."

"Nice to meet you. Follow me." She kept talking while leading him to wherever Callie's things were. "So weird the way she took off and forgot her phone. Who forgets her phone?"

"It was probably out of charge. Callie never remembers to charge it." Shawn wondered if his affectionate tone was fooling the waitress. She looked smart, smarter than his fucking wife.

At the employee room, she pointed at an open cardboard box sitting on top of one of the tables. "It's only her phone and a couple of Aussie T-shirts. We all keep spares just in case. People are so clumsy. Someone can bump into you while you're carrying a tray, and boom, you're covered in BBQ sauce."

Shawn shook his head in fake commiseration. "Tell me about it. I also work with customers. What a nightmare."

"What do you do?"

He was glad that Callie hadn't told them anything about him. The question was why? Had she been ashamed of him?

Nah. He was handsome and made good money. Any other woman would've been bragging about what a catch she'd landed.

"I sell luxury vehicles."

Kati put her hand on her hip. "Rich people are the worst, treating everyone as if they are beneath them, and they don't tip well. Unless they are celebrities. Those are the best tippers because they still remember being poor, just like us."

The waitress was talkative, which was good, but Shawn didn't know how to steer the conversation to Callie and whoever she'd been meeting at Aussie.

After mulling over it for days, he decided there was no other place she could've managed a secret affair. He'd known where she was every minute of the day, and she'd never spent long at the supermarket or even clothes shopping. She hadn't gone to nail salons or gotten facials either, and she'd had her haircuts at Supercuts. She must've been meeting her lovers at Aussie.

"Who was your best tipper? Anyone famous?"

"I'm not sure he was a celebrity, but he left a huge tip. In cash. He looked like a rock star, with long blond hair and a body to die for. You should know him. Callie said he was her cousin from Scotland."

"Right. That cousin. I think he plays in a band." Shawn was putting on the best performance of his life. He deserved a fucking Oscar for keeping his murderous rage bottled up and smiling like an idiot. "I keep forgetting his name. Do you remember it?"

Kati scratched her scalp. "Nope. Nothing comes up. It's like a black hole in there. Let me ask Susan. Maybe she remembers."

"Much appreciated. It's so embarrassing. Callie must've told me his name at least ten times and I still keep forgetting it."

As Kati walked out, Shawn paced the small room, counting numbers to keep himself from exploding. His face felt hot.

A few minutes later Kati came back. "Sorry, Shawn, Susan doesn't remember his name either. She doesn't even remember what he looks like, which is really strange because a guy looking like that sticks in a woman's memory." She winked. "But she remembered something about him that I forgot. Susan says he sounds like a robot or a computer. Flat."

Something about a guy who sounded like that tugged at Shawn's memory. But when he tried to focus, it felt as if needles were being shoved into his brain. Shaking his head, he tried again, but again lost the thread and the headache got worse.

"Anything else I can help you with?" Kati asked.

"Thank you. You were most helpful. I'll just take the box."

"Tell Callie we miss her and to come say hi when she's back. Also, that I pray for her father's health."

"I will. You're a good friend."

## 33

## CALLIE

Thank God it was the middle of the week, and the club was closing at two in the morning. Callie was counting the minutes until Franco turned on the lights and called it a night.

After their dinner at Gino's, Brundar had brought her home just in time for her to change into her uniform, then dropped her at the club and headed for his night rotation. Which meant that tonight he was free and could walk her home. Or drive her. But she preferred the walk even though her feet were killing her after seven hours of running around taking orders and delivering drinks.

Breathing the fresh air and enjoying the quiet was calming. It helped her sleep better, but not always. Some nights she was plagued by nightmares about Shawn finding her; others, she kept tossing and turning because of wet dreams about Brundar doing all kinds of wicked things to her.

"What are you still doing here?" Miri asked on her way out.

"Waiting for Brad."

"What's the matter, Donnie can't take you?"

The barmaid still wasn't convinced nothing was going on between Callie and the bouncer, and Callie didn't have the heart to tell her that Donnie had his eyes on someone else.

"I'm sure he can, but I want Brad to take me tonight." In more ways than one. At the end of their walk, Callie intended to invite Brundar up to her apartment and have her way with him.

Miri shook her head as if Callie was deluding herself. "Goodnight. I'll see you tomorrow."

"Goodnight to you too."

To pass the time and not look like she was waiting to catch him, which she was, Callie got busy helping the busboys clear the tables.

A few minutes later, Donnie walked in. "What's up, Callie?"

Crap. She should have told him he didn't need to wait for her and could go home. "Sorry. I forgot to tell you that I'm waiting for Brad tonight."

Donnie lifted a brow. "Does he know that you're waiting for him?"

"Nope. But he is going to find out."

"What if he can't take you?"

"He will have to if you're gone. Don't worry. I'll tell him I sent you home."

Donnie plopped down on a bar stool and crossed his arms over his chest. "I'll wait."

Stubborn man. "Why?"

"First of all because I don't want to lose my job. No offense, but Brad is my boss, not you. And secondly, Miri is outside, lying in wait for me. I told her I need to take you home. I hope she gets tired of waiting and drives off."

*Poor Miri.* Callie knew all about pining for a guy who wasn't interested. But at least Brundar was attracted to her. He just didn't want a relationship. Donnie didn't find Miri attractive.

"Just tell her you're not interested."

Donnie grimaced. "I can't say it straight out like that. I don't want to hurt her feelings. Besides, she is scary. I don't want to go on her shit list."

Callie chuckled. "I know what you mean. That's one more reason why you should go after Fran. When Miri sees you with someone else, she'll give up."

"It's happening this weekend."

"Good for you." Callie patted his shoulder.

"What's happening at the weekend?" Brundar asked, startling both her and Donnie.

Hand on her racing heart, she turned around. "Could you please make more noise when you walk? You scared the bejesus out of me."

There was no amusement in his tone as he stared daggers at the bouncer. "Donnie?"

The guy looked so extremely uncomfortable that Callie decided to come to his rescue.

"Donnie is going to ask someone out."

"Is it someone who works here?" Brundar was still staring at Donnie who seemed to be shrinking under that intense scrutiny.

"Yeah. It's Fran," he finally admitted.

Brundar relaxed. "Good luck with that. Just remember to keep your hands and other body parts to yourself on club grounds. Anywhere else it's none of my business."

"Yes, boss."

Callie rolled her eyes. First of all, considering what went on down in the basement, telling Donnie to keep his hands to himself was hypocritical. And secondly, Fran hadn't said yes yet. She might prove to be a snooty little bitch and turn sweet Donnie down.

"Are you taking me home?" She turned to Brundar. "Donnie waited to make sure I have an escort."

"Yes."

"Good." She turned to Donnie. "Thank you for waiting. I hope the coast is clear."

The bouncer pushed to his feet. "Me too."

"What was that about?" Brundar asked after Donnie left.

Forgetting his aversion to touch, Callie threaded her arm through his, but surprisingly he didn't pull away.

"It's a soap opera. Miri is waiting for Donnie outside because she likes him, but he likes Fran. He was hiding inside under the pretense of waiting for you to make sure I had an escort, hoping she'd give up and go home."

They stepped out into the cool night. Callie huddled closer to Brundar. It was a little windy, and her light jacket didn't offer enough protection.

He wrapped his arm around her and held her tight against his side. "You're cold. We should take my car."

"I like to walk home. It's soothing after the hustle and bustle of the nightclub. Helps me sleep better."

He frowned as he looked down at her. "You have trouble sleeping?"

"Sometimes. I have nightmares about Shawn finding me and threatening to kill me." She couldn't tell him about the other types of dreams that had been keeping her awake.

"Would you feel better if I slept by your side?"

Wow. That was such an unexpected and wonderful offer. "Of course. But what about your night rotation?"

"It's every other day. I can come in the morning after my shift ends."

She stopped and turned her face up to him. "That would be amazing. I hate sleeping alone."

He grimaced, and she immediately regretted her words. The only other person she had slept with had been her husband and the number one threat to her life. Sleeping with him hadn't felt safe in a long time.

"Perhaps you should get a dog. A big one."

"That's not a bad idea. But what about the times when I'm at work? Who is going to take care of it?"

"True. I hadn't thought of that." He wrapped his arm around her waist as they kept walking.

"I can get a cat. They don't need as much company."

"A cat is no protection."

"I don't even know if pets are allowed in the building." Brundar should know. She was certain that he'd rented the place and not his imaginary friend, and it still bothered her that he'd lied. But she didn't want to confront him about it. Their relationship was too tenuous to withstand a big blowup over a lie that was rooted in good intentions.

The problem was that it sat like a nasty sediment at the pit of her stomach. If she could somehow get Brundar to confess and explain why he'd done it, she could get rid of that bad feeling.

"Did your friend have a pet?"

"What friend?"

"The professor. The one who's teaching abroad. By the way, you never told me which university he's teaching at. Or even in what country."

Brundar shrugged. "I don't know. I can ask the manager if pets are allowed. Did you see any of your neighbors walking a dog?"

"No. The only neighbor I've talked to was the lady in the apartment right next to me."

Brundar frowned. "I thought she was always traveling."

"She is. But she came back, and we had lunch together."

Callie was watching Brundar's expression closely. The changes were so minute, it was easy to miss them. Except, she'd learned to pay attention. Brundar might be a closed book to everyone else, but not to her.

There was the slight tightness of his jaw, the crease on his forehead, and sometimes she caught his eyes glowing. Or at least they seemed to when he got angry or sexed up.

"Did you like her?"

"I did. She knows your friend. The professor. But she is convinced he moved out and is teaching somewhere else in the States. Not abroad."

Brundar stopped walking and put both hands on Callie's waist. "She must be mistaken."

Pulling her against his body, he kissed her, his lips smashing over hers, his tongue slipping inside her mouth without preamble, taking, possessing as he backed her against a block wall fence.

She knew what he was doing, but his distraction tactic was working. His aggression turned her on, making her feel boneless, needy, hungry.

When his palm closed over her breast and kneaded, the neighbor and the lie suddenly seemed unimportant.

"Brundar," she breathed.

Pressing his hard length against her, he pushed his hand under her club T-shirt and tweaked her nipple through her bra. Hard. "Let's go back to the club and play. Everyone has left already." His words came out sounding like a hiss—as if he was in pain.

Brundar was in a dangerous mood tonight, and Callie knew that whatever he was planning to do to her, he wasn't going to be gentle, and it turned her on even more.

"Okay," Callie whispered.

She was more than ready to play.

## 34

# BRUNDAR

Calypso's heartbeat had been drumming a rapid beat throughout their short walk back to the club. It accelerated as Brundar opened the door to his favorite playroom, the one he'd taken her to their first time together.

"Do you think they've had time to clean it up already?" Her voice shook a little.

Some of it was nervousness; most of it was excitement. His girl was in the mood for something darker. She was eager to play.

Good, because so was he. Typically, he didn't care one way or another. As long as his basic requirements were met, he was game for most kinds of play, but it was more like willing to eat a treat than craving it.

Tonight he was craving it.

Because it was Calypso, and because she'd pushed him to his limit and he needed to assert his dominance over this feisty female who was trying to turn him into someone he was not.

In here he was the teacher, and she was the pupil. He instructed, and she obeyed. The beauty of it was that he wasn't going to hear any arguments from her. On this subject, they were in agreement.

In here she accepted his authority without question.

In her bedroom he had let the boundaries slip.

It wasn't working for him. He had caved, wanting to satisfy her need for intimacy, but he could provide it after the scene was over and the sexual energy released, when he was no longer sporting two-inch-long fangs and glowing eyes and could let her see him.

"The room was cleaned. It's on the chart outside the room."

"That's smart," she mumbled, eyeing the equipment. Now that she knew what it was for, it must've looked more ominous to her.

"Strip," Brundar commanded, watching Calypso's eyes widen.

He hadn't used that tone on her before because she'd been a newbie, and he'd thought she was fragile and vulnerable. He'd learned since that Calypso was neither. She was a fighter, she didn't cower, she plotted and schemed, and she got her way one way or another.

Not tonight. Not in this room.

The only say she had about what was going to happen was either submit or abort by safe-wording out of the play.

Leaning against the door, Brundar crossed his arms over his chest and waited.

Unmoving, Calypso stared right back at him.

He wasn't going to repeat his command. He wasn't going to do anything until she obeyed. He had the patience of a sequoia tree.

The standoff didn't last long. With a slight nod, Calypso walked over to one of the nightstands and put her purse down, then gripped the bottom of her T-shirt and yanked it over her head.

Watching her strip, the smile tugging on his lips made keeping up the stern expression difficult.

Calypso was obeying him, but in the most defiant, non-submissive way possible, while at the same time careful not to cross the line into giving him an excuse to punish her.

Although baring her body to him was arousing no matter how it was done, she wasn't making the slightest effort to make it a sexy striptease. Undressing unceremoniously as if she was about to step into the shower, she didn't let her eyes leave his for a moment.

The woman was a force to be reckoned with.

When she was bare, she mimicked his stance, crossing her arms over her breasts in a futile effort to hide them from his eyes.

"Arms by your sides, Calypso."

She closed her eyes for a couple of seconds, then did as he commanded.

"Get in position on the bench."

A hurt look flitted through her beautiful green eyes, tempting him to drop the charade and take her into his arms. But a moment later, it was gone and she tilted her chin, straightened her back, and walked over to the bench.

When she got in position, he walked over to her, pulled her hair to one side and kissed her exposed neck. "Good girl," he said in a soothing tone as his palm traveled down her back, caressing her incredibly smooth skin, then kneading her taut buttocks.

With a sigh, she relaxed the tension in her shoulders.

"How come your palms are not calloused?" Calypso blurted out of the blue.

His hand stilled on her body. No woman had asked him that even though he'd listed fencing as his main hobby on the questionnaire. No one had ever wondered how come his hands were smooth despite supposedly playing a sport that was known to produce callouses. No one had paid enough attention, or cared.

*Damnation.*

Two things were obvious. One—the woman was dangerous if she was so observant. Two—he was doing something wrong if this was what she was thinking of during play.

"I use gloves." A lie, but the alternative was some bullshit about a hand moisturizer. Not very manly. Especially given where they were, and what they were doing.

He delivered a hard smack to her butt. "No more talking."

"Not even please more, or this is so good?"

*Impudent girl.*

He delivered another smack, then leaned against her back. "That's allowed. But no more questions. Is that clear?"

"Yes, sir."

To her credit, Calypso stayed in position, not looking back or reaching to rub her stinging ass even though he hadn't restrained her yet. Something he was about to remedy right away.

It took him less than a minute to have her secured to the bench, the blindfold going on last. He didn't ask if she was okay. By now he knew Calypso wouldn't hesitate to tell him if anything felt uncomfortable.

That was the advantage of playing with a woman who wasn't a true submissive. Calypso wouldn't endure excessive discomfort or pain just to please him. A relief. He didn't have to keep checking and reassessing to make sure she wasn't suffering. Or rather not suffering more than she wanted to.

In that regard, she was the perfect playmate for him. Hell, in every regard.

She took to bondage like a pro. As soon as he'd fastened the last restraint, she relaxed into the bonds holding her body, and as soon as he'd finished tying the silk scarf around her eyes, she uttered a contented sigh.

Beautiful.

Brundar caressed her back, kissing one side of her neck down to her shoulder then moving to the other side.

Calypso purred like a kitten, and when he cupped her butt cheeks and kneaded the warmed up flesh, she laid her head back on his shoulder and purred even louder.

A little mewl of protest left her throat when he stopped touching her to pull his T-shirt over his head and toss it behind him. But when he leaned over her back, covering it with his bare chest, she once again let her head drop back on his shoulder and sighed.

The contraption she was strapped to supported her front only up to her breasts. There was an extension he could've pulled up, a narrow beam that went between the breasts and terminated in a padded chin support, but he didn't think Calypso would have liked it even though it would've made her more comfortable. The strap that went around the neck would've prevented her from leaning her head back on his shoulder.

Besides, it required a level of submission he didn't think she had in her.

Palming her breasts, he rubbed his erection against her soft bottom, regretting that he hadn't shucked his pants along with the T-shirt.

For a few moments, he was gentle, kneading and stroking, thumbing her nipples, stoking her need and her hunger for something spicier.

## 35

## CALLIE

Callie was on fire.
His rhythm unpredictable, Brundar moved from drawing lazy circles around her areolas to plucking at her nipples, then pinching, then gently stroking again. She never knew what would come next, a zing of pain or a soft caress.

Everything about tonight felt different.

Brundar was different, and yet the same. Not as careful or gentle as before, his touch rougher and more demanding, he was nevertheless in full control of his emotions. It was still about her pleasure, Callie didn't doubt that for a moment, but he was upping the ante and testing her limits.

Apparently, he'd been right. Painting the experience a shade darker was pushing all of her buttons.

Bound and blindfolded with Brundar's hard length rubbing against her bottom, her whole body singing to the tune of his torment, she was on the brink of orgasm before he even touched between her legs.

"Please," she groaned.

As his grip on her stiff nipples tightened, she pushed forward to escape the rough treatment, but the restraints allowed her no more than an inch of wiggle room.

The realization that she was at Brundar's mercy finally hit home.

Until tonight, he'd been holding back, his treatment of her more gentle than what she would've liked. Even the spanking had been more playful than painful. This was different. He was pushing her boundaries, testing her willingness to submit.

It should have scared her, but it didn't.

With a throaty moan, she relaxed into the pain, trusting that Brundar's cruel touch was a means to an end. It wasn't about inflicting pain for pain's sake, it was about helping her unlock a place inside herself for which this was the only key.

Pulling a shocked gasp out of her throat, his grip tightened.

The buildup was more of a leap than a gradual climb. Before she was done processing the confusing messages her body and her mind were sending, Callie snapped, lights exploding behind her closed eyes and her mouth opening on a scream.

If not for Brundar's body pressing against her back and the bonds that were holding her up, the force of the climax would've brought her down to her knees.

As bliss slowly receded, she registered Brundar's warm palms cupping her breasts, soothing, and his muscular chest glued to her sweaty back. He was unbuckling the restraint on her left wrist, then moved to the right.

Disappointed, Callie whispered, "Are we done?"

A few moments to recuperate were desperately needed, but she didn't want their play to be over yet. As tired as she was, Callie had another climax or two in her.

"Not by a long shot." His warm chest abandoned her back as he bent to tackle the restraints holding her thighs spread wide. When he was done with those, he moved to the ones strapping her calves to the lower supports.

"That's good to know." Despite the incredible release, she was still craving a spanking, and the tiny sting from the two smacks he'd delivered before was long gone.

The blindfold remained as Brundar lifted her into his arms, cradling her to his chest and carrying her to the bed. It felt amazing to be held like that. Like she was precious, and he didn't want to let go.

She refused to dwell on the fact that Brundar didn't have feelings like that. He was holding her tight only because her body was so limp that he was afraid she would fall. The rest was the product of wishful thinking and her imagination.

Laying her on the bed, Brundar's palm tenderly cradled the entire back of her head. His lips were soft and warm as he kissed her, his tongue parting hers and gaining access without waiting for her permission.

It seemed that he was done asking.

Callie had thought it was his style, but apparently, he'd only been testing her and learning her responses until he had her figured out.

She liked that he was letting the dominant in him take over. It added a level of excitement to their play. As long as he dropped the autocratic attitude outside the bedroom, she was perfectly fine with being his willing subject in here.

Guiding her arms over her head, he once again restrained her hands with the soft Velcro ties. This time, though, he didn't tie each one individually to an opposite corner of the headboard. He bound her hands together and tethered them to a central post.

Her legs were left unbound.

Was he going to flip her around on her tummy? Maybe she would still get the spanking she'd been craving?

Just imagining that wrested a moan from her throat, and new moisture seeped from her still untouched core.

"Brundar?"

She heard him kick off his boots and unbuckle his jeans.

"What is it, sweetling?"

"I need you."

"I'm right here." He climbed on the bed. Lying on his side, his hand slowly caressed her from collarbone to hip as if there was no urgency, but his ragged breathing told a different story. It was amazing how much could be discerned from sound, smell, and touch when sight was not available.

Even if the evidence of his arousal weren't pulsing against her thigh, Brundar's labored breathing told her everything she needed to know. The guy was in such incredible shape that he could run a marathon and his breaths would come out as calm and as even as if he were taking a casual stroll.

He was turned on. Big time.

Callie smiled. Brundar could huff, and he could puff, but the real big bad wolf in this bed was her. Well, not really, but they could take turns.

"What's that smile about, beautiful?"

With his palm circling from her hip to her stomach and traveling south, so close to where she needed him, it was hard to formulate words.

"Touch me," she commanded.

His hand halted. "Who is in charge in here, sweetling?"

His stern tone had woken a flurry of butterflies in her stomach.

Damn it. She didn't like these kinds of games.

Or did she?

Hadn't he told her that this was all about her? And that ultimately she was the one in charge?

One word from her could stop everything. She could use a safe word, while Brundar couldn't.

She needed to remember, though, that her pleasure depended on keeping her head in the game and not in the real world. Out there, Callie would have never tolerated him talking to her like that. But this was not the real world. It was a fantasy. The rules were whatever they wanted them to be for this particular game. Other games would have different ones.

"You are." Should she have added 'sir'?

Maybe next time she would. After all, there was no sense in playing the game if she wasn't going to use all its pieces.

"That's right, sweetling." Mercifully, his hand returned to her stomach. "In here, I decide when to touch you and how."

Callie held her breath as his palm finally made it to her aching center, but he only cupped her, holding her there as if her feminine center belonged to him.

She almost issued another command before catching her lower lip between her teeth to keep herself quiet.

Brundar leaned and licked at the lip she was chewing until she released it, then sucked it into his mouth, at the same time parting her folds with his finger and pushing it in.

Her hips arching off the bed, Callie groaned.

"Please..." He'd said it was okay to plead, just not to command.

His finger left her sheath, and she was about to cry out her protest and complain when he seized her by her hips and flipped her around onto her stomach. A moment later he tucked a pillow under her belly, then another one, until he was satisfied with the angle.

Oh, God, was he going to spank her?

Could she at least hint that she wanted him to?

Would he stop their play if she did?"

Brundar had discovered that the most effective punishment for her disobedience wasn't his hand on her ass, but the lack of it, there and everywhere else.

Experimentally, she wiggled her butt a little and arched further up.

Crap, she must've looked like a cat in heat. How embarrassing. Her behind was high enough propped up as it had been. Immediately, she lowered herself back down until her pelvis rested on the pillows.

When she heard a drawer open, Callie wondered what Brundar was looking for—a condom or an implement of punishment?

A condom was fine. But a paddle or a strap was not. She specifically marked those as hard limits. Listening intently for a clue, she heard him remove the wrapping from something that sounded a lot bigger than a condom.

Her butt cheeks clenched a moment before something that felt like soft strips of suede touched her back.

"It's a flogger," he said, dragging the strips down her to her bottom. "It's very soft, and is meant for pleasure, not pain." He waited for her to okay it or not.

Apparently, when introducing something new, Brundar was still going to ask.

She was willing to try an implement of pleasure. And if it proved unpleasant, she could always tell him to stop. But what if she didn't want their play to stop, just the use of the flogger?

"I want to add another color to red, yellow, and green."

Brundar chuckled and kept caressing her with the flogger, not an unpleasant sensation. "That should be interesting. Why would you need another color?"

"In case I don't like the flogger or some other implement you want to try on me, and I want you to go back to using only your hands, which you know is my preference, I will say purple."

"Does that mean you're giving me the green light to try other things?"

"Yes." Even if Brundar decided to use one of those horrid paddles, or a strap, or even his belt, one smack wasn't going to kill her or her mood, but it could satisfy her curiosity.

He chuckled again. "Purple is officially added to the list of safe words."

The tails dragged in a slithery caress up across her shoulders, then down again to wrap around her inner thighs. Brundar's palm followed, with two fingers seeking her moist entrance from behind and pushing in, retreating and then pushing back.

She clenched around his fingers, trying to hold them in, but he withdrew. A moment later she tensed at the sound of the tails swinging, but the flogger struck gently, slapping her bottom with barely any force.

It didn't even sting.

Callie relaxed, relieved, but also a little disappointed. The flogger retreated again. Its caress was gentle as it landed on her left shoulder blade, then the other, then going back to her bottom, a little more forceful this time, but still just a little more than a caress.

She knew where it was going and welcomed it.

Finding his rhythm, Brundar landed soft strokes on her shoulders and thighs, heavier ones on her bottom, playing her like a musical instrument.

Her soft moans sang the perfect tune to accompany the steady beat.

She was writhing now, her lower body moving to the rhythm of the flogger, her skin tingling, her bottom stinging but not hurting. Awash in sensation, Callie decided she liked the flogger and the man who wielded it so expertly.

Through the haze of arousal, Callie was dimly aware of a drawer opening. A moment later, she heard the unmistakable sound of a condom wrapper tearing.

Brundar's rhythm never faltered. The flogger landed several times in quick succession on her upturned behind before delivering one last hard sting, then getting tossed to the floor. A split second later, Brundar surged inside her, filling her in one powerful thrust and detonating the orgasm that he'd been steadily building.

She cried out, the exquisite pleasure like an electrical current pulsing through every part of her body.

Without pause, Brundar pounded into her, his groin smacking against her warmed up behind, each thrust into her soaking sex making a lewd wet sound and bringing her closer to another climax while his own rushed to the front.

Hanging on for dear life, Callie was barely aware of Brundar's mouth latching onto her neck. A split second later, his teeth pierced her skin. There was a distant sensation of burning pain, and then she climaxed again.

## 36

# BRUNDAR

Brundar discarded the condom, grabbed a few washcloths and came back to bed. Releasing Calypso's wrists from the restraints, he wondered whether he should thrall her while she was still out of it, or wait to see if she remembered his bite.

He removed her blindfold and examined her neck. The bite marks were already gone, so there would be no evidence of it, and even if she remembered, he might be able to talk his way out of it.

Damnation. He hated all the lying necessary to keep his people safe.

Except, it was for a very good cause, and he would do so as long as he had to in order to preserve Calypso's sharp mind. Even every other day or every third day could cause irreversible damage to a human's brain. He had developed a good system that allowed him to refrain from using the thrall too often, and it worked well in the club, but Calypso wasn't as easy to fool.

She didn't miss much.

After a quick wipe down with a washcloth, he tucked her into his chest and held on. So soft and so perfect. Nothing had ever felt as good and as right.

She opened her eyes and looked up at him with a smile. "Did I pass out again?"

"Just for a few minutes." Her body was getting accustomed to his venom. Soon, she wouldn't black out at all.

"You must be so proud of yourself," she teased. "It takes skill to have a woman pass out each time you make love to her."

The phrase making love grated on his mental synapses. Why did humans have to use euphemisms when talking about sex?

He didn't like the word fucking either; there was a demeaning connotation to it that he wanted nowhere near Calypso. Plain old sex worked best. Not making love, not sleeping together unless they were actually sleeping, and not fucking or screwing either.

He and Calypso had sex.

But he wasn't going to correct her. Calling the act of sex making love obviously meant something to her, and if he commented on it, she would get offended, maybe even start crying. The petty peeve he had with the euphemism wasn't worth ruining her orgasm afterglow over.

"Did you enjoy the flogger, sweetling?"

"A lot. I'm so glad we added purple as a safe word. Now I feel like I could get adventurous and try new things. Nothing is so bad that I can't endure a few seconds of it."

"You can always say red and everything stops. Isn't that enough?"

Calypso eyed his chest, then leaned forward and kissed it. "Is this okay? Or is it the same as touching?"

He cradled the back of her head and kissed her forehead. "It's okay. You can kiss me anywhere you want."

"Anywhere?" She waggled her brows.

He slapped her behind. "Answer the question I asked you."

She made a pouty face. "Meanie. What was the question?"

Perhaps she was still loopy and unfocused from the venom. "Why do you need purple when red stops everything?"

"Because I don't want everything to stop. It's a downer. Purple is about implements only. There are so many of them that they deserve a color of their own."

There was some logic to it, though he doubted it would make sense to anyone but the two of them. But then the two of them was what mattered. Until he could no longer stay around, Brundar wasn't going to play with anyone else, and neither was Calypso. Which meant the condoms could and should go.

"I want you to go on the pill. I don't want any barriers between us. I'll get checked up and bring you a letter from the doctor as proof that I'm clean."

"How do you know you are? Were you always safe?"

"I was. But I don't want you to take my word for it. Never do that with any guy no matter how much they swear on it. Always ask for documents."

Her smile vanished, her chin quivering a little. "How can you talk about me with other men?"

He couldn't. The words had left his mouth before he had time to let the implications sink in. "It's hypothetical. I want to make sure that no matter what the future holds, you're always careful and protected."

Calypso nodded. "You're right. But by the same token, you should also ask me for a certificate. What if I'm infected?"

Brundar chuckled. "You married the first guy you had sex with, was with said guy for two years, and I'm the second one. I don't think there is a chance you caught something."

Calypso chewed on her lower lip. "What if Shawn cheated on me?"

"You think he did?"

"Why else would he be so suspicious of me cheating on him all of the time? Everyone judges others by their own standards or lack thereof."

He nodded. "Yeah. That's why it never crossed my mind that the lowlife could've brought diseases back home to you."

She kissed his chin. "You're a good man, Brundar."

Was he?

Not really. But he was honorable. He would've never cheated on a life mate even if their match wasn't a true love one.

"I can arrange an appointment for you with my other cousin who is a doctor." Bridget would do it for free, saving Calypso unnecessary expense.

Calypso chuckled. "Not another cousin, Brundar. I want to do this one on my own."

"Why? My cousin would do it for free."

She shook her head. "Not this time. I'm going to find a nice doctor and make an appointment like everyone else."

"I'll drive you to the appointment."

She rolled her eyes. "We will talk about it later."

Which in Calypso speak meant forget it.

He didn't understand why she'd refused getting checked up by a relative of his, or why she wanted to do this without him.

Was she trying to hide something?

Nah. Calypso was like an open book. Whatever bothered her about his involvement must have been something else. Probably one of those strange female-specific issues no male would ever understand.

## 37

# RONI

"How do I look?" Roni pulled down on the skin under his eye, stretching out the dark circle that had formed there.

Sylvia straightened his shirt collar. "Sickly, but at least presentable."

"Tell me more about that Kian dude, so I can mentally prepare."

She shrugged. "I don't know him that well. From what I hear he is cranky and short-tempered but not a pompous ass. The Guardians all admire him."

"Anandur is a Guardian, right?"

"Yes, and Onegus is the chief Guardian."

"How many Guardians do you have?"

She hesitated. "I'm pretty sure it's classified information."

"But you know."

"I do, but I'm not supposed to talk about it."

Sylvia seemed distraught by the situation he'd put her in. As his girlfriend, she should have no secrets from him, but some secrets were not hers to share. He didn't want to make her uncomfortable.

"It's okay, baby." He pulled her into a hug. "I love you."

She kissed him lightly on the lips. "I love you too."

He took her hand. "Let's go. I don't want to be late."

"You don't want to be early either. He gave us fifteen minutes, not because he is a megalomaniac, but because he really doesn't have time."

That remained to be seen. People in positions of power usually didn't get there by playing nice.

Roni was surprised to see Sylvia press the button for one of the underground levels. "Where is his office?"

"Down in the basement. Most of our facilities are there. There is a gym, a swimming pool, a movie theater, classrooms, a grand hall, a commercial kitchen. The list goes on. Oh, and the catacombs. And a dungeon."

Roni wiped a hand over his mouth. "I'll be damned. A dungeon? Can I see it? Is it like a medieval torture chamber or a place to have kinky sex?"

Sylvia slapped his arm. "You're so juvenile. The dungeon is a level with several holding cells that are supposedly pretty nice. Nothing medieval about them. You can ask Anandur to show you. I don't think there is anyone there at the moment."

They exited the elevators and continued down a wide corridor, identical to the one leading to the clinic. Anandur was waiting for them outside a set of glass doors.

"Hey, Roni, my man." The big guy's hand landed on Roni's shoulder with a surprisingly light touch. "How are you feeling? I hear you got a place all to yourself."

"It's temporary. Ingrid told me she would have to pair me with someone."

Anandur scratched his beard. "Yeah, we are a little short on lodging here. But pretty soon we will have room to spare in a village-like atmosphere with lots of green stuff to look at." He leaned to whisper in Roni's ear. "Personally, I'm tired of the concrete jungle."

Sylvia sighed. "That's why my mom refuses to move into the keep. She says it's depressing."

Anandur glanced at his watch, then knocked on the door. "It's time, kids." He pushed the door open.

"Are you coming in?" Roni asked. No one had asked Anandur to come talk on behalf of Roni, but it seemed the guy had volunteered. Andrew, who was the ideal candidate for the job, was still playing chicken and refusing to get anywhere near Roni until Bridget reassured him that the virus was no longer contagious.

"Yes, I am. But I'm going to be quiet. With that big mouth of yours, I'm sure you can manage on your own."

Sylvia groaned. "That's what I'm afraid of."

"That's what I'm here for." Anandur winked. "To kick him under the table if he forgets his manners."

"Are you guys going to be standing out in the corridor much longer? Because I have shit to do," came a gruff voice from inside the room.

Roni liked the guy already.

He strode inside, ready to offer his hand for a handshake, when the guy pushed up to his feet and rounded his desk.

Holly shit, the dude was good-looking. Like in movie-star, girls throwing their panties at him good-looking.

Roni swallowed. Jerks with attitude didn't intimidate him, but guys like Kian did. Too attractive, and too full of themselves because every female in their vicinity drooled like an idiot.

"I'm Kian." The guy offered his hand, and Sylvia nudged Roni to reciprocate.

Falling back on years of experience dealing with people who thought he was easily intimidated because he wasn't big and buff, Roni shook Kian's hand. "It's good to meet you, Kian. I heard a lot about you." He was proud that his voice came out sounding steady and professional.

Kian regarded him with a pair of eyes that were the most intense Roni had ever seen.

"Let's all sit at the conference table." He pointed to the oblong thing that was taking most of the floor space of his office.

The boss sat at the head of the table, Anandur to his left, and Roni took the seat to his right. Sylvia sat next to him. Evidently, Kian intimidated her as well, though not sexually.

Roni felt ridiculously grateful that sexual relationships between clan members were prohibited. According to Sylvia, it was something about all of them sharing the same bloodline. Because there was no way any woman who wasn't a blood relative wouldn't be attracted to that dude.

"What can I help you with, Roni?"

"I need to know what my status here is. If I transition, that's obvious, I join the clan. But at the moment it seems doubtful."

Kian nodded. "I understand that you prefer to stay on, even if it means you're a prisoner here."

"You understand correctly. I want to be with Sylvia. We love each other."

A pitying look flitted through Kian's eyes. "A relationship between an immortal and a human is doomed from the start. But you're young. You still have many years ahead of you even as a human. On the other hand, you can have a full life outside of here. I can arrange for a new identity, a new place to settle in, and we can even use your services without you knowing who and what we are. The problem is that erasing your memories would be next to impossible. You've accumulated a shitload of those with Sylvia."

Kian cast her a reprimanding glare. "You shouldn't have done it. Not for so long. I understand we are talking months, right?"

Sylvia nodded without looking Kian in the eyes.

"We face several challenges here. Completely wiping Sylvia from your memory is impossible. I can give it a shot and erase just the part about her being immortal, but I doubt it would work on you. Your brain is too powerful. Which brings me to the next complication. I would hate to damage it even slightly. It's like ruining a one of a kind work of art. Unforgivable."

"Thank you. I appreciate the compliment. But that leaves only one option, and that's of me staying on. I'm fine with that. I was a prisoner where I was before, so that's not a big change. Hopefully, I'll be treated better here. It was so fucking lonely there. I'm not going to miss that."

Sylvia gasped in horror, but Kian grinned.

"I think you're going to miss those days when you realize what a bunch of fucking busybodies your new friends are. Privacy? Forget about it. Keeping secrets? Only if you don't tell a soul."

Roni felt a heavy weight lift off his chest, and it had nothing to do with the pneumonia. "Does it mean I can stay?"

Kian shook his head, scaring the crap out of Roni, but then he nodded. "There is a precedent. Andrew was allowed in because of Syssi, his sister and my wife. Syssi transitioned, so we knew Andrew was a Dormant as well, but he was older, and there was a fear he wouldn't make it. It all ended well, and he transitioned, but the point of the story is that we welcomed him regardless. You don't have a blood relative who we know has transitioned, but you have Sylvia. Not as strong of a case as Andrew's, but I can work with that."

Roni slumped in his chair. "Thank God."

Kian lifted a finger. "But, I have to take precautions to ensure the safety of my people. You will be fitted with an unremovable cuff that will track your location at all times and sound the alarm if you try to leave."

Unable to stop himself, Roni snorted. "With all due respect, Kian, do you think I can't disarm a thing like that?"

Kian's smile was part conceited, part evil. "You might be smart, even brilliant, but our William is just as smart and has the advantage of advanced technology you've never even heard about. Try to mess with that cuff and it will explode, taking your arm with it."

Roni gulped and instinctively cradled his forearm.

His expression menacing, Kian leaned toward him. "Just think about it, Roni. How are you going to do all that hacking of yours with only one hand?"

## 38

## JACKSON

A box of pastries under his arm, Jackson walked into the keep's café and scanned the small crowd. It was late morning, after the breakfast rush was over and before the lunch one began, and yet four out of the café's twelve tables were occupied, most by more than one immortal.

Mid-morning coffee break for those working in the keep.

He put the box down on one of the barstools. "Hi, Carol, how are things going?"

She shrugged. "Business as usual. What about you?"

"Same, though not for long. Everything is going to change after the move to the new place."

She nodded. "I'm still stuck with running the café unless someone volunteers to take it off my hands. I don't think Nathalie is ever coming back. Not until little Phoenix is old enough to go to preschool." Carol shook her head. "The little darling will have a long commute. I don't know how far it is to the nearest school, but my guess is about an hour's drive. The place is so isolated that it will make socializing with people outside the clan difficult."

"Do you prefer it here?"

"No. I prefer my own little home, which I'm renting out."

So did Jackson's mother. As a therapist, she worked mostly with humans and shared a clinic with several other therapists in an office building that wasn't anywhere near the keep but was ten minutes' drive from their home.

Her home, he corrected himself.

Jackson no longer lived there, and he had no intention of going back. The next place he was moving into was the house he and Tessa were going to share in the village. Which would make his commute a nightmare too.

"I've been thinking. What if I take over the new café?"

Carol's eyes widened. "What about Nathalie's old café? I hear it's doing very well."

"It is. But I'm thinking about the commute too. Besides, Vlad and Gordon are starting college. Vlad is staying in town so he can work part-time, but Gordon is going out of state."

"You can hire humans."

Jackson swiped his long bangs back. "I will, if I have to. But what do you think about my idea?"

Carol tilted her head, taking a few moments to think. "If Nathalie doesn't mind about the other place, then I'm all for it. I can work part-time too, help you out until you get settled." She sighed. "I would love to reclaim my old life and chill a little. I miss the clubs and the partying and inviting friends over for dinner."

Fates, he knew the feeling. Ever since he'd taken over the café and then started dating Tessa, everything else had become less of a priority, which meant nonexistent. When was the last time he'd chilled with his friends? Except for performing and practicing their music?

With the guys leaving for college, even that would be over.

It hit him then that he and Tessa were like an old married couple. Tessa didn't know any better, since she'd missed the entire high school experience and started working for Eva at sixteen or seventeen, but he did. They should get together with other couples. Go out dancing or something. For Tessa's sake more than his.

There was a whole chunk of life she'd missed out on, and it was up to him to help make up for that.

Jackson opened the large box and pulled out a smaller one. "Here are your pastries." He closed the bigger box and tucked it under his arm. "I'm going to restock the vending machine."

"We are all out of muffins."

He patted the box. "I have plenty of them here."

The vending machine needed to smarten up and send messages when it was running low on something. The technology was available. He should check it out. Someone must've thought of that and already built smart vending machines.

Perhaps he should suggest it to Kian. Unless they were available for lease, Jackson couldn't afford to buy even one. But the good thing about Kian was that he was generous with money if he deemed the expense justified. Given that automation was the only alternative to employing humans, which Kian was refusing to consider, Jackson had a feeling the boss would be all for getting the new and improved vending machines.

Not that he could blame the guy. Jackson didn't like working with humans either. It was a constant strain to watch himself and not let on that he could hear conversations from across the room, or lift things that took the strength of two human males.

Opening the machine, he started filling up the slots with wrapped pastries, when a pair of legs stopped next to him.

"Is it going to take long?"

Jackson lifted his eyes. "Sylvia? What are you doing here?"

"Same as everyone else. I want to grab something to eat."

"I meant in the keep."

"I came to be with Roni."

"Who?" He didn't know any Roni.

"Didn't you hear about him?" Sylvia rolled her eyes. "Where have you been, on the moon? I thought everyone knew."

Jackson went back to filling the machine. "Apparently not everyone."

"I thought you were tight with Andrew. Roni is, or rather was, a hacker for the government who worked with Andrew. He found Eva's trail. That's how Bhathian knew to look for her in Brazil."

"Now I know who you're talking about."

"Long story short, Roni's maternal grandmother, who had supposedly drowned when Roni's mom was a young girl, applied for a driver's license not once but twice since, looking the same way she did at twenty-something. So naturally, we assumed she was an immortal and that Roni was a Dormant, right?"

"Right." Jackson closed the vending machine.

"So we staged this elaborate setup, a dojo where he was supposed to train, and Anandur pretended to be the instructor. He got bitten several times, and after the last time, he developed a fever and we thought he was transitioning, but it turned out to be pneumonia. So now he is here, and Kian agreed for him to stay even though he is a human."

Jackson rubbed his jaw. "I'm obviously missing some important parts of the story. Why the elaborate setup? And since when are you working for Kian?"

For some reason his questions caused Sylvia to blush. "I don't work at the keep. I'm Roni's girlfriend. And the reason we needed the dojo excuse was that Roni wasn't free to go as he pleased. When he was a kid, he hacked into some classified information, got caught, and instead of going to prison, or a juvenile correction facility, he was offered a job. He couldn't go anywhere without his handler. Andrew convinced the bosses that Roni needed physical activity to keep his mind sharp, which was obviously important to them as he was their top hacker, so they agreed, and we staged the dojo."

That was one hell of a story, and there was probably much more to it. But Jackson couldn't spend all day chatting with Sylvia. The guys needed him back at the café. Still, there was one quick question that could satisfy his curiosity for now.

"How old is your Roni?"

"About your age."

"You don't say." Jackson smiled, an idea forming in his head. "And he now lives here in the keep?"

"Yes."

"Did you move in with him?"

"Not yet. But I'm here a lot."

"How about we all get together? My girlfriend and me, you and Roni."

"Roni is not allowed to leave the keep."

"We can hang out at his place. Who is he rooming with?"

"For now, no one. And that's a wonderful idea. Roni could use some friends his age. He spent the last few years surrounded by agents who were way older than him."

This was just perfect. Both Roni and Tessa had missed a big chunk of normal growing up. They should get along splendidly.

Jackson pulled out his phone. "Let's exchange numbers. Check with Roni when is a good time and let me know. We'll come over, and I'll bring the pastries."

Sylvia frowned. "Who's your girlfriend? I'm not aware of any girl who has recently transitioned."

"She didn't. Tessa is a Dormant just like your Roni, and Kian gave me permission to tell her who we are."

Sylvia put her hands on her hips. "How come your girlfriend knows about us and is free to come and go, while my boyfriend is a prisoner?"

Damn. Telling her about Tessa's special situation was the last thing he wanted to do. Having a good time with people their age didn't involve sharing her horrific past with them.

"How about we talk about it when we get together? I have to go back to work."

"Fine." She pointed a finger at him. "But you owe me an explanation."

Not really, but he didn't want to argue the point with her. Before the four of them got together, he would think of a good excuse that didn't involve revealing Tessa's past.

## 39

## TESSA

"How do I look?" Tessa asked.

"Amazing." Jackson grabbed her by her waist and lifted her up for a kiss.

Usually, she loved when he did that, but they were right outside Eva's house. "Stop it. Put me down."

"No one is looking. And if they are, they are jealous." Instead of letting go of her, Jackson carried her to the other side of his car, letting her slide to the ground only because he needed his hand to open the passenger door for her.

"Your car always smells of pastries." Tessa buckled up and turned her head to glance at the back seat. A big pink box was the source of the smell.

"I told Sylvia I'd bring some." Jackson turned the ignition on and eased into the street.

"How many people are going to be there?" She was mentally prepared to meet two new people. Not a big bunch of them.

"Just us, Sylvia and Roni."

It would be fun to spend an evening with another couple. Especially since one was an immortal and the other still a human. The human boy was Jackson's age, and the girl was a few years older than Tessa. The reverse age difference was another thing they had in common.

She wondered if Roni was as mature as Jackson. He had to be for a twenty-five-year-old woman to find him interesting. But then the guy was some kind of a genius hacker, so naturally he must be fascinating.

Except, Nick was a great hacker too, and he wasn't mature at all. All he cared about was scoring with girls and watching sports or reality shows on TV. Tessa loved him like a brother, but that didn't mean they had anything to talk about other than job-related stuff.

"I think you overdid it with the pastries. Unless that box is mostly empty."

"It's full. My motto is that it is always better to bring too much than too little. They can put some in the freezer for later."

At the keep, the security guy waved them in with no questions asked. She could understand Jackson getting in without showing identification. After all, he or one of the other guys were delivering pastries to the café on a daily basis, but it was strange that they had let her through without asking her to show her identification or frisking her for weapons or having her pass through a metal detector. The keep's security was supposed to be top notch.

"How come no one asked me who I am? Did you call ahead of time?"

Jackson shook his head. "You were entered into the system the first time you came here, and apparently given a security clearance to come and go as you please. Kian must've been really impressed with you."

Or had felt really sorry for her. Jackson claimed he'd never told Kian any details about her ordeal, but Kian seemed like a guy who didn't shy away from the ugliness of this world. He must've known what her captivity had entailed.

When Jackson knocked on the door, the young woman who opened the door smiled wide and pulled Tessa into a hug. "You have no idea how happy I am to meet you, Tessa."

"And what am I? Chopped liver?" Jackson squeezed by them with the big box. "You forget who is holding the pastries, woman."

Sylvia let go of Tessa. "I happen to love chopped liver." She sauntered over to Jackson and kissed his cheek.

A sick-looking guy waved at them from the couch. "Excuse me for not getting up. This fucking pneumonia is killing me."

"Roni!" Sylvia gasped.

"What? If we are all supposed to get friendly, I'd rather be myself."

Jackson walked over to Roni and offered his hand. "I have no problem with cussing, and neither does Tessa. She only looks fragile, but she can kick butt."

It was Tessa's turn to gasp. "Jackson!"

Jackson plopped on the couch next to Roni and wrapped his arm around the guy's narrow shoulders. "Let's make a deal. There will be no pretending to be anything other than who we really are. Deal?"

Tessa and Sylvia exchanged glances in female solidarity.

Sylvia shrugged. "You guys want an excuse to cuss, then be our guests. But Tessa and I are ladies."

For a moment, Tessa was afraid Jackson would snort a *yeah right*. But apparently he was smarter than that and so was Roni. Both guys nodded in agreement.

"Who wants tea and who wants coffee?" Sylvia asked.

"Coffee," Roni said.

"I'll have whatever soft drink you have." After a day at the café, the last thing Jackson wanted was another cup of coffee.

"I would love some tea. Do you have herbal?" Tessa followed Sylvia to the kitchen.

Sylvia pulled out a box from one of the cabinets. "I'm afraid we don't have much. Roni moved in just a couple of days ago, and I'm still working on stocking this place with food."

"How is he feeling? Jackson told me he has pneumonia."

"He's better, but as you can see, he is still sick."

They walked back into the living room with Sylvia carrying two cups of coffee and Tessa her tea and a can of ginger ale for Jackson.

He took the can from her. "Ginger ale?"

"Roni gets nauseous. The ginger ale helps."

Sylvia went back to the kitchen and came back with a plate loaded with pastries.

Jackson popped the lid and took a sip. "Not bad."

There was an uncomfortable moment of silence, with each of them pretending to be busy with their beverages.

Tessa put her tea on the coffee table. "So I know that Roni is a hacker. What do you do, Sylvia?" Talking about work was always a safe subject. Even she knew that.

"I'm a student."

Jackson lifted a brow. "In what field?"

Sylvia smirked. "Several. I figured there is no rush, so why not study whatever I'm interested in, like literature, psychology, criminology, philosophy, ancient languages, archeology, etc."

Must be wonderful to have no financial worries and be an eternal student. Except, Jackson had told her that clan members didn't start getting a share in clan profits until they were twenty-five.

"What did you do for money before you turned twenty-five?"

"I see Jackson told you about that silly rule. But there is a loophole. Those who finish a bachelor's degree get their share when they graduate. Annani is big on education, and that's her incentive for clan members to get it. I finished my first bachelor's degree at twenty."

"My woman is smart." Roni patted the spot on his other side. "Come sit with your man."

Tessa stifled a smile. Roni was so thin and young looking. Calling himself a man was a stretch.

But apparently to Sylvia, he was. She got up and went to sit with him, lifting her legs and tucking them under her as she snuggled up to him.

Cute.

It was apparent the two were in love.

"What about you, Tessa? What do you do?"

"I work in a detective agency."

Roni looked impressed. "Must be exciting."

"Not really. I'm just the personal assistant and bookkeeper."

"You never get any field work?" Sylvia asked.

"When Eva, my boss, needs someone who can pull off looking like a twelve-year-old, she calls on me."

The look-over Roni gave her made it clear he thought she was all woman. It used to make Tessa uncomfortable, sometimes even scared, when men gave her appreciative looks, but Roni seemed so harmless that all she felt was flattered.

"You look all grown up to me," he concluded his assessment.

To say that Jackson was not too happy about Roni's appraisal was a huge understatement. The glare he directed at the guy was murderous.

She patted her hair. "It's the haircut and makeup. Take those away, and I can play the role of a kid easy."

Jackson shifted in his seat. "What do you do for fun, Roni?"

"Hacking."

"Other than work."

"I love hacking. I listen to music while I'm hacking. When I can't hack, I read and listen to music."

Roni's love of music softened Jackson's attitude. "What do you like listening to?"

By the time Roni was done reciting all the groups he liked, Jackson was regarding him like he was his best friend. "You have good taste in music, bro. Do you play any?"

Oh, so now Roni was a bro. Men were so weird. Even the good ones.

"When I was a kid, I used to play the drums. But that was years ago."

Jackson perked up. "Were you any good?"

Roni puffed up his chest. "I'm good at everything I do."

"I'm asking because I have a band and our drummer is leaving for college. I can use you."

Sylvia cleared her throat. "You're forgetting the small detail about Roni not being allowed to leave the keep."

Both guys' moods plummeted from their temporary high.

"You can perform here," Tessa offered. "And later in the village square. It looks like the perfect place for a rock concert."

Roni and Jackson exchanged looks.

"I like it," Jackson said. "We will have to get Kian's approval, but I'm sure he will be okay with that."

Roni groaned. "I don't have a drum set to practice on, and until I get paid, I can't buy one."

Sylvia caught his chin with her fingers and turned his head to face her. "I can loan you the money."

Roni shook his head. "No. You already bought me clothes and filled up the fridge and the pantry. The drums can wait."

For a moment, Sylvia looked like she was going to argue, but then she seemed to have decided against it. For now. Tessa had a feeling she would raise the issue as soon as she was alone with Roni.

"Fuck," Roni exclaimed. "I forgot to talk money with Kian." He turned to Sylvia. "You think he would agree to see me again?"

"How about you send him an email? He is so busy he might get annoyed by another request for a meeting."

Roni banged his head against the back of the sofa. "I'm such a fucking moron."

Sylvia patted his hand. "No, baby. You're brilliant. You are just not well."

Roni turned a pair of smitten eyes on his girlfriend. "You're so good to me. I love you so much." He leaned and kissed her as if Tessa and Jackson weren't there.

"I love you too," Sylvia mumbled into his mouth.

Tessa cast Jackson an amused glance. "I think that's our cue."

# 40

# ANANDUR

Sitting in the old truck he'd borrowed, the same one he'd used when pretending to be a lowly deck boy to get close to Lana, Anandur waited for Brundar's Escalade to leave the underground garage and hit the street.

It was an underhanded, dishonest, and all around crappy thing to do, but Anandur was sick and tired of his brother's secrecy. Today, he was going to check out the mystery woman who had his brother wrapped around her little finger.

The guy was so inexperienced with women that a smart one could've taken advantage of him. Having plenty of sex, even the kinky kind, didn't make Brundar an expert on female manipulation or immune to the magic some women wielded.

On the contrary. All those silly contracts and agreements they insisted on in those places defined the rules of the game and left little to chance.

Real life didn't work like that.

And if all Brundar was familiar with were hookers who did what they were asked to, and/or kink partners who did what was written in their contract, he was in for a very rude awakening.

Out in the real world, where emotion ruled supreme, Brundar was like a helpless little lamb. It took acumen and experience to decipher women's intentions. They were so much more careful and subtle in their scheming than men. Anandur wasn't going to let some shrewd manipulator take advantage of his brother.

He didn't have to wait long.

The good thing about Brundar's rigidity was that he tended to follow an exact timetable, and his routine made it easy to anticipate his moves. That was how Anandur had discovered his brother was a regular visitor to a nightclub, which had seemed odd until Anandur had learned about the basement level, which housed a secret kink club.

Naturally, Anandur kept pretending that he didn't know. It wasn't a big deal. Brundar was entitled to his privacy, and his sex life was none of Anandur's business. He just wanted to make sure his brother was safe.

One slip was enough for a lifetime. It had cost Brundar his soul, and laid a burden of guilt on Anandur that he was still carrying around every day of his goddamn life. Even though Brundar was more than capable of taking care of himself, Anandur couldn't let go of the constant worry.

Thank fuck Brundar's car was a monster. It made following him from a good distance easy. Not that it would be a big deal if Brundar caught him spying on him. Anandur could always claim it was a lark.

Heading in the direction of the club, Brundar stopped a couple of blocks away from it and parked his car next to an apartment building. A few moments later he came down with a girl who was wearing the nightclub's T-shirt.

Was he picking up a waitress? Or was this the mystery woman?

She was a looker, that was for sure, but a bit too skinny and delicate for Anandur's taste. He liked his women sturdier, but then his size demanded it. Brundar, on the other hand, wasn't as big or as bulky, which made the girl perfect for him.

Just like her body, her face was small and delicate. Her honey-colored hair was pulled in a ponytail, but he could tell it was long. It wasn't straight either. The ends curled up.

He'd parked a considerable distance away, so other details like her eye color and the exact shape of her lips remained a mystery.

Not a problem. Once Brundar left for his rotation tonight, Anandur would go in and have a talk with the little missy.

Heck, he didn't even have to follow them to the club. He would come later after Brundar left.

AT NINE O'CLOCK, Anandur parked in the guest parking lot of the club and headed for the entry. He nodded at the bouncer, who nodded back, a professional courtesy from one guardian to another. Different positions, and yet similar. They were both keeping the good guys safe.

The receptionist was cute, and Anandur flirted with her because he always did. When she took his money, she gave him a coupon for one free drink, and he felt bad about leading her on.

"Enjoy," she said.

"I will."

She looked disappointed that he didn't take his flirting further than that. It was too bad. If he weren't on a mission, and this wasn't his brother's playground, he would've asked when she was getting off and arranged for a hookup.

It was mid-week, so the club wasn't packed, or maybe it was still too early. Whatever the reason for the sparse clientele, it made it easier locating the two waitresses and figuring which area Brundar's girl was in charge of.

He took a seat and waited.

A few minutes later she arrived. The tag attached to her T-shirt identified her as Calypso. An unusual name, but he liked it.

"What can I get for you?" she asked with the pleasant smile of a professional waitress.

He took a good look at the girl as she placed a napkin on his table. Beautiful, in a fragile small-boned way. Except, he had a feeling she was anything but. There was strength in those small bones that had nothing to do with their physical composition.

*Nice.* Brundar had good taste.

"Chivas, please."

For some reason, his choice of drink made her narrow her pretty green eyes at him as if she was trying to figure out where she'd seen him before. He was about to crack a joke when she waved a finger at him.

"I know who you are."

"And who might that be?" He leaned his elbows on the table and cast her a flirtatious glance from under his long lashes. Not that he had any intentions of hooking up with Brundar's woman, but he wanted to see what she would do.

Calypso bent a little and lowered her voice. "You're Brundar's brother. Right?"

That took him by surprise. "How did you know?"

She smirked. "He described you as really big with lots of crinkly red hair all over your face and body. I doubt many guys fit that description."

"Busted. I'm Anandur."

He offered his hand, and she shook it, pointing to her name tag. "Calypso."

"Nice to meet you, Calypso. May I ask why are you whispering?"

She leaned closer. "He uses the name Brad around here. Besides, I don't want anyone to notice us talking. He would get mad if he knew you came spying on him."

"I'm not spying on him. I just happened to stop by for a drink."

She shook her head. "Right. And I'm Sleeping Beauty."

Anandur couldn't help himself. "A beauty you are, just not a sleeping one."

She waved her finger at him again. "Flirting with your brother's girlfriend is against the bro code."

Anandur grinned. He liked the girl, but he wasn't done poking at her. "Are you his girlfriend?"

That must've hit a nerve because she grimaced. "Sort of. We are exclusive, but he told me not to get my hopes up because he is married to his job."

The girl had just done a clever role reversal, milking him for information.

Anandur nodded. "He is, and so am I. Did he tell you what we do?" He was curious how much his tight-lipped brother had revealed to the girl.

"He said you both work as bodyguards for your cousin who is an important businessman. But I know it's more than that. Your brother has contacts everywhere." Her eyes holding his with an unwavering gaze, she waited for him to spill some more information.

Gutsy girl. Clever too.

What Anandur wanted to know, however, was who Brundar had mentioned to her and why.

"We've been in this business for many years, so naturally we got to know a lot of people. Anyone specific you're referring to?"

Calypso narrowed her eyes again. "I don't know if it's okay for me to talk about it. I know you're his brother, and you work together, but I'm not going to drop names without asking him if it's okay first."

Gutsy, smart, and loyal. Anandur approved.

He clasped her delicate hand. "I prefer he didn't know I came here. Brundar is a secretive bastard. I just wanted to make sure he was okay."

She shook her head. "You guys and your appalling choice of words. You're not bastards. You're love children."

Anandur laughed. "Did you tell him that?"

"You bet I did."

She was just too cute. "Good for you. Our mother is sending her thanks."

Pulling her hand out of his grasp, she glanced around. "Let me get you your drink and see what those guys want." She tilted her head toward the next table over. "I've been standing here for too long. We'll talk some more when I come back."

"I'll be here."

When she returned with his Chivas, it was just the way he liked it. Straight, no ice. Brundar had taught her well.

"Can you take a break so we can talk outside?"

"I can, but it's not a good idea. Donnie, the bouncer outside, is keeping an eye on me for Brundar. He would tell him I talked with a big red-haired guy and you'd get busted."

"We are talking now."

"Not the same. Lots of guys like to talk." She winked. "And we are not supposed to be rude to customers unless they get handsy."

He nodded. "I wish we could talk some more."

"Me too. I wanted to invite you to dinner, but Brundar said no. He is a tough nut to crack."

Anandur pulled out a pen and wrote his phone number on a napkin. "For emergencies." He handed it to her. "Or if you just need someone to talk to. I know my brother is not easy to be with. He has his issues, but he is a good man."

"What issues?" Calypso took the napkin and stuffed it in the back pocket of her black jeans.

"Oh, you know." Anandur waved a dismissive hand, regretting his slip of the tongue. Brundar's secret was safe with him. No one knew what had happened all those years ago, not even their mother. He'd sworn to take it to his grave. "He is brooding and rigid and has no sense of humor. It takes a special girl to stick around a *charmer* like him."

Calypso put a hand on her hip. "He is also honorable, loyal, and brave."

Anandur liked her even better for defending Brundar. She was a keeper. For a little while, at least. What a shame the girl was a human.

"That he is."

# 41

# CALLIE

Callie filled a pot with water and put it on the stove to boil.
After their lunch at Gino's, she'd promised Brundar an Italian dinner to outshine anything he'd ever had at that restaurant. Not that it hadn't been good, but her lasagna was better.

It was a complicated recipe that took about an hour and a half to make, and she planned to have everything done at least half an hour before Brundar arrived. It should be enough time for a quick shower and the rest of her minimalistic beauty routine. A little mascara, a clear lip gloss, and that was it.

The dress would have to be the same strapless one she'd worn before because she didn't have anything else nice.

Clothes shopping was in order, but the thing was, Callie felt odd about using an Uber to get to the mall and back. Seemed frivolous.

She really needed a car.

Tomorrow, she would have no choice but to take a taxi or an Uber to get to her doctor's appointment. On second thought, she couldn't use Uber.

Brundar had provided her with new identification but no new credit cards. The ones she had were joint with Shawn. She couldn't use them. In fact, she should cut them up and get rid of them, together with everything else that was left over from her marriage. The fewer reminders, the better.

Hopefully, the taxi driver would have no problem with her paying cash.

Another solution was to buy one of those prepaid credit cards. Yeah, that was better. Tomorrow morning she would stop by the supermarket and get one.

There were so many details to remember when hiding and on the run. She'd almost made the mistake of booking the doctor's appointment under her real name.

The best thing would be to switch identities entirely and get used to the new name. Heather Wilson. The problem was that everyone at the club knew her by her real name. Perhaps she should find another job.

Crap. She liked working for Franco, especially since Brundar was there. The best part was access to the basement when no club members were there.

God, the basement.

Remembering their time there, Callie felt shivers rock her body—the good kind. So intense. So amazing. She wanted more of that.

Except, she didn't need to work at the nightclub for Brundar to sneak her into one of the playrooms down below when no one else was there.

Did Anandur know about his brother's involvement in the club?

Did he know about the kinky sex?

She should've asked him. No, she should not have. That would have been one heck of an awkward conversation. Especially since she was willing to bet Anandur was pure vanilla.

The brothers were each other's opposites. Brundar was shrouded in darkness while Anandur basked in the light. Brundar's perfect features were hard—like a statue's. Anandur was all smiles and flirtation.

The one who snagged Anandur would be a lucky woman.

And yet, Callie would never trade her brooding, dark angel for his sunny counterpart. Or anyone else for that matter.

Brundar was the one for her. The one she was destined to be with. Callie felt it with every fiber of her body and soul. That being said, she would have loved having Anandur as a brother.

*Brother-in-law.*

Feeling silly, Callie shook her head. Next thing she would be doodling her name with Brundar's inside a heart and drawing flowers around it.

It was way too soon to be thinking about anything permanent. Especially since Brundar had made it clear that it wasn't going to happen.

## 42

# BRUNDAR

*A* good bottle of wine in hand, Brundar knocked on Calypso's door. The smells coming from her apartment were mouth-watering, as was the woman who opened the way.

That strapless black dress would be the death of him.

As hunger seized him by the throat, not the kind that could be satisfied by the appetizing smells, he reached for her with his free hand and pulled her into his arms. She melted into him, parting her lips and sucking his tongue in as if her hunger was just as potent as his.

There was an easy solution to that. Lifting her up, he stepped in and kicked the door closed, then marched in the direction of her bedroom.

Calypso laughed. "Put me down. I didn't spend all this time cooking for it to go to waste. Save that enthusiasm for after dinner."

Brundar growled, but the sound that would've terrified a grown man had no effect on this woman.

She pushed on his chest. "Save that growling for later too. I prepared a feast for you, and I'm going to feed you first."

Reluctantly, he put her down. "I would rather feast on something else."

"Hold that thought." She reached for the wine. "Let's add this to the table. You didn't even look at it."

Fuck. Who could think about the table setting with her looking like that?

*Women.*

Sulking, he followed her back to the living room. It looked like Calypso had set the table for a romantic dinner for two, complete with candles and flowers and cloth napkins.

"It looks nice," he said, thinking Calypso expected him to say something about it. Brundar couldn't care less. He would've enjoyed this dinner just as much or even more if they were eating it at the kitchen counter.

She pulled out a chair. "Sit down. I'm going to serve you the best Italian food you ever had."

He shook his head. "I should be the one pulling it out for you, not the other way around."

She patted the back of the chair. "I'll make you a deal. Whenever you take me out to a restaurant, I'll wait patiently for you to do the gentlemanly thing."

"Can't I help in the kitchen or something?"

She chuckled. "Nope. You stay here and uncork the wine. That's the only thing I'm allowing you to do other than eating and praising the cook. A few moans of pleasure are acceptable as well."

"Mine or yours?" Relenting, he took the seat.

"Mine will come later." She winked.

Brundar moaned. A lot. First when Calypso served the minestrone soup, which was the best he'd ever had, then his eyes rolled back in his head when he took the first bite of her lasagna. Even the salad was terrific, and he wasn't big on salads or any other kinds of greens.

When she served the tiramisu, he was so full he felt his stomach had doubled in size.

Calypso smiled with satisfaction. "Well? Is my Italian better than Gino's?"

"The food definitely. The language, I'm not sure. I've never heard you speak Italian."

She poured him coffee from the carafe. "I'm afraid Gino wins in this department. I don't speak anything other than English and a tiny bit of Spanish. Do you?"

"I know a few languages. Not well enough to speak, but I understand." For some reason, absorbing new languages was easy for immortals. Naturally, some were better at it than others, but most were better than the average human.

"How about your brother, is he good with languages too?"

"Yes." The last thing he wanted was to talk about Anandur.

"How about other family members?"

"I guess so."

"I would really like to invite your brother to dinner. He doesn't have to bring a date when it's here."

"No."

"Why not?"

"Because I don't want him here."

"Why?"

Stubborn woman. What did he have to do to make it clear that meeting his family wasn't on the table?

He couldn't tell her she was a forbidden pleasure he shouldn't have let himself indulge in, and that his family wouldn't be happy about that indulgence. As long as him having a woman was just a rumor or a guess, no one could demand that he forsake her. As it was, he was living on borrowed time with her, and he had no wish to shorten it.

"It's complicated. I'm not supposed to have a relationship. It's one of the conditions of my job. If anyone found out, I would be ordered to stop seeing you."

Calypso's lips tightened into a thin line as she glared at him.

"You're lying."

Her words felt like a punch to his gut. He might have omitted things and had twisted the truth when he had no choice, but he'd never outright lied to her.

"Are you really accusing me of being a liar?"

She crossed her arms over her chest. "That's exactly what I'm doing. You're lying straight to my face and not for the first time. Though I'll be damned if I know why."

"What in damnation are you talking about?"

"Your friend the professor. He is not your friend. You never even met him. The landlady told you about him when you rented the apartment for me. You could've told me the truth. You should've told me the truth. Why make up the story? So I will feel less guilty about accepting your generosity? I don't understand."

Fuck. He should've known Calypso would eventually find out. Except, when he'd come up with the story, he'd had no intention of having a relationship with her. All he'd wanted was for her to accept the apartment without argument, and if she later discovered the truth, it wouldn't have been a big deal.

"I didn't have any friends who needed a house sitter. But you needed a place to stay, and I knew you would refuse the apartment if you knew I was paying for it."

"So you decided to lie about it."

His palm landed on the table with a thud. "I did what I thought was right at the time. I wanted you safe, and frankly, I didn't care if you learned about it later. I had no intention of having a relationship with you. I still don't."

"Why?" There were tears in her eyes.

Brundar was too angry to care.

She should be grateful and thank him for his kindness and generosity, not attack him as if he'd done something despicable. Other than the fucking apartment, which was a non-issue as far as he was concerned, he had been upfront with her as much as he could've been under the circumstances.

"Because I can't, and I told you that time and again. I'm breaking the rules by being with you."

"Why?" The tears were running freely down her cheeks. "Why are you breaking the rules for me?"

The woman was driving him mad, using her tears and her incessant questions like weapons and spurring his aggression.

An enemy holding a sword to Brundar's throat would have been less of a provocation.

He did the only thing he could to regain control. Brundar retreated into the zone—the cold and unfeeling place that was his safe haven, where nothing could touch him. Including Calypso's tears.

"It was a mistake." He pushed his chair back and stood up. "Thank you for dinner." He walked out.

Her sobs followed him all the way to his car. Intellectually, he acknowledged them and regretted causing her sorrow. Emotionally, he felt nothing.

## 43

# CALLIE

A full bladder forced Callie out of bed. She didn't want to wake up, she didn't want to feel the pain, she wanted to stay asleep and pretend her heart hadn't been broken into a million shards.

After Brundar had left, she'd cried for hours, had called in sick and cried some more, until finally falling into an exhausted sleep.

Trudging to the bathroom, she relieved herself, then went back to bed. But sleep wouldn't come back. How could it when her mind was racing, and her heart was aching, and her soul was crushed?

How could he have turned so cold?

It had happened in front of her eyes. Brundar had shut down, his shields slamming down with an almost audible thud, his eyes becoming flat. No emotion, nothing. Like he wasn't even there.

And the worst part was that she couldn't help blaming herself. What had possessed her to push him like that? Accuse him of lying?

But it hadn't been a false accusation. Brundar had lied to her face.

If his employment terms prohibited him from having a relationship, Anandur would have said so.

That was the second lie she'd caught him in, and he'd admitted the first one. How many were there?

Was he married with a bunch of kids, and had all his talk about being married to his job been a smokescreen? Did he want to keep her as a mistress? Would Anandur have told her if that was the case?

God, she felt like a loser playing the 'what if' game.

Her mouth felt disgusting, she needed to brush her teeth, and she desperately needed to get some caffeine in her. Everything would look better once she had her morning coffee.

As Callie waited for the coffeemaker to provide her salvation, her thoughts kept jumping around like a bunch of helium balloons in a cage, bouncing from the walls to the ceiling and the floor, chaotic.

Coffee helped her put some order into the mess.

It didn't make sense to think Brundar was married. Anandur would've been much less accepting of her, or would have at least looked uncomfortable on behalf of his brother. Unless he was a cheater himself.

But that was a far-fetched scenario, and she pushed it aside.

His explanation about wanting to ensure her safety sounded true. She hadn't known him then, and accepting his offer of a place to live was much easier the way he'd presented it. She would've refused to let him pay for the apartment, and according to the neighbor, Callie could not have afforded the rent.

The question was why. He'd been attracted to her from the start but had resisted her not too subtle advances. Which was consistent with the story about his job and not being allowed ongoing relationships.

But what kind of a job demanded such a thing? Even commandos and other Special Forces soldiers could have girlfriends and wives. Many probably chose not to, given the constant danger they were in, but it certainly wasn't prohibited.

Brundar and Anandur's situation was most likely the same. Getting involved in a long-term relationship wasn't recommended, but it was not forbidden.

Which left her with the conclusion that Brundar just didn't want that. It was about time she accepted that the man was emotionally handicapped and incapable of sharing his life with anyone.

Even before his brother had hinted at it, she'd known that Brundar had issues. It was quite obvious.

Her mistake was a classic female pitfall.

Callie had deluded herself that she could fix him. The worst part was that she'd convinced herself that it wasn't what she'd been doing. She'd called it pushing, helping him out of his shell, teaching him to communicate better.

All of that boiled down to her trying to fix him.

Except, the man didn't want her to fix him. Furthermore, she knew that trying to change someone was futile. But she'd listened to her heart, and that little liar had made her believe that love conquered all.

It was time to face the facts.

She was in love with the idiot. But she wasn't going to waste her life trying to fix the unfixable. Callie had made that mistake before, and it had landed her in her current predicament. She should've learned her lesson.

Only an idiot kept making the same mistakes and hoping for different results.

If Brundar wanted her, if he was willing to make an effort, he knew where to find her. At least until she found a new apartment. And a new job. Because she wasn't going to hang around and live off his charity.

Today was as good a day as any to start.

It was a little after nine o'clock in the morning, and her doctor's appointment was at eleven, which meant she would probably be done by twelve. Plenty of time to go apartment and job hunting.

If only she had a car.

Change of plans. After her doctor's appointment, she was going to get herself a car—a used one she could buy for cash. Heather Wilson had no credit history, and no employment record, so leasing one was out of the question even though she would've preferred to keep her money for emergencies instead of buying a car with a good chunk of it.

But it was okay. She was young and healthy and hard working. She had plenty of time to save up for future emergencies.

Flipping her laptop open, Callie Googled Craigslist and started going over the used cars section.

A few phone calls later she had a couple of good options she was going to check out.

## 44

## LOSHAM

"Which one is the human you wanted me to take a look at?" Losham asked.

Rami pointed at a tall, handsome man. "His name is Shawn Davidson. He is a car salesman, a good one. Whenever he talks, the others listen. He has a commanding presence."

Taking a seat at the back of the group, Losham spent the next hour observing the guy closely. The quack psychologist was doing a decent job of spurring the men on without going as far as inciting them to commit violence against their exes. Shawn kept throwing around crude jokes and making comments that had the other men laughing and nodding in agreement.

As the meeting drew to a close, Losham leaned toward Rami's ear. "He has potential."

What the other men saw was a confident, charming, and easy-to-smile young man who entertained them. But underneath was a seething rage. Losham didn't like the guy. Shawn was emotionally unstable, and therefore dangerous and unpredictable. The opposite of what Losham valued in a man. But the human fit perfectly into Rami's plan.

Provided they could harness all that rage and control it.

They didn't need a loose cannon, they needed a charismatic leader. One who could turn a bunch of suburban rejects into Satan-worshipping fanatics who dressed up in robes and performed idiotic rituals, believing wholeheartedly that they were the evil one's chosen.

The question was whether the human was not only charismatic but also capable of managing the cult and growing its numbers. Losham was willing to finance the operation, but he wanted to hand the management over to a competent human.

His and Rami's time was too valuable to waste on this smokescreen operation.

As it grew, the cult could start collecting membership fees, and Losham would no longer need to finance it. Maybe he could even make a profit. After all, that was what cults were for—to make their leaders rich by convincing the brainwashed members to surrender their money, and sometimes even their women.

They could keep the females. Losham wasn't interested in their subpar stock, only in the profits.

"Bring him to me," he told Rami.

"Yes, sir."

The human smiled confidently, even though he was clearly suspicious, and offered his hand. "Shawn Davidson at your service."

Losham shook the guy's hand. "Logan Foresight. Could I have a few minutes of your time, Shawn? I want to make you an offer, but I'd rather not do it here."

Shawn chuckled. "Me neither. If you want to talk, let's do it over beers."

"Excellent idea. Do you have a place in mind?"

When Losham and Rami arrived at the bar Shawn Davidson had chosen, the human was already there, clasping hands with the bartender as if they were old friends. They probably were. Mr. Davidson smelled like a guy who liked to drink. Since he hadn't started his drinking yet, his body odor was too faint for a human to detect, but not to an immortal. It was the ever-present scent of a heavy drinker.

Shawn showed them to a booth at the end. "I ordered beers. Domestic okay?"

Losham wouldn't touch the thing if he could help it, but he smiled and nodded as if it was fine.

"How are you enjoying our support group?" Losham started.

Shawn shrugged. "The shrink is good. No bullshit from that guy. He knows we all have been wronged and doesn't try to sugarcoat it."

Losham nodded. "That's right. We have been wronged, and we need an outlet to express our anger."

The waitress arrived with their beers and a bowl of mixed nuts. Shawn didn't even pretend to pull out his wallet, waiting for Losham to pay. Good. The guy was cheap and greedy. He would do anything for money.

"So what's your story, Logan? Your wife left you? Cheated on you?"

"Something like that. That is why I founded the support group. I like helping other men get their lives back in order. The right order." He glanced at Shawn meaningfully. "Where I come from, women are not free to do whatever they want like they are here. They are owned. The way it's supposed to be."

Shawn lifted his beer bottle. "Amen to that."

Encouraged by Shawn's response, Losham pushed forward with Mortdh's age-old propaganda that had worked its magic on countless generations of humans. "Life is so much simpler that way. There can be only one leader in the family, and naturally, it's the male. Women should obey and serve their husbands."

Shawn lifted his bottle again. "You're my kind of guy, Logan." He emptied the bottle and signaled the bartender to bring him another one.

"You are probably wondering about the offer I mentioned."

Shawn nodded while stealing glances at the bartender, impatient for his next drink.

"I'm a busy man, and I don't have time to manage this little pet project of mine. I need someone to lead the group and grow it into a club. I recognize leadership ability when I see it, and you have it in spades. To start with, I'm going to compensate you for your time, generously. When membership grows and becomes more substantial, we will start charging fees and you'll get a cut of the profits. Basically, I'm handing you a business and financing it. I'm sure a man as smart as yourself recognizes that this is a once in a lifetime opportunity."

The wheels in Shawn's head were turning, calculating, appraising. The guy's expression was guarded, but his eyes betrayed his thoughts—starting with greed and ending in doubt. A few moments later, he admitted he had no idea how to go about it. "What exactly do you want me to do?"

Losham leaned back in his chair. "Men need an ideology to serve as the glue that binds them together. If we want to grow this thing into a profitable business, it needs to become a cult. People like rituals, they like feeling special, better than others. We need to sell them on a belief system."

Shawn rubbed his jaw. "I'm a salesman. I can sell anything. But I'm not good at making up that kind of crap."

The waitress arrived with Shawn's beer. "Can I get you guys anything?"

"No, thank you." Losham lifted his untouched beer as if he was going to take a sip.

"Don't worry about that part. I can supply you with the script and the agenda. Do you want to have a say in what it would be?"

Losham was leading up to this. It was where Shawn was supposed to spill his own set of beliefs if he had any.

"I like your attitude toward females. That's something I stand a hundred percent behind and have no problem promoting. Other than that, as long as you don't ask me to preach turning the other cheek, I don't care what it is. If you want me to convince a bunch of guys to chant prayers to Satan or some other crap like that, I'll do it. I don't have a problem with inciting them to violence either. What I want is to grow this shit into a profit making machine and get revenge on the whoring cunt who left me and stole my money."

Losham patted Rami on the back and offered Shawn a wide grin. "Then we have a deal, Mr. Davidson. How does ten thousand a month starting salary sound?"

Shawn's eyes popped wide open. "Sounds good, what about profit sharing?"

"Once the cult starts making money, I only want to keep twenty percent. The rest will go to you, but naturally, your salary will get deducted from your share."

Shawn whistled. "One hell of an offer, Logan. When do I start?"

"You need to give notice at your current place of employment. Are two weeks good?" Losham needed time to formulate the new religion that Shawn would be preaching. Otherwise, he would've demanded an earlier start.

Shawn offered his hand. "Let's shake on it, but I would like to get this in writing too. No offense, Logan, but I don't want to leave my job for empty promises. I make good money selling luxury cars."

"Naturally."

Losham lifted his palm and Rami put a checkbook on it together with a pen. "Would the first month's pay put you at ease?"

The guy's eyes were on the checkbook when he nodded. "Sure."

Handing the human a check for ten thousand dollars, Losham held on to it for a moment longer. "One more thing, my friend. The time for your revenge will come, but not yet, and not without my permission. I don't want my new manager getting in trouble with the law."

The guy didn't like it, but the allure of a ten thousand dollar check was apparently stronger than his need for immediate revenge.

"I will not do anything illegal."

"Good enough."

## 45

# CALLIE

The waiting room at the clinic was depressing. Out of the six women waiting to be called in, Callie was the only one not pregnant. The woman next to her was with her husband, and the two were holding hands, whispering in each other's ears, and smiling like a couple of teenagers in love.

She felt like crap.

*You're only twenty-one*, she kept repeating in her head like a mantra. She had plenty of time to start a family. Her heart, though, had other ideas. It wanted her to be the woman sitting next to her with her loving husband and a baby on the way.

Grabbing a magazine, Callie searched for something interesting to read, but every other story was about nursing or baby development and how to stay healthy while expecting. She dropped it on the table and grabbed another one.

"Heather Wilson?" the nurse repeated.

It took a moment for the name to register as hers.

"That's me." She jumped to her feet. "I'm so sorry for keeping you waiting. How are you doing?"

The nurse smiled. "I'm great. How about you? A lot on your mind?"

*You have no idea.* "I'm good. I was just reading an interesting article."

The nurse guided Callie to her station. "Please take a seat."

"Thank you." Cradling her purse in her lap, Callie sat down. She had five thousand dollars in there for the car she was going to buy later, and she needed to keep it close.

"I see you are here about contraceptives."

Callie nodded.

"Do you remember the date of your last period?"

Five minutes later, she was in the doctor's room after having been weighed, her height measured, and her blood pressure recorded. There had been an uncomfortable moment when the nurse asked about Callie's previous doctor and her medical record. Callie had mumbled something about it being in Alabama, and the nurse had dropped the subject. Perhaps she needed to write a fake history for Heather Wilson and memorize it. It would make it easier to come up with answers on the spot.

The energetic knock on the door made her jump and hastily tuck the thin sheet around her naked lower half.

"Can I come in?" A woman's voice.

That was a relief. On the phone, Callie had gotten only the doctor's last name. It didn't matter, a doctor was a doctor, but Callie preferred a female gynecologist.

"Yes."

Dr. Stone was a tall, middle-aged woman with cropped silver hair and a no-nonsense attitude.

"Have you ever taken oral contraceptives before?"

"No."

"You opted for the shot?"

"No. I never used any contraceptives other than condoms."

The doctor nodded, looking over the chart the nurse had prepared.

Callie wondered what the doctor was thinking. Until she read the part about the marriage and the miscarriage in Callie's file, she was probably assuming Callie was entering her first exclusive relationship and was ready to discard the rubber.

In a way, it had been true at the time Callie had made the appointment, but that was no longer the case. God knew when she was going to have sex again. She should wait to start the pills. It didn't make sense to stuff her body with unnecessary hormones until she had a partner again. Which was not going to happen anytime soon.

For the foreseeable future, Callie was done with men.

"You have several options. One is a pill that you need to remember to take every day. There are two kinds of pills, and I'll explain the differences later. The second is the shot which you need to remember to come for every eleven to twelve weeks. The third is an IUD which is an implant good for about ten years. Other than that there are patches and—"

By the time the doctor was done, Callie felt more confused than informed. There were too many options and possible side effects. Everything from weight gain to tender breasts to bleeding between periods and a long infertility period after the shot, which scared her the most.

"I'm starting to think I should stick with the condoms."

The doctor smiled indulgently. "I don't blame you. But you need to realize that those are only possible side effects. You may not get any, or only a mild case of a few. My job is to make sure you are aware of them and the risks involved with each method. Condoms have their problems too."

Callie knew it better than most.

"What do you recommend?"

"If you trust yourself to remember to take the pill every day, I would start with that. Out of all the options, it has the fewest side effects."

"The pill it is, then."

"Good choice. Keep using the condoms for the first seven days. But if you have reason to suspect your partner isn't clean, don't stop using them."

Callie looked down at her hands, gathering the nerve for her next question. "How do I know that I'm clean?"

The doctor turned around from the keyboard where she'd been typing in her notes. "When was the last time you had unprotected sex?"

"Over a month ago. With my ex-husband," she added, not wanting the doctor to think she was irresponsible. "At the time, he was the only one I ever had sex with, but I'm not certain of his fidelity."

The doctor looked unfazed. Probably not the first time she'd heard that particular concern.

"I can perform two tests. One will give you a rapid result, the other takes longer but is more accurate."

"Can I do both?"

"Sure."

Callie was afraid to ask how much all of that was going to cost. Several hundred for sure. But whatever it was, her peace of mind was worth it.

Thank God, the rapid test came out negative.

The doctor gave her a free pack of pills and a prescription. "Call me if you have any concerns, or if you experience bothersome side effects. There are many other brands you can try."

"I will. Thank you."

The free sample saved Callie a trip to the pharmacy, which meant she could go straight to see the first car on her list.

She pulled out her phone and called the owner. "Hi, it's Heather. I can be there in half an hour. Is that okay?"

"Yeah, no problem."

Callie called a taxi, which took fifteen minutes to pick her up, causing her to arrive a little late at her destination.

The owner was waiting outside when she got there, and after a short negotiation, she was the proud owner of a 2009 Chevy Aveo. The guy agreed to shave off two hundred dollars of his asking price because Callie was paying cash, which brought the cost down to thirty-five hundred dollars. Not a bad deal for a car that was in good condition and had low mileage given that it was eight years old.

Now it remained to be seen if her fake documentation would pass the test of registering the vehicle in her new name. She also needed insurance.

One thing at a time.

The important thing was that she'd taken the first step toward her independence. A new job and a new apartment were next.

## 46

# ANANDUR

*Finally.* Anandur smiled as his phone chimed with the ringtone he'd assigned to Carol. He'd known she was going to cave in. The mission, although dangerous in the extreme, was too tempting for her to give up just because she was squeamish about killing an animal.

"Carol, what's up?" He was already thinking about where he should take her hunting.

"You need to come down to the gym."

He frowned, switching the phone to his other ear. "Why? What's going on? Is anyone giving you trouble?"

Taking over the self-defense classes when Carol herself was still a trainee must have been difficult. There were always assholes who liked to mouth off to the instructor, especially when she was a small, soft woman like Carol.

"It's Brundar. He's been training for hours, and he looks like he is going to drop any moment but pushes himself to keep going. No one dares to approach him, but maybe you can talk sense into him. Do you know what's eating him?"

Anandur had an inkling that it had something to do with a certain green-eyed girl.

"I'm coming down. In the meantime, clear the gym."

"Already did."

Anandur had seen his brother in that state before. Not lately, though. It hadn't happened in decades, but he knew the signs.

When Brundar couldn't handle his emotions, he retreated deep into himself. His pale blue eyes, which looked cold and unfeeling on any given day, turned so flat and deadened that he looked soulless.

But he wasn't. Brundar was hurting, and the only way he knew how to deal with emotional upheaval was to beat it into submission either by storming into battle or keep training until he dropped.

The thing was, there was not much Anandur could do about it besides watch over the guy and make sure he didn't attack any innocent bystanders. When he got like that, Brundar turned into a machine, oblivious to the fact that his body was made of flesh and bone and not titanium, and that not everyone around him was the enemy.

When he got there, Carol was waiting for him outside the gym, her big eyes showing her worry. "Do you know what's wrong with him?"

He patted her shoulder. "When other guys drown their sorrows in booze or go brawling, Brundar trains, or fights if there is an enemy who needs killing. He is too dangerous to indulge in what other dudes do to relieve stress."

Carol nodded. "Is it safe for you to go in there?"

"Don't worry, I'm not going to fight him. Not unless he is so far gone that he attacks me."

"That's what I'm worried about."

"It hasn't happened yet, and I've seen him in this state before."

"I'll stay here in case you need me." She patted the handgun strapped to her thigh. "As a last resort."

"Good idea. Aim for the knees. But only if it looks like he is about to take off my head." Carol was an excellent shot. She wouldn't miss.

Entering the gym, Anandur stayed near the entrance. He leaned against the wall, crossed his arms over his chest, and watched his brother.

Bare-chested and barefoot, his pale skin covered in a sheen of sweat, Brundar wielded his sword with the fluid grace of a dancer, executing each series of moves flawlessly even though his arms must've been killing him. Anandur was well familiar with the burn that came from swinging a heavy sword for hours.

Being ambidextrous, Brundar could go on wielding it for much longer. He kept switching, letting one hand rest while using the other. His brother hadn't been born with the ability. He'd trained until he achieved mastery with either hand.

Oblivious to Anandur's presence, Brundar kept going until his movements began slowing, imperceptibly at first, then gradually getting more and more laborious. When he couldn't lift his arms anymore, Brundar braced the tip of his sword on the floor, cutting a deep indent into the matting as he leaned on it.

Anandur had been waiting for that moment patiently. "Do you want to talk about it?" he asked.

Brundar shook his head.

"You should've realized by now that it's impossible to kill invisible demons with a sword, no matter how many times you imagine taking off their ugly heads."

Brundar nodded. "Do you have anything to say that is actually helpful, or do you just like to hear yourself talk?"

"I can't help you if you don't talk to me."

For a couple of minutes, it seemed Brundar wasn't going to respond.

But then, looking down at where his sword cut into the matting, he said quietly, "It's getting harder."

"What is?"

"Living in the zone. It used to be easy."

Brundar's accursed zone. The place inside his head he hid in to avoid living. "Was it ever fun? That desolate emptiness you call the zone?"

For the first time since Anandur had arrived, Brundar turned and looked him in the eyes. "It's peaceful. I need the quiet to function at my best."

Anandur shook his head. "People, even top athletes, don't live in the zone, Brundar. They slip into it when they need to. What you're doing is hiding from life."

Brundar shrugged. "It works for me."

"Does it? Because it doesn't look like it from where I stand. You're a high-functioning walking dead."

Yanking the sword out of the floor, Brundar walked over to where he'd left its scabbard, and sheathed it. "If that's all, I'm going to hit the shower."

*Not today, buddy. Today you are going to talk whether you want to or not.* If necessary, Anandur was going to follow the guy under the spray.

"Life is messy, and it stinks, and it hurts, but it's also beautiful and exciting. Hiding from it to avoid the pain, you're missing out on all its fucked-up glory. It's worth enduring tons of crap for a few moments of wonderful."

Brundar picked up his stuff and started walking. "Not for me."

Anandur followed. "That's what you've convinced yourself of, but it's a lie."

Stopping, Brundar turned around, his eyes blazing with fury. "Are you calling me a liar?"

With a smirk, Anandur crossed his arms over his chest. "What if I am?"

In the blink of an eye, the sword was out of its scabbard, with the rest of Brundar's stuff hitting the floor. "Do you want to repeat that?"

Anandur lifted a brow. "First, drop the sword and lift your fists." With a weapon in hand, Brundar was undefeated, but he wasn't as good in hand to hand, for the simple reason he never trained for it.

The sword clanked to the floor.

With a big grin, Anandur leaned forward and enunciated, "Liar."

# 47

# SHAWN

The first thing Shawn had done after talking to Logan was to deposit the check. It hadn't bounced, the money went into Shawn's account, and he immediately withdrew it. Just in case.

Good to his word, Logan had brought the papers to the next group meeting.

Shawn hadn't been surprised that it said nothing about the group's agenda and Logan's plans for it. It wasn't something that should ever go in writing. The agreement only referred to the financial side of things and appointed Shawn as the manager.

The following day, Shawn quit his job at the dealership. There was no point in giving notice, it wasn't like he needed to train a replacement. The other salespeople would snatch up his shifts like a bunch of vultures, happy to be rid of the best closer on the lot. More money for them.

No more sweating in his suit and tie on hot California days. No more smiling at old farts with limp dicks who thought a luxury car would compensate for their impotence. No more sucking up to his manager to get the best hours on the best days of the week. The only thing he would miss were the hot cunts who had often accompanied the limp dicks. Some had been more than happy to ride his stiff, thick cock behind their sugar daddies' backs.

Whores, all in it for the money.

Now that he had time on his hands, Shawn was going to resume the search for his lying, cheating whore of an ex-wife.

The cunt hadn't even called her father or her best friend to tell them she was leaving. He knew that for a fact since he'd had their home lines and her cell phone bugged. She'd told no one. She'd gone underground and had yet to surface.

Except, there was one place he knew he would eventually find her.

The university.

There was no way she'd given up on that stupid dream of hers. Getting accepted wasn't easy, and Callie would never throw away the chance she'd been given.

In the back of his mind, Shawn suspected that one of the reasons she'd run out on him was because he'd refused to let her pursue her silly dream. But apparently, it hadn't been the only one. It had been the last push she needed to run away with her lover. The soon to be dead lover.

That morning, he'd tried calling the university's administrative offices, but he couldn't get anyone to talk to him.

There was no way around it. He needed to drive over there, which wasn't a big deal since he had nothing better to do until Logan supplied him with the agenda for their new business venture.

In person, Shawn had a better chance of getting the information he needed. Bitches responded to his charm, willing to do all kinds of favors for him to get into his pants.

Swaggering into the admissions office, he plastered his best smile on his face. "Good afternoon, pretty lady." He leaned on the desk belonging to the flustered thirty-something soccer mom type. Those were the easiest to manipulate, their dried-up pussies yearning for a young dick to make them wet. "My sister misplaced her papers and asked me to stop by and get her another copy. Calypso Davidson is the name."

The woman shook her head. "I'm sorry. She would have to come in person."

He leaned closer. "Come on. All the way from Alabama? She can't."

"Then she could call and provide her social security number to verify it's really her."

If that was all the bitchy receptionist needed, then he was good. "I have her social. Please, the girl is going crazy. She is so worried she'll miss her chance. Studying here is her dream."

The woman relented, giving him a post-it and a pencil. "Write down her name and social security number."

He scribbled it down and handed it back.

A few keyboard clicks later, the woman shook her head. "I'm sorry. I don't have anyone under the name Calypso Davidson or under that social." She handed him the post-it back. "Maybe she spelled her name differently, or you wrote the wrong number."

Shawn double checked his notes, but the number was correct. Maybe she applied under her maiden name?

"Try Calypso Meyers."

The woman typed it in and shook her head again. "Sorry, no Calypso Meyers either."

"Try Callie. She goes by Callie." It was a long shot. She would've used her legal name on the application.

"Nope, sorry. No Callie Davidson or Meyers either."

What the hell was going on? Had she made up the whole story about getting accepted to UCLA? Had she even applied? And why would she lie about that?

Shawn ran his fingers through his hair. "Thank you. My sister is such a scatterbrain. She probably applied to a different university and sent me here for nothing."

As he walked out and headed for his car, Shawn felt like he was in an episode of *The Twilight Zone*. Nothing made sense. Was he losing his fucking mind?

Back at home, he upended every drawer and searched every cabinet for any scrap of paper Callie might have left behind. There was no trace of any paperwork. Not the acceptance letter, and not the multiple scholarship forms she'd filled out right before his eyes.

She had either taken everything with her or destroyed them before leaving.

Either that or he'd imagined the whole thing. Could too much booze and drugs induce hallucinations?

Had he even been married? Or had it all been in his head?

Except, of that he had proof. The fucking divorce papers were exactly where Shawn had left them. On the coffee table.

A constant reminder of how the cunt had screwed him over.

## 48

# CALLIE

Going home with her new car had felt liberating.
Callie felt like she'd turned a new page, and even though she was still mad as hell at Brundar, she no longer felt like crying.

Keeping busy as heck had helped.

Between the doctor's appointment and the car buying, yesterday had been a full day. She had barely had enough time to grab a bite to eat and put on her club T-shirt before driving to work.

Brundar, the coward, hadn't shown up at all.

He hadn't called or texted either.

Whatever.

She was moving on.

Today, she was going to find a new job.

A list of steakhouses in hand, Callie stopped next to the first one. It wasn't that she had an overwhelming love of steaks, but the tips were better the higher the tickets, which they were in most steakhouses. The other requirement was a full bar. Besides the quality of meat, it was the most crucial factor in a steakhouse's success.

"Hi, can I speak to the manager? I'm looking for a waitressing job." She smiled sweetly at the host. The guy was about her age, but he was still a kid while she was not. Hadn't been for a long time.

The guy smiled back, his expression all about trying to look cool and flirt with her. "I'll get him for you. I don't think we need anyone, but I hope he hires you anyway." He winked.

God, it was good to feel young and free again. A cute guy was flirting with her, and it felt great even though she wasn't interested.

A few moments later, he came back with a man who she presumed was the owner and not just a manager. The guy was in his late fifties, balding, and with the belly of someone who loved to eat. Managers were usually much younger.

He offered his hand. "Damian Gonzales."

"Heather Wilson." She shook what he offered.

He motioned for her to follow him into his tiny office. "Do you have any experience as a waitress, Heather?"

"Plenty. I worked at a steakhouse for over a year."

"Which one?"

Damn it. She couldn't use Aussie as a reference. She would have to lie.

"It was in Alabama."

He eyed her suspiciously, probably noting the blush that had crept up her cheeks. She was a terrible liar.

"Would they give you references?"

*Crap.*

Callie locked stares with the owner, then decided to go for the truth. "I really worked in a steakhouse, and I'm a damn good waitress. But if you called and asked for references they wouldn't know who you're talking about. I just got divorced, and my ex is a dangerous man. For my protection, I've been given a new identity."

Damian still looked skeptical. "Why should I believe you?"

"Because it's the truth. Give me one shift, and I'll prove it to you. I'm good under pressure; I don't panic when I have to cover two stations at once because someone didn't show up for their shift, and I can charm even the shittiest of customers. You will never hear any complaints about me."

Damian chuckled. "Of that, I have no doubt. A pretty girl like you can get away with murder. You're lucky to show up when you did. One of the girls just called in sick. I'll give you her shift, and we will take it from there."

"What, like now?"

The owner lifted a brow. "Do you have a problem with that?"

"No, not at all. But I need to be at my other job by seven."

He nodded. "Do you intend to work two jobs?"

"Not for long. I'll quit the nightclub when I have another full-time job."

"What do you do there?" He gave her a once-over as if suspecting she was a pole dancer or something.

"I serve drinks. The tips are good, but the noise is not. I want to quit before my hearing gets damaged." It was partially true. The other part about a jerky boyfriend who wasn't a boyfriend was none of Damian's business.

"I'll tell you what. I'll test you. And if by six you prove you're as good as you claim to be, I'll hire you. How long of a notice do you need to give the other place?"

"A week or two should do it."

Franco didn't really need her, and the other servers would be happy to pick up more hours.

The owner rose to his feet and turned to the shelving unit behind him. Pulling out a T-shirt and an apron from a neatly folded stack, he handed them to her. "You can change in the ladies room. Tyler, that's the host, will show you Brenda's tables—the waitress you are covering for. Grab a menu and learn it by heart. It should be a breeze for you after working in a steakhouse for a year. We serve every cocktail imaginable and carry all the major brands. The drinks menu is three times the size of the food menu, but if a customer asks for something, we most likely have it. Just write it down, and the bartender will take care of it."

Callie tucked the garments the owner had handed her under her arm and offered him her hand. "Thank you for giving me a chance. You're not going to regret it."

He took her hand, covering it with his other one, but it wasn't a come-on gesture, more like fatherly. "I hope everything works out for you, Heather. It's a shame a young woman like you has to run and hide from some abusive asshole. If you're half as good as you say you are, you got the job."

# 49

# BRUNDAR

As he got dressed in the morning, Brundar checked his reflection in the mirror, relieved to see that his eyes were back to normal with only a slight purplish hue serving as a reminder of the beating he'd taken.

Having the shit pounded out of him by his brother had been oddly therapeutic. Brundar hadn't practiced hand to hand in ages, which was a mistake, as Anandur had proven.

Several good things came out of having his face busted, not the least of which was him and Anandur getting closer than they had been in years. After his brute of a brother had proven that Brundar wasn't as invincible as he'd thought he was, the two of them had actually embraced, then had gone back to their apartment and proceeded to demolish a bottle of whiskey each, while reminiscing about the old glory days of the Guardian force.

Anandur had managed to do something extraordinary. Not only had Brundar been nowhere near the zone while fighting his brother, but he had felt great about it. In the zone, he felt nothing, good or bad.

Yesterday, even the pain had been good because it had made him feel alive.

But that was the physical pain. The other kind didn't feel good at all.

The echo of Calypso's sobs had haunted him throughout the night. He'd hurt her for no good reason. She'd had every right to call him a liar because he was. She hadn't done it to spite him or to hurt him; she'd done it to force the truth out of him.

Regardless of the fact that he couldn't have given it to her, he could've been much more understanding and forgiving about her accusation.

Bottom line, he needed to go to her and beg for forgiveness. Even if she refused to take him back, which would be the best for both of them, he needed to atone for the way he'd behaved. Brundar wanted the memory of their time together to be something they could both cherish, untainted by how badly it had ended.

He should've called, but talking, especially on the phone, wasn't his forte. He sucked at it. Besides, an apology needed to be done face to face.

Pulling out his phone he did the cowardly thing and texted her.

*Can I come over this afternoon?*

There was no response.

She was probably still sleeping. Or what was more likely, she was mad at him, and rightfully so.

He hadn't gone to the club after leaving her apartment. The following day he'd spent working, then training, then having the crap beaten out of him, and later, after he and Anandur had spent some quality time with their friends Jack Daniels and Chivas, he'd gone on rotation.

Two days of radio silence.

What did he expect? That she would text him back with hearts and kisses?

He fired off another one. *I want to apologize.*

No response.

Fuck, that was bad.

As little as Brundar knew about females, it was a known fact that they were more forgiving than males, especially when said males were offering to grovel at their feet.

His duties calling, he had no choice but to stuff the phone in his pocket and head to Kian's office. He kept checking for messages all throughout Kian's three-hour morning meeting with Turner, and then during lunch with two dudes who needed funds for their startup and were trying to convince Kian to invest, then back at the keep.

A little before three in the afternoon she finally answered. *I was busy running around all morning. You can come anytime before my shift starts.*

Busy all morning? Doing what?

Never mind. It was none of his business.

*I'll be there in an hour.*

*Fine. If you want to eat, bring food.*

In Calypso speak, it was like telling him to go screw himself. She was making a point, informing him he didn't deserve her making an effort for him and feeding him.

Damnation. Did he have time to stop by Gerard's and beg the guy to make him a to-go dinner?

The restaurant wasn't open this early, and Brundar didn't have a membership, but he was Brundar, and very few dared to refuse him anything. Except for one green-eyed spitfire who he could lift with one finger but wouldn't dare.

A few phone calls later, and a string of profanities in French—Gerard's—Brundar headed for Calypso's apartment with a fancy dinner for two packed in an insulated food carrier and a bottle of wine.

She opened the door wearing pajama pants and an old T-shirt, her hair pulled up in a messy ponytail and no shoes—her way of telling him that she didn't give a damn.

The thing was, she looked even sexier in her homebody attire than when all decked out.

"What's all that?" She eyed the big square carrier.

"You said to bring dinner, so I did."

"I meant burgers or Chinese." She moved back to let him and his bulky cargo pass through.

Brundar put the carrier and the bottle of wine on top of one of the dining room's chairs, then pulled out another for Calypso. "My lady?"

She quirked a brow but took the seat he offered.

Gerard's crew had packed everything needed for a fancy dinner, including a tablecloth, plates, utensils, napkins, and goblets. All he had to do was to set it up.

Calypso watched as he pulled things out one after the other, doing his best to make the table look as nice as she usually did. Gerard had numbered the containers so Brundar wouldn't mess up the serving order, but there was nothing about what was in them. Supposedly, everything the guy made was as excellent as what he'd prepared for Syssi and Kian's wedding.

As he opened the first container, marked number one, and lifted the appetizer plate, Brundar understood why each individual serving came with its own plate and was packed separately. The artistic presentation wasn't something Brundar could've ever managed.

Calypso's eyes widened as he placed the small plate in front of her. "Where did you get this?"

He smirked. "I told you I have a cousin who's a renowned chef."

"Right. Another cousin."

Brundar pulled out the second appetizer plate and sat next to Calypso. "Don't ask me what this is because I have no clue."

She lifted one of the three forks that came with the place settings and held it above the small stack of unidentifiable ingredients. "I'm dying to taste it, but I feel bad about ruining this work of art."

Brundar waited until she finally poked it with her fork and took a tiny bite. "Oh, wow. That's amazing." She narrowed her eyes at him. "How long have you been planning this?"

"Since you told me to bring food."

"Impossible. That was an hour ago. No one can prepare a gourmet meal like that on such short notice."

Brundar cast her one of his stern looks. "Are you calling me a liar again?"

Calypso let her head drop, sighed, then looked up again. "I'm sorry. Calling you a liar was rude."

She wasn't retracting her accusation, just apologizing for calling him out on it. Still, he appreciated it. It must've been difficult for her to do.

"I lied about the apartment, so I deserved it. But I didn't lie about the other things."

"What about this?" She waved a hand over the table.

Brundar smirked. "I bullied my cousin into it. He was preparing dinner for a private party tonight, and I twisted his arm to part with some of it."

"What is he going to do?"

Brundar couldn't care less. Some of those French profanities Gerard had hurled at him were quite colorful. "He has enough time to fill the shortage."

Calypso took another small forkful but didn't bring it up to her mouth. "Why did you leave the way you did? And more importantly, why did you come back?"

He admired her directness. No beating around the bush for this gutsy girl.

The thing was, he didn't know how to answer that. But he was going to try. She wouldn't let him get away without at least making an effort.

"I was doing my best under the circumstances, but it wasn't enough for you. You kept pushing for more until I snapped. I've never been in a relationship. I don't know how to play this game. It's hard to explain, but in a situation like that, when I need to calm down, the best thing for me to do is to slip into the unfeeling, cold place I call the zone. That is where I function the best. I don't need anyone when I'm there."

Calypso put her fork down. "So if I understand correctly what you're trying to say, you felt threatened, retreated into your safe place, and stayed there. That's why you didn't call or text?"

"Right."

"What has changed?"

"Anandur beat the shit out of me."

Calypso gasped. "What? Why? How? Aren't you the best?"

"I am the weapons master. Anandur is the champion of hand to hand. He challenged me, and I accepted, thinking I could best him at that too, but he proved me wrong."

"I still don't understand what sparring with your brother has to do with you coming back to me."

"A wake-up call. While he was beating me up, he talked some sense into me. He made me realize that living in the zone wasn't living. To avoid pain, I was giving up on life."

Calypso's eyes softened. "He is a smart man." She chuckled in an obvious attempt to lighten the mood. "From your description of him, I thought he was a silly clown. But apparently, he has depth."

"He is a good man."

A crease in her forehead warned him that another question was coming. "I thought you never let anyone close enough to touch you. That's why you always fight with weapons. Is it different with your brother? Is it okay for him to touch you?"

"No. That's why we never sparred like that before. I thought I wouldn't be able to tolerate it, but I did. We even embraced when he helped me up, and it was tolerable. I guess enough time has passed."

"Enough time from what?"

*Damnation.* Brundar pinched his forehead between his thumb and forefinger. He hadn't told anyone about what had happened all those years ago. He'd never even talked about it with Anandur, who was the only one who knew.

The last thing he wanted was to reopen those old wounds and let anyone in on the humiliation and guilt that had been eating at him for years. But for some reason, he felt compelled to tell Calypso. Not the entire story, he could never do that, but maybe a highly modified and censored version.

She was the first person he'd let get close to him since the event that had changed him irrevocably.

"Something bad happened to me when I was twelve. Someone who I thought of as a friend, whom I loved as a brother, betrayed me in the worst possible way. I got hurt, but I wasn't the only one. My entire family suffered as a result. That's all I can tell you. Please don't ask for more. Not now, and not ever."

## 50

# CALLIE

Callie's heart broke for Brundar, and that was without knowing what exactly had happened to him.

Her best guess was that he'd gotten beaten up severely.

That explained why he'd become such an incredible fighter, but it didn't explain his aversion to being touched. Had it been a sexual assault? Had his so-called friend been a much older boy?

It was hard to imagine a twelve-year-old committing such an atrocity.

But then some people were just born evil.

Callie would've liked to believe differently. It was much more palatable to theorize that all babies were born pure and good and that the only reason some of them became monsters was because of external factors like neglect and abuse. But it wasn't true. Genetics played a much larger role in a person's makeup than previously believed. In recent years, the old nature versus nurture argument was leaning more and more in favor of nature.

Besides, any mother could tell that each of her children was born different. Starting from day one, kids' unique personalities were quite obvious.

Callie wasn't sure she believed in souls, leaning more toward the scientific explanation that consciousness and sense of self emerged from biological functions and not some mystical reservoir of souls. It left genetics to account for the marked differences between one child and the next.

"I won't ask, I promise. But you need to talk to someone about it. It's not healthy to carry it all bottled up inside."

Brundar shook his head. "You can't help yourself, can you? You always have to push. Let me rephrase. I don't want to talk about it, period. Understood?"

Crap. He'd opened up to her and she repaid him by offering unsolicited advice. When was she going to learn to shut up and just listen?

Was he ever going to tell her anything after that?

"I'm sorry. It will not happen again. Scout's honor."

He lifted a brow.

"I swear. Do you want me to write it a hundred times? I will. I will write a hundred times: Callie will mind her own business and not stick her nose where it doesn't belong."

Brundar chuckled. "I'll believe it when I see it."

Mission accomplished. He looked amused, which meant he wasn't angry anymore.

"Let's eat this amazing dinner before it gets cold."

When they finished the appetizer, Brundar refused to let her help serve the next dish. "It's my treat today, from beginning to end."

She leaned back in her chair. "I can get used to that."

He kissed her forehead as he put the main course in front of her. "Then do. Because I plan on pampering you as much as I can."

The change in Brundar was so drastic that Callie was almost glad about their spat. He was even talking about a future. She'd learned her lesson, though, and kept her mouth closed, not daring to make a comment that would start a new argument.

After the main course, Brundar made coffee and served it with the dessert.

Cup in hand, he leaned back in his chair. "What have you been doing this morning that has kept you so busy?"

It was on the tip of her tongue to tell him that she was entitled to her secrets the same way he was, but that would have been petty. Besides, it wasn't like she could hide it for long.

"I went apartment hunting."

He frowned. "Why?"

"Because I don't want to keep living off charity. I want to stand on my own two feet. You helped me a lot, but I'm ready to take my life into my own hands."

"Did you find anything you liked?"

"I did. It's a studio apartment, not nearly as nice as this one, but I can afford it on my salary, which is my main objective."

"I don't want you living somewhere unsafe. And how are you going to get to work? Is it nearby?"

She was about to ruin the newfound peace, but there was no way around it. Better to yank the Band-Aid in one go.

"I also bought a car and found a new job."

"You were really busy."

Brundar didn't seem angry, but he didn't look happy either. Maybe the next item would make him happier.

"I also went to the doctor and got birth control. I'm on the pill, which means we can say goodbye to condoms in about a week. I also got tested for sexually transmitted diseases. Some of the results were immediate, all clear, but some will take up to two weeks. So I guess we will have to wait until everything is in. Did you get yours?"

"Not yet. But I will."

The frown remained.

"What's wrong? Aren't you happy about finally doing away with condoms?"

"I am. But I'm not happy about you moving out of here or working somewhere else. I want you safe, and I want to keep an eye on you."

That was rich. As if he'd been doing such a great job of it for the last couple of days.

*Take a deep breath, Callie, and keep your cool. He is reacting better than expected to the news.*

"I went looking for a new job because of safety concerns, not because I didn't like working in the club or bumping into you on occasion. Everyone there knows me by my real name, and that's not safe. I used the fake name to apply for the new job—a steakhouse, like Aussie. I should be earning about the same as I did there. I also bought the car under the fake name, and I made the doctor's appointment as Heather, not Callie or Calypso. The fewer people who know me by my real name, the better."

"I agree."

"So you're not mad?"

"Mad? No. Why would I be mad? You did the right thing. Except for the apartment. It's rented under my name. There is no reason for you to leave."

"I can't afford the rent, Brundar. I checked. It's twice as much as what I'll be paying for the studio."

"I'll share the rent with you."

"You already have an apartment you're paying for."

"With my brother, and it's paid for by our boss. If I'm going to be spending a lot of time with you, it's only fair that I share in the expenses. And that goes for groceries and everything else as well."

He was making a convincing argument. But what would happen the next time they fought? Would she get stuck with an apartment she couldn't afford?

On the other hand, life didn't come with guarantees. Shit would no doubt happen, and she would have to deal with it. Besides, she hadn't heard back from the leasing agent yet. Without references, she might have not gotten it.

"I'll agree to stay here on the condition that you'll really let me pay half of the rent."

"Starting next month."

"Fine." There was no point in sweating the details. Especially since pushing Brundar beyond what he considered as reasonable seemed to always backfire.

As it was, he'd been much more accommodating than she'd expected.

Heck, he'd implied that he intended spending more time with her, had made arrangements for sharing rent and grocery bills with her. This wasn't how a guy who planned to bail talked.

It was too good to be true.

What happened to the prohibition on relationships?

Had he gotten approval from his boss?

Or was he rebelling?

Callie burned with the need to ask these questions but knew better than to succumb to it. Too much had been achieved today to jeopardize because of impatience. Eventually, she would have the answers, but not today.

## 51

# BRUNDAR

*B*rundar felt as if he was digging a hole for himself he would never be able to climb out of. What had possessed him to make all those promises to Calypso?

He'd made it sound as if he was staying.

The thing was, he wanted to, and for once in his life, he was going to do the unthinkable.

Fuck the rules.

Calypso was everything that was good. Hell, she was the only good thing that had happened to him throughout his adult life.

She made him feel.

He wasn't going to give her up for anything. Fuck the rules, and fuck his goddamned honor. None of it mattered to him anymore. He was going to keep her and fight to the death anyone who would threaten to take her away.

She was his, as he was hers.

What were they going to do to him? Fire him from his Guardian job? Sentence him to entombment?

He snorted. Who and what army was going to accomplish that?

If need be, he would grab Calypso and run. It would be hard to part with Anandur, but there was a time in a man's life when he needed to make a choice between his past and his future.

Calypso was his future.

"What are you thinking so hard about?" she asked. "You're frowning as if you're trying to solve an unsolvable problem."

Very perceptive of her.

But as far as Brundar was concerned, he no longer had a problem. He'd made up his mind. Others might disagree, but then it was their problem, not his.

"I'm thinking of the best and quickest way to get you naked and under me. I wonder if this table is sturdy enough."

"You should have said so." Calypso pushed to her feet, gripped the bottom of her T-shirt, and pulled it over her head. "I would have offered solutions." She hooked her thumbs in the elastic of her pajama pants and pushed them down. "Race you to bed." She stepped out of the loose pants, which had pooled at her feet, and sprinted for the bedroom.

Didn't she know not to run from a predator?

In a split second, Brundar was out of his chair and leaping after her. Calypso managed two steps away from the dining table when he grabbed her by her waist, twisted her around, and draped her over his shoulder—fireman style.

Or was it caveman style?

Calypso laughed and pushed back.

He smacked her upturned behind. "Stay. Don't wiggle."

The more she struggled, the more turned on he became. Brundar's imagination produced images of the kinds of games they could play if she were an immortal. He would take her somewhere wild and give her a head start, then hunt her for hours as she hid and tried to evade him.

The things he would do to her once he caught her...

Yeah, if Calypso were an immortal, a lot of things would be different.

But she wasn't.

She was perfect the way she was. Human, fragile, beautiful, feisty, independent, assertive, yet willing to yield to him and offer her complete surrender.

On top of all that, to wish she was also an immortal was greedy and ungrateful. It was good Brundar didn't believe in the Fates. Otherwise, he would have feared their retribution for regarding their gifts with such ungratefulness.

Laying Calypso gently on the bed, he quickly divested her of the last two scraps of fabric still covering her body.

With a smile, she stretched her arms over her head, arching her back and pushing her perfect breasts up. "Are you going to tie me up?"

He shook his head. "Just grab onto the headboard and don't let go."

Unfortunately, he could not forgo the blindfold. Already, his fangs were making his speech slur, and the only reason Calypso didn't notice the glow coming from his eyes was that it was still daytime and her bedroom was drenched in sunlight.

He pulled out one of the five silk scarves she kept in her drawer next to the stash of condoms. The nylon stockings he'd used the first time were there as well. He loved it that she was prepared for him, that she not only accommodated his quirks but planned for them by keeping the things he needed close by.

Scarf pulled between his hands, Brundar sat on the bed next to Calypso. "Lift your head, sweetling."

She obeyed, the smile never leaving her lush lips. Did she love the game as much as he did?

"Do you like it when I blindfold you?" he asked as he tied the ends behind her head, careful not to snag any of her beautiful hair in the knot.

"I love all the games we play, and I'm looking forward to learning more."

Gutsy girl.

"Should I buy you your own personal flogger?"

She caught her lower lip between her teeth and nodded.

"The same kind I used on you in the club?"

"Yes," she said on a moan, the scent of her arousal permeating the air and turning his erection into a steel rod.

"Soft suede?"

She nodded.

Damnation. What a shame he didn't have one with him. It seemed Calypso was craving it. Or maybe she just enjoyed talking about it?

He caressed her side, lightly brushing his knuckles against her left breast. "Perhaps I should buy a lot of different toys and bring them here for you to experiment with?" He put his hand on her stomach, feeling the small tremors his version of dirty talk was sending through her body.

"Yes. I want to have my own, brand new toys to play with."

Brundar stifled a chuckle. His girl was rushing forward faster than he'd ever imagined she could or would want to.

Feisty, brave, adventurous.

"There are online catalogs." He cupped her hot center, then leaned to nibble on her ear. "Imagine how wet you'll get just from browsing and imagining what I could do to you with each toy."

"Oh, God." She arched her back. "Keep talking like that, and I'm going to come all over your hand."

This time he couldn't suppress the chuckle. "That would be a first for me. I've never had a woman climax just from the sound of my voice."

A sly smirk twisting her plump lips, she rubbed her center on his palm. "No wonder. It would've required you to actually talk."

## 52

## CALLIE

Callie waited for a comeback that never came. Instead, Brundar leaned forward and clamped his hand on the back of her head, lifting it and crushing his lips over hers.

As his tongue pushed in, she parted for him, moaning into his mouth, desperate to lift her arms and hold him close to her.

What would he do? Tell her to put her hands back up? It wasn't enough of a deterrent. She could steal a moment, pretending she'd acted on instinct.

Her fingers were in the process of loosening their grip on the metal scrollwork when Brundar reminded her of the rules of the game. Still kissing her like he was drowning in her, he brought his other hand to her throat, caging it, two fingers pressed against her pulse points as if he wanted to feel the effect his kiss and possessive grip had on her heartbeat.

It sped up, not in fear, but out of pure lust. Everything felt too tight; her jaw, her nipples, her stomach muscles, her quivering sheath.

Brundar's kiss was telling her all the things he wouldn't or couldn't say. By hungrily sucking on her tongue, he was telling her that he could never get enough of her, and by gently caging her neck with his fingers, he was telling her that she was his, and he would always keep her safe, even from his own darkness.

"Brundar," she whispered as he let go of her mouth to let her suck in a breath. "Make love to me."

Callie was all in for Brundar's rough and wild eroticism, but today she craved his tender loving touch. Today she needed reassurances. Today she wanted him to show her with his body what he couldn't say with words.

## 53

# SHAWN

"Motherfucker!" Shawn woke up, a string of vile curses spilling out of his mouth.

The divorce papers lay scattered on the floor next to the couch where they had slipped from his hands when he'd fallen into a booze-induced stupor. He'd been watching *The Lord of the Rings* on Netflix, dozing on and off and sipping out of a bottle of vodka, until his eyes had closed, opening with a start when he'd woken up from a very vivid dream.

It was him—the elf lookalike fucker.

The guy who over a year ago had thrown Callie and Shawn out of the kink club. The same one who'd delivered the divorce papers, and the same one who had roughed Shawn up.

The weirdo with the long blond hair must've been some sort of a hypnotist. He must've fucked with Shawn's head. That was the only explanation for why he hadn't remembered him. Not the first time, or the second, or the third.

Shawn had collided with the motherfucker three times, and he hadn't remembered any of them until everything came back to him in the dream.

*Not old enough*, Shawn seethed.

The fucker had thrown them out of the club with the excuse that Callie had been too young. But apparently, she was old enough for the guy to slip her his phone number and pork her behind her husband's back.

The cunt must've been fucking the asswipe for over a year, and then he'd convinced her to leave Shawn and run away with him.

Fuck, maybe he had hypnotized her the same way he'd done to Shawn. Maybe it wasn't her fault that she'd let him bang her. Because come on, why would she leave a man like Shawn for a girly-looking pretty boy like that?

That first time in the club, Shawn had been convinced that the guy was a homo. What man let his hair grow down to his ass? Only one who wanted that ass fucked, that's who.

The fucker sure was pretty enough for even some straight guys to give it to him. Not Shawn, his dick would never touch some guy's hairy ass, not even for revenge.

Well, maybe in vengeance. But that would be the only reason.

Still, if the asswipe was banging Callie, he was either straight or went both ways.

Shawn glanced at the clock on the wall, one of the cheap junky knickknacks Callie used to buy at the discount store to hang over the holes he'd made in the walls. He should get a trash bag and get rid of all that junk, then hire someone to patch up the walls. Why live as if he were poor when he was making so much money?

It was ten after eight at night, a perfect time to visit a certain club, find the girly motherfucker, and get him to confess.

The thing was, together with the other recollections, Shawn also remembered how fucking strong the bastard was. He'd lifted Shawn's two hundred and twenty pounds as if it was nothing.

What a freak.

But even the strongest freak would sing with a bullet in his gut, or even better, his knees, but those were harder to hit. The gut was a bigger target, one Shawn couldn't miss.

Fuck, his head was pounding with the mother of all hangovers, and he needed to piss. Otherwise, he would have been in his car already. But acting without a plan and with a sluggish brain was stupid.

A long cold shower and five Advils later, he was good to go.

Shawn still wasn't clear on what exactly he was going to do once he got there, except scare the crap out of the motherfucker and get him to spill where Callie was hiding.

Armed with his two Colt Cobras, Shawn got into the car and programmed the nightclub's address into its GPS.

Shawn had been practicing with the twin beauties for years, even before his father had gifted them to him to start his own vintage gun collection. He had kept them in perfect working condition just as his father had taught him.

Most often he'd practiced in a shooting range, but sometimes he'd ventured out into the mountains. Hunting wasn't allowed just anyplace, so he'd bought silencers to avoid getting caught. He never took his kills home, leaving the carcasses to be eaten by other predators.

As he stashed the guns in the glove compartment, Shawn envisioned two possible scenarios for their use.

One was to threaten the scumbag screwing his wife, watch him as he pissed himself in fear, and get him to confess Callie's whereabouts. The other was to drive him out to the mountains, kill him, and leave his carcass for the wild animals to dispose of, the same way Shawn had done with the critters he'd killed.

Or both.

## 54

## CALLIE

"What's up, Callie?" Donnie asked as she joined him outside on her break. "I miss our walks."

She leaned into him, putting her head on his bicep. "Me too. But I like having a car and driving myself places. You can't live in Los Angeles without a car."

"That's true." Donnie pulled out a cigarette and offered her one, even though she always declined.

Callie eyed the pack. "You know what? I'll give it another try. I feel adventurous lately." She took the Marlboro Light, waiting for Donnie to light it up for her.

"Be careful. Don't inhale too much."

She chuckled. "I won't. I learned my lesson."

It still tasted awful, but she decided to give it a chance. Some things took getting used to before they felt good. Even amazing.

Callie blushed. Like the flogger. It had been such a surprise that a scary-looking instrument like that with even a scarier name could be used for pleasure. A lot of pleasure. It wasn't harmless. If Brundar had applied more force, she would have no doubt felt the sting despite how soft those suede strips were.

Maybe someday she'd be brave enough to try. A little pain enhanced the pleasure. But as she was discovering, it sometimes worked for her and sometimes didn't. She needed to be in the right frame of mind to enjoy it.

"You're getting the hang of it," Donnie commented.

Lost in thought, she'd smoked one-third of the cigarette. "I'm getting light-headed. I think that's enough for my virgin voyage."

Stifling a chuckle, Donnie shook his head as he took the cigarette from her. "You say the damnedest things, Callie. I have to bite my cheek every time."

She waved a hand. "Feel free to say whatever is on your mind. I'm not a delicate flower."

"Maybe not, but your boyfriend may not approve."

"He is not here." It didn't escape Callie's notice that it was the first time she hadn't denied Brundar was her boyfriend. Maybe because yesterday had been the first time he'd acted like one. He'd even texted her today, twice. Once to tell her he had a busy day and wouldn't be able to come over, which was a shame since he also had a rotation tonight. The second time he'd texted her just to ask how she was doing and promised to sneak into her bed when he was done with his rotation in the morning.

Callie was soaring on a happy cloud.

"That is true. But you never know what he can hear. I swear the dude has bat hearing."

She'd noticed that. Sometimes she would mumble something in the kitchen, and he would answer her from the living room as if she was right next to him. Just one more oddity to add to the mystery that was Brundar.

But who was counting?

Donnie pulled out several folded pages from the inner pocket of his jacket. "I finally came up with an idea for a comic strip starring Fran. She is an investigative reporter, looking for vampires. I only have a few pages done. What do you think?" Moving closer to the light, he held up the first page.

"It's Fran all right. Just better looking. It's obvious that you're smitten with her. But that's good. What girl doesn't like to be drawn as a gorgeous bombshell?"

"I was following your advice. But I didn't need to enhance much. She is already beautiful." Donnie's smile was wistful.

Leaning closer, Callie tried to read the tight writing enclosed in the bubbles, when a shadow darted behind Donnie.

Was someone trying to sneak into the club behind the bouncer's back?

She put her hand on his arm to alert him when she heard a heavy thud.

As Donnie groaned and started crumbling down to the sidewalk, her ponytail got yanked from behind, and she stumbled.

It was all happening so fast.

The moment Callie opened her mouth to scream, a meaty fist connected with her jaw, then something rigid hit the back of her head, and it was lights out.

## 55

# BRUNDAR

"Can you do me a favor?" The words tasted like sawdust in Brundar's mouth. He hated asking for anything, favors in particular.

Anandur fought to stifle a smirk and lost. "What type of favor?"

To his credit, his brother refrained from making his typical comments, which must've cost him real effort. The guy lived for opportunities like that.

"Can you switch rotations with me?"

"Just tonight, or in general?"

"Tonight." He would've loved to fob off all of his rotations on someone else, but the other Guardians were in no position to take on any additional load.

"Any special reason?"

Evidently, it was too much to hope for Anandur to just do it without asking questions and commenting.

"My reasons are my own. Can you do it, or not?"

"I'll do it. And if you tell me what it's about, I'll take over all of your rotations for the next month. Hopefully, by then the murders will stop, and there will be no more need for us to do it."

It was tempting.

It was extremely fucking tempting.

"I've stuff I need to do in the evenings and nights. Stuff I've been doing for a long time. This thing with the rotations is putting a real strain on my time."

Anandur crossed his arms over his chest. "Not good enough, bro. I need details."

Damnation. What to do? Confide in his brother, or keep going on the fucking rotations?

Contrary to what everyone thought of him, Anandur was good with secrets. He wouldn't rat Brundar out.

"This stays between us."

Anandur nodded. "Naturally."

"And I don't want to hear any comments or remarks from you. I don't find them funny."

Anandur tapped his chest over his heart. "You wound me, but then you have no sense of humor, and my jokes are wasted on you."

"Are you done?"

"Yes."

"I bought half of a club I'm a member of. The owner is a shitty businessman, and it was about to go under. I liked the place, so I decided to save it, thinking of it as an investment. But my money is not going to keep it afloat unless things change and it starts turning up a decent profit."

Anandur eyed him curiously as if he was seeing him in a whole new light. "My little bro is a businessman, who would've guessed?"

"Are you going to take over my rotations, or not?"

Anandur lifted a finger. "One last question."

Brundar tensed. There was no doubt in his mind what his nosy brother's question would be about. He'd been trying to get information on Brundar's mystery woman since the first day he'd guessed her existence.

"Is it working? Did you make the place profitable?"

*Hell and damnation.* This wasn't the question Brundar had been expecting. He was more than happy to answer this one.

"At this point, I'm glad it's no longer bleeding money. There is a small profit, but I'm working on making it bigger."

"I'm proud of you." Anandur clapped him on the back. "It's good that you're showing interest in things other than your sword, and that you're good at it too. I always knew you were smart."

As Anandur geared up and left their apartment, Brundar changed into his club attire, which consisted of black jeans and a black T-shirt. Thinking about his conversation with Anandur, it occurred to him that his brother had never asked what type of club it was.

Brundar frowned. It was not like Anandur to leave a detail like that unanswered. His brother was too shrewd for that. Which made Brundar suspect that Anandur had known about it all along. Maybe not the part about him owning half of the place, but about his membership.

Sneaky bastard had probably planted a tracker on Brundar's Escalade. The first thing he was going to do when he got down to the garage was to check every inch of that car until he found it.

Damnation. What if Anandur made a habit of spying on him and knew all about Calypso?

## 56

# CALLIE

*G*roggy and confused, Callie opened her eyes and saw a familiar room. In front of her, next to the front door, was the clock she'd bought two months ago to cover yet another hole in the wall; to her right was the couch and to her left the kitchen.

Callie's head hurt something awful, and so did her jaw. She tried to move it a little, but it hurt like hell.

The sharp pain cleared the fog in her head enough for her to realize she was tied to a chair. Duct tape secured each wrist to an armrest, her torso to the back of the chair, her calves to its legs, and her thighs to its seat. It was one of the stacking chairs they kept in the garage for when Shawn invited his buddies from work to watch a football game. The frame was aluminum. Unbreakable.

She was going to die in that chair. Shawn was going to kill her.

How had he found her? She and Brundar had been so careful.

"You're awake. Good. I want you to watch me kill your boyfriend."

Shawn entered the living room with another chair and put it down right next to her. He then walked over to the coffee table and picked up two handguns. Taking a seat, he had one gun loosely gripped in his hand, the other on his lap.

"Are you comfortable?" He wasn't expecting a response. "You should thank me for arranging a front row seat for you. You're not going to miss a thing. I hope his blood sprays your tits, same way you've let his cum do."

He looked crazed, but his tone was calm as if he was talking about the weather, which was much more worrisome than if he was shouting and raging. She'd never seen him like that before. The hatred, the cruelty, had turned his handsome face into a monstrous mask. Or had the face he'd shown her before been the mask, and this was his real one?

She'd married a monster.

Cold sweat trickled down Callie's back. Her life was forfeit, but she wouldn't let Brundar sacrifice his on her behalf. She was going to lie and plead like her life depended on it, even though she had a feeling nothing was going to save her.

"What boyfriend? What are you talking about?"

Calmly, as if he was swatting a fly, Shawn backhanded her. Pain exploded in her cheek, stars blinking behind her tears.

"Don't lie to me, bitch. Your fucking elf lover is going to come for you, and I'm going to shoot first and ask questions later. I'm not going to give him a chance to hypnotize me again."

She had no idea what he was talking about but was afraid to say so. He was obviously delusional. There was something in the elf reference, but not the one about Brundar hypnotizing him.

"You're such a stupid cunt, Callie. You could've lived like a queen. I was saving up for us to move to a nicer place. You think what I put in our joint account was all the money I made? Just shows how stupid you are. I would have never put all my money where you could put your grubby little hands on it. I have hundreds of thousands stashed in different bank accounts. Accounts no fucking divorce lawyer could've found, so don't you get any ideas."

Did it mean he wasn't planning on killing her? A dead woman couldn't contact a divorce lawyer.

"If you were just a little more agreeable as a wife, you could have had everything a woman could want. But no, you had to argue about every goddamned thing instead of listening to your husband. Your older and much smarter husband."

Delusional indeed.

As if she'd argued about anything. Throughout their marriage, Shawn had treated her as his personal maid, expecting her to do all the cooking and the cleaning and the picking up after him even though she worked too and put all of her money into their joint account, not just a small portion of it like he had done.

But there was no sense in arguing the point with a madman. He would just hit her again, and she was already in so much pain that she was fighting to stay awake and not to black out.

He turned to her. "What did you lack? Were you embarrassed about being married to a car salesman? Just so you know, I got a new job." He smiled evilly. "A very well-paying managerial job. I'm the top guy and what I say goes. They chose me because I'm a natural born leader. But only my whoring cunt of a wife couldn't see it!"

He lifted his hand again, and Callie flinched, expecting a blow, but it didn't come. His hand was gentle as he cupped her bruised cheek. "You were so young. Maybe if I slapped you around from the start, taught you to obey, none of this would have happened." He waved the gun between them.

He slapped her then, lightly, but it was over the big bruise he'd left before, and the pain was too much for Callie to keep the tears from leaking.

Shawn wiped her tears with his thumb. "I like this look on you. Beaten and defeated. You'd better get used to it because you'll be wearing it every goddamned day until the day you die."

## 57

# BRUNDAR

It was ten o'clock when Brundar parked his Escalade in the club's parking lot.

Calypso was going to be so surprised. She wasn't expecting him until the early hours of the morning. He'd wanted to bring her a nice meal like he'd done yesterday, but he'd been in a rush to get to the club. Besides, nothing could top Gerard's culinary genius.

Instead, Brundar had emptied the vending machines of all the remaining pastries. Callie was going to love them for breakfast.

He smirked thinking of all the pissed off immortals who were going to find the machines empty. They would probably blame Jackson for not restocking them in a timely manner.

Perhaps he should bring her one now? A little energy boost to help her through her shift?

Taking a pastry out of the paper bag, Brundar searched his glove compartment for a clean cloth. He always kept several on hand in case he needed to clean his weapons.

He wrapped the pastry in the cloth, put it in his leather jacket's roomy pocket, got out of his car, and locked it, activating the alarm. This wasn't the best of neighborhoods, and his brand new Escalade was too tempting of a target.

Brundar saw Donnie as soon as he rounded the corner, sitting on the sidewalk and rubbing the back of his head. A feeling of dread raised the small hairs on the back of his neck as he sprinted toward the bouncer.

"What happened?" He crouched next to him.

"I don't know. One minute I was showing Callie my comics, the next someone hit me over the back of the head. By the shape of the lump, I think it was a gun." He patted his pants pocket. "Weird, my wallet is still here. Someone must've scared the guy off."

"Where is Calypso?"

"I don't know. Maybe she went inside to get help?"

Brundar had a bad feeling. Whoever had knocked Donnie out was obviously after something other than his wallet. He ran inside, stopping by the receptionist. "Did Calypso come in?"

The girl pointed at the door. "She is taking her break outside with Donnie."

"She is not. I'm asking again. Did you see her coming in?"

"No. I thought she was still outside. What's going on?"

"Call Franco. Donnie was hit over the head and needs to be taken to the hospital. I'm going to look for Calypso."

He didn't wait for her response as he dashed out, stopping momentarily by Donnie. "Franco is coming, and he is going to take you to see a doctor. I'm going to look for Calypso."

Donnie staggered to his feet. "I'll come with you. I'm fine."

"You're not fine, and I don't need any help." Brundar sprinted to his car.

He had a good idea who had taken Calypso and where. The thing was, to get her out alive, he might need help after all. The jerk had a gun. Shawn couldn't kill Brundar, but he could incapacitate him.

Brundar needed backup.

For the second time in one day, he was going to ask his brother for a favor, and he didn't care what it was going to cost him.

To save her life, he would pay any price.

Hopefully, he wasn't too late already.

## 58

## CALLIE

Shawn wasn't going to kill her.

He was going to keep her locked up and make her life a living hell. Callie had read several stories about women who'd been held captive for years, rotting in some basement with no one suspecting the psychos who'd kidnapped them of anything. The difference was that in all of those cases the abductors were strangers, not ex-husbands or ex-boyfriends.

Severe cases of spousal abuse usually ended in the woman's death, not her imprisonment.

It seemed the perpetrators of the respective crimes didn't share the same psychosis.

Except for Shawn.

Either that or the stories of spouses kept under lock and key didn't make the news.

For the past several minutes, Shawn had been quiet, staring intently at the door, waiting for Brundar to show up. He was going to wait for a long time.

Thank God, Brundar was on rotation tonight. He wouldn't even know she was missing until he came to her apartment in the early hours of the morning.

Crap. When Donnie regained consciousness, which he had most likely already done or was about to, he would sound the alarm. She had no doubt someone would call Brundar.

Would he know where to look for her?

If the roles were reversed, she would've figured it out immediately. There was only one person after her. The chances that Shawn had been the one who'd taken her were far greater than her falling victim to some random act of violence. Someone as experienced as Brundar would come to the same conclusion.

Which meant that he was either on his way or would be shortly.

*God, make him call the police and not barge in here like some avenging hero.*

He would, though.

The guy thought of himself as the best fighter, and maybe he was, but he wasn't fast enough to dodge a bullet fired from less than ten feet away, no matter how good he was.

She should scream for help.

No, she shouldn't.

The moment she did, Shawn would punch her again and then gag her, and the chances that someone would respond to one scream for help were slim. Shawn would hide her in the bedroom, and smile charmingly at whoever knocked on the door, telling them a story about a loud movie.

People would believe him because it was human nature to believe in what they hoped was true, and not what they feared.

Gagged, she would lose her chance to warn Brundar or plead with Shawn for mercy. Not that she harbored much hope for either, but it was better than nothing. Better than feeling completely hopeless and defeated the way Shawn was planning for her to spend the rest of her life.

Callie would welcome death with open arms rather than live like that.

# 59

# BRUNDAR

*D*riving like a bat out of hell, Brundar's mind was calm. Thanks to years of practice, he was able to slip into the zone even under the most difficult circumstances.

And these were the most disturbing he'd ever experienced.

Shawn showing up at the club meant that he'd somehow remembered their first encounter, as well as the others, and had connected the dots.

The bastard had already suspected Calypso of cheating on him, and now he had a face to put on her imaginary lover.

Well, not imaginary, but Calypso hadn't been unfaithful although she'd had every right to be. Her husband certainly hadn't refrained from it, as Brundar had witnessed in his memories.

Parking his car a few houses down the block, he removed his boots and sprinted the rest of the way barefoot. A stealth approach would give him the element of surprise. A split second difference was all he needed to disarm Shawn.

He'd expected to hear loud arguments, maybe even Calypso crying, but the house was eerily quiet, and all the blinds were pulled down, blocking him from peeking inside.

Imagining the worst, Brundar's pulse quickened.

He prayed he wasn't too late.

He prayed he hadn't misjudged the situation and Calypso wasn't somewhere else altogether.

Far from a criminal mastermind, Shawn was a simple-minded thug. He wouldn't have thought to take Calypso to a motel. Besides, he needed privacy for what he intended.

But what were his intentions?

To hurt Calypso was one, that was for sure. Brundar had seen into the guy's mind. The other was to kill her lover.

He was waiting for Brundar. Which was excellent because it meant Calypso was alive. Probably gagged.

By holding her hostage, Shawn could force Brundar to submit. The jerk could actually manage to kill Brundar. The right kind of bullet, shot point blank to the heart or the brain, would end him.

It was good that backup was coming. He only hoped Anandur hadn't mobilized the entire Guardian force. He'd said he wouldn't, but he hadn't sworn on it.

Circling the house to the back, Brundar checked every window and door, but they were all locked. Not only that, they were all wired. Shawn had either activated the alarm or not, but Brundar couldn't take the chance that he had.

Not with Calypso's life on the line.

That left coming through the front door. If Shawn was waiting for him, he would be sitting in his living room and facing the door with a gun in his hand.

The question was whether he was going to shoot first and talk later or the other way around. Brundar was hoping for the second one. The guy had probably taken all of his villainous ideas from the movies, where the bad guys delivered long speeches before firing a single bullet.

A knife in each hand, Brundar kicked the door in, zeroing on his target, who was hiding behind the terrified Calypso, a gun aimed at her temple, and a second one pointing at the door.

She was tied to a fucking chair, and the only part of the coward's big body sticking from behind it was his left shoulder. Brundar could've hit it easily, but the jerk would press the trigger and kill Calypso on the spot.

It was back to the original plan—serving as a pincushion for the guy's bullets until Anandur arrived.

"You don't want to do that, Shawn." Brundar imbued his tone with as much influence as he could muster.

"None of that, asshole." Shawn pressed the trigger, hitting Brundar in one knee, and then immediately going for the other. Brundar's legs collapsed. He would've powered through the pain, but the mechanics simply were no longer there.

His knees were shattered.

It was one of the rare injuries that took weeks of regeneration instead of minutes or hours. For some reason, re-growing bones and tendons was harder than internal organs and muscle tissue.

Calypso screamed. Shawn put an end to it with a blow to her face, sending her toppling sideways together with her chair.

With Calypso out of the way and no longer providing cover for her ex, Brundar let his knives fly, both hitting the same target—Shawn's blackened heart.

The knives bounced back and clunked to the floor.

Laughing, the guy tore his shirt open, showing Brundar his makeshift armor —a large cast iron griddle strapped to his torso, protecting all of his vital organs.

Fuck, he should have aimed for the knees, same as the motherfucker who wasn't as stupid as Brundar had thought he was.

It also made sense now why he'd aimed at Brundar's knees without having any way of knowing Brundar's vital organs were less vulnerable than his joints.

Shawn had assumed Brundar had come prepared the same way he had, with something to shield his heart.

The guy calmly walked around him, keeping his distance as if sensing that Brundar wasn't as incapacitated as he looked, and closed the door Brundar had left open.

Brundar tried to concentrate and effect a thrall, but the pain was too intense. He managed a weak one, only to feel it disintegrate before he was able to coalesce enough mental power to hurl it at Shawn.

Besides, the guy had somehow figured it out, probably assuming hypnosis, and was ready for it, actively resisting.

Even in peak performance, Brundar would have had a hard time thralling an actively resisting human.

"I could kill you right now, motherfucker, but I want my whore of a wife to see her lover die."

He grabbed Calypso's hair, lifting her up together with the chair she was strapped to.

Thank the merciful Fates she was still unconscious and didn't feel it.

"Wake up, bitch." He slapped her bruised cheeks, first one, and then the other.

As if yanking her by the hair wasn't enough to wake her if she could've been awakened. Brundar could hear her steady heartbeat, which meant she was first and foremost alive, but also that she was mercifully spared the pain and anguish.

"You've got the situation all wrong. I'm just a friend." Brundar was trying to stall, and he wasn't above using the misconceptions people had about him. "I'm gay. She has nothing I want. I swear."

Shawn frowned, contemplating Brundar's statement and eyeing him suspiciously.

Then he waved his gun and smiled.

"Nice try. Is that why you delivered the divorce papers in person and roughed me up? Because she has nothing you want? Is that why you are here facing death? Because she has nothing you want? I don't think so. You were thinking with your dick, buddy, not your brain. And your dick is dumb as fuck."

*Hell and damnation.*

Where in the name of the bloody Fates was Anandur?

# 60

# CALLIE

Callie came to with a start, her pain immediately forgotten as she saw Brundar on the floor with both his knees looking like they'd been blown to pieces, his pale face paler than she'd ever seen it. Shawn was standing next to her, pointing both of his guns at Brundar. He had silencers on them. No wonder none of the neighbors had called the police yet.

Or maybe they had, and help was on the way.

Not letting on that she was awake, she listened to the exchange between Brundar and Shawn. If the situation weren't as dire as it was, she would've laughed at Brundar's attempt to convince Shawn he was gay. Given his looks, it was a good try, but Shawn wasn't buying it.

She needed to come up with something else to stall.

Something that would stroke Shawn's ego. Maybe she should tell him she'd been only using Brundar, and that he meant nothing to her. She could say that she'd filed for divorce because she'd been mad about the school situation but had regretted it immediately because she missed him. Where could she ever find another man as sexy and as manly as Shawn?

Callie was about to open her mouth and start her pleading when she caught Brundar's nearly imperceptible head shake. When she closed her mouth, he closed and opened his eyes several times until she understood what he was trying to tell her.

He wanted her to pretend she was still out.

Callie closed her eyes, forcing her body to go limp and letting her head loll down.

"Say your final prayers, asshole. As soon as she wakes up, you're history."

"Don't do it, man. You don't want to spend the rest of your life in jail because of a woman, do you? She's not worth it. No woman is."

Shawn chuckled. "You're preaching to the choir. But no one betrays me and cuckolds me without paying the price. I'm not going to jail for ending your miserable life either. I'll drop your carcass in the mountains for the predators to dispose of. The bitch over here will tell no one because I'm going to keep her naked, chained to the bed, and gagged."

Callie suppressed a shiver. She had no doubt Shawn meant every word.

Brundar closed his eyes again, signaling her to keep playing possum.

"Don't you dare pass out, asshole," Shawn spat in Brundar's direction. "Or are you praying?"

"I'm praying."

"Good. Make peace with your maker, motherfucker. Pray for the Lord's forgiveness for you have sinned. God is on my side. As the cuckolded husband, it's my right and obligation to kill you and my whore of a wife. But I prefer to let her live out the rest of her life in misery."

*Crap, don't let the tears fall, don't cry, dead possums don't cry...please God, if you can hear me, please help us, we don't deserve to end like this.*

Callie was losing the battle against her tears. Any moment one would slide down her cheek and Shawn would kill Brundar. She scrunched her eyes, holding tight, hoping Shawn couldn't see her face because her chin was practically down to her chest.

Boom!

The door burst open, ending Callie's pretense as she instinctively jerked her head up and opened her eyes.

Her first thought was the Terminator. Her second and more logical one was that it was a guy wearing a futuristic soldier's body armor like the ones she'd seen in Sci-Fi movies.

Shawn fired at the soldier until both guns clicked on empty, but the guy kept on advancing in his slow lumbering strides, probably unable to go any faster because of the heavy suiting.

Shawn backed away, but the soldier reached with a long arm and grabbed him by the neck. A split second later, she heard a snap, and Shawn's body crumbled to the floor.

"What took you so long?" Brundar asked.

Putting both gloved hands on his helmet, the soldier pulled it off, revealing a headful of crinkly red hair.

"Anandur!" Callie called out.

He turned to her with an apologetic expression on his face. "I hope you don't mind." He tilted his head toward Shawn's body. "After seeing what he did to you and to my brother, I couldn't help myself."

"It was self-defense," she offered. Callie wasn't going to shed a single tear for that monster. Anandur had done the world a favor by getting rid of him. She would testify in any court that it was done in self-defense.

"Nope, not really. I was wearing a protective suit. But I can't say I'm sorry I did it." Anandur removed his gloves and gently unwrapped the duct tape from Callie's wrists, causing her as little discomfort possible. A gentle giant.

"Go help Brundar, I can do the rest."

"Don't worry about him. He is going to be fine." Anandur kept unwrapping, removing the tape around her torso and upper arms.

"God, how can you say that? I don't know if your brother will ever walk again."

Brundar groaned, but Anandur's big body was blocking him from her view. "He is right, Calypso. I'll be fine. I've had worse. But it hurts like a son-of-a-bitch."

Anandur turned his head toward his brother. "Don't be a pussy. Suck it up like a man."

"Up yours."

He turned back to Callie and started working on the tape around her ankles. "I apologize for my brother and myself. That's no way to talk in front of a lady."

"I heard much worse tonight. Thank you for coming to our rescue."

He nodded, tackling the tape around her thighs.

"We need to call the police."

Anandur shook his head. "No, we don't."

"Are we going to just leave him like that? They will eventually find him and come asking questions. If we don't report it, we will look guilty."

"I'm going to make it look as if he hung himself, and we are going to clean up Brundar's blood from the floor. Case closed."

She threw him an incredulous look. "Do you think anyone would buy it?"

"Scatter the divorce papers on the floor next to where you hang him," Brundar suggested from behind Anandur's back. "They are on the coffee table."

He sounded awfully calm for someone who was in lots and lots of pain.

"All done." Anandur removed the last piece of tape and helped Callie up.

She swayed on her feet, catching herself by bracing on his bicep. He wrapped his arm around her waist, which elicited a peculiar growl from behind him.

"Cut it out, moron. The woman can barely stand."

Brundar responded with a grunt.

"I'm fine. Just a little woozy. I want to tend to Brundar." She took a couple of wobbly steps and plopped down on the floor next to him. He was lying on his back, looking as pale as a ghost. "You look terrible." She caressed his cheek, finally letting the tears flow. She'd been holding them in for so long, there was a lake of them ready to spill.

Brundar lifted his arm and wiped her tears away with gentle fingers. "You don't look so hot yourself. But you're always beautiful to me."

"Oh, that's so precious. I'm going to cry." Anandur affected a Southern belle tone and accent while hefting Shawn's body over his shoulder.

"How can he joke while carrying a dead body?"

Brundar rolled his eyes. "Don't get me started on that. In the dictionary, next to the terms inappropriate and crude, you'll find a picture of Anandur with a goofy smirk on his face."

She shook her head. "I don't get how you can joke at a time like this either."

Clasping her hand, he brought it to his lips and kissed the inside of her palm. "I'm a happy man. You're alive, I'm alive, and we get to live another day. What else could I ask for?"

# DARK ANGEL'S SURRENDER

# 1

# ANANDUR

Sometimes, the best of things happened at the worst of times, Anandur mused as he hoisted the body up, looping the noose fashioned from the guy's leather belt around the corpse's neck.

Mortal danger had a way of bringing out the worst or the best in people.

Love could flourish even when surrounded by pain, blood, and death. But then this was no news to him. Anandur had always been a romantic, and today's events had just proven what he'd already known.

But it was no doubt shocking news to Brundar. Poor guy was completely out of his element. The love part, that was. Brundar was no stranger to blood, pain, or death.

Taking one last look at the body swinging from the noose, Anandur admired his handiwork. An excellent job if he said so himself. The angle was consistent with the way he'd snapped the ex-husband's neck.

*I wonder how long it will take until he's found.*

Did the psychopath have friends? A family that gave a shit?

Calypso should know.

To spare her the gory sight, Anandur had loaded the girl and his brother into Brundar's Escalade. Later, he would drop Callie at her home, deposit Brundar into the capable hands of Doctor Bridget, and then take an Uber back to the scene of the crime for his Thunderbird.

The neighborhood seemed safe enough to leave a car overnight. Besides, he had one hell of an alarm system, and a tracker he'd installed himself on top of the LoJack. Whoever dared to steal his baby wouldn't get far with her.

His next task was to clean the blood off the tiled floor. A roll of paper towels in hand, Anandur got down on his knees, not an easy feat given the protective suiting he was still wearing, and got to work. It was a good thing Brundar hadn't made it past the entry and onto the carpet before getting shot. Nothing save torching the place would've eliminated all traces of his blood if any of it had gotten on the carpet.

He finished the job with a thorough wipe down, using up an entire container of bleach. When the cleaning was done, including the ex's guns, Anandur put the empty bleach container into a large trash bag, then filled it with the wadded paper towels.

The guns went into a dresser drawer in the bedroom.

Trash bag in hand, he walked out the door. The fireplace in his and Brundar's apartment would finally be put to good use.

Dropping the bag in the trunk, Anandur glanced at the back seat, where Brundar was lying propped against the door with his legs resting in Calypso's lap. Apparently, the girl wasn't scared of a little blood. As badly bruised as she was, her main concern was to keep Brundar as comfortable as possible throughout the drive.

The thing was, after dropping her off at her apartment, Brundar would have to manage without her support for the rest of the ride.

"How are you holding up?" he asked his brother.

"I'll live," Brundar said. "The bleeding's stopped."

"That's good. I don't think you could've gotten any paler." Anandur turned to the girl. "I need your address, Callie."

"What for?" She lifted her chin and threw him a challenging look. "I'm not going home. Wherever Brundar goes, I go."

With a slight tilt of his head, Anandur signaled Brundar to take it from there and explain why it wasn't possible.

Instead of doing the smart thing, Brundar did the opposite. "Bridget should take a look at her bruises."

"I can take Calypso to a hum—" Anandur stopped himself in time "—hospital before I take you to Bridget."

Brundar shook his head. "They will ask questions."

"So what are you suggesting we do? If we bring an outsider in, Kian is going to tear us new asses."

"I have clean strips of fabric in the glove compartment that I can use to blindfold her."

Calypso snorted. "Aren't you guys going a little overboard with this? I'm sure your cousin is not that mean."

"He is," Anandur and Brundar said simultaneously.

"Maybe we can sneak her in to see Bridget and then I'll take her home."

"I'm here, guys. Don't talk about me as if I'm not."

"Sorry," Anandur said.

Brundar shifted, a pained groan escaping his throat. "Call Bridget and tell her we're coming in."

To make that sound, Brundar must've been in unbearable pain. Anandur punched the glove compartment open and pulled out one of the soft white cloths. "I don't want to know why you keep this in your car." He tossed the fabric to Brundar.

"To clean my weapons. What do you think I use it for?"

"Never mind." Anandur turned the engine on and eased into the street, then called Bridget once he reached the freeway.

"What's the emergency?" She sounded tired.

"I'm bringing Brundar and his lady friend in. He was shot in both knees, and his friend is badly bruised. They are both in the car with me, and you're on speakerphone."

"ETA?"

Smart woman. Not that he'd left much room for misinterpretation. "Fifteen minutes or less."

"I'll bring a gurney."

"Much obliged." He ended the call.

In the back, Calypso took the cloth from Brundar's hands, folded it on the diagonal to fashion a blindfold, and then tied it loosely around her eyes.

"Everything hurts too much for me to tie it securely, but I promise not to peek."

"It's fine. I trust you." Brundar took her hand and brought it to his lips for a kiss.

Anandur barely managed to stifle a shocked gasp, forcing himself to look at the road instead of spying on his brother in the rearview mirror. But what he'd just witnessed had been a fucking miracle. Brundar acting affectionate?

Anandur had thought he would never live to see the day.

The woman deserved sainthood for pulling that off.

It was imperative that he keep her safe from Kian and anyone else who might think to separate her from Brundar. Given what she'd accomplished, her humanity was almost irrelevant.

Brundar needed her.

"Listen, Calypso. When we get there, don't wander away from us. You stay glued to either Brundar or me, and you do exactly what we tell you. Understood?"

"Yeah. I got that. I have to hide from the big bad wolf."

"You have no idea."

2

# CALLIE

The blindfold kept sliding down Callie's nose and, even though the fabric was incredibly soft, it hurt every time she had to move it back up. Pushing it into position one last time, she leaned against the headrest, hoping to anchor it in place.

The guys were most likely exaggerating their cousin's hostile disposition. Either that or he was indeed a terror of a man.

She couldn't imagine those two cowering before anyone.

On the other hand, it might have not been fear. The brothers held their boss in the highest esteem, and breaking his rules didn't sit well with them.

Whatever.

As long as she got to be with Brundar, she didn't care what she had to do.

Besides, a blindfold was nothing new. Except, she associated it with hot sex and not clandestine operations. Callie was almost grateful for the all-consuming pain she was in, which prevented the Pavlov-like sexual response to the blindfold. Under the circumstances, getting horny would've been grossly inappropriate.

She wondered how come she was so calm. Everything hurt, from her bruised face to her scraped wrists to her arms and legs and everything in between. But she was alive and free, which less than an hour ago seemed like an impossible dream.

Oh God, Shawn was dead.

Callie still couldn't wrap her head around it, nor could she summon even a smidgen of sorrow or regret. After all, she had some memories with him that weren't horrible. She should've felt something. But there was nothing, not even shock. Not even horror at what had transpired over the last couple of hours.

Maybe it was a typical response for survivors—feeling euphoric for the simple reason that they were alive. Especially when that survival was nothing short of miraculous.

Brundar's cold hand closed around hers, reminding her that they weren't out of the woods yet. Her injuries were superficial, and the most she had to worry about was some scarring. But, despite his and Anandur's reassurances, Brundar might never walk again.

If he ended up crippled because of her, she would never forgive herself for getting him involved in her crap.

"Are you okay, sweetling? Are you in pain?" Brundar asked.

Her injuries were nothing compared to his, and yet he was concerned about her. God, she loved this man. The thing was, if she told him that, he would run off, or crawl away as was the case.

Hey, maybe this was the perfect opportunity to spring it on him.

In his condition, he couldn't get far.

"If you're smiling, I assume it's not so bad. Want to tell me about it? I could use a distraction."

If he only knew.

"I'm worried about you. I would never forgive myself if your injuries crippled you. But as shameful as it is to admit, I smiled thinking that there is one advantage to you being in this state. You can't run away from me. You can try crawling away, but I will have no problem catching you."

He squeezed her hand. "I'm not going anywhere. I'm done running."

Anandur sighed. "Oh, man. We are in a shitload of trouble."

It made her angry to think that what she and Brundar shared could be considered a problem. It was like they were stuck in a story from a different age or place, where social status and other crap like that stood in the way of love. "Why do you work for a tyrant like that? You can quit and find better employment, where you are free to be with whomever you choose."

"It's complicated," Anandur said.

Evidently.

Did their cousin hold something over their heads? Or did they owe him a debt of gratitude? It had to be something huge to justify such sacrifice on their part.

She wondered what on earth could merit such loyalty to a guy who didn't allow them to have a life. The thing that bothered her most, though, was that Kian was happily married, meaning the rules against relationships didn't apply to him. That wasn't fair. If he demanded it from those in his employ, he should at least abide by the same rules.

The car slowed and turned, then went through a series of downward spirals until it stopped. Callie heard what sounded like the pneumatic hiss of a mechanism, then the screech of a heavy door sliding on rails. When the noise stopped, Anandur pulled forward, driving for a few feet before coming to a full stop.

Brundar patted her thigh. "You can remove the blindfold."

"Thank God." She untied the loose knot at the back of her head and let the cloth drop to her lap. A blindfold wasn't fun when it had nothing to do with sex.

As she'd guessed, they were in an underground parking lot. It was dimly lit, and even though her eyes had been closed throughout the drive and therefore accustomed to the dark, it took Callie a moment to notice the small form standing next to the entry to the building proper.

The shadowy figure detached from the wall she'd been leaning against and headed their way, pushing a wheeled gurney in front of her. As she got closer, Callie saw more details. The woman was young, mid to late twenties at the most, and was dressed in jeans and a T-shirt. And yet, Callie had no doubt that the woman was the doctor Anandur had spoken to before. She had that unmistakable air of confidence and competence about her.

Anandur got out, and, after exchanging a few words with the doctor, he opened the back door. "I'm going to lift you up and place you on the gurney," he told Brundar.

Brundar nodded.

"Wait, can't the doctor give him something for the pain before you move him?" Callie asked.

Anandur hesitated for a moment, looking from the petite doctor to Brundar and back.

"Just do it." Brundar leaned forward, then groaned and fell back against the door.

"Let me." The doctor put her hand on Anandur's bicep, motioning for him to move aside.

"Hello. I'm Doctor Bridget." She offered her hand to Callie as if there was no injured man in the vehicle, waiting for her to alleviate his pain.

"Callie," she said as she offered the doctor her hand, which the woman shook quickly.

"I'm going to squeeze by you, okay?"

"Sure." Callie cast the woman a puzzled look. Was she going to get inside and give Brundar a shot for the pain?

"Anandur, push the gurney up to the seat and adjust the height until it's level with it. We are going to slide Brundar over."

Callie lifted her hand. "Aren't you going to give him a shot first?"

"No." The doctor snaked her arm under Brundar's back. "When I say go, Callie, scoot as gently as you can toward the gurney, one inch at a time. I'm going to push Brundar at the same rate, so there is no pressure on his knees. When you reach the end, Anandur is going to lift you together with Brundar's legs. You'll provide the support while I lift his torso from behind."

Callie cast her an incredulous look. "How are you going to lift him?" The woman looked to be no more than an inch or two over five feet, if that, and delicately built. She could never lift a big guy like Brundar.

"Don't worry about that. I'm stronger than I look. Just do exactly as I say, and we will have him on that gurney with minimal pain. Understood?"

Neither guy argued with the doctor about her plan, so they must know something that Callie didn't. Like maybe Bridget was moonlighting as a bodybuilder.

"Yes, ma'am."

"Small movements, Callie. On three. One, two, three!"

3

# BRUNDAR

Brundar gritted his teeth as Bridget moistened his pants and then cut them off him, all without giving him anything for the pain. Was she punishing him for involving her in harboring a human?

"Bridget."

"What?" She didn't look up from her task of examining his knees.

"Can I trust you to keep Calypso a secret?"

"Anandur said he is taking her home as soon as I'm done treating her."

"He is."

"Then it's all I'm going to say if asked. As a doctor, it is my obligation to treat her. But nothing more."

"Thank you."

"I need to knock you out to reset your knees, which I will have to do without the help of a nurse because there is a human here I can't allow her to see. The bones are already mending, but not in the right way."

"Can I have a local shot? I don't want to be out completely."

"Fine," she grumbled. "You're lucky that I just discharged Roni and no new patients have come in. I don't know what possessed you to bring her in here. You're aware that you can't hide her for long. Even if she is hidden from sight, her scent and her heartbeat are going to give her away."

"I know. But I couldn't leave her alone after what she's been through."

"I'm still waiting to hear all about it, like how the hell the clan's best fighter got both of his knees shot by a human. It's not very confidence inspiring."

He had never heard Bridget talk so nastily to anyone, let alone a patient.

"Why are you angry?"

She waved a hand. "I don't have all night. Talk to me."

By the time Brundar had finished telling Bridget a very condensed version of the night's events and what had led up to them, the anger in the doctor's eyes had subsided.

"Callie must be traumatized. Even if she hated the guy, his violent death must have been difficult for her. After I'm done with you, I'll see if she needs anything for the shock."

"Thank you."

As always, Bridget worked quickly and efficiently. It took her about thirty minutes to administer the local epidural, reset his knees, and put them in braces to keep him from accidentally moving them.

When she was done, Bridget put her hands on her hips and glared at him. "Don't even think about putting pressure on your knees until I tell you it's okay. Your brother will have to carry you to the bathroom and back for a couple of days. After that, you can use a wheelchair, and crutches to the bathroom."

"How long?"

"As long as it takes."

Bridget was still in a nasty mood.

He rephrased his question. "When can I go back to work?"

"After your knees are fully mended, which should take about two weeks. I don't want to have to re-break and reset them again because you didn't listen to me." She looked evilly at him. "I will do it the old-fashioned way, with a belt between your teeth to bite on and no painkillers."

Fuck, he'd been there, done that. It was easy to forget how bad it used to be.

"I promise you that I'm going to follow your instructions to the letter. Contrary to popular belief, I'm not into pain."

That got a smile out of her. "Good boy." She patted his shoulder. "Rest here while I treat your girlfriend." Bridget stepped out of the room and closed the door.

A moment later it opened again, the irate redhead letting Calypso and Anandur in. "She wants to check on you first." Bridget grimaced.

Calypso's face looked bad. Splotches of purple and yellow and black covered most of it.

Had it gotten worse, or had he been in too much pain to notice it before?

"You need to let the doctor treat you, Calypso."

"I will in a minute." She walked up to his bed. "What's the prognosis?"

"He is going to be as good as new in a few weeks," Bridget said from behind her.

Callie lifted a brow. "I'm not a doctor, but even I know it's impossible to heal from such severe injuries so quickly."

Bridget put her hands on her hips and glared at the three of them. "I used a new experimental procedure that speeds up the healing process significantly. You have my word. In a few weeks, there will be no sign of the injury."

Calypso smiled for the first time that night. "Thank you, Doctor. That's the best news I've ever gotten." She leaned to kiss Brundar's cheek. "Now I'm ready to get treated."

Behind her back, Bridget rolled her eyes and mouthed, "You owe me big time."

He nodded. Bridget had lied for him. She sure as hell hadn't enjoyed it.

Calypso pushed up and turned to the doctor. "Any chance you can pull a miracle treatment like that for me? Something to get rid of those bruises overnight so I can go back to work?"

"Sorry. That procedure works only on bones and tendons and cuts, not bruises."

To Bridget's credit, she handled Calypso with way more care than she had him, touching as gently as she could and apologizing for hurting her every time Calypso winced.

"Nothing is broken. I'll give you something for the pain. How are you holding up emotionally?"

Calypso shrugged. "Surprisingly fine." She tugged her T-shirt down. "Is there something wrong with me? Shouldn't I feel something?"

"I'm not a psychologist. I guess that you didn't have time to internalize what happened yet and that it will hit you later. I'll give you a mild relaxant in case it does."

The doctor walked out, returning a few moments later with three containers of pills. "The instructions are right here." She showed them to Calypso, then waved her hand in Brundar's direction. "Okay, people. It's late, and I want to get some sleep tonight. You're free to go."

Anandur pointed at the gurney. "Am I taking him up with that?"

"Unless you want to carry him in your arms, then the answer is yes."

"I'll take the gurney."

"Smart move. Goodnight, guys. Call me if you need me."

"Thank you, doctor," Calypso said.

As soon as Bridget had left, Anandur closed the door behind her and walked over to the bed. "Am I taking Calypso home now, or is she staying the night?"

"Is that an option?" She looked hopefully at Brundar.

He didn't want her to go. Not now, not ever. But that wasn't on the table. The next twenty-four hours was the best bargain he was going to get. "She comes with us. You can sneak her out tomorrow night."

"That's what I thought." Anandur leaned over him, lifting him an inch off the bed and repositioning him as far as he could go to the right.

"Up you go." He motioned for Calypso to get on.

Brundar extended his arm, pulling her to him as soon as she climbed up. With Calypso pressed against him, he inhaled her scent, taking his first deep breath of the day.

Anandur grabbed a blanket, shook it out, and covered them both with it. "Not much of a plan, but that's all I got."

"There are no cameras in the clan's elevators," Brundar offered.

"True. This is just in case we bump into someone."

As if a blanket would help.

Even if they managed somehow to mask Calypso's scent, an immortal would immediately pick up on the additional heartbeat. But Anandur was right that there wasn't much to be done about it. They were taking a risk.

His brother opened the door and then took up position behind the gurney. "Let's roll, kids. May the odds be ever in our favor."

4

# CALLIE

The painkillers Bridget had given her hit Callie on the way up to Brundar's apartment. With the gurney sliding quietly on its wheels, and her tucked against his side, warm and safe, she closed her eyes and let herself drift off, waking up only when Anandur lifted the blanket.

She shivered at the loss of warmth and cuddled closer to Brundar.

"Up you go, Calypso." Anandur showed her no mercy.

Brundar was as reluctant to let her go as she was to get up. "Can we sleep here?" She grabbed for the blanket.

Anandur yanked it off. "You'll be more comfortable in the bed, and I bet you would like to shower first."

Right. She vaguely remembered being dragged over the pavement. Her clothes were covered with dirt, and her hair was all tangled up. Going to bed without a shower was not happening no matter how exhausted she was.

As Callie waited for Anandur to pull down the railing on her side of the gurney, she took a look around the apartment. It was a typical bachelor pad, complete with a big screen, correction, a huge screen, open boxes of pizza with leftovers sticking to the cardboard and empty beer and whiskey bottles galore.

In short, it was a pigsty.

"Don't look at the mess, Calypso. All of it is Anandur's doing. I refuse to clean up after him. I'm not his maid."

Anandur humphed. "Yeah, as if I was eating pizza and drinking beer by myself. Half of this mess is yours."

Brundar ignored his brother. "Come to my room, and you'll see. It's spotless."

Frankly, Callie couldn't care less about the state of cleanliness of their bedrooms, what she cared about was the bathroom. She was too tired to start cleaning it, but if the brothers were as disgusting as Shawn had been, and the toilet was covered in pee, she would have no choice but to clean it first.

"Can you guys point me in the direction of the bathroom?"

Heck, she needed a clean towel and a change of clothes as well.

Brundar must've noticed her despondent expression. "You can use my bathroom, and I have brand new T-shirts and underwear you're welcome to."

"Thank you. What about you? How are you going to shower?"

Brundar glanced at his brother.

Anandur patted his shoulder. "It won't be the first time I had to wash his ugly butt."

"And I washed yours, more than once. I think we're even."

"Yeah. When you're right, you're right. Come on, Calypso, let me show you where he keeps his underwear." He took her elbow and leaned to whisper in her ear. "I wonder if he keeps his lacy thongs in there too."

Callie laughed. Imagining Brundar wearing women's panties was hilarious, but Anandur deserved some of his own medicine back. "I bet his butt looks better in a thong than yours."

Anandur waggled his brows. "There is only one way to find out. Should I demonstrate?"

"Over my dead body!" Brundar called out from the living room.

The guy really had bat ears.

She took the pack of T-shirts and another one of boxer shorts Anandur had handed her. "I don't know how he does it. He hears everything."

"Maybe he is a mutant," Anandur deadpanned as he opened the bathroom door. "There are extra toothbrushes and soap in there." He pointed at a tall cabinet. "As well as clean towels."

"Thank you."

Thank God the bathroom was spotless, and she didn't need to clean a thing. Avoiding her own reflection in the mirror, Callie took off her clothes and folded them on top of the vanity. A glimpse of her face in the clinic's bathroom had been enough.

Awful didn't begin to describe it.

Stepping into the shower, she was relieved to find that Brundar had great hair products, including conditioner. Her scalp was tender from having been dragged by her ponytail. Even after the double dose of conditioner she'd applied, and the ten minutes she'd let it sit and work its magic, combing her hair out hurt like hell.

When she was done, she put on one of Brundar's plain white T-shirts and a pair of his boxer shorts. It was long enough to cover her butt, with only a fraction of the shorts showing, but regrettably too sheer to forego the bra.

"Here you are," Anandur greeted her as she walked into the living room. "Come grab something to eat."

The guy had been busy.

Gone were the empty pizza boxes and beer bottles. He'd even wiped down the coffee table, which was topped with readymade sandwiches, an assortment of pastries, and a coffee carafe. She wondered where the food came from. Only gas station minimarts and Denny's were still open this late at night.

Brundar, who looked showered, was sitting in an armchair with his legs propped up on an ottoman and eating a sandwich.

"The coffee smells divine." She walked over and poured herself a cup, then debated where to sit. Next to Anandur on the couch, or try to squeeze next to Brundar in the armchair, which was what she wanted to do.

"Come sit with me," Brundar said.

"I don't want to make you uncomfortable."

"You're making me uncomfortable just standing there. Come." He lifted himself by bracing his arms on the chair's armrests, then moved over to make room for her.

Callie grabbed a muffin and her coffee mug and squeezed her butt into the tiny space, nestling against Brundar. As he wrapped his arm around her, they uttered a simultaneous sigh of relief.

Anandur put his hand over his heart and batted his eyelashes. "You guys are just too adorable."

He was so funny, mimicking the accent and hand gestures of a southern lady, that Callie couldn't help the laugh exploding from her mouth together with the sip of coffee she'd just taken.

She wiped her mouth. "God, Anandur, living with you is a health hazard. Don't joke while people are drinking or eating."

"I'm sorry. I'm so used to him reacting to nothing, I sometimes forget that other people find me funny." He threw Brundar a mockingly accusing glance.

"They don't. They are just polite," Brundar grumbled.

It dawned on her then why the two were such opposites. Callie was willing to bet that what had triggered their polar opposite dispositions had something to do with what had happened to Brundar as a kid.

With the younger brother losing the ability to find joy in life, the older one had turned himself into a joker in a desperate attempt to bring it back.

Did Brundar know how lucky he was to have a brother who cared for him that much?

Did he know Anandur was clowning around for him?

Probably not.

## 5

## CALLIE

"Let go!" Callie screamed, trying to pry off Shawn's vise-like grip on her arm.

"Never. You're mine, you little bitch." He lifted a fist, pulling his arm back to deliver a blow.

Callie cowered, covering her face with her hands, but the punch never came. Instead, he began shaking her.

"Wake up, Calypso!"

*Calypso.*

Shawn never called her that. And it wasn't his voice either. She was dreaming.

Callie forced herself to wake up, lifting off the bed and commanding her eyes to open. Her angel was there to keep her safe. Brundar was hovering over her, a worried expression on his handsome face. Even injured he would never let anything happen to her.

His name a whisper on her lips, she closed her eyes and dropped back on the bed. "Brundar."

"I'm here, sweetling. It was just a nightmare."

"Tell me about it. I dreamt Shawn had me."

His eyes blazing with a strange inner light, Brundar kissed her forehead. "Never again. Anandur made sure of that."

"Thank God. Am I a horrible person for saying that?"

Tenderly, Brundar brushed a strand of sweaty hair from her cheek. "Shawn was evil. Anandur did you and the world a favor."

As a shiver ran through her, Callie covered her eyes with her hands. "I can't believe I lived with a man for two years and didn't see it. I mean I did, but I didn't internalize how bad it was. Or maybe I just didn't want to admit that I married a monster. I convinced myself that Shawn just had anger issues, and that he was controlling, but it was so much more than that. Why did he hate me?

Do you know?" She removed her hands to look at her angel through a mist of tears.

"He didn't hate you. He hated everything and everyone. Don't ask me why. There was no reason. You said he came from a normal middle-class family, right?"

"He did. I don't think Shawn was ever abused. On the contrary. He told me he used to be a bully who terrorized others just because he could. But he wasn't stupid. He'd kept up his charming façade until after the wedding. Before that, I only had a gut feeling that something about him wasn't right. I should've trusted it instead of brushing it off. But I was young and pregnant, and I thought I was doing the right thing."

It felt cathartic to let it all spill out, to admit the guilt and self-loathing she'd carried with her for so long.

"You can put all of that behind you. I'm not telling you to forget it, that's never going to happen, but you can enjoy your freedom and safety without feeling guilty about it."

Freedom.

No more hiding. No more staying away from the people she loved. Callie could have her identity back. "I don't even need the fake name anymore. Do you think your hacker can change the name back in the university records so I can go as Calypso and not as Heather?"

"I'm sure he can."

Wow, she could have her life back. She could call her father and Dawn. Even go visit them. Having the freedom to just be herself and enjoy her family and friends was intoxicating. Heck, she could even go back to working at Aussie.

Except, too much had changed.

She could have her life back, but she wasn't the same woman she was a month ago. Her priorities had shifted, with the man leaning over her being number one. She owed him and his brother her life.

For some reason, the realization calmed her racing mind as if the cogs had finally realigned to work in perfect harmony. The problem was that once her mind had quieted, she started paying attention to her body's aches and pains.

"I think I'm going to take one of those pills Bridget gave me. How about you? Do you need yours?"

Brundar grimaced. "I do. But first I need to take care of another pressing need."

It took her a split second to realize what was bothering him. The poor guy needed to use the bathroom. "I'll get Anandur."

He looked so miserable. "Thank you."

Callie padded down the corridor to the other bedroom and knocked on the door.

A moment later the door flew open with Anandur in all his naked glory staring down at her. "Brundar okay?"

She averted her gaze. "He needs to use the facilities." As did Anandur, judging by the involuntary glimpse she'd gotten.

"I'll be right there." He closed the door in her face.

Apparently, the joker slept in the nude and was grumpy in the morning.

She rushed back to Brundar's bedroom, ducking straight into the bathroom to empty her bladder before Anandur got there. She'd even managed to brush her teeth before hearing Brundar's groan of pain from the bedroom.

Quickly, she opened the door, holding it for Anandur who was carrying his brother in his arms, thankfully, wearing jeans but no shirt.

He must've worked out a lot. Callie felt horrible for noticing. The guy was her boyfriend's brother, and she liked him, but she wasn't attracted to him. Still, a woman had to be either blind or dead not to notice all those muscles.

"I'll wait outside." She closed the door behind her and went into the living room to search for the pills.

They were on the kitchen counter where she'd left them last night. Callie filled up a cup with tap water and took two.

While waiting for the guys to be done, she decided to start the coffeemaker and make breakfast. Those two needed a lot of food to maintain their bodies. She knew Brundar's appetite was healthy and was willing to bet that Anandur's was even healthier. He was a big guy.

The problem was, they had nothing to make breakfast from. The fridge was stuffed with beer bottles, but food-wise she found only a half-eaten pack of sliced bread and two jars of peanut butter, one of them empty.

It seemed the brothers either ate out or dined with their boss, enjoying his butler's vegan cooking. Or not. What was more likely, they didn't care what was served as long as someone else cooked it.

Brundar liked steaks, not veggies.

The coffeemaker was spewing the last of the brew when the brothers emerged, Anandur carrying Brundar and depositing him in the same armchair he'd sat in last night. It was touching to see how careful the big guy was with his younger brother. Anandur's heart was as big as his body.

She poured the coffee into three mugs, fixed hers with sugar and cream, and Anandur's with one cube of sugar like she'd seen him do last night, then brought them out to the living room. "I made breakfast if you can call peanut butter sandwiches that. You guys have nothing in the fridge aside from beer."

Anandur took his mug. "That's the important stuff. We stock up on Snake's Venom because it's not available in just any store. Food you can get anywhere."

Callie handed Brundar his coffee. "Then you won't mind doing a little shopping so I can make you guys a decent lunch?" She walked back to the kitchen to get the sandwiches and handed them out. "This is a travesty of a breakfast."

Anandur bit into his sandwich, taking half of it into his mouth and chewing with gusto. Apparently, he didn't share Brundar's refined table manners.

"I need to get Brundar a wheelchair from Bridget. If she doesn't have one, I need to find a place that sells them. But I can get more stuff from the café downstairs."

Callie shook her head. "No more sandwiches. To heal, Brundar needs proper food in his body. Wouldn't you prefer to eat Chicken Piccata with a side of spaghetti and a lettuce salad, to yet another sandwich?"

Anandur salivated.

"Calypso is an amazing cook," Brundar said.

"You win. It's good that today is Saturday and I have time. What I'm really glad about, though, is that I don't need to report to Kian yet, and inform him that both Brundar and I are out of commission. He will go ballistic when he hears that."

"I'm sure he is going to understand."

Anandur humphed. "Trust me, he will not. But never mind that. I know how to handle him." He waved a hand. "Make a list of what you need."

Callie smiled, the small victory feeling surprisingly good, giving her some sense of control in a situation where she had none. She was trespassing, hiding, and counting the minutes she had with the man she loved until forced to leave.

"I'm going to make you a list of items for meals to last you guys a week. Also, if you don't mind, could you stop by the club and bring me my purse?"

Crap, a split second later she realized that Anandur wasn't supposed to know where she worked. "I'll give you the address and the combination to my locker. I'll call to let them know you're coming."

Anandur rolled his eyes. "Anything else?"

There was, but she shook her head. "That's all."

The purse was a must. Callie's birth control pills were in there, and she didn't want to miss a day when she'd just started taking them. A change of clothes would've been nice, but it wasn't a necessity. Asking Anandur to pick up some stuff from her apartment on top of everything else was too much.

"I'll get you something to wear from Walmart. Don't put on your list things they don't carry. I'm not going on a shopping expedition. I'm getting everything on the list from there."

Stifling a grimace, Callie nodded. "I'll make sure of it." She didn't mind clothing from Walmart, but their fresh produce wasn't the best.

6

# TESSA

Saturday mornings at Jackson's café, or as the sign over the door still proclaimed, Fernando's Café, were busy. That was why Tessa preferred to come over much later in the day. But she'd slept over at Jackson's, and he'd insisted she stay for breakfast even though he couldn't spare a minute to be with her.

Sitting at the back and watching the customers was kind of fun but felt awkward. People standing in line and waiting to be seated were giving her the hairy eyeball for taking up an entire booth to herself.

Maybe she could join Vlad in the kitchen.

Tessa pulled out her phone and texted Jackson even though she could see him standing behind the register. If she moved from her booth even for a moment, someone was going to claim it.

*Can I sit with Vlad in the kitchen? I'm lonely.*

She saw him typing away on his phone. *Of course. I'm sorry I can't be with you.*

Tessa grabbed her plate and her cup and headed for the kitchen, stopping by Jackson to give him a quick peck on the cheek. He was hers, and she wanted all those horny customers ogling him to know that.

"Hi, Vlad. I hope you don't mind some company. I don't like eating alone, and Jackson is busy." She sat on the only stool in the kitchen, using a corner of the worktable to put down her plate and cup.

"Saturday is busy all day long. But it's going to get a little easier in an hour or so."

Vlad worked like a machine, preparing plate after plate of sandwiches with sides of salads, then handing them over to Gordon who was running around taking orders and making deliveries.

"What happened to the girl who used to work for you guys?"

"She quit."

"Without notice?"

"Took her paycheck, said thank you it was nice, and walked out. No explanation, nothing." Vlad shook his head. "Humans." He blushed and cast her an apologetic glance. "Other than you, Tessa. You're awesome."

"Thank you."

Tessa watched for a few more minutes before deciding to help out. It wasn't as if she had anything better to do. The only thing on her agenda for today was Karen's class, which was much later in the day.

Walking up to the row of pegs, she lifted the last apron off and put it on. "What do you need help with the most? Making sandwiches, or delivering them?"

Vlad hesitated for all of thirty seconds. "Delivering. I need to stay here. Customers get weird when they see me out there."

She frowned. "Assholes, all of them. You're one of the nicest guys I know."

He blushed again. "Thank you."

A moment later he handed her a plate. "Table four. Table one is the one next to the window and table two is the one across from it, and so it goes."

"Got it." She headed out with the plate.

Jackson stopped her. "What are you doing?"

"Helping out until it quiets down a bit."

He looked like he was about to argue, but the smile on Gordon's face when he saw her wearing the apron must've convinced him otherwise.

"It should get better after ten," he said.

The moment it did, Jackson walked over to her and untied her apron. "Thank you for your help, but now I want you to sit down. I'll join you for a cup of coffee for me and tea for you."

"Sounds awesome. I wouldn't mind a chocolate croissant with my tea."

Apparently, working on her feet had awakened Tessa's appetite. After years of sedentary office work, running around with plates and cups had been surprisingly invigorating. Especially since she was in pretty good shape thanks to her intensive Krav Maga training.

All in all, her life was getting good. She had a great guy for a fiancé, new friends, and thanks to Karen she was in great shape. The most significant change, though, was that she wasn't as anxious as she used to be.

Instead of a constant state of alert, her panic attacks were becoming less and less frequent. Occasionally, something would trigger her fight or flight response, and after that happened her adrenaline level would take forever to return to normal, but it was happening less and less. If she were to give herself a grade, Tessa would say that she was ninety-five percent okay. A vast improvement from the mere thirty she'd estimated not so long ago.

Jackson sauntered over with two cups and a plate, moving in that sensual and yet all male way of his.

*Sigh.*

She was one lucky girl.

"Hi, beautiful." He leaned to kiss her cheek the same way she'd done to him before, and only then put the cups and plate down. "I'm sorry I couldn't sit with you this morning. And for making you work for free."

"I'll collect my dues later." She winked.

Jackson lifted his coffee cup and leaned against the booth's upholstered back. "What do you have in mind?"

"I'll think of something. But whatever it is, I can't say it here."

His eyes started glowing, betraying his excitement. "Whisper it. I'll hear."

That's right. She kept forgetting her guy wasn't an ordinary human. Tessa leaned forward, making sure no one could read her lips other than Jackson. "I'm ready."

Jackson's expression turned serious. "I don't know about that."

"I am. This time I'm sure. I have never felt so good about myself as I do now. Not even before, you know." She didn't want to spoil the moment by bringing up the nasty part.

"You're right. This is not the time or place to talk about it."

"Then when?"

"Later. After closing."

"Here?"

He shook his head. "I'll think of somewhere with a better atmosphere."

"We need privacy. How about my place?"

He lifted a brow. "Your place and privacy is an oxymoron. Unless Eva and Bhathian are out."

"Right. What about your place?"

"The guys are not going out tonight."

Tessa slumped. "I wish we had our own place already."

"Yeah, me too."

## 7

# JACKSON

"I feel like a teenager in one of those coming of age movies." Tessa chuckled. "Sneaking stolen moments in a car because we have no place of our own."

"I am a teenager, but I don't feel like one." Jackson was uneasy about Tessa's idea to stop at the deserted parking lot of the park. During the day it was okay, and he had even taken Nathalie's father on walks there, but at night the place turned into a different kind of playground. All sorts of dirty deeds were done in parks after dark. Gang meet-ups, hookers, drug dealers.

His eyes were busy scanning the area instead of focusing on the beautiful girl sitting next to him. Tessa had brought him here to talk him into having sex with her, and he still wasn't sure it was the right time to take the final step, cross the barrier, to boldly go where Jackson had never gone before with Tessa.

He had to admit that her confidence level was at a record high, as evidenced by her choice of location for their talk. The old Tessa would've been hyperventilating from a panic attack if he'd brought her to a dark, deserted place like this. The new Tessa seemed perfectly comfortable parking in the darkest spot of the small parking lot, while he was nervous as fuck. Maybe because it was up to him to defend her in case any one of those denizens of the night decided to bother them.

"What are you looking at?" Tessa followed his eyes as he snapped his head in the direction of a shadow darting behind the recreation building.

"I don't like it here. All kinds of shady characters come here at night. It's not safe."

She leaned her head against his bicep. "But you're Jackson--an immortal with superpowers. They need to fear you, not the other way around."

"I'm not afraid. I'm uneasy. You're still mortal, Tessa, and I'm just one guy."

Reaching out a hand, she caressed his cheek. "I don't want you to feel uncomfortable. We can go somewhere else to talk."

*Hallelujah.* "We can park across the street from the café and still have privacy. Gordon and Vlad's hearing is good, but not that good."

"Okay."

As Jackson let out a relieved breath and put the car in reverse, executing a K-turn, the shadow from before darted from behind the building, running toward the playground and then hiding behind the slide.

When he left the parking lot and turned into the street, Jackson took one last glance in his rearview mirror. The shadow hadn't moved.

Tessa turned to look back. "Did you see someone?"

"Yeah. Someone was definitely there, skulking, darting from one shadowy spot to another. I could tell he was up to no good." To put it mildly. It was all over the news that there was a serial killer on the loose. The rumor spreading throughout the keep was that he might be an immortal.

Tessa glanced at the new weird-looking ring she'd gotten from Karen and fisted her hand, so the ring's triangular tip pointed out. "This can double as a weapon." She jabbed the air in front of her, then relaxed her fist and flexed her fingers.

"I bet it can. But it wouldn't do you much good against a guy with a gun or a knife, or against two guys coming at you at once."

Her heartbeat speeding up, Tessa sucked in a breath, then another.

Fuck, he shouldn't have said anything. Way to undermine her newfound confidence. "But what are the chances of that, right?" Jackson forced a smile.

"No, you're right. Bhathian told me that there is a serial killer on the loose and to be careful."

Damn. He'd thought Tessa didn't know.

Normally, Tessa avoided reading or watching the news because anything and everything triggered her anxiety, but she was getting stronger by the day, and he wouldn't be doing her any favors by shielding her from everything that might upset her.

"Did he tell you they think it's an immortal male?"

Tessa frowned. "Are you sure? He didn't mention it. I would think that as a Guardian he would know."

"That's what I've heard. The police are not releasing details, but apparently, the victims bleed to death from twin punctures to their necks."

Her hand going for her throat, Tessa smoothed it over his latest bite. "I thought a male couldn't harm a female that way. I never bleed after you bite me."

"Obviously, he is doing it on purpose, hitting the right artery and then not closing the wounds with his saliva." Jackson shook his head. "Unless it's a human who wants the murders to look like a vampire attack."

The more Jackson thought about it, the more he was inclined to believe it was a human copycat. A nutcase with vampiric delusions.

Tessa sighed. "We are sitting in your car, and instead of talking about how I'm finally ready to have sex with you, we are talking about murders. I don't know about you, but I'd rather talk about sex."

Jackson chuckled and pushed his chair back. "Come here." Releasing her seatbelt, he lifted her into his lap. "I'd rather talk about sex too. But talking is overrated." He cupped the back of her neck and kissed her.

Her arms going around his neck, Tessa kissed him right back, their tongues not so much dueling as dancing. When her need for air forced her to release him, she took in a deep breath.

Looking at his mouth with hooded eyes, she rubbed her thumb over his lips. "I'm so ready, Jackson, it's not even funny."

A smile tugging at her lips, she leaned and whispered in his ear, tickling it with her warm breath. "Do you want to hear a secret?"

"Yeah."

"Do you want to know why I'm so sure I'm ready?"

"Please, don't torture me like that. Spit it out already."

She blew air into his ear, then nipped it playfully. "For the past week, every night when I went to sleep without you, I played with myself."

"Fates, Tessa, that's so hot."

She whispered, "Do you want to know what I fantasize about when I finger myself?"

"What?" Jackson hissed through elongated fangs. He was so turned on he was about to come in his pants like some runny-nosed preteen.

"I imagine you on top of me, inside me, making love to me."

"And?"

She blew another puff of air into his ear. "I climax every single time."

He was so ready to be inside her, right there and then, in the car, parked on the street where anyone could see them. All it would take was to push his pants down, and her skirt up.

*Fuck no.*

Their first time wasn't going to be in his car, or even his bedroom, or hers.

They had waited so long for this moment, and their joining was going to signify so much more than sex, the occasion called for an appropriately elaborate setup. He wanted it to be special for them. Like a honeymoon, special.

But that didn't mean they couldn't make love. He could still pleasure his girl with his fingers and his mouth and his tongue, bringing her to one climax after another.

Jackson pushed his hand under Tessa's skirt and slid his finger under her soaked panties.

She moaned even before he touched her folds. "Oh, yes!" She sounded triumphant.

"Baby, we are not going to do it here."

"Let's go up to your room." She made a move to slide back into the passenger seat.

Jackson held on. "We will go up, and we will make love to each other, but not all the way."

"Why not?"

"We've waited for so long, we can wait a little longer and make our first time super special. I want to find us a romantic inn and rent the honeymoon suite. I want to fill the room with flowers and candles and music. Can you let me do this for us? Can you wait until next Sunday?"

Tessa cupped both his cheeks. "I love you so much, Jackson. Of course, I can wait. I want the honeymoon suite and the flowers and the candles. I want our first time to be romantic and sweet and uniquely ours, a memory to cherish forever."

"I love you, kitten, and I want to give all of that to you, but I can't promise that all of it is going to be sweet." He waggled his brows.

"Neither can I. We will start with sweet, continue to hot and sweaty, and finish with fireworks."

"I like your plan."

## 8

# ANANDUR

Bridget didn't have a wheelchair.
Apparently, since she'd opened her clinic in the keep, there had never been a case of an injury that required the use of one.

Luckily, his trusted old Walmart had one. Typically it was an order-only item, but someone had returned theirs to the store.

Anandur loved the place. One-stop shopping for all his needs. His snob of a brother would never set foot in the discount store, but the joke was on him. Brundar was going to use their wheelchair.

He'd even found another nifty item for the snob. A portable urinal. Brundar could pee in the plastic bottle instead of waiting for Anandur to carry him to the bathroom.

What other store could have had him in and out, his entire shopping list fulfilled, in less than thirty minutes? Altogether the round trip, including the stop at Brundar's club, had taken him a little over an hour.

In the keep's parking garage, Anandur unfolded the wheelchair, loaded it with all the shopping bags, then wheeled it into the elevator.

The lift stopped at the lobby level, and Andrew walked in, holding a paper bag with pastries. "What's that?" He pointed at the chair.

Fuck, Anandur had hoped to have a little more time before the keep's rumor machine started spinning and someone told Kian.

"Brundar got injured."

"How?" Andrew sounded incredulous, as would everyone else once they heard the news.

The invincible warrior having been incapacitated by a human was big news, and not good news, which meant that the rumor was going to spread even faster. For some reason, people hungered for drama much more than they hungered for good news and certainly more than comedy.

*Fools.*

There wasn't a shortage of drama in the world, while the other two were in short supply.

"It was a hostage situation. It was either him or the victim. Brundar chose the nobler path."

Andrew rubbed his jaw. "Damn. That's a nasty situation I'm well familiar with. How is he doing?"

"Cranky. You know how proud Brundar is. He doesn't want anyone to see him like that. So don't tell a soul. The last thing he wants is to entertain well-meaning visitors."

Andrew nodded. "I understand. No one will hear about it from me. But you can tell Brundar that I'm proud of him. That is if you think he is up to hearing that. Some men don't like praise for what they consider their duty."

"I'll tell him. The worst thing he can do is growl at me, which I'm used to."

Andrew slapped his shoulder. "You can take it, big guy."

"Say hi to your girls for me," Anandur said as the elevator stopped on Andrew's floor. "And kiss the little one's cheeks."

Andrew grinned. "Will do."

As soon as the doors closed, the smile slid off Anandur's face. Andrew was a good man, but he would no doubt tell Nathalie, swearing her to secrecy. But then she would do the same with Syssi, and *boom*—the news would get to Kian.

They needed to get Calypso out of the building as soon as possible.

The trouble was, to sneak her out they needed to wait until it was late at night, when there was less of a chance of bumping into someone.

Exiting on his floor, Anandur glanced at the third elevator door, the one dedicated to the penthouse level. As Kian's bodyguards, he and Brundar had access to it. If he made sure Kian was asleep, he could sneak Calypso into it.

The thing didn't stop at any of the other floors, not unless those inside it commanded it to do so.

The thing was, Kian was known to occasionally wander between his basement and home office, sometimes in the middle of the night. Doing business with companies across the Pond often required him to make phone calls when he was supposed to be asleep.

No wonder the dude was always so grumpy.

The guy needed a vacation, but Anandur wasn't the fool who was going to suggest it. Kian fumed whenever anyone even mentioned the word.

"I'm home!" Anandur called out as soon as he opened the door. Given Brundar's injuries, he doubted his brother was up to getting busy with Calypso, but it wasn't completely outside the realms of possibility. The girl was hot. This morning, she hadn't had a bra on, which meant that he'd gotten an eyeful of her impressive breasts, perfectly outlined under Brundar's white T-shirt.

Looking had been wrong on so many levels. First of all because Callie was Brundar's, and second of all because she'd been traumatized and beaten the night before and certainly wouldn't appreciate anyone ogling her breasts.

Especially not her boyfriend's brother.

Anandur had done his best to keep his eyes on her face, but that one glance had been enough to make him feel like a lecher. He would have to learn to do better, think of her as a sister, or a cousin.

Fates knew he'd had enough practice with that.

Callie pushed up from the armchair she had been sitting in snuggled up to Brundar. "Let me unpack the groceries, so I know what I have to work with."

He lifted the bags off the chair and put them on the counter. "Here is your purse." He handed it to her together with a bag of clothes. "I got you a pair of leggings, a couple of long T-shirts, a pack of panties, and a bra."

Brundar growled but said nothing.

Callie might have blushed, but with all the different colors on her face it was hard to tell. She reached into her purse and pulled out a wallet. "How much do I owe you?"

"Nothing. You can make us lunch, and I'll consider your debt paid in full." He winked, then leaned closer. "I'm getting one hell of a deal here. I'm sure your cooking is worth much more than the few bucks I spent on the clothes."

She smiled. "You need to taste it first."

"I can't wait. Chicken Piccata sounds so appetizing."

He left her to deal with the groceries and wheeled the chair to Brundar. "Want to test drive this beauty?"

"No, but I have to. I need to pee again. I think the painkillers Bridget gave me have a diuretic effect."

"Aha! I got something for you!" Anandur pulled out the portable urinal, presenting it to Brundar like a trophy.

Brundar grimaced but took the thing. "Thank you. It will make my life easier. Help me to the chair?"

Lifting his brother, Anandur gently lowered him to the wheelchair, then adjusted the leg supports. "Be careful navigating the corners, so you don't bang your legs into anything."

Brundar handed the bottle back to Anandur, grabbed the wheels and moved the chair forward, then backward and sideways. "I think I got it. Hand me back that bottle. I'm going to give it a try in the bathroom."

"I'll help you. It takes time to learn how to move in this thing." Anandur leaned closer and whispered, "We need to talk."

Brundar nodded. "But only this one time," he said for the benefit of Callie's ears.

"You got it."

Anandur pushed the chair down the corridor and into Brundar's bedroom, then waited until Brundar was done in the bathroom.

"I bumped into Andrew on the way up," he said as Brundar wheeled himself back. "He asked what's the chair for and I told him you got injured in a hostage situation. Which is the truth. I asked him to keep it to himself because you're grumpy and don't want anyone visiting, but I don't trust him not to tell Nathalie, who in turn might feel compelled to tell Syssi. Bottom line, we have to get Calypso out of here as soon as possible."

"Agreed. You need to sneak her out tonight."

"I have a feeling she is going to resist."

"Most likely."

"Are you man enough to stand up to her?"

Brundar cast him one of his more deadly glares. "Calypso is traumatized and bruised, and every instinct I have screams for me to keep her safe by my side. So if she resists, and I cave in, it is because I *am* a man."

Anandur was so proud of his little brother he wanted to pull him into a crushing bro embrace. He didn't, and not only because Brundar was injured. Instead, he inclined his head. "I stand humbled and corrected."

## 9

# BRUNDAR

"This is so good." Anandur paused for a moment to compliment Calypso, then shoved another piece of chicken into his mouth.

She smiled. "I'm glad you like it. What about you, Brundar?"

"Superb as always."

Calypso didn't look convinced. "Tell me the truth. I know you like beef."

He did, but whatever Calypso made tasted great. "I do. But I like sampling your creations even more."

Anandur reached for the platter and jabbed his fork into another piece of Chicken Piccata, put it on his plate and added a heap of spaghetti. "I wish we could keep you. I could get used to eating like this. But I'll have to double my workout time if I want to fit through the door."

Brundar felt his gut clench uncomfortably. He didn't like the reminder that Calypso was leaving tonight.

"If I stayed a little longer, you could get back to work while I kept an eye on Brundar. Wouldn't your cousin like that? Having both of his bodyguards out of commission must be worse than having harmless little me stay in his building."

Her logic was solid, and it would be hard to argue without giving away the real reason why she couldn't stay. Brundar exchanged glances with Anandur, hoping his brother would come up with something that sounded even remotely logical.

Anandur wiped his mustache with a napkin. "Unless Kian and his wife want to go out, he doesn't need us during the weekend. By Monday, Brundar is going to be okay to stay here by himself."

That had sounded very logical, but it had also given Calypso an opening for a new argument.

"In that case, I see no reason why I need to leave tonight. I can spend Sunday here, and you can take me home Sunday night."

Anandur scratched his beard. "It's risky, but maybe it's worth it. For me. If you stay with Brundar tonight, I can go out and have some fun. He can manage now that he has a wheelchair and a bottle to pee in."

Calypso ignored the comment about the urinal and smiled triumphantly. She lifted her hand, palm up. "There you go. I stay, and everyone is happy. As long as the big bad wolf doesn't sniff me out, that is."

A chuckle bubbled up from Anandur's chest. "An apt analogy."

"I can make dinner too, for today and tomorrow. And a Sunday brunch."

Poor girl, trying to justify her stay by cooking for them. Naturally, he wasn't going to phrase his objection like that because it would offend her. She would deny it and make up all kinds of reasons for why she just had to spend the rest of the weekend cooking. He would have to come up with an excuse, like her need to rest. In fact, it was the truth. Calypso was pushing herself too hard. He should not have agreed to her cooking lunch either. But then she would have felt bad.

Brundar shook his head. Calypso was changing him. A few weeks ago he wouldn't have thought twice about saying what was on his mind regardless of how it would've been received.

Reaching over the dining table, he clasped her hand. "Slow down, Calypso. Anandur was just joking. You need your rest too. Takeout will do."

Anandur started to open his mouth, most likely to protest, but Brundar threw him a warning glance. His brother shut it without saying a thing, but his crestfallen expression and slumped posture spoke louder than words.

Something in Brundar's stern expression must have affected Calypso, either that or her fatigue had finally gotten the better of her, and she nodded. "I love having someone, two someones, to cook for who appreciate and enjoy it. But you're right. I need to take it easy."

He knew Calypso and waited for the catch. She never capitulated without a fight. Outside the bedroom, that was.

"When I make dinner tonight, I'll make double. It's not more work, and we will have dinner for tomorrow too." She eyed the empty platter with a satisfied smirk. "On second thoughts, I'll make it quadruple. I thought I made enough for lunch tomorrow as well."

He wasn't going to get a better deal than that.

"On one condition." Brundar cast his brother a warning glance. "You let Anandur help you. He can peel and cut and do other stuff like that."

Anandur shook his head. "I don't know about that. Having me around the kitchen is like the proverbial bull in a china shop."

"Can you wash dishes?" Calypso asked.

"I can do that."

"That's all the help I need. Cleaning up takes almost as much time as cooking, and it's my least favorite part of the process."

"Then I shall be your humble dishwasher, madam. I've already played a lowly deck boy, I can do this."

Calypso's eyes widened. "Are you an actor?"

"Not professionally. It was part of an undercover assignment."

Her eyes got even wider. "Can you tell me about it, or is it classified information?"

Anandur leaned back in his chair and rubbed his stomach. "I guess I can tell you the story without revealing any identifying details."

Brundar rolled his eyes. Anandur enjoyed drama. He could've told Calypso the name of each participant, and it still would have told her nothing. It wasn't as if the story had made the news.

"We suspected the owner of a luxury yacht of smuggling drugs, and since his crew was all female, I pretended to be a deck boy, offering my services to yacht owners in the marina." He winked suggestively.

It took a moment for his meaning to sink in, and when it did, Calypso gasped. "You didn't." She giggled.

Anandur inclined his head with pride. "Oh yes, I did."

## 10

# CALLIE

After Anandur had left, Callie leaned against Brundar and sighed. This was one of the best days of her life, and the good news was that the day wasn't over yet. She'd never felt such a sense of belonging, of family, even though she and Brundar were barely a couple, and she'd only met Anandur recently.

But then traumatic events had a way of creating a bond between people.

She'd read that people working in emergency rooms felt it, as well as soldiers in commando units. Superficial differences that meant something outside of those intense environments went up in smoke when people fought as a unit for survival, either their own in the case of commandos, or patients in the case of emergency room personnel.

But it was more than that.

Listening to Anandur tell his stories with Brundar's arm wrapped around her, holding her close, Callie had felt at peace. She had felt at home.

What a shame it was an illusion.

Tomorrow night, her carriage was going to turn back into a pumpkin, but she wasn't going to leave a glass slipper behind.

"When is Anandur coming back?" she asked.

"Why? Do you miss him already?" There was an edge to Brundar's voice, his body tensing next to hers.

Did he think she was interested in his brother?

Silly man.

"He is fun, and I like him, but that's not why I'm asking. I'm trying to figure out how much alone time we have left."

Brundar relaxed back into the couch. "Plenty. He probably won't be back until the early hours of the morning. Do you have something in mind?"

"Maybe." If Brundar was up to it.

Though judging by how he'd gotten himself out of the wheelchair and onto the sofa, Brundar wasn't exactly helpless despite his injuries.

She still marveled at his incredible upper body strength.

Using the coffee table and the sofa's armrest for support, he'd lifted himself off the wheelchair and onto the couch with his feet never touching the floor.

Brundar hooked a finger under her chin and turned her head to look up at him. "Tell me what you want, sweetling."

She didn't want him to look at her battered face up close. It wasn't a pleasant sight, but he wouldn't let go. "Don't look at me like that."

"Like what?"

"Like you think I'm beautiful. I know what I look like and it ain't pretty."

He dipped his head and planted a chaste kiss on her lips. "You're always beautiful to me."

Who knew the guy was a closet romantic. "That's sweet of you to say, but I look like crap. If I didn't, you wouldn't be kissing me like I'm sick."

"I don't want to hurt you. Your face is so badly bruised that I'm afraid that even the gentlest of touches will cause you pain."

He was right about that, and it wasn't only her face. Her whole body was one big ache, but for some reason, it didn't make her any less lustful. Was it a survivor's thing? Wanting to celebrate life because she'd almost lost it?

"I want you. Is it wrong to feel horny when both of us are such a mess? How can we even go about it without hurting each other?"

"You can sit on me," he suggested with a smirk.

The idea had crossed her mind, but there was a problem with that. "I can't do it with my hands tied up. I need them for balance."

"Can you do it with a blindfold?"

"I guess. Does it mean I can touch you?"

"Given the circumstances, I'll allow it this time."

"Maybe we could do without the blindfold as well?"

"No."

"Why not? I want to see the expression on your face when you climax."

By the sudden tenting of his loose pajama pants, the idea wasn't abhorrent to him, which made her hopeful.

"That's not negotiable, Calypso." Brundar's tone changed from playful to commanding, which had the desired effect on her.

So much for hope, but she had to give it one last try. "Please?"

"Go to my bedroom and get one of the ties from my closet."

"Yes, sir." She mock saluted him.

"And put a chair against the front door in case Anandur comes back early."

"As if a chair would stop him. I don't think a grand piano would."

"It will give us a second to cover up."

She could live with that. Besides, there was something exciting about doing it in the middle of the living room when there was a chance they could get caught. A small chance, but then if she thought it was likely for Anandur to show up in the next hour or so, she would've insisted on moving the fun to the bedroom.

"I'll bring a blanket."

After picking a dark silk tie from Brundar's small collection, she put it on top of the blanket she'd folded on the bed, and reached for her purse which Anandur had kindly delivered. The birth control pills hadn't been the only reason she'd needed her purse; the pack of condoms she had in there was the other.

After all, that antsy feeling had been dogging her since morning, and there had been little else she'd been thinking about while cooking lunch and then dinner. It was either a survivor's need to embrace life, or Brundar's pheromones.

It was a good thing her bra was the padded kind, not because she needed enhancement, but because it did a great job of concealing her stiff nipples. That was why she'd worn her own and not the one Anandur had gotten for her at Walmart.

It was the right size, which made her realize that he'd been sneaking peeks at her breasts, but it was one of those thin fabric ones that would have covered nothing.

With everything ready, there was one last thing she needed to do—get naked and try to renegotiate from a position of power. Brundar would have a much harder time sticking to his guns while staring at her bare breasts.

## 11

# BRUNDAR

Brundar's breath caught when Calypso entered the living room without as much as a single strip of fabric on her.

The woman was perfection. From her high breasts and pink nipples, which were begging to be sucked, to her slim waist and narrow hips, to her long, toned legs. Except, it pained him to see the large bruises on her left hip and shoulder.

The memory of Calypso falling together with the chair she'd been strapped to would be forever etched in his brain, as would the backhand to her face that put that in motion.

If Shawn weren't already dead, Brundar would have taken great pleasure killing him, not with a quick and merciful snapping of the neck, but a slow and excruciating death. For every iota of pain the motherfucker had inflicted on Calypso, Brundar would have made him pay that times a thousand.

She stopped in front of him and put a hand on her hip. "Why are you glaring at me?"

He leaned forward and reached for her hips, pulling her to him.

"Careful," she said, resisting his pull when her thighs touched his.

"Straddle me," he commanded.

She put her bundle of a folded blanket, one of his silk ties, and two wrapped condoms on the couch next to him.

Brundar smiled at that. Apparently, Calypso had faith in his ability to satisfy her despite his injuries.

Climbing with her knees on the sofa, she lifted one knee over and lowered herself, so her naked core was on top of his aching, pajama-pants covered cock.

"At least someone is happy to see me," she said.

Brundar caressed her back. "The bruises on your arm and your hip reminded me of how you got them. I wish I could kill him again. But I wouldn't have granted him a merciful death like my brother did. I would've made him suffer."

Calypso frowned. "Your eyes, they look as if they are glowing."

Damnation. He should not have allowed himself to get carried away like that. The glowing eyes could be explained away, but he could feel his fangs elongating as well.

"It's an illusion created by the angle of the light fixture." He cupped her breast to distract her and reached with his other for the tie.

Calypso moaned and closed her eyes, giving him the perfect opportunity to slip the tie over her eyes.

"Sneaky," she said. "You know, I put down some hard limits, like paddles and other instruments of torture, but then moved some of them into the soft limits category. I don't see how the blindfold is any different."

"If you call paddles and floggers instruments of torture, you obviously don't know what those are." He thumbed both nipples.

Calypso arched her back. "Tell me," she breathed.

Naughty girl. Just from reading over the questionnaire in the club she should have a good idea, but, apparently, talking about it aroused her.

"Nipple clamps, for one." To demonstrate, he pinched her nipples hard.

"Ouch!" She pushed his hands aside and cupped her breasts protectively. "Never. There is nothing sexy about those nasty things."

Her scent agreed with her proclamation. No nipple clamps. Good. He didn't like them either.

"Okay. Those are crossed out."

"What else?"

"There are small vibrators to stimulate a woman for hours. In my opinion, when used like that those are worse than the nipple clamps. But in small doses they can be pleasurable."

"I agree. What about plugs?"

"Those are supposed to be more pleasurable than not, but I don't play with them."

"Good. They don't sound like fun to me either."

This time her scent didn't agree with her statement. Calypso was curious about that form of play. Regrettably, he wouldn't be satisfying that curiosity. He could never associate pleasure with that.

Deflecting again, he continued, "And then there are the real instruments of torture that deliver only pain, such as whips and the like."

"Masochists find pleasure in pain."

"True." He ran a finger through her wet folds. "But you're not one of them."

She shook her head. "No. I just like it when you boss me around. In bed, I mean."

He delivered a soft smack to her behind. "And you like being spanked."

"Yes. But not today."

"I know, sweetling. I was just teasing."

She leaned forward and kissed him, her tongue seeking entry he couldn't grant. He couldn't pull her hair either; her scalp was too tender from the assault. Instead, to stop her, Brundar wedged a finger between their lips.

"Turn around, Calypso," he commanded.

She hesitated for a moment, but then did as he asked, straddling him with her back to his front.

Brundar lifted up and pulled his pants down, freeing his cock, then lowered her to rub her moist center against it.

"I like it. Feeling you like that against my skin is so much better than through the rubber."

"How much longer before we can toss those out?" He cupped her breasts, holding her to him and letting her have all the control over their lower halves.

"Four days. And I don't even care that you didn't bring me a letter from your doctor yet."

"I'll get her to write it when she comes to check up on me."

"As much as I'm enjoying this, I have to ask you to please put the condom on and get inside me before I spontaneously combust."

"Your wish is my command."

She snorted. "Aren't those supposed to be my words?"

"Normally, yes." Brundar tore the wrapper and sheathed himself. He lifted her by her hips and pushed in an inch. "I'm making an exception today."

"Oh, yeah?" Calypso lowered herself another inch. "Doesn't feel like it to me. You're still calling the shots."

"Just the way you like it, sweetling." He surged all the way in.

"Oh, yes!" She threw her head back, her lush hair covering his chest.

He lifted her up, then lowered her, then did it again a couple of times. "You want to give taking over a try? I'll just provide the prop." He pushed up to demonstrate.

"Okay."

Brundar let go of her hips and put his hands behind his head, lacing the fingers. "I'm ready to be ridden by my lady jockey."

Calypso gave it all she had. For about a minute and a half before tiring. "I like it better when you do it."

"Of course."

## 12

# ANANDUR

*A*nandur leaned back in his chair and popped open the top button of his pants. "I'm so full, I can't move."

Calypso was one hell of a cook. As she'd promised Brundar, dinner today was made from yesterday's leftovers, but she'd fixed it up, so it tasted like something new.

Dabbing his mouth with a napkin, Brundar cast him a hard look. "Too bad, because you're doing the dishes."

"I know. Just give me a moment to catch my breath."

Calypso started pushing to her feet. "There is no rush. Let's have coffee first."

Brundar reached for her hand and pulled her back down. "Anandur can make coffee."

She patted his shoulder. "It's okay. Let your brother rest. I don't mind."

Glaring, he didn't let go of her hand. "Please, sit down. You've done enough. Anandur is perfectly capable of making coffee and serving it."

Bossy little fucker, but he was right, and it wasn't as if Anandur could tell him to do it himself. Brundar was taking advantage of his temporary disability.

No matter. Payback was a bitch. Once he was back on his feet, Anandur was going to make him wash dishes and serve coffee for weeks.

"I'm all rested." He pushed his chair back. "And I'll bring cookies."

Calypso chuckled. "I thought you said you were full."

"I am. So what? There is always room left for dessert." He headed for the kitchen.

A loud knock on the door startled all three of them, freezing them in place.

"Fuck." Anandur rushed back. "You need to hide," he whispered as he caught Callie's elbow, helping her up.

This time Brundar didn't pull her back.

Where could he stash the girl so whoever was on the other side of the door wouldn't hear her heartbeat? Given the cooking smells permeating the apartment, her scent was less of a problem.

"The balcony," he whispered in her ear as he propelled her toward the sliding glass doors.

"Give me a moment!" Brundar called out to stall their visitor. "I'm in a goddamned wheelchair!"

Anandur slid the balcony door open and pointed to the farthest corner. "Stand flush against the wall."

She nodded and did exactly as he'd instructed. Anandur closed the door and pulled the curtains closed.

Brundar motioned for him to duck into the corridor, then continued wheeling himself clumsily toward the door while banging into everything in his path to make as much noise as possible.

In his room, Anandur went a step further, going to the bathroom and flushing the toilet.

"Kian," he heard Brundar say.

Fuck. Out of everyone in the keep, Kian was the last person Anandur wanted to see this evening. He'd thought they had made it through the weekend, and that later tonight he would sneak Calypso out of the keep with no one any the wiser.

Yeah. Neither he nor Brundar were that lucky.

"How are you doing?" Kian asked.

"Have been better," Brundar grumbled.

"Aren't you going to invite me in?"

"Yes, of course. It's hard to maneuver this damned thing. I can't wait to be out of it."

Anandur walked into the living room as Brundar pushed himself back, letting Kian in.

*Fuck, fuckety fuck.* The dining table was set for three.

Anandur moved to block it with his body, leaning against the table and motioning for Kian to take the couch.

"I heard you were injured. How come you didn't report it to me?"

"It wasn't in the line of duty, and I didn't want to bother you on the weekend."

Kian lifted a brow. "What happened?"

Anandur crossed his arms over his chest. "Brundar decided to play the hero and rescue a damsel in distress."

Kian ignored him, focusing his intense eyes on Brundar instead. "Care to elaborate?"

"I do not. It's a private matter."

"When my best fighter is put out of commission for two weeks, I think I'm entitled to an explanation, and for your sake, I hope it's a good one, like saving a bus-load of school children from certain death."

Brundar returned Kian's glower with one of his own. "The life of a friend was on the line. In my book that's a good enough reason."

Kian glared for a few seconds more, then took in a deep breath and let his shoulders relax on the exhale. "I can't argue with that. Especially since I would've done the same thing."

He rose to his feet. "I'm sorry for interrupting your dinner. I'll let you guys go back to it." He took a sniff. "Something smells amazing. Where did you order the food from? Syssi and I should give it a try."

Anandur was about to come up with a lie when Kian peeked at the table behind him, immediately noticing the three place settings.

"Who is your guest?" He took another sniff. "You have a woman here?" His chest inflated with anger. "How many times do I need to repeat that no one is allowed to bring their hookups up here?"

Anandur let out a quiet breath. Kian's assumption would make this much easier to explain.

"I'm sorry, boss. My bad." Anandur took the blame. "When she offered to cook for me, I couldn't resist." He inhaled deeply. "Can you blame me? The girl is a wizard in the kitchen."

Kian didn't smile. "Where is she? Where are you hiding her?"

"Come on, boss. No need to scare the panties off the little thing. Right after dinner, I'm going to take her home and scrub her memories. She doesn't need to see you."

"If you care for her feelings, bring her out from wherever you've stashed her before I do. And just so we are clear, Monday morning I want you in my office for a formal reprimand. You're not getting away with harboring a human without penalty."

"Yes, boss." Anandur inclined his head in acceptance but didn't move toward the balcony. Maybe now that Kian had huffed and puffed he would leave.

"I'm waiting. Bring. Her. Out."

Fuck. He was going to smell Brundar all over Calypso and know that she wasn't Anandur's. Unless he held her close. It would be hard for Kian to tell where Brundar's scent was coming from. After all, he was right there with them.

Anandur walked to the door, slid it open, and stepped out onto the balcony. He found Calypso shivering from the cold, her arms wrapped around herself.

Damn. For a human, it was way too chilly and windy to be standing outside in a T-shirt.

"I'm sorry, love. Come here, and I'll warm you up." He winked and tilted his head toward the inside, urging her to play along, then wrapped his arm around her and walked her in.

"Kian, this is Calypso. Calypso, this is Kian."

Kian's angry expression turned furious. "Who did this to you?" He pointed at her face.

Fuck, Anandur felt like such an idiot. He'd forgotten about Calypso's bruises.

As opposed to just playing along, she huddled closer to him, seeking shelter from Kian's anger.

Brundar growled and wheeled himself between Kian on one side and Anandur and Calypso on the other. "Enough. Come to me, Calypso."

He extended his hand, and she took it.

Pulling to bring her close against his side, he turned his head to look at Kian. "Calypso is with me, not with my brother."

Kian kept glaring.

"Her ex-husband did this to her." Brundar pointed at her bruises. "And he would've done much worse if not for Anandur's and my intervention."

Kian looked at Calypso's battered face, then pinned Brundar with a hard stare. "Is he dead?"

"Yes."

"Good."

## 13

## CALLIE

It wasn't often that Callie felt so grossly intimidated. Brundar's boss had a commanding presence, saturating all the air in the apartment with his anger.

He was blindingly beautiful, and usually she would have been attracted to a guy who was that good-looking, and who exuded such a powerful vibe, but all she felt now was fear.

As Donnie had said, the devil was beautiful because he used to be an angel. From now on, whenever Callie thought of the devil, he would be wearing this guy's stunning face.

*You're being silly,* the voice of reason in her head whispered. She had experienced evil. He had left ugly, painful marks all over her body. This guy was intense, but she was willing to bet that he'd never in his entire life hit a woman.

As he turned to look at her face again, Kian's expression softened and he raked his fingers through his hair, which she suspected was a nervous habit. "Are you okay?"

She nodded, not trusting her voice not to quiver.

"I'm sorry for what happened to you, but I can't allow you to stay."

"Why?" She managed a tiny whisper.

"I don't need to share my reasons with you." He said it matter-of-factly, not in anger, or in any way condescendingly.

"Can I come visit Brundar? I mean while he is recovering and can't drive?"

Kian shook his head. "I'm sorry, but no."

Evidently, Brundar hadn't been lying about his boss's eccentric demands.

Tears pooling at the corners of her eyes at the thought of not being allowed to see Brundar, Callie nodded in resignation. She was going to miss him so much. Maybe she could convince Anandur to drive him over to her apartment.

"Do you have somewhere to go?" Kian surprised her.

Would he let her stay if she said no?

"I can arrange an apartment for you until you get back on your feet."

So sweet of him to offer. Callie felt guilty for comparing him to the devil. "Thank you, but that won't be necessary. I have my own apartment and a job that pays the bills." She knew better than to add that she had those things thanks to Brundar.

"Good. I'm glad to hear that." He turned to Anandur. "Take Calypso home today, and make sure to do whatever is necessary to help her get settled."

"It will be done, boss."

For some reason she had a feeling there was a double message in Kian's command. Why would he tell Anandur to help her get settled in her own place? She had the absurd notion that Kian was telling Anandur to get rid of her.

Permanently.

Crap, she'd been reading too many crime novels.

Kian inclined his head in her direction, then turned on his heel and walked out without saying goodbye or any of the other conventional niceties.

As soon as the door closed behind the guy, Anandur plopped down on the couch. "Do you think he is going to invent some new creative torment for me as punishment for aiding and abetting?"

Brundar shrugged, appearing significantly less rattled by Kian's unexpected visit than his brother was. Anandur looked like he'd been in a boxing match and lost. "You know him. Kian gets all riled up and then calms down after letting the steam out."

Callie sat on the couch next to Anandur. "I don't know how you can stand working for him. It must be like holding a live wire in your hands for hours every day. So draining."

"Nah. Kian is okay. Most of the time his electrical hum is low and steady, and when it gets a bit intense it is usually for a good reason," Anandur said.

She cast him a sidelong glance. "A bit intense? Are you serious? It's like calling a woman giving birth a bit pregnant."

Anandur laughed. "The lass has a sense of humor. Tell me, Callie, how can you tolerate that dry stick over there?" He pointed at Brundar.

She wasn't about to allow anyone to belittle her guy. Not even his brother, and not even as a joke. Lowering her voice, she waggled her brows. "Brundar compensates in other areas."

Brundar cleared his throat as if he was uncomfortable with their banter. Funny, as a part owner of a kink club this little sexual innuendo shouldn't have bothered him.

"We need to figure out what to do. I have no intention of being stuck in this apartment until I can walk again."

"You can come stay with me," she offered on the remote chance that he would agree.

"Not a good idea," Anandur said. "You can't lift him or hold him up in the shower."

If that was the only objection, she'd already won the argument. "There are handicap attachments we can install next to the toilet and in the shower. The shower in my apartment is big. We can fit a sturdy chair in there."

Anandur threw her an amused glance. "What's all that about, we can do this, and we can do that? Are you handy with a drill?"

"We, as in a joint effort. I'll buy the accessories, and you'll install them."

"I was just teasing, lass. I'll get the stuff and put it in."

That was good because Callie wasn't sure what to get and where, and she was very glad to fob it off on the big, strong guy sitting next to her. Her style of feminism wasn't about doing everything herself to prove she didn't need men for anything. Of course, she could do that, but why should she, when she could utilize them to do the things they were good at, like lifting heavy stuff and tightening screws.

Good managers delegated, they didn't do everything themselves. Not only that, though, they put the task on the schedule to make sure it was going to get done, and then inspected the completed product.

"When? Can you do it tomorrow?"

"The sooner I do it the better. With Brundar staying at your place, I can go back to work." He glanced at his brother. "First, though, you need to go see Bridget and ask her if it's okay."

"I'll do it later after you take Calypso home."

She was a little sad that he wasn't coming home with her tonight, but knowing he would be there tomorrow or the day after to stay, at least until he got better or maybe longer, was good enough.

Maybe she could keep him there. Tie him to her bed.

Callie smiled at the thought.

There was just one problem with her pleasant fantasy. "What about Kian? He is not going to approve."

Brundar shrugged. "He can kiss my ass. What is he going to do, fire me?"

Anandur's eyes peeled wide. "You're willing to leave everything behind for the lass?"

God, what a lack of sensitivity. With that remark, Anandur was putting them both on the spot.

"Slow down." She lifted her hand. "No one is firing anyone, and no one is quitting either. How about we take one day at a time and see what happens?"

Anandur shook his head. "What's going to happen is shit hitting the fan. But then it wouldn't be our first shit storm. I'll get my umbrella ready."

## 14

## BRUNDAR

The quiet in the apartment felt oppressive. It hadn't been even half an hour since Calypso had left with Anandur, and Brundar was missing her already.

If he were out in the field, the separation would've been tolerable, but sitting in the damned wheelchair in the middle of the living room and staring at the wall was making it worse. Much worse.

Being alone had never bothered him before. On the contrary, he used to enjoy the quiet whenever Anandur was out and he had the apartment all to himself. He would put on some classical music and read.

Not that he'd done either lately.

Brundar had no time to indulge in leisure activities. Since buying into Franco's, those moments had become scarce.

The thing was, right now he didn't feel like listening to music or reading. He craved what he'd had for the last two days.

Calypso.

How the hell was he going to make it until tomorrow?

Come to think of it, there was no reason to wait. He could go see Bridget right now.

Damnation. The doctor wouldn't be in her office on a Sunday night. Bridget was probably partying somewhere. He could call her and complain about something. She would drop everything and come check up on him.

Brundar chuckled. If he told her his heart was acting up and his blood flow was all screwed up, he wouldn't be lying.

Where the hell was his phone?

Did he have it on him when they'd gotten home Friday night?

Damn. It was probably in the pocket of the jeans Bridget had cut off him. Hopefully, she hadn't tossed the pants with the phone in the trash.

Brundar wheeled himself to the kitchen counter, grabbed the house phone, and dialed the clinic's number. It was worth a shot. If there was no answer, he would call her apartment. Her cell phone number was programmed into his shortlist of favorites, but he didn't remember it.

She answered after a few rings. "Bridget here."

"What are you doing in the clinic on a Sunday night?"

She chuckled without mirth. "Research. Whenever I'm in a shitty mood I dive into my research. What can I do for you? Are you in pain?"

"I don't remember if I left my phone in the pants you cut off me. Did you throw them away?"

"I put them in a zipped plastic bag in case you wanted them as a memento."

"Could you check to see if my phone is in one of the pockets? After that burn them."

"Not a sentimental guy, are you?"

"Did I ever give you the impression that I was?"

He'd spent most of his life trying to forget things, not remember them. Most of his experiences had been of the kind better forgotten, but then some he needed to keep as a reminder of what not to do next time in similar situations.

"Hold the line while I check your pants."

He waited, listening as Bridget opened a drawer, then the rustle of plastic and the whoosh of unzipping, until she picked up the receiver again. "It's here. Do you want me to bring it up to you?"

"I can come down. Anandur got me a wheelchair."

"That's okay. I will come to you. I need a break anyway, and I'll check your knees while I'm at it."

"Thank you."

He'd been looking forward to wheeling himself out and into the elevator. It would have given him something to do other than staring at the walls. Now he was going to pass another ten minutes or so in inactivity.

The next two weeks were going to be hell. Even when he finally replaced the wheelchair with crutches, he would still be stuck doing nothing.

An injured Guardian was worthless.

Maybe he could dedicate this time to focusing on Franco's.

In fact, if he stayed at Calypso's she could drive him there and back, and it would be nice to spend his days and nights with her. It would sure make the coming weeks more tolerable.

Would she tolerate his presence twenty-four-seven?

Brundar knew he was going to love every minute of it. But that was because Calypso was all sunshine. In contrast, he was the dark cloud to dim her light. She might soon get tired of him.

The thought obliterated the temporary spark of good mood.

Brundar was glad to hear the knock on the door announcing Bridget. For the next few minutes, he would be too busy to brood.

"Come in. It's open."

Bridget entered, holding her old-fashioned doctor's bag. She pulled his phone out of her pants pocket. "Here you go. Nothing broken."

"Thank you."

"Let's see those knees of yours. Can you wheel yourself next to the couch?"

He nodded and followed her.

"You're doing as well as expected," she said when she was done. "Tomorrow, you can start putting a little pressure on them. Not walking, but you can put your feet down on the floor while bracing most of your weight on your arms to move from the wheelchair to the bed or the sofa."

"That's good to hear because I'm moving in with Calypso until my knees heal completely. We don't have enough Guardians for Anandur to play nurse to me."

"That's a big mistake, and you know it. It was semi-okay to pretend like this was going to work before your injury. Callie saw your knees get shot to pieces, and she is not stupid. Even with my bullshit explanation, she would know no one can recover from an injury like that in two weeks. What are you going to do when there is no trace of it? Keep your pants on so she won't see your perfectly healthy knees?"

Brundar's lips curved in a smirk. "I got that part covered."

Bridget frowned. "How?"

"I have my ways."

"Oh, yeah." She blushed. "So the rumors are true? You're into that bondage thing?"

He'd been hiding it for so long and for no good reason. There was no shame in what he did. But then it was no one's business how he liked things in bed. However, he could make an exception in Bridget's case. It would ease her mind to know how well he was hiding his nature.

"A blindfold is a great tool for an immortal male. I don't need to worry about my eyes glowing or my fangs showing. And now I can add perfectly healed knees to that."

She shook her head. "I agree that it's an excellent cover. In fact, you may suggest it to some of the guys who need help in that department. But the more time you spend with the girl, the stronger the emotional entanglement will become. You're sentencing both of you to misery. And don't forget the addiction part. It can happen with a human female as easily as with an immortal. Think how difficult it would be for her once you leave."

What did she think? That he hadn't gone through all those scenarios in his head already and still felt powerless to resist?

Maybe he was losing his ever-loving mind, but he was willing to sacrifice everything for a few good years with Calypso until he could no longer hide the fact that he wasn't aging.

Except, he was not ready to challenge the clan yet. There was time for that. In the meantime, he was going to lie.

"It's just until I'm healed. I'll end it then."

Given the doubtful expression on her face, Bridget wasn't buying it. But she wouldn't go as far as accusing him of lying. Most likely, she thought he was delusional.

"I want to see you tomorrow before you put any pressure on your knees. If everything is okay, I'll give you a different kind of braces that allow for more movement."

"What time do you want me here?"

"Late afternoon or early evening. Do you have a way to get back here?"

"I'll have to ask Anandur to pick me up."

"He might be busy. Give me Calypso's address, and I'll come to you."

He shook his head. "I don't want you to get in trouble because of me. Kian knows that we snuck Calypso in. He caught us. But I'm not going to tell him I'm staying with her. If I'm lucky, he won't know until the two weeks are up."

Bridget put a hand on her hip. "I'll keep your secret, Brundar. He is not going to hear it from me."

"I know. But if he finds out, you'll get in trouble."

She waved a hand. "I'm not scared of him. He is all bark and no bite. What is he going to do? Fire me?"

Brundar smiled. "Funny that you should say that. That's my stance as well."

Bridget put her hand over her heart. "Oh Fates, Brundar, are we talking mutiny?"

"We are a family, Bridget, not a ship crew. We cooperate because it's in our best interest. Sometimes, though, it is not."

## 15

# RONI

Roni looked at the cuff William had secured around his wrist and grimaced. "It looks like women's jewelry. Don't you have anything more manly?"

William snorted. "Dalhu and Michael didn't complain, and those two are as manly as they come."

Roni shook his wrist from side to side, testing the cuff's fit. "I don't know those guys, but I'll take your word for it. What happens when I gain weight? Can you adjust it?"

"I'll make you a new one."

"If I never take it off, how am I going to clean the skin under it? It's going to get gross."

William sighed and gripped Roni's arm. "Look, it's loose enough so you can push it up for washing. Do you always complain this much?"

"Yeah, I do. It's a good strategy. The squeaky wheel gets the grease."

"And gets annoying, but what do I know?" The guy shrugged. "I'm not so great with people either. I talk too much. They get bored and scurry away."

William talked fast, but Roni didn't mind. Everything the guy had told him was fascinating. "That's because they are a bunch of morons who don't understand half of what you're talking about, and even if they do, they can't follow because you talk so fast. You're too smart for them, man."

William cracked a smile. "Thank you. Let's see how you're going to talk after working with me for a couple of weeks. Kian told me to make room for you in my lab."

That was the best news Roni had had in a while. "Are we going to work together?"

"Yep. Side by side." William collected the tools he'd brought with him to cuff Roni and put them back in a blue fabric pouch.

"Can I come see the place?"

"Do you feel well enough?"

"I'm much better, thank you for asking." For some reason, Roni felt like being polite to the guy and curbing the snarky attitude he treated almost everyone else with. Not because William was a good guy, and not because he was inviting Roni to share his kingdom, but because he sensed vulnerability in him.

Most of the time Roni was too self-absorbed to notice other people's emotional states, but William's eyes had a haunted look to them that bothered Roni. He had a feeling it was something that happened recently because everyone who mentioned William had commented what a cheerful and friendly guy he was. The dude was friendly for sure, but he was far from cheerful.

"Then let's go. Now that you have the cuff, I can have your thumbprint programmed into the scanners."

"Right, I was wondering when I'd be allowed out of this apartment." Not that he was going anywhere.

Roni's computer equipment was right there, and Sylvia made sure he had food in the fridge. Other than work and necessities, the only reason to leave would be to go visit someone, but he knew only a few people: Andrew, who still kept his distance; Kian, who Roni wasn't going to visit unless his life depended on it; and Jackson and Tessa, who didn't live at the keep. And William, of course.

Sylvia had told him about the gym and the movie theater, but he was still too weak for exercising, and watching a movie all by himself in an empty theater was as appealing as telling jokes to himself in the mirror. Some things had to be done in company. Even a loner like him knew that.

The first thing that struck Roni as odd was that the door to William's lab was unlocked. Apparently, the guy trusted his fellow clan members not to sabotage his work.

"You should lock the door when you leave the room," he said as he followed the guy inside.

"It's safe down here."

"Yeah, until it's not." Roni took a look around, underwhelmed by what he saw. It was a disorganized mess of epic proportions. How the hell did the guy work in a dump like that?

William frowned. "What do you mean? Only family is allowed in here."

"And you trust every one of them implicitly? There are bad apples in every family. Imagine if someone holds a grudge for something and decides to retaliate by sabotaging the keep's brain, which I assume is all in here."

"It is." William pushed his glasses up his nose. "I never considered the possibility, but you're right. It's not like it couldn't happen."

"Exactly. Put in a retina scanner. Those are impossible to trick. Better than thumb scanners."

William's lips lifted in a crooked smirk. "I can do better than that. I can use my facial recognition program to grant entry only to those who need to be here, and I'll have a record of everyone entering the lab."

"Perfect."

William walked over to his messy station. "So, what do you think? Nice setup, right?"

Roni liked the guy, but it didn't mean he was going to lie about something as important as his future working environment to spare his feelings.

"It's a dump. Your equipment is good, but I don't know how you can work here. First of all, all those cables lying around on the floor are a safety hazard. This super expensive equipment is piled up like it's a junkyard. Then there is your desk and your chair. No considerations at all to ergonomics. I know that you're an immortal and that you heal fast, but sitting in that crappy chair all day must do a number on your back. I'm sure it hurts."

William glanced around his domain, once, then again, as if he was trying to see it through Roni's eyes.

"There are no pictures on the walls, either," he added to Roni's list of things that needed improvement.

Roni nodded. "The walls could use a fresh coat of paint before you hang pictures on them. Look at the smoke stains over there. Did something catch fire?"

William rubbed his neck. "Yeah, I had a small accident a couple of years ago."

"Wow. Your maintenance crew sucks, man. You should hire a new one."

"We have no maintenance crew. We have my ramped up Roomba, but because of the wires I can't let it loose in here."

"You don't hire maintenance people because of the secrecy?"

"Naturally."

"How about your own people?"

"No one wants to do a job like that. We each clean and perform upkeep on our own work spaces. Except for Kian, that is. He has a butler that does it for him. But then Kian is the hardest working person in the keep."

Roni glanced around. "I'm sure not everyone does a good job of keeping things clean."

William cast him a sheepish glance. "Any ideas on how to improve things? From what Andrew tells me, you worked in the heart of hearts of the government's computer network."

"I did. Anything I wanted I put in a request for, and it was delivered or done. I called it my throne room and treated it as such."

"I like it. A throne room. In here, if the procurement requires serious funds it goes through Kian. I'm authorized to spend up to twenty thousand a month at my own discretion. Usually, it's enough."

It was Roni's turn to look uncomfortable. "I can make a list of what we need to transform this place, but I have no clue how much it's going to cost. I worked for the government. Our department had unlimited budget."

"Let's start with that list and go from there."

# 16

# ANANDUR

Anandur wiped the drill shavings from the bathroom floor with a wet rag, then stood back to examine his work. If Kian ever kicked him out of the Guardian force, he could have a career as a handyman.

Installing the special handicapped rails and supports hadn't been a complicated job. If he could do that with no training, after watching two YouTube vids, he could learn how to do other things just as quickly. It boiled down to having the right tools and figuring out how to use them.

As the idea took on a life of its own, Anandur grinned at his reflection in the vanity mirror. He could imagine himself with a tool belt, fixing things for lonely ladies in need of small home improvements and big orgasms.

He could be known as the fixer-upper gigolo. He'd charge for the improvements and throw in the orgasms for free.

"What are you smiling about?" Calypso asked, handing him a tall glass of lemonade.

"A job well done." He moved back so she could inspect his work.

"Looks awesome. I'll tell Brundar to come give it a try."

Last night, his stubborn brother had made Anandur take him to Calypso's even though her apartment wasn't ready for him and his special needs. The guy had it bad, or good, depending on which end of the prism one chose to look through.

"You'll have to clear the bathroom," Brundar said from the entrance. "It's not that I'm modest, but there isn't enough room for you and me and my wheelchair."

Anandur stepped out, and Calypso followed.

Brundar wheeled himself inside, maneuvered the chair next to the toilet, grabbed the bars and hoisted himself up. "Okay, going in. Now let's see if it works the other way around." He hoisted himself up again and sat back on the chair.

"Dude, you need to check if you can take your pants down as well."

Brundar ignored him and wheeled himself toward the shower, where Anandur had put in a sturdy chair designed especially for that purpose. With his brother's upper body strength, it was really no challenge, but Anandur wondered how injured or paralyzed humans handled situations like that. They probably couldn't do it at all without assistance.

"Thank you," Brundar said as he got himself back into the wheelchair. "I owe you."

"No, you don't. I did it for me as much as for you. I want to get back to work knowing you can manage on your own."

Brundar nodded. "Still, it's appreciated."

Calypso nudged Anandur's arm. "I'm making lunch. Wash your hands and come join us."

He would've loved to, but he'd already spent the entire morning on the installation and needed to get back to the keep before Kian decided to pay them another visit, finding no one home.

"I wish I could. But I have to get back to work." And whatever torment Kian had planned for him.

"I'll put the cutlet inside a sandwich so you can eat it in the car on the way."

"Thank you. That would be great."

Anandur was falling a little in love with his brother's woman. Not romantically, but as someone he was happy to know. Calypso was awesome. Pretty, funny, feisty, and a goddess in the kitchen. But most importantly, she made Brundar smile.

After collecting his new tools and washing his hands, Anandur walked out the door with a kiss on his cheek and a sandwich packed in a paper bag.

He could get used to that. Would his brother mind if he moved in with him and Calypso?

Yeah, he would.

Bummer.

Even though Brundar's knees were busted and he was in a wheelchair, the guy looked happy for the first time since he was a little kid. Anandur was adamant about keeping it that way. If need be, he would slay dragons and fight Kian, or the other way around, to guard Brundar's little slice of happiness.

His brother deserved it.

Back in the keep, Anandur headed straight for Kian's office to report for duty. As far as he knew, Kian had no outside meetings scheduled for today, but things often changed.

He knocked on the door and walked in. "I'm back and reporting for duty."

Kian lifted his head and cast him a hard look. "Who is taking care of your brother?"

"He is doing fine by himself. A few grab bars solved the bathroom problem." He wasn't lying, he just wasn't being specific. Kian didn't need to know that the grab bars were not in Anandur and Brundar's apartment.

"What about the girl?"

"She is back at her place." Again, not a lie.

Kian shook his head. "What are you not telling me, Anandur? I can smell your guilt."

Damn. He'd forgotten about Kian's super-nose. His sense of smell was superior. Perhaps because he was as close genetically to the gods as it got, or maybe it was his special talent, but the guy could differentiate between the slightest nuances.

"Brundar has feelings for the girl. You know him, you know how closed off he was, pushing everyone away, including me. He was living on autopilot, like a zombie. I'm sure you realize what a breakthrough this is for him."

"I do. But it changes nothing. Even if he decided to run off with her, what would happen in a few years when she ages, and he doesn't? He would have to leave her, and it'd destroy him. I've been in that movie. The pain I carried with me for years was much worse than if I had given the girl up right at the beginning."

"I like Calypso."

"I'm sure you do, but it has nothing to do with anything."

"But it does. Amanda has a new theory about immortals and Dormants feeling affinity toward each other. Maybe Calypso is a Dormant?"

"If she were, she would've transitioned already. I'm sure Brundar hasn't kept their relationship platonic. He is behaving like a mated male."

Yeah, there was that. Anandur suspected Brundar had been involved with Calypso for a long while. All that secrecy, all those days and nights he would disappear from sight, not telling anyone where he was going.

No doubt some of it had to do with the club he'd acquired, but not all. Kian was right. Brundar and Calypso acted like a mated couple.

And yet, Jackson and Tessa were another couple in a similar situation, and Kian was allowing them to be together. Not only that, he let Tessa live away from the keep, free as a bird while privy to all their secrets and its location.

It wasn't right, and Anandur was going to confront Kian about it even if it got him in deeper shit than he already was. "How come you went out on a limb for Tessa and Jackson, a teenage boy and a human girl with no Dormant indicators, but you're refusing to do the same for Brundar? A man who has served you faithfully for centuries?"

Kian's eyes started glowing dangerously. "I have my reasons, and I don't need to share them with you."

Anandur should have known to back off, but he was too riled to back down. "You're playing favorites, Kian, and not for the right people. I don't care what your reasons are. If anyone deserves happiness, it is my brother."

"Get out," Kian hissed from between tight lips, his fangs getting so long they were protruding below his upper lip. "You chose a bad day to question my leadership and show disrespect for my authority."

As if there were ever a good day for that.

Anandur rose to his feet. "I'll be in the gym if you need me." He still had a duty to perform, even if his boss was a monumental jerk with a God complex.

Well, he happened to be an actual demigod, but that was beside the point.

It took all of Anandur's self-restraint to walk out of Kian's office without throwing a punch into one of the walls and to not slam the door behind himself.

Imagining the punching bag in the gym helped.

Alone in the elevator, Anandur let out the growl he'd been holding. It shook the small cabin. A disembodied voice came through the loudspeakers. "Is there a problem?"

The shaking must've alerted security.

"No problem. I was just releasing some steam."

The voice chuckled. "Is the elevator still in one piece?"

"Yeah, no worries."

"I'll take your word for it, Anandur."

Damn it. Everyone working in security knew him, but Anandur hadn't expected his voice to be so easily recognizable.

As the elevator came to a stop at the gym level, Anandur stepped out and walked straight into Amanda. He caught her shoulders, steadying her.

"Sorry, princess. Are you okay?"

"It's my fault. I was checking messages on my phone and not paying attention. What's going on? You look flustered."

"Do I?" Anandur touched his hand to his cheek. It was warm. One of the many disadvantages of being a redhead was that cursed fair skin that became ruddy with every heightened emotion and after a couple of drinks.

"You do. Is it about Brundar? I heard what happened to him. In fact, I came home for lunch with the intent of paying him a visit."

Anandur closed his eyes. The plot was thickening. Pretty soon every goddamned clan member would want to come visit poor injured Brundar, only to discover that he wasn't there.

"Brundar doesn't want to see anyone. You know how proud he is. Getting bested by a human is not something he wants to talk about. He wants to forget it ever happened."

Amanda put her hand on her hip. "That's the thing. No one knows what happened. Or how. I want details, Anandur."

"I'm sure you do."

# 17

# AMANDA

"I'm going to talk to Kian," Amanda said after Anandur had filled her in on what was going on. She'd practically muscled him into one of the empty classrooms and forced the story out of him.

It was so much bigger than Brundar getting shot. The ice prince was in love. Not that Anandur had mentioned the word love, but the words fate and mate and affinity had been thrown into the mix of his otherwise matter-of-fact account.

"Don't. And please, for the love of everything that's dear to you, don't spread the story. Especially since it is not my story to tell. You trusted me with yours way back then, and I'm trusting you with this."

"You're not the only one who needs to fight for Brundar. I'm going to fight for him too."

"I appreciate the sentiment, I really do. But your brother is in one of his shite moods today. He told me to get out when I dared mention Tessa and Jackson and the leeway he is allowing them. He will just blow up at you."

"Tessa and Jackson have nothing to do with Brundar and his girl. Each story is different. It was a strategic mistake on your part to bring them up."

"In hindsight, yes. But I don't understand why."

Amanda re-crossed her legs in an attempt to get comfortable on the desk she was sitting on. "Tessa is like Eva's daughter. She would never do anything to betray the woman who saved her life and raised her as her own."

Anandur tilted his head. "That's a story I would like to hear."

"I bet. But it's not my story to tell."

"I told you Brundar's."

"Nice try. It's not the same. I barely know Tessa, while Brundar is your brother and you're trying to build a team to fight for him."

"I am?"

"Sure you are. That's why you told me his story. You want my help."

"Honestly, I wasn't thinking in that direction at all. I just needed someone to hear me out, and as I said before, I trust you."

"And I owe you. Don't think I've forgotten what you did for me when I was fighting for my right to be with Dalhu."

Anandur let out a sigh. "Why is your brother such an ass?"

"He is not an ass. He is stressed out and overworked, and he needs to take time off. I think he is nearing a breaking point. He snaps at everyone, except Syssi, that is. She is the only one who can calm him down."

"In that case, we need her on our team."

"We need my mother."

Anandur crossed his arms over his chest. "I don't know about that. You are her daughter, so naturally, she was inclined to assist you. But Brundar is just one more clan member, no more special than the next. She will not go against Kian for him."

Amanda smirked. "Men think so linearly. I will not ask her to come here for Brundar. I'll ask her to come to help Kian. He needs a vacation, and she is the only one who can force him to take one."

Anandur looked doubtful. "And who is going to run things when he is vacationing?"

"I can take time off from the university and run things for him while he is gone."

Anandur tried to stifle his snort but failed. "With all due respect, Amanda, you're a smart and capable woman, but you can't fill Kian's shoes. He's been running this conglomerate since its creation. You wouldn't know where to start."

"True. But contrary to what Kian believes, the world will not come to an end if he is not holding it up on his shoulders twenty-four-seven. Our business empire will not crumble during the two weeks he is gone, and World War III will not start because he abandoned his watch."

"Dream on, princess. You'll be lucky if he takes the weekend off. Don't even mention two weeks if you want your head to stay attached to your shoulders."

She shrugged. "I'm not afraid of him."

"Yeah, that's why you're thinking of pulling out the big guns, meaning your mother."

"It's not because I'm afraid, but because I know she is the only one he is going to listen to. He has no choice."

Anandur sighed. "I have a feeling we are getting carried away. Conspiring against Kian, asking Annani to come, it's like we are preparing for war. I don't want that."

Amanda put a hand on his bicep. "I was meaning to ask my mother to come and stay with us for a while even before you told me about Brundar. Andrew and Nathalie are dragging their feet about taking little Phoenix up to Annani's sanctuary. They are leaving that child vulnerable for no good reason. So instead of harping on at them to take their daughter up there already, so the goddess can induce her transition, I figured Annani can come for a visit and spend time with the baby, which she loves doing. Phoenix can transition right here without leaving the keep."

"I like it. It will look less like a conspiracy if Annani comes for the baby, but then notices that Kian is at the end of his rope and needs a vacation."

"Exactly."

"You are a deviously brilliant woman, Amanda."

She lifted an eyebrow. "And that's news to you?"

He chuckled. "No, not really. But I keep forgetting that you are so much more than your gorgeous face."

"A mistake a lot of people live to regret."

"So let me get this straight. The goddess comes and forces Kian to take a vacation. How is it going to help Brundar's cause?"

Amanda rolled her eyes. "Darling, did you forget already that Kian needing a vacation is only the excuse I'm going to use to lure her in?"

He frowned. "I thought it was the baby."

"Both. She will ask what's going on with Kian, and I'll give Brundar's situation as an example of Kian being unreasonable. Annani is a sucker for romance. She will intervene on your brother's behalf."

Anandur crossed his arms over his chest. "I'm not sure you're right. She might be a sucker for romance, but she is the one who made the rules about staying away from humans. Not that she wasn't absolutely right to do so. I happen to believe that an exception needs to be made in Brundar's case because it is crucial for his mental health, but I'm not sure Annani will share my opinion."

"That might be. But do you have a better idea?"

"Can't say that I do."

"That's what I thought. We will do the best we can, while praying to the Fates to smile upon us. It is better than doing nothing and hoping everything will turn out fine on its own."

"True."

## 18

## CALLIE

Callie applied another coat of makeup and took a step back to examine her face. The bruising was still visible. But maybe in the club's dim light no one would notice.

As much as she enjoyed spending all day with Brundar, she needed to get back to work. The thing was, customers didn't want their waitress to look as if someone had used her face as a punching bag. Franco would take one look at her and send her home.

"No one expects you to go back to work yet," Brundar said from behind her.

She turned and smiled at him. "Maybe so, but I need to go grocery shopping. I have nothing to make dinner from."

"We can order takeout."

Callie put a hand on her chest. "Blasphemy. Do not utter the word takeout in this house." She tried to sound stern.

"Takeout," he deadpanned.

Frowning, she waved a finger at him. "You're not a God-fearing man."

"I'm not. I worship a different deity, and its temple is the Golden Palace."

"Chinese food?"

He nodded.

"Does your brother know that you actually have a sense of humor?"

Brundar's lips lifted in a crooked smile. "I'm experimenting with it. Am I doing it right?"

Callie giggled. He reminded her of a cyborg in one of her sci-fi romance novels. Part machine part man, the guy was trying to assimilate into human society by attempting humor and slang.

Was that what Brundar was trying to do? Assimilate?

"You're doing it perfectly. I like dry humor. I think jokes that are told with a straight face are the funniest."

"Then you must find me very funny."

"Not yet. But you're getting there." She leaned to kiss his cheek.

Ever since Brundar's injury, Callie had been sneaking a little touch here, a kiss there, and gauging his responses. He was either not noticing them, or humoring her. In either case, it was progress she was very pleased about.

"Are we ordering Chinese?" he asked.

"Fine. But don't get used to that. Tomorrow morning I'm going grocery shopping, and you're going to eat what I make for you—healthy food your body needs in order to heal. Not crap that is loaded with MSG and oil."

"Yes, ma'am."

She liked it when he obeyed so nicely. In some small way, it evened the score between them a little.

Callie loved submitting to Brundar sexually, but despite all her self-talk and the famous *love as thy wilt* that she'd adopted as her mantra, it still bothered her on some level that she did.

That was why hearing him saying 'yes, ma'am' felt so good. It made her feel better about saying 'yes, sir' during their play time.

"Do you have their number?"

"On speed dial."

She waved a hand. "Then dial away."

"What would you like?"

She shrugged. "I don't know what's on their menu, and I'm not a big fan of Chinese food. Order what you like, and I'll nibble."

"I can order from somewhere else."

"No. If you find their food worth worship, I have to check it out. Just make sure there are some veggies in there, not only meat."

Brundar cast her an amused glance. "Why don't you go online and check out their menu and decide what you want?"

She sauntered toward him, braced her hands on his wheelchair's armrests and leaned forward, giving him a good glimpse of her cleavage. "I want you to order for me, and later order *me*."

"Order you what?" His tone got deeper.

"Order me to strip, order me to pleasure you with my mouth or my hands, or both. You decide."

His hands closed on her ass and squeezed. "I would like to reverse the order."

"You would?"

"You first, Chinese later."

"Hmm, that's not a bad idea. We can work up an appetite."

"Are you ready for your first order?"

"Yes, sir."

"Get the blindfold and bring it to me."

Crap. She'd been hoping he would forget about the damn blindfold for once. Not that it wasn't a turn-on for her, it was, but she wanted to see Brundar's face while he climaxed, at least once. After that, he wouldn't even have to remind her to put on the blindfold.

He followed her to the bedroom, watching as she pulled out the scarf from the nightstand's drawer. The condom packets peeked at her from under the other scarves. Callie reached for one then paused.

It hadn't been a week yet, and Brundar hadn't provided her with a clean bill of health like he'd promised, but she'd seen the doctor treat him without gloves. If Bridget deemed his blood safe to handle with her bare hands, then she must've known he was clean.

She could still get pregnant, though, and as someone who'd experienced an unwanted pregnancy and its consequences, Callie knew better.

With a sigh, she closed her hand around the packet.

"What's the matter, sweetling?"

"Nothing." She turned around with a smile and handed him the scarf, then dropped the packet on the bed where he could see it and remember to use it.

Brundar's eyes followed the plastic square. "Right. I don't know why I keep forgetting to ask Bridget for that letter."

"I'm not worried about that. It hasn't been seven days yet. I can still get pregnant."

He looked like he was about to say something but then changed his mind. Brundar did that a lot, and she always wondered what he was about to say and why he decided not to.

If only she could read minds.

Yeah. Life would've been so much easier.

She would've known not to marry Shawn despite the pregnancy. It would've been infinitely better to be a single parent than to tie herself to a monster.

If she were a mind reader, she would know what Brundar was hiding from her and maybe avoid making another catastrophic mistake. In her gut and in her heart she knew Brundar was a good man, but Callie didn't trust her instincts. Not fully. Not after they had led her astray before.

Well, that wasn't exactly true. Her instincts had screamed at her not to marry Shawn, but she'd chosen to ignore them and do what everyone had expected her to.

It seemed her heart and her gut were better judges of character than her mind because they didn't have the capacity to come up with excuses and lies.

"Bed or couch?" Brundar asked.

"Bed."

# 19

# BRUNDAR

After three days in the damned wheelchair, Brundar was a pro at getting himself out of the thing and onto the bed.

That didn't make it any less of a turn-off, though, for him as well as for Calypso. His usually graceful movements were clumsy and laborious.

Regrettably, he couldn't blindfold her yet to keep her from watching him perform those maneuvers. It would've been counterproductive to do so while he still needed her help to pull off his pants.

Everything had to be done with utmost care not to disturb his knees—a task impossible to do blindfolded. Hopefully, when Bridget got there later, she would approve more freedom of movement for him and replace his knee braces with ones that were more flexible.

Sensing his discomfort, Calypso got busy taking off her clothes, letting him watch her instead of her watching him.

And what a sight she was. Even battered and bruised, she was perfection.

Thankfully, the pain was keeping his arousal at bay. Without her blindfold on, he had to be mindful of his eyes starting to glow and his fangs starting to grow, which was difficult while watching Calypso's beautiful, nude body.

He removed his shirt and folded it on the nightstand beside him, then popped the button on the wide, carpenter-style jeans Anandur had gotten for him from Walmart, of course, and lowered the zipper. When Calypso got in position, he braced on his arms and lifted himself off the bed a couple of inches, while she carefully pulled his pants and boxers down to his thighs.

Her eyes lingering on his shaft, she paused. It twitched in greeting, lifting away from his belly.

"I love this sight," she said. "Do you realize that this is the first time you let me see it? I always had a blindfold on before." She smoothed a finger from the tip down to the base. "Perfect, like the rest of you."

Damnation. Having her look at his shaft with such admiration in her eyes was hotter than hell, but if he didn't blindfold her in the next second, she would get an eyeful of much more than his dick.

He could just imagine the horror replacing that reverent expression.

"Come closer," he commanded, lifting the scarf.

Calypso wasn't happy about that, her beautiful, expressive face showing her disappointment, but she obeyed.

"Can I at least touch you?" she asked when he finished tying the scarf around her eyes.

"You may." It would be a first for him. No woman had ever touched his manhood with her hands or her tongue. To allow it required trust he hadn't felt toward anyone.

But he trusted Calypso, deeply, implicitly. In fact, he couldn't wait to feel her hands and her mouth on him. Should he tell her that she was going to be the first?

He fisted his cock. "No one but me has ever held it. No one has tongued it either. You're the first." He wanted to add that she would also be the last, but she wouldn't believe him.

For a moment, Calypso remained speechless, but then she smiled. "Good, because with no one to compare me to you'll think I'm amazing."

"You are incomparable."

"I hope so." Starting from his thigh, she smoothed her palm up to his groin.

He let go of his erection, relinquishing control.

She cupped it gently. Her palm soft and warm on his skin, she leaned down from her kneeling position at his side and gave him a tentative lick, then another, and another. Emboldened, she swirled her tongue around the bulbous head, pulling a ragged groan from his throat.

It felt good. Better than good, but the taste she'd given him only whetted his appetite for more. Cupping the back of her head, he pulled her a little lower.

Calypso didn't need any further encouragement. Taking him into her mouth, she sunk lower to envelop as much of his length as she could before retreating back up and swirling her tongue around the tip.

His eyes rolled back in their sockets. He threaded his fingers in her hair, fanning it out so he could watch his cock going in and out of her hot, wet mouth. The sight was so erotic he could've climaxed just from that. But he didn't want it to end, not yet.

Unhurried, Calypso bobbed her head in a steady rhythm, prolonging his pleasure and not pushing for his release. Did she love pleasuring him with her mouth as much as he loved eating her up?

Given the intensifying scent of her arousal, she did.

Which was good, because he never wanted her to do anything just to please him. If she didn't find pleasure in whatever he wanted to do to her, or her to do to him, then he couldn't find pleasure in it either.

"This is so good, sweetling."

She moaned around him, sending another electrical pulse through his nervous system, priming his balls and his venom glands for action.

Brundar didn't want to come in her mouth, and he definitely didn't want to come before she did.

He cupped her cheek. "That's enough, love."

She let his cock slip out of her mouth. "Did I do something wrong?"

"No, you were perfect. But I can't wait any longer to have my mouth on you. Turn around and straddle me, then bend down and lift your sweet ass up so I can eat you up."

She smiled. "I like the way you think."

Careful around his knees, she did exactly as he'd asked, but the moment her ass was in the right position, she leaned down and took him back in her mouth.

He chuckled as he clamped his hands on her butt cheeks, his thumbs seeking her entrance. "I like the way you think even better."

She was drenched as if he'd been the one pleasuring her and not the other way around. He was one lucky bastard to have a woman who enjoyed giving as much as she enjoyed receiving. In that, they were perfectly matched.

He squeezed her buttocks and pulled her closer to him, so he could lap all that nectar up.

She moaned against his shaft again.

If he didn't hurry, Calypso would have him climax before she did, and that was unacceptable.

It was a catch-22. The more excited Calypso became, the more she moaned, and the more she moaned, the more excited he became. If he weren't injured, he would've flipped her around and fucked her, but that was not in the cards.

Shite. He couldn't pull on her hair to let go of him either because her scalp was still very sensitive. The only option was to grit his teeth and hold back while giving it all he had so she could reach the finish line first.

## 20

# LOSHAM

*L*osham paced the spacious living room of his hotel suite, listening to his assistant's report while his mind was racing ahead.

"Any news from Grud?" he interrupted Rami.

"No, sir. He is still MIA."

That wasn't good. First, the human they had chosen to lead their so-called cult hadn't shown up to a meeting, and then the next one, and he wasn't responding to phone calls either.

Now one of his men had gone missing too.

No one had heard from Grud since he'd gone out last night to search for a suitable victim.

Grud was a good man, not the type Losham would have suspected of desertion. Not that any Doomer was stupid enough to attempt it. The warriors' lives might not have been perfect, but they were much better than what they could've hoped for on the outside.

Besides, the men knew they would be hunted until found and then tortured horrifically and publicly as a deterrent to others.

No. Doomers didn't desert. Something must have happened to Grud. Somehow he had met with misfortune.

Since fangs were all that was needed for the nightly missions, the men didn't carry firearms with them. Grud could have succumbed to a group of humans. But unless they had shot him execution style, emptying a chamber straight into his head or his heart, he wouldn't have died.

Besides, without a body, Losham couldn't be sure the guy was dead.

Had he been captured?

Was he being held by Guardians and tortured for information?

Again, it was a remote possibility. But not one that Losham could ignore.

"We need to move the men to a new location and rent a new warehouse for our meetings."

Rami lifted his head from his tablet. "You think Grud was captured?"

"It is a possibility we need to consider." Losham was glad about choosing to lodge separately from his men. His decision had been motivated mainly by costs and in deference to his status, but it had proven to have strategic value as well.

"I'll get right on it."

"Yes. Time is of the essence."

The human wasn't as important as Grud. He didn't know anything about Losham or his organization. Whatever misfortune he'd met with was regrettable only in the sense that they had wasted ten thousand dollars on the drunkard and would now need to search for a new candidate.

A setback, but a minor one. No operation ran smoothly from start to finish. There was always something to contend with. A smart leader didn't allow those small annoyances to distract him from his goal.

Except, Losham's analytical brain abhorred unsolved mysteries and unlikely coincidences. The human disappearing could be explained in a lot of ways, but not Grud's, and not the fact that they had happened only several days apart.

As much as his mind raced and churned trying to come up with plausible scenarios, Losham was coming up with nothing.

Obviously if the answer eluded him, a mastermind, he was missing vital information.

Perhaps the human's disappearance was worth investigating after all.

## 21

# BRUNDAR

"When is the doctor coming?" Calypso asked.

"She should be here any minute." Brundar glanced at his watch. "Bridget called around four o'clock and said she'd be here within an hour."

"I'll set up the table for three."

After an epic afternoon of lovemaking, they had worked up quite an appetite. He was hungry, and the food smelled delicious. Brundar wanted to dig into the boxes right away and not wait for Bridget. "It will get cold by the time she gets here. Let's eat."

"You said she would be here any minute. How would it look if she gets here and we are munching away and not inviting her to join us?"

"Like we are hungry and she is not a dinner guest."

Calypso put her hands on her hips. "If you want to be rude, do it while you're not with me."

"Fine. Just give me one of the boxes to tide me over. You can't deny a hungry, injured man food."

"I can do that." She looked at the labels until she found the beef dish. "Here you go." She handed him the box. "Chopsticks or fork?"

"Chopsticks."

She pulled out a pair from the delivery bag.

Brundar opened the box and picked a piece, but it felt wrong to eat while Calypso didn't. He knew she was hungry too.

"Come here." He beckoned with the chopsticks. "Open your mouth."

She hesitated for a couple of moments but then bent down and took the piece he was holding up for her. The next piece went into his mouth, and then another one because she was still chewing.

"Hmm, it's really good," Calypso said.

"Told you. Here, take one more." He held out another piece.

She ate that one as well, but then refused the third. "You can finish the rest."

He wanted to argue, but the buzzer went off, announcing their visitor.

Calypso buzzed Bridget in, then opened the door and waited for her to exit the elevator.

"Hello, guys." The doctor walked in, holding her black bag in one hand and a big plastic one in the other. "It smells good in here."

"We were just about to sit down for dinner. Please, join us." Calypso motioned for Bridget to take a seat at the dining table.

Bridget shook her head. "I should check on my patient first."

"The food will get cold. Let's eat first."

Bridget didn't need more convincing. "I would have loved to politely decline, but I'm hungry, and I love Chinese." She took the seat Calypso pointed to.

"Brundar ordered enough to feed a small village. Dig in."

"Don't mind if I do. But I'm going to stick to the fried rice. I don't eat meat."

Calypso opened all of the boxes and pushed some toward Bridget. "There is also an eggplant dish, and one with green beans and tofu."

"Fantastic."

Brundar dumped his empty container in the trash and wheeled himself to the table, where Calypso had already prepared a plate for him, heaped with an assortment of different dishes, including the green bean one and the one with the eggplant.

"*Bon appetit*," Bridget said and dug into her plate. For a small woman, the doctor sure had a big appetite.

"Your face looks much better," she commented as she refilled her plate.

"Makeup does wonders. I'm going back to work tomorrow."

"What do you do?"

"I'm a waitress at a nightclub."

"Then I would advise you to stay home for one more day and rest. If you had a desk job, it would've been okay to go back to work. But you're not ready for a job that keeps you on your feet for hours."

Brundar wiped sweet and sour sauce from his chin. "That's exactly what I've told her. Maybe she will listen to you because she sure doesn't listen to me."

Bridget grinned from ear to ear. "Good for you." She winked at Calypso but then wagged a finger at her. "This time, though, I have to agree with Brundar. One more day of rest. Doctor's orders."

"Is everyone in your family bossy?" Calypso grimaced, and he knew they would be arguing about it later.

Bridget smiled. "Yep, pretty much."

"How do you manage not to kill each other?"

"With difficulty and a lot of love." Bridget winked.

When they were done, the doctor stood up and lifted her plate. "I'll help you clear the table and then check up on Brundar's knees."

"Leave it." Calypso took the plate from her hand. "Go check up on Brundar. I'll take care of the cleanup."

Bridget shook her head. "And you call us bossy."

Fifteen minutes later the table was clean, and the doctor was done adjusting the new braces she'd brought for him.

"Tell me again what I can and can't do with these."

"Keep using the wheelchair and brace on your arms when you want to sit on the couch or go to bed. But it's okay to put your feet down and put a little pressure on them. In two days you can go to the bathroom using crutches. But nothing longer than that. After a week, you can walk with the crutches, but, again, only short distances around the apartment."

"Got it."

Brundar's phone rang where he'd left it to charge on the kitchen counter. Calypso disconnected it from the wire and brought it over.

Glancing at the display, he frowned. What the hell did Amanda want from him? Hopefully not to pay him a visit.

"Amanda," he answered.

"Syssi and I are coming over, and don't you dare say no to us. We are bringing pastries."

"I'm not feeling up to it."

"We don't care."

He rolled his eyes. "I'm not home."

"I know. I got your girlfriend's address from Anandur."

He was going to strangle his brother. The idiot was supposed to keep quiet about Brundar staying with Calypso.

"Is there any way I can convince you not to come?"

"Nope. I called just to let you know we are coming. Not to ask your permission."

Brundar groaned as he clicked the call off.

Bridget patted his shoulder. "Don't worry about that. They are on your side."

He lifted his eyes to her. "Why? Did you hear anything?"

She shrugged. "No. But I know those two, and I bet they are up to something. It's good to have powerful allies, Brundar."

Yeah. The question was whether they were really on his side or not. If they were coming to try to convince him to leave Calypso, he was going to throw them out.

## 22

# CALLIE

"I should leave." Bridget picked up her things.

"What's the hurry? We are going to have a fucking party here," Brundar grumbled.

"Stay." Callie put her hand on the petite doctor's arm. "It's going to be fun." She winked. "Four girls and one poor Brundar, no wonder he is not happy about it. Maybe we should call Anandur and ask him to join us?"

"He is on rotation tonight," Brundar said.

Bridget put her bag back down. "Okay, I'll stay. I'm curious to hear what those two are planning."

"What do you mean?"

The doctor regarded her as if she was dim-witted, which rankled. "Kian's sister and his wife are paying you a visit after he kicked you out. Why do you think that is?"

"They are curious? They want to check out Brundar's new girlfriend?"

"Yes, but not only that."

"What else?"

Bridget winked. "That depends on whether they like you or not."

Great, now she wasn't as happy about the visit as she was a moment ago. What if they didn't approve?

Callie touched her face. "Tell me the truth, do I look horrible?"

"No, Callie, you're a beautiful girl who was criminally assaulted. After five minutes with you, Amanda and Syssi will forget all about the bruises. They are going to like you."

"How can you be sure?"

"Because I am. What's not to like?"

Callie could think of a thing or two or three, but she wasn't going to spend valuable time convincing Bridget that she was far from perfect. "If you excuse me, I'm going to freshen up a bit."

She practically ran into the bedroom. Was there time to curl her hair? When it was all puffed up, it could hide some of the bruising. It would also make her look a little bit older and better put together.

Hot iron on dry hair could do only so much, but she managed to give herself a little bounce. Another layer of foundation helped hide some of the hideous coloring, and she framed her eyes with a dark green pencil, hoping to draw attention to her best feature and away from the ugly bruises.

She'd already put on her best pair of jeans and nicest T-shirt before Bridget came, so there was no need to change clothes. Maybe she could put on her black pumps? They made her legs look longer and her butt look tighter, but then she would look as if she was trying too hard. In the end, she chose to keep her flip-flops on.

So what if her toenails weren't painted.

The buzzer went on in the living room, and Bridget answered, letting the two women come in.

Callie opened the door and took a deep breath, waiting for the elevator doors to open.

A stunning, tall brunette and a much shorter beautiful blond came out of the lift. The brunette smiled like a movie star and extended her hand. "Hi, I'm Amanda. And this is Syssi, my sister-in-law."

"Nice to meet you both. I'm Callie." She shook Amanda's hand and then Syssi's.

Amanda looked like she wanted to give Callie a hug but then reconsidered. Which meant that the bruising was still visible despite her best efforts to hide it.

"We brought pastries. I hope you have coffee." Amanda walked in and put the box she was carrying on the counter.

"Bridget, what a nice surprise." She pulled the tiny doctor into her arms and gave her a big hug. "I'm so glad you're here. We are recruiting if you care to join us."

"Are we planning a war?"

"No, just a friendly takeover. " She winked.

"Oh, my."

"Where is our injured hero?"

Just then Callie noticed that Brundar wasn't in the living room. Where had he escaped to?

A flutter of curtains gave his hiding place away.

"I think he is on the balcony, getting a breath of fresh air."

"More like hiding from us, but that's okay. We are here mainly to see you."

"Well, in that case, please take a seat."

"In a moment. First, I need a plate for the pastries, and second, where is your coffeemaker?"

"I'm in charge of the coffee," Syssi said.

It was strange how the four of them felt comfortable with each other as if they had been friends for years.

Amanda was even more blindingly beautiful than her brother and had the confidence to match. She was dressed simply, but Callie could tell it was all very expensive stuff. And yet she wasn't off-putting or intimidating. Her high energy was infectious.

Syssi was beautiful too, but in a more approachable girl-next-door way. Less outgoing than Amanda, and definitely not as dramatic, she was sweet and friendly and exuded a sort of calm that was soothing. How could she stand being married to Kian? The guy was all pent up anger and frustration.

An ogre of a man, only gorgeous instead of green and ugly.

But then Brundar wasn't a cheerful cherub either, and still, Callie would not have traded him for anyone. Maybe Syssi was the cool water to Kian's inferno, the soothing balm on his rough edges.

The redheaded doctor was somewhere in between the two. Confident, but not at all dramatic, beautiful and curvy in all the right places, but not as stunning as Amanda. No woman was. Callie wondered what Kian and Amanda's mother looked like. Was she even more beautiful than her children? Was it even possible to outdo perfection?

Next to these women, Callie felt quite plain. And yet, not uncomfortable.

"Coffee is ready," Syssi said. "Let's take everything to the living room."

Brundar was still out on the balcony, and Callie decided it was time for him to stop playing chicken and get inside.

"Come on, Brundar, please come back. You're being rude."

He shrugged. "They are used to me being like this. They don't expect anything else."

"That's not an excuse. Those are your relatives, and you're leaving me alone to entertain them."

That finally got to him, and he wheeled himself inside. "Amanda, Syssi, how nice of you to drop by." He sounded as sincere as a used car salesman.

Bad analogy. Shawn was a car salesman. Or rather had been. She shivered, remembering the terrible hours that had led to his death.

As always, Brundar noticed everything. He turned his wheelchair around and closed the balcony door, probably thinking she was cold. "Do you want me to get you a sweater, Calypso?"

That was so sweet of him to offer, especially since he was the one with limited mobility.

"Thank you, but I'm okay." She lifted a cup of coffee off the table and handed it to him. "Which pastry would you like?"

"I'm good. The coffee will do."

"So, Calypso, or is it Callie? Tell us how you and Brundar met."

Callie glanced at Brundar, who retreated into his impassive mask. He shook his head slightly, letting her know not to tell them their story. But which parts?"

"Calypso is my given name. My friends call me Callie, but Brundar prefers Calypso."

"I like Callie," Amanda said. "I'm so curious to hear you guys' story."

"We met at a nightclub," Brundar said.

"And when was that?" Amanda kept pushing.

"About a year ago," Callie said, sneaking a glance at Brundar.

He shrugged.

"You've been together for an entire year?" Syssi asked.

"No. We met a year ago in passing. Then again about a month ago."

*Please let them be happy with that and not ask more questions.* Perhaps she could turn the tables on them.

"What do you do, Amanda?"

"I teach at the university."

Callie's eyes widened. "I want to be a teacher too, but not in the university. I want to teach kindergarten, maybe go into special education. I have not decided yet. I'm starting UCLA in the fall."

"That's marvelous," Amanda said.

Did she mean it, though? On top of the way she looked, she was also a freaking professor? How many gifts could one woman have?

*Unfair.*

Syssi put her coffee cup down. "You must love children."

"I do."

"I do too."

"Do you have any?"

Syssi's eyes looked sad, but she put on a smile. "Not yet. Working on it, though."

Amanda snickered. "That's the fun part."

Callie couldn't imagine Kian as a father. He would terrorize his kids just by looking at them. "Well, I wish you good luck. In the meantime, though, have fun practicing."

Syssi blushed.

Amanda chuckled. "I like this girl."

"Me too," Bridget said.

## 23

# BRUNDAR

"I had a really good time. I hope we can do this again sometime." Calypso hugged Bridget and then Syssi.

Amanda was the last one at the door. She pulled Calypso into a gentle embrace and kissed her forehead. "I would've kissed your cheek, but I didn't want to hurt you. The forehead seemed like a safe place."

"Yeah, it's probably the only spot on my face that is not damaged. Thank you for coming. It was fun."

"Thank you for having us. Good night, Callie." She looked over Calypso's head and waved at him. "You too, Brundar. Don't overexert yourself." She winked.

"You have a very nice family," Calypso said as she closed the door.

"Busybodies."

She started picking up cups and plates from the coffee table. "Maybe, but they mean well."

"They are annoying."

She put the dishes in the sink and returned with a rag to wipe the table. "And you're grumpy."

He grunted in agreement.

"I would love to hang out with them some more, also with Anandur. Are Bridget and Amanda married?"

"Amanda has a mate. Bridget doesn't."

Calypso threw him a puzzled look. "A mate? What does that mean?"

A slip of the tongue, but easily corrected. Calypso didn't expect him to express himself clearly or correctly, which worked to his advantage in situations like this. "She has a life partner whom she didn't marry in an official ceremony."

"A live-in boyfriend."

"No. A boyfriend implies a temporary arrangement. Amanda and Dalhu's is permanent."

Calypso sighed. "Nothing is permanent, not even marriage."

"In their case it is."

"You're awfully sure of that. What if you're wrong?"

Damnation. The woman was impossible. He would have to either lie or tell her that the discussion was over.

Unless he managed to deflect again. He was becoming an expert at it. "You can call your father now and let him know you're no longer in danger."

Calypso plopped down on the couch, flipped off her flip-flops and put her legs on the ottoman. "I almost did, but then thought better of it. I don't know if Shawn's body's been found yet. I can't call my dad and tell him Shawn committed suicide because how am I supposed to know that, right?"

"Good point. I'll call my contact in the government and have him check if it was reported. Not every suicide makes the news."

"You mean Andrew, Syssi's brother?"

"Yeah."

He didn't know what game Amanda and Syssi were playing. They had blabbered freely as if Calypso was one of them and had divulged too much information. If he were ever forced to thrall away Calypso's memories, it would be one hell of an impossible job. As long as he was the only one she remembered, the clan's secret was safe. She didn't know he was different, and Brundar wasn't about to let her find that out. But his connections to Amanda and Andrew were like a trail of breadcrumbs. Someone determined enough could find where a professor named Amanda taught. Cross-referencing it with a government employee named Andrew would narrow the search.

"If your cousins and your tough boss's wife can tell me people's names, I'm sure you can too."

"Not really. One is his sister, the other is his wife. I don't hold the same sway over him."

"Could be. But you no longer need to talk in code about things they already told me."

That was true, but old habits were hard to break, as was remembering what she already knew and what not. The safest thing for her and for his clan would've been to keep them separated and for Calypso to know nothing about them. She already knew too much.

Tomorrow, he would ask Anandur to drive him back to the keep so he could have a talk with Amanda and Syssi. They meant well, but those good intentions might lead straight to hell.

"Did you call the steakhouse and tell them that you're not coming in to work?"

"No, I didn't. Why would I? They don't expect me for another week."

"Now that you no longer need to hide, you can keep working at Franco's."

"You're right. I didn't think of that. It's a hard decision, though. I like the people at Franco's, and I don't know anyone at the new place, but the pay is going to be a little better and so will the hours. I wouldn't have to work late nights anymore. What will happen once the school year starts and I have early morning classes? On the other hand, a late shift means I have all day for studying."

"You're forgetting one thing. At Franco's you have me."

Calypso huffed and crossed her arms over her chest. "Yeah, right. You disappear into that basement, and I'm lucky if I get to see you after closing time."

She had a point. Brundar wheeled himself closer to the couch, and using the armrest and coffee table to brace most of his weight, hefted himself to sit next to Calypso.

"What if I promise to come see you at least once during your shift?"

She shrugged. "Not good enough. Besides, I have my hearing to think of. I'm sure I've already done enough damage."

"That's what earplugs are for." He wrapped his arm around her and pulled her closer to him.

"I tried. But I can't take drink orders when I can't hear the customers."

"There are special earplugs that filtrate certain wavelengths. You can still hear people talking, but the ambient noise is reduced."

"Earplugs are uncomfortable."

Calypso was proving to be a tough negotiator. There was something she was hoping to get out of it. Was it a raise? More shifts?

"Tell me what would sweeten the deal for you, and I'll make it happen."

Her triumphant smile proved that he'd been right. "I want to participate in the classes and demonstrations you guys hold down in the basement. I'll schedule my breaks accordingly."

"Only watching, nothing more."

"That's what I want." She snorted. "I don't want to be the test dummy for your whip."

"I might allow it as long as you sit quietly and don't ask any questions. I don't want the club members to notice you."

She narrowed her eyes at him. "Why? Are you embarrassed by me?"

Silly girl. "No, I'm proud of you. More than you can imagine. But I don't want any members to get ideas about you. I don't want them to look at you and imagine what they would like to do to you. If I catch them leering, I'll have to kill them, and their blood will be on your hands."

He'd meant every word, but Calypso thought he was joking.

"I wouldn't want that. I promise to be as quiet as a mouse. I'll slink in after the class or demonstration begins, sit in the back, and then slink out before it ends. No one will see me."

He smiled and offered her his hand. "It's a deal. You stay at Franco's, and I'll allow you to sit in on the classes and demonstrations but only if you keep your presence unobtrusive."

Calypso squealed happily, wrapped her arms around his neck and jumped on him, brushing against his knees as she straddled him.

Brundar winced.

Her face fell. "I'm sorry. I forgot about the not touching rule." She dropped her arms to her sides.

"It's not that." He lifted her arms and put them back around his neck. "You brushed against my knees."

Her eyes widened in horror. "I'm so sorry. It was so careless of me. What can I do to make it better? Do you need an ice pack? Painkillers?"

He shook his head. "Your lips will do." He pulled out the scarf he stashed in his pocket just for such occasions. After their afternoon lovemaking session, he'd been struck by the brilliant idea of always having it with him. "But first, the blindfold."

## 24

# RONI

"Do you really need me in there?" Roni asked William.

William patted Roni's shoulder. "Don't worry. He is not going to eat you for breakfast. You're too skinny."

"And sour. He is going to eat you first."

William laughed.

Kian wasn't on Roni's list of favorite people. Not that the dude was evil or anything. Roni had met his share of self-entitled pricks, and Kian wasn't like them either. But he made Roni feel like a nuisance.

Maybe he was like that with everyone, but that didn't make Roni any happier about having to sit in front of the guy again.

No one had treated him like a nuisance in his previous job. They might have not liked him, and some had resented a teenager holding so much power, but everyone had respected him and vied for his services.

He was one of a kind, goddamn it, an irreplaceable asset any organization would have killed for, and he deserved to be treated as such.

William knocked on the door and then pushed it open and walked in. Roni followed behind him.

This time Kian wasn't alone in his office. A tall, gangly guy was sitting at the conference table with several files spread out in front him.

"Hi, Shai." William and the guy clapped hands.

Kian pointed at the two chairs in front of his desk. "You have two minutes. Talk."

William took a seat and looked at Roni.

Damn it, he'd been hoping William would do the talking. He was older, loved to talk nonstop, and he knew Kian better. Maybe that was why he wanted Roni to present their request. He knew Kian was going to be nasty about it.

Roni pulled out the list of supplies he needed and handed it to Kian. "William's lab is a mess and a health hazard. He's also missing some components. This is the list of what I need to transform it into a decent workspace. At the bottom is a rough estimate of how much it is going to cost." His presentation had taken about thirty seconds.

Kian took the list, skimmed through it, and then handed it back. "Approved. Shai is going to take care of the rest. Good day, gentlemen."

"Thank you."

Well, that had gone well. Kian had been curt, but he'd approved the acquisition request, and that was what they had come for—not to socialize over coffee and canapés.

As they stood up and turned to Shai, William cast Roni an appreciative look, but it wasn't until they were done with Kian's assistant and on their way back to the lab that he commented on Roni's performance. "From now on you are in charge of dealing with Kian. He likes you."

Roni snorted. "If that's how he treats people he likes, I don't ever want to get on his shit list."

William rubbed his chin. "He is not always like that. When he is not so stressed, he even jokes around. But there is a lot going on right now."

"The move to the new place?"

"Yes. It's a very complicated project, and it's taking longer to complete than Kian would've liked. Then there are the murders that are keeping the Guardians busy. Other than that he still needs to run the business side of things, and one of the two people he hired to manage parts of it couldn't handle the pressure and quit."

Roni shook his head. "I feel for him, but you know that it's all in his head."

William gave him one of those condescending looks adults tended to throw at him before realizing that Roni wasn't a typical teenager. "Those are real problems, Roni. He is not imagining them."

"What I meant wasn't that the problems do not exist but that the urgency is in his head. He can slow down on everything except the murders. Nothing will happen if the village is completed a month later than scheduled. And all the corporate crap can be done at a slower pace as well. Other than that, he should wait with further expansion until he has the current business running smoothly with good people at the helm."

"Good advice, kid. But not so easy to implement. Good people are hard to find. But you are right about one thing. Kian is a perfectionist, and a lot of the stress he is under is his own doing. I wish I could help. I can design programs that would make his life easier. But to do so I need his input, and he doesn't have the time to spend."

"What about his assistant, Shai? The dude probably knows everything that's going on."

William stopped and turned to Roni. "Why didn't I think of that? It's such an obvious solution. I can have Shai explain how they do things and work from that."

Roni felt incredibly smug but covered it up with fake modesty. "Sometimes it takes an outsider to see things those on the inside are blind to."

## 25

# KIAN

"What's new with the murder investigation?" Kian opened the Guardian meeting by addressing Onegus.

"There were no new murders in the past week."

Interesting. It wasn't because the Guardians were patrolling the streets, because they weren't. They were waiting in a central location for the command center to alert them to suspicious activity caught on the surveillance cameras.

But there had been several false alarms. Two involved street-walkers getting into an argument with clients, and the rest were drunk couples making out on the streets. Could the murderer have seen a Guardian arrive at the scene?

Not likely.

Something else was going on. But what?

"Let's keep the rotations for another week. If nothing happens, we can assume that's the end of it."

"What if it is not?" Onegus asked.

"We can't keep it up forever. We knew that at some point the rotations would have to stop. I just hoped we would catch the murderer first."

The guys looked grim. With Brundar out of commission, they'd each had to take on more hours. Anandur had volunteered to do both his and Brundar's shifts, but Kian had forbidden it. Everyone shared the burden equally.

He needed more Guardians.

The thing was, when nothing was going on, there was barely enough work to keep the seven he had busy. But then when something happened, they were short on warriors. The retired Guardians would not come for anything less than a full out war or a rescue operation. Kian had had a hard time convincing them to come in for one week of training a year to keep up their skills.

He needed more Guardians on a permanent basis, and if they had nothing to do, so be it.

"Onegus."

"Yes, boss."

"I want you to stay after the meeting."

Onegus nodded.

Later, when everyone was done reporting and had filed out of his office, Kian walked over to the fridge hidden behind the wooden doors of the buffet and pulled out two beers.

Onegus took one with a raised brow. "Beer for breakfast?"

"Are we Scots or are we not?"

"Aye, we still are." Onegus took a swig.

"I want to get at least two more permanent Guardians. Any ideas on who might be open to negotiation? I'm willing to pay handsomely."

"You can't pay them more than you pay the other Guardians. It wouldn't be fair."

"So I'll pay everyone more. What else?"

"More vacation time. Especially after weeks of rotations."

"If we have more people, then they can take vacations whenever they want. Unless there is a crisis, that is."

"How many do you want?"

"As many as I can get, but I'll settle for two. Give me names of possible prospects."

Onegus regarded him with a frown. "Don't tell me you want to make the phone calls yourself."

"I'd be more than happy to leave that job to you."

"Good, because you're too grumpy to convince anyone to join."

"What's that supposed to mean?"

Onegus scratched his head. "If anyone needs a vacation it's you."

"If you can find someone to do my job, I'll gladly take one."

## 26

# BRUNDAR

*F*ucking crutches. Brundar dropped his butt on the couch and threw them on the floor in disgust.

He'd thought they would make moving around more manageable, but they were a nuisance and made him feel even more disabled than the wheelchair had. Sitting in one was not so much different from sitting in an office chair with wheels.

Not really, but he could pretend.

It wasn't only that. The inactivity was getting to him. For a man who was used to long grueling days, doing nothing was maddening.

So yeah, he'd made love to Calypso four times yesterday and then had felt guilty as hell because it was too much for a human girl to take, especially one who was recovering from an ordeal herself.

She hadn't complained, but that didn't mean it had been okay to exhaust her like that.

He should've asked Anandur to bring him a book. Except, Brundar was too agitated to focus on anything. Even the stories of epic battles that he usually enjoyed reading would probably not hold his interest. It was an activity reserved for the end of a satisfying day in the field. That left the television, which was the only form of entertainment in the apartment, and he hated the thing. He couldn't find anything worth watching. Even the news reported nothing of substance. It was mostly sensationalized nonsense.

Calypso emerged from the bedroom, her hair wet from the shower. "I called Franco and told him I'm coming back to work today."

Brundar couldn't blame her for wanting out of the apartment. "I'll come with you."

She put her hands on her hips. "Bridget said not to overdo it with the crutches."

"I'm going to sit in the wheelchair with a beer in my hand, watching your sexy bottom as you run around serving drinks."

Calypso sauntered closer and leaned over him, her ample cleavage on display in the flimsy, low-cut shirt she had on. "It's been a week."

"It's only Wednesday." His injury had happened Friday night.

"I'm not talking about that. I'm talking about the birth control. We can throw the condoms away, or donate them to a worthy charity." She winked.

His male anatomy responded with enthusiasm, but his male ego not so much. The first time he made love to Calypso without a bloody rubber between them, he wanted her under him, which was impossible at the moment. On the other hand, he didn't want to wait another week and a half either.

Her smile wilted. "Why are you frowning?"

"It doesn't feel right to celebrate our first time while I'm like this." He waved a hand over his knees.

"Oh, baby." She cupped his cheek and kissed him.

It hadn't escaped Brundar's notice that each passing day she was touching him more and more, or that he was getting more and more comfortable with her doing so.

In fact, he craved her touch.

That didn't mean that he wouldn't tie her up as soon as he was back to normal, but it would be for fun, not because he couldn't do it any other way.

Calypso was healing him.

Without breaking the kiss, he wrapped his arm around her and pulled her to sit next to him. She moaned, and he pushed his hand under her shirt and cupped her breast, thumbing the stiffening nipple.

Eyes hooded with desire, Calypso arched into his hand. "It would be silly to keep using condoms until you get better," she said when he let go of her mouth.

It was. But the only way they could have sex now was with her straddling him, and they both craved more than that.

"I know."

"We will make it special in some other way." She waggled her brows. "Missionary position is not a prerequisite."

"What do you have in mind?"

"I'll think about it while you are in the shower."

Trying to imagine what Calypso could possibly come up with, Brundar let the water pelt him as he sat on the shower bench. Whatever it was, they were still limited to the one position of him either sitting or lying, and her straddling him.

He was just about finished when Calypso walked into the bathroom and opened the shower enclosure, holding a large towel in front of her. "Are you done, your lordship? I was sent to towel you dry."

Brundar cocked a brow. What kind of a game was she playing?

"By whom?" he asked.

"The head maid, of course. May I turn the water off and pat you dry with this big, fluffy towel?"

With a smile curving his lips, Brundar leaned against the shower wall. "You may."

"Thank you, my lord." Still holding the towel in front of her, Calypso curtsied.

She was hiding something. Was she naked? Waiting for her to come closer, Brundar yanked the towel out of her hands.

Wow. The girl was sure creative. She had taken her plain black cooking apron and fashioned a tiny French maid one out of it. The front was cut in the shape of a heart and barely covered her nipples, and the bottom was cut in an arc, with its lowest point barely covering her mound.

Sexy didn't begin to describe it.

Tossing the towel on the bench, he reached for her and cupped her ass. She had nothing on other than the apron.

Playacting wasn't his strong suit, but he was going to give it his best because Calypso's idea was brilliant. His injuries limited the physical possibilities, but there was no limit on imagination.

"You are a naughty, naughty maiden. Did you come in here to try and seduce your master?"

Calypso lowered her head in pretend shame and nodded. "Are you disappointed in me, my lord? Do you think I deserve punishment for my presumptuousness?" Worrying her lower lip, she peeked at him from under her long eyelashes.

Aha, so that was where she wanted to take this. It hadn't crossed his mind to spank her, even playfully, while she was still bruised and hurting. But apparently, Calypso was ready for some play. He should be able to satisfy her wish while being very gentle. After all, it was all an act, the excitement having more to do with the mindset than the physical sensations.

"Turn around, young miss. And present your bottom."

Calypso barely managed to stifle her smile as she pretended remorse. "Yes, my lord."

She turned around, braced her hands on the shower wall, pushed her lovely bottom out, then gave him a sexy come-hither look over her shoulder. "Is that how you want me, my lord?"

Oh yeah, he did. Calypso assumed the perfect position for him to reach her bottom from where he was sitting. The minx had thought of everything.

He rubbed her left butt cheek first, then the right. "You have to keep your eyes closed tight. If I catch you peeking, you're going to be a very sorry young lady. Is that clear?"

"Yes, my lord," Calypso breathed.

"You are going to keep your eyes closed until I tell you to open them."

"Yes, my lord. I swear I'm going to obey your commands."

Even though it was pretend-play, he knew her promise was sincere. Calypso was trustworthy. She wouldn't open her eyes until he told her it was okay.

"Good girl." He caressed her butt cheeks. They were soft and smooth and so small that he could cover both with one hand, but it didn't make her shape any less feminine. Her narrow hips tapered into an even narrower waist, giving her a beautiful hourglass form.

"You are a very beautiful girl, Calypso."

"Thank you, my lord. Does it mean you forgive me for coming in here with illicit intent?"

"I do. But I'm going to spank you anyway because you need to be taught self-discipline."

"Thank you, my lord. I'm looking forward to your correction."

## 27

# CALLIE

Callie was having a blast. When she'd concocted her plan, she'd been worried that Brundar was too rigid to enjoy playacting, or even to participate, but her guy was full of surprises.

He was doing great.

It was like he was reading her mind and doing everything exactly as she'd envisioned it.

What a turn-on.

The first smack shocked her, not because it was hard or painful, it was neither, but because of the magnifying effect of the shower enclosure creating an echo chamber. The gentle slap had sounded like a thunderclap.

It was good that her next door neighbor was out of town again, or she might have imagined the worst and called the police.

"It's very loud in here," Brundar said, probably worried about the neighbors as well.

"There is no one in the adjoining suite of rooms, my lord. No one can hear you disciplining me."

He rubbed the spot he'd slapped. "In that case, I shall continue."

"If you please, my lord."

A volley of light smacks ensued, warming her behind and delivering just a smidgen of a sting. It was exactly what she wanted. Nothing overly taxing or intense, just playful.

"As this is your first offense, young lady, I think it is enough. Have you learned your lesson?"

Callie hesitated. Did she want more?

Yeah, she did. He hadn't spanked her in so long.

"I'm a little bit thick-headed, my lord, and sometimes I need a lesson repeated before it sinks in."

Brundar chuckled. "I see. Very well." He continued the playful smacking, adding ten more, then switched to rubbing.

His caresses were getting more intimate by the second. "You're very wet, sweetling. Are you aching for me?"

"Yes, sir."

"Hmm." He pushed a finger inside her. "Are your eyes still tightly closed?"

"Yes, sir."

He pulled on the tie holding her apron. "Then turn around." With a quick tug, he took it off, baring her body.

Breasts swollen and nipples aching, Callie waited for Brundar to touch more of her, but he was doing something with her apron. Was he folding it?

When he tied the blindfold he'd fashioned from it over her eyes, she found out.

Didn't he trust her? And why was it so important to him? Was he going to tell her one day?

In the beginning, she'd suspected Brundar had some deformity he didn't want her to see. He'd never gotten fully naked unless she was blindfolded. But since the injury, she'd seen every inch of him, except for his knees that were bandaged, and everything was perfect. Maybe they had been deformed even before the injury?

It didn't make sense though, because he still insisted on the blindfold even though his knees were always covered.

"It's not that I don't trust you. But you might forget in the throes of passion."

It was what it was, though, and at the moment she was more interested in continuing their playacting than solving all of Brundar's mysteries.

For all she knew, he turned into a werewolf when he climaxed. But then he would have felt hairy, which he didn't. The man had very little body hair, none on his chest and only sparse pale blond hair on his arms and legs.

"I understand, sir."

"Good girl." He tugged on her hand, guiding her to straddle him by placing her knees on the bench, then wrapped her in his arms and just held her.

It was such an intimate pose, chest to chest, face to face, even though she couldn't see him. She felt his warm breath on her skin as he whispered in her ear, "You are precious to me."

Callie melted into a puddle. Brundar had called her beautiful, he'd called her sweetling, but not precious, and not like that. It wasn't just a term of endearment, it was his way of telling her he loved her.

Her dark angel had surrendered. The ice around his heart had melted.

"You're precious to me too." She found his lips and kissed him, but he immediately took over the way he always did.

It was fine. She loved his gentle dominance.

Cupping her buttocks with one large hand, Brundar lifted her up and guided his shaft inside her, wedging just the head and waiting for her to adjust to him.

She took over from there, sliding down slowly, enjoying the feeling of his velvety smooth skin, the warmth of him. It felt so different without the barrier between them. Perfect. The fit was as tight as always, but not uncomfortably so. It felt as if they were made for each other.

When he was fully seated inside her, she didn't move, and neither did he.

Being connected like that was so magical that neither of them uttered a sound, not even a moan.

For a few moments, they just held on tight to each other, connected in the most intimate of ways. But eventually, the need to move became overwhelming.

Clasping her bottom in his strong hands, Brundar lifted her up and then lowered her down. Pretty soon, though, he changed tactics. Holding her glued to his chest, stationary, he was thrusting into her as if he weren't injured and had full use of his legs.

There was no way he could lift his buttocks and piston into her with such force without bracing his feet on the tile floor. She was too far gone to object, though, and it seemed that he was too far gone to feel pain.

When his shaft swelled inside her, he latched onto her neck and bit down. Pain exploded where his teeth pierced her skin, but a split second later the pain just wasn't there anymore, and she was climaxing like a woman possessed. On and on her inner walls convulsed around him, milking what seemed like a never-ending geyser of semen.

The last coherent thought Callie had before blacking out was that if she weren't on the pill, Brundar would've most definitely planted a baby in her.

Surprisingly, she felt a pang of sorrow that it was not to be.

## 28

# RONI

Roni glanced through the balcony glass doors at the darkening sky. What was keeping Sylvia?

He'd been waiting impatiently, not counting the minutes, but glancing at his watch every so often. He missed her. Yesterday, she had been studying for a test and couldn't come, and today she was running more than an hour late.

After a day at the lab, he was drained even though he hadn't done much aside from finishing the task William had assigned to him. There had been a few surveillance cameras he'd missed, and he'd added them on to the extensive array he'd already assembled.

Except, it seemed that all that work had been a waste of time because there were no more murders. Unfortunately, the killer hadn't been found, so there was still a chance it wasn't over yet.

Roni had a feeling that the area they had defined wasn't big enough, and he would need to expand their reach. As long as he could play a part in preventing more murders, he didn't mind how hard he had to work, or how tedious the task was.

Lives were at stake.

The pneumonia was still taking a lot out of him. The good news was that Bridget had declared him no longer contagious, and he was looking forward to getting together with Andrew. Meeting Andrew's wife and the baby would also be fun. She'd been an angel, sending him home-cooked meals every day. If it weren't for her, he would've been surviving on those disgusting frozen dinners that he found barely edible.

Roni got up and shuffled to the kitchen for another ginger ale. Sylvia had been harping on him to drink water instead of the fizzy sweet drink loaded with sugar and chemicals, but he didn't like drinking plain water. Besides, the ginger ale helped with the headache and the nausea.

As he was shuffling back to the couch, the door opened, and Sylvia walked in with a huge grin splitting her face.

Turning back, Roni's steps were much livelier. He wrapped his arm around his girl and kissed her cheek. "Where have you been, and what are you so happy about?"

"I have a surprise for you. Come." She took his hand and headed for the door.

"A surprise?" It wasn't his birthday.

"Yeah. You're going to love it."

They entered the elevator, and she pressed the button for one of the underground levels. Maybe she was taking him to watch a movie in the keep's theater? He hadn't seen it yet.

"Can you give me a hint?"

"No. We are almost there."

Where was there? He followed her out of the elevator and down the corridor. The doors on this level had small square windows on top. Some were empty, and some were set up as classrooms. He wondered what was being taught in there.

"Here we are." Sylvia opened one of the doors and walked inside.

It wasn't a classroom, but it wasn't empty either. Big cardboard boxes of varying sizes were stacked in the middle of the room, and several utilitarian chairs were haphazardly scattered throughout. He counted six.

"What is this?"

Sylvia grinned. "Open one of the boxes."

He chose the smallest one from the top of the pile and tore the tape off. There was another box inside, and he pulled it out.

"Drumsticks?"

"Open another one."

Roni could already guess what he would find in the other boxes.

"You got me a drum set?"

She nodded enthusiastically. "The guy that helped me in Guitar Warehouse said that this is the base set and that you can add other things to it. He started asking me all kinds of questions about the kind of music you play, but I didn't know what to tell him. I'll go back and get you whatever else you need."

For once, Roni was speechless. He'd told Sylvia not to do it, but was touched beyond words that she had done it anyway.

Pulling her into his arms, he kissed her. "Thank you. But I have to pay you back. In a couple of weeks, I should be getting my first paycheck, or however money things work here. I don't have a bank account I can use safely, but maybe Andrew can cash them for me."

Sylvia didn't look happy about that. In fact, she appeared offended. "Can you accept it as your birthday present?"

"It's not my birthday, and even if it was I couldn't accept something so expensive."

"What if you buy me something expensive back?"

"Like what?"

"Like a diamond ring. A diamond engagement ring."

For the second time in one evening, Roni was rendered speechless. Was Sylvia proposing?

She punched his chest playfully. "Say something."

"Yes."

"Yes, what?"

"Yes, I'll marry you. Wasn't that a proposal?"

"It was, but for a very long engagement. You're too young to be getting married. You're not ready."

"The hell I'm not. If that's what it takes for you to move in with me, I'm ready today. Your mother can't object to you moving in with your husband, am I right?"

There was hesitation in Sylvia's eyes. "I don't like rushing into things, and my mom is not good with sudden changes. Let's give it some time. Okay?"

Roni nodded, but his jubilant mood had plummeted. He knew exactly what Sylvia was thinking. She wanted to wait and see whether he turned or not, and she wasn't ready to fully commit to their relationship as long as his future wasn't clear.

Not that he could blame her. If he didn't turn, he would grow old and eventually die while Sylvia remained young and healthy and sad. If she loved him, and he was pretty sure she did, the heartache would be unbearable.

Although if the roles were reversed, he would've chosen to be with her even if their time together was finite. If the pain of losing her proved too much to bear, he would've found a way to end his life after she was gone.

"Do you want to start putting the set together? I have no idea what goes where, but you can tell me what to do."

The sad reality was that in his current state Roni was too weak to do it himself and needed her help. Sylvia was strong, was stronger than him even before the pneumonia. Lifting the heavy drums would be nothing for her.

But he didn't want to put his feebleness on display. Not while she was watching. He would get William to help him, or maybe Andrew.

It was about time the guy came to see him, and Roni could guilt him into helping with the assembly.

"I'm too tired, baby. I'll get one of the guys to help me tomorrow."

Sylvia looked disappointed. "You can tell me what to do, and I'll do it by myself while you sit on a chair and supervise."

He shook his head. "And miss out on the fun of assembling it myself? I don't think so."

She pouted. "Fine. Be like that. But once it's up I want to hear you play."

"It's a deal."

## 29

## CALLIE

"Ready to go?" Callie asked.

Leaning on his crutches, Brundar nodded.

Yesterday's bareback sex had been epic, but Brundar had paid for it dearly with his knees. In the height of passion, he'd been oblivious to the pain, but once the endorphins and adrenaline levels had subsided, it hit him full force. It had been so bad that he'd even agreed to go back on the painkillers. The man was too stubborn and too macho to take them unless the pain level was intolerable.

He hadn't even argued when she'd called Franco and told him they were not coming in.

"Are you sure? Because if you are still hurting, I can call Franco again and cancel. He was very understanding yesterday."

"I'm good."

"Do you have the painkillers with you?"

He shook his head.

Of course not. Silly man. He would rather suffer than, God forbid, admit he was taking anything for pain.

Callie turned around, snatched the bottle of pills from the counter, and threw it inside her purse.

"Now we can go." She held the door open for Brundar.

"You could've gone yesterday. I didn't need you to stay and watch me sleep."

Brundar falling asleep after taking a hefty dose of the little white pills was the reason she'd stayed. Fearing that he'd overdosed on those pills, Callie wouldn't leave his side. Reading to keep herself awake, she'd checked every few minutes that he was still breathing.

"Yeah, yeah. As if you'd have left me alone at home if the roles were reversed."

"You got me there."

As she opened the passenger door for him, Brundar handed her one of the crutches and got inside, then gave her the other one.

"Thank you," he said when she dropped them in the back seat.

His face appeared as expressionless as always, but by the slight tightening of his jaw muscles, she could tell that he was either irritated or in pain or both. Probably both. Depending on others for his basic needs must be difficult for a man like Brundar.

Easing out into the traffic, Callie cast him a sidelong glance. "Everyone will have a ton of questions for us. What do we tell them?"

"A mugger wouldn't have dragged you with him. We will have to go with a would-be rapist."

"And what happened to him after he shot you?"

"He heard a police siren and ran away."

She shook her head. "They didn't report the incident because they thought we did. The weakest link in this story is why we didn't. Your injuries needed hospitalization, and no one will believe the emergency room personnel didn't call the cops."

"Right. I can claim a criminal record. They would believe it about me."

That was too extreme. Callie was wracking her brain for a better story when an idea struck her.

"Did you talk to Franco or anyone else from the club after the incident?"

"No. You called Franco. Remember?"

"Yes, but I wanted to make sure that you didn't talk with anyone."

"Why?"

She smirked. "Because I only told Franco that you were injured while rescuing me from the lowlife. I said nothing about you getting shot. We can say that you broke your knees while chasing the assailant. He jumped over a wall, and you followed, but your shirt got caught on something, and you fell badly, breaking both knees."

Brundar smiled. "That might work. No one will check what's going on under my knee braces."

"Exactly. In fact, I don't think anyone would've believed that you were shot in both knees and could walk already. I witnessed everything with my own two eyes, and I still find it hard to believe. Your healing is nothing short of miraculous."

Brundar turned to look out the window. "I'm lucky to know Bridget. Without her revolutionary procedure, it wouldn't have been possible."

Callie still had her doubts, but she couldn't argue with the evidence. Brundar was walking less than a week after getting both of his knees shot to pieces. Bridget was a miracle worker.

How the heck had a woman so young achieved so much? She must have been some kind of a prodigy. One of those kids who graduated high school at twelve and got a master's degree at sixteen. She'd seemed pretty normal, though.

"Is Bridget a genius? Did she finish medical school at eighteen or something? How does someone so young become an expert in her field? And not only an expert but an innovator?"

"She is very smart. But I don't think she invented that new procedure."

"I see." That made more sense. Tomorrow, Callie would search the Internet for a new and revolutionary knee reconstruction surgical procedure. Something like that was big news. Someone must've written an article about it in one of the scientific journals.

What was she hoping to find out, though?

That a procedure like that existed?

What if it did not?

Things didn't add up.

Heck, they hadn't been adding up since the beginning. For some reason, Donnie's remark about Brundar's long teeth came to the forefront of her mind. She could've sworn Brundar had bitten her yesterday when they had both climaxed. She had a vague memory of a sharp pain, and what was more, it hadn't been the first time that she'd looked for teeth marks the next day.

But she'd never found any.

It was possible to discount them as phantom bites created by her imagination, except aside from the imagined bites, there were other things. Like Brundar's superhuman hearing, and now his miraculous healing.

He turned to look at her. "So that's the story we are sticking with. I was chasing the would-be rapist and took a bad fall. There was nothing to report because other than hitting you in the face he didn't manage to do anything, and neither of us saw his face. He was wearing a ski mask."

"Sounds good to me."

At the club's parking lot, Callie helped Brundar out of the car, holding the crutches for him, and again he looked irritated by his dependence on her.

Well, tough. That was his reality for the near future, and he'd better get used to it.

"Callie!" Donnie rushed up to them as soon as they rounded the corner, his arms open and ready to envelop her.

"Careful, big guy. I'm bruised everywhere," she forestalled him, holding her palm out.

Donnie slowed down and hugged her with utmost care. "I'm so glad you're okay. You are okay, right?" His eyes roamed her body.

"I am. Thanks to Bru… Brad."

Crap, she'd almost forgotten he went under a different name in the club. Just one more oddity to add to the long list.

Up until now, Donnie hadn't even noticed Brundar standing a few paces behind her. Eyeing the crutches and the braces on Brundar's knees, the bouncer shook his head. "You should have let me come with you, man. What happened to you?"

"A bad fall."

Donnie tilted his head as if trying to figure out what kind of a fall could cause injuries like that. "How far down did you fall?"

"About thirty feet."

Donnie whistled. "You should count yourself lucky for not breaking your back."

"He saved me." Callie diverted Donnie's attention to her. "He chased the scumbag away. I don't want to think what would've happened to me if Brad hadn't shown up on time."

Inside the club, Callie had to repeat the story once to Franco and then again to Miri who wanted more details. At some point, Brundar ducked into the hallway leading down to the basement, leaving her alone to deal with the curious staff.

She was relieved to put on her little apron and get back to work. Lots of makeup combined with the nightclub's dim lighting hid her bruises from the customers, and for the first time in a week, she felt as if things were getting back to normal.

Or as normal as they could get with Brundar in her life.

## 30

# BRUNDAR

*C*alypso was quiet on their way home, either introspective or perhaps tired. Brundar certainly was.

As someone who was used to relying on his body to always function at peak performance, it was difficult for him to accept his new reality. Thank the Fates it was temporary. The crutches were a nuisance, clumsy and chafing at his armpits, but that hadn't been the only problem. His body's rapid healing required him to rest and let it divert energy to where it was needed most. Instead, he'd shuffled through the basement trying to prove, mainly to himself, that his injuries weren't a hindrance to his performance.

No one else expected him to do much. Franco had tried to stick him in the office to go over the books, probably to get him off his feet. Naturally, Brundar had refused, which had been stupid. No one needed a cripple to act as a monitor, but Franco sure as hell needed someone with a head for numbers.

Hell, he could've done it at home.

Yeah, as if he could ever do that. His pride aside, Brundar couldn't stand being apart from Calypso. During the evening, he'd climbed up the stairs twice, a taxing maneuver for someone relying on crutches, just so he could watch her work for a few minutes. It was like taking a deep breath before diving underwater again. It could sustain him only for so long before he needed to surface and take another breath.

"I'll get your crutches," Calypso said as she cut the engine.

He opened the passenger door and swung his legs out. She pulled the crutches from the back seat and handed them to him one at a time.

He hefted himself up, his knees protesting any further pressure. Gritting his teeth, he followed Calypso to the elevator. "You can take the stairs if you want." He knew how much she hated being stuck in the small lift.

"No. I go where you go, big guy. You're not getting rid of me."

He leaned and kissed the top of her head, relieved by her teasing. Her silence in the car had worried him. It wasn't like Calypso to stay so quiet, especially after her first day back at work and most likely plenty of new gossip to share.

"I'm going to grab a snack," she said as he plopped tiredly on the couch. "Do you want something?" she asked a few moments later, whispering for some reason.

Naturally, he'd heard her perfectly well.

"A cup of water, please." He was contemplating taking a couple of pills to numb the throbbing pain so he could sleep.

"Here is your water." She handed him a tall glass.

Her tone was different than usual, and he wondered what this was about. Did she resent waiting on him? Maybe she'd whispered before because her throat hurt. Was she coming down with a cold or flu?

"How are you feeling?" he asked.

"I'm great. It was good to be working again."

Now she sounded like her old self. He must've imagined things before, projecting his less than optimal condition on her. "Could I bother you again? I need the pills. I overdid it tonight."

"Of course." Calypso's eyes immediately softened, and she rushed to bring him the container from her purse. "How many do you need?"

"Three."

She shook them out on her palm and handed them to him.

"Thank you." He popped the pills into his mouth and followed with a long swig of water.

Calypso remained standing, casting him a suspicious look. "How did you hear me from the kitchen? I whispered so low I barely heard myself."

Damnation. This was unexpected and worrisome. She was starting to get suspicious and was testing him.

He shrugged, pretending nonchalance. "I have very good hearing."

She shook her head. "This is not good hearing. This is extraordinary hearing."

"If you say so." He winced, exaggerating the expression to distract her from her line of inquiry.

"I'm sorry. You're in pain, and I'm bothering you with nonsense. You need to shower and get into bed."

He sighed. "Sounds like a plan to me. I'm exhausted."

"Let me help you take off the bandages."

He couldn't wait. Up until tonight, he had showered with waterproof covers over his bandages, but Bridget had called earlier today telling him it was okay to take them off and replace them with the compression knee sleeves she'd left for him. In fact, it had been okay since Tuesday, but she'd forgotten to tell him. He had been supposed to come in for a checkup but had skipped it.

Brundar lifted his butt and pulled down his pants. "I'm all yours."

"I'll get a wet washcloth."

Calypso came back a moment later with a plastic bowl filled with water and a couple of washcloths. "Just in case the bandages are sticking to your skin."

They weren't, but he would let her discover it on her own.

With gentle fingers, Calypso carefully unwrapped the first bandage. Her eyes widened as she bared his knee. "I can't believe it. Look at this. There is barely any sign of the injury. How is it possible?"

Damnation. He hadn't expected it to look so good so fast. "The skin is healed. But the tendons and bones are not. That will take much longer."

"Even so. I was expecting to see scars and stitches, but all that remains are thin white lines." She touched a finger to one of them. "How?"

Brundar let his head drop back on the couch. He was so tired of lying. Maybe he should just thrall Calypso and get it over with. But he'd already thralled her yesterday after biting her, and he was loath to do so again so soon.

"I'm not a doctor. I don't know what kind of magic Bridget performed. You should address all these questions to her. I'm tired. I want to shower and get into bed."

Brundar didn't want to imagine how Bridget was going to retaliate for the hot potato he was dropping at her feet. But he could deal with that tomorrow when he had more energy.

"Do you need my help in the shower?" Calypso looked remorseful.

Brundar had detected notes of both hope and apology in her request, but he needed a few minutes to himself. "I'm fine. Finish your snack. I'll be quick about it. I know you want to shower too."

"Let me finish your other knee first."

"I can do it myself."

"Please?" Her sad eyes pleaded with him from where she was kneeling on the floor.

He couldn't deny her when she looked at him like that. "Fine."

When she was done, Calypso gathered the used bandages and took them to the trash, while he shuffled with the help of his crutches to the bathroom.

Sitting on the bench, Brundar closed his eyes and let the hot water soothe his strained muscles. The nightclub's smells lingered on clothes and skin but mostly the hair, necessitating a shower even if they'd done so before during the day.

He heard her open the bathroom door and a few moments later she entered the shower.

"Do you mind if I join you?" Her eyes looked haunted.

"Come here." He patted the spot next to him on the bench.

She snuggled up to him. "I don't like it when we fight."

He wrapped his arm around her and kissed the top of her head. "We didn't fight. I'm just tired and in pain, and it makes me cranky."

"Would it help if I massaged your scalp?"

No one had ever done that for him. It sounded pleasurable.

"It might."

"I've wanted to wash your hair for so long. It's so beautiful."

# 31

# CALLIE

Brundar closed his eyes and surrendered to Callie's massaging fingers.

"Can I use shampoo? It would make the massage feel even better."

"By all means."

He was really enjoying this, which made her feel so much better.

So what if he was a bit strange. Maybe fast healing was a genetic trait his family was keeping a secret. No one wanted to be poked and probed, perhaps even imprisoned and experimented on.

It was a far-fetched scenario, but it was better than believing Brundar was an alien pretending to be human.

Or a vampire.

Provided creatures like that really existed, which was an absurd notion, Brundar with his long canines could have been one. But even if they did exist, he had no problem with sunlight, so that was out. On the other hand, Callie was almost sure he'd bitten her and then made her forget it.

Shawn had accused Brundar of toying with his mind, but then Shawn had been insane.

Callie shook her head. She needed to stay with what made sense and away from crazy ideas. A hereditary genetic trait was a scientific possibility, while the other ones were pure fiction. Perhaps there were other intelligent species in the vast universe and aliens existed somewhere, but they didn't come to visit Earth, and vampires were a myth.

A dollop of shampoo in her palm, she started massaging Brundar's scalp.

"Your hair is so thick and glossy. Women spend a fortune on hair products, professionally done highlights, and Brazilian blowouts to get that look and fail."

Brundar's jaw muscles tightened, and he didn't respond to her compliments. Maybe he didn't like comments about his hair. Which didn't make sense. By growing it out so long, he was practically inviting them.

He was so touchy about so many things that she wasn't sure which topics of conversation were safe anymore. And to think people accused her generation—the millennials—of being too sensitive.

She stopped her massaging. "What's the matter? You don't like me talking about your hair?"

"It's not that. Please continue."

Resuming her kneading, she asked, "Then what? You can't shut me out whenever I ask you a personal question."

He sighed. "As a kid, I was bullied because of my hair. The boys called me a girl."

Kids could sometimes be so cruel. No wonder all her talk about women wanting hair like his reminded him of the taunting. "Was that why you became a fighter? So you could beat up the bullies?"

When he didn't respond, Callie assumed he didn't want to talk about it, but a few moments later he said, "No, only after I was attacked. I vowed to never be weak again. I refused to be a victim."

"Good for you." She kept massaging. "Was your hair as long then as it is now?" It was wrong to put the blame on the victim, but if he had been bullied and taunted for it, he should've cut it short. It would have saved him so much misery.

"Back then it was only chin length. It was a popular style. It was no different than that of most boys."

Callie frowned. When Brundar was a child, long hair hadn't been in style for boys. But maybe things had been different in the small Scottish village he'd grown up in.

After another moment he continued. "I let it grow out when I was older. It was both a reminder to never let my guard down and a reverse taunt. If I'd been targeted because of supposedly looking feminine, I made myself a more obvious target. But if anyone thought to bully me again, I would teach them a quick and painful lesson. But no one dared."

She rolled her eyes. "Duh, you look lethal. No wonder no one dared to bully you when you were older. But isn't long hair a hindrance to a fighter? Someone can grab you by the hair and drag you. I know how painful it is." The memory of Shawn pulling her by her ponytail and dragging her on the pavement was still fresh in her mind,

Brundar chuckled. "Not to me. No one can ever get close enough to grab it. I'd cut them down first."

Callie nodded even though he couldn't see her. She understood.

"I love your hair. Not for a single moment did I ever think that it made you look feminine. You're the manliest man I've ever met. Bullies will always find something to taunt other people about, and if there is nothing they can latch on to, they'll invent something. And I'm not referring to kids only. Adults can be bullies too. Sometimes those who have nothing they can be proud of put other people down to feel superior."

Brundar covered her hand on his shoulder with his. "True words."

## 32

# KIAN

The house phone rang, once, twice.

Kian ignored it. After the third ring, someone picked up. Either Syssi or Okidu.

If anyone needed him, they knew to call his cellphone. The Guardians didn't use the landline, and no one else had his home number except for his mother and sisters.

Alena never called, and on the rare occasion that Amanda and Sari did, they used his cell number. Which left his mother. But he wasn't expecting a call from her.

It was probably someone in the keep looking for Syssi.

Kian went back to looking over the proposal Shai had summarized for him so he didn't have to sift through pages upon pages of technical and financial stuff that could be boiled down to a few paragraphs.

Shai had been the one to come up with the idea, and it was a life saver, cutting hours off Kian's workday. The problem was, he always found more things he could fill them with. Good for their business, but bad for him and Syssi.

The woman was a saint, tolerating his shitty moods and not complaining about having too little time with him.

The phone line went from blinking red to green, and a second later Syssi called using the intercom. "It's your mother. She wants to talk to you."

"Thanks."

Fuck. A call from his mother was never good news. Annani didn't call to chitchat. She called to issue orders and demand reports. Not often, thank the merciful Fates.

"Hello, Mother."

"How are you doing, Kian?"

Was he imagining it, or did he detect a note of true concern in her tone?

"Busy as usual. I'm in the process of acquiring several new enterprises. Our growth for the last quarter was in the two digits."

"I did not call to inquire about our holdings. I wanted to know how my son was doing."

Great. Someone must've told Annani that he'd been stressed lately. Suspect *numero uno*—Amanda. No one would ever suspect a woman who looked like her to have a yenta personality, but she did.

"I'm doing fine, Mother."

"Fabulous. I want you in a good mood while I am visiting."

"The village is not ready yet." Annani was supposed to come for the grand opening ceremony.

"I know, dear, but I need to come because of Phoenix. That little girl should have been turned already."

A good excuse. But Kian knew it wasn't the reason his mother was coming.

"Shouldn't her parents bring her to you?"

"Indeed they should. But Andrew cannot take another long vacation, and Nathalie refuses to come without her husband."

The door opened quietly, and Syssi walked in. She sat across from his desk and mouthed, "What's going on?"

"Annani is coming for a visit," he mouthed back.

Syssi's eyes brightened, and she did that silent hand clapping to show him she was excited about the news. His wife was probably the only woman in the universe who couldn't wait to spend time with her mother-in-law. Yet another reason to adore her.

"When should we expect you?" he asked Annani.

"The day after tomorrow. I will notify you when I board the plane."

"Very well. I'll send the chopper to pick you up from our landing strip."

"Thank you. I am looking forward to spending time with you and Syssi and Amanda and her mate."

"We are looking forward to it too." Not really, but he was doing his best to sound polite. "Goodbye, Mother."

Ending the call, Kian put his elbows on his desk and dropped his head into his hands. "As if I don't have enough to contend with, the last thing I need is my mother visiting. I don't have time for that."

Syssi waved a dismissive hand. "Don't worry about it. Amanda and I are going to keep her busy. Besides, she will be spending most of her time doting on Phoenix. You know how your mother adores babies."

"That is the reason she gave for coming. Phoenix needs to turn as soon as possible, but her parents are in no hurry." He wagged a finger at her. "I blame your brother for that."

Syssi shrugged. "It's going to be okay. I for one am happy she is coming. Your mom is so much fun."

That was part of the problem. Hosting his mother was like hosting a mischievous teenage girl who needed constant supervision, but who he had no control over whatsoever and had to treat like the celebrity prima donna she was.

Kian raked his fingers through his hair. "Where are we even going to put her? Can she stay at Amanda's again?"

Syssi shook her head. "I don't think she is going to be comfortable with

Dalhu there. Or let me rephrase, I don't think Dalhu is going to be comfortable with her there. She still intimidates the hell out of him." She leaned back in her chair and crossed her arms over her chest. "Annani can stay with us. We have plenty of room, for her and her Odus."

"I can send Amanda and Dalhu on a vacation, and she can stay at their place," Kian suggested.

"Really? Is having your mother over so terrible?"

He sighed. "Normally no. But I'm hanging by a thread, and Annani is not easy to deal with."

"Was there a time you weren't stressed? That's your normal."

"I'm not always stressed."

Syssi uncrossed her arms and leaned forward. "Oh, yeah? Give me a recent example."

"Easy. When we make love, and for about half an hour after."

She laughed. "Great. So while your mother is here, all we have to do is have plenty of sex to negate the extra stress her company causes you."

"Aha. But she is going to hear us, and you're still shy about that."

"True." Syssi frowned. "We can't put her in one of the lower level apartments, she will be offended by that, and we can't put her in a hotel for the same reason."

That gave him an idea. "You're right. We can't put her anywhere other than our or Amanda's penthouse without offending her, but we can stay wherever the fuck we want."

"Like the Four Seasons?"

"Sure."

She waggled her brows. "The last time we stayed there, I had dream sex with you. This time we can have the real thing."

He still remembered the scent of her arousal that had permeated the presidential suite. "What exactly did you dream?"

"I'm not going to tell you."

The hell she wasn't. "Tell me!"

Syssi's lips twitched as she pretended to be upset with him. "Tsk, tsk, Kian. We've discussed this before. You're only allowed to boss me around in the bedroom."

"No. I'm allowed to boss you around in any sexual situation. Talking about sex qualifies."

"I could tell you, but I'd rather show you." Syssi winked.

He was out of his chair before the last word had left her mouth. "Come." He reached for her hand.

"Not here, silly boy. At the Four Seasons!"

"Fine. Come with me, and I'll show you *my* dreams."

"You dream about me?"

"Every fucking minute of the day." He pulled her up and wrapped his arms around her. "Let's go."

## 33

## BRUNDAR

An hour of sitting in Franco's ugly office was more than enough for Brundar. He could work on the numbers upstairs while keeping an eye on Calypso. Not in the sense of keeping her safe, the danger was over, but for his own selfish reasons.

He was addicted to her.

Dropping the tablet inside a plastic bag that he'd tied to one of the rungs on his right crutch, he was ready to go. There was no other way for him to carry the damned thing. It was too big for a pocket, and he couldn't stick it under his arm because that was where the crutches went.

If not for Bridget's threat to reset his bones without the benefit of anesthesia, which wasn't an idle one, he would've tossed them aside and walked like a man even if it killed him.

Franco should install a goddamned elevator from the basement to the nightclub. Climbing the stairs with crutches was a circus act Brundar was getting tired of.

In fact, he was getting tired of the whole scene. The basement didn't hold his interest anymore. There was nothing for him down there. The only one he wanted to play with was running around and serving drinks at the surface level, and that was where he wanted to be.

Hence the tablet. Crunching numbers was the one thing that he was still good for.

Brundar shook his head. He'd been transformed from a fighter with a kinky bent to a boring accountant who wanted nothing more than to take his woman home and make love to her.

Yes, make love.

Not have sex, not fuck, not shag, but make love.

Fates, he used to pity Kian for spending his days behind a desk and being so wrapped up in his woman that he could barely function without her.

Was he turning into a version of Kian?

The thing was, it didn't bother him as much as it should. Brundar had discovered that he liked playing with numbers. He was good at making estimates, profit and loss predictions, and calculating returns on investments. And what's more, he found it interesting. For centuries he'd watched Kian conduct business, all along thinking that it was an uninspired, boring job.

He'd been wrong.

Now he understood the rush Kian was getting out of the wheeling and dealing. He was one of the top players in a game only the select few were good at.

Brundar was nowhere near Kian's caliber and would probably never be, but he could play a scaled down game and test his abilities without risking too much.

By the time Brundar reached the top of the stairs, he was winded, and his knees were in agony. Unfortunately, it would be two more hours before he could go home. Calypso's shift didn't end until two in the morning, and she was his ride home.

"Brundar." She ran up to him as he shuffled out of the side corridor and into the club proper. "Are you in pain? You look pale. I mean paler than usual."

With Calypso, he didn't feel the need to pretend that a tough guy like him didn't need relief from pain. She would've called him on his bullshit right away. "I could use a few of those pills. Did you bring them?"

"Of course. First, let me find you a place to sit, and then I'll go get them."

He nodded, following behind her as she pushed her way in between the many bodies crowding the floor. Friday night was one of the busiest days of the week. The place was packed. Good for business, not so good for Calypso's prospects of finding him a place to sit. Not a single table was vacant. Maybe she could get him a seat at the bar.

Except, Brundar had forgotten that by law a table had to be reserved for people in his situation. The table set aside for the disabled happened to be free.

After Calypso had helped him get settled and run off to get his pills, a couple of girls sauntered over with come-hither smiles plastered on their heavily made-up faces. They were eyeing the two vacant chairs at his table, obviously more interested in the seats and maybe a free drink than in him.

He treated them to one of his more severe stares and pushed with a little thrall, convincing them that sitting next to him was a really bad idea. They kept on walking, searching for their next victim.

Calypso got back and handed him the glass of water, then pulled the pill container out of the pocket of her pants. "If you don't want to be bothered, I can take away these two chairs and add them to another table."

"Good thinking." He dropped four pills into his palm, popped them into his mouth and followed with water.

Regrettably, Calypso couldn't stay long, and Brundar was left all alone at his table with no extra chairs to tempt unwanted company. Pulling out the tablet from the plastic bag, he tried to go over his projections for the month and compare them to what the two clubs actually pulled in. It wasn't a difficult task to perform, but doing so with the loud music playing and people constantly jostling against his chair and his table was proving difficult if not impossible.

Brundar closed his eyes and slipped into the zone. Nothing disturbed him there. Sounds and visuals faded into the background, leaving only one thing to focus on. On the battlefield, it was usually an opponent with a weapon in his hand, but today it was a tablet with numbers to crunch.

Time went by fast or slowly in the zone, depending on which way Brundar needed to stretch it. He lost track of it, shifting from one spreadsheet to another, writing notes, and making estimates for next month. Things were looking good, and with the additional space they were going to add they would look even better.

"Brundar." Calypso's voice reached him from afar.

He closed his eyes again and abandoned his quiet space, his surroundings coming into focus like tunnel vision in reverse. He was expecting a rush of noise, but the music had stopped, the lights were up, and only the staff remained, tidying up and preparing the floor for the cleaning crew.

"Ready to go?" Calypso asked.

"I have been ready for hours."

She frowned. "Why didn't you say so? I would've taken you home."

He took her hand and kissed the back of it. "To leave me there and go back to work? I don't think so."

"Well, I could've asked the boss to let me go early." She winked. "I'm sure he would've okayed it."

## 34

# RONI

"No way. I'm not going to play." Roni took one of the paper bags out of Sylvia's hands. Full of refreshments, including bottles of beer and cans of ginger ale, they were quite heavy. He couldn't carry them all, but he could at least appear as if he was helping.

"You don't have to. But it could be fun. No one expects you to be any good after one hour of practice."

Yesterday, Roni had guilted Andrew into helping him assemble the drum set, meaning Andrew had done all the work while Roni had sat on a chair and gave instructions.

He'd played for as long as he could, but drumming was physically demanding, and after an hour he'd had to quit and go up to his apartment to lie down.

They stepped into the elevator. "I'm rusty as hell. Besides, I don't have the energy."

Sylvia leaned and kissed his cheek. "Then you can just sit and enjoy yourself. I hope." She grimaced. "I've never heard them play. They might be awful."

That was a possibility, but judging by Jackson's taste in music a remote one. "If they get gigs in clubs they can't be too sucky."

"There is no accounting for taste. People listen to heavy metal and love it, while all I hear are screams."

They reached the basement level and exited the lift, heading for what Roni had started calling his music room. By the sound of it, the guys had already started jamming.

"Not bad," Roni said.

Sylvia nodded. "Thank the merciful Fates, I don't hear any screeching screams."

As he opened the door for Sylvia and followed her in, the guys stopped playing.

"Sweet set of drums." The band's drummer pushed up to his feet and walked over. "I'm Gordon." He offered his hand.

"Roni."

The tall, gangly, goth-looking dude leaned his bass guitar against a chair and came over to introduce himself as well. "Vlad." He offered a pale hand with long fingers. His nails were painted black.

"Have you been jamming long?" Roni asked as he shook the guy's hand.

"We've just started." Jackson strummed his guitar. "Want to join us on the drums?"

"Not this time. Today I'm in the audience."

Tessa walked over and gave Roni a hug. "Come and hang out with Sylvia and me. We will be drinking beer and munching on goodies while the guys play."

"Right." He turned to Sylvia who got busy taking things out of the paper bags and arranging them on the table someone had dragged into the room. "Why didn't you wait for me to help you?" He hated feeling useless.

"Don't worry about it. I've got it. It's not like I'm preparing a gourmet meal here. Pretzels, nuts, fruit, beers, and ginger ale."

"Don't forget the pastries," Tessa said.

Sylvia glanced around the room. "Where are they?"

"I'll get them." Tessa walked over to where the guys had left their guitar cases, and lifted a big pink box from behind them.

"Did you bring any cheese Danishes?" Roni peeked into the box as Tessa started pulling the pastries out and arranging them on paper plates.

She handed him one. "Freshly baked. We ran out, but I remembered how much you liked them and asked Vlad to make more."

Roni turned to the band and lifted the half-eaten Danish. "Thanks, man. I appreciate it. I mean it. No one ever baked anything for me. Not even my mom."

Vlad smiled shyly. "Enjoy."

"I will." He grabbed a can of ginger ale and popped the lid. "I'm in heaven."

The band started playing again, this time with Jackson singing. The guy had a decent voice, and he and his friends played well. Not bad for teenagers, but they needed someone to write better music for them, and lyrics. Still, Roni had to admit that their performance was surprisingly professional.

Taking a seat at the table, he helped himself to another Danish. Sylvia and Tessa were trying to talk over the loud music, but Tessa kept asking her to repeat what she'd said, and eventually, the girls gave up.

The guys played one more song and then decided to take a break, apparently tempted by the food and beers.

"Snake's Venom. Awesome." Jackson helped himself to one. "Where did you get them?"

"In the store. Where else?" Sylvia said.

"They are not easy to find and pricey. We need to split the bill for those."

Sylvia waved a hand. "Forget it. Next time is going to be your treat."

Jackson lifted the beer in a salute. "Deal."

"Who writes your music?" Roni asked.

"Vlad writes the lyrics, and I write the music. Gordon is the ideas man. He comes up with all kinds of weird shit our audiences eat up."

"Would you mind if I wrote something for you guys?"

Jackson lifted one blond brow. "What are you saying, Roni? Do you think our music sucks?"

Fuck. Had he offended them? For a change, he hadn't meant to. "No, of course not. You guys are good. I just want to give it a shot."

Jackson clapped his back. "Don't worry, man. No hurt feelings here. I would love to get new material that I don't need to sweat creating. Besides, you are going to join our band, right? We need you." He wrapped his arm around Roni's shoulders as if they were the best of buddies.

Given that Roni had none, Jackson had no competition for the position. It was his if he wanted it.

With everyone at the table looking at him expectantly, there was only one way to answer that. "Sure. But I'm nowhere near Gordon's level."

Jackson squeezed his shoulder. "You will be. You're a perfectionist and competitive as hell."

With a frown, Roni straightened in his chair. "How do you know that about me? You've known me for what? Two whole hours?"

Jackson shrugged. "Simple. You don't get to be the best in your field unless you have an uncompromising drive and ambition. Whatever you do, you strive to be the best at."

Roni dipped his head. "True. But aside from my obvious genius, which admittedly makes learning new things very easy for me, drumming requires a lot of practice. I have no doubt that eventually, I will get to be as good as Gordon or even better, but it's not going to happen by the time he leaves for college."

His genius remark drew snorts and chuckles from everyone other than Sylvia, who knew he hadn't meant it as a joke.

He was a damn genius, and he didn't believe in fake modesty.

"Okay, guys." Jackson put down his empty beer bottle. "Now that I have food in my belly, we can go back to jamming." He rose to his feet and offered his hand to Tessa. "Your turn, kitten."

She looked up at him with a puzzled expression on her face. "To do what?"

"Sing, of course."

She shook her head. "Oh, no, no, no. I'm not going to sing in front of people."

Jackson waved a hand at everyone present. "What people? Gordon and Vlad have heard you sing before, and Sylvia and Roni are our friends, soon to become part of the band."

Sneaking a glance at Sylvia and then at Roni, Tessa smiled sheepishly. "One song."

"Awesome. Sylvia is going to sing the next one," Jackson said.

Roni expected his girlfriend to object, same as Tessa, but she surprised him by accepting the challenge.

As the band started playing and Tessa took the microphone, Roni leaned back in his chair and crossed his legs at the ankles.

Tessa had a lovely voice, but weak. Jackson kept adjusting the amplifier connected to the mic, but it didn't help much.

When Tessa was done, he and Sylvia clapped, causing her to blush."

Sylvia didn't need any encouragement to take the mic next. "I don't know any of the songs you guys play. Do you know *'You're Gonna Miss Me when I'm Gone'*?

"Sing a few bars and we will improvise," Jackson said.

Wow. Sylvia could sing. He hadn't known that. She had a sweet voice, similar to the original singer of that song. It was clear and strong, and her pitch was perfect. Roni felt his heart swell with pride, and with something else that was new and unexpected.

He liked these people, and they seemed to like him back.

They wanted to hang out with him, not because of his hacking skills, but because they enjoyed his company. These guys wanted him to jam with them, a fun activity people did with friends.

Friends.

For the first time since he was a toddler, Roni had actually made friends.

## 35

## JACKSON

Jackson's hands were sweaty on the steering wheel, and he had a feeling that sweat stains were spreading under his armpits.

It was ridiculous. Neither he nor Tessa was a virgin, and he believed that this time she was truly ready. So why the hell was he so nervous?

Apparently, cool Jackson was gone, replaced by an insecure eighteen-year-old. Almost nineteen, he reminded himself.

Tessa didn't look anxious, thank the merciful Fates, but she seemed contemplative. They'd been on the road for over an hour, and she'd barely said a word to him.

"What are you thinking about?"

She shrugged. "This and that. Just random thoughts."

"Care to share them with me?"

Tessa threw him a sidelong glance. "Are you sure? It's mostly girl stuff that will bore you."

"Try me."

"I was thinking about Sharon. She is cool and pretty and smart, but she's never had a boyfriend. She has plenty of hookups, but that doesn't count. I asked her about it, and she said that none of the guys she's been with was a mensch, and most were just meh—boring to talk to and boring in bed. So I was wondering if she was going to like any of the immortals Eva and Bhathian were planning to introduce her to. If she is that picky, she might not like any of them, and there aren't that many to start with. Right?"

Jackson rubbed his jaw. "Frankly, I didn't give it much thought. But yeah, it's possible she won't find what she is looking for."

Tessa nodded. "If she doesn't find an immortal guy she likes and who likes her back, is Kian going to allow these guys to sleep with her and try to induce her transition? And what about telling her the truth? Are they going to do it without her knowledge? If she turns, fine, and if she doesn't, no harm done?"

"I don't know." He chuckled. "I'm very happy I'm not Kian. When I was a kid, I wanted to be just like him—a leader, a successful businessman. But I don't want to be faced with these kinds of decisions."

She was quiet for a few moments. "When I was a kid, all I wanted was a family. A mom and a dad who loved me."

Jackson reached for her hand. "You have a family. Me and Eva and Bhathian, and Nathalie and Andrew and Phoenix, and everyone else in the clan."

"I can't allow myself to think about them that way. Not until after my transition. Except for Eva, of course. She will always be there for me no matter what. Even Kian can't command her to forsake me. He might think he has authority over her, but he doesn't and never will. Eva answers only to Eva and to some extent to Bhathian. That's it."

"What about me? I'll never leave you. You must know that."

She turned her face to the window, looking at the frosted scenery they were passing on their way to the cabin he'd rented for them in Big Bear.

"If I don't turn, I will not stay with you. I love you too much to cause you that much pain. I know I wouldn't want to see you get old and die, while I stayed young and healthy. I'm a firm believer in not doing to others what I don't want done to me."

Jackson shook his head. They were on their way to what he considered an equivalent of a honeymoon, and Tessa was talking about leaving him.

"Then I'm not like you. Because I would rather be with you for as long as I can than not at all."

"What if the roles were reversed and you were the human and I the immortal?"

He grinned. "Then I would've been doubly happy because I would have had a forever hot woman by my side. What guy doesn't want that?"

Tessa crossed her arms over her chest. "If Eva's ex didn't suffer from dementia, you could've asked him. He had a gorgeous, young-looking wife, and he still cheated on her with others."

"Idiot."

"Yeah. I agree."

"Finally we agree on something. I didn't plan this romantic getaway so we can contemplate every catastrophic scenario imaginable." He cast her a sidelong glance. "I'm a firm believer in the glass half full as opposed to half empty."

"You're right. Let's talk about something else. Where are you taking me?"

"To a magical place."

"Seriously. I know it's up in the mountains because you told me to pack a sweater and we've been climbing for the past forty-five minutes."

If Tessa were a native Californian, she would have known where he was taking her, so there was no harm in telling her the destination. The cabin he'd rented, though, he was going to keep a surprise. He wanted to see her face as she entered.

Jackson had paid for the honeymoon package, which included the fanciest cabin in the resort, fresh flowers, a bottle of champagne, and a fruit basket. In addition, he'd asked for candles to be lit before their arrival but had been refused. Apparently, candles were considered a fire hazard.

It put a little dent in his plans, but he had it covered. There was a bunch of assorted candles in his travel bag, three bottles of wine, and enough Godiva chocolates to land Tessa in a hospital. Naturally, he was going to portion those out so she wouldn't overdose. The girl had no self-control when faced with those sweet treats.

"We are going to Big Bear. I rented us a cabin. It's summer, so there will be no snow, but the place is beautiful all year round."

Tessa frowned. "That sounds expensive. I hope you didn't spend too much on the cabin."

Given the state of his finances, it had cost a fortune, but he and Tessa were going to have their first time together only once. He needed to get it right because there were no re-dos on that.

"No, not too much." Not a lie. Nothing was too much to make this day and night special.

"How did you manage to take a day off tomorrow?"

"Our wayward waitress came back."

"Oh, yeah? Where was she?"

"Got another job. They promised her better pay but ended up paying her less. So she is back."

"And you took her back? She is unreliable."

"True, but I know she is not going to disappear at least until she gets her paycheck, which is in two weeks. She needs the money."

"What if she doesn't show up tomorrow? What are Vlad and Gordon going to do?"

Jackson shook his head. "Glass half full, kitten. I have to stick with that."

Twenty minutes or so later, they arrived at the resort.

"Stay here. I'll get us checked in."

"Okay."

It was good she had no problem staying in the car. He didn't want Tessa to come with him in case the clerk at the reception started blabbing about the honeymoon suite and spoiled his surprise. After checking them in, Jackson made reservations for dinner in one of the restaurants the guy at reception had suggested, then headed back to the car.

"Our cabin is a short drive from here," he told Tessa.

Even from the outside, it looked bigger and fancier than all the other cabins they had passed on the way.

Dropping their bags on the front porch, Jackson pulled the key out of his pocket and unlocked the door but opened it only a tiny crack.

"Close your eyes," he told Tessa.

She smiled. "Okay."

Lifting her into his arms, he pushed the door open with his foot. "You can open your eyes now."

"Jackson, it's beautiful." Tessa turned her head this way and that, taking in the ultra luxurious cabin. "This must have cost a bundle. And you said you didn't pay much for it." She cast him an accusing glance.

"You asked me if I paid *too much*, and I said no because nothing is too much to make this day special for you. For us." He kissed her tenderly.

Eying the huge bed, Tessa worried her lower lip. "What now? Is there a protocol for how this should be done?"

"Item number one on the agenda is to feed the bride so she'll have the energy for a long night of great sex."

He turned her in his arms, so her chest was pressed against his and kissed her again.

After letting him cuddle and kiss her until he had his fill, Tessa shimmied down his body. When her feet touched the floor, she tugged her shirt down. "I bet you made reservations."

"Of course. I leave nothing to chance."

## 36

# TESSA

Dinner ended up being a drawn-out affair.
Tessa had ordered a glass of wine, and then another one, sipping on them as slowly as she could. It wasn't that she'd changed her mind, or felt that she wasn't ready after all.

She felt pressured. For lack of a better term, Tessa was suffering from what she suspected was the equivalent of performance anxiety.

What Jackson hadn't realized was that the elaborate setup was more of a hindrance than an aphrodisiac. Things would have been simpler if they had done it in his room atop the café. There was no pressure there. They would have started with kissing and fondling, and one thing would have led to another, and things would have progressed naturally to where they were supposed to.

But Jackson wanted to make it special, and she had no heart to tell him that all that preparation was making her anxious.

"Are you ready to go, kitten?" he asked when the last drop of wine in her glass was gone.

No more stalling. "Yes." She rose to her feet, or rather to her six-inch platform shoes. Several guys glanced her way, but the new Tessa was able to interpret their appreciative looks as a compliment and not a threat.

Tessa expelled a breath. She could do it. She wasn't a scared little girl anymore. She was a confident young woman who could kick ass when necessary, and who was secure in her own sexuality. Not only that, she was going to make love to an amazing guy who loved her to pieces, and whom she loved back just as much.

On the front porch of the cabin, Jackson opened the door and lifted her in his arms again, then carried her over the threshold. She wrapped her arms around his neck and snuggled closer. For a slim guy, he was always warm—her own personal blanket for whenever she got cold, which was often.

"Where do you want to go, bed or bath?"

"Bath, definitely. I bet they have a jacuzzi in there."

"They do. A two-person whirlpool spa."

Oh, goodie. Jackson was going to get in the tub with her. They would start with a little fondling and continue to bed.

Jackson set her down on the counter, then turned around to start the water for their tub.

Her legs dangling over the edge and her arms propped on the marble countertop, Tessa felt like a little girl again. A naughty girl who was planning on doing naughty things with her hot fiancé all night long.

She was getting all hot and bothered just looking at Jackson as he crouched next to the tub. With his broad back, his powerful thighs, and the tight ass that was a work of art, he was a man any woman would've loved to call her own.

He was also three years Tessa's junior.

She should be the one babying him, and not the other way around. The thing was, she loved how he always took care of her.

Age was irrelevant.

Their personalities dictated the roles they assumed in their relationship. Jackson was the caretaker, and she was the one being taken care of, and they both enjoyed the roles they played.

So what was the harm in that?

She would do anything for him, and if Jackson ever needed her to take care of him, she would. But in their day to day life their default modes suited them perfectly well.

Satisfied with the temperature of the water, Jackson straightened up and turned to her. "Is my kitten waiting for me to undress her?"

"Yes." She treated him to a bright smile, letting him know she liked the direction this was going.

"My pleasure."

He started with her shoes, the very tall ones he'd bought for her, removing one at the time and then massaging her toes and her arches until she purred like a real cat.

Next, Jackson tackled the buttons of her white, silk blouse, opening each of the tiny fake pearls with nimble fingers. When the last one was done, he parted the two halves of the shirt and slid the sleeves down her arms, letting it fall on the counter behind her.

"Very nice." He trailed his fingers over the top of her breasts, leaving goose bumps in the wake of his feather-light touch.

"A new bra?"

"Yeah." Tessa cupped the undersides of her bra-encased small breasts. "The latest in bridal lingerie. Adds two cup sizes." It was also embroidered with tiny fake diamonds on the sides. Apparently, Jackson hadn't been the only one who thought of this as their honeymoon. Tessa had gotten the bra because she needed a white one under the sheer fabric of her new blouse, but there were many others she could've chosen, and yet she'd been drawn to the bridal model.

Jackson's eyes started glowing. "Did you get the matching panties?"

She waggled her brows. "You'll have to find out."

Wrapping an arm around her waist, he lifted her a couple of inches off the counter and pulled her tight stretchy pants off with his other hand. His eyes zeroed in on the tiny lace triangle covering her mound. "Very nice indeed." He trailed a finger over her cleft. The lace panties were useless as far as absorbing any moisture, and the evidence of her arousal had already seeped through.

Jackson lifted his wet finger to his mouth and licked it clean. "There is no better taste in the world." His speech was getting slurred.

His fangs were such a turn-on.

But they were nowhere near their full length yet. She knew exactly how to get them there. "There is a surprise for you in the back."

"Show me."

Oh, she was going to have fun with that. Sometimes, being small was an advantage, because a tall woman could not have done what Tessa had in mind. The ceiling was too low for that.

Bracing on her hands, she lifted herself and pulled her legs up. When her feet were on the counter, she pushed up and turned around, leaning against the mirror and pushing her ass out.

The panties were thong style, tied with a little bow at the back. All Jackson had to do was tug on that bow, and they would fall off.

After all, it was a bridal set.

Jackson gasped. "Dear Fates. I have to take a picture of that."

What the hell? That wasn't what she'd expected. "Don't you dare! I don't want pictures of my butt all over the Internet."

"I'll erase it as soon as I show it to you. I bet you have no idea how hot you look."

Naturally, she'd checked herself in the mirror when she'd put them on, but not from the angle Jackson was seeing now. "Okay. Just one."

He pulled out his phone and snapped three in quick succession, then handed her the phone. "You can erase them yourself when you're done."

Wow, that was one hell of a view. Slightly lewd, since the thong didn't cover much, but sexy as hell.

Damn, she was turning herself on.

Tessa erased the pictures, crouched down on the counter, and reached behind her to hand Jackson his phone back.

"Stay like that," he hissed, cupping her butt cheeks in his large hands.

She looked at him over her shoulder. "Are you going to pull on the bow?"

He answered with a growl, catching the little white bow between his front teeth, which were now framed by his huge fangs, and pulled. The thong fell off, leaving her naked save for the bra.

"I'm going to eat you up like that." Holding her in place, Jackson dipped his head, extended his tongue, and treated her to a long lick. "Yum. So tasty."

Panting, Tessa leaned her head against the mirror and surrendered to pleasure.

## 37

## JACKSON

Tessa was trembling with the aftershocks of her orgasm as Jackson lifted her off the counter and hugged her to him, careful not to squash her. But it was hard not to tighten his arms around her when he was overflowing with emotions.

Every time he brought her to a climax felt like a triumph, hers as well as his. Especially one that had left her boneless like she was now.

"Ready for your bath, kitten?"

She opened her bliss-glazed eyes and cupped his cheek. "Could you take off my bra first?"

He bent to plant a soft kiss on her lips. With his fangs at full length, he needed to be extra careful not to nick her. "Of course."

Holding her with one arm, he snapped the bra open with his other and tossed it on the counter next to those sexy panties he was going to keep as a souvenir.

"I'll dip your tush first. Tell me if the temperature is okay." He lowered her gently into the water.

"It's good."

Jackson lowered Tessa all the way until she was sprawled comfortably in the bathtub, then shucked his clothes and joined her. Slipping in behind her instead of taking the spot across from her as the tub's design suggested, he hugged her close and nuzzled her neck. His cock was hard enough to hammer nails with, but he didn't want to rush her. It wouldn't be the first time he'd suffered a woodie and the way it was nestled between her ass cheeks it was getting even harder.

Tessa rested her head on his chest and sighed. "You're so good to me."

"And you are to me."

She chuckled. "Not really. You just treated me to an orgasm that left me boneless, while you're still sporting a boner."

"I'm a patient man."

"Yes, you are. And a wonderful one." She turned in his arms, pressing her breasts against his chest. "How about we get out of here and put that king-sized bed to good, rigorous use?"

He kissed her cute little nose. "You can barely move. I think you need to rest a little."

"Not necessarily. It's not as if I'm going to do much work out there. My only job is to moan loudly as you pound into me."

The image she'd just painted in his mind had his cock twitch and release a bead of moisture. Tessa was definitely over her aversion to sex and anything that had to do with it.

A few weeks ago he would've never believed she could talk like that.

"Is that what you want? Just a pounding?"

"Is there anything else?"

There was still so much he could teach her. "Plenty. Though eventually it all leads to that."

Even through the water, he could smell the flare in her desire that his words brought about.

Her eyes hooded, she trailed a finger down his chest. "I want everything. But most of all I'm looking forward to the pounding."

Jackson didn't need any more prodding. Lifting Tessa with him, he stepped out of the tub and grabbed a towel.

"I love how strong you are." She had her arms wrapped around his neck.

He put the towel on the counter, then set Tessa on top of the folded towel, and grabbed another, wrapping it quickly around her.

His girl got chilled easily. He couldn't allow that to happen.

Once he had Tessa cocooned in two towels with only her head peeking out, Jackson pulled one for himself.

"I can't move my arms," she complained.

"But you're warm. I'll unwrap you when you're under the blanket."

"Can we light the fire?"

Done toweling himself dry, Jackson dropped his bath sheet on the floor and lifted Tessa up together with her towel cocoon. "Good idea. It will make the room all warm and cozy for my girl who doesn't like to be cold."

Stretching her neck up, she kissed the underside of his jaw. "Did I tell you how much I love you?"

"Once or twice. But I can never get enough." He put her down on one side of the bed, lifting the thick, down-filled comforter with the other. "Okay, kitten, on three." He helped her out of the towels and under the blanket.

"It's cold. Can you get in and warm me up?"

"Don't you want me to start the fire first?"

"Later."

He was fine with that. Getting under the blanket with a naked Tessa wasn't a hard sell.

"Come here, baby." He wrapped himself around her small body. She was so tiny. At six feet two inches, he was a tall guy. Were they going to fit?

He would've been really worried if Tessa were a virgin.

"Jackson?"

"Yeah?"

"I'm not on any contraceptives. Are we going to use a condom?"

"No. I told you what Bridget said. The bite has to come together with intercourse."

"I thought she meant the act."

"I have to get my seed inside you at the same time as my venom."

"What if I get pregnant?"

"Very unlikely. Immortals don't procreate much."

"I'm still a mortal."

"But I'm not. And I haven't gotten anyone pregnant yet."

"You did it without condoms?"

He shrugged. "I can't get or transmit diseases. All I had to do was push a little thrall to let them think I had protection when I didn't, and no one got pregnant."

"That's because all those girls are on the pill or something else."

It was going to kill him, but if she wanted to get contraceptives first, he was okay with going home without consummating their union. They had managed up until now, they would manage a few more days.

"Do you want to get pills first? We don't have to do it tonight. What's one more week, right?"

"No way in hell. If you're willing to chance it, then I am too."

Fates, what a relief. "I am. And if by some miracle I put a baby in you, I will not mind it at all."

"Me neither," Tessa whispered into his chest.

## 38

## TESSA

*A* baby. Images of her and Jackson with their baby popped behind Tessa's closed eyelids, and there was nothing but joy in them. She would finally have a family of her own. Not an adopted family, not a foster family, but totally hers.

It would be wonderful.

That didn't mean she would be devastated if she didn't conceive on their first try. They had plenty of time, and Tessa wanted to transition first.

Nathalie and Andrew had had a hell of a time worrying about the baby because Nathalie had gotten pregnant as a human. On the other hand, conception was much more difficult for immortals. Tessa's chances would drop significantly after her transition.

She kissed Jackson's chest. "Whatever happens, happens. Your Fates are going to decide."

He cupped her breast and thumbed the nipple. "I don't trust them. They do as they please, and our prayers fall on deaf ears, but there isn't much I can do about it other than helping them along with lots and lots of sex, that is." He waggled his brows.

She could live with that. "Starting tonight."

"Yes." His eyes blazed in the dark room. "Are you all warmed up?" He started pulling the blanket down, exposing her breasts.

"I am, but my nipples are getting cold."

"Not for long."

With a gentle push, Jackson turned her on her back, and covered her body with his. Bracing on his forearms, he looked into her eyes and waited.

It took her a moment to realize what he was waiting for.

He was on top of her, his big body pressing hers into the mattress, a position that used to freak her out because she couldn't stand being trapped under a man's body. Except, the fear was so completely gone that she'd forgotten she'd ever had a problem with that. All she felt was love, acceptance, and simmering arousal.

Tessa smiled and wrapped her arms around Jackson's neck, pulling him even closer, so his entire weight was pressing into her. He wasn't too heavy, he was just perfect, feeling wonderful on top of her. She could stay like this forever. "Kiss me," she breathed.

He took her lips gently, his tongue flicking over them in a playful request for entry, then getting bolder when she granted it. His kisses were still gentle as he moved to her neck, then her collarbone, and then slid down her body to take one aching nipple into his hot mouth while his fingers teased the other.

How the hell was he doing it? Being so patient with her and holding back the inferno she was seeing in his blazing eyes?

His erection hadn't eased since he'd brought her to a shattering climax in the bathroom. Jackson was no doubt desperate to get inside her, but he was taking the time to give her slow and sweet, showing her love with every touch, every caress.

Threading her fingers through his silky blond hair, she whispered, "I love you."

His mouth left her nipple with a plop. "I know, kitten. I love you too."

"I'm ready," she said.

He shook his head. "I'll be the judge of that."

Even if she wasn't before, she was now. Bossy Jackson was sexy as hell, especially since his bossiness was always about ensuring her pleasure.

He was such a giver.

Resuming his suckling on her other nipple, he pushed a hand down to her center, first just cupping it possessively, then trailing a finger down her drenched folds.

She groaned as he pushed a finger inside her, the muscles in her sheath clamping around it. He pulled it out, dragging the moisture up to her throbbing bundle of nerve endings, then circling it without actually touching. A moment later, he came back with two fingers, pumping a few times, and then pulling out to smear more juices before resuming the maddeningly slow circling.

Waiting for his invasion, she was on the verge of climax, panting breathlessly. But instead of his shaft, he used three fingers to stretch her wide.

Tessa knew he was doing what he thought was best to prepare her, but fingers weren't what she needed.

"I want you inside me when I come."

As he lifted his head from her breast and looked up at her, Jackson's conflicting emotions were all over his face. There was lust, and need, and love, but also fear. He didn't want to hurt her, to trigger a panic attack, and she didn't know how to reassure him that it wasn't going to happen.

Cupping his cheeks, she held his gaze as she gave it her best. "Right now, there is nothing in the world I want more than for you to fill me so completely that I wouldn't know where you end and I begin. Make us one, Jackson, I don't want to wait another second."

She watched as the last of his fears dissipated from his eyes, and all that was left was love and lust.

That was how she wanted him to look at her for the rest of their lives. No longer as the broken doll who had to be handled with care, but a woman who loved him and lusted after him.

A true partner, not a fix-up project.

Jackson fisted his shaft and guided it to her entrance, but he didn't immediately push in, as she'd expected. Rubbing the velvety smooth hard length over her slit, he coated it in her juices, teasing her for a few moments longer before pushing in with just the very tip.

There was no panic, just an intense craving for more.

His eyes were locked on her face as he pushed another inch in.

It was a tight fit, but delightfully so. Her own eyes hooded with desire, she let out a moan that was a mix of pleasure and relief.

Finally, Jackson was inside her, and it felt perfect.

Encouraged by her moan, he pushed a little deeper and stopped again.

Was she half full or half empty?

Tessa lifted her butt off the mattress, impaling herself on another couple of inches before he stopped her with a hand on her chest, pushing her back down. "Patience, kitten."

"I'm all out." She clutched at his shoulders, letting him feel her short nails.

That broke the last of Jackson's resistance, and he surged all the way in, filling her completely.

For long moments, they just clung to each other, savoring the unbelievable feeling of connection, of oneness. It was more than desire, more than love, it was magical.

"I love you so much," Jackson breathed.

He was so tall that lying down they couldn't be face to face unless he folded himself. As it was, her face was pressed against his pecs. Tessa put her lips on them, kissing, licking, nipping, she couldn't get enough of him.

Bracing on his forearms, he lifted his torso and looked down at where they were joined. Moving with shallow thrusts, he watched himself going in and out of her, his expression one of awe.

His blue eyes shining with inner light and his fangs long and pointy, Jackson would've looked terrifying to anyone but her.

To Tessa, he was just breathtakingly beautiful. There was nothing about him that she feared. She loved everything, accepted everything, and would have not changed a single thing about him.

There was only one of him in the world, and he was hers.

As Tessa spread her legs wider, taking more of him inside, Jackson lifted his head and dipped it again to kiss her, the force and tempo of his thrusts increasing.

His control was admirable.

Still holding back, he was increasing the ferocity in small increments instead of going all out, making sure not to overwhelm her. His reserve was sweet and considerate, but at the same time, it implied that he still saw her as a broken doll.

Tessa felt a tinge of disappointment, but then pushed it away. It might have had nothing to do with her past. After all, she was still a fragile human, while he was a super strong immortal who could easily break her if he weren't careful.

She bucked into him, meeting every thrust with one of her own and spurring him on.

He threw her a wicked grin before adding a slight spin to his forward thrusts that had him rubbing against an ultra-sensitive spot inside her.

"Oh, my, God, oh, oh!" she exclaimed as her climax started building up momentum at a ferocious pace. Reaching the point of no return, she let it wash over her in wave after wave of electrical currents that were shocking in their intensity.

As her inner walls clamped around his shaft, Jackson emitted a feral snarl, and his restraint snapped. His hard pounding wringing another orgasm out of her, he erupted inside her, pouring his essence into her for long moments until she was overflowing with it.

But that wasn't the end of it. Just when she thought he couldn't have any more in him, Jackson cupped her head, tilted it sideways, and with a hiss struck her throat.

A split second of pain, and then unimaginable bliss.

# 39

# KIAN

Up on the roof of his keep, Kian awaited his mother's arrival with Syssi at his side.

He was grateful. Syssi could've easily wriggled out of having to welcome his mother, but she hadn't, taking the day off and in doing so forcing Amanda to do the same.

After all, the daughter could do no less than the daughter-in-law.

His sister, however, was late as usual. Not much of a welcoming committee if she arrived after Annani had landed.

"Are you cold?" Kian glanced down at Syssi who huddled close to him.

She wrapped her arms around his middle and pressed her cheek to his chest. "A little. But mostly I'm tired. Someone didn't let me sleep much last night."

He smirked. "Guilty as charged." In preparation for his mother's impending visit, Kian had been in desperate need of lowering his stress levels a notch, and there was nothing that could do it better and faster than a night of wild sex with his wife. "Do you want to go back inside? I'll tell Annani that you are waiting to welcome her in the penthouse. You could lie down for a few minutes. Fates know you will not get a chance once she is here."

His mother was a very demanding lady and an attention-hogger. He was so glad he had Syssi to take some of the burden of dealing with her off his shoulders.

Annani would've driven him crazy. She still might.

"I think I hear the chopper," Syssi said.

"I'll call Amanda and tell her to hurry up."

"Tell her to bring me a jacket."

He nodded and speed-dialed his sister. "The chopper is landing. You better hurry up. And bring Syssi a jacket, she is cold."

"I'll be right there."

Kian ended the call and put the phone back in his pocket.

A few moments later, Amanda joined them on the roof and handed Syssi a leather coat.

"What is it?" Syssi put it on. The coat was black, shiny, and long, reaching down to her calves. "I feel like I'm in *The Matrix* movie and should have machine guns under here."

Amanda smirked. "Are you warm?"

"Yes, thank you."

"I figured you were cold all over and this is the only long coat I own."

Kian lifted a brow. "I find that hard to believe."

Amanda crossed her arms over her chest. "I donated the rest to charity."

That explained it. "What happened? Long coats been out of fashion for the last couple of days?"

"The past year. I don't keep anything for longer than that."

Well, at least she was donating all of it to charity. It was probably selling well in second-hand stores specializing in fine clothing and bringing in good revenue to whatever charity Amanda had chosen.

"Here it is." Syssi pointed to the black dot getting larger as it got closer.

Kian took in a long breath and prayed for patience.

When the chopper landed, Kri exited first, then offered her hand to Annani to help her down.

Nimble as ever, his mother took Kri's hand, but then jumped down in a flurry of silk as the bottom of her midnight blue dress was caught in the wind created by the chopper's slowing blades.

Syssi leaned closer. "No matter how many times I see her, I can't help my reaction to her beauty. It's literally breathtaking."

"She is a goddess," Kian said. No further comment was needed. Her kind had been perfect in every way. Physically, at least. According to Annani, all the gods had been incredibly beautiful, though not all of them had been sane, or kind.

"That makes her even more awe-inspiring. It's easier to think of her as just an incredibly beautiful woman."

"Come on, we need to meet her halfway, or she'll be offended." With his hand on the small of her back, he propelled Syssi toward Annani.

As they reached her, Syssi bowed her head. "Clan Mother, it's an honor to receive you."

"Oh, none of that, child. Come here." She opened her arms, and Syssi walked into the embrace. "To you, I am just Annani." She kissed Syssi on the cheek and then on the other one. "If you keep up that Clan Mother nonsense, I will start calling you she who is my son's mate."

Syssi laughed, which had been Annani's goal.

His mother let go of her daughter-in-law to embrace Amanda next. "You look lovely as ever, my sweet little Mindi."

"You too, Ninni." *Little Mindi* had to bend considerably to align herself with their petite mother.

When his turn came around, Kian knelt in front of the goddess, in part to save them both from body acrobatics, and in part because it pleased her. The more pleased Annani was, the less likely she was to pester him.

"Welcome, Mother. Thank you for coming to spend time with Phoenix. We will all worry less once this baby transitions."

Annani smiled and cupped his cheeks, then kissed his forehead. "She is not the only reason I am here. I want to spend time with the rest of my family as well."

He rose to his feet, towering over her physically, and yet feeling dwarfed by her power. "Let's get you settled. This time, you're staying with Syssi and me."

"Thank you. I am going to have the best time."

Annani threaded one arm through Syssi's and the other through Amanda's, and the three walked into the vestibule. Behind them, Annani's two Odus followed, each carrying two large pieces of luggage.

That was a worrisome sight.

How long was she planning on staying that she'd brought so much clothing with her?

Kian raked his fingers through his hair and sighed, then joined the procession back to his and Syssi's penthouse.

Okidu had a welcome feast prepared for the immediate family, which besides Kian and Syssi, included Amanda and Dalhu, Andrew and Nathalie and their little daughter.

Thank the merciful Fates for that cute baby.

As soon as Annani saw Phoenix, she squealed with happiness and forgot about everyone and everything.

"Who is this beautiful little girl?" She took her from Andrew's arms.

Phoenix regarded Annani with curious eyes, then reached for her red hair, clutched a handful, and pulled.

Nathalie jumped up to help the goddess, but Annani would have none of that. "I am used to the little ones pulling on my hair. The color fascinates them."

Annani refused to give the baby back, eating dinner with one hand while holding Phoenix with the other. Andrew and Nathalie looked nervous. As small and as charming as Annani was, she was also intimidating.

But the baby seemed unfazed by the powerful vibe emanating from the woman holding her. Kian regarded it as a good sign. That little girl would grow up into a strong woman who wouldn't be easy to intimidate.

When they were done, Nathalie cleared her throat. "May I ask you a question, Clan Mother?"

"Of course."

"How long does Phoenix need to spend in your presence to turn?"

Annani smiled at the baby and offered her a finger to chew on. "Every child is different. For some, it takes a few days, for others, weeks."

Everyone at the table accepted her statement at face value. Only Kian knew the truth his mother and older sister were hiding. It wasn't the goddess's magnificent presence that turned the little girls, it was her blood. The same blood that had saved Syssi's life during her transition.

With Andrew and Nathalie constantly hovering over their daughter, the trick would be to get the child alone with Annani long enough for her to administer the tiny transfusion.

## 40

# ANANDUR

Anandur put the case of Snake's Venom on the conference table and started pulling out the beers he'd chilled overnight in preparation for Uisdean and Niall's welcome party. It wasn't every day that two new Guardians, or rather old ones, came back to fortify the force.

The seven would become nine.

"Are we having a party?" Kian said as he walked in.

"Yes, we are. I'm doing my part in making Uisdean and Niall feel at home."

Kian clapped his back. "Good. Then you won't mind being in charge of their training."

Great. As the saying went, no good deed went unpunished.

"I'm already doing double shift rotations. How am I supposed to find time to train them?"

"Being in charge doesn't mean you need to do everything yourself. It means you test them, determine what they need to work on, and then make a schedule. These two are experienced fighters, they don't need babysitting while running on the treadmill or practicing in the shooting range."

"What about hand to hand?"

Kian lifted a brow. "Do you want to assign that part to someone else?"

"No. I'll do it."

"That's what I thought."

As the champion of that form of fighting, Anandur considered it his duty to refresh these old timers' skills. Besides, they needed a reminder who was boss lest they'd forgotten.

"Good evening, gentlemen." Arwel walked into the conference room carrying four bottles of Chivas, and put them on the table next to the beers.

Kian shook his head. "You really want to get everyone drunk, don't you?"

Arwel grinned. "I'm aiming for joyous. That's not enough booze to get nine Guardians and one Regent drunk."

"Too bad," Kri said as she put a covered tray on the table. "I was hoping everyone would be too drunk to care that I burned the pizza pockets."

It took a special talent to burn ready-made snacks, but then Kri had never pretended to know her way around the kitchen. He'd been hoping Michael would do it, but apparently the kid had been busy.

Anandur lifted the lid and took one out, then popped it into his mouth. It was a little burned and crusty but still edible. "It's good. Don't worry about it."

Looking at the burned pockets with disdain, Kri shook her head. "I hope Niall and Uisdean are as easy to please as you are."

"We've eaten worse." Anandur grimaced.

"When are they going to get here?" Kri asked.

Kian glanced at his watch. "Niall called over an hour ago to let me know they had landed. Luggage, customs, and immigration should take an hour or so, and then they still have to battle the traffic."

Anandur frowned. Kian's time was too valuable to waste waiting for the two Guardians to arrive. "You're early."

"Yeah. A good excuse to leave the other welcoming party."

Aha, Kian was hiding from his mother. "I assume her Highness's visit is to remain confidential?"

"I prefer it this way. Thankfully there are no weddings for her to preside over so I can sleep at night without worrying about too many people knowing she is here. We can't provide adequate protection for her. It maddens me to be in this situation. I wish we had an army of Guardians."

"Who would be scratching their balls with nothing to do."

"True, but how is it different from any army during peacetime? The USA is not sending all of its soldiers into early retirement because there is no war to fight at the moment. They train."

Anandur scratched his beard. "Yeah. It's even true for the Doomers. They maintain a huge force, but they haven't participated actively in any of the recent wars. They send a few units here and there, but most of the force stays home."

"Exactly. But we can't manage to build up a force despite all of our efforts. I had to promise the moon to get two additional Guardians."

"What did you offer them?"

Kian's lips twisted into a grimace. "A huge recruitment bonus and a month's paid vacation a year."

Anandur whistled. "Are the rest of us getting the same deal?"

"Do I have any other choice?"

Kian would have a mutiny on his hands if he didn't treat them all equally. But if each took a month off, they would actually have fewer Guardians on duty at each given time than without the two new ones, and with the two weeks' vacation they were getting currently.

"How does that math work for you?"

"It doesn't. But I hope more Guardians will take the bait." Kian grabbed a beer, popped the cap, and taking a long swig, he then walked over to his desk and booted up his computer.

Bhathian and Yamanu joined them a few minutes later, the first one with the box of pastries he'd picked up from Jackson, the second with a huge bag of trail mix. Not a bad spread for an impromptu party Anandur had decided on a couple of hours ago.

Onegus arrived last and took a seat across from Kian's desk. "How is our esteemed Clan Mother doing?" he asked.

Kian glanced up. "Harping on at me to take a vacation."

Onegus inclined his head. "Wise as always."

"Oh, yeah? Do you want to take over for me while I'm gone?"

"I can give it a try."

Kian dismissed him with a wave of his hand. "Right."

Anandur walked over, leaned his butt against the desk and crossed his arms over his chest. "I wouldn't mind a short visit to our resort in Hawaii and to say hi to Lana in person. We can depart Thursday morning and return Sunday night. Just a long weekend."

Kian drummed his fingers on the desk. "I like your idea. I can do a tour of the property, and if needed I could commandeer an office and work from there. Annani will be happy I'm vacationing, while I can still put in the work."

Anandur offered a silent prayer of thanks to the Fates. With Kian away from the keep, he wouldn't have to worry about the boss discovering that Brundar was spending his recovery time in his human girlfriend's apartment.

Besides, a trip to Hawaii, even as Kian's bodyguard, was still a trip to Hawaii. He rubbed his hands. "I can't wait. Are we going surfing?"

"You can surf. Syssi and I will watch while sipping tropical drinks on the beach."

"Sounds good."

Kian frowned. "But if I take you with me, who is going to be in charge of Uisdean and Niall's training?"

Onegus lifted a finger. "I'll do it. Until Anandur comes back, that is. The important thing here is to make the Clan Mother happy. Am I right?"

Kian smirked. "Yes, you are. And it's also a perfect opportunity to convince her that I don't need more than one bodyguard. I'll make it a condition for taking the fucking vacation. I can't take two Guardians away from the keep, especially not during her visit."

Onegus grinned. "Every cloud has a silver lining, eh?"

Anandur clapped the chief Guardian's back. "I hope there are no clouds where we're going."

## 41

# CALLIE

*Life is good*, Callie thought as she cracked another egg into the bowl. With the absence of the constant fear, she finally felt free. Brundar's guy had hacked into the university's computers again and changed her name back to Calypso, and Meyers instead of Davidson.

She'd also applied for a new driver's license under her maiden name.

It bothered her that there was no mention in the news about Shawn's *suicide*. Not only because she couldn't call her father and her best friend to let them know she was no longer in danger, but because it was awful if Shawn's body was still rotting in that house.

"Brundar, can you call Andrew again and ask him if there is any news about Shawn?"

"I don't want to call him at work. I'll do it when I know he is home." He walked over to her and wrapped himself around her back. "What are you making?"

"A mushroom omelet." She looked at him over her shoulder. "Where are your crutches?"

"I don't need them anymore."

Callie put the spatula down and turned around in his arms. "Did you ask Bridget if it's okay?"

"Yes."

"And?"

"She approved."

"That's a cause for celebration." Callie threw her arms around Brundar's neck and kissed him long and hard.

"Your omelet is burning," he said when she let go of his mouth.

"Oh, crap." Callie grabbed the pan by the handle and moved it away from the burner. "I'll make a new one."

Brundar reached behind her and took the pan. "I'll eat it."

"No way. I'm making a new one."

She tried to take it away from him, but he lifted the pan up so she couldn't reach.

"I'll eat this one and the new one you make."

The guy would eat anything. Except for seafood, that was. "Fine."

Brundar took out a plate and dropped the slightly charred omelet onto it, then returned the pan to the stove.

Leaning against the counter, he folded the omelet in half and ate it as if it was a taco.

"You must be hungry."

He finished chewing the last bite and wiped his hands and mouth with a paper towel. "I need to feed this body to heal."

Callie still couldn't wrap her head around his miraculous recovery. She'd searched the Internet for revolutionary knee reconstructive surgery techniques, and had even found a few articles, but none promised new knees in two weeks.

Maybe Bridget had used something experimental that was not approved for publication yet. Whatever it was, a new procedure or marvelous genetics, Callie was grateful for it. Brundar's knees had healed, and he was walking without crutches.

"Let's invite your family over to celebrate. Syssi, Amanda, Bridget, and Anandur." She cracked several more eggs into the mixing bowl.

Brundar groaned. "Why? I'd rather celebrate just with you."

"I know. But you need to be more social. We are talking close family, not a bunch of strangers."

"I don't know if Syssi would want to come without Kian, but we can't invite him because he doesn't know I'm staying here, and we want to keep it that way. Amanda may want to come with her mate, though."

Again with the mate thing. Must be Scottish slang for significant other. The same as it was slang for friend or buddy for the English and the Australians.

"Then let's invite him too." Callie poured the mixture into the pan.

"On second thought, scratch that. He is not comfortable with new people."

She snorted. "Must be hell for him to live with an extrovert like Amanda. What does he do when she invites people over, hide in the bedroom?"

Brundar shrugged. "I don't know. She never invited me."

Callie felt offended on Brundar's behalf. How come he'd never been invited to his cousin's place?

"Is there a reason for that? Did you have a falling out?" She folded the omelet over the mushroom and onions mixture and transferred it to a plate.

"No. I don't think she invites people over that often. And we are not close."

"Here you go." She handed Brundar the second plate. "Close enough for her to come visit you when you got injured."

Brundar snorted. "That's because she is nosy and wanted to check you out."

Callie poured the rest of the mixture into a pan for another omelet. "I hope I passed."

"With flying colors."

She glanced at him over her shoulder. "How do you know, did she say something to you?"

"No, but the way all four of you were chatting away and then hugging and kissing, it looked like you were old friends."

It was true. Callie wasn't socially awkward and befriended people easily, but not as easily as she had those three. For some reason, she'd felt comfortable with these women almost like she did with Dawn, whom she'd known for years.

"That's another reason to invite them over." She put the omelet on a plate and joined Brundar at the counter.

"I see that I can't talk you out of this."

"Nope."

"It will have to be today, though. Anandur has rotation tomorrow, and the day after that he is off to vacation with Syssi and Kian. Theirs, not his. He is going as the bodyguard."

If Brundar thought to dissuade her from inviting his family for dinner by not giving her enough time to prepare, he had another thing coming. "Make the calls and tell me who is coming and who is not. I can have everything ready by five."

Brundar cocked a brow. "And what about work?"

She leaned and kissed his cheek, then whispered in his ear, "Don't tell anyone, but I'm sleeping with the boss. I can take a day off whenever I want."

That got a chuckle out of him. "What do I tell Franco when he asks why you are not coming in tonight?"

Callie pretended to think it over. "You can tell him that you're giving your girlfriend the night off."

## 42

# BRUNDAR

"It's a shame Syssi and Amanda couldn't come." Calypso cut an avocado in half and scooped the flesh out with a spoon.

"Syssi is packing for their trip to Hawaii, and Amanda didn't want to leave Dalhu alone at home."

Calypso reached for the next avocado. "She could've come with him. Is he as scary as Kian?"

Brundar chuckled. "That depends on what you find scary. Dalhu is even bigger than Anandur, and he lacks my brother's sunny disposition."

Callie started mashing the avocado flesh she'd scooped out with a fork. "Amanda is tall. I figured her guy would be tall too. Is that why she doesn't want him to come? She thinks he'll intimidate me?"

"No."

"Then why?"

"As I told you, Kian doesn't know that I'm not staying at the keep. Amanda and Syssi are okay with keeping my secret. They think of it as a game. The thing is, if Kian finds out, he will have no choice but to forgive them because one is his wife and the other his sister. Dalhu is not in the same position."

"I see. So Amanda prefers not to get him involved."

"That's right."

Crouching down, she disappeared behind the counter to reach into one of the bottom cabinets, then reappeared with a large cutting board in hand. "To tell you the truth, I'm relieved. I didn't have time to prepare anything elaborate, and I would've felt bad about serving fajitas to Syssi and Amanda. Especially Amanda. She seems so fancy. Next time, when I have a few days to plan, I can really wow them with my culinary skills."

There wasn't going to be a next time.

In a few days, he would be back at work and have a talk with the few people who knew about Calypso.

He would keep her for as long as he could, but he knew better than to delude himself that it would last more than a few weeks, or maybe a few months if he were incredibly lucky.

The less talk there was about Calypso, the longer his time with her could be. Amanda and Syssi and Bridget needed to pretend that they had never met her. Perhaps he should thrall her to forget them. Her memory of Anandur coming to their rescue was too traumatic to suppress, but he trusted Anandur to keep his mouth shut and act as if he knew nothing if asked.

Amanda was pretty good at that too. But if confronted, Bridget and Syssi would spill the beans.

"I'll set the table," he offered.

Calypso lifted a brow. "Do you know how?"

"I think I can manage." He might have had zero skill in the kitchen, but he could manage a tablecloth and four place settings.

An hour later, Brundar welcomed their two guests and showed them to the table.

"It smells good," Anandur said, clapping Brundar on the back, then headed to the kitchen to pull Calypso into a brotherly hug, which was how Brundar forced himself to think about it to stop the growl building up in his chest from coming out of his mouth.

"Hello, Brundar." Bridget entered. "Hi, Callie." She waved at Calypso then turned back to him. "I see you're moving around without the crutches. Any pain?"

"Only when I bend my knees."

Bridget nodded. "Let me take a look."

Sitting on the couch, he lifted a leg and propped it on the coffee table. Bridget took hold of his ankle with one hand and put the other one on his thigh, a little above his knee.

"I'm going to bend your leg, and you need to tell me when it starts to hurt." She eyed him with a stern expression on her face. "And don't try to be macho about it and pretend like you don't feel any pain. I need to know exactly when it becomes uncomfortable."

After checking both knees, Bridget lowered his feet to the floor. "You're doing very well. I want you to exercise bending your legs a few times every hour. This will speed up your recovery." She leaned closer and whispered, "If you were a human, I would have said to do it once a day, but at the rate you're healing, it needs to be done every hour."

Brundar cast a sidelong glance at Calypso. Her frown indicated that she'd seen Bridget whisper in his ear, and she didn't like it one bit.

Damnation. Later, she would put him through one hell of an interrogation. In fact, once the dinner was done, she would probably have a long list of things to ask him about. Bridget and Anandur would have to be very careful with what they said around her.

"Just don't say anything you're not supposed to," he whispered to Bridget. "Calypso is very bright. There isn't much that escapes her notice."

Bridget nodded, then crossed her arms over her chest. "I'm your doctor, Brundar," she said loud enough for Calypso to hear. "Whatever you choose to share with others is your prerogative. My job is to keep your health issues confidential." She winked at him.

A good coverup, but he expected many more would be needed before this get-together was over.

"Dinner is served. To the table, everyone," Calypso called out.

Anandur took a seat and rubbed his hands. "I hope you made enough to feed this." He waved over his middle.

"Don't worry. I made enough to satisfy even your and Brundar's appetites."

"Is that a challenge?"

Calypso laughed. "I think Bridget and I should load our plates first. Otherwise you boys are not going to leave us anything to eat."

As dinner progressed, Brundar enjoyed watching Calypso chatting with Anandur and Bridget and laughing at Anandur's jokes. Admittedly, spending time with his family wasn't as bad as he'd expected. His contribution to the conversation was limited to a few nods and grunts, but Calypso was so animated and happy that nothing more was needed to keep the lively atmosphere going.

Unfortunately, as pleasant as this evening was, it would probably be the last. Brundar would eventually have to choose between his family and Calypso.

Coexistence was impossible.

He knew better than most that humans and immortals didn't mix. The two could coexist only if the immortals kept to themselves and didn't befriend humans. Romantic entanglements were not the only kind of human and immortal interactions that were fraught with danger.

Brundar had once thought he could be friends with a human. The results had been disastrous not only for him but for his clan as well.

Knowing that as soon as the villagers discovered the bodies, they would come after their number one suspect—their strange neighbors—his family had had to pack up and run.

Back then, the clan had been much smaller, poorer, and scattered throughout the countryside. Escaping in the middle of the night, they had left behind everything they had worked so hard for, with only the clothes on their backs and the few provisions they could amass on such short notice.

After that incident, Annani had gathered the clan, announcing that they were all going to live together in one defensible location, far away from the humans.

It had taken them decades of back-breaking work and all of their combined resources to build their Scottish fortress. The Scottish Highlands were freezing cold in the winter, and living in temporary shelters while every able-bodied male and female worked on building the fortress had been miserable.

Even the food had been scarce.

One stupid mistake had cost the clan decades of misery. How they had managed to forget and forgive Brundar was beyond him. Other than Anandur, none of them knew what had been done to him. All Anandur had said was that his little brother had been attacked and Anandur had killed his assailants. The violation Brundar had suffered remained a secret he and Anandur were going to take with them to their eventual graves.

## 43

## CALLIE

"I had fun," Callie said after Anandur and Bridget had left.

Brundar nodded.

He hadn't said much throughout dinner, but while he'd looked as if he was enjoying himself at the start of the evening, a gloom had settled over him toward the end.

Maybe he was in pain.

The guy had pushed himself too hard on his first day of walking without crutches. He should've taken it easy as Bridget had told him to.

Typical man. Less than two weeks after having his knees blown to pieces, he couldn't wait to prove that he was back to his old self.

Freaking Doctor Bridget was a miracle worker. Or a witch.

Brundar and his family were all a bit strange, but as far as she could trust her judgment, they were good people. So what if sometimes it had seemed as if there were two separate conversations going on at the table, one of which she hadn't been privy to. All families had secrets, some more than others.

Brundar came up behind her and wrapped his arms around her. "Andrew texted me while we were having dinner, but I didn't want to spoil the mood."

Callie stilled. "Shawn's body has been found?"

"Yes. Apparently, he was found a week ago. But because it was a clear case of suicide, it didn't make it to the news."

"How did Andrew find out?"

"He checked the morgue records."

"I see," she whispered. "I feel sorry for Shawn's family. I don't think they knew he was insane."

"You should call your father."

"Yeah, I should." Shawn's parents had probably contacted Donald looking for her. Hopefully, he hadn't told them anything.

Callie left the dirty dishes in the sink and dried her hands with a paper towel. "I'll finish these later."

"I'll do it. Make the call."

"Thanks."

Callie walked to the bedroom on shaky legs and retrieved her phone from her purse. Sitting on the bed, she wondered what exactly she was supposed to say. With Shawn's suicide not making it into the news, how was she supposed to know that he was dead?

Should she pretend she was calling to let them know she was okay and wait for her dad to break the news to her?

That was probably the only way.

Her dad, who'd always been happy to let Iris get the phone, answered on the first ring as if he was sitting and waiting for her call. "Hello?"

"Hi, Daddy."

He released a breath with an audible whoosh. "Callie, thank God you called. I've been so worried."

"I'm fine. Sorry I didn't call before."

"That's okay. You had a good reason. Did you hear about Shawn?"

Callie hated to lie to her father, but there was no other way. "No, is it anything that I need to worry about?"

"Not anymore. He committed suicide."

"Oh, my God."

"Good riddance, that's what I have to say."

Amen to that. "Did he leave a note?"

"No, but they found the divorce papers on the floor, right under where he hung himself."

Callie sighed. "I feel so sorry for his parents."

"Don't. They had some choice words to say about you."

"I hope you didn't tell them what I've told you."

"I'm not a heartless bastard. They were out of their minds with grief. I wasn't going to tarnish the memory of their son. I just told them the regular crap about fifty percent of marriages ending in divorce. I also said that you were devastated by it, and that was why you left on a long trip to meditate over the breakup, leaving your phone behind."

"Thank you. I appreciate it. I don't think I could've gone to the funeral."

"I understand. So now that the coast is clear, when are we going to see you?"

"I'll come when the baby is born. I just started a new job, and I don't want to ask for time off right away."

"Sweetheart, your baby brother was born three weeks ago."

Callie gasped. It was as if ever since she'd fled Shawn, she'd existed in some parallel universe, imagining that the life she'd left behind remained frozen in the same time frame she'd last remembered.

"Oh, my God! How is he? How is Iris?"

"They are both fine. Justin was born a healthy seven pounds and seven ounces." Her dad sounded proud. And happy.

She hadn't heard that upbeat tone in his voice for as long as she could remember.

"Justin. I like it. I wish I could hop on a plane and come see him right away. You need to warn him that his big sister is coming to kiss him all over."

Her dad chuckled. "Don't do anything rash just because you're excited about the baby, and don't jeopardize your new job to come see him. Right now he doesn't do much besides sleeping, eating, and pooping. Come when the time is right for you."

"I'll see what I can do. I'll talk to my boss."

"Don't if you think it will upset him. Or is it a her? And what kind of job is it?"

"I serve drinks at a nightclub that is owned by two very nice guys." Callie rolled her eyes as she waited for her father to disapprove of her new job.

"Do you like it there? Are the tips good?"

"Excellent. And I like the people I work with. We are like one big happy family."

"I'm glad. What about school?"

"I start in the fall."

"I'm so happy to hear that." Her father sighed. "I feel like the rainbow has finally come out after years upon years of nothing but dark clouds."

Callie felt tears well in the corners of her eyes. "Kiss Iris and Justin for me."

"I will. Take care of yourself."

Ending the call, Callie flopped down on the bed and closed her eyes for a moment, opening them when she heard Brundar enter the room.

"Here, take this," he said, handing her a tall glass.

She sat back up. "What's in it?"

"Your favorite cocktail. I think a toast is in order." He lifted his own glass.

A drink was exactly what she needed. "What are we toasting?"

"New beginnings."

## 44

## BRUNDAR

"To new beginnings." Calypso clinked Brundar's glass and took a long sip. "You made it exactly how I like it. Thank you."

He nodded. "Congratulations on your new brother."

"Thanks. I would've asked you how you knew, but I'm not going to, Mr. Bat Ears."

Her scent was a mixture of happiness and anxiety. The happiness was because of the baby, but why the anxiety?

"How are you feeling, Calypso, everything okay?"

"Happy, relieved, excited about the future but also sad." She touched a hand to her stomach. "I feel uncomfortable here. I know it's because of Shawn and his death and his funeral and his poor parents, and I also know that what happened wasn't my fault, but I still feel guilty. So horribly guilty. If he'd never met me, he wouldn't be dead now."

"True. He would've most likely been tormenting some other woman. Someone who didn't have friends like my brother and me to rescue her. With no one to stop him, he would have had a lot of years to make someone else's life a living hell."

Calypso's hand moved from her stomach to her heart. "When you put it like that, it almost sounds as if I should feel lucky and not guilty. Maybe I was put in Shawn's path and then yours for a reason. Maybe Fate maneuvered us into place so we could take him out and save his next victim."

The bitter undertone had dissipated from her scent, leaving behind only the familiar scents of sweetness and sunshine that Brundar associated with Calypso.

"Feeling better?" he asked even though he knew the answer.

"Much. What about you? You seemed a little down toward the end of dinner. Are you in pain? Are your knees bothering you?"

Brundar took the glass from her hand and put it on the nightstand. "Let's celebrate life the way it should be celebrated." Pushing her back on the bed, he pulled down her sexy black dress. Underneath, Calypso had her beautiful breasts bound in that torture device he'd told her not to wear.

"Tsk, tsk. You disobeyed me." He reached around her back and unclasped the bra. "I told you I never want to see you wearing this painful contraption again." He tossed it behind him.

Calypso's scent became musky with her nascent arousal. "I couldn't entertain your brother and Bridget braless, and this is the only strapless one I have. Nothing else works with this dress."

"Then it's time you went shopping, sweetling."

"Yes, sir." She saluted.

He gently massaged the bra's angry red compression lines. "Marring your perfect skin like this is a punishable offense."

Calypso's arousal intensified. "Are you going to spank me?" She sounded breathy and excited.

"I could take you over my knee at last. But I have other ideas." He glanced at the melting ice cubes in the glass on the nightstand. But first things first, he needed to blindfold her before his own arousal pushed his alienness to the surface.

In one swift move, he divested her of her panties and lifted Calypso up to reposition her in the center of the bed.

"You shouldn't lift heavy things. It's too much strain on your knees."

"I didn't lift anything heavy." He pulled the silk scarf from the drawer.

Calypso lifted her head without him having to ask her to, holding it up until he was done tying the blindfold over her eyes.

"I love it and hate it at the same time." She dropped her head on the pillow. "I love how every sensation is amplified by the lack of sight, but I hate not seeing you. I've never seen you truly aroused."

"It's not a pretty sight. I drool," he said to make her laugh, which was so unlike him. Brundar didn't know what had possessed him to do it.

But it worked. Calypso giggled. "No way. I know you don't."

He pulled out the stockings and tied them to the four corners of the bed. "I do. I can't help it. You're so drool-worthy. Whenever I see you naked, my tongue lolls out like a dog's. A visual not at all conducive to your arousal." He secured her left wrist with the stocking, then moved to the right.

She cooperated beautifully, stretching her arms and legs, spread-eagled for him. "Do you really? Because I can't hear you panting."

Brundar leaned over her and kissed her lips. "You're going to hear me panting very soon." He nipped those perfect puffy pillows. "When I'm buried deep inside you."

Calypso was stunning all over, but her lips were his favorite. No, that wasn't true, her green eyes were, especially when they were smiling. But the lips were a very close second.

Her perky nipples were third.

Dipping his head, he took one into his mouth, sucking it in and licking round and round, then repeated the same on her other side while reaching for the ice cubes.

He pulled one out and touched it to the nipple he'd just finished warming up with his mouth.

Calypso hissed and arched her back. "That's cold. You're mean."

He moved the ice cube to her other breast and took the chilled nipple into his mouth. Going back and forth, Brundar fell into a predictable rhythm, letting Calypso learn the sequence and relax into the contrasting sensations.

When the ice cube melted, he pulled another one out of the glass and slowly trailed it down her belly until he reached the juncture of her thighs. Calypso hissed again, but then sighed with pleasure as his tongue replaced the ice.

"Oh, that's much better."

He replaced his hot tongue with the cold ice, then his tongue again, lapping up the melted water together with her juices, then chilling her again until the ice cube was no more.

Calypso might have hissed and whined, but the powerful scent of her arousal betrayed the pleasure she derived from the torment.

"You like this, sweetling, don't you?" He pushed a finger into her wet heat.

She shook her head, then quickly nodded when he removed his finger. "Don't stop, please."

He chuckled, returning with two and curling them up to touch that sensitive spot that had her arching off the bed as far as her restraints allowed her.

"Beautiful," he whispered as he took his clothes off. "I can never get enough of looking at you." He covered her with his body, his heavy length wedged between her thighs.

Calypso panted, her hips swiveling under him, urging him on. "Don't tease me, Brundar. I need you inside me."

Turned on by her frantic gyrations, he cupped her cheeks and kissed her long and deep. "Poor, baby, I think I've teased you enough." He surged into her.

"Yes." She threw her head back, her arms straining against her bonds which aroused her and frustrated her at the same time.

Brundar knew Calypso wanted to touch him, and the truth was that he wanted that too. He craved her arms around him, her fingers digging into his back and holding him tight, and her nails leaving small moon-shaped gouges on his skin.

It was too late to do anything about it now. Sheathed inside her wet heat, he could do nothing other than move, faster, harder, until he was pounding into her without holding back, mindlessly driven by a primitive urge to claim, to possess, to plant his seed inside her.

As Calypso shouted her climax, Brundar kept going, wringing another one from her. When his own erupted, his guttural groan sounding more animal than human, he clamped his fangs on her neck and bit down.

Calypso climaxed again.

## 45

## TESSA

"Ladies, can I have your attention please." Karen clapped her hands. "Please form a circle around me."

She waited until everyone was in position. "Today, you are going to practice on each other. I'm going to pair you up according to skill, not size. Because what is my motto?" She put a cupped hand to her ear.

"Size doesn't matter!" they all responded—some mumbling in obvious disagreement, and some, like Tessa, shouting it out with conviction.

"That's right," Karen said. "Skill compensates for size." She smirked. "And not only in a fight, eh?"

Again, the responses were mixed.

Karen waved a hand. "Those who disagree haven't experienced real skill yet. When you do, you'll come back here and tell me, Karen, you were right."

Tessa hid her smile. Being small had caused many of her insecurities, but thanks to Jackson and Karen she'd gotten over them. Karen had taught her that she could be a good fighter despite her size, and Jackson found her sexy and desirable even though she was small all over.

And as to what Karen had hinted at not too subtly, Jackson was the whole package. He was both big and skilled. The perfect lover. They had made love three times in the cabin, and two times last night, and each time she'd climaxed, sometimes more than once.

Five sessions of lovemaking, seven or eight orgasms, but only two bites.

Apparently, once a day was the limit on venom bites as far as Jackson was concerned. Though she couldn't understand why. He didn't need to thrall her after biting her, and she wasn't aware that the venom on its own could cause any damage.

It was supposed to be a miraculous elixir, delivering fast healing, euphoria, and a string of orgasms.

She'd wanted to ask Jackson if it was a physical limitation but then decided not to. After the wonderful weekend he'd treated her to, the last thing she wanted was to accidentally hurt his feelings.

Still, she couldn't help wondering if more venom bites would have resulted in a faster transition. Two were probably not enough to trigger it, so there was no reason to worry yet, but Tessa couldn't help but feel the tension mounting.

*It's only Tuesday,* she reminded herself. *Give it at least a week.*

"Tessa, you are with Megan." Karen pulled on both Tessa's and Megan's hands, leading them to where the other pairs were waiting.

When everyone had a partner, Karen waved her hands wide. "Okay, girls, let's spread out. Let's start with the mugger move."

After half an hour, Tessa was sweating buckets, but Megan was in no better shape. In fact, she was panting so hard Tessa was afraid the woman might pass out.

"Let's take a break. I need a drink of water," she said, more for Megan's benefit than her own.

Megan glanced at Karen for approval. The instructor nodded and clapped her hands. "Good work, ladies. Take a five-minute break to hydrate."

The class was divided into two camps. One comprised of those who were serious about self-defense, women who had worked their asses off for the past thirty minutes and looked no better than Tessa and Megan. The other camp, the one Sharon belonged to, joined the class to get in shape or just to hang out with friends, and had barely broken a sweat.

Megan filled two paper cups with water from the cooler and handed one to Tessa. "I thought it would be easy to go up against you. But you're proof that Karen is right and skill trumps size." The woman was in her mid-thirties, heavier than Tessa by at least twenty pounds and half a head taller.

But then Tessa had youth and energy on her side.

Not that she felt very energetic at the moment. Her head was spinning, and she was a little nauseous. Blaming dehydration, Tessa gulped down the water, then refilled the cup and downed it too.

It didn't help. "I need to sit down for a moment." She barely made it to the chairs lined up against one side of the room.

Karen rushed to her. "Feeling dizzy?"

"Yes."

"Put your head down." She pressed on Tessa's back until her head was between her spread knees. "Breathe in, and out, slowly, don't force it. In and out."

Sharon crouched in front of her. "Do you want another cup of water? Do you have a headache? Because I have some Motrin in my purse."

Tessa shook her head, which worsened the dizziness. "I'm fine. Just give me a moment to catch my breath."

"Does she look pale, or am I imagining it?" Sharon asked Karen.

"Don't fuss so much. The girl pushed herself too hard, that's all." The instructor turned her back to Tessa, blocking her from the others' view. "Back to work, ladies. Megan, you're with me."

Thank God for Karen's no-nonsense attitude. A few moments without anyone hovering over her would be golden.

Trying to contain the nausea, Tessa closed her eyes and continued the careful breathing. For a few minutes, it seemed like it was helping, but then a violent twist in her stomach stole her breath and pushed everything out in a geyser of mostly water.

A moment later she blacked out.

"Oh, my God. I'm calling an ambulance." Tessa heard Sharon as if she was talking through a tunnel.

"Calm yourself down, Sharon. It's just puke. My commandos puked all the time after I made them run on the sand for hours. The poor guys couldn't keep up with me, but they sure as hell tried. That's how endurance is built."

As consciousness returned, Tessa found herself lying on the floor with a towel folded under her head. Someone must have cleaned up the vomit, but the smell lingered, bringing the nausea back.

Tessa's stomach contracted again, and she lifted her torso, turning her head sideways, ready to hurl on the floor, when Karen stuck a wad of paper towels under her.

"Just let it all out, girl." Karen held her head up and pushed her hair out of the way. "You'll feel better."

A little stinky liquid was all that she managed to purge.

"Is she pregnant?" Tessa heard one of the women ask.

She couldn't be. Even if she were, she wouldn't be puking a day or two after conceiving. It was either a virus or something she ate.

"I'm calling Eva," Sharon said.

Tessa was too weak to protest. Besides, it might be a good idea for Bhathian to come pick her up. At the moment, walking to the car seemed like mission impossible.

Someone came with a wet towel and gently wiped her face.

"Thank you," she managed feebly, struggling to stay awake.

One by one the women left, with only Karen and Sharon remaining by her side.

"Eva and Bhathian are coming to take you to a doctor," Sharon said.

Tessa knew better than to shake her head. Instead, she lifted her hand. "I want to go home. It's just a stomach flu."

"The doctor will decide that."

"I stink."

"I'm sure you won't be the first stinky patient or the last one the doctor sees."

Ugh, she was too weak to argue, and the temptation to close her eyes and drift away was too powerful to ignore.

She must've dozed off, or maybe she'd blacked out again, because the next time Tessa opened her eyes, she was being carried by a pair of powerful arms. "Bhathian?"

"I'm here, and so is Eva."

"You're going to be fine, sweetheart." Eva took her hand.

"I want to go home," she said as Bhathian laid her down on the back seat of his car.

Eva slid in and lifted Tessa's head to rest on her lap. "We are taking you to see Bridget."

"Why? It's just flu."

"It might be, but I want Bridget to take a look at you. Bhathian called Jackson, and he is going to meet us at the clinic."

"Do you think it can be the transition?"

"I don't know, sweetheart. That's up to Bridget to decide. Now enough talking. Rest."

If she weren't feeling so shitty, Tessa would've smiled. Even at twenty-one she still liked it when Eva treated her like a child.

Being cared for was precious, reassuring. It proved that Tessa wasn't alone, and if Eva had a say in it, she never would be.

## 46

## JACKSON

"I'm leaving." Jackson threw his apron on the counter. "Close up for me."

Vlad cast him a worried glance. "What happened?"

"Tessa is not feeling well. Eva and Bhathian are taking her to Bridget."

Vlad's pale face turned even paler. "Is it, you know, the transition?"

"I don't know." Jackson grabbed his keys and opened the back door. "You'll have to deal with whatever happens in here. I'm not leaving Tessa's side even if the place is on fire. Not until she is well again, that is."

"Don't worry about a thing. Gordon and I will manage. Let us know how Tessa is doing."

Jackson nodded. "Thanks."

It was probably flu. Vomiting wasn't one of the typical symptoms of transition. Bridget had told him about fever and chills, and about passing out, but nothing about an upset stomach and puking.

He stopped at Eva's house to collect the overnight bag Sharon had packed for Tessa, deflected questions about where Bhathian and Eva had taken her, and rushed back to his car.

Twenty minutes later he knocked on the clinic's door and walked in.

"Hi, Jackson. She is over there." Bridget pointed.

"How is she?"

"Waiting for you impatiently. I told her that she can't take a shower without assistance, and she doesn't want anyone's help but yours."

"I meant healthwise."

Bridget shrugged. "I don't think it's anything serious. She has no fever and her blood pressure is stable."

Jackson let out a relieved breath. "So it's not the transition."

"I didn't say that. It might be."

"But you said it usually comes with a fever."

"We have a very small group of transitioned Dormants, and each case was different."

Great. If the clan's doctor didn't have answers, who did?

"I'll go check on Tessa."

The door to her room was ajar, and he knocked on it while pushing it open.

Tessa's eyes brightened. "Jackson, you're here. Did you bring me a change of clothes?"

"Hello, Jackson." Eva got up from the chair she'd been sitting on and gave him a quick hug.

"Hi." He barely spared Eva a half smile.

His entire focus was on Tessa. She looked pale, and the dark circles under her eyes were more pronounced than usual, but she was sitting in bed and smiling at him.

"And here I thought you were happy to see me." He walked over and leaned to kiss her.

She stopped him with a hand to his chest. "I stink of puke. Help me into the shower, will you?"

"Of course." He dropped the overnight bag on the floor.

"I'll leave you two alone and go find Bhathian." Eva made a hasty exit.

Tessa swung her legs over the side of the bed, but Jackson had no intention of letting her walk to the bathroom and scooped her into his arms.

She looked away. "Close your nose. I don't want you to smell me."

"Don't be silly. It's not like I never puked myself. Did I tell you about how Vlad and Gordon and I got drunk at Syssi and Kian's wedding?" He marched into the utilitarian bathroom adjacent to the room and lowered Tessa to the stool inside the open shower.

"I remember you telling me something about it."

Jackson pulled Tessa's exercise shirt over her head. "We stole several bottles of whiskey and hid in one of the underground classrooms." He crouched in front of her and pulled her leggings down. "We missed the whole party while getting shit-faced in there."

Tessa unclasped her bra and threw it on the floor outside the shower.

Jackson helped her get her panties off. "We thought we were so tough and grown up, forcing that vile stuff down our throats to prove we were so cool."

"You don't like whiskey?" she asked.

"I hate it." Jackson kicked off his shoes and removed his socks, then grabbed the handheld and turned the water on.

"You are going to get wet. Take off your clothes."

Good point. "Here, hold this." He handed her the shower head, got rid of his clothes, and got back into the shower with her.

"Damn, I forgot to bring the bag in here. Sharon packed your shampoo and conditioner. I'll be right back." He grabbed a towel, wrapped it around his hips and ducked back into the room.

"That's a good look for you." Bhathian chuckled. "You rock the Egyptian."

Jackson pointed a finger at him. "You didn't see a thing."

"Right. How is Tessa?"

"She seems fine. Just weak."

"Take care of her."

"I'll do my best." Jackson lifted the overnight bag and returned to the bathroom.

Tessa was holding the handheld over her head, letting the water drench her chin-length hair.

Rummaging through the bag, he pulled out her shampoo and conditioner.

"Are you going to wash my hair?"

"Do you want me to?"

She nodded.

Jackson wondered why he'd never thought of doing so before. Taking care of Tessa filled him with a sense of satisfaction, of purpose, he was meant to do that.

Squirting a dollop into his hand, he stood behind her and gently massaged the shampoo into her hair.

Tessa leaned back against him and sighed. "This feels heavenly."

"Tilt your head back, kitten." He took hold of the handheld and rinsed the shampoo out of her hair, then repeated the process before applying conditioner.

Her eyes closed, Tessa sat limply on the stool, letting him soap her and rinse her. By the time he was done, she was almost asleep.

"Hang in there for a few moments longer." Jackson was thankful for his long arms allowing him to reach for the towel without moving away from Tessa. He had a feeling she would fall over the moment he let go.

With the big towel wrapped around her, he lifted her up and carried her to the bed. While they had been in the bathroom, someone had replaced the sheets with fresh ones. He laid Tessa on top of them, then went back for another towel and her overnight bag.

Jackson found a long sleep shirt in the bag and pulled it over Tessa's head, then fitted her limp arms through the sleeves. By the time he tucked the blanket around her, she was fast asleep.

With only his pants back on, he sat on the chair Eva had vacated and watched Tessa sleep. She was so small, so fragile. She seemed bigger when awake. But that was okay. He was there to guard and protect his treasure—small but priceless.

# 47

# KIAN

"I will have another cup of coffee, Okidu," Annani said.

"Of course, Clan Mother." He bowed, then lifted the thermal carafe to refill her cup.

Kian cut another piece of waffle, piled it with strawberries, and popped it in his mouth. He hadn't seen his mother the entire day yesterday, working in his basement office until late at night.

He was trying to spend as little time around her as possible, but that hadn't been the reason for his late-night session in the basement. With the noise levels in his penthouse, working from his home office had been impossible.

Since Annani's visit was kept on a need to know basis, Nathalie had to bring Phoenix to her instead of the goddess going over to Andrew's apartment. Only the penthouse level was fully restricted to its occupants. Even the Guardian floor wasn't forbidden to other clan members. Which meant that his home had been invaded by a baby and her array of baby toys. The question was whether Annani had managed to get Phoenix alone for long enough to administer the transfusion.

The goddess wasn't going home until that mission was accomplished.

Later, when he'd been sure the coast was clear and was about to head home, Kian had gotten a call from Bhathian about Tessa and had gone to pay her a visit. The girl had been asleep, but Jackson had looked so distraught that Kian had stayed with him for an hour or so.

By the time he'd gotten back home, Annani had retired to the guest room.

"How did it go yesterday? Did you have fun with the baby?" he asked.

Annani smiled, her intense eyes growing soft. "She is such a sweet little darling. I got to hold her and play with her for hours. Poor Nathalie hovered like a mother hen, worried I would somehow hurt her daughter as if I had not handled countless generations of babies before her."

Translation, Nathalie hadn't left the baby alone with Annani for a moment.

"It will pass. She'll see that you're capable and that Phoenix is happy in your arms." He turned to Syssi. "Maybe you could suggest an adults-only outing to Nathalie."

Syssi put her coffee cup down. "I don't think Nathalie will agree to leave Phoenix with Annani. Not yet." She glanced at the frowning goddess. "It's not that she doesn't trust you. Phoenix doesn't know you well, and she might get scared if her mother leaves her with you. You're still a stranger to her."

"Maybe in a day or two?" Kian pushed.

Syssi threw him a puzzled look. "Why is it important?"

"For the child to bond with me, I need some alone time with her," Annani said.

It had sounded so well rehearsed, that it was probably what she said to all the new mothers.

"I'll test the waters later today. Maybe I'll suggest visiting Amanda. Nathalie won't mind if it's only a short visit across the vestibule."

"It is a splendid idea," Annani agreed.

Nathalie's reluctance to leave the baby with Annani could be the excuse he needed to cancel the vacation his mother was forcing him to take. "I think Syssi and I need to stay. Nathalie will not feel comfortable alone with you."

Unfortunately, Annani was too smart and too stubborn to fall for that. "Nonsense. She will get used to me, and if need be, I will summon Amanda."

It was a long shot, but Kian had another ace up his sleeve. "I can't leave anyway. Tessa, a young woman we believe is a Dormant, is down at Bridget's clinic, and we don't know if she is transitioning or just sick. I have to stay until we know she is okay. The vacation will have to be postponed."

Annani pinned him with a hard stare. "There is nothing you can do for the girl, Kian. You are not a doctor, and Bridget does not need your assistance taking care of her, so it does not matter if you are here or on vacation when you receive updates about her condition."

Fuck. His mother was the most stubborn, difficult woman on the face of the earth. Hell, probably in the entire known universe.

He crossed his arms over his chest. "I'll be too worried to enjoy my vacation."

Annani looked down her nose at him. "You have nothing to worry about while I am here. I will give the girl my blessing to ensure her safe transition."

Checkmate. Kian had lost, but he was going to try one last thing. Annani didn't like leaving her sanctuary for too long. "Will you stay until we are back?"

She nodded. "Yes. How long are you going to be gone?"

"We are coming back Sunday night," Syssi said.

Annani's lips compressed into a thin line. "I thought I told you the vacation should be a week long at the minimum."

"You did. And I said I can't be gone for so long. This is a compromise." Annani was big on compromising. She would have a hard time arguing that.

For a moment, she just glared at him, then a beautiful smile bloomed on her face, scaring him way more than her glare. "That means you will have to take another vacation soon."

As long as it wasn't now, he was good. "We will discuss it when the time comes."

"You can be sure of that, my son." She took one last sip of her coffee and put her cup down. "I am going out on the terrace to soak up some sun. Call me when Nathalie gets here."

Kian pushed to his feet in deference to his mother and remained standing until her Odu closed the door behind her.

Syssi poured herself another cup from the carafe. "Why are you fighting this vacation so hard? It's only a few days, and we are going to have fun. Hawaii, sandy beaches, me in a bikini..." She waggled her brows.

Kian growled. "Only on our private beach, unless you want to leave a trail of mutilated males in your wake."

Her eyes widened. "We have a private beach?"

"We are not staying at the hotel. I purchased a house with a stretch of beach inaccessible from either side. So yeah, it's private."

"I can't believe it. Did you buy it just for our vacation?"

"No. I got it even before we bought the property for the hotel."

She let out a breath. "Good, because talk about extravagant gestures. Are we taking anyone other than Anandur with us?"

"The pilot, but he is going to stay at the hotel."

"Is the house big?"

"Pretty big. Why?"

She shrugged. "To tell you the truth, I was looking forward to staying at the hotel and getting some human interaction."

Kian raked his fingers through his hair. "I don't like being surrounded by humans. We can go out to restaurants and visit the sights and do all the tourist things people do when they vacation in Hawaii. But I need a place where I can relax and be myself."

Syssi got up and sat on his lap. "Be honest." She smirked. "You don't want to stay in the hotel because you don't want the other guests to hear my moans of ecstasy."

He cupped her head, holding her still as he took her lips. As always, she melted into him, her hands going under his shirt to caress his skin.

"You got me," Kian said when he let her come up for air. "I also don't want anyone calling security because of the ruckus we are making."

The scent of her arousal flaring, she wiggled in his lap. "We are going to have so much fun."

Looking into his wife's beautiful eyes, Kian smiled. Why the hell had he been fighting the idea of a vacation for so long? Four days of just him and Syssi, relaxing, having fun, sounded like paradise.

"I've been a fool for objecting. I can't wait to have you all to myself for four days straight."

"Are we being selfish?" Syssi wrapped her arms around his neck. "Leaving Tessa to her fate and Nathalie to deal with your mother?"

"Yes, we are. But so what? Annani is right. Us staying here will not affect the outcome either way, and tomorrow it will be another thing, then another. It never ends."

"True. We have to make us a priority."

"My woman is smart and beautiful. How the hell did I get so lucky?"

## 48

# LOSHAM

"This was the last one," the doctor said.

Losham pulled out the wad of cash in the amount they had agreed on. "Thank you, Doctor. It was a pleasure doing business with you." He offered the human his hand.

The man shook it. "The pleasure was all mine." He stuffed the four thousand dollars inside his leather briefcase.

"My assistant will take you back."

"Yes, thank you."

The guy followed Rami out.

Implanting his men with trackers was one of Losham's better ideas. In fact, he should recommend that all Doomers be implanted with them. No more defections, and no more loss of men in mysterious circumstances.

In addition to the human, two out of his twelve men were missing.

The human was dead. An obituary had been posted in one of the newspapers. The cause of death hadn't been mentioned, and it didn't matter enough to merit further investigation. The only thing that bothered Losham was the money he'd lost.

His two missing men, however, could have either defected or been captured by Guardians—either imprisoned or dead.

Not knowing what had befallen them was eating at him. Losham almost hoped they had been captured. There was no shame in that. But defecting? That was shameful, more for him than his men because it implied lack of leadership.

Regardless of what had happened to the missing men, his official story would be that they'd been taken out by Guardians.

He could get away with losing two, but no more. That was why he had halted the operation. Now with the implants, he could resume the murders. If another man went missing, he would track the son-of-a-bitch, and if the man had indeed defected, Losham would make an example out of him in the most gruesome way.

Not that any of the men would be stupid enough to try to run now.

Not with the implants in their backs.

His ten remaining warriors were recuperating in the back of the warehouse. It shouldn't take more than a couple of hours for the muscles to close over the trackers and the skin to knot itself back to its pre-operation pristine condition.

While waiting, Losham sat down with his laptop and began a new search for rumors and theories about the murders. Most speculated that it was a madman who believed himself a vampire. Not bad as far as alerting the clan, but not great. He needed two murders to occur at the same time in two separate locations for the authorities and the clan to realize it wasn't the work of a single man. Perhaps he should send half of his remaining crew to San Francisco. Two simultaneous murders, one in Los Angeles, the other in San Francisco, would put an end to the lone madman theory.

The thing was, could he trust them to operate independently?

"Sir?" Gommed knocked on the door to the warehouse's dusty office.

"Come in."

"We have a problem, sir."

"Yes?"

The man turned his bare back to Losham. "Our bodies are rejecting the trackers."

The device projecting from the guy's back was almost completely out.

Losham rose to his feet, gripped the protruding tracker with his fingers, and yanked it the rest of the way out.

Blood trickled down Gommed's back, but the warrior didn't move or utter a sound.

"That's what is happening with the others as well?"

"Yes, sir."

It wasn't as if Losham hadn't considered the possibility. After all, immortal bodies pushed out bullets and blades as they healed. But the dealer who'd sold him the trackers had sworn that they were made from a special material the body didn't recognize as foreign and therefore didn't reject.

Losham should have known not to trust the human. Or maybe it was true for human bodies but not immortal.

He hated having wasted more money for nothing.

Between the cost of the trackers and what he'd paid the doctor, Losham was out another ten thousand dollars or so.

"What's going on?" Rami asked as he walked in.

"Their bodies are rejecting the trackers."

"What are we going to do, sir?"

Indeed.

"Did you thrall the doctor?" he asked Rami.

"Of course. But just to be on the safe side, tomorrow I'll go to his office and do it again."

"If he retains any of the memories, get rid of him."

"Yes, sir."

As the two left him alone in the warehouse's office, Losham sat behind the desk and began working on a new plan.

Failure wasn't the end of the story. It was the beginning of a new one. Successful people failed as many times if not more than those who didn't achieve much. The difference was that they didn't let failure bring them down. They got up and started anew—again, and again, and again.

# 49

# CALLIE

Brundar leaned against the kitchen counter. "I'm going to work today."

"Why? Aren't you on leave until Monday?" Callie cracked two eggs into the mixing bowl.

"I need to go over the schedule and get updates."

She had no doubt it could have waited for Monday, but it was obvious that being cooped up at home was making Brundar antsy. His work at the club didn't provide him with a sense of purpose like his day job did.

Brundar was a defender, and he prided himself on keeping his people safe.

Besides, ever since he'd gotten injured, he seemed to have lost interest in the club scene and was spending barely any time in the basement. Instead, he occupied himself with drawing plans for the expansion that he and Franco had planned, and crunching the numbers.

Callie wasn't sure what had caused his change of heart. Was it the injury? Or was it her?

Apparently, Brundar was a one-woman man, and once he'd committed to her, in his noncommittal way, he'd lost interest in the activities of the club's lower level.

A pity.

She was glad he didn't want to play with anyone else, but that didn't mean he had to give up the entire thing.

Callie was still curious as hell, but without Brundar to watch over her, there was no chance he and Franco would allow her to attend any of the demonstrations or classes.

But that was a worry for another day.

Her only worry for now was the state of her wardrobe. It was good to have such mundane, everyday problems. No more psychotic husband to fear, no more hiding, no more fake identity.

She felt years younger—carefree for the first time in forever.

"I need to go shopping," Callie said while folding the omelet over a spinach and mushroom sauté.

"Perfect. You can do it while I'm at the office." Brundar took the plate she handed him.

She started on the second omelet. "I'm not talking about a quick run to the supermarket. I need to go clothes and shoe shopping."

Brundar poured them both coffee and put the mugs on the counter. "How long do you think it will take?"

"At least a couple of hours."

"That's how long I need too. Do you want to meet for lunch?"

The offer was as wonderful as it was unexpected. So unlike Brundar, who still struggled with the very basics of couple interactions. Except for sex, of course; that part he'd mastered. Hell, he was so good he could teach it.

But wait, he already did.

"I would love to." She slid the other omelet onto a plate and took it to the counter. "I'll text you when I'm done with shopping. Any place in particular you have in mind?"

He shrugged. "No. You choose."

"Does it have to be someplace fancy?" Other than steakhouses, she wasn't familiar with high-end restaurants.

"Whatever you choose is fine with me. Hamburgers and fries will do."

They had only been out once to that Italian restaurant Brundar had taken her to. Their one and only date. The other time, when Brundar had brought her a gourmet meal from his cousin's place, didn't count because they'd eaten at home. Besides, it had been a reconciliation gesture, not a romantic one.

Today, they were going to have their second actual date, and she didn't want to waste it on hamburgers and fries even though she loved them.

"I'll think of something."

After spending every hour of the day for the past ten days with him, it was weird to kiss Brundar and watch him leave.

Alone in the apartment, Callie realized that the strange sensation in her gut was separation anxiety, which was ridiculous. In ten days she'd gotten addicted to Brundar's presence and dreaded being away from him.

This wasn't healthy.

Callie shook her head. It was probably the result of the trauma. She and Brundar were like survivors of a catastrophe, clinging to each other for dear life. Once things went back to normal, that feeling should pass.

Hopefully.

Because if it didn't, she would need to see a shrink about it. A grown woman shouldn't feel anxious when separated from her partner for a few hours.

Shopping should take her mind off Brundar.

Callie needed a nice new dress, a pair of high-heeled shoes, and a new strapless bra that didn't dig into her skin—if such a thing existed.

At the mall, Callie found the dress first. Another black one, but with wide shoulder straps to cover a regular bra. It was simple, with a square neckline that didn't reveal too much, and not too short, just a couple of inches above the knees.

"May I suggest the jacket that goes with it?" the salesgirl asked.

"Is it also on sale?"

"Everything in the store is thirty percent off until the end of the weekend."

"Then let's see that jacket."

*Nice,* Callie thought as she looked herself over in the mirror. Waist length, with three-quarter sleeves, the jacket made the outfit look like something from a sixties fashion magazine—a Jackie look. The outfit was very elegant. Perhaps she could wear it to her lunch date with Brundar.

"Do you have shoes that go with this?" she asked the girl. After all, she couldn't wear an outfit like that with socks and sneakers. That look might work in New York but not in Los Angeles.

"What's your size?"

"Seven."

"I'll be right back."

The girl brought back a pair of black, three-inch-heel pumps. Perfect. Not too extreme to finish her shopping, and not too plain for the dress. The best part was that all three items ended up costing her less than a hundred dollars, which left enough of her budget for another bra on top of the strapless, maybe a sexy number with matching panties.

It would be fun to have something beautiful to surprise Brundar with. Most of Callie's underwear was made from cotton and came in packs of six. Not that she thought Brundar cared one way or another, but she wanted it for the way it would make her feel. A femme fatale.

Unfortunately, her favorite lingerie store was closed for remodeling, which left her with two options—try to find what she needed in one of the department stores, or drive over to another mall.

Difficult decision.

The thing was, a beautiful set in black satin and lace had caught her eye in one of the advertisements the store was running, and now that she'd decided to splurge on it, Callie didn't want to compromise on something else. Heck, the next mall was only twenty minutes away, and besides, she had plenty of time before lunch, even if she made it an early one.

On the way back to the parking lot, Callie's new outfit earned her a few appreciative glances, and one guy even went as far as whistling. Rude, but at the same time flattering.

Working as a drink server in a nightclub, she couldn't consider every inappropriate glance and remark a harassment, even if she was inclined to. But she wasn't. Flirting was okay unless the guy crossed the line, becoming offensive or persisting without any encouragement on her part.

It happened sometimes, but she had no problem dealing with the offender herself. A stern look or a snide remark was usually enough.

Callie dropped the bag with her old clothes and her purse on the floor of the passenger seat, turned the engine on, and backed out from her parking spot. She turned left at the first light.

Idling at the next intersection, Callie closed her eyes for what seemed like a couple of seconds when someone behind her honked the horn.

"What's your problem, asshat?"

The light must've turned green right at that moment, and the driver was very impatient.

"People."

She continued down the boulevard, deciding to use surface streets instead of going on the freeway.

When someone honked at the next red light, Callie began to worry. Why was she closing her eyes at all? She wasn't tired.

Furthermore, the honking implied that she was closing them for longer than she thought she was.

Should she pull over?

Nah, she needed to find a Starbucks and get a double-shot cappuccino. That would wake her up.

A few blocks later it happened again.

This time, though, Callie wasn't idling at a red light, she was driving, and it wasn't a honk that woke her up, but the sound of screeching tires.

She had a split second to panic before the impact, and then everything turned black.

## 50

# BRUNDAR

"Stop looking at your watch every goddamned minute." Anandur rolled his eyes.

They had finished the Guardian meeting with Kian an hour ago, going over everything he wanted them to do and not do in his absence. The guy was going away for a long weekend but was preparing as if he was leaving for at least a year.

"And stop looking at your phone too. Your fidgeting is making me nervous."

Brundar couldn't help it. Calypso had planned to leave the apartment shortly after he had, which was a little after ten in the morning. She'd said that shopping would take her no more than two hours, but it was already after one in the afternoon, and she hadn't texted him yet.

"I should call her." He selected her contact.

Anandur stayed his hand. "Don't. You told me that this is the first time since the incident that she is taking some time to herself. Let the girl shop in peace."

"I worry about her."

"That's exactly why you shouldn't call her. You'll make her feel guilty and cut her fun time short."

Maybe, but if Brundar didn't hear from her in the next fifteen minutes, he was going to lose his shit.

Something was wrong, he could feel it in his gut. "I'm calling her."

"What if she's driving? Does she have Bluetooth in her car?"

"No. It's an older model."

"Then she would have to reach into her purse to find the damn thing, and that's not safe."

Brundar put the phone back, pulled one of his knives from its holster, and started twirling it between his fingers.

"I hate it when you do that. I know how sharp you keep them."

"I've never nicked myself before." Brundar twirled faster, the knife turning into a blur as he tried to quiet the unease churning in his gut by keeping his focus on the sharp blade.

"You should've put a tracker on her car. Then you would have had peace of mind."

Yeah, he should have, but it hadn't crossed his mind. "I'm calling her."

Anandur shrugged. "You do what you have to do. But don't say I didn't warn you."

The phone rang and rang and rang, finally going to voicemail. Brundar dialed again with the same results.

"She is not answering."

"It's noisy in the mall. She probably can't hear the ring."

Brundar typed a quick message. *Call me as soon as you can.*

Pacing the corridor in front of Kian's office, Brundar waited for Calypso's response.

Ten minutes later he was done waiting. "Fuck it. I'm going to look for her."

"Where? It's a big city."

Brundar called Calypso's number again, but again it went to voicemail. "What else can I do?"

"Do you know her license plate number?"

"No. How the hell should I?"

Anandur scratched his beard. "Maybe Roni can get it from the security camera footage in her apartment building. Does the building have one in the parking garage?"

"It does." Brundar started walking toward the elevators.

"Stop. Roni is working in William's lab now."

Brundar reversed direction and headed for the lab, with Anandur following closely behind him.

The kid lifted his head from an array of monitors. "How can I help you, gentlemen?"

"I need you to find a license plate number." Brundar typed the address, Calypso's car model and color, then handed his phone to Roni. "This is her address. See if you can find the parking lot feed."

"Was it parked there last night?"

Brundar nodded.

It took the kid five minutes to find the feed, then enlarge it so he could copy the number. "Here you go." He handed Brundar a piece of paper.

"You're not done. I need you to check if that car was involved in an accident. Check reports from ten o'clock this morning until now."

Roni frowned. "What happened?"

Anandur waved a dismissive hand. "My brother is overreacting. His friend went shopping, and he can't get a hold of her."

Brundar gritted his teeth. "I have a bad feeling."

"You should have said so." Anandur's tone changed from mocking to worried in an instant. The big oaf had always been superstitious. He believed in omens and lucky numbers and all that shit.

Roni's fingers were a blur on his keyboard. If Brundar hadn't known better, he would have thought the kid was an immortal. Humans just didn't operate at speeds like that.

"Got it. You were right."

Brundar's gut flipped and then twisted in a tight knot. "Talk."

"She was involved in an accident, another car hit her when she didn't stop at a red light. She was taken to the nearest hospital with a broken arm, a light concussion, and some superficial cuts. Nothing life-threatening."

"Thank the merciful Fates." Anandur clutched at his heart.

Brundar wasn't going to thank the sadistic bitches. As if she hadn't suffered enough, Calypso was hurting again. But at least she was alive.

"Which hospital?" he asked.

Roni scribbled the name and address on a note and handed it to Brundar.

"I'll come with you," Anandur offered.

"No. I'm going to get Bridget. You stay here. I don't want to stir up a storm that would reach Kian."

Anandur scratched his head. "Bridget is kind of busy at the moment. Tessa is at the clinic."

"Is she transitioning?"

"Bridget doesn't know yet."

"I'm going to the hospital with Bridget or without."

Anandur nodded. "Give Callie my love."

Brundar dialed the doctor's number. "Can you drop everything and come with me? Calypso was in a car accident."

"What's the damage?"

Fucking Bridget and her cold heart. He'd been expecting a gasp, or an 'oh no', but all he got was a fucking 'what's the damage?'

"A broken arm, a concussion, and some superficial cuts."

"She doesn't need me. I'm sure the human doctors can handle that."

*Cold-hearted woman.*

"I'm asking a favor. I want you to examine her and then decide whether she needs your help or not."

"I'll meet you in the parking garage in fifteen minutes."

## 51

## JACKSON

"How are you feeling?" Jackson asked the moment Tessa's eyelids fluttered open.

"It hurts all over."

He pushed out from the chair and moved to sit next to her on the bed. "I'll call Bridget to give you something for the pain." He brushed a strand of hair away from her cheek.

"It's not so bad. It's not an acute pain. Did you eat anything? You've been sitting in this chair since last night."

Sweet girl, worrying about him even when she was the one in a hospital bed and hurting.

"Bhathian brought me a sandwich from the café this morning."

"What time is it?"

"Around one o'clock."

"And you haven't eaten since breakfast? Go get yourself something to eat." She waved a hand, shooing him away.

Jackson leaned and kissed her damp forehead. "Sylvia is on her way, and she is bringing me lunch. What about you? Are you hungry?"

Tessa hadn't been able to keep anything down, not even water, and was hooked up to an intravenous drip, but maybe after so many hours of sleep, her stomach had settled.

"No. I don't want to puke again."

Smoothing his hand over her hair, he kissed her forehead again. "Poor baby. Is there anything I can do to make you more comfortable?"

"You're here. That's enough. Who is running the shop?"

"Vlad and Gordon. I told them to close up if they can't manage. I'm not leaving your side."

Tessa's smile was a feeble attempt at one. "Thank you. I know I'm being selfish, but I don't want to be alone here."

"Nonsense. You couldn't get rid of me even if you tried."

She cupped his cheek. "I love you."

"Ditto."

"Ditto? That's it?"

She was teasing, which was a good sign. If she were in a lot of pain, humor would've been the last thing on her mind.

"I love you this much." He spread his arms wide.

"Then hug me."

It was a request Jackson was happy to oblige, provided he could figure out a way around all the tubes and sticky pads attached to her. He ended up wrapping his arms over everything and lifting her very gently to his chest.

Tessa sighed. "That feels so good."

Holding her to him with one hand, he caressed her exposed back with his other. Was it his imagination or had she gotten even thinner overnight? The girl was all bones.

A quick knock on the door was all the notice they got before Bridget strode in.

"I'm sorry to interrupt, kids, but I want to run a quick check on Tessa before I have to leave."

"You're leaving?" he asked.

"I won't be gone long, and Hildegard is here if you need anything."

Jackson laid Tessa back on the bed. "Do you need me to move?"

"Yes, please."

Leaning against the wall, Jackson crossed his arms over his chest as he watched Bridget perform her checkup.

"Tell me what you feel, Tessa," Bridget asked.

"I hurt everywhere, not like in unbearable pain, but a constant low-level pain."

"Is it a stabbing sort of pain, or does it feel like pressure?"

"I think, it's more like pressure."

"Does it feel like pins and needles or like a squeeze?"

"Not a squeeze. More like my skin is too tight and everything inside me is swelling."

He was no doctor and knew nothing about human ailments, but that didn't sound good.

Bridget nodded as if she knew exactly what Tessa was complaining about and pulled a measuring tape out of her white coat's pocket.

She'd measured Tessa last night, and now again? What was she expecting to find?

Once the doctor was done taking dozens of measurements and notating them on her tablet, she put the tape back in her pocket and smiled. "I have great news for you, Tessa. Since last night, you've gained one-eighth of an inch in height."

Tessa looked confused, and so was he.

"What does it mean?" Tessa asked.

"It means that you're transitioning."

They had suspected it, but it was just a possibility. Now Bridget sounded as if it was a done deal.

"Can you explain a little bit more?" Tessa squeaked her question.

"I had a feeling that your growth had been stunted for some reason. I could've made sure by taking X-rays of your joints, but I was waiting for your stomach to settle first. Now I don't need to. The fact that you're growing means that you're transitioning and your body is working on reaching its full potential. Andrew gained a couple of inches during his transition, though in his case I don't think he would've reached that height as a human even under perfect conditions. It's just the size he was supposed to be as an immortal. The difference is that he was unconscious for days during his transition, most likely because of his age."

"Did Nathalie grow taller?"

"No. She didn't change at all. Every person is different."

Tessa closed her eyes. "I can't believe it is actually happening," she whispered.

"Congratulations." Bridget pushed to her feet. "Before I leave, do you want anything for the pain?"

Tessa shook her head. "No. Now that I know why it hurts, I want to savor it. My body is fixing itself."

"If you change your mind, Hildegard can help you."

"Thank you, Doctor."

Bridget patted Tessa's slim shoulder. "You're welcome."

As Jackson took Bridget's place on the bed, his smile grew into a face-splitting grin that was almost painful. "Is my kitten going to turn into a cat?" He clasped Tessa's hand and brought it to his lips for a kiss.

"Would it bother you? I know you like it that I'm small."

"I love you. Small, big, average, it doesn't matter. You'll always be my kitten."

Tessa smiled sheepishly. "I wouldn't mind being a couple of inches taller, or a couple of cup sizes bustier." She glanced down at her small breasts, their outline barely visible under the loose hospital johnny.

Jackson would've loved nothing more than to show her how much he worshiped her breasts, but it would have to wait for when she felt better.

"As I said. It doesn't matter to me. You're perfect the way you are, and you're going to be just as perfect after your transition."

Tessa opened her arms. "Come here."

He embraced her gently, careful not to dislodge any of the tubes and wires. "Do you realize that all of our dreams will now become a reality?"

"Don't tempt the Fates, Jackson," she whispered in his ear. "Nothing is guaranteed, not even for immortals."

Unfortunately, it was true.

The Fates bestowed and the Fates took away, and no one's life was without trials and hardships. Except, Tessa had already paid her dues and then some. For the rest of her immortal life, she deserved nothing but good fortune and happiness.

Jackson, on the other hand, had been blessed with a wonderful life. At some point, the Fates might decide it was his turn to pay up.

## 52

# BRUNDAR

"How is your thralling ability?" Bridget asked as they stepped through the hospital's sliding doors.

"It's above average. Why do you ask?"

As she looked up at him, Bridget's expression was condescending, but he was too anxious to care.

"We are not Callie's family. They might not let us in. I need you to make them believe you're her husband and I'm her sister. My thralling ability is decent but not excellent, and I don't get much practice."

He nodded.

"What name is she using now?" Bridget asked.

"She is back to Calypso. Calypso Meyers, that's her maiden name."

"Is that the name on the driver's license she is using?"

Damnation. He wasn't sure. She'd registered her car under Heather Wilson, and Brundar doubted she'd had time to transfer ownership to Calypso Meyers. She might've been using the fake driver's license.

"Let me check with Roni. He was the one who found out where she was."

Since he didn't have the kid's number, Brundar texted William his question.

The answer came a few moments later. *Calypso Meyers.*

"It's Calypso. Let's go."

"Does she have medical insurance?"

"Yes." Franco had all of his employees covered even before it became mandatory, including the part-timers.

They walked over to the reception, where Brundar didn't waste time with niceties, taking over the receptionist's mind right away. "I'm looking for my wife. Calypso Meyers. She was admitted about an hour ago."

Eyes glazed over, the woman nodded and typed the name into the computer.

Brundar had used brute force, too much for such a simple task, but he wasn't in the right frame of mind for delicate probing. Bridget remained silent beside him, but he sensed no disapproval from her.

The woman gave them Calypso's room number, together with two visitor passes to clip on their shirts.

"She is not in the emergency room, which is a good sign," Bridget said as they entered the elevator. "If her injuries were severe, they would have kept her there for observation."

On the fifth floor, they passed the nurses' station and went straight into Calypso's room.

They found her sleeping, her mouth slightly agape and drooling.

Brundar winced. Calypso's face hadn't had time to recover from the previous abuse she'd suffered, and now it was covered in new bruises and shallow cuts. Her left arm was in a cast and her forehead was bandaged, probably hiding a bigger gash.

Bridget walked in and opened the chart.

"She was given mild pain medication, that's all. The arm was reset without an operation." As Bridget kept reading, her eyebrows dipped in a frown. "She is scheduled for a CT scan. Apparently, she fell asleep or blacked out while driving." The doctor cast him an accusing sidelong glance. "Did you keep her up all night long?"

"She had an adequate number of sleeping hours for a human," he said quietly. "There was no reason for her to fall asleep at the wheel. Something must be wrong."

"I agree. We should take her to the clinic."

"Why?"

"She might be transitioning," Bridget whispered.

Brundar shook his head. "She is not a Dormant. Quit thinking of her as one. Focus on finding what's wrong instead."

Lately, Bridget had been dealing almost exclusively with transitioning Dormants. No wonder that was the direction her mind went for answers. But unfortunately, in Calypso's case, there had to be some human biological malfunction that had caused her to black out.

"I can do both at the clinic. But if she is transitioning, it is imperative that we take her out of here."

"And how do you suggest we do it?"

"One of us carries her out while the other thralls the staff and has one of the doctors write her a release."

"What about Kian?" It was the middle of the day, and there was no way they could sneak Calypso into the clinic without anyone noticing. Besides, with Tessa there, people would be coming to visit the girl, and it would be impossible to hide the extra patient in the room next to her.

"I have the authority to override him when it comes to medical emergencies. This certainly qualifies as one."

"What emergency?" Calypso startled them both.

Brundar sat on the bed next to her and took her uninjured hand. "Your accident, sweetling. How are you feeling?"

"Like I was hit by a truck, which I was."

"How did it happen?"

Calypso tilted her head to look at Bridget. "Hi, it's so nice of you to come, but it looks worse than it is. They need to run some more tests, but after that, they are going to let me go home tomorrow."

Bridget came closer. "I know. I read your chart. Can you tell us what happened?" She repeated Brundar's question.

Calypso touched her hand to the bandage on her forehead. "I don't know. I remember closing my eyes while idling at a red light, twice. Both times people behind me honked, and when I opened my eyes the light was green. I thought they were impatient. But what if I had my eyes closed for longer than I thought I did? I must've done it again, this time not with the brake on, but I don't remember anything. One moment I'm driving, the next one I'm on a stretcher and paramedics are hovering over me. They later told me that I ran a red light, just kept on driving. Lucky for me, the guy that hit me wasn't going fast."

A tear slid out of the corner of her eye. "My car is totaled, and so is the guy's truck. We are both lucky to be alive."

Brundar leaned over her and took her into his arms. "You're okay, and the other guy is alive. Right?"

She sniffled and nodded.

"Then nothing else matters. Your injuries are mild, and you'll be okay in no time. The car is just a piece of metal. It's replaceable."

"I know, but I still feel like crap. Why is it happening to me? Why can't I catch a break?" Calypso started sobbing openly.

Lost, Brundar cast a pleading glance at Bridget. Maybe as a female and a doctor she had the right words to soothe the crying woman in his arms? Because he sure as hell had no idea what to do.

Taking pity on him, or maybe on Calypso, Bridget said, "Would you feel better recuperating in my clinic? I have all the equipment needed to run tests and find out why you blacked out. It might be something as benign as dehydration, or a vicious virus."

Calypso nodded. "I would love that. But I don't think they are going to let me go without first running those tests the doctor ordered."

"I can call the doctor in, and you can say that you want to be discharged. No one can keep you against your will. They'll just have you sign papers releasing them from liability."

"Should I?"

"Yes, you should."

"Okay. But I don't have anything to wear. I think they cut off my clothes."

"I'll get you something from the gift shop while Brundar deals with the doctor. Right, Brundar?"

"Right. I'll go get him. Or is it her?" Brundar asked.

Bridget looked at the chart. "Her. Doctor Belinda Hernandez."

"Got it."

It took over an hour for all the paperwork to get filled in and signed, but in the end he didn't even have to thrall anyone to get Calypso out of there. Doctor Hernandez wasn't happy about it, but apparently, she had no choice. It was Calypso's prerogative to release herself. They even provided an orderly with a wheelchair to take Calypso to Brundar's car.

"I'll drive," Bridget volunteered. "You guys sit together in the back."

"Thank you," he and Calypso said at the same time.

"I need you to hold me," Calypso whispered in his ear as he lifted her off the wheelchair and into the Escalade's back seat.

"And I need to do the holding."

Up front in the driver seat, Bridget sighed, and then mumbled quietly, "Always the bridesmaid, never the bride."

## 53

# CALLIE

Callie opened her eyes to a dimly illuminated room. Was she in the hospital?

She had a hazy recollection of being taken to an ambulance, and another one of someone telling her that her arm was broken. She lifted her right arm, then the left. The left was much heavier—the one with the cast.

Had she dreamt about Brundar holding her? Taking her away?

But she was still in a hospital room, so it must've been a dream. It had been daytime when she'd last closed her eyes. Apparently, night had fallen because it was dark in her room. Maybe someone closed the blinds.

Her head felt as if it was stuffed with cotton balls. Her thoughts couldn't travel freely or connect. Bits and pieces were stuck in random places, not coalescing into something that made sense.

She must have hit her head pretty bad. Evidently, the airbag hadn't deployed. Callie remembered hitting the steering wheel, not the impact itself—she'd blacked out before it had happened—but she remembered anticipating it.

As proof, her head was throbbing with pain. She reached with her uninjured arm and lightly touched her forehead, or rather the bandage covering it. Even that feather-light touch caused her to wince.

Callie closed her eyes and took in a shallow breath in case her ribs were broken too. It hurt a little. Her ribs were bruised but not broken.

Thank God. If the damage was limited to a broken arm and a cut on her forehead, she should count herself lucky.

It could've been worse.

In the adjacent bathroom, she heard the toilet flush, then the water run as whoever was using it washed their hands. Probably the patient in the next room with whom she was sharing the bathroom. Once that lady was done, Callie needed to use the facilities herself.

Should she call the nurse to help her?

Nah, first she would try without anyone's aid. If that didn't work, and she felt dizzy, she could then call for the nurse. Carefully, Callie pushed to a sitting position, waited for a moment to see if that was okay, then dropped her legs over the side of the bed.

So far, so good.

The question was whether she could stand.

The bathroom door opened, spilling light into the room, but the silhouette that appeared in that doorway was way too big to be a woman.

"What are you doing?" asked a familiar gruff voice.

"Brundar?"

He crossed the distance in two long strides, stopping in front of her and blocking her way. "Where do you think you are going?"

Why did he sound so agitated? Was she still dreaming? "The bathroom."

"I'll carry you."

She was in his arms before she had a chance to object. "When did you get here?"

He looked at her with a puzzled expression on his face. "I never left."

Now that her eyes had gotten used to the sudden burst of light, she could see his features more clearly, but that didn't help with her confusion. "I don't understand."

"What is the last thing you remember?"

"The doctor saying something about my arm being broken."

Brundar frowned, his puzzled expression turning worried. "Let's get you to the bathroom first, and then we will talk."

"Okay."

As he set her down on the toilet, Callie took a look around. The bathroom looked familiar and yet strange at the same time. But the mystery would have to wait for later. First, she needed to empty her bladder.

"Can you turn around, please?"

When he did as she asked, Callie lifted the flaps of her hospital johnny, expecting to be naked under it, but someone had put panties on her.

Crap. Pushing them down with one hand proved to be much harder than she'd expected, but after some wiggling, she finally managed.

Putting them back, though, was a different story. "Um, Brundar? A little help, please?"

He turned around, crouched at her feet, and gently pulled her panties up. "Good?"

Callie smiled, reminded of how he used to ask her if she was okay every step of the way on her sexual journey of exploration. "Yeah. Though I think that maybe I shouldn't be wearing panties at all. It would make going to the bathroom easier."

"Do you want me to take them off?"

"Maybe before you have to leave. When are the visiting hours over?" She pushed to her feet and turned to the sink to wash her hands.

"Visiting hours? There are no visiting hours. I can stay as long as I want to."

"That's nice. Most hospitals have rules about that. I think ten o'clock is the latest. Unless you're the spouse, but we are not married." She dried her hands with a paper towel.

"You're not in the hospital, Calypso. You're in Bridget's clinic. Don't you remember getting yourself discharged so you could come with us?"

Callie turned around and leaned against the vanity. "I don't. Maybe, I don't know. I'm so confused." She had no reason to doubt him, which meant that her brain was playing tricks on her. "Maybe they gave me something at the hospital? Some drug that I had a reaction to?"

Brundar scooped her into his arms and carried her back to the bed. "I'm no expert. But I think that your brain couldn't handle yet another trauma so soon after the last one, and decided to take a vacation. But I might be talking nonsense. We should consult Bridget."

Actually, what he'd said made a lot of sense. During her previous short stay in Bridget's clinic, Callie remembered the doctor telling her that she hadn't fully internalized what had happened to her. Maybe it had finally caught up with her.

"What time is it?" she asked after he tucked the blanket around her.

"Early. It's a little after five in the morning."

"Crap, how long was I out? I thought it was still yesterday evening."

Brundar sat on the bed next to her. "Bridget and I got you out of the hospital at around three in the afternoon, you fell asleep in the car, and I carried you here. You've been asleep ever since."

"No wonder I'm so thirsty. Is there anything to drink here?"

"I'll get you water."

Her lips twisted in distaste. "I was thinking coffee. But I'll start with water."

"I'm not giving you anything other than that until Bridget approves it." He went outside the room and a moment later returned with a paper cup filled with water.

"When is she coming in?" Callie let the water wet her dried out, cracked lips before gulping it down.

"I don't expect her to be here before seven. She stayed late, taking your vitals several times until she was sure you're fine."

"I need to thank her." She finished the cup and handed it to Brundar. "Could you get me another one?"

"Of course."

Her eyelids felt heavy, and Callie let them drop as soon as Brundar had left the room to fill up her cup.

*Just for a few seconds until he comes back.*

## 54

# BRUNDAR

When Brundar returned with the water Calypso had asked for, he found her sleeping again. Something wasn't right, but all he could do was wait and worry until Bridget got there.

It had been her idea to put Calypso in the after surgery recovery room. With the OR and lab separating it from the front of the clinic, it was secluded and as far away from Tessa as possible.

Security was well aware of the visitor, but Bridget had told them to keep it quiet. Whether they'd informed Kian or not was anyone's guess. But since the guy hadn't called to chew Brundar or Bridget's heads off, they probably hadn't. It made sense that they had instructions not to bother him on his vacation unless it was an emergency.

In either case, it was important to keep Calypso hidden from the clan members, or rather the other way around.

Yesterday, with people coming to visit Tessa throughout the afternoon, Brundar had done his best to stay out of their way. Now, there was no one there except for Jackson, who refused to leave the girl's side even for a moment.

In a way, Brundar envied the kid. Tessa wasn't a secret stowaway like Calypso. Jackson's friends and his mother had brought him a change of clothes and food and whatever else was needed.

Brundar had only Anandur and Bridget to help him out, which wasn't much.

Anandur had stopped by last night, but he'd left early that morning for Hawaii. And Bridget had her hands full with two patients. Besides, it wasn't her job to take care of him.

If Brundar wanted to eat, he had to slink out like a thief, get something from the vending machine upstairs, and then sneak back in without any of Tessa's visitors seeing him, which wasn't an easy feat given that they were all immortals.

At seven-thirty, Bridget walked into the recovery room. "Did she wake up at all?"

"She woke up early in the morning, used the bathroom, and had a drink of water. But when I went to refill her cup she fell asleep again. That's a lot of sleeping even for a human."

Bridget put a finger to her lips, shushing him. Calypso was sleeping, not unconscious, and he should watch what he said in front of her.

The doctor adjusted the lights in the room, making it a little brighter before checking on her patient.

"Brundar, come over here." She motioned for him to get closer. "Look at the cuts on her cheeks. They are almost gone."

Brundar hadn't noticed before, but now that he was paying closer attention, he saw that not only were the cuts much less visible, but her bruises had faded too. Even the old ones. His gut flipped and twisted into a knot. Did it mean that she was transitioning? But Calypso wasn't a Dormant.

"How is it possible?" he whispered.

Bridget patted his shoulder. "The Fates have smiled upon you, Brundar. Your woman is a Dormant, and she is transitioning. Offer them your thanks."

He shook his head. "I don't get it. Unless you count superb culinary skills, she has zero special abilities."

"Affinity, my dear Brundar. You felt it, I felt it, your brother felt it. It's the immediate connection we rarely feel for anyone outside our family. It doesn't even have to be a liking. Fates know there are some clan members I can't stand, but I still feel connected to them. Do you get what I'm trying to say?"

He shook his head. "I'm afraid not." It wasn't easy for him to talk about his shortcomings, but confiding in Bridget wasn't like talking to just anyone. She was a doctor and therefore bound to keep it confidential. "My emotional intelligence is subpar. I don't feel connected to anyone aside from my brother to an extent, and now to Calypso. Even my own mother feels like a mere acquaintance to me."

Bridget threw him a pitying look, then quickly masked it with her all-knowing doctor expression. "When you open yourself up to it, you'll get it."

She leaned over Calypso and gently started unwrapping the bandage over her forehead. "Look at this. It's nothing more than a scratch. Give it a couple of hours, and it will fade completely. I bet her arm is going to be as good as new by the end of the day or tomorrow morning."

"What is going to be as good as new?" Calypso asked.

"Your arm," Bridget answered.

With her eyes still closed, Calypso smiled. "I'm dreaming, right?"

"No, you're awake." Bridget walked over to one of the cabinets and pulled out a mirror. "Take a look." She handed it to her, then lifted the back of the bed to a reclining position.

Calypso opened her eyes, but it was too dark for her to see. Apparently, her eyesight was still human. "What am I looking at?"

"Get the lights, Brundar," the doctor ordered.

He turned them up, but not all the way. There was no reason to flood the room with a bright light that would hurt Calypso's eyes.

"Oh, wow. My bruises are gone. What did you give me, a magic potion?"

"Not a single thing."

Calypso frowned and looked closer. "I thought the cut on my forehead was deep. But look at this, it's only a scratch. I don't know why they made such a big fuss about it."

Her mind was looking for an explanation within her frame of reference. Unless someone told her what was going on, she would never think in that direction.

But damn, where to begin?

Bridget took the mirror away. "Let me show you something, Callie." She loaded a tray with a few packets of sterile gauze and a small surgical knife.

"Give me your hand."

Calypso eyed the tray suspiciously. "What are you going to do?"

"A little test."

She offered the doctor her uninjured hand. Bridget held it, palm up, then struck fast, making a tiny cut.

"What the fuck? Why did you do that?" Calypso tried to yank her hand out of Bridget's grasp.

"Just look at the cut, Callie." Bridget wiped the blood off with a gauze square.

It wasn't closing as fast as it would for an immortal, but it was much faster than humanly possible. She was still transitioning. Her body would probably get more adept at healing itself when the process was completed.

"I'm dreaming." Calypso dropped her head on the pillow and closed her eyes. "Some really fucked up dreams. Where the hell is my brain coming up with that?" she mumbled, talking to herself.

Bridget rose to her feet and threw away the soiled gauze. "I did my part, but she is still in denial. Now it's your turn."

Brundar swallowed.

"Where do I start?"

"At the beginning, of course." Bridget cast him a smile over her shoulder as she headed out the door.

Right. At the beginning.

## 55

# CALLIE

*B*ridget had told Brundar to start at the beginning. What had she meant by that?

The beginning of what?

Brundar sat on the bed next to Callie and kissed the palm Bridget had nicked with her wicked knife. "You're not dreaming. This is all real, and after I explain, it will all make sense. But first, you need to drink some more. You were thirsty before you fell asleep again."

"I still am."

Heck, even if it was a dream, it was for sure interesting. She would play along and see what her mind was capable of inventing.

Brundar got up and walked over to the sink, filling her cup with tap water. "All the water in the keep is filtered." He handed her a cup.

Did he say the keep? Like a castle? Both times Callie had been taken to this place, she hadn't seen where it was. The first time she'd been blindfolded, the second time asleep. But from the one she'd been conscious for, Callie remembered that the drive wasn't long. As far as she knew, there were no castles within driving distance of her old house.

"Thank you." She gulped the contents in one go.

Brundar sat on the bed again and clasped her hand. "Remember how you wondered about my incredible recovery? It wasn't because of some revolutionary new procedure. I heal fast because I am immortal. And so are Anandur and Bridget and every other member of my family. That is the real reason I couldn't be with you, and it's also the reason Kian was so angry about us bringing you to the keep. Our existence must be kept secret from the human world. Can you imagine what would happen if word got out that there are people who don't age?"

If they were real, they would be hunted and collected like the most precious treasure in the world, and experimented on. But of course, they weren't. Brundar would not be talking about it so openly either.

"So if it is such a big secret, why are you telling me about it now?"

"Some humans carry our dormant genes. They are very rare and almost impossible to find. Typically they exhibit some paranormal abilities, like precognition or telepathy."

Callie frowned. "I remember you asking me if I had any." Immortals were not a new concept, there were plenty of movies and books featuring some sort of creatures that couldn't die, but she didn't remember ever reading anything about Dormants, and it was unlikely that her mind had conjured that idea out of nothing. Could it be that it wasn't a dream after all?

He nodded. "I was hoping against hope that you were one of these rare humans. Because if you were, I could activate those dormant genes and you would turn immortal, which would mean a possible future for us."

Lifting her palm, Callie glanced at the spot Bridget had nicked with her surgical knife. It was completely healed as if it had never been injured. "Are you telling me that I am one of those humans who carry immortal genes and that you accidentally turned me into an immortal?"

She had one hell of an imagination to come up with a story like that. Nice story, though, where she and Brundar could live happily ever after. Forever. Which brought her back to the dream theory. This was the sort of fantasy she was capable of inventing.

"That's exactly what I'm saying. The Fates have smiled upon me. There is no other explanation for you appearing in my life. Dormants are extremely rare, and finding a true love match is even rarer. It cannot be a coincidence."

As crazy as it sounded, Callie held similar beliefs. From the very start, she'd felt that her meeting with Brundar had been fated. Except, she'd thought it had to do with him rescuing her from Shawn.

But what if the picture was bigger than that?

"What is the catalyst for activating those dormant genes?"

Brundar smiled. "Kiss me, and I'll show you." He lowered his head and took her mouth in a gentle kiss. She wrapped her good arm around his neck and held him close, savoring his warmth, his solid chest.

There was nothing in her world that compared to the feeling Callie got every time their bodies touched like that, and it wasn't only the attraction. It was a coming together.

They were like two halves that needed to fuse in order to breathe easy.

"Open your eyes," he said as he let go of her mouth.

The lights must be playing tricks on her because it looked as if Brundar's eyes were glowing from the inside.

And then he smiled.

"Oh, my God!" She pointed. "You have fangs." Now Callie was certain she was dreaming.

"That's what happens when I am aroused, or when I get aggressive. That's why I insisted on the blindfold. Obviously, I couldn't allow you to see me like this."

Why did it make so much sense?

Maybe because she was the one making it up?

But what if all of it was real?

How would she know?

"Are you in shock?" Brundar asked when she remained quiet.

Callie shook her head. "I have to find a way to ascertain if I am dreaming or hallucinating. If this is real or not. But I can't think of anything that would prove it beyond a shadow of a doubt. I often have very realistic dreams."

"Would it help if I pinched you?"

"Not really. If pain were a convincing sign, then Bridget cutting into my palm would've been proof enough. I've dreamt about pain, and I've dreamt about pleasure, and both felt very real."

Brundar rubbed his jaw. "If I tell you my clan's history, and it will be a tale that you could've never imagined on your own, would you believe me then?"

"I have to hear it first."

Brundar took in a deep breath. "I'm not the best at telling stories, but I'll give it a try. The gods you've learned about in mythology were real. The furthest back our known history goes is ancient Sumer. The mother of our clan—"

More than an hour passed until Brundar was done with his story. And one hell of a story it was. Callie had about a thousand questions, but she'd asked none, listening to Brundar's tale from beginning to end without interruptions. Here and there she'd tried to guess where the story was going, but most of the time had gotten it wrong, proving to herself that it wasn't a product of her imagination.

"I have so many questions that I don't know where to start."

"Do you believe me, though? That this is not a dream?"

She nodded, fighting the tears stinging the back of her eyes. "It's such a sad story. Poor Annani, to lose her one true love so tragically and then everyone else she'd ever loved. To be all alone in the universe. She was so incredibly brave."

"Indeed, she is. But the most amazing thing about her is her heart and her joy in life. After all that she's been through, she should be bitter and jaded, but she is not."

Callie hoped to meet the goddess one day, even if only to see her from afar. After all, it wasn't likely that a powerful being like Annani would deign to talk to a simple ex-human like Callie. "Annani could be such a fantastic role model. Especially for girls. It's a shame her story can't be taught in schools."

With a smile, Brundar pulled her into his arms for a gentle hug. "You're amazing, Calypso. Always thinking of others. I'm so proud to call you my mate."

She cleared her throat. "About that mate thing. Can we call it something else?"

Brundar pulled back, amusement dancing in his glowing eyes. "Would you prefer wife?"

"Is that a proposal?"

"Only if you want it to be."

## 56

# BRUNDAR

*I*t wasn't the most romantic proposal, even Brundar knew that. Calypso would probably say no, or not yet. She hadn't grown up with the myth of a true love match, and she might not realize the gift they had been given.

In time, she would.

Except, with her history of being pushed into a marriage that had resulted in a catastrophe, she might never be ready.

It didn't matter. Brundar didn't need a ceremony to bind him to Calypso, or her to him. They were bound by much stronger forces than that.

Love and fate.

But she was so damn young.

What if she decided to follow the advice he'd given her about not rushing into another commitment before partying for a while?

Over his dead body, or rather that of any male she partied with, which now included his immortal clansmen.

He should dissuade her from that idea. "You don't need to answer me yet. But just so you know, the venom is addictive. You'll be repulsed by other males. Human and immortal alike."

Calypso cupped his cheek. "Since you and I are never going to have other partners, that's not a problem. You are it for me, and I am it for you."

"So, is it a yes?"

"If you can find someone to marry us now, I'll do it here in this hospital room with Bridget and the nurse as witnesses."

He shook his head. "First, you need to get well, which fortunately is not going to take much longer now that you're immortal, or rather on your way to becoming one. According to Bridget, it takes up to six months for the body to complete the transition."

Calypso lay back on the pillows and closed her eyes. "Yeah, you're right. I don't want to black out in the middle of the ceremony. I keep falling asleep."

"That's because of the transition. The first stages wreak havoc on the body, and it tries to preserve energy by becoming inactive. You're lucky to only fall asleep. Syssi was unconscious for over a day, and Andrew for several days."

Calypso's eyes widened. "Syssi was a human? No wonder she seemed so normal."

"She was the first Dormant Amanda found. And what do you mean, Syssi seemed normal? Amanda and Bridget didn't?"

"Not really. I felt a different vibe from them, same with you and Anandur."

Brundar frowned. As far as he was aware, humans couldn't detect immortals unless they were showing glowing eyes and fangs. If something was giving them away, he needed to know about it. "Different in what way?"

"It's hard to explain. I thought it was because you guys were all originally from Europe, and Europeans have a different vibe than Americans. But maybe that's not it. I really can't put my finger on it."

"If you come up with something later, please let me know. Staying hidden and undetectable is crucial to our survival."

"I'll try. Maybe this is my special talent? Sensing immortals?"

"Could be. But, apparently, there is another Dormant here who exhibits no unique abilities. So maybe it's not a prerequisite."

When Calypso didn't respond, Brundar realized she'd fallen asleep again. Except, now that he knew why this was happening, he was no longer worried. She needed the sleep.

Careful not to disturb the bed, he got up and walked out. Leaning against the wall of the reception room outside the recovery area, he pulled out his phone and called his brother.

Anandur answered before the first ring ended. "What happened?"

"Everything is all right," Brundar calmed his brother. No wonder Anandur assumed he was calling with news of some disaster. He never called unless it was an emergency. "I have good news. Calypso is transitioning."

Aside from Anandur's heavy breathing, the line was silent for a long moment. "How?"

"Apparently, she is a Dormant."

"Are you sure she is transitioning?"

"Positive. Bridget performed the cut test. Calypso blacked out while driving because she was transitioning. I thank the merciful Fates for her getting away with only minor injuries. She could've been killed." His gut clenched uncomfortably at the thought.

"Right. But you were together for weeks, and I assume it wasn't a platonic relationship."

"Where are you going with that?"

"She should've transitioned a long time ago. Why only now?"

Brundar rubbed his jaw, trying to figure out what had been different about last week. Well, since he'd been staying with Calypso, they had been having sex more frequently. That could've been the difference. "Before my injury, we hadn't had sex as often."

"Nothing else?"

"Calypso started using birth control. Could that have anything to do with it?"

"What did you do before that? Did you thrall her every time to make her think you had protection?"

What kind of a man did his brother think he was?

"Of course not. I tried to keep the thralling to a minimum. I used condoms. And thanks to the blindfold, I didn't need to thrall her after every bite either."

"You need to tell Bridget. It might be important."

"True. I also wanted to tell you that I asked Calypso to marry me and she said yes."

"Yes!" Anandur shouted.

"Keep it down. Is Kian with you?"

"He and Syssi are taking a nap. But, bro, we no longer need to keep it a secret. Do you want me to tell him? Or do you want to do the honors yourself?"

"I'd rather wait until he is back."

"Do you have a date? Or is it just in the agreement stage?"

"You know who is here. It's an opportunity." Even though their sat phones were using a secured and heavily encrypted connection, Brundar preferred not to mention the goddess's name.

"Right. Are you going to wait for me to come back?"

"Of course I will, you moron. I'm not getting married without you. Besides, Calypso needs to heal completely first, and then she would probably want to get a nice dress and maybe plan a party or something."

"Aha, so it's not that you are waiting for me to come back because you want your brother to be your best man. It's all about a dress."

Brundar chuckled. "Of course, it's about the dress. You can't come to my wedding wearing jeans."

Anandur gasped dramatically. "Brundar, you told a joke! You are cured!"

## 57

# JACKSON

It was the middle of the night when a small cloaked figure practically floated into the room and closed the door behind her. Even with the cloak's hood hiding her face and her inner glow subdued, Jackson knew who it was.

He pushed to his feet and bowed. "Greetings, Clan Mother."

"Shush." Annani pulled the hood back and put a finger to her lips. "No one knows I am here." She smirked. "I was supposed to stay in Kian's penthouse, but I wanted to give my blessing to the new member of my clan. How is the girl doing?"

Jackson bowed again, moved by Annani's concern for Tessa, a girl she'd never met. "Thank you. Tessa is doing well. She is sleeping."

The goddess glided closer and put her hand on Tessa's forehead. "She is not unconscious. This is good. I was worried, but I see that she is very young. The young fare better through the transition."

"Could you bless her anyway?"

Annani smiled. "Of course, child." She glided toward him and lifted a small palm to his cheek. "Such a handsome boy."

"Thank you." Jackson dropped to his knees so the goddess wouldn't have to look up.

She sighed, but it wasn't a sad sigh. "I sense so much love in you. Your heart has a boundless capacity for feelings. I hope the Fates bless your union with many children. They will be loved and cherished."

Jackson looked into the goddess's warm, smiling eyes. "Is this a blessing, or a prediction?"

"Both." She leaned and kissed his forehead. "Do not tell anyone I was here. My presence in the keep is known only to the Guardians and council members, and it needs to stay that way."

Tessa would've loved to see the goddess. But now he couldn't even tell her.

Jackson hesitated for a split second before asking, "Can I tell Tessa? Knowing that you came to see her will mean so much to her."

Annani turned her head to look at the sleeping girl. "I will do better than that. I will wake her."

Jackson was speechless. He hadn't expected Annani to be so accommodating. The rumors painted her as unyielding, a prima donna that had to have her way in all things—as was her due. After all, she was the last remaining goddess and the mother of their clan. They were lucky she wasn't a tyrant, and that her demands weren't too outrageous.

As Annani walked over to the bed in that floating way she moved, Jackson looked down at her feet, checking if they were even touching the floor, but her cloak was too long, dragging on the floor behind her.

She leaned and kissed Tessa's forehead. "Wake up, sleeping beauty."

Annani laughed at her own joke, the sound of her laughter so sweet it sent shivers up and down Jackson's spine. There was an unearthly quality to her voice, especially when she sang or laughed.

From the other side of the bed, Jackson saw Tessa crack her eyes open, and then open them wider. "Am I dead? Are you an angel?"

Annani laughed again. "If I am, then I am a very naughty one."

"Your voice is so beautiful. It sounds like little crystal bells." Tessa reached out a hand to touch a lock of Annani's hair. "So soft." She lifted her eyes back to Annani's face. "Are you here to escort me to the other side?"

The Goddess smiled and patted Tessa's cheek. "You are not dead, child, and I am not an angel. But I am a goddess. I am sure you have heard about me. I am Annani, otherwise known as Clan Mother."

Tessa gasped and pushed back on the bed. "Oh, my, God. I mean Goddess." She turned frantic eyes to Jackson. "What am I supposed to do?"

Annani patted her cheek again. "Nothing at all except get better. I came to give you my blessing, but you are doing splendidly without it." She leaned closer. "You and Jackson are already blessed beyond measure. Your love for each other shines like a thousand suns."

## 58

## BRUNDAR

*A* text arrived at three in the morning, or rather night, waking Brundar from the short nap he'd allowed himself. Calypso was still sleeping for long stretches at a time, and he was afraid that during one of them she would slip into unconsciousness. Which meant that he kept checking on her throughout the night.

He pulled his phone out of his pocket and looked at the screen.

The text was from Kian. *Congratulations. Best news I've got in a long time,* Kian wrote at midnight Hawaiian time. An apology for the way he'd kicked Calypso out was apparently too much to expect from the guy.

Fucking Anandur. He was supposed to keep his mouth shut.

Brundar dozed off for what seemed like a few minutes when another text came in, jarring him awake. This time from Syssi. *I'm so happy for both of you. This is a miracle, and it deserves a grand celebration. Tell Callie we are going to have one as soon as I'm back from Hawaii.*

Apparently, Anandur hadn't told them about the wedding plans. Maybe he'd misunderstood, thinking that he wasn't supposed to talk about the wedding but that telling Kian and Syssi about Calypso's transition was okay.

He would give him the benefit of the doubt. After all, he owed his brother not only his life but Calypso's as well. For as long as he lived, Brundar was never going to forget Anandur's arrival at the scene at Shawn's house.

He fired a couple of quick *thanks* to both and closed his eyes again. When he opened them again, it was seven in the morning.

Frantically, Brundar pushed to his feet and clasped Calypso's hand, relaxing when she squeezed back.

"What time it is?" she mumbled.

"Seven."

"Morning or evening? I lost track of time."

"Morning."

Calypso swung her legs over the side of the bed and got up.

He was at her side in the blink of an eye. "What do you think you're doing?"

"I'm going to the bathroom."

"Let me help you."

"No, I can do it. I feel strong."

"Can I come with you anyway? I know you need help with your panties."

She smiled. "If I can't manage, I'll call for you to come in. Okay?"

He didn't have much choice. The woman was trying to prove something. "I'll stand outside the door."

Calypso rolled her eyes. "Fine."

He listened as she used the toilet, then washed her uninjured hand and brushed her teeth, all while having only one arm to work with. Stubborn woman. He could've made it so much easier for her.

"Brundar," she finally called out.

He opened the door.

"Can you find me a hairbrush? My hair looks like a bird's nest."

"I'll ask Bridget. But first I want to see you get in bed without falling down and breaking more bones."

She smiled sheepishly. "If everything heals as fast as those cuts and bruises, then I have nothing to worry about. Look at my face." She pointed with her good hand. "Perfect."

"I agree." He guided her back to the bed and helped her up.

"Can you find me a cup of coffee too?"

"I'll ask Bridget if it's okay."

"Ask Bridget what?" The doctor walked in.

"I want coffee," Calypso said. "And food. I'm starving."

"All taken care of." The doctor turned her head towards the door. "You can come in, Amanda. Callie is awake."

Amanda sauntered in pushing a loaded cart in front of her. "Good morning, darlings. My butler prepared breakfast for you."

Calypso eyed it hungrily. "Thank you and your butler. I would kill for a cup of coffee."

Amanda lifted the carafe. "No need to kill anyone." She poured dark liquid into the cup. "Cream and sugar?"

"Yes, please."

She fixed Calypso's coffee and handed it to her. "You take yours black, right?" she asked Brundar.

He nodded.

"Here you go." She handed him a steaming mug.

Calypso took a few grateful sips, then looked at Bridget. "Do you have a hairbrush I can borrow?"

"I got you covered, girl." Amanda pulled out a large paper bag from the cart's lower shelf and put it on the bed. "A brush and a change of clothes. No bra, I'm afraid. Mine wouldn't fit you."

"Thank you. You're awesome." Calypso got off the bed with surprising ease. "I'm going to change and brush my hair. I need to feel human again." She giggled. "But I'm not, am I?"

Bridget lifted a hand. "Not yet. I want to remove your cast, and it will get messy. You'll need a shower after that."

"Are you sure the bone is already mended?"

"If you still need a little support, I'll give you a sling. Eat something first, though. You said you were starving."

A few minutes later, when Calypso was done with a sandwich and another cup of coffee, Bridget shooed Brundar and Amanda out. "And take the cart with you. I need room to move."

"How did you know we were here?" Brundar asked as they stepped out into the waiting room.

"Anandur told Syssi, and Syssi told Nathalie and me, and we told everyone else. You know how the rumor machine works."

Damnation. Now he wouldn't have a moment's peace.

As if to prove him right, there was a knock on the waiting room's door.

"Come in," Amanda said.

The Guardians piled into the small room, sucking up all the air, or at least it felt like it to Brundar. The anxious knot in his gut refused to ease even though Calypso was doing exceptionally well. Everything was happening so fast and so unexpectedly, Brundar was having a hard time adjusting to his new reality.

Yesterday morning Calypso was a human, and they had zero prospects as a couple, and now they were talking forever.

Several embraces and backslaps later, the questions began.

"How did you find her?"

"Did you know she was Dormant?"

"Did you suspect?"

He tried to answer them patiently. After all, these men and Kri were almost like brothers and sister to him.

"When can we see your mystery woman?" Bhathian asked.

Amanda crossed her arms over her chest. "Not today, gentlemen and lady. Give the girl a breather. Once she is ready, Brundar will invite you over to his apartment. Right, Brundar?"

"Right." As long as it got them to leave as soon as possible, he was willing to promise a lot of things.

Amanda uncrossed her arms and headed for the door as well. "I need to get going, or I'll be late to my morning class. I'll call you when I'm back. Oh, and Annani told me that she wants to talk to you. Not right now, but at your earliest convenience."

Brundar frowned. "Do you know what she wants?"

"Probably to give you some words of wisdom and ask about a wedding date." She winked.

He was going to strangle Anandur. "Why? What did you hear?"

"Nothing. But Calypso is your true-love match, and I assume you would like to make it official at some point."

"What about you and Dalhu? You guys don't seem in a hurry."

"We are very comfortable the way we are." She pushed the door handle down. "Do whatever feels right for you and Calypso. You can get married tomorrow, or next week, or in a year, or never. It doesn't matter. The bond between you is indestructible."

For some reason, Amanda's words managed to ease the knot in his gut. He didn't know whether it was the reassurance that he and Calypso would never have to part, or the realization that they didn't need to rush into a wedding only because Annani was there. They had all the time in the world.

He was about to head back into the recovery room when there was another knock on the door. Who the hell was it this time?

He yanked it open. "Carol. You heard too?"

She flung herself into his arms, and he had no choice but to catch her. What had gotten into her? She knew he didn't like to be touched.

Surprisingly, though, he felt no revulsion, not even the slightest discomfort.

Carol was family, and she was excited for him. He hugged her back.

He hadn't expected her to burst into tears. "What's the matter? Aren't you happy for me?"

"I'm ecstatic." She pulled away and plopped down on one of the chairs. "Those are tears of joy, Brundar. Sometimes females get overemotional, and the only way to let the pressure out is to cry."

He sat next to her. "Are you still trying to teach me how to interpret emotions?"

She shrugged. "You need it now more than ever. This is just the beginning for you. Relationships need constant work."

"Calypso knows who and what I am."

Carol threw him a sidelong glance. "Does she, now?"

He frowned. "What are you trying to say?"

She sighed. "I get you, Brundar. More than you realize. We are both survivors. I haven't told anyone the complete story of what was done to me. I can't. Not because I'm ashamed, or anything like that, but because to talk about it would mean to relive it. But if one day I'm lucky enough to find my true love match, I'll have to tell him."

"Why?"

"True love means true acceptance. The good, the bad, and the ugly."

## 59

# CALLIE

Callie's arm was healed.

In fact, she hadn't felt so good in a long time. After what she'd suffered at Shawn's hands, the visible bruising had been only part of the story. She'd been aching all over and putting a brave face on it because it was nothing compared to Brundar's injuries.

"I think I'll head into the shower now," she told Bridget.

"By all means. As far as I'm concerned, you're free to go. But just in case those blackouts return, I want you to stay in the keep for a few days, and absolutely no driving."

"I know. I wouldn't dare."

"Good, and please stop by my office on your way out. I'll print out a list of instructions for you."

"Thank you."

"You're welcome." Bridget patted her shoulder.

In the bathroom, Callie dropped the johnny on the floor and examined what she could see in the vanity mirror. The bruising was all gone, but she had somehow lost a lot of weight over the last twenty-four hours. Her skin was stretched over her protruding ribs. Not a sexy look. She needed to go on a calorie-dense diet.

Other than that she was still the same Callie. Same color eyes, same messy hair, same everything. Apparently, the change didn't make people look better.

*Don't be greedy, Callie. You're an immortal, and so is the man you love.*

*Immortal.*

*Wow.*

Life was sure stranger than fiction.

Except, standing in front of the mirror and staring at her reflection wasn't going to help her wrap her head around this new reality she'd found herself in.

In the meantime, life went on, and she needed to get busy to keep from freaking out.

Step one, shower.

When she was done, Callie put on the clothes Amanda had so thoughtfully lent her. They were nothing fancy, a pair of black leggings and a black T-shirt, but the labels were enough to make Callie suck in a breath. She'd never even tried on anything like that. A pair of new panties with the price tag still attached, another sticker shocker, but no bra. No big deal. The T-shirt was loose and the fabric substantial. Unless someone looked closely, it was hard to tell Callie wasn't wearing one.

She pulled her wet hair back, tucking it behind her ears, and opened the door to the recovery room.

Brundar was leaning against the wall, his arms crossed over his chest and his legs at the ankles. "You look good."

"Thank you." She looked down at her outfit. "I've never worn anything so expensive in my life."

"I'm not talking about your clothes." He pushed off the wall and sauntered toward her, the predatory gleam in his eyes giving her pause. He'd told her a lot yesterday, but that was only the tip of the iceberg. She knew so little about the man she'd fallen in love with.

God, he'd proposed last night, but he hadn't told her he loved her yet. Not that she doubted he did, but she needed to hear him say it.

As he pulled her into his arms and kissed her, hungrily, savagely, crushing her to him, Callie realized that he'd been holding back until now, mindful of her human fragility. How strong was she anyway?

Suddenly, she was reminded of Donnie's story about Brundar lifting an SUV with one hand. How strong was he?

"Ready to go home?"

"Bridget said I need to stay here for a few days."

"I know. I was talking about my and Anandur's apartment."

"Oh. Let me just pick up my things." Using the same bag Amanda had brought her change of clothes in, Callie put in the sweats and underwear Bridget had gotten for her in the hospital's gift shop and her purse that the paramedic had pulled out of her wrecked car, then went to the bathroom for the toothbrush Bridget had given her.

"Now I'm ready." Sort of.

Callie still felt as if she'd been transported into a parallel universe.

On their way out, they stopped at Bridget's office for the set of instructions.

Bridget handed them to Brundar. "Make sure she follows this. Especially the part about the food." She pointed a finger at Callie. "Your body needs a lot of calories for what it is doing. This is not the time to think about your figure."

Callie waved a dismissive hand. "Don't worry. I don't like seeing my own ribs. I'm going to indulge in every sinful dish I skipped over because it was too fattening."

That had proven to be a bit of a problem, as she'd discovered looking into Brundar's empty fridge. "I see that Anandur went back to his old ways after I left. All you have is beer and peanut butter. Nothing else."

"I'll get us something from the café downstairs."

She shook her head. "I don't want more sandwiches. I want real food. Can you stop at a grocery store and get me some supplies?"

"I want you to rest, not cook. I'll bring takeout from wherever you want."

Given the stubborn expression on his face, it was pointless to argue. She would let him win today, but tomorrow she was going to cook no matter what. She would find someone to bring her groceries. Perhaps Amanda could lend Callie her butler.

"Can you also stop by our apartment and bring me more clothes? And my lotions and my hairbrush."

"Anything else?"

"Shoes. And socks. My nightshirt. And don't forget panties and bras."

A smile tugged at the corner of his lips. "Is that all?"

"I can't think of anything else right now. I'll text you if I remember. But please, stop by a supermarket and at least get some eggs and butter and bread and a few vegetables. Maybe some cookies. If I'm to stay here for a few days, I don't want to depend on takeout alone."

He nodded. "I can do that."

"Thank you." She wrapped her arms around his neck and stretched to give him a kiss. "It's strange to adjust to the reversal of roles. Again. First, you took care of me, then I took care of you, and now you're taking care of me again."

"That's what people who love each other do."

Did Brundar just say the L word?

"Say it again."

He lifted a brow. "What? That people who love each other take care of each other?"

"Yes, that. You said love."

"I know what I said."

"That's the first time you told me that you love me."

Brundar frowned. "I might have not used that specific word, but I think it was pretty obvious."

"Yes, but I still needed to hear it."

He smiled. "I love you, Calypso."

"And I love you, Brundar. Forever."

He nodded. "Forever."

## 60

# BRUNDAR

By the time Brundar finished unloading his car, the elevator was full of grocery bags, clothes bags, and Chinese takeout. He'd emptied Calypso's closet and brought everything that was there, which wasn't much. It was time the girl started thinking about herself, and stuffed her closet full of clothes like any other female.

Perhaps he could ask Amanda to help Calypso out. Even better, he could give the princess his credit card and ask her to order things online. That way Calypso couldn't argue or fuss over the prices.

He would get rid of the price tags before she saw them. Brundar wanted her to have the same kind of luxuries Amanda took for granted and take them for granted as well. He hadn't liked the way she'd referred to the borrowed clothes as if they were things she could never have.

The thought of taking care of his mate filled Brundar with a profound sense of satisfaction. Living as long as he had and spending very little, he'd amassed a small fortune. He could spoil Calypso with fancy stuff until she forgot ever living without it. There was nothing he wouldn't get for her.

He was Calypso's mate, and therefore she could no longer refuse his support or his gifts.

*Mate.*

Fates, the word felt good on his lips. He had a mate. His true love match.

Brundar had never thought he would get that lucky. Even when Amanda had discovered Syssi, and the entire clan had been buzzing with hope, he'd never believed one would be found for him. And later, when it had become clear that Amanda had been overly optimistic and finding Syssi and Michael had been a lucky fluke, he hadn't been disappointed because he'd never expected to have one.

Calypso was a gift.

Which reminded him that he still owed Annani a visit, and making the goddess wait was never a good strategy.

Both hands holding multiple bags, he kicked the door to his apartment. "Calypso, open up," he said without raising his voice, hoping her hearing had improved with her transition.

It had. A moment later he heard her footsteps and then the door opened. "Need help?" she asked.

"I've got it." As if he would let her lift anything.

He dropped everything on the floor and went back to bring the rest of the stuff from the elevator.

Calypso was already pulling things out from the bags. "Did you bring every last piece of clothing from the apartment?"

"Just about. There wasn't much."

"Yeah. And the new beautiful outfit I bought at the mall got ruined in the accident." She looked sad.

He pulled her into his arms. "We will get you a new one. A lot of new ones. One ruined outfit is no reason for sorrow."

She hugged him back, holding him tight to her. "I know. But it was a nice one. You would've liked it."

He caressed her back, noting how thin she'd gotten in the span of one day. "I brought Chinese takeout. You need to eat." He let go of her.

Her stomach rumbled in agreement. "It smells amazing. Let me set up the table."

He caught her hand. "We can eat straight from the boxes. I have a meeting I have to get to. I don't have time."

For a change, Calypso didn't argue. She was either too hungry or too tired to bother with plates.

Sitting at the counter, they demolished the six different dishes he'd brought, including all the rice and the fortune cookies.

"Look." Calypso handed him the thin strip of paper with her fortune.

He read it out loud. "Out of misfortune, a blessing will arise."

"Creepy," she said.

"Very apt." He put the piece of paper inside his pocket for safekeeping.

"What are you going to do with that?"

"I don't know yet, but I want to keep it. Maybe frame it. Or perhaps put it inside one of those little decorative boxes."

Calypso lifted a brow. "I didn't peg you as sentimental."

He leaned and kissed her lightly. "I didn't either. But I find myself feeling and doing a lot of things I never did before."

"Because of me?"

"Thanks to you."

## 61

# CALLIE

Her belly full to bursting, Callie felt like taking a nap, but the bags on the floor bothered her. Until she put everything away and made sure the place was nice and tidy, she wouldn't be able to sleep.

Besides, Brundar's meeting was a perfect opportunity to clean up and organize without him fussing and demanding that she rest and not touch a thing.

Callie poured herself another cup of coffee and got to work.

After putting the groceries away, she took her things to Brundar's closet, which had enough unused space to accommodate all of them with plenty of room to spare. The guy didn't have much, but what he had was neatly organized. Obviously, he used some laundry service because everything was professionally pressed.

She picked up a sweater and brought it to her nose for a sniff. It had been laundered, but some of Brundar's unique scent remained. Closing her eyes, she buried her nose in it and breathed his scent in, a sense of calm suffusing her.

Was it part of the addiction he'd told her about? Or was it normal for a woman in love?

She was still sniffing and pondering that question when someone knocked on the door. Brundar would have just walked in, and Anandur was in Hawaii. So who could it be?

Maybe Amanda. Or Bridget.

It turned out to be Amanda and another woman Callie had never met before, who was holding an adorable baby girl.

"Callie, meet Nathalie and her daughter Phoenix. Nathalie, meet Callie." Amanda made the introductions as the two women stepped in.

Nathalie offered her hand. "Hi. I'm a new immortal too. I thought you would like to talk with a kindred spirit."

Callie shook what she was offered, but her eyes remained glued to Phoenix's toothless smile. "She is adorable."

Nathalie adjusted the baby to a more comfortable position. "Thank you."

"Please come in and take a seat. Can I offer you a cup of coffee? I have some freshly brewed."

"I'll get it." Amanda waved a hand. "You sit with Nathalie and have a chat."

For some reason, Callie had a feeling that it would be just as pointless to argue with Amanda as it was with Brundar.

"There are cookies next to the coffeemaker."

"I'll get them."

"How are you feeling?" Nathalie asked. "Amanda said you had no idea you were a Dormant and that the transition took you and Brundar by surprise."

"It happened while I was driving. I'm lucky to be alive."

"By the way," Amanda said as she came in with three cups of coffee. "Bridget is on her way as well. I wish Syssi were here, then the welcoming party would be complete. She is also an ex-human turned immortal. Our first one." She handed Callie her coffee mug and put Nathalie's on the coffee table.

"Brundar told me. We had a very long talk yesterday. Or rather he talked, and I listened."

Amanda shook her head. "I wish I could've seen that. I don't think I ever heard Brundar string more than two words together."

There was a knock on the door and Amanda, who was still standing, opened the way. "Bridget. You're just in time for coffee."

"I need one. With two Dormants transitioning at the same time, I've hardly had any sleep."

"How is Tessa doing?" Callie asked.

"She is still down in the clinic. Your transition went pretty smoothly, aside from the accident that is, but her body is going through more changes so it will take longer."

"Why is that?"

"I have a theory. I think that during the transition the body reaches its full potential. Tessa should have been a bit taller, but growing up she didn't get proper nutrition. She is compensating for it now."

Callie frowned. "I looked myself over in the mirror, and I look exactly the same as I did before."

"So do I," Nathalie said. "My butt is still too big and my boobs too small. I guess I was destined to be disproportioned."

Callie chuckled. "I have the opposite problem. My butt is too small, and my boobs are too big."

Amanda looked at the two of them as if they were nuts. "You girls are being silly. You are each beautiful in your own way. The world would have been a boring place if we all looked the same."

"Says the most gorgeous woman in the universe," Nathalie mumbled.

"I am not. That title belongs to my mother."

The goddess. Kian and Amanda's mother. No wonder the brother and sister were so inhumanly beautiful.

"I have a question," Callie said. "My father and stepmother just had a baby boy. Is he a Dormant like me?"

"Not likely," Bridget said. "If you had the same mother then the answer would have been yes. The immortal genes come from the mother. Are your parents divorced?"

"No. My mother was killed in a car accident when I was a toddler."

Nathalie patted her knee. "I'm so sorry."

Callie shrugged. "I don't even remember her. All I have are a few pictures and home movies. My dad never really got over her death, and it was very difficult for him to talk about her, so I don't even know much about what kind of a person she was. She seemed nice in the home movies, and happy. My father did too."

"That's so sad," Nathalie said.

"He is better now. Iris, his new wife, brought the smile back to his face, and now with the new baby, he sounds really happy. I can't wait to see my baby brother." She glanced at the little girl in Nathalie's arms. "I absolutely adore babies."

Bridget cleared her throat. "Did you think about what you are going to tell him?"

"I'm not going to tell him anything." Callie snorted. "If I come up with a story like that, he will have me committed to a mental institution."

"Eventually he will notice that you're not aging," Bridget said.

Right. But there was plenty of time to think about that. Callie was only twenty-one. Her father would not expect to see wrinkles on her face for many years to come.

## 62

## BRUNDAR

"Good evening, Clan Mother." Brundar bowed.

"Come sit with me." She patted the spot next to her.

He did as she asked, but sat as far away from her as the couch allowed. It wasn't that he feared her, but sitting so close to the goddess seemed disrespectful.

She smiled. "I heard the wonderful news. Congratulations."

He bowed his head again. "Thank you, Clan Mother."

"Please." She waved a hand. "Call me Annani. We are not meeting in any official capacity. This is family business."

"As you wish." He would swallow his own tongue before using her given name.

"It is very fortunate that I happen to be here. If you so wish, I can perform a joining ceremony for you and your beloved."

The goddess's eyes sparkled with enthusiasm. There were two things that made the Clan Mother especially happy. One was babies, and the other was weddings. He would have to disappoint her.

"I thank you for your offer, but it's too early for us to be talking about a wedding." Hopefully, Anandur had kept his yap shut and hadn't told Kian or Syssi about Brundar's proposal.

The last thing he needed was to antagonize the goddess. If she'd heard from Kian or Syssi about his proposal, she would think he was lying to her on purpose.

Annani frowned, and his gut twisted in a knot. Did she know?

"Why is that? Are you not sure that she is the one and only for you?"

He shook his head. "It's not that. I know Calypso is my true love match. But we haven't been together long. I need her to get to know me better first."

"I see." The spark in the goddess's eyes dimmed a little. "You are not sure of her love for you."

"It's not that either. I know Calypso loves me."

Frustrated, the goddess lifted both hands in the air. "So what is the problem, young man?"

He wasn't going to tell Annani his deepest secret, but maybe he could ask her advice. "Do you believe that mates need to know everything about each other?"

A naughty smile brought back the sparkle in her eyes. "Well, not everything. Some mystery makes the relationship more interesting."

It was obvious that she was not talking about his type of secret. "What about traumatic events that happened a long time ago? Things that might affect the way she sees me?"

Annani's expression turned somber. "You are a warrior, Brundar. Whatever you have done in the line of duty is nothing to feel ashamed of. Your beloved should know who you are, including your past deeds, and accept you, warts and all. If she does not, then she is not worthy of you."

Again, Annani had mistaken his question to mean something else. Brundar was not ashamed of his past deeds as a soldier. He hadn't told Calypso any details, but she knew he had killed in defense of his clan and had no problem with that.

Still, the goddess had it right. If he never told Calypso about what had happened to him, he would always wonder if it might change the way she saw him. It was better to get it over with, and not let it fester indefinitely.

"Thank you for the advice, Clan Mother. I will tell Calypso everything there is to know about me. But I need to find the right time to do it."

The goddess put her tiny hand on his thigh. "Do not delay. The more you think about it, the harder it will become. Things of this nature always seem worse than they actually are."

"Words of wisdom."

She smiled. "I have not always been so wise. It comes with age. Talk with your Calypso. If you change your mind about the wedding, do so soon. I am leaving the day after Kian and Syssi are back."

"I will. Thank you." He pushed to his feet.

"I want to meet your mate when she feels better. Perhaps tomorrow?"

That was unexpected. He hadn't told Calypso about Annani staying at the keep because it was supposed to be classified information. "I'm under orders to keep your presence here a secret. Only the Guardians, the council members, and Phoenix's parents are allowed to know."

Annani waved a dismissive hand. "I am amending your orders to include Calypso in that shortlist. As long as I am here, I want to meet the new additions to my clan. I already met Tessa, and now I want to meet Calypso."

He bowed again. "Of course, Clan Mother."

She sighed. "I see that it is no use with you. Hopefully, your mate will soften you some. You are too rigid."

"Yes, Clan Mother."

## CALLIE

"I'm scared," Callie said. Her, plain Callie Meyers, meeting a real freaking goddess face to face?

*Someone please wake me from this insane dream.* What was she saying? *No, please don't. If this is a dream I never want to wake up.*

"Don't be. Annani is powerful, but she is kind. She just wants to get to know you."

"What if she doesn't like me?"

"Why wouldn't she? You're smart and kind and brave and beautiful. What else is there?"

"I'm a waitress, for God's sake." She chuckled. "I guess I need to change that to a for Goddess's sake."

"So what? What's wrong with being a waitress?"

She shrugged. "A lot of people look down on waitressing because it doesn't require education."

"Not Annani. She is smarter than that."

Callie nodded. "I guess I have no choice either way. It's not like I can refuse a summons from a goddess."

"No, you can't. Can I knock on the door now?"

"Yeah." She sucked in a deep breath and forced her hands to stop fidgeting with the bottom of her shirt.

Crap, if only she had something nicer to wear. But the strapless black dress was not appropriate for a formal meeting, and everything else she had was limited to jeans, leggings and T-shirts. The outfit she'd bought before the accident would have been perfect, but unfortunately, it hadn't made it.

A short, kind of square-looking man wearing a suit opened the door and bowed. "Greetings, master and mistress. Please enter, the Clan Mother is awaiting you."

A strange little man, but then everything in Callie's new reality was.

Brundar's hand on the small of her back propelled her forward as her eyes darted around for her first glimpse of the goddess.

She found her sitting on the couch. A small woman with a massive head of hair, soft red curls cascading down her back and front and pooling around her. Callie had never seen hair like that.

But then the woman turned toward them, and Callie's knees buckled. She barely stifled the "Oh, my God," she felt compelled to exclaim.

Amanda had been right. As stunning as the daughter was, her mother, who at first glance looked much younger than her daughter, was incomparable. It was hard to put her finger on what exactly made the goddess so inhumanly beautiful. Callie had a feeling that a mere picture could have never translated all this otherworldly creature was. Her beauty emanated from the inside, striking Callie like a force field.

An immense power was contained in that small package.

"Calypso, come sit with me." She patted the couch next to her.

Callie glanced at Brundar.

He encouraged her with a nod, and when she didn't move, led her to the couch. She lowered herself down to sit on the very edge, looking down at her feet instead of facing the nuclear power plant sitting next to her.

What if the radiation made her face melt off? Callie felt like giggling hysterically at the absurd notion. Or was it? The goddess was glowing. Didn't it imply some form of radiation?

Brundar nudged her, reminding her of her manners.

"It's an honor to meet you, Clan Mother." She whispered the words Brundar had instructed her to say.

The goddess reached for her clammy hand and clasped it. "Call me Annani. Clan Mother is a title I tolerate at ceremonies. I am not too fond of it in private."

"Oh," was the only response Callie could come up with. Brilliant.

The goddess turned to look at Brundar. "You may leave us. I want a few moments alone with your mate. I will summon you when we are done."

He bowed, ignoring Callie's panicked expression. "As you wish, Clan Mother." He turned on his heel and left.

*The traitor.*

When the door closed behind him, the goddess sighed. "You have your work cut out for you, child. That boy needs to loosen up, and you seem like the right girl to pull that stick out of his backside."

Shocked, Callie looked up at the goddess's smiling face.

The goddess waved a hand. "Do not look so shocked. You know I am right."

Callie swallowed. "I guess," she whispered.

"Use your outside voice, Calypso," the esteemed Clan Mother singsonged the tune from a *Saturday Night Live* skit.

Callie giggled, the frog in her throat shrinking. "I would've never expected a goddess to watch television."

Annani rolled her eyes. "How else am I going to learn all about popular culture? Besides, I enjoy a good laugh. That skit is so funny."

"It is." It was also vulgar, but apparently, the goddess was no prude.

"You are probably wondering why I wanted to see you."

Callie nodded. "Brundar said you wanted to get to know me."

"Yes. It is a rare opportunity for me to welcome a new member to my clan who is not of my line. A new blood, if you will. I do not know if Brundar explained how important it is to us to find people like you. Especially females who could become the mothers of new genetic lines."

"He told me a lot, but I don't remember everything. It was so much to absorb. But I understand that those who are your descendants can't intermarry, and that up until recently there weren't any other known immortals other than your clan and your enemies the Doomers, who are all male and are obviously not considered good marriage material."

"That is it in a nutshell. You understand perfectly. Now tell me about yourself, including how you and Brundar found each other." The goddess smirked. "If I ask him, I will get a three-word answer at best. I would rather hear the story from you."

Callie took a deep breath and decided to tell the goddess everything. After all, she had nothing to hide or be ashamed of, and even if she had, it would be foolish to tell half-truths to a goddess who might be able to read her mind.

"You are a very brave young woman," Annani said after Callie was done.

She felt herself blush at the undeserved compliment. "It's very kind of you, but I'm not. I just did what I had to do to survive." She looked into the goddess's warm eyes. "You are the brave one. I know you are a goddess and that you are very powerful, but from what Brundar told me I understand that you were still a young girl when you lost the love of your life and then your entire family. If I were you, I would've crawled into a hole and waited to die."

As sadness replaced the mirth in Annani's eyes, Callie regretted letting herself blabber like that.

"That is exactly what I did, child. But at some point, I realized it was selfish. I was the only survivor of an advanced civilization, and without me and the knowledge I carried humanity would be lost for thousands of years. I had to do all I could to preserve my people's legacy and help humanity evolve."

"As I said, you were incredibly courageous to take on such a monumental task, and at such a young age, despite the despair that must've weighed you down."

"My despair was illuminated by a tiny glimmer of hope, and it was enough to keep me going. It still does."

"The hope for humanity?"

Annani tilted her head as if deliberating whether she should answer or not. "Not only that. It was more personal than that."

What could it be? Brundar had said that the goddess had vowed to never love again. So that could not have been it. "Do you hope some of your people survived? Or maybe got away?"

"No, child. At the beginning I did. But after I'd learned all the facts I knew they were all gone."

The goddess sighed and smiled a sad smile. "It happened before I escaped, while I was still in mourning and inconsolable in my grief. An old human fortuneteller came to see me. She was quite famous for her abilities, so I agreed to hear her out even though I did not want to talk to anyone other than my parents and my best friend, Gulan."

Annani let go of Callie's hand and wiped a lone tear from the corner of her eye. "The fortuneteller told me not to despair because all was not lost. I cannot say more because she made me swear to never repeat this to anyone, and I am not foolish enough to disregard the words of a seer, even a human one."

Callie could understand that. If the foretelling was so important that it had kept Annani going for thousands of years, she was right to follow the seer's instructions to the letter and not jinx it in any way.

"I hope it was okay for you to tell me even this little."

Annani nodded. "I do not know why I did. I never told anyone." She smiled. "There must be something special about you."

Callie put a hand over her heart. "I will never repeat this to anyone. Your secret is safe with me."

The goddess leaned over and kissed her cheek. "I know, child."

## 64

# BRUNDAR

Calypso didn't say much as Brundar picked her up from Kian's penthouse. She seemed dazed, which was understandable following her first encounter with Annani.

The goddess's presence was unnerving even to her own descendants, let alone to a girl who'd known nothing of their world up until the day before yesterday.

"Are you okay?" he asked as they entered the elevator.

"Yes. I don't know how my head didn't explode yet, but somehow I'm holding it together."

He pulled her into his arms. "You are stronger than you realize."

She leaned her forehead on his chest. "I'm not all that strong. I have you to lean on."

Her words filled him with immense satisfaction. "Always." He kissed the top of her head.

Calypso lifted her eyes to him. "And you have me to lean on too. I hope you realize that. It's no longer just your brother and you. I'm your family too."

Brundar tightened his arms around her, then let her go as the elevator doors opened.

Hand in hand, they walked down the corridor to what would be, from now on, their home. At least until he applied for a house in the village.

Would Anandur stay with them? Did he want to keep his brother as a roommate?

Brundar didn't mind, but those kinds of decisions were no longer his own. It would be up to Calypso. His future was with her.

However, there was one more thing Brundar needed to do before he could think of a future with his mate without a dark cloud hanging over his head.

Back in the apartment, he had Calypso sit on the couch and then poured himself a hefty serving of whiskey.

She lifted a brow. "Isn't it a bit early for that?"

"Anytime after five in the afternoon is not too early."

She laughed. "I guess for Scots it never is."

"Aye." He saluted. "I would offer you a drink, but all we have are beers and whiskey."

"I'll settle for a glass of water."

He went back to the kitchen, filled a tall glass for her, then came back to sit next to her on the couch.

"I need to tell you something, and it's not going to be easy for me."

She put a hand on his thigh. "You don't need to tell me anything that makes you uncomfortable."

He shook his head. "There should be no secrets between mates. Not big ones, anyway. If I don't tell you, it will keep bothering me until I do."

She nodded, but her eyes betrayed her trepidation. He wondered what Calypso was imagining his big secret was to make her so fearful.

"Remember when I told you about what happened to me when I was a kid?"

"Of course." She let out a breath, which he took to mean that this wasn't what she'd thought he was about to tell her.

"I didn't tell you everything. No one other than Anandur knows what happened. Not even our mother."

She frowned. "Are you sure you want to tell me?"

The more outs she was giving him, the more determined he was to tell her. "Yes, I am. It was more than a severe beating. I was violated by someone I thought of as my best friend."

She nodded as if his confession didn't come as a surprise to her. "I guessed as much."

It was a tremendous relief. The worst part about telling Calypso was fear of her reaction. If she'd responded with horror or pity, it would have crushed him.

"How did you know?"

"Your aversion to touch. A beating, no matter how severe, wouldn't have caused it." She took his hand and lifted it to her lips for a kiss. "Thank you for telling me. Your trust means a lot to me."

He closed his eyes for a split second, thanking the Fates for the gift that was Calypso. Somehow she'd managed to turn this difficult moment and the memory of a vile act into something positive—a gift of trust.

"That's not the end of the story. Anandur saved me from further violation by the rest of the gang that had attacked me. He killed them all."

"How old was he?"

"He was already a grown man, a warrior. If not for him, I would've died. It was before my transition, I was still human, and a weak human at that."

Calypso's lip quivered, and tears pooled at the corners of her eyes before spilling down her cheeks. "I'm sorry. I wanted to be strong for you, but imagining a young boy tortured and murdered, I just can't handle it. I'm so sorry."

He pulled her into his arms. "Thanks to Anandur it didn't happen. But my family had to flee in the middle of the night, leaving everything behind. The villagers were coming to avenge their sons, and there were too few of us to defend our homes. After that, Annani decreed that we all needed to move to one location, far away from any human settlements. It took us decades of hardship to build our home in Scotland. And it was all my fault."

She pushed on his chest. "It wasn't your fault. You were a boy, a victim."

He shook his head. "If I had listened to my mother and stayed away from the humans, none of that would have happened."

"First of all, you were a young boy. Show me one preteen who listens to his mother. Secondly, it might have saved your clan from worse things. What happened to you was tragic and awful, but it forced your family to build a strong, defensible home. So maybe you should think of it as thanks to you and not because of you."

She was so adorable when berating him for putting himself down.

At that moment, he loved her more than ever. "I love you, Calypso. You are like an explosion of light that obliterates my darkness. I couldn't hold on to it even if I tried."

The indignation in her eyes gave way to the sweetest expression. She cupped his cheek. "This is the power of love. It is the antidote to darkness."

"I agree."

As long as he was on a roll, he should get it all out. "There is more."

Calypso flinched.

He squeezed her hand. "No more tragedies, I promise. But you might get angry after you hear my last confession."

"What is it?"

"When I first met you at the club, I couldn't just let you go. You were married, off limits to me, but I peeked into Shawn's mind and knew you weren't safe with him. I've watched over you ever since." He smoothed his hand over his jaw. "It was straight out stalker behavior, but I couldn't help myself. I guess I knew on a subconscious level that you were my fated one."

Again, Calypso didn't look shocked or surprised. "Did you park across the street from my house?"

He nodded.

"I felt it. I would look out the window and get this peaceful feeling as if someone was watching over me. I thought it was just my imagination."

"So you're not mad?"

"Mad? No way, I'm grateful. Knowing that I was never really alone during those hard times is such a relief."

"You are never going to be alone again. Not as long as I breathe. We are one."

She cuddled up to him. "Always and forever."

## 65

# TURNER

*D*eath.

The bastard finally came to collect, much earlier than Turner had been expecting him.

Forty-six was too young to die.

For a civilian.

As a soldier in an elite commando unit, he hadn't expected to live long, but then he was no longer one—hadn't been for a long time. Turner had been retired for a good number of years, and even before that, his field days had been a distant memory. His tactical abilities had become apparent early on in his military career, making him a much more valuable asset with a pen and paper behind the desk than with a rifle behind enemy lines.

The irony wasn't lost on him.

With a rifle, he would have had much less blood on his hands than what he'd accomplished from behind the fucking desk. As a brilliant tactician, Turner had no doubt that his missions had resulted in lower casualties compared to missions planned by others, but that didn't mean he hadn't sent many to their deaths.

Knowingly.

He had an uncanny ability to predict the precise outcome of every mission. Unfortunately, he could count those with no lives lost on the fingers of one hand.

Over the course of his military career, and later as a civilian operator, Turner had fed the Grim Reaper countless lives. But the monster wasn't satisfied with that offering. He came back for Turner with one of his most deadly hatchets.

Lung cancer.

Turner had never smoked, had never shared an office with a smoker, and as far as he knew, he hadn't been exposed to any toxic substances either. He watched what he put in his mouth, kept a gruelingly intense workout routine, and was a black belt in several martial arts disciplines.

One of the advantages of being a single man who didn't date much was plenty of free time. His lifestyle had been Spartan. He'd kept to his strict regimen, believing it would keep him in good shape and healthy into old age.

But fate was a vindictive bitch.

The disease had come out of the blue. A persistent cough that had finally prompted him to see a doctor, leading to the diagnosis less than a week later.

Not that death was imminent. With treatments he could forestall the fucker for years, maybe even for good, but Turner refused to live under his dark shadow.

He wasn't ready to go.

What had he done with his life?

A lot for others, but very little for himself.

And yet, if Turner cared to be honest with himself, he had to admit that this wasn't entirely true. Even though his job had been about the most complicated rescue and extraction operations, seemingly a noble task, he'd done it because he'd loved the game.

Outsmarting the enemy had given him the kind of satisfaction he couldn't derive from anything else; he lived for the thrill, and the collateral damage hadn't bothered him too much.

He was an analytical man, not an emotional one.

Even now, facing the possibility of his own premature death, Turner didn't feel despair or anger. He wasn't even overly surprised. But that didn't mean he was going to throw in the towel and accept defeat. That wasn't his style.

He was Turner, the guy who always found another angle, another solution.

There was no cure for what he had. The doctor had talked about treatment and remission, not a cure. But that didn't mean there was no other way to cheat death.

Permanently.

It was a long shot.

Turner had always suspected that there were hidden forces at work behind the seemingly unpredictable machinations of global affairs, and that what was considered occult often had a scientific explanation, albeit one yet to be discovered.

Apparently, the mythological gods hadn't been the construct of human imagination, but an advanced species that had become extinct.

Kian and Andrew hadn't shared many details with him, but after further investigation, Turner had deduced the rest by putting the puzzle pieces together.

A very small portion of the human population carried their immortal genes. Those lucky humans tended to exhibit a wide array of paranormal talents with varying strengths.

The only thing that had made Andrew special was his ability to tell truth from lie. A useful trick that Turner had exploited on more than one occasion during the years Andrew had served under him. But that little trick was nothing in comparison to what Turner could do.

Of course, that didn't mean he was a Dormant carrier of immortal genes, but there was a small chance that he was.

A chance was all he was going to ask for, and Kian was going to give it to him.

Willingly or not.

Turner wasn't above blackmail. On the contrary, it was one of the better tools in his arsenal. Kian needed to keep his people's existence secret, and Turner was more than happy to comply.

For a price.

A chance at immortality.

Victor Turner still had a lot of living to do.

---

Dear reader,

Thank you for joining me on the continuing adventures of the **_Children of the Gods_**. As an independent author, I rely on your support to spread the word. So if you enjoyed the story, please share your experience, and if it isn't too much trouble, I would greatly appreciate a brief review on Amazon.

Click **HERE** to leave a review

Love & happy reading,
Isabell

## COMING UP NEXT
### Dark Operative Trilogy

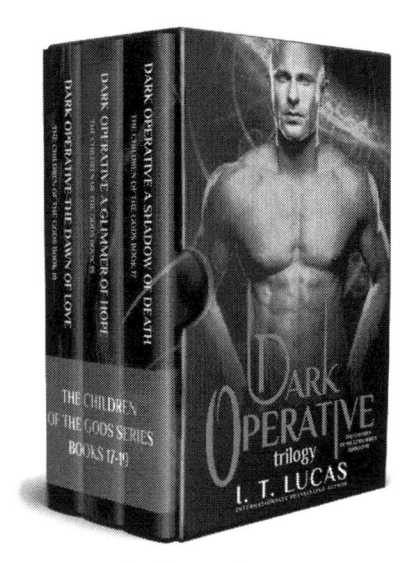

*Read the enclosed excerpt*

### Includes
**17: Dark Operative: A Shadow of Death**
**18: Dark Operative: A Glimmer of Hope**
**19: Dark Operative: The Dawn of Love**

### Don't miss out on
## THE PERFECT MATCH SERIES
**Perfect Match 1: Vampire's Consort**
**Perfect Match 2: King's Chosen**
**Perfect Match 3: Captain's Conquest**

## FOR EXCLUSIVE PEEKS AT UPCOMING RELEASES
Join my *VIP Club* and gain access to the VIP portal at itlucas.com
**click here to join**

(If you're already a subscriber and forgot the password to the VIP portal, you can find it at the bottom of each of my emails. Or click **HERE** to retrieve it. You can also email me at isabell@itlucas.com)

# DARK OPERATIVE A SHADOW OF DEATH

## EXCERPT

### KIAN

"After you, my love." Kian held open the door to the rooftop vestibule for Syssi.

"Your mother was in an awful hurry to get back home this time," she said. "Do you think something happened while we were away?"

As soon as they'd returned from Hawaii, Annani had been in such a rush to leave the chopper's engines hadn't had a chance to cool off after shuttling them back from the clan's airstrip.

"She doesn't like to be away from her sanctuary for too long."

And thank the merciful Fates for that. Kian couldn't wait to reclaim their penthouse. At last, they had the place to themselves, with no family members invading their space and demanding his attention.

Guests, even loved ones, stretched his patience to the limit. His home was his sanctuary, the one place he could let go and just be Kian—not the regent, not the head of the keep or the clan's business empire—just a guy chilling at home with his wife.

Besides, the sooner his mother was back at the sanctuary, the better. Kian had enough on his mind without adding concern for the goddess's safety to the mix.

Just as he'd known she would, Annani had failed to keep her presence a secret. His mother had visited Tessa in the clinic, not at all concerned about bumping into someone who wasn't on the need-to-know list.

But then Annani considered his insistence on secrecy an overkill. After all, she could pull a number of tricks her immortal descendants couldn't, like sneaking into Tessa's room under the cover of a shroud with no one any the wiser.

The goddess had the power to manipulate human and immortal minds with ease, while he and the other immortals could only affect those of humans. Thankfully, she refrained from using those powers on her family.

His mother was manipulating them the old-fashioned way. Like any other mother worth her salt, Annani guilted and bullied them into doing her bidding.

"She visited the catacombs again," Syssi said.

Not a big surprise. Every time the goddess graced his keep with her presence, she paid her respects to their dead.

Thank the Fates the catacombs in his keep housed only a few. The final resting place for most of those they had lost over the years was at the clan's old Scottish stronghold.

Kian shrugged. "Annani is sentimental."

"I know. It's just strange that she includes the Doomers in her walkabout."

"Tell me about it. My mother holds on to the naive belief that one day the entombed Doomers she forbade us to kill could be resurrected and brought into the clan's fold."

"I understand her reluctance to kill them. Even though they are brainwashed to hate her and seek her demise and her progeny's demise, she feels that they are still her people and there aren't many of you left."

"Us," he corrected her. "You're part of the clan."

Syssi waved a hand. "Naturally. But I meant your family. I wasn't born into it. Though you are right, I should say us."

He wrapped his arms around her. "You are my family first. The clan comes second."

"I love you too." Syssi reached for his cheek and cupped it in her soft palm. "I would never tell Annani this to her face, but I agree that her thinking they could be reformed is naive, especially for someone who is older than most civilizations and should know better. She should never put her family in danger like that."

"Don't worry. I would never let her do something so idiotic. It's like freeing a bunch of deadly vipers inside your home, hoping they will play nice and go peacefully about their business."

Syssi nodded. "The moment they are able, they will attack."

"Exactly."

Not on his watch.

Letting Syssi out of the cocoon of his arms, Kian walked over to the bar and poured himself a shot of whiskey. "Do you want a drink?" he asked.

"No, thanks. I want to go visit Brundar and Anandur and welcome Callie into the clan. You need to come too."

"Why? Can't you go as my representative?" Kian grimaced. "I was quite rude to the girl when I caught her hiding in their apartment."

"It wasn't her idea to sneak into the keep. It was theirs. You should have been nicer to her." Syssi shook her head. "Poor girl. She'd been through a horrible trauma, and then you had to go and scare her even more. Do you know how terrifying you are when you're angry?"

Kian raked his fingers through his hair.

If Syssi was trying to make him feel guilty, she was succeeding. Except, his anger had been justified and he had done nothing wrong. The girl was a human, and humans were not allowed in the clan areas of the building. Kian was willing to relax the rules for a potential Dormant, but even Brundar hadn't suspected her of that. Callie had none of the indicators. Her transition had taken all of them by surprise.

"I did what I had to. There is a reason no humans are allowed on the floors occupied by the clan. I don't make up rules to make everyone's life more difficult; they are there to ensure the safety and survival of my people."

Syssi waved a hand. "Before Amanda met Dalhu, she'd been bringing guys up to her penthouse and breaking your rules all the time. I'm sure many of the others are doing so as well. They are just better at hiding it from you."

Anger, hot and sharp, filled his chest. What else was happening right under his nose that he wasn't aware of?

"I'm going to fire the entire goddamned security department. They should have informed me of what was going on. It's not like the rules are unclear. It's their fucking job to monitor who goes where!"

"How would they've known?" Syssi rolled her eyes. "Amanda parked in the clan's private garage and used the penthouse's dedicated elevator, which has no surveillance cameras. That's a big gaping hole in your security protocol, Mr. Regent in charge of everyone's safety."

Fuck. Syssi was right. But to put cameras in the parking garage and in the clan's private elevators was an invasion of privacy he wanted to avoid. "I'm walking a very thin line between ensuring safety and a big-brother-watching type of security."

Syssi sighed. "I know, my love." She walked over to him and wrapped her arms around his waist. "These kinds of problems will no longer be an issue once we move everyone to the village."

He held her to him, burying his nose in her hair. "Then there will be new ones. I feel like I'm in charge of a kindergarten full of misbehaving children, instead of people who've lived long enough and have experienced enough to know better. And what's worse, my own mother is the ringleader."

Syssi caressed his back. "After living with danger for so long, people get tired of hiding and worrying. They just want to live normal lives. You can see it on the news when a terrorist bomb explodes in a busy café, killing and maiming dozens of innocent civilians. The next day, the same street is teeming with people again. Life goes on."

"And I bet the security personnel in charge of keeping all those civilians safe are going nuts."

She chuckled. "Probably. But I don't want to talk about depressing subjects, especially when we have reason to celebrate. We have two new clan members—two new females to start two new hereditary lines. Not so long ago, you would've been jumping with joy at such news."

True words. With his lack of gratitude, Kian was probably courting the Fates' wrath. Instead of complaining, he should be offering his thanks. After millennia of turning their capricious backs on his family, recently the Fates had bestowed a bounty of gifts on his clan.

He, in particular, had a lot to be grateful for.

The Fates had been incredibly kind to him, bringing him Syssi, the love of his life, his truelove mate, and the first Dormant ever discovered.

Kian kissed the top of his wife's head. "What would I have done without you? Who would have called me out on my bullshit?"

She chuckled. "Your mother, Amanda, and your two other sisters."

Yeah, he was surrounded by smart women who he couldn't intimidate no matter how hard he tried, and who had no problem chewing him out whenever he deserved it. "Let's go and get the visit over with. Is Callie staying at Brundar's?"

"They plan to live here until the village is ready."

"What about Anandur? Did he move out?"

"The three of them are staying together." Syssi laughed. "I don't think they could've gotten rid of him even if they wanted to. Callie is an amazing cook, and you know how Anandur loves it when someone makes food for him, especially when it's not vegan."

"That didn't stop him and his brother from taking every opportunity to show up just when Okidu was serving lunch or dinner. They kept complaining about it being vegan and eating it anyway."

"As I said, having someone else cook for him is more important to Anandur than what is served."

No wonder the guy wanted to stay. Having a cook at home who had no problem with preparing meat dishes was a dream come true for him.

The question was whether Brundar was happy with the arrangement. Kian would have hated having one of his nosy siblings around. A mated couple needed their privacy. Anandur needed to move out.

Perhaps the girl should ruin a couple of dishes on purpose.

Except, her cooking might be a source of pride for her. Kian wondered what her level of skill was. Had she studied the culinary arts, or was it just a hobby?

"How do you know Callie is a good cook?"

"Bridget told me." Syssi's cheeks were getting pinker by the minute.

Kian cocked a brow and looked down at his wife, who was trying to avoid his gaze. "And how did Bridget learn of the fact?"

Syssi looked away. "Hmm, Callie invited her and Anandur to dinner."

"So soon after her transition?"

"It was before that."

"I knew it, the bastards kept hiding her in their apartment even after I ordered them to take her home. I'll have those two whipped."

Syssi paled. "The dinner wasn't there. It was at Callie's apartment."

He didn't smell a lie, but it didn't make sense for Bridget to accompany Brundar to his girlfriend's place. It wasn't as if the doctor and Brundar were close friends. Unless, she'd gone there to check up on him, which meant that he'd been staying with Callie while pretending to be in the keep.

Since Kian hadn't asked, he couldn't even accuse the guy of lying, but apparently the conspiracy to keep this from him involved more than Brundar and his brother.

"Who else knew that Brundar was staying at Callie's?"

Syssi's pale cheeks flushed with color again. "Bridget and Anandur."

"And who else?"

She chewed on her lower lip.

"Spit it out, Syssi."

She sighed. "Amanda and I knew as well. Amanda even dragged me over there to check Callie out. She is very nice. All of us liked her even when she was still a human, which should have clued us in about her being a Dormant. We all felt an affinity for her."

He cast her a stern look. "Tsk, tsk. You kept a secret from me."

"I know, and I'm sorry, but it wasn't my secret to share, and besides, you would've gotten mad and demanded that Brundar return to the keep. We all thought he needed to be with her, for his sake and for hers. They helped each other heal. She didn't know who we were, just that we were Brundar's family. There was no harm in that. I didn't break any clan laws."

It was all true, but there was still the matter of Syssi practically lying to him by not telling him that she'd gone to visit Callie.

"I think you earned yourself a spanking to remember, my love."

Without looking up at him, Syssi nodded, but for the first time ever, she didn't seem excited by the prospect. Instead of arousal, Kian smelled fear.

With a frown, he hooked a finger under her chin. "Look at me, sweet girl."

She raised a pair of worried eyes to him.

"I can't believe that the promise of a spanking makes you anxious. Did I ever hurt you?"

"No, but you were never mad at me like this either."

He shook his head. "I'm not mad, and this is still the same game we love to play for the enjoyment of both of us and nothing else."

Syssi expelled a breath. "For a moment there, I wasn't sure. You looked so disappointed."

"I am disappointed. Apparently, you don't trust me. The omission of truth is almost as bad as a lie, but thinking that I could ever do anything to hurt you is worse."

Tears pooled in the corners of Syssi's eyes. "I'm sorry. Can you forgive me? What can I do to make it up to you?"

Damn. When Syssi looked so remorseful, it was impossible to stay even slightly peeved at her or pretend that he was.

Wrapping his arms around his wife, Kian lifted her so their faces were aligned. "I'm glad to finally have something to be disappointed about. You're so damn perfect all of the time, while I'm so utterly flawed, that it's a relief to catch you doing something wrong."

As he kissed her, she melted into him, her anxious scent dissipating.

"I love you, my sweet girl, with everything that I am, and with everything that I've got."

Love shining in her beautiful eyes, Syssi cupped his cheeks. "You keep saying that you are not a romantic and that you're not good with words, but you always find the perfect ones for me."

## TURNER

Turner knocked on the door of the suite that had become his and Kian's usual meeting place. With both of them keeping the locations of their real offices secret, they needed a neutral territory to conduct their business. Coffee shops and restaurants didn't provide the necessary privacy, so Kian generously offered this vacant room in one of the clan's many office buildings.

Naturally, Turner had it under surveillance.

The space was used for nothing else, which was quite wasteful since they weren't meeting all that often. Kian was losing good money by not renting it out. But then he could afford it.

At the start of their business association, when Turner had done the background check on his new client, he'd been surprised to find out how extensive their holdings were. It had been difficult to track everything the clan owned, but then Kian wasn't Turner's first client to run an international conglomerate under myriad shadow companies. The clan's, though, was definitely the largest.

One of Kian's bodyguards opened the door. The redhead Viking smiled broadly, his whole face lighting up as if he was welcoming his best friend. "Turner, my man, come in. You're early as usual."

"And as always, you're already here."

The giant slapped his back. "Wouldn't want to keep an important man like you waiting." He stepped aside.

Kian rose to his feet and offered his hand. "Good to see you, Turner."

"You too. How are things going?" He shook the guy's offered hand.

"Busy."

"Busy is good." Turner sat in one of the two leather chairs.

Kian took the other one, while the Viking leaned against the desk and crossed his arms over his chest, doing his best to look formidable. Not that he had to work hard at it. Take away that charming smile and what was left was a killer.

The other bodyguard, the more dangerous of the two, was absent this time, making Turner wonder whether Kian had sent the blond on an errand, or had decided that Turner wasn't dangerous enough to merit two bodyguards.

"What happened to Brundar?" Turner asked.

Kian lifted a brow. "I'm surprised that you remember the names of my men."

"You shouldn't be." Turner paid attention to details others ignored and committed everything to memory. Every seemingly insignificant tidbit could prove useful in the future.

The guy's lips showed a shadow of a smile. "You're right, I shouldn't. So, what do you have for me?"

Turner appreciated that Kian didn't waste his time beating around the bush. The immortal had as much patience for idle chitchat as he had.

Pulling a laptop from his briefcase, Turner put it on the desk. "Your initial plan is not going to work. You might be able to take out some of the smaller operators, but the next day others would take their place. Slave trafficking is painfully easy to do, and where big money can be made with nothing more than lies and manipulation, the scum of the world jumps to fill the void."

"What about the ones who run the operations?"

"Frankly, I can't see anyone taking them down. Countless operators, big and small, are spread all over the world, and some of the organizations are so big, powerful, and ruthless that they make your dreaded enemies the Doomers with all their immortal tricks seem like small fry."

Kian leaned back in his chair and crossed his arms over his chest. "If I didn't know you, I would dismiss your statement as uninformed nonsense. The Doomers are extremely powerful, not only as a mercenary army with thousands of nearly invincible immortal warriors, but with immense resources, including many politicians they hold in their pockets either with bribes or extortion."

"Other than the immortality, some of those slave traders have all of that and more. And unlike your Doomers, who are concentrated in one location, they are spread all over the world. Not only that, they don't function as an army or even as guerrilla forces like drug and arms dealers. The structure is economical in nature, and some of the big ones operate like franchises. I don't know of any army or government that can deal with that effectively."

Turner smoothed his hand over his bald scalp. What he'd found out bothered him, which was unusual for him, and quite disturbing. His professional success depended on his cold and calculated detachment. Emotions were just as bad as alcohol or drugs at compromising the thought process. Probably worse.

"I didn't know how widespread it was until I started digging. It's a plague, and most of it isn't even about abductions. In Third World countries, false promises of employment or marriage coerce desperate families to sell their daughters for a few bucks. And I'm talking about girls as young as twelve and sometimes younger. Abductions are more of a problem in the West. They use promises of love and romance to lure the girls themselves."

Kian shook his head. "Unbelievable."

"Later, when they sell the girls to brothels or individual pimps, they ensure cooperation by sending a small portion of the girls' earnings to their families in the case of Third World countries, and by threatening to harm loved ones in the West. In both cases, severe beatings and starvation are often used to break the girls' spirits."

"Fuck." Kian uncrossed his arms and leaned his forearms on the desk. "So what are we supposed to do? Nothing? Thinking about all those young lives destroyed haunted my nights even before I knew how widespread this vile trade is. Now I won't be able to sleep at all."

As Turner observed Kian's distress, he wondered how the guy had managed to survive as head of his clan for so long. Despite his centuries' long experience, Kian hadn't mastered the detachment that would've helped keep him sane in an insane world. Feelings that strong were not only a burden but also a hindrance to a leader.

First of all, he was inviting competition from within, but that was only part of the problem. Kian wasn't nearly as ruthless as he needed to be in order to win the war against his enemies of old. To fight and actually win, even the good guys couldn't afford compassion.

It wasn't that Turner was indifferent. The world was a fucked up place, but to feel sorrow for all the suffering and injustice was pointless and counterproductive.

After all, he'd spent most of his life rescuing people from bad situations, but for him it meant acknowledging the wrong and trying to fix it to the best of his ability. It didn't affect him emotionally as it did Kian.

Nothing did.

His lack of feelings would've been considered a disability by most, but Turner counted it as one of his most valuable assets. Logic and analytical thinking necessitated detachment. Emotions led to rushed decisions and half-baked actions, which often resulted in more lives lost.

After examining the issue from all angles, the plan he'd come up with was quite extreme and didn't provide the fast solution Kian had hoped for, but it was the only course of action that could actually achieve measurable results. "There is something we can do," he said.

Kian cocked a brow. "And that is?"

"We become the buyers."

The guy leaned away. "You can't be serious. That would contribute to the trade instead of putting a stop to it. I have no intention of lining the traders' pockets with more cash."

Turner shrugged. "You asked me what can be done, and I offered you a solution. I didn't say you were going to like it."

He pinned Kian with a hard stare. "Our goal is to save those girls in any way we can. Until a better solution presents itself, buying and freeing them is better than sitting on our asses and scratching our heads. Your clan is rich, and this is a most worthy charity. Hell, I'm not a philanthropist or an activist, but even I'm willing to contribute to the cause. I'm sure we can find others who would too."

Kian glanced at the open laptop. "I assume you made initial estimates?"

"I did. But contrary to what you may think, the monetary side isn't the most problematic. Our biggest concern is keeping our true intentions secret from the traffickers. To them, we must appear as legit buyers, which means that we can't return the girls to their families. Besides, in the case of Third World countries, the families don't want the girls back. They prefer to think of them as dead rather than have them come back and shame the family."

It was indeed a fucked up world, and young girls had always been its most vulnerable and abused victims. In ancient times virgins had been sacrificed to idols, and in modern times they were sold like commodities then considered tainted and unwanted when used for the purpose they'd been sold for.

Kian shook his head. "What are we supposed to do once we get them? With all due respect, Turner, your plan is too ambitious. We are talking about thousands of girls. The increased demand will only make the traffickers rub their hands with glee and double their efforts. We will solve nothing."

"If buying out the girls was the only thing we did, you would be right. But I'm even more ambitious than that. We approach it from both ends. We buy the girls, and at the same time eliminate the competition, either by outbidding the individual buyers, or stealing girls away from the brothels and then reducing the brothels to rubble. The buyers are a much easier target than the suppliers."

Kian didn't seem convinced; in fact, he regarded Turner as if he'd lost his mind—a reaction Turner was used to since most people had a hard time following his logic. His ability to weave complicated webs in his head without getting lost in the maze allowed him to see clearly what others couldn't.

An example could help Kian understand.

"Imagine that one day your Doomers decide that they want to establish a chain of brothels exactly like the one they have on their island. Will they try to take over the world's slave market? Or will they buy out the entire supply by outbidding their competitors?"

"If taking over is as impossible as you imply, then they would outbid the competition."

Turner nodded. "They buy all the supply, but then they realize that it costs them too much. They want to renegotiate the terms, but the slavers refuse because they know that there are plenty of other buyers. It's in the traffickers' best interests to sell to the highest bidders. What do the Doomers do?"

Given the glow emanating from Kian's eyes, the wheels in his head were gaining momentum. "They take out the other bidders and become the only game in town. Or at least try to."

"Right. Does it surprise anyone?"

"Not really. That's what they do."

"And what will the slavers do when the Doomers are the only remaining bulk buyers and negotiate the prices down?"

Kian tilted his head. "Either live with that or try to take out the Doomers."

"Correct." Turner leaned back in his chair and waited for the gears in Kian's head to do the rest.

The guy shook his head. "I don't get it. Are you suggesting that we establish a chain of brothels or pretend to do so? What's the point?"

Turner had thought the guy was smarter than that. But then it was possible that Kian's do-gooder nature prevented him from seeing the big picture that Turner had so carefully painted for him.

"Let me recap and elaborate. Over time, we become the only game in town by outbidding the competition and then taking everyone else out. Supposedly, we are buying all the stock to create a chain of exclusive brothels in secret locations, when in fact we are stashing the girls somewhere safe. At the same time, we are deflecting suspicion by pointing the big dogs toward your enemies. If you are lucky, the traffickers might help you win your war without you having to lose a single soldier. It's a long shot, but it's a possibility."

The glow emanating from Kian's eyes intensified, making him look even more alien than usual, and when he smiled, he flashed Turner a pair of gleaming white, pointy fangs. "You are a fucking genius, Turner. Your idea is absolutely fucking brilliant. Crazy, probably impossible, but still brilliant."

"It's not impossible. If you can take care of the financial side, I can take care of the tactical one. Between the two of us, we can make it happen." Provided Turner lived long enough to see it through.

This wasn't a short-term plan. It would take years or even decades—time that Turner didn't have unless Kian agreed to grant him his wish.

He stifled a grin.

If Kian chose to proceed with the ambitious plan, he would have one hell of an incentive to do everything in his power to keep Turner around.

## KIAN

Turner's idea was insane.

Even with their combined resources, Kian couldn't see how they could pull it off. It was incredibly costly and involved and would take years if not decades to implement. The part about it that he liked the most was getting the victims out, starting right now.

At least some of them.

He needed Turner to prepare a detailed plan and estimate the rate of acquisitions. If Kian were to divert significant clan resources to the project, he had to get the clan's approval first. As long as he was using their money to grow more of it, he could spend it at his discretion. But he couldn't undertake a humanitarian effort of the magnitude Turner was talking about without a majority vote.

That was only one part of the problem, though, and not the biggest one.

The clan's resources were traditionally used to invest in new scientific research and the development of new technologies. By doing so, they were helping the advancement of humanity while amassing more money to fund more research and more new technologies. If he were to siphon funds away, he would be slowing that progress.

Was it worth it?

Billions of people across the globe would have to wait longer for their lives to improve because the clan was dedicating resources to rescuing mere thousands and providing them with a life worth living.

A tough choice.

Saving the girls was akin to treating the symptoms, while pushing for the advancement of all humanity was akin to eliminating the pathogens of the disease.

The people now living in such abject poverty that some were reduced to selling their children would in the long run benefit from better and cheaper farming equipment, easier and cheaper access to medical treatment, and better education. All of that was possible with the help of technology. Taking resources away from that would slow down the process, which wasn't going fast enough as it was.

Except, the immediate problem was too devastatingly tragic to be allowed to continue. Logic dictated that the needs of millions outweighed the needs of thousands, but the heart didn't agree.

What Kian found peculiar, though, was that a purely analytical man like Turner was the mind behind a plan that required a heart. Perhaps he wasn't the cold-hearted bastard everyone believed him to be.

"I need to sleep on it," he told Turner.

"Do you want me to start working on the plan? I don't want to waste my time if you feel it is not a project you want to undertake."

"I'm inclined to move forward with this, but I need to sell the idea to my clan first. As shareholders, they have the right to refuse an endeavor that is about to make all of them poorer. Furthermore, by diverting resources from investing in new technologies, we are veering away from our main goal, which is to push forward all of humanity's progress."

Turner nodded. "I understand. Do you need help convincing your people? I can prepare a killer presentation. Something so heart-wrenching that no one would refuse you after hearing it."

Kian doubted Turner would know how to achieve that. One needed to have a heart to know how to tug on its strings. This was a project for Amanda.

"Give me a rough draft, and I'll have someone who is excellent at manipulating emotions edit it."

"No problem."

As always, Turner's poker face revealed nothing, but the faint scent emanating from him hinted at disappointment. Usually, Kian's sense of smell was superior, but Turner was either in complete control of his emotions or just didn't feel strongly about anything. Perhaps Andrew was right, and the guy was a borderline sociopath.

"Is there anything else you wish to discuss?"

Turner glanced at Anandur. "There is. But I'd rather not discuss it in front of an audience."

"Anandur is privy to all my business dealings. I vouch for his discretion."

A slight grimace was the first emotion Turner had ever displayed in front of Kian. The guy shifted in his chair. "The matter I wish to discuss with you has nothing to do with business. It's private." He pinned Kian with his hard grey eyes. "All I'm asking for is a few minutes of your time. Do you really need a bodyguard in here? I pose no threat to you. You're faster and stronger than me, and I'm unarmed. Your guy is welcome to search me."

"That won't be necessary." Kian glanced at Anandur, who was shaking his head.

To send him away was a breach of protocol, but Turner was right that Anandur's presence was unnecessary. "Fifteen minutes," he said.

The guy inclined his head. "More than I need."

Anandur pushed away from the corner of the desk he'd been leaning against. "I'll be outside the door."

Turner cleared his throat. "I know how good your hearing is, and I really need this to be private."

Kian was impatient to hear what the guy had to say. "Very well." He looked up at Anandur. "Would you mind getting us coffee? There is a Starbucks in the next building over."

Anandur waved his hands in the air. "I'm getting demoted from a bodyguard to a delivery boy. Why would I mind?" He walked out the door without looking back.

"I guess that's the trouble with employing family," Turner said.

"Tell me about it. But there are advantages too."

"I bet. They are very loyal to you."

"That they are."

"It speaks volumes about the kind of leader you are. They respect you."

Kian smiled. "Okay, now that you've stroked my ego, you can tell me what you need from me."

Turner shrugged. "Regardless, it's the truth."

"What do you want, Turner?"

The guy took a deep breath, then looked Kian straight in the eyes. "I have cancer."

Kian was taken aback. Turner looked as healthy as a horse and was in great shape. "I'm sorry to hear that, but I don't see how I can help you. If we had the cure for cancer, we would've shared the knowledge with humanity."

"I'm not asking you for a cure. I'm asking you to do for me what you did for Andrew."

That was unexpected. As far as Kian was aware, Turner had been told only what was necessary for him to help them. "What do you know about that?"

"I know he was human and now he is not. He gained about two inches in height, and his scars are gone."

"Do you know how it was done?"

"No. But it's not important. If you did it for Spivak, you could do it for me."

"Andrew already carried our genes. All we had to do was to activate them."

"I might have them too."

"Dormant carriers of immortal genes are extremely rare. What makes you think you're one of them?"

His jaw hardening, Turner narrowed his eyes. "Let's cut the crap, shall we? I'm not the best in my field for nothing. Andrew's sister works in a lab with a professor who researches paranormal abilities, and who happens to look a lot like you. A sister, I assume?"

Kian's blood turned cold. If Turner could follow the breadcrumbs to Amanda, then others could too. "Did you have Andrew followed?"

"Naturally. And you too." He waved his hand at the office they were using for their meetings. "We can drop the charade. I know exactly where you live and work. From now on, we can meet over there."

"Fuck. I should've known you'd do that."

"Yes, you should've. But don't worry, your secrets are safe with me."

"What about your people? I assume you didn't do the following yourself."

"No, I didn't. But I don't share with my people the reasons for sending them on assignments. They have no idea why I need the information they collect, and no one person gathers all of the pieces. I'm the only one who puts the puzzle together."

Fuck. Turner had discovered a major flaw in their defenses. The breach had to be addressed as soon as possible.

How much did he know already?

"And what did you learn from putting those puzzle pieces together?"

"Dr. Amanda Dokani is testing people for paranormal abilities, which both Andrew and Syssi have. Andrew has his lie-detector skills, and his sister has visions of the future. I've known this for years because Andrew didn't keep it a secret. You are obviously interested in finding people with paranormal abilities. My guess is that you believe they are good candidates for what you did with Andrew, and I assume with his sister as well."

This was bad. This human, who had no personal alliance with them, knew too much. He was too smart and too cautious to be affected by a memory-suppressing thrall, and he was too valuable to get rid of.

In short, Turner was in a position to blackmail them. He'd maneuvered things so that Kian would not be able to refuse his request.

"Even if we assume that you are a dormant carrier of our immortal genes, which is highly unlikely, you are way past the safe age to attempt transition. Andrew almost died during his, and he is several years younger than you. The older the person, the harder the transition. In addition, you're sick, which in our very limited experience prevents the body from going into transition. If you're not a Dormant, the process will probably not harm you, but if you are, you are most likely going to die from it. Instead of sacrificing the years you still have for an impossible dream, my advice is to get treatment and try to enjoy your life."

Turner shook his head. "I've made up my mind. I'd rather end this quickly than drag it out. I don't want to live in the Grim Reaper's shadow. I'm willing to take the chance. All I'm asking is for you to give it to me."

Fuck. Kian couldn't turn the guy away, but he didn't want to sign Turner's death warrant either. There was a lot of good Turner could still do for them. It would be a shame to lose a valuable asset like that.

Except, Turner was most likely not a Dormant, which meant that they could go through the motions of inducing his transition and nothing would happen. Who knew? Maybe the injection of venom would help with the cancer? They'd never tried it before.

"I'll tell you what I'm willing to do for you. I'll arrange a visit with our in-house doctor. She will evaluate your general health and determine your chances of successfully completing a transition. We will abide by her decision."

Turner narrowed his eyes. "The doctor is working for you, and she will do whatever you tell her."

A snort escaped Kian's throat. "You obviously don't know Bridget. But even if she were inclined to listen to me, she outranks me in everything that has to do with medicine."

The guy didn't look convinced. "But you outrank her in everything that has to do with security. In every organization, safety concerns trump everything else."

Kian spread his arms. "You already know everything that has to do with our safety. If I wanted you dead, I would tell the doctor to approve your request. Your death would solve the security breach you represent, and your blood would not even be on my hands because you asked for it."

That seemed to appease Turner. "Where and when?"

"I'll let you know."

Turner pushed to his feet and offered Kian his hand. "Thank you. You're not going to regret it."

Kian shook what he was offered. "If you die, I certainly will. We need you."

### Dark Operative Trilogy
#### or
**17: Dark Operative: A Shadow of Death**
**18: Dark Operative: A Glimmer of Hope**
**19: Dark Operative: The Dawn of Love**

# THE CHILDREN OF THE GODS SERIES

## THE CHILDREN OF THE GODS ORIGINS

### 1: Goddess's Choice

When gods and immortals still ruled the ancient world, one young goddess risked everything for love.

### 2: Goddess's Hope

Hungry for power and infatuated with the beautiful Areana, Navuh plots his father's demise. After all, by getting rid of the insane god he would be doing the world a favor. Except, when gods and immortals conspire against each other, humanity pays the price.

But things are not what they seem, and prophecies should not to be trusted...

## THE CHILDREN OF THE GODS

### 1: Dark Stranger The Dream

Syssi's paranormal foresight lands her a job at Dr. Amanda Dokani's neuroscience lab, but it fails to predict the thrilling yet terrifying turn her life will take. Syssi has no clue that her boss is an immortal who'll drag her into a secret, millennia-old battle over humanity's future. Nor does she realize that the professor's imposing brother is the mysterious stranger who's been starring in her dreams.

Since the dawn of human civilization, two warring factions of immortals—the descendants of the gods of old—have been secretly shaping its destiny. Leading the clandestine battle from his luxurious Los Angeles high-rise, Kian is surrounded by his clan, yet alone. Descending from a single goddess, clan members are forbidden to each other. And as the only other immortals are their hated enemies, Kian and his kin have been long resigned to a lonely existence of fleeting trysts with human partners. That is, until his sister makes a game-changing discovery—a mortal seeress who she believes is a dormant carrier of their genes. Ever the realist, Kian is skeptical and refuses Amanda's plea to attempt Syssi's activation. But when his enemies learn of the Dormant's existence, he's forced to rush her to the safety of his keep. Inexorably drawn to Syssi, Kian wrestles with his conscience as he is tempted to explore her budding interest in the darker shades of sensuality.

### 2: Dark Stranger Revealed

While sheltered in the clan's stronghold, Syssi is unaware that Kian and Amanda are not human, and neither are the supposedly religious fanatics that are after her. She feels a powerful connection to Kian, and as he introduces her to a world of pleasure she never dared imagine, his dominant sexuality is a revelation. Considering that she's completely out of her element, Syssi feels comfortable and safe letting go with him. That is, until she begins to suspect that all is not as it seems. Piecing the puzzle together, she draws a scary, yet wrong conclusion...

### 3: Dark Stranger Immortal

When Kian confesses his true nature, Syssi is not as much shocked by the revelation as she is wounded by what she perceives as his callous plans for her.

If she doesn't turn, he'll be forced to erase her memories and let her go. His family's safety demands secrecy – no one in the mortal world is allowed to know that immortals exist.

Resigned to the cruel reality that even if she stays on to never again leave the keep, she'll get old while Kian won't, Syssi is determined to enjoy what little time she has with him, one day at a time.

Can Kian let go of the mortal woman he loves? Will Syssi turn? And if she does, will she survive the dangerous transition?

### 4: Dark Enemy Taken

Dalhu can't believe his luck when he stumbles upon the beautiful immortal professor. Presented with a once in a lifetime opportunity to grab an immortal female for himself, he kidnaps her and runs. If he ever gets caught, either by her people or his, his life is forfeit. But for a chance of a loving mate and a family of his own, Dalhu is prepared to do everything in his power to win Amanda's heart, and that includes leaving the Doom brotherhood and his old life behind.

Amanda soon discovers that there is more to the handsome Doomer than his dark past and a hulking, sexy body. But succumbing to her enemy's seduction, or worse, developing feelings for a ruthless killer is out of the question. No man is worth life on the run, not even the one and only immortal male she could claim as her own…

Her clan and her research must come first…

### 5: Dark Enemy Captive

When the rescue team returns with Amanda and the chained Dalhu to the keep, Amanda is not as thrilled to be back as she thought she'd be. Between Kian's contempt for her and Dalhu's imprisonment, Amanda's budding relationship with Dalhu seems doomed. Things start to look up when Annani offers her help, and together with Syssi they resolve to find a way for Amanda to be with Dalhu. But will she still want him when she realizes that he is responsible for her nephew's murder? Could she? Will she take the easy way out and choose Andrew instead?

### 6: Dark Enemy Redeemed

Amanda suspects that something fishy is going on onboard the Anna. But when her investigation of the peculiar all-female Russian crew fails to uncover anything other than more speculation, she decides it's time to stop playing detective and face her real problem —a man she shouldn't want but can't live without.

### 6.5: My Dark Amazon

When Michael and Kri fight off a gang of humans, Michael gets stabbed. The injury to his immortal body recovers fast, but the one to his ego takes longer, putting a strain on his relationship with Kri.

### 7: Dark Warrior Mine

When Andrew is forced to retire from active duty, he believes that all he has to look forward to is a boring desk job. His glory days in special ops are over. But as it turns out, his thrill ride has just begun. Andrew discovers not only that immortals exist and have been manipulating global affairs since antiquity, but that he and his sister are rare possessors of the immortal genes.

Problem is, Andrew might be too old to attempt the activation process. His sister, who is fourteen years his junior, barely made it through the transition, so the odds of him coming out of it alive, let alone immortal, are slim.

But fate may force his hand.

Helping a friend find his long-lost daughter, Andrew finds a woman who's worth taking the risk for. Nathalie might be a Dormant, but the only way to find out for sure requires fangs and venom.

## 8: Dark Warrior's Promise

Andrew and Nathalie's love flourishes, but the secrets they keep from each other taint their relationship with doubts and suspicions. In the meantime, Sebastian and his men are getting bolder, and the storm that's brewing will shift the balance of power in the millennia-old conflict between Annani's clan and its enemies.

## 9: Dark Warrior's Destiny

The new ghost in Nathalie's head remembers who he was in life, providing Andrew and her with indisputable proof that he is real and not a figment of her imagination.

Convinced that she is a Dormant, Andrew decides to go forward with his transition immediately after the rescue mission at the Doomers' HQ.

Fearing for his life, Nathalie pleads with him to reconsider. She'd rather spend the rest of her mortal days with Andrew than risk what they have for the fickle promise of immortality.

While the clan gets ready for battle, Carol gets help from an unlikely ally. Sebastian's second-in-command can no longer ignore the torment she suffers at the hands of his commander and offers to help her, but only if she agrees to his terms.

## 10: Dark Warrior's Legacy

Andrew's acclimation to his post-transition body isn't easy. His senses are sharper, he's bigger, stronger, and hungrier. Nathalie fears that the changes in the man she loves are more than physical. Measuring up to this new version of him is going to be a challenge.

Carol and Robert are disillusioned with each other. They are not destined mates, and love is not on the horizon. When Robert's three months are up, he might be left with nothing to show for his sacrifice.

Lana contacts Anandur with disturbing news; the yacht and its human cargo are in Mexico. Kian must find a way to apprehend Alex and rescue the women on board without causing an international incident.

## 11: Dark Guardian Found

### What would you do if you stopped aging?

Eva runs. The ex-DEA agent doesn't know what caused her strange mutation, only that if discovered, she'll be dissected like a lab rat. What Eva doesn't know, though, is that she's a descendant of the gods, and that she is not alone. The man who rocked her world in one life-changing encounter over thirty years ago is an immortal as well.

To keep his people's existence secret, Bhathian was forced to turn his back on the only woman who ever captured his heart, but he's never forgotten and never stopped looking for her.

## 12: Dark Guardian Craved

Cautious after a lifetime of disappointments, Eva is mistrustful of Bhathian's professed feelings of love. She accepts him as a lover and a confidant but not as a life partner.

Jackson suspects that Tessa is his true love mate, but unless she overcomes her fears, he might never find out.

Carol gets an offer she can't refuse—a chance to prove that there is more to her than meets the eye. Robert believes she's about to commit a deadly mistake, but when he tries to dissuade her, she tells him to leave.

## 13: Dark Guardian's Mate

Prepare for the heart-warming culmination of Eva and Bhathian's story!

**14: Dark Angel's Obsession**

The cold and stoic warrior is an enigma even to those closest to him. His secrets are about to unravel...

**15: Dark Angel's Seduction**

Brundar is fighting a losing battle. Calypso is slowly chipping away his icy armor from the outside, while his need for her is melting it from the inside.

He can't allow it to happen. Calypso is a human with none of the Dormant indicators. There is no way he can keep her for more than a few weeks.

**16: Dark Angel's Surrender**

**Get ready for the heart pounding conclusion to Brundar and Calypso's story.**

Callie still couldn't wrap her head around it, nor could she summon even a smidgen of sorrow or regret. After all, she had some memories with him that weren't horrible. She should've felt something. But there was nothing, not even shock. Not even horror at what had transpired over the last couple of hours.

Maybe it was a typical response for survivors--feeling euphoric for the simple reason that they were alive. Especially when that survival was nothing short of miraculous.

Brundar's cold hand closed around hers, reminding her that they weren't out of the woods yet. Her injuries were superficial, and the most she had to worry about was some scarring. But, despite his and Anandur's reassurances, Brundar might never walk again.

If he ended up crippled because of her, she would never forgive herself for getting him involved in her crap.

"Are you okay, sweetling? Are you in pain?" Brundar asked.

Her injuries were nothing compared to his, and yet he was concerned about her. God, she loved this man. The thing was, if she told him that, he would run off, or crawl away as was the case.

Hey, maybe this was the perfect opportunity to spring it on him.

**17: Dark Operative: A Shadow of Death**

As a brilliant strategist and the only human entrusted with the secret of immortals' existence, Turner is both an asset and a liability to the clan. His request to attempt transition into immortality as an alternative to cancer treatments cannot be denied without risking the clan's exposure. On the other hand, approving it means risking his premature death. In both scenarios, the clan will lose a valuable ally.

When the decision is left to the clan's physician, Turner makes plans to manipulate her by taking advantage of her interest in him.

Will Bridget fall for the cold, calculated operative? Or will Turner fall into his own trap?

**18: Dark Operative: A Glimmer of Hope**

As Turner and Bridget's relationship deepens, living together seems like the right move, but to make it work both need to make concessions.

Bridget is realistic and keeps her expectations low. Turner could never be the truelove mate she yearns for, but he is as good as she's going to get. Other than his emotional limitations, he's perfect in every way.

Turner's hard shell is starting to show cracks. He wants immortality, he wants to be part of the clan, and he wants Bridget, but he doesn't want to cause her pain.

His options are either abandon his quest for immortality and give Bridget his few remaining decades, or abandon Bridget by going for the transition and most likely dying. His rational mind dictates that he chooses the former, but his gut pulls him toward the latter. Which one is he going to trust?

### 19: Dark Operative: The Dawn of Love

Get ready for the exciting finale of Bridget and Turner's story!

### 20: Dark Survivor Awakened

This was a strange new world she had awakened to.

Her memory loss must have been catastrophic because almost nothing was familiar. The language was foreign to her, with only a few words bearing some similarity to the language she thought in. Still, a full moon cycle had passed since her awakening, and little by little she was gaining basic understanding of it--only a few words and phrases, but she was learning more each day.

A week or so ago, a little girl on the street had tugged on her mother's sleeve and pointed at her. "Look, Mama, Wonder Woman!"

The mother smiled apologetically, saying something in the language these people spoke, then scurried away with the child looking behind her shoulder and grinning.

When it happened again with another child on the same day, it was settled.

Wonder Woman must have been the name of someone important in this strange world she had awoken to, and since both times it had been said with a smile it must have been a good one.

Wonder had a nice ring to it.

She just wished she knew what it meant.

### 21: Dark Survivor Echoes of Love

Wonder's journey continues in *Dark Survivor Echoes of Love*.

### 22: Dark Survivor Reunited

The exciting finale of Wonder and Anandur's story.

### 23: Dark Widow's Secret

Vivian and her daughter share a powerful telepathic connection, so when Ella can't be reached by conventional or psychic means, her mother fears the worst.

Help arrives from an unexpected source when Vivian gets a call from the young doctor she met at a psychic convention. Turns out Julian belongs to a private organization specializing in retrieving missing girls.

As Julian's clan mobilizes its considerable resources to rescue the daughter, Magnus is charged with keeping the gorgeous young mother safe.

Worry for Ella and the secrets Vivian and Magnus keep from each other should be enough to prevent the sparks of attraction from kindling a blaze of desire. Except, these pesky sparks have a mind of their own.

### 24: Dark Widow's Curse

A simple rescue operation turns into mission impossible when the Russian mafia gets involved. Bad things are supposed to come in threes, but in Vivian's case, it seems like there is no limit to bad luck. Her family and everyone who gets close to her is affected by her curse.

Will Magnus and his people prove her wrong?

### 25: Dark Widow's Blessing

The thrilling finale of the Dark Widow trilogy!

### 26: Dark Dream's Temptation

Julian has known Ella is the one for him from the moment he saw her picture, but when he finally frees her from captivity, she seems indifferent to him. Could he have been mistaken?

Ella's rescue should've ended that chapter in her life, but it seems like the road back to normalcy has just begun and it's full of obstacles. Between the pitying looks she gets and her mother's attempts to get her into therapy, Ella feels like she's typecast as a victim, when nothing could be further from the truth. She's a tough survivor, and she's going to prove it.

Strangely, the only one who seems to understand is Logan, who keeps popping up in her dreams. But then, he's a figment of her imagination—or is he?

### 27: Dark Dream's Unraveling

While trying to figure out a way around Logan's silencing compulsion, Ella concocts an ambitious plan. What if instead of trying to keep him out of her dreams, she could pretend to like him and lure him into a trap?

Catching Navuh's son would be a major boon for the clan, as well as for Ella. She will have her revenge, turning the tables on another scumbag out to get her.

### 28: Dark Dream's Trap

The trap is set, but who is the hunter and who is the prey? Find out in this heart-pounding conclusion to the *Dark Dream* trilogy.

### 29: Dark Prince's Enigma

As the son of the most dangerous male on the planet, Lokan lives by three rules:

Don't trust a soul.

Don't show emotions.

And don't get attached.

Will one extraordinary woman make him break all three?

### 30: Dark Prince's Dilemma

Will Kian decide that the benefits of trusting Lokan outweigh the risks?

Will Lokan betray his father and brothers for the greater good of his people?

Are Carol and Lokan true-love mates, or is one of them playing the other?

So many questions, the path ahead is anything but clear.

### 31: Dark Prince's Agenda

While Turner and Kian work out the details of Areana's rescue plan, Carol and Lokan's tumultuous relationship hits another snag. Is it a sign of things to come?

### 32 : Dark Queen's Quest

A former beauty queen, a retired undercover agent, and a successful model, Mey is not the typical damsel in distress. But when her sister drops off the radar and then someone starts following her around, she panics.

Following a vague clue that Kalugal might be in New York, Kian sends a team headed by Yamanu to search for him.

As Mey and Yamanu's paths cross, he offers her his help and protection, but will that be all?

### 33: Dark Queen's Knight

As the only member of his clan with a godlike power over human minds, Yamanu has been shielding his people for centuries, but that power comes at a steep price. When Mey enters his life, he's faced with the most difficult choice.

The safety of his clan or a future with his fated mate.

### 34: Dark Queen's Army

As Mey anxiously waits for her transition to begin and for Yamanu to test whether his godlike powers are gone, the clan sets out to solve two mysteries:

Where is Jin, and is she there voluntarily?

Where is Kalugal, and what is he up to?

### 35: Dark Spy Conscripted

Jin possesses a unique paranormal ability. Just by touching someone, she can insert a mental hook into their psyche and tie a string of her consciousness to it, creating a tether. That doesn't make her a spy, though, not unless her talent is discovered by those seeking to exploit it.

### 36: Dark Spy's Mission

Jin's first spying mission is supposed to be easy. Walk into the club, touch Kalugal to tether her consciousness to him, and walk out.

Except, they should have known better.

### 37: Dark Spy's Resolution

The best-laid plans often go awry...

### 38: Dark Overlord New Horizon

Jacki has two talents that set her apart from the rest of the human race.

She has unpredictable glimpses of other people's futures, and she is immune to mind manipulation.

Unfortunately, both talents are pretty useless for finding a job other than the one she had in the government's paranormal division.

It seemed like a sweet deal, until she found out that the director planned on producing super babies by compelling the recruits into pairing up. When an opportunity to escape the program presented itself, she took it, only to find out that humans are not at the top of the food chain.

Immortals are real, and at the very top of the hierarchy is Kalugal, the most powerful, arrogant, and sexiest male she has ever met.

With one look, he sets her blood on fire, but Jacki is not a fool. A man like him will never think of her as anything more than a tasty snack, while she will never settle for anything less than his heart.

### 39: Dark Overlord's Wife

Jacki is still clinging to her all-or-nothing policy, but Kalugal is chipping away at her resistance. Perhaps it's time to ease up on her convictions. A little less than all is still much better than nothing, and a couple of decades with a demigod is probably worth more than a lifetime with a mere mortal.

### 40: Dark Overlord's Clan

As Jacki and Kalugal prepare to celebrate their union, Kian takes every precaution to safeguard his people. Except, Kalugal and his men are not his only potential adversaries, and compulsion is not the only power he should fear.

### 41: Dark Choices The Quandary

When Rufsur and Edna meet, the attraction is as unexpected as it is undeniable. Except, she's the clan's judge and councilwoman, and he's Kalugal's second-in-command. Will loyalty and duty to their people keep them apart?

### 42: Dark Choices Paradigm Shift

Edna and Rufsur are miserable without each other, and their two-week separation seems like an eternity. Long-distance relationships are difficult, but for immortal couples they are impossible. Unless one of them is willing to leave everything behind for the other, things are just going to get worse. Except, the cost of compromise is far greater than giving up their comfortable lives and hard-earned positions. The future of their people is on the line.

### 43: Dark Choices The Accord

The winds of change blowing over the village demand hard choices. For better or worse, Kian's decisions will alter the trajectory of the clan's future, and he is not ready to take the plunge. But as Edna and Rufsur's plight gains widespread support, his resistance slowly begins to erode.

### 44: Dark Secrets Resurgence

On a sabbatical from his Stanford teaching position, Professor David Levinson finally has time to write the sci-fi novel he's been thinking about for years.

The phenomena of past life memories and near-death experiences are too controversial to include in his formal psychiatric research, while fiction is the perfect outlet for his esoteric ideas.

Hoping that a change of pace will provide the inspiration he needs, David accepts a friend's invitation to an old Scottish castle.

### 45: Dark Secrets Unveiled

When Professor David Levinson accepts a friend's invitation to an old Scottish castle, what he finds there is more fantastical than his most outlandish theories. The castle is home to a clan of immortals, their leader is a stunning demigoddess, and even more shockingly, it might be precisely where he belongs.

Except, the clan founder is hiding a secret that might cast a dark shadow on David's relationship with her daughter.

Nevertheless, when offered a chance at immortality, he agrees to undergo the dangerous induction process.

Will David survive his transition into immortality? And if he does, will his relationship with Sari survive the unveiling of her mother's secret?

### 46: Dark Secrets Absolved

Absolution.

David had given and received it.

The few short hours since he'd emerged from the coma had felt incredible. He'd finally been free of the guilt and pain, and for the first time since Jonah's death, he had felt truly happy and optimistic about the future.

He'd survived the transition into immortality, had been accepted into the clan, and was about to marry the best woman on the face of the planet, his true love mate, his salvation, his everything.

What could have possibly gone wrong?

Just about everything.

### 47: Dark Haven Illusion

Welcome to Safe Haven, where not everything is what it seems.

On a quest to process personal pain, Anastasia joins the Safe Haven Spiritual Retreat.

Through meditation, self-reflection, and hard work, she hopes to make peace with the voices in her head.

This is where she belongs.

Except, membership comes with a hefty price, doubts are sacrilege, and leaving is not as easy as walking out the front gate.

Is living in utopia worth the sacrifice?

Anastasia believes so until the arrival of a new acolyte changes everything.

Apparently, the gods of old were not a myth, their immortal descendants share the planet with humans, and she might be a carrier of their genes.

### 48: Dark Haven Unmasked

As Anastasia leaves Safe Haven for a week-long romantic vacation with Leon, she hopes to explore her newly discovered passionate side, their budding relationship, and perhaps also solve the mystery of the voices in her head. What she discovers exceeds her wildest expectations.

In the meantime, Eleanor and Peter hope to solve another mystery. Who is Emmett Haderech, and what is he up to?

---

For a FREE Audiobook, Preview chapters, And other goodies offered only to my VIPs,

### JOIN THE VIP CLUB AT ITLUCAS.COM

---

TRY THE SERIES ON

### AUDIBLE

2 FREE audiobooks with your new Audible subscription!

# THE PERFECT MATCH SERIES

### Perfect Match 1: Vampire's Consort

When Gabriel's company is ready to start beta testing, he invites his old crush to inspect its medical safety protocol.

Curious about the revolutionary technology of the *Perfect Match Virtual Fantasy-Fulfillment studios*, Brenna agrees.

Neither expects to end up partnering for its first fully immersive test run.

### Perfect Match 2: King's Chosen

When Lisa's nutty friends get her a gift certificate to *Perfect Match Virtual Fantasy Studios*, she has no intentions of using it. But since the only way to get a refund is if no partner can be found for her, she makes sure to request a fantasy so girly and over the top that no sane guy will pick it up.

Except, someone does.

**Warning:** This fantasy contains a hot, domineering crown prince, sweet insta-love, steamy love scenes painted with light shades of gray, a wedding, and a HEA in both the virtual and real worlds.

Intended for mature audience.

### Perfect Match 3: Captain's Conquest

Working as a Starbucks barista, Alicia fends off flirting all day long, but none of the guys are as charming and sexy as Gregg. His frequent visits are the highlight of her day, but since he's never asked her out, she assumes he's taken. Besides, between a day job and a budding music career, she has no time to start a new relationship.

That is until Gregg makes her an offer she can't refuse—a gift certificate to the virtual fantasy fulfillment service everyone is talking about. As a huge Star Trek fan, Alicia has a perfect match in mind—the captain of the Starship Enterprise.

# Also by I. T. Lucas

## THE CHILDREN OF THE GODS ORIGINS
1: Goddess's Choice
2: Goddess's Hope

## THE CHILDREN OF THE GODS

### Dark Stranger
1: Dark Stranger The Dream
2: Dark Stranger Revealed
3: Dark Stranger Immortal

### Dark Enemy
4: Dark Enemy Taken
5: Dark Enemy Captive
6: Dark Enemy Redeemed

### Kri & Michael's Story
6.5: My Dark Amazon

### Dark Warrior
7: Dark Warrior Mine
8: Dark Warrior's Promise
9: Dark Warrior's Destiny
10: Dark Warrior's Legacy

### Dark Guardian
11: Dark Guardian Found
12: Dark Guardian Craved
13: Dark Guardian's Mate

### Dark Angel
14: Dark Angel's Obsession
15: Dark Angel's Seduction
16: Dark Angel's Surrender

### Dark Operative
17: Dark Operative: A Shadow of Death
18: Dark Operative: A Glimmer of Hope
19: Dark Operative: The Dawn of Love

### Dark Survivor
20: Dark Survivor Awakened
21: Dark Survivor Echoes of Love
22: Dark Survivor Reunited

### Dark Widow
23: Dark Widow's Secret
24: Dark Widow's Curse
25: Dark Widow's Blessing

### Dark Dream
26: Dark Dream's Temptation
27: Dark Dream's Unraveling
28: Dark Dream's Trap

### Dark Prince
29: Dark Prince's Enigma

## ALSO BY I. T. LUCAS

30: Dark Prince's Dilemma
31: Dark Prince's Agenda

### Dark Queen
32: Dark Queen's Quest
33: Dark Queen's Knight
34: Dark Queen's Army

### Dark Spy
35: Dark Spy Conscripted
36: Dark Spy's Mission
37: Dark Spy's Resolution

### Dark Overlord
38: Dark Overlord New Horizon
39: Dark Overlord's Wife
40: Dark Overlord's Clan

### Dark Choices
41: Dark Choices The Quandary
42: Dark Choices Paradigm Shift
43: Dark Choices The Accord

### Dark Secrets
44: Dark Secrets Resurgence
45: Dark Secrets Unveiled
46: Dark Secrets Absolved

### Dark Haven
47: Dark haven Illusion
48: Dark Haven Unmasked

---

## PERFECT MATCH
Perfect Match 1: Vampire's Consort
Perfect Match 2: King's Chosen
Perfect Match 3: Captain's Conquest

---

### The Children of the Gods Series Sets

Books 1-3: Dark Stranger trilogy—Includes a bonus short story: **The Fates take a Vacation**
  Books 4-6: Dark Enemy Trilogy —Includes a bonus short story —**The Fates' Post-Wedding Celebration**
    Books 7-10: Dark Warrior Tetralogy
    Books 11-13: Dark Guardian Trilogy
    Books 14-16: Dark Angel Trilogy
    Books 17-19: Dark Operative Trilogy
    Books 20-22: Dark Survivor Trilogy
    Books 23-25: Dark Widow Trilogy
    Books 26-28: Dark Dream Trilogy

ALSO BY I. T. LUCAS

Books 29-31: Dark Prince Trilogy
Books 32-34: Dark Queen Trilogy
Books 35-37: Dark Spy Trilogy
Books 38-40: Dark Overlord Trilogy
Books 41-43: Dark Choices Trilogy
Books 44-46: Dark Secrets Trilogy

**MEGA SETS**

The Children of the Gods: Books 1-6—includes character lists

The Children of the Gods: Books 6.5-10—includes character lists

---

**TRY THE CHILDREN OF THE GODS SERIES ON
AUDIBLE**
2 FREE audiobooks with your new Audible subscription!

## FOR EXCLUSIVE PEEKS AT UPCOMING RELEASES & A FREE COMPANION BOOK

Join my *VIP Club* and gain access to the VIP portal at itlucas.com

[CLICK HERE TO JOIN](http://eepurl.com/blMTpD)

### Included in your free membership:

- FREE Children of the Gods companion book 1
- FREE narration of Goddess's Choice—Book 1 in The Children of the Gods Origins series.
- Preview chapters of upcoming releases.
- And other exclusive content offered only to my VIPs.

**If you're already a subscriber**, you can find **your VIP password** at the bottom of each of my new release emails. If you are not getting them, your email provider is sending them to your junk folder, and you are missing out on **important updates, side characters' portraits, additional content, and other goodies.** To fix that, add isabell@itlucas.com to your email contacts or to your email VIP list.

Printed in Great Britain
by Amazon